THE RISING STORM

Also by Suzanne Goodwin

SUZANNE GOODWIN

THE RISING STORM

WARNER BOOKS

A WARNER BOOK

First published in Britain by Macdonald in 1992

This edition published by Warner in 1993
copyright © Suzanne Goodwin 1992

The moral right of the author has been asserted

A CIP catalogue for this book
is available from the British Library

ISBN 0 7515 0044 5

Printed in England by Clays Ltd, St Ives plc

Warner
A Division of
Little, Brown and Company (UK) Limited
165 Great Dover Street
London SE1 4YA

PART ONE

1

A sense of well-being, a surge of optimism, were often harbingers of bad luck, but Roz did not remember that. The day was brilliant and sharp, a sunny end to a cold rainy March, and the whole of Oxford was on the move. The city would have no true meaning again until the undergraduates came flooding back for their summer term, the last of the year. There was a start-of-vacation sound in the voices of passers-by in the street, distant shouts and the rev of car engines. Roz's face wore a holiday expression, and there was an untidy carefree air about her as she packed. She threw armfuls of books into a long orange-coloured bag the shape of a monstrous sausage and crammed T-shirts into a plastic carrier. Wearing the inevitable tracksuit, which was pink and fought violently with the orange sausage, Roz was pale, red-headed, freckled and almost beautiful. Or beautiful occasionally.

The other tenants of the house had gone long ago, determined to make the best of every moment, like children who wake at six on the morning of a holiday. Alice and Huw, who each had rooms on the ground floor, had set off to the station at an unearthly hour. The speechless tenant from the attic bedroom under the roof, who lived only to work and worry over future examinations, had cadged a lift to Bristol. No 10, Erith Road, was empty except for Roz, and quiet except for the distant noises from the road. Silence did not suit her; she was used to loud music, shouts of laughter, slammed doors and sudden arguments, and conscious of the hush pervading the little house she began to hurry as she completed her packing. Well-being continued to fill her. Because it was strong she remembered, just then, the demon in the corner of her mind, the belief that to feel like this did sometimes mean bad luck. Oh, superstitious claptrap, thought Roz.

Her bags were heavy and she kicked them out of her room on to the landing, then stood trying to be sure she had forgotten nothing. Wasn't there a book she had bought for her grandmother, where was that? Still in its Blackwell's bag in the sitting room. Leaving her luggage at the top of the stairs she ran down just as the front door opened.

A man peered in. Seeing Roz, he pushed the door wider but did not come into the house. He stood leaning against the doorpost, hands in his pockets. There was the usual exchange, a mutual 'Hi?' In Roz's case it was a query, in the young man's a pleasant non-committal greeting. They gave a grin, using a particular kind of meaningless friendliness they both felt necessary. They did not know each other well.

'Well, come in,' said Roz impatiently, as he continued to lean against the door. 'You're just what I need. You can bring my things down. I was going to kick them, but supposing one of them split.' Roz was much mocked at university for allowing – inviting – men to wait on her, even occasionally letting them pay for her. She broke a good many of the female rules. And she enjoyed annoying her girl friends.

'I take it,' said the young man, whose name was Michael Chance, 'that they weigh a ton.'

'Not really.'

'I don't believe you,' he said, obligingly going up the stairs.

'It's the books, mostly, I have to work like a dog all Easter,' shouted Roz after him.

He gave an incredulous smile. He was as slender as she was, with the thinness of the young which thickens later, like the trunks of growing trees. He was dark, with a short nose slightly blunted at the end, naturally curly hair which was boyish, which he was not. His eyes were steady, and too observant. Roz, watching him as he bent over her luggage, had not made up her mind about him. He loaded himself with her bags, stowing some of them under his arms like an old-time station porter, and came somewhat gingerly down the stairs.

'Ally keeps telling me not to ask men to do the heavy jobs,' Roz called from the bottom of the stairs. 'I don't see why not.'

'Because Ally would rather shoulder a piano than ask a guy to help her.'

'She asks Huw all the time.'

'No, she doesn't,' replied Michael Chance, speaking with a slight effort, the weight was appalling. 'He manages to do what she wants just before she tells him not to.'

'You're too clever by half.'

To Michael Chance, this young woman, almost a stranger in spite of their casual meetings in Oxford pubs or parties, was alluringly full of life. She represented the mystery of a woman with whom he had never been alone. He felt disturbed by her, drawn to her, annoyed with her. When he saw her unexpectedly, his heart lifted. When she waved at him from a distance, and did not stop to speak to him, there was a hollow somewhere.

She was watching him piling the bags painstakingly by the front door. She had a small pang of contrition: his head was bent and she liked his hair. Then he looked up. 'Now you want all this stuff bunged into your car?'

'Sure. Oh,' remembering, 'I never asked why you're here. Is it social or is there the usual reason, like will I give you a lift to London?'

'How did you guess?'

'Those massive hints you kept dropping last night. I didn't pick up one of them.'

'I noticed.'

'Oh dear. Am I horrible? I'm driving to Chiswick. Will that do?'

He said yes, and thanks, speaking over his shoulder, already going out towards the car.

Roz was by nature impulsive, carelessly generous, and still

3

at twenty had a trusting belief that the world was her close friend. Too often she acted and then regretted afterwards, which was monotonous to those who loved her and would have her develop more sense. Her confidence was a matter of awe to some, resentment to others; it came from the certainty of being loved. This surprised the curious when they learned that she had no parents and had been brought up for the last eleven years by a widowed grandmother. 'Spoilt rotten' was the verdict when Roz was at her most insensitive. 'Generous to a fault' was the other side of the coin.

She had not reacted with her usual warmth on the previous evening when she had met Michael Chance while having farewell drinks with her friends. She had believed Alice and Huw, her closest friends and flat-sharers in Erith Road, would be coming to London with her. Her grandmother liked them, and Roz had imagined a celebration supper: her grandmother enjoyed spending money and there might be champagne. But her friends unexpectedly changed their plans. Alice, who took life with rueful seriousness, had appeared in Roz's bedroom at five this morning, looming up, a ghost in white cotton.

'Roz? It's me. Sorry to wake you. But Huw has decided, he is a pain, that we've got to go to Wales after all. Isn't it frightening?' Sad and regretful, she remained standing by Roz's bed. She had a thick cloud of spiralling hair, great eyes, a luminous skin, she was fascinatingly like Elizabeth Siddall at her most consumptive. Alice was strong as a horse. 'Welsh parents,' she muttered and remained motionless, looking through the half gloom (the curtains were thin) in Roz's direction.

'Huw says as we're serious about getting – you know—'

The word 'married' stuck in Alice's throat. She never managed it.

'Welsh parents,' she repeated.

'You'll be a big success.'

'Oh no. I feel sick.'

With the gap left by her friends, Roz was not unwilling to have Michael Chance as her companion. But she did not offer to drive him to wherever he was heading. She had been caught out too often by that; one young man, an Oxford acquaintance with an aura of misfortune, had begged a lift from her on a previous occasion and Roz had found herself forced to drive through nearly impenetrable traffic as far as Kilburn. She remembered a favourite maxim of her great uncle's when he had lived in London. 'Never have friends who live in Hampstead.'

He had lived near Sloane Square.

'Chiswick would be fine,' said Michael Chance, as they climbed into the car. 'I plan to bum a room from a man I know in Hammersmith.'

'So you're not going home?'

'Scarcely. My parents are living in South Carolina.'

'Wow,' said Roz.

He smiled. 'My mother and stepfather have been there for five years. He's taken up painting and it's a good place for that. All the water, and the odd alligator.'

'My grandmother taught me how to run if you're pursued by an alligator. From side to side, like this,' said Roz, demonstrating.

'Because they only go in straight lines. Don't you believe it.'

It was already mid morning when Roz's muddy and ill-kempt car drove away from Erith Road. At the corner by the Baptist Chapel, six people, four young men and two girls, were piling into another shabby car; it looked as full as a police car in an old Keystone Cops movie. Roz waved as she went by and was answered by grins and shouts of goodbye. She smiled, forgetting the demon.

She drove out of the cheerful city into the cheerful sunshine. 'Shall I put on a tape?' she asked, and when Michael agreed, pleased, she chose a tape her grandmother had given her, a lighthearted 19th century operetta, filled with the absurd gallantry of confident males and flirtatious girls. She scarcely listened to it as she left an Oxford on the very edge of spring and drove towards London. Her own music was for crazy dancing or as a drumming background to work. At present she was simply driving, occupied with the task and her own thoughts. Neither she nor Michael Chance talked much. When they did, it was in the same meaningless comradely tone they always used when they met.

Roz asked herself if she found him attractive. Well – yes. But she was not in the mood for a love affair, supposing it was in his mind. She was aware that most of her friends had more experience than she, they were good at sex, they said. It sounded to Roz like the claims of a ballet dancer or an athlete. Ally had told her more than once that *she* was, and so was Huw. Roz had not been able to decide whether to giggle or envy them. Her own love affair, only one, had happened the previous year and it had not lasted. The young man, his name was Peter, had been a few weeks in London before leaving for a job in Australia. She had found him physically alluring and the fact that he was going away had added to his attraction. 'Our love is doomed' she used to say melodramatically and they smiled together. He was tall, rangy, foxy, thin-lipped, his physical appearance affected her almost without any act of imagination on her part; they spent most of the month before he left England in bed. Doomed, thought Roz. She sometimes wondered, and would never know the answer, whether the affair would have lasted had they known each other in Oxford, as striving, hopeful, difficult, complicated beings; and not just as partners in tumultuous sex.

The miles slipped away, the traffic grew thicker, the country began to lose its battle with the creeping city. Yet the verges of the road were juicy green, and they drove past a budding cornfield. In the distance, the spire of a church rose up, sadly pointing to a heaven Roz was pretty sure did not exist.

'I expect my grandmother will manage lunch,' she remarked, after a long silence, 'or are you keen to get to Hammersmith right away?'

'Why should I be?'

'In case that friend gives the room to somebody else.'

'I can stay there anytime I want,' said Michael Chance, nettled. He did not know why she annoyed him. He was clever with women, preferred their company to that of his own sex. He liked being with women, liked their softness, their scent, enjoyed the things they talked about. Human things. Women were more adult than men, so many of whom remained children all their lives. In his turn, he felt attractive in female company. But this girl got between himself and his self-confidence.

'I'd like to lunch if your grandmother would put up with me. That's very kind.'

'Not really. She loves visitors.'

'Rare in an old lady.'

'Oh, she's not old,' said Roz, surprised.

The journey was nearly over, they were almost in Chiswick, driving past lines of neat houses which with their scraps of garden and clean curtains somehow managed to exist, even to bear, the deafening motorway. Roz slowed down at a junction and turned into a broad suburban road. It was edged with cherry trees which for a short period in late spring behaved like brides. But it was too early yet for white blossom; in the gardens the daffodils were out, although many were past their prime. Turning to the right, Roz drove into a road which ran by the side of the Thames. It was at the short interval when the tide neither ebbed nor flowed, the great greenish stretch of water brimmed, with here and there a little group of Canada geese. After heavy rains recently, the path was flooded and one or two spreading pools reflected the sky. Along their edges was a debris of dead leaves, willow branches, twigs, and one or two of those unexplained lumps of white plastic which get washed up on winter beaches.

'You never said you lived by the river!' exclaimed Michael, much interested, as Roz drew to a stop.

'I haven't told you anything, actually.'

'No you haven't.'

'So. This is home. Ta-rar!' said Roz, as they climbed out of the car. She indicated the house, like a man at the circus announcing a wonder.

The house was very old and looked rich, thought Michael Chance. It was early 17th century, the front door under a portico guarded by thin white pillars, the elaborate front

7

railings of wrought iron curved into thick loops. Up the front of the house grew a wisteria, hanging with grey buds. Michael took the luggage from the back of the car, but Roz, her face alight with expectation, ran up the path and slapped her hand flat on the front door. She pushed, but it did not respond.

'Imagine her forgetting,' she said irritably, 'she's only started all this locking of doors recently. Some drunks from the pub tried to get in one night. The police arrived and told her she had to lock up more securely.' She gave the door another push, then scrabbled in her shoulder bag for a Yale key. She fitted it into a lower lock and turned. She had to turn the key twice. Above was another lock. That, too, needed to be turned. Puzzled and frowning, she kicked the door open.

'It would be nice,' said Roz, beckoning him indoors, 'if she'd happened to remember her granddaughter was arriving home today.' She ran ahead, yelling, 'Gran! Hi!'

Michael Chance remained in the entrance hall, looking round. How exquisite these very old houses were. The marble floor was hollowed by feet which had walked across the black and white tiles over a period of hundreds of years. The staircase was as delicate as the curve of a violin. In the high window at the back of the staircase was crimson and yellow stained glass.

'Gran!' repeated Roz, emerging from a large drawing room to the left.

'Where's she got to?' She continued to run around and to shout.

Michael said nothing. The sun slanted through the glass and threw jewels on the stairs. The house was very quiet. He had a feeling that it was empty.

Muttering that she would look in the garden, Roz, with a pale face, brushed past him. But returned a moment later giving what seemed like an angry shrug. 'Damn it,' she said. 'Where is she?'

'Out, I suppose. Would she have left you a note, perhaps?'

Roz's face cleared at once. 'Of course. How ridiculous of me. When she's had to go out she always leaves one on the salver over there—' As she spoke she darted across to an oak chest, on which, dead centre, was a large silver salver. There was nothing on it. In the pause that followed, Roz remembered the demon in the corner.

Michael Chance had been watching her, not surprised at the lack of a note, most of his friends gave no explanation for their absences, but touched by something in the girl's face. She almost looked scared. Because he liked her and was attracted to her, he wanted to banish the look. He spoke in a deliberately relaxed way, 'There's always a perfectly obvious explanation when people aren't where they're supposed to be.'

'But she *always*—'

'Nobody does anything "always", Roz. That's what makes life intriguing.'

'I don't want it to be intriguing. She always—'

He interrupted her with a laugh. 'Look, why don't we nose around and see if we can find a clue?'

She did not react, did not share his smile, and he went over, put his hands on her shoulders, and gave her a slight shake.

'Now, Roz, you can't be upset just because your grand-mother isn't here laying out the red carpet. There's nothing to look so doleful about – have a sense of proportion. Come on. She probably wrote a note and forgot to put it in its usual place. Okay?'

For once Roz was not the leader, the sought-after girl whose beauty affected her men friends so that they did what *she* wanted. Looking dismal, she followed him. He went into the drawing room to start the search – another beautiful ordered place of books and paintings and panelling, with windows overlooking a walled garden. The room smelled of woodsmoke and the bowls of pot-pourri. But there was nothing to be found, no clue as to where the missing Mrs Lingard might have left her letter. Not on the chimney piece, the windowsills, chests of drawers. Nowhere. Next they went into a dining room. They looked under the silver candlesticks, on the sideboard, and under a blue and white bowl planted with just-emerging hyacinths. Men in full-bottomed wigs,

9

with lecherous faces and supercilious eyelids, watched them. Michael opened the lid of an inlaid tea-caddy.

'As if she'd stuff it in there,' said Roz, sounding more like herself.

'Absent-minded people do absent-minded things.'

'She's never been like that.'

'Then we'll find a note, won't we?'

'Of course!' said Roz suddenly, 'I know where it'll be. In her bedroom on the dressing table. She did that once.'

'See?'

She made a friendly face at him, and ran out – he heard her hurrying up the stairs.

Affected by her certainty, Michael stopped his search and wandered back into the hall, thinking this really was a remarkable house. His interest in Roz quickened because her setting enhanced her – she was more fascinating because she belonged in this strange old place. He walked down a passage and found the kitchen, which overlooked a garden of surprising size. There were lime trees and lawns shaggy with early spring growth, the brick walls were decorated with long parallel lines of espaliered fruit trees, the beds filled with the now-dying daffodils. He glimpsed a sundial.

The kitchen was too tidy, and standing with his hands in his pockets, he had the idea that nobody had been here for some time. Not recently. Not even a day ago. When he went over to the sink, it was bone dry. A cloth, neatly folded on the washing-up board, had hardened into ridges like cardboard. And then he saw an envelope propped against the window.

He ran to the bottom of the staircase. 'Roz!'

'What is it?'

'*I've found it!*'

He had no time to tell her that there was a letter in the kitchen, she came pelting down the stairs jumping the last three steps. 'Where? Where?'

'On the kitchen window-sill—' he began, following her as she rushed ahead, skidding into the kitchen and snatching up the letter. She was already smiling in relief. He watched her tear it open. And waited. She stood with the letter in her hand.

10

'Well?' prompted Michael. 'When's she due back?'

'What?' said Roz, not listening.

She stood for what seemed a long time, simply looking at the letter, her face blank.

'When's she back, Roz?' he repeated.

She looked up then, conscious that he had spoken to her, and without a word passed him the letter. Michael had a moment of pleasure at being taken into her confidence. The letter, written in a bold somewhat over-flourishing hand, was short.

'Roz darling,

Did you get the message I left at College? I left two but I know you've often said the porter is hopeless and forgets. How I *wish* Erith Road had a telephone.

I feel guilty at springing this on you without us talking, but you're such a resilient creature, you may even be rather pleased by my bombshell – in a way. I've decided on a rather sudden holiday. An impulse, really. It's a bit of a rush and I'm leaving at once, so won't be here when you get home. But *do* enjoy your vac. and have people to stay etc. I've fixed for you to use my food accounts in local shops, I know how penniless you always are at the end of term! Oh yes, and I've upped your allowance so your bank balance will be quite healthy for a change. Jack will cope with any other money matters if you need him.

Don't know when I'll be back, darling, but take care. I shall think of you.

Always your affec.

Gran.'

He returned the letter, saying non-committally, 'Not very enlightening.'

'Enlightening! What does it mean? Where has she gone? Why hasn't she told me? *She never does things like that.*'

He grimaced at another of her certainties.

'I suppose it's a bit of a surprise, but elderly people sometimes get bees in their bonnets and —'

'For Christ's sake!' she was furious, 'you've never clapped

11

eyes on her. She's a bloody sight more level-headed and a thousand times cleverer than you are.'

'Thanks.'

'Well, she is,' said Roz, and seeing his offended face couldn't help laughing. The laughter vanished from her face like a screen wipe. She was angry and alarmed again.

'Sorry. I'm sorry I shouted at you but I can't make it out. Make *her* out. She's disappeared, doesn't tell me where. And –' She stopped. The kitchen was very quiet. Michael waited, while emotions he could not interpret struggled in her face. Then, with something like a sob, she pushed open the kitchen door and ran out into the garden, throwing herself on the ground. With nobody to console her but a man she scarcely knew. Nobody to explain the pain away. She stared blindly at the flowers which had begun to turn brown and to stoop on thin stems. You only realize how much you want somebody when they've gone, she thought. I want Gran. Where is she? I need her. She felt ice-cold in the merry March sunshine.

Both her parents had been dead for the last eleven years, they had been killed in a tragic air crash in Italy; the plane had hit a mountain-side in a fog. Roz had been nine years old, the only child of doting parents, spoiled and petted and well aware she was the centre of the world. Even now across the vast gap of half her life, the day she learned of their death remained in her mind. Her nature had been burned that day like the poor victims of the crash. And the person who had brought the awful news, who had come to the house and scooped her into her arms and her life, had been her grandmother; Roz's mother. Polly had been her only daughter.

Since that day, Roz's life had been lit, enriched, warmed and ruled by her grandmother. Sophy Lingard was energetic and still almost beautiful in her sixties, a strong, fiery woman who ran towards life like a boxer who knows how to bend when the real blow comes. She suffered excruciatingly over her daughter's death but had no time to shout aloud with pain. She made a life for Polly's child who grew to love her. Such dependent love had changed and in the last two or three years Roz had grown up and in a sense grown away. But looming finals had brought back a hunger for the old days. She needed her grandmother again. Now, sitting with her back to the house, she ached.

Michael remained in the open doorway, rather as he'd stood in the door at Erith Road, awaiting events. There were things about all this that he did not understand, but then neither did the miserable figure in the garden. There was a childlike despair about Roz's back – it touched and surprised him. He had never seen such a demonstration of family love. Most of his friends did not rate their parents, and as for his own – living in the States, they were too absorbed with their own lives to make much of his. When Roz finally stood up and came over to him, he put his arms round her. She neither resisted nor rejected him, but merely stood still.

When she looked up, her face was very white and he said, 'I suppose it's useless to tell you not to worry.'

'Yeah. Useless.'

'But that's what your grandmother obviously wanted. Didn't she call you resilient?'

'I don't give a f—' she swallowed the obscenity which was out of tune, 'I don't care what she called me or how she felt, she knew perfectly well what she was doing. It was horribly selfish of her.'

'Roz. Be reasonable. She tried to telephone you.'

'And didn't get me. Great.'

He persisted. 'But she has a perfect right –'

'Who has a perfect right? If you're truly fond of somebody you have no rights. Gran had none, and left me flat.' The voice was desolate.

'Surely you can at least give her some freedom in your mind,' he said gently, 'she must have thought out whatever it is she decided to do. One imagines it was important. If you're so fond of her, can't you let her go?'

The girl sighed. 'You don't understand,' she said, and began to disengage herself from his arms, but gently, as if she didn't want to offend him.

'Then telephone somebody. Your grandmother must have friends.'

'She has lots of friends.'

'Okay, so ring the best of them.'

'She'll only say exactly what Gran says in that letter.'

'How can you know that? Don't make up the answers before you've asked the questions. And who's "she"?'

'Mary DuCann. She lives in Kensington and they see each other all the time.'

'Fine. So where's the telephone?'

The number rang for a short time and then Mary DuCann's voice answered.

'It's me,' said Roz without preliminary, 'Mary, *where's Gran*?'

'Don't you know?' was the surprised answer.

'No, nothing, but I gather you do, so thank God for that.'

'But Roz, I don't. Didn't she ring you before she went?'

'Apparently left a message at College, and much good that did. I never got it. All the letter says is that she's off.'

There was a moment's silence. 'That's exactly what her letter to me said. Roz, didn't she give you any information at all?'

'Nothing. She called it a sudden holiday.'

'Yes. The same phrase to me.'

Roz paused and then burst out. 'Mary. What is going on?'

Mary DuCann's sigh came over the telephone. 'My dear, I wish I knew. Of course Sophy is inclined to go at things like a bull at a gate, but only ordinary things, never something important like this. William and I can't make head nor tail of it. At dinner a week or two ago, she did mutter something to him about a holiday and when he said "where to?" she only laughed and said it was a big world or something. Nothing very ominous about that. Did your letter say she hoped you wouldn't be cross?'

'Yes. Didn't she *know* how I'd feel?'

'Oh poor Roz. I was hoping she'd at least have told *you* something, but I had this horrid feeling she hadn't. I'm so sorry, I'm no help, am I?'

'Of course you are,' said the girl. It was not true.

'I'm afraid it's no use ringing your great uncle,' added

Mary DuCann. 'I tried, after I got Sophy's letter. What do you think? He's now ex-directory.'

'Typical,' said Roz. She had never liked him.

Mary laughed in a shocked middle-aged way. 'I suppose he is rather an old curmudgeon, but he and Sophy have always been so devoted. The infuriating thing about him being incommunicado is that if anybody knows what's happened to Sophy, it is Jack. Oh yes, I did have one other idea. I rang Carmen's digs. It seems your grandmother gave her a month's paid holiday and Carmen has swanned off to her family in Madrid. Her flat-mate told me Sophy asked Carmen to go on doing the house when she's back from Spain and Carmen agreed. The bank are to pay her salary or something.'

Roz wished she'd thought of her great uncle and the Spanish daily help. 'You have done a lot, Mary.'

'But all of it useless. Don't be too upset, Roz. I'm sure Sophy thought you'd take it in your stride.' Mary was echoing Michael. 'What I can't make out is – why the mystery? It's my guess Sophy is doing something silly and doesn't want us telling her so. She never was one to take advice from anybody except her brother.'

They promised to be in touch if either should get any news. They sounded as if they expected none. During the conversation Michael had gone back to the garden, sitting down by the sundial. He lifted his face to the sun and shut his eyes. Hearing her step, he opened them and stood up. 'What's happened?'

'Not a thing. Mary had the same sort of letter. She is as flummoxed as me.' She looked at him gloomily for a moment and said she supposed he wanted something to eat. In other circumstances the remark and its manner would have made him laugh but she filled him with pity just then. How unsuitable freckles were on a face which was angry and sad. Freckles belonged to American boys of seven years old, wearing peaked caps and playing baseball with adoring fathers.

He said he ought to get to Hammersmith after all and she

nodded vaguely; she did not bother to hide the fact that she wanted to be alone. She went with him through the house to the front door and down the path to the elaborate gate made by an ironworker three hundred years ago. Michael was in two minds. He found it extraordinary that in this day and age a letter from somebody's absent grandmother, even if it omitted the interesting fact as to where the hell the lady had gone, could have such an effect. Roz was in pain. She had the screwed-up distant look of a person who can just about bear the ache. He stood hesitating at the gate.

'Are you sure you'll be all right?' he said, trotting out the cliché of the one about to escape.

'Don't be stupid.'

'If there's anything I can do.'

'*Oh, just go.*' She turned round and ran back to the house, slamming the door.

He walked along the towpath, reflecting about the girl he had just left. Half an hour ago she had been a sexually inviting young woman he'd had his eye on at Oxford. She was more beautiful than most of the girls, and there was always a crowd of men after her. Yet she seemed to prefer the company of those two somewhat earnest friends, Alice and Huw. And whenever he did happen to see Roz accompanied by a man, it never seemed to be the same one twice. That had decided him that there was nobody, at present, she was serious over. There were girls who shied away from the usual Oxford affairs, the usual Oxford heartaches. Such girls were cautious or nervous, and Roz seemed neither of those things. He looked at the river flowing by, hurrying out to sea, covered with a thousand reflections and shadows and ripples and shimmers. Two ducks went by, letting the fast tide hasten them along.

Every step he took was further from the rich deserted house, and the girl with her unhappy white face. What can I do about it? About her? Nothing. One must be like the ducks, he thought. Let fate take you along with the tide. She doesn't need me. Why should she? We're nothing to each other.

When he arrived at the row of workmen's cottages off King

Street in Hammersmith where his erstwhile schoolfriend lived, he saw the houses had been transformed. They were no longer places for the poor, but had been turned into 'dwellings' with crimson or navy blue doors, over-bright brass bells and doorknockers and French enamel numbers on gate posts. He let himself into number 27. The hallway smelled of garlic and positively shuddered with music.

A girl in jeans, wearing a Greenpeace T-shirt, looked over the banisters. 'Are you Mike? Great. Jeff is out but he'll be back later and he says there's a note on the TV.' Today was full of notes from absentee hosts.

Two miles away at Bowling House, Roz was wandering about like a ghost doomed for a certain term to walk the night. She went from one room to another. Made herself some coffee and finally ended up in the drawing room, lying on the divan by the empty fireplace to read her grandmother's letter over and over again. If you read a letter too often, she thought, you begin to see meanings under every word. What did 'a sudden holiday' mean? Why should a holiday be sudden unless somebody invited you out of the blue in which case why not say so? But 'an impulse' did not sound like an invitation. What would have happened if she'd been given Sophy's message and had rung back? I suppose there would have been some kind of argument, thought Roz, certain that would never have changed her grandmother's mind. The call would have got nowhere. Sophy had already made her plans.

Roz belonged to today. She was proud of being independent, making her own decisions, choosing her own friends, being mistress of her own future. She was as poised and cool as any young woman in the country, and more beautiful than most. She despised herself now because inside her heart she was a mess of tears. She longed for Sophy. For the worn sardonic face, the smell of French scent, the sudden laugh on an upward scale, the passionate interest, the very look of Sophy sitting as untidily as a girl. She loved her grandmother's appearance, the wide brow and the hair, still thick but grey with only strands here and there of its once-bright copper, her short upper lip, the determination of a rounded chin in which a dimple was set dead centre. She wanted Sophy. Too much. And uselessly. She picked up her mug of coffee. It was stone cold.

The afternoon dragged by and there were footsteps on the towpath and now and again voices were raised as they had been in Oxford this morning – a century ago – raised and laughing. Oppressed by solitude, the letter in her lap, she fell asleep.

She woke slowly and saw with amazed surprise that it had grown dark. For one moment she did not remember what had happened and was her natural sanguine self. Then she became violently and cruelly aware of solitude. She shivered, stood up and went round the room switching on all the lamps. Outside the street lights were shining down on the deserted towpath. Bowling House was far enough from the popular pubs for visitors to take another road through gardens at the edge of the river. Tonight everywhere was eerily quiet.

She picked up the letter which had fallen on the floor, said aloud 'Bloody hell' and pitched it into the fireplace where it lay on top of the mass of pine cones she and Sophy had collected last autumn.

There was a ring at the front door. A surge of unthinking hope shot through her as she ran to the door and threw it open. It was Michael Chance. 'Don't say "oh, it's you again",' he said, 'I can see it's what you're thinking. I've come to take you out to a meal. I bet you haven't eaten anything since you threw me out. May I come in?'

'Sure. But —'

'But you won't have supper with me? Then come to The Dove instead. It's jam packed and there's one hell of a din. Better than an antique silence.'

He saw the crushed cushions and the screwed-up letter. Her cheek had a mark like a scar where she'd slept against a braided cushion.

She hesitated. 'It's kind of you, but—'

'But nothing. I'm not leaving you alone in this place. You've been asleep. What good did that do? One sleeps to get

18

away from things and wakes and they look worse. Look, shall we have a drink here – is there some? – and then go to The Dove and eat shepherd's pie.'

He went into the dining room, opened a sideboard and found various bottles which in the way of the elderly had not been hospitably on display. He poured out two vodkas and returned to the drawing room. Roz had fished the letter out of the fireplace and was smoothing it out on the table. He wished the sight of her did not touch him so. She wakened feelings he did not welcome. Sex, yes. But not this curious sensation as if his heart was being gently and painfully squeezed.

Glancing up, she gave him for the first time a real smile. 'You're very good. Coming back when I pushed you out.'

'You were miserable and wanted to wallow.'

'Much good it did me. You think I'm making the most ludicrous fuss about something quite unimportant, don't you?'

'As it happens,' he said judicially, 'I don't.'

They sat and talked. He fetched the bottle of vodka and they drank some more. She told him about herself, in a voice which was worrying because it was so flat. She described her parents' death, her grandmother rescuing her – a parentless child. She told him about her mother and father, who were now drifting from her memory, and described the life her grandmother had given her, as safe as this house itself. She'd been loved. Protected. Listening, Michael began to wonder if the responsibility of bringing up this girl had begun to die out of Sophy Lingard in recent years. Roz was poised. In command of herself. She knew what she wanted. Mightn't Sophy Lingard have begun to see she was no longer needed?

The evening was lengthening into spring night when Roz finished a story in which there had not been a single over-statement. It had been unemotional, deliberately matter of fact. Yet she finished by saying, 'So you must see I have to find out where she's gone.'

'Even though she doesn't want you to.'

'She may be ill.'

'And gone off like an elephant to die by herself in the jungle.'

'I wasn't making a joke,' she said in a solemn voice. Her grandmother had had a Sealyham called John, of all unsuitable names for a dog. He had been called after an MP who'd admired Sophy and bought the dog for her. The dog was scarcely two years old when he caught distemper and was very ill. Sophy and Roz nursed him night and day, but one morning when Roz came down to the kitchen, the dog basket was empty and the door to the garden had been left open. She ran out and looked everywhere, calling desperately for him. Finally she discovered the poor creature hiding behind a pile of grass cuttings at the very end of the garden. He was lying flat, four legs splayed out, and when she knelt beside him, he looked up at her, showing the whites of his dark brown eyes.

'It was so awful.'

'He died?' enquired Michael, unmoved by tales of animals.

'No, he did not,' said Roz, annoyed at the lack of sympathy. 'I picked up the poor old boy and carried him into the house, and I yelled for Gran. And we gave him brandy in an eye dropper, and she wrapped him up in a shawl and sat with him on her lap. She scarcely stirred all day, and John slept and slept. Then in the evening a bit more brandy and milk, and the next day we could *see* he was a little better. Apart from anything else, he started growling at me, rather weakly, but he showed his teeth when I came too near. That was because he was still on her lap. He was a jealous little bastard.'

'Happy ending?'

'Yes. That time.'

'I don't exactly see where the story leads to. Apart from liking to hear about your grandmother, of course.'

She looked at him then, and shook her head pityingly. 'You do miss points, don't you?'

But she did feel better, knowing very well it must be the vodka. She agreed to go to The Dove for supper with him. As they walked along by the river, she was comforted by

20

her companion. Michael was relaxed, and now and again managed to make her laugh. But wasn't he the sort of man to look relaxed, whatever he was truly thinking? He'd said he understood her anxieties. She wasn't being panicky or unreasonable. Doubts and questions came flooding back. But she swam over them. There was nothing to be done until the next day.

Michael was right, the crowded pub, the noise and festivity, were what she needed. They bought plates of shepherd's pie and Roz found to her surprise that she was hungry. They returned to Bowling House arm in arm. There was a sliver of moon showing through the budding trees, the tide was out, revealing acres of gleaming mud and pebbles and brave masses of grassy stuff like reeds.

'How are the Hammersmith digs?' asked Roz, stopping at the gate of the house.

'They're okay. The houses have been tarted up, though. Very cutesie. However, I'm not staying in Hammersmith tonight. I'm not letting you sleep here alone. You'll frighten yourself into fits.'

'Of course I won't!'

'I know, I know, you think it's years since girls were scared by empty houses, don't you? Ally would come on very hot and strong about that. Okay, so girls aren't scared when they're alone at night in a dam' great place like this. Well, you may not be, but I am. You feel fine now but it won't last, food and drink and chat never do. I'm staying. So you can forget your feminist principles for the moment.'

Roz shrugged with the air of a girl who thought him unnecessarily silly. She said nothing as they went into the house. The thought uppermost in her mind wasn't fear of being alone but the question of whether Michael wanted to make love to her. Most men seemed to. But she never used sex like that, as a solace, a balm for a bruised heart. In spite of beginning to feel miserable again she decided that if he did make a move, she would say no.

She did not switch on the lights and moonlight poured through the high stained-glass window with the colours of St

21

Agnes's Eve. Michael looked solid, thought Roz. Which was more than Sophy was.

'Roz?'

'Mmm?' She was standing staring at nothing.

'Could you just indicate where I am to sleep?'

'Okay.'

They went up the stairs not touching, each conscious of the other's physical nearness as if they could feel the warmth. She took him down a corridor into a comfortable pleasantly furnished bedroom. There was even a private bathroom. Michael peered into it, admiring the thick pale blue carpet, the mirrors, luxury.

'Slightly different from my sleeping bag in Hammersmith. Your Gran seems somewhat rich.'

'I suppose she is.'

'And you're spoilt rotten.'

'No such thing. She can be quite strict about money. Generous, you know, but only up to a point. She and her brother, my great uncle, inherited a lot years ago from some relative or other. That's my great uncle, Jack Hayward.' She indicated a framed pen and ink sketch over the fireplace. The drawing was in a Topolski-style, thick lines and squiggles, and Michael took in a man who was elderly and tough. He was in profile, with combed-back hair and spectacles; a pipe between his teeth. He looked sturdy and strong.

'What is he like?'

'I dunno. We've never had anything to say to each other. Now I think of it, I don't believe we've had a conversation alone in our lives.'

'You don't like him?'

'I didn't say that.'

'Your voice did. It was cold. Anyway,' he continued, sitting down on the bed, 'how come he's your grandmother's brother and you and he don't talk?'

'I only see him at Christmas. Gran goes to the Cotswolds – that's where he lives – alone the other times. When I do get dragged there and Gran happens not to be in the room, he manages to leave before I speak. Or else puts his head into the drinks cupboard and you can't talk to somebody's back.'

'You can if you're determined to.'

Roz stood looking at the man in the drawing, head thrust forward, pipe at an angle. She had never since her childhood been able to guess a single one of her great uncle's thoughts. She yawned. She was tired and the drink made her head spin. The squiggles in the drawing danced in front of her eyes.

Next morning Michael Chance slept late. The bed was comfortable, the room which overlooked the garden was extraordinarily quiet for London; walls built long before Vanbrugh or Hawksmoor designed the homes of the nobility, were as thick as the walls of a palace. When he woke the sun was edging the curtains. He groped for his watch and saw with surprise that it was almost ten o'clock.

He fell out of the bed, remembered he was wearing nothing, pulled on his jeans and opened the bathroom door to the smell of coffee and the beat of Radio One.

Roz was in the kitchen, wearing jeans and a jacket; her pallor had not left her. Everything was in order. There were biscuits, jam, and some dried milk mixed in a jug. She was sitting at the table cradling a mug.

'I forgot to shop but at least there's coffee. I looked in at eight and you were still dead to the world.'

'Sorry.'

'Why?' said Roz, more relaxed than on the previous evening. The first shock had gone and her youth had persuaded her that her grandmother was not, like the Sealyham, crawling away to die. Sophy, Roz decided, would make a big scene about dying, there had always been a melodramatic quality in her. Like a Victorian duchess she would leave detailed instructions about her own memorial service and choose sentimental poems to be read. Besides, a person who disappeared as thoroughly as Sophy had done was scarcely likely to be ill. You needed energy to organize a vanishing. You needed forethought and probably air tickets. If you're ill, there is the problem of an ambulance. One way and another Roz had argued herself into a better frame of mind. But she was still miserable over Sophy, and hollow in her stomach.

She moved over to make room for him at the kitchen table, pulling up a stool. He sat down, accepting the hot coffee with a smile. His hair was in spikes, he was unshaven and because he was dark, resembled an Italian gangster in some old-time movie, thought Roz with faint approval. When he had eaten and drunk in silence for a while he said, 'I feel more human now. Well? What's our plan?'

'*We* haven't one.'

'You mean you'll take the letter at its face value. Jolly good. You can stay here in style, and run up bills on asparagus and champagne.'

'Oh, funny joke. I'm leaving in half an hour.'

'Where are we going?'

'*We* are going nowhere, Michael. Thanks for the offer but I shall do this alone.' She spoke without gratitude. 'And since I ought to go soon, if you want a bath you'd better hurry.'

He put down his coffee mug and said mildly, 'Might one ask where you're going?'

'To see my great uncle.'

'What makes you think that will do any good?'

'Oh, come *on*,' she said irritably. 'It's obvious, Mary DuCann doesn't know any more than I do where Gran's gone, but she agreed with me that my great uncle is the one who's sure to know. Gran always confides in him. She tells him everything. And I've often thought she's the only woman in the world he rates, he thinks the rest of us real idiots. I ought to set Ally on him. Anyway, that's where I'm going. I've packed some stuff in case I stay the night at his house and I'm driving there this morning. It's near Chipping Norton.'

Michael Chance digested the news. Conscious that a man in a grubby vest and with last night's beard usually lost any arguments but those helped by violence, he went upstairs. Roz followed him a moment later, flourishing an electric razor.

'Who does *that* belong to?' He was surprised.

'I use it to shave my legs.'

'Then I'm not sure I'm going to use it,' he said and she made a face at him. The razor was newish and in a black leather case. Taking it, he said without thinking, 'This house has everything except its owner.' And was sorry when he saw her face.

When he returned downstairs, feeling and looking considerably better, Roz's luggage was on the oak chest in the hall. It was not the heavy stuff he had lugged for her yesterday but a neat zip bag of the kind he used for squash. He found her in the garden, picking the deadheads off the daffodils.

'Oh good. Now I can go,' she said, standing up and stretching, looking, with her marmalade-coloured hair, like a cat. Her mouth was half open as if she were drinking the sunlight, and for a moment he badly wanted to kiss her.

She yawned. 'Thanks for stopping last night. Maybe it was a good idea after all. I'll call you when I get back. *If* I get back.'

'Let me come with you, Roz,' he suddenly said.

She gave a slight laugh, saying it was kind of him but out of the question. Her great uncle wasn't going to be at all pleased at her turning up out of the blue. If she arrived with somebody he did not know, it would make things worse.

'Don't take me along, then. I'll wait at a local pub or something.'

She shook her head and refused a second time. At the way she said no, he asked himself why he was bothering. She was brisk and ungracious in spite of what he'd done for her yesterday. She could get on with it, he thought. Yet as they left the house in all its empty beauty he felt slightly desolate. She went to her car and, climbing in, wound down the window to say goodbye. Did he think he saw the same desolation in her pale face? 'Let me give you my Hammersmith number. I shall be there for two or three days,' he said, scribbling it on the back of an envelope and handing it to her. 'You'll call me?'

'Okay, if there's anything to tell. There may not be.'

'But call me anyway,' he said, and touched her cold hand.

Roz was relieved when she drove away. Michael Chance disturbed her. She didn't want to think about love at present.

She didn't want to think about it at all. She was occupied, preoccupied, with Sophy's desertion. Why did it make her feel so sad? She had completely persuaded herself that Sophy could not be seriously ill, that had been a daft idea. Yet now she was sure Sophy was in good health, the pain at her going seemed worse.

Roz had no experience of being thrown over; her only lover, Peter, had gone to Australia, but that had been arranged months before she ever met him. Their affair had been, in a way, based upon goodbyes. No other man since then had touched her heart, she had been free of love. But how many girls she'd known, and men too, had been rejected. How many hours she had spent trying uselessly to comfort them. It seemed to Roz that they did not only suffer from loss but from surprise. They would ask forlornly, 'Why couldn't he or she love me?' As if they were so lovable that to be abandoned was a mystery, a tormenting mystery. Now it was her turn. Why couldn't Sophy have loved her enough to share whatever reason had made her vanish into thin air? This one action, cruel, sudden, seemed to have destroyed the very foundation of their affection, as if Roz had discovered that the house of her life had rotten floorboards in every room. Until she found out why Sophy had gone, Roz knew that she couldn't forgive her.

It took nearly two hours to reach Chipping Norton; it was a fine Saturday morning and everybody who owned a car, which meant everybody, was merrily driving out. Roz was not free of traffic until she had left Chipping Norton behind and driven into the country where the hedges still grew, thorny and high, and the ditches had begun to fill with buttercups. She passed a mansion whose owner bred racehorses; there were three or four of the delicate creatures standing under a chestnut tree. At last she reached the long sloping road which led to her uncle's house. Fields and woods spread away into a distance hazy and blueish, it was a glorious day. When she opened the car window, she could smell the spring.

At a dip in the long incline was Fuchsia Cottage, where Jack Hayward had lived for as long as Roz could remember.

Sophy had once told her he had bought the house at the end of the war from a friend who needed ready money: it had cost him five hundred pounds.

The house, incorrectly named a cottage, was a sturdy building of local stone, dove-coloured, unremarkable, with rambler roses growing contentedly under the windows, and a well-kept smallish gravel drive. A passer-by would imagine it a typical family house, full of children whose parents, leaning from upstairs windows, would shout instructions to small figures mounting bicycles or digging in flower beds which should be left untouched. Some little girl ought to trot up on a pony. But no parents leaned out from the first floor, no mufflered children stood, faces upturned, and no bicycle bells annoyingly rang. There wasn't the sign of a pony. Fuchsia Cottage was as quiet as a church, except for the sound of a tiny stream which ran, non-stop, in a ditch in front of the drive. In summer it sprouted yellow irises. There was a half-acre or so of garden at the back of Fuchsia Cottage, which was where Sophy's brother spent most of his time. At Christmas when Roz was on her duty visit, Jack would make excuses to go out into the freezing garden to look at frost-bitten bushes or pick up iron-hard dead leaves.

Turning into the drive, Roz felt nervous. She had never been here alone before. Don't be wet, she told herself, it's true you don't like him, and he doesn't like you, but so what? You are not visting Dracula. She had a sudden image of her great uncle in a black silk cape lined with scarlet, his eye-teeth very long, grinning at her. She grinned back. He must be at home, for his car, oldish and winkingly clean, was parked outside the house. She pressed the bell.

In her thoughts she saw him, hearing the sound, looking up from *The Times*, then returning to it again. Typical, thought Roz. Nobody came to the door, and she wondered why Mrs Matthews, who did some housework for him, hadn't answered. She was always there to greet Sophy and Roz when they arrived at Christmas; a prim elderly body, devoted to Jack Hayward and the reason the house was so well kept. But of course it was Saturday. Mrs Matthews never came to

Fuchsia Cottage at weekends. Roz rang again. At her third ring, she kept her finger deliberately on the bell for a long time Still there was no answer, except from a thrush in the bushes. And then she realized how stupid she was being. The sun shone down, warming the top of her head; it blessed the young leaves of the roses, the air was chattering with birds. Where else would her great uncle be than in the garden?

There was a wrought-iron gate on the left of the house, it was unlocked, and Roz went along a paved terrace and arrived in a garden with one of the loveliest views in the Cotswolds. Fields. Woods. A church spire. A sort of dream in the country which pretended that nothing had changed. A man was by the rose beds, with his back to her: a broad stocky back, clad in an old-fashioned checked jacket, with two vents as if for riding. He straightened up, to lean towards another bush, and for a moment she saw her great uncle in profile: the steely hair, inexpressive face, thick neck, glasses. She always marvelled, when she saw him, that this thick-set old man, this Dutch burgher, could be the brother of her radiant grandmother.

'Uncle Jack?' she called, coming towards him across the wet grass. He turned around, the pruning clippers open in one hand. In the other he held a long shoot of soft green rose leaves.

'Hello,' he said.

2

He betrayed no surprise at seeing the girl who never came to his house except once a year, never in his life by herself and always by arrangement. He faced her with a vague smile. But Roz saw that his eyes were wary.

'Popped in on your way to town, have you?' he said, making it perfectly plain that he wished to go on with his pruning. Before Roz could reply he added, 'End of Hilary, is it? How are you getting on at Oxford, none too well, I imagine.'

He chuckled, adding, 'The distaff side of our family have never been much cop at their books.'

'I'm not doing so badly, I like my subjects and I'm lucky to have one smashing tutor. Haven't seen the others for the last two terms.'

'Good. Good.' He wasn't really listening. His eyes strayed towards the roses.

'I came to ask your advice,' said Roz winningly. She found she could not be blunt with this man. Talking to Jack Hayward was like standing by an animal's den and keeping very still until it poked out its head.

'Not sure I'm qualified to give advice any more. Used to charge for it. They tell me lawyers' prices are shooting up. They weren't too merry and bright in my day unless you happened to be Birkett.' She had no idea what he was talking about.

They stood blinking at each other in the dazzling sun, a girl with bright hair and a white face, dressed in the universal clothes of today, jeans and shabby jacket which could be a man's; and her elderly relative shabby in a different way, immortally so. He had once worn an 18th century peruke.

'Like some instant coffee?' he enquired, apparently relenting. Or capitulating since it was clear the young woman intended to stay. She had a look of his sister this morning; he knew that set of the chin and it did not please him. The weather was just right for pruning.

They went into the house through a back door which in summer was absurdly wreathed in Dorothy Perkins roses like bunches of pink grapes. Jack had green fingers: Sophy always said if he put a piece of firewood into the ground, it would sprout. The kitchen was tidy, not a dirty cup or saucepan in sight: it had a bachelor look. He busied himself switching on the electric kettle and taking from a china cupboard two flower-wreathed cups, one decorated with violets, the other with pansies. Flowers, thought Roz, had taken her uncle over. Not people, though.

He made the coffee in silence, placed the cups on an antique mahogany butler's tray and stepped back for her to precede him into the sitting room. It was sunny, and the French windows were open on to stone steps leading to the side of the house. The bookshelves were built in on either side of the fireplace and divided Jack Hayward's life neatly into two. On one side were huge old volumes, leather-bound, some with their spines beginning to crumble, and every single one connected with the law. On the other side were bright-covered books, big and small, on trees, flowers, on rockeries, bulbs, annuals, perennials. These were much-read and the vivid covers worn and torn.

'Might as well make yourself comfortable,' he said, pulling up the best chair. He gave her a place with her back to the sun which dazzled somewhat; he himself sat down in its glare, blinking and taking off his spectacles to polish them. Immediately he removed them, his face lost its power. He looked as helpless as a baby, even the deep lines down the sides of his nose appeared effaced. He gazed myopically at the glasses, finished the polishing and replaced them. A formidable man then looked at her.

'Uncle Jack. You must know why I've come.'

He said nothing to that, but stirred his coffee, adding some kind of sugar substitute from a silver snuff box he took from his jacket pocket.

'Of course it's about Gran who's upped and gone,' said Roz.

He stirred his coffee with concentration like a woman stirring a Christmas pudding.

'Uncle Jack, you *know* she's gone, don't you?'

He glanced up at last. 'She did inform me. As she apparently informed you or you wouldn't be here, would you?'

'But *what* did she inform you, as you call it?'

'I don't think I understand,' he said. He never called Roz by her name and he didn't now. 'She said she was going on some kind of holiday. She told me she was leaving you a word and you could make yourself comfortable in the house, look after yourself, mm? What more is there? It is all perfectly reasonable.' He finished with the bland expression of somebody who had given a completely satisfactory reply. He'd told her nothing. But had she ever thought he would?

She resented the old man sitting there in the sun, drinking coffee, the pruners sticking out of his pocket and dragging the jacket out of shape. She didn't recall a single occasion when she and Jack had exchanged a sensible remark. Sophy always laughed when Roz complained about him. That was how Jack was: born secretive and shy.

'Shy!' cried Roz in derision. 'Yes, shy,' repeated Sophy. Her brother always had been; why, when he was a boy ... and she told stories of the past in which Roz could not recognize her great uncle. To Roz people were as they were: to quote an Australian friend at Oxford, they were set like a jelly. She could never imagine some antique don as young and passionate, some fat woman JP as a long-legged beauty. She could not accept that Jack Hayward had ever been other than abrupt and bloody-minded, courteously rude and farcically selfish. Sophy once told her Jack had been deeply in love; that had made Roz laugh.

Now when he remarked that what her grandmother had done was 'perfectly reasonable' Roz wanted to shout and swear. She knew that would get her nowhere except possibly back into the car. Her opponent was studying her impassively.

'I was very upset when I found Gran had gone. It was a shock. It's so unlike her. So worrying. Aren't *you* worried?' she said accusingly.

Jack Hayward made the kind of sound rarely heard today, a sort of 'Pshaw'.

'No, I am not and neither should you be. Your grandmother does silly things on occasions. Very silly things. This – ah – holiday is one of them. Take no notice. Get on with your own affairs. Like doing some work during the vac,' he added with malice.

'I can't take no notice! There's something horrible about her just disappearing – it's eerie—'

'What a song and dance about a woman taking herself off for a few days.'

'Will it be a few days?' She had spoken too quickly.

He rubbed his chin with the flat of his hand.

'Can't say that exactly. Not sure.'

'What *are* you sure about? What did Gran tell you?'

He was bored. He stood up, shambling over to take the coffee cup, saw she had not finished and apologized. Roz said thank you but she had had sufficient. He picked up her cup.

'Don't you like the way I make it?' Taking the tray he went out in the direction of the kitchen.

Roz sat looking at the law books. Some of them were enormous. She wanted to creep out behind her great uncle and throw the largest at his head. He infuriated her. What *was* all this? Where was Sophy and why wouldn't he tell her? And why did he treat her like an idiot? But that was nothing new. He always had. She guessed he had now escaped out into the garden. Sure enough, when she went to the kitchen window, with its heart-stopping Cotswold view of gentle hills and rolling fields and a lonely church spire, there he was bent over the roses again.

I'm damned if I'm going to leave, she thought. He wants me to, so I shan't. I'll hang about and annoy him.

For all his abruptness, selfishness, unbreakable habits, set face and half-blind yet steady eyes, for all the reserve he'd built round him like a palisade, she had noticed from the time she was a child that Jack had an extraordinary politeness.

His manners were wonderful. When she thought of her own friends with their 'Hi's' and 'Okay, fines', and the equality which Ally and Co demanded, which meant that when you were on a bus you never got a seat and young men and fat men did, Roz found Jack's manners almost beautiful. They interested her. His past did not. She couldn't believe he had ever been young. She knew, of course, that he had been a brilliant barrister; when he spoke there was a resonance in his voice, you wanted to listen to it. Once, five years ago, he had given a lecture at a literary club on Fiction and the Law and Sophy had taken her to hear him. He had been superb. But it was not Jack's career which intrigued Roz, it was the courtesy; it ought to be sold at Sotheby's. 'A fine last-century essence of particular interest to collectors. Unique. Am I offered a hundred thousand pounds?'

Jack's good manners meant that if she wanted to stay here at Fuchsia Cottage, although he was longing to see the back of her, she could. As a gesture, she washed up the sentimental cups and put them carefully away. Then went back into the garden. He had nearly finished pruning the smaller rose bed and was standing with his hands on his non-existent waist, studying the bushes he had clipped.

'Hello,' he said as if she had only just arrived. 'These are Gallicas. Old shrub roses. They're supposed to thrive on poor soil and mine's nothing to write home about. That one,' pointing at a bush about four foot high, 'is a Belle De Creçy. Only produces solitary flowers, and then only in late June and July. Not worth the trouble, I shall grub it out.'

'I've heard of Belle de Creçy. Doesn't it have a wonderful smell?'

'Not bad. But it's got to go.'

'Poor thing, it looks so healthy. Couldn't you give it to somebody?'

'Who'd want it except some rose fanatic and I don't know any of those, thank heaven. The great thing in life is to cut your losses. It's a rule I always follow. Cut your losses.'

Roz was always floored when Jack trotted out his clichés, quotations, catchprases and aphorisms. He would murmur Softly Softly Catchee Monkee if Roz appeared impatient, or Sufficient Unto the Day when his sister wanted to make plans. He liked to quote Omar Khayyam when he gave Sophy a drink: 'Before Life's Liquor in its Cup be dry'. He used the phrases in conversation like a cricketer blocking a ball.

'Uncle,' said Roz, after a pause by the rose beds. Her voice had the offhand casualness of the young. 'I wonder if I could stay the night?' Before he could reply she added that she would like to go and look at the bluebell wood, and perhaps call on the people at The Linden Arms while she happened to be here.

'Why not?' said her great uncle, 'why not? Make yourself at home. Spare room's always ready, Mrs Matthews tells me. Says she airs the bed. God knows why, seems to be expecting me to have visitors. Well, for once she's right.'

Good manners prevailed. He must realize very well that she was only hanging about to try and coax him into telling her something. But the wily old bird appeared quite willing for her to stay. He had the air of a man amused at the impertinence of the chit who imagined she would succeed in making him change his mind.

'I'll take my bag upstairs, then,' said Roz.

'Good, good. Oh, by the by, can't take you out for a bite this evening, I'm afraid. I'm dining with Lionel White, old sparring partner of mine. Remember him?'

'Yes. He makes Gran laugh.'

'His jokes aren't bad, but he's a fox. Curious when you come to think of it, that's what he named his house. Foxholes. Could you get a chop at The Linden Arms, do you think?'

'Of course.'

He nodded and turned back to his contemplation of the doomed Belle de Creçy.

Roz spent a curious day. They had bread and cheese in the kitchen for a late lunch, and then her great uncle returned to work in the garden until dusk. She sat on the terrace in a deck chair he had dragged out of a rickety summerhouse for her. Wisely, she had brought books. Oxford books. She spent two profitable hours on work, followed by half an hour on a new paperback as a reward.

When twilight blurred the colours of grass and trees, and the birds loudly whistled and it was chill, Jack came across the grass, rubbing earthy hands, and said hospitably, 'Time for a drink.'

'Great.'

'Put back the chair, would you? And – here's the key – lock the summerhouse.'

What's in it to nick? thought Roz. She carried the chair into a gimcrack shed-like structure, where it joined a rustic table and some stools and a large spider immobile in his perfect web.

In the house, Jack turned on the lights and put a match to a fire expertly laid by the absent Mrs Matthews: it crackled into welcome. He went to a high corner cupboard with double doors and disappeared inside, his head and shoulders hidden, while he prepared Roz a Cinzano, and a Scotch for himself.

'But still the Vine her ancient Ruby yields,' he remarked, handing her the glass, with a smile, 'except that it's the wrong colour.' He sipped his drink and added that this was the best moment of the day.

'Yes. It's good,' agreed Roz.

The fire made a small drama, rushing at the bone-dry twigs.

'Uncle Jack. About Gran.'

'Oh, come now,' he said, 'we have settled that. She's gone off to have some time to herself and you're on your own, and that's how it is. You do surprise me.'

'Why?'

'Fussing. At your age. Nothing to fuss about.'

The girl thinned her lips. She detested the word, felt frustrated and to a degree foolish and knew that was what he wanted. She drank her drink, looking across at him while he looked into the fire. The inscrutable face was hiding something.

'I can't understand why you won't tell me,' she suddenly said. 'I know you want me to shut up but I *can't*. Where is she? What's happened? Why am I not allowed to know?'

'What a lot of stuff,' he said, his tone as disapproving as a schoolmaster's. 'Your grandmother is fine. I have told you so. I explained why she is not at Bowling House, she wants some time to herself. I can only presume there is another reason for this agitation of yours. However, in answer to your questions, I have already told you that Sophy is perfectly well, that you should get on with your own affairs and spend your time profitably. We'll close this subject now, if you please.'

Apart from her previous longing, to pull out the big law book and heave it at him there and then, Roz was out of ammunition.

'Money, of course,' said Jack suddenly.

His voice changed, it had more life in it and Roz had a moment's wild hope that she was about to learn something. She leaned forward, gripping the stem of the empty glass.

'The little matter of your finances,' he said.

Hope dropped like a stone.

'I meant to tell you earlier, but it slipped my mind. Now that my sister's away, I have power of attorney. She's asked me to up your allowance, which I've done, and of course it will continue to be paid into your bank. If you have any extra expenses – reasonable ones – of the kind Sophy used to help with, you can call on me.'

He waited for a reply. For thanks, perhaps. All the girl said, in an empty voice and after a long pause, was, 'That means she really has gone.'

Jack Hayward was a man who went in for sniffs, grunts, pshaw's, expressive coughs. He'd used the techniques when he was a barrister. He now made a blowing sound rather like that made by a hippopotamus, an animal with the same powerful figure and wrinkled skin as himself. He crossed the room to disappear into the drinks cupboard, asking her, with his back turned, if he could pour her a second Cinzano? She refused. He came back to his chair with another Scotch, looked first at the fire and then at his great niece. She was controlling herself, but only just, and put him in mind of those occasions when highly strung women came to consult him at his chambers and he was landed with them. They would burst into sobs. Women were the devil.

'Repetition is a bore,' he mildly remarked. 'But you appear to require it. I repeat. Your grandmother is perfectly all right but behaving in a way I consider silly. She has gone off on her own. I can tell you no more. Now. Change your mind and allow me to fill your glass. In quarter of an hour, I fear, I must go and change.'

Later, he returned downstairs to say goodnight and to enquire if she would need a hot-water bottle. 'These spring evenings are parky.' He gave her a front door key. 'Don't be late, you need your beauty sleep.' He drove away.

Roz had a bath, washed her hair, changed into a clean shirt and drove to the nearby village, and the smart restaurant-cum-pub where she and Sophy stayed when they spent Christmases with Jack.

The Sinclair-Groves, husband and wife, were making more money than they had imagined in their wildest dreams and becoming grander all the time; they were pleased to see her. She had a delicious but expensive meal, read her paperback, had coffee by yet another log fire and drove back to Fuchsia Cottage. The house was in darkness.

The trouble with me is that I'm sorry for myself, she thought. It was an unusual emotion to Roz, and she considered it a despicable one. But she hadn't known, until her grandmother had left her, just how much Sophy was the centre of her life. Roz's parents had become ghostly figures now. It was eleven years since the plane crash when they had been killed. Polly, Sophy's only child, had not resembled her in the least; she had been fair, selfish, a little cold. Roz, when very young, had always noticed that when her mother embraced her, the kiss was so quick. It never seemed to last. After Polly was dead, Roz used to think about those kisses and wonder whether she had misjudged her mother. Perhaps Polly just wasn't the sort of person who liked to hug. Roz's father Tom had been a journalist, clever and over-busy. He drank too much, but he was funny and lively and his wife had adored him. They had been mutually devoted and although they had made a fuss of Roz, it was perfunctory, like the kisses. They only needed each other.

Roz had expensive nannies, probably paid for by Sophy, and was sent to expensive schools. When her parents were gone, so tragically, so suddenly, the shock to the little girl had worn off soon. People said the child would suffer later, she was sure to; she never had.

It was Sophy who had rescued her, warmed her. Sophy was everything Roz's mother was not. She was impulsive and demonstrative and difficult and demanding and fond. She was cross and irresistible. Roz grew up from the age of nine warmed by a personality bright as fire. Now a bucket of water had doused the flames. There was nothing to look at but wet ashes.

Like a girl waiting at a window, a woman waiting by the telephone, a man rushing to the post, she mutely asked the lost beloved excruciating questions. Where have you gone? Why did you leave me? How could you give me up? Why did you never love me? Because she was now sure Sophy was not ill – in duty bound Jack would have at least told her that – the desertion seemed worse. And how could she blame Jack for his discretion? He was a lawyer by nature as well as trade. It was Sophy she blamed.

The house was quiet but not unfriendly. She let herself in and climbed the steep staircase to her own bedroom, peering into her great uncle's with a spark of curiosity. It was tidy, but so was the rest of the house. It wasn't grand like her grandmother's luxurious and feminine bedroom in Bowling House. The bedcover was as old as the hills and faded with laundering. There was a photograph of Sophy on her wedding day on a desk in the corner, a desk too small for a man. Roz did not bother to look at the picture which she knew by heart. It showed Sophy, beautiful and old-fashioned in 1940s gear, veil, satin, arriving at the church on her father's arm, her veil down, carrying lilies and wearing white for purity. I bet *that* wasn't the truth, thought Roz, although she knew little of her grandmother's past life.

She went down the corridor to her own room. The double bed looked large and lonely.

And quite suddenly she remembered Michael Chance. She sat reflecting, but only for a moment, before reaching for her shoulder bag. She returned down the stairs to the telephone and dialled his Hammersmith number. She listened to it ringing, hoping, quite longing for him to be there. But people never were when you wanted them to be.

When a voice answered she said at once, 'Michael?'

'Roz! What a surprise. A good one. You're back home already. So what happened?'

'No, I'm still in the Cotswolds and nothing's happened. I'm staying the night with my great uncle. He's out at present. He won't say a word.'

'Surely he told you something?'

'Not he. He obviously knows what's happened and where she is, and all he said was she was okay and not to worry. Stuff like that.'

A very small pause.

'Do you think you might take his advice?'

'No. I can't let it go. I'm such a fool.'

'Never. When am I going to see you?'

She chewed a strand of her hair.

'Do you want to?'

Why did the question, used in such games, give him a slight pang of the heart? Did she only want a reaction because she was at a loose end, and her great uncle wouldn't help her, and things were in a mess?

'Sure. I want to see you very much. You know that.'

'I wanted to hear you say it. I'd like to see you too.'

'When? Are you staying on there, Roz?'

'Only till tomorrow.'

They talked for a while and nothing they said was what they meant or what they heard in each other's voices. Sex came over the telephone wires.

Upstairs, she undressed and climbed into the big bed. She lay down and shut her eyes, thinking that she had been right. There had indeed been a demon in the corner yesterday at Oxford, waiting to make her unhappy.

When Jack Hayward drove back to the house just after eleven, and went carefully up the stairs which creaked, he opened her door and looked in. It was the old habit from when his sister had been a child – as if to be sure she was asleep and safe. The light from windows across which Roz had forgotten to pull the curtains was half-starry, and fell on the bed, the humped pillows, the sleeping face and disordered tawny hair. She was breathing like a child.

He nodded to himself and crept off to his own room like a man treading on glass.

Daylight woke Roz, and in the first moment of consciousness, looking up at an unfamiliar ceiling and an old-fashioned centre light, she wondered where the devil she was.

Ah, she thought, remembering. Of course. I'm in Uncle Jack's spare room and my Gran has gone.

She lay for a while, thinking about things, seeing how pitiful her struggles had been up until now. Jack had won hands down. But she had slept for nearly nine hours and felt strong again. How strong will *he* be, she thought? She made up her mind that she would have one final try. Why not, after all she was still here. I think this time I'll nag, thought Roz. He looks like a man no woman would dare to nag; it'll surprise him.

She went downstairs in search of breakfast; there was no sign of her elderly relative, not a sound or indication that he had come home last night. But she had seen his car in the drive so he must be upstairs asleep. It was surely unusual for somebody of his age to sleep so well and for so long: Sophy was always wide awake and making tea at half past six.

In the kitchen Roz made toast, found some home-made marmalade, brewed coffee and looked through the kitchen

40

window at a morning as untouched as the beginning of Saxon history. Oxfordshire was waiting for her out there and she couldn't resist it. She almost ran out of doors.

She had told Michael Chance that she only visited her great uncle once a year at Christmastime, but there had been a single occasion when Sophy had brought her here in the spring. Roz had never forgotten the visit because of a certain walk with her grandmother to Stirrup's Wood. Now on this perfect morning she made a pilgrimage, taking the same road, turning after ten minutes or so in to a narrow rutted lane thick with mud from farm tractors. She looked about for the gate. There it was, after all those years, locked with the same padlock she and Sophy had examined; covered with rust it had begun to look as if it belonged in the Tower of London. The gate, too, was in a bad way, some of its bars green and beginning to split from their nails. Roz climbed the gate and jumped down into squelchy grass.

Through the thin leaves the sun threw freckled light broken by patches of shade. In a moment of superstition, as in games played by children, Roz thought: 'If the flowers are out, it means Uncle Jack will tell me.'

She made her way into the wood.

As far as she could see, threaded in and out among the trunks of many trees, in places thick as lakes of mauveish blue, in places beginning to bud in dark purple, were bluebells. They were everywhere. They bent their heads. They sprang erect like spears of folded green buds. They grew through the brambles, round the logs and at the lumpy boles of the larger trees. They *were* the wood. She sat down on a blackened log round which they ebbed and flowered and saw the good omen and smiled.

Hope had sprung up in her. Here were Sophy's bluebells, and a few minutes away was Sophy's brother, who would – who must – give Roz the comfort she needed. And it was spring, and in London there was Michael Chance. She stooped down and picked a few flowers, scarcely enough to fill a tea-cup. Their scent was fainter, but as sweet as cultivated hyacinths. She swung back to Fuchsia Cottage, almost running.

The front door was open and her great uncle was standing, hands in his pockets, sunning himself like an old dog. He wore the same tweed jacket, the same baggy grey trousers. He looked as if yesterday and today had been rolled into one and there had been no dinner party, no night's sleep or bath or shave. Time did not bother to touch him.

'Bluebells, eh?' he said. 'You've brought good weather.'

'Haven't I, just?'

'I suppose you got yourself some breakfast. Couldn't tell by the state of the kitchen, Watson. Not a single clue for Holmes to discover.'

'I mustn't leave dirty dishes or you won't ask me again,' Roz said gaily.

He laughed like a man who thought the idea of a return visit sufficiently idiotic, and they went into the house.

The fire was freshly burning in the drawing room, piled with small logs. A tray of coffee was laid.

'Sit down, sit down, I thought we'd have elevenses,' he said, ruining the effect by adding that he supposed she would be gone before lunch.

'Unless you offer me bread and cheese again,' said Roz, still euphoric, and sniffing the flowers.

'Well, I'd like to. But today I am lunching with the Savages. That's good, isn't it? Lunch with the savages. Might end up in the pot myself. Nice couple, came to the district two years ago, retired of course. She's a pretty woman. Actress once, I believe.'

'I'm sorry we can't lunch, Uncle.'

Strengthened, vital, she said rashly, 'I know you think I'm being really stupid – but oh, please reconsider! Surely you know how I feel? Can't you at least tell me *something*?'

She looked straight at him and it was like facing something carved out of stone. Modern, or thousands of years old and discovered in a lost temple on the far side of the world. Rounded, mysterious, polished, slippery. Marble? Granite?

He felt for his pipe, filled it, lit it and began to smoke. She was unused to the smell which was pungent and not unpleasant, with a tang like ginger.

42

'You're making a bit of a nuisance of yourself, aren't you? You remind me of Sophy sometimes. Now, why not look at this sensibly, as I suggested last night. You're in your last term at Oxford with mountains of work to get through, if I recall rightly. You've enough money. And your grandmother has let you have the run of Bowling House, which is damned generous of her. It seems to me the only reason you keep asking questions I don't intend to answer is vulgar curiosity. Just vulgar curiosity.' He repeated the phrase as if it pleased him. Roz expected him to add that it killed the cat. She said nothing and he continued, puffing at the pipe.

'You must stop, you know. Stop asking me, stop asking *yourself* where she's gone. If you're a free agent, isn't she? If a woman wants to take a holiday and tell nobody about it but her lawyer, no reason why she shouldn't. Call it a truce. You go your way, Sophy goes hers. She's done her duty by you. More than done it, in my opinion. Now, I must toddle. Angela Savage asked me to turn up early, she's invited some gardening people she thinks will interest me. I doubt it. Gardening chaps are usually a damned bore. Ah well ...'

He got to his feet as if to say 'Off you go.'

'But, Uncle –'

He looked at her, then, straight and strong. His eyes were dark brown like the eyes of an Italian or a Greek, the only thing he had in common with her grandmother. The glance was as steady as a rock and it held a warning. Roz literally quailed. Hadn't Sophy told her once that Jack was almost never angry but woe betide anybody who made him so. The girl muttered, with ill grace, that she supposed she had better shut up. She didn't seem to be getting anywhere.

'No. You're not,' he agreed cheerfully.

'All I can say is, you're as bad as Gran,' she burst out.

The remark took the elderly man's fancy for a moment. He appeared to consider it in the same way that he had considered the Belle de Creçy, looking at its possibilities and finally rejecting them. He noticed the girl was pale in the face again, although she had not looked too bad when he saw her coming back from the wood. The little bunch of bluebells, poor things, were wilting on the table. He pointed at them.

'Best put those in water. They never last.'

'Do I have to go *now*?' She sounded fourteen.

Good manners returned in a surge; he looked quite shocked.

'Stay as long as you like.' He spoke like a victor. 'Stay tonight if you wish.'

She shook her head at that and he continued, more cheerfully, why didn't she have an egg or something and then drive back to London? He took her to the front door and showed her a pot of jasmine behind which he and Mrs Matthews always hid a spare set of keys.

'Double lock before you go. Don't forget. And see the back door is bolted in case you happen to go into the garden while you're still here.'

Her closed face and ungracious manner had as little effect on him as if he'd seen a spider scuttling across his path. He turned to say goodbye. Roz did not kiss his elderly cheek. He looked quite disappointed.

'Damn, damn, damn,' said Roz when his car had driven away. She damned everything. Her great uncle for being bloody immoveable, her grandmother for being cruel, herself for being an optimistic fool. She would have damned Michael Chance if she could think of a reason to do so. She was furious and frustrated. What was there to do now? Pack and go. She felt much worse than when she had driven here yesterday. At least then she had half believed her affection and concern for Sophy would persuade her uncle to tell her something. What a pathetic idea. All he'd done was made her feel like a naïve and nosey relative eaten up with curiosity.

She walked angrily round the room and her eye fell on the bluebells. They had lost their solidity and seemed to die as she watched. She marched out to the kitchen, hammered the juicy stems and put them in a tall glass of water where they stood, a miniature blue clump, on the windowsill by the mops and cloths.

Upstairs, she made her bed, a duvet, replaced a bed cover which had been a lace curtain years ago. She packed her bag

44

and still in an evil mood paused at the top of the stairs and pitched it straight down into the hall.

She stood scowling.

And then the idea occurred.

It came like a whisper in her ear, a pull at her sleeve, a muttered 'Idiot! You aren't using your brains.' Wasn't it possible that somewhere in this house she could find the answer to the tormenting question? Her great uncle had said he would not be home until late afternoon – now it was scarcely midday. She was perfectly safe to hunt about. And it was Sunday, she could hear the church bells ringing across the fields this very moment; Sunday meant no Mrs Matthews.

Roz metaphorically rolled up her sleeves.

She spent over an hour behaving like a detective in a TV serial. She combed her great uncle's house room by room, systematically going through drawers and cupboards. She riffled through files and folders, painstakingly went through letters – most of them simply arrangements made by old friends to see him – and clips of bills. She was impressed with Jack Hayward's exactness. The bills were in date order, with comments marked upon them. '? too high. Check c.heating account 6 months ago.' 'Check milk. Surely wrong here?'

She began, logically, with the big desk in the study in the front of the house. It was her main hope and when she began opening drawers she kept thinking she would be certain to find something – anything – to give her the longed-for clue. But the desk held nothing but folders of letters from old colleagues, barristers, a judge or two. There were reports on his shares, and a good many bank statements. Roz was astounded at how much money there was in his current account.

Putting the files carefully back, she imagined how angry he would be if he caught her. She felt like a criminal for a moment or two: until she thought about Sophy again.

There was one excited minute at the desk when Roz caught a glimpse of her grandmother's handwriting and shouted 'At last!' Sophy's writing, bold, rather fanciful, was unmistakable. Roz snatched the letter out, her hands trembling. But the letter was merely a scrawl, six months old, asking Jack what he wanted for his birthday.

'Hopeless you are. I know, I know. Gloves again! And how many pairs have I given you, my darling, and how many *single* gloves have you lost?'

'My darling,' said Roz aloud. How could her grandmother use such an endearment to that old curmudgeon?

Roz went upstairs into his bedroom. She opened drawers filled with shirts, striped or plain white. Underclothes. And suits, old as history, well-pressed and smelling of the dry cleaners. There was nothing in any pocket – no telegram, no scribbled note. Nothing.

At last she gave up. Her search had been an inspiration – and a miserable failure. Fortunately, she was neat-fingered, and nervously careful when she replaced everything she handled. She put the smallest items into their appointed places. A box of paper clips. A roll of Sellotape. A cardboard box full of old seed packets. A piece of green string tied round some pencils, and a rubber which couldn't have been used for years. It was all shiny.

She stood adrift on the landing of the second floor, after going through the boxroom in which there were empty trunks, mouldering luggage made of real leather, a step ladder and some religious pictures with their faces to the wall.

Roz gave a sigh so loud that it reverberated down the stairs like a groan.

Only one room was left – its door ajar. It was what used to be the maids' bedroom, a glorified attic with inward sloping ceiling. Entering the room she saw it had been used as a storing place for junk. The divan bed, hard as iron, looked as if, like Jack's india rubber, it hadn't been used for half a century. There was a white chest of drawers, an old swing mirror, a heap of faded garden cushions, and a positive mountain of books which more thoughtful people would have taken to Oxfam. Long ago, housemaids giggling about the admiring eyes of butchers' boys, had squeezed into this room, sleeping in truckle beds, rising at six to light fires and clean shoes. It was difficult for Roz to accept that her grandmother had known such a time. As well as the books piled in corners there was a long bookshelf-full, the spines faded with the years. Black had turned grey, red to a muddy orange. There was a *Scarlet Pimpernel* with a split back, a French/English dictionary with no back at all, novels by authors Roz did not recognize and a series of *Highways and Byways of English Counties*. On a bottom shelf was a tidier line of volumes all matched in height. There were five. They were stout navy-blue faded into grey and when she knelt down to look at them she saw that on the spine of each was a figure marked in almost-vanished ink.

'1939. April to July.'

'1939. July to Dec.'

'1940 – till F of F.'

And finally the thickest of the volumes,

'1940/41! with the addition of words almost indecipherable, 'the rest.'

Roz squatted on the ground. From student's habit, she started in chronological order, took out the first volume and opened it at the first page. It was a diary. But not only a diary: the book also contained newspaper cuttings, theatre tickets, sketches, pressed flowers whose petals had metamorphosed into thinnest brown paper.

The writing was Sophy's.

'I shall have to hide this if I'm going to tell the truth in it. I must think of somewhere clever. But the fact is I've got to write it down or I shall burst. I've been at the parents for weeks. I'm determined to go to Anne-Marie, and since Bob doesn't mind, why are they being *ridiculous*?

But I shall go! I've made up my mind, and that's all there is to say about that. I shall go and they can't stop me.'

Sophy's voice spoke just then. Vibrant and determined and angry and full of sparkling glittering life. She was nineteen.

PART TWO

3

Everybody kept playing tennis. Sophy liked the game well enough and was entertained when, to her surprise, she pulled off a tricky if erratic shot. But tennis was not a passion with her; it was with her father. Every summer evening after returning home on the London train and driving from the station, he changed into white clothes and went straight out into the garden to the tennis lawn. Friends were invited to partner him, mostly middle-aged friends who lived locally. Their wives, Sophy noticed, never played tennis after reaching the vast age of forty. If there was nobody else on hand, her father demanded that Sophy should join him on the court; he liked playing opposite her because he usually won. On the few occasions when her wild game worked, he was thoroughly put out. He was a very bad sport.

It was May, a perfect evening, gentle and sunny, ideal for the beastly game, thought Sophy. She could hear from her open bedroom window her father's voice calling the score. If she leaned out she could see white-clad figures running to and fro. How long would the game last? She was impatient to speak to her parents, bursting to announce a decision she had made. It was not going to be popular and she wanted to get it over. But while tennis was in progress she would have to wait. This evening her father was playing against Bob Lingard – and Sophy knew in advance who would win. That was a good thing about Bob: he never fudged the score or deliberately missed shots to allow her father to be victor. There were a good many things about Bob which Sophy affectionately approved. She'd had a cavalcade of admirers in the last three years, and most of them had been invited to play tennis with her father. They then had the pathetic idea that by letting Herbert Hayward win, they would earn Sophy's smiles as well as her father's. Men really are boobies, thought the girl. Her father wasn't, but then she didn't respect him either.

She disliked the way he treated her mother, for a start. Herbert behaved like a lord with a serving-maid in some Victorian-medieval verse. Of course it was her mother's own fault, she pandered to him. It was as if her husband unnerved her.

'Herbert will be down in a minute,' she would say at breakfast, nervously cutting the bread.

'Herbert's going to the masonic dinner tonight, Sophy. Could you put in his gold links?'

'No! no! no!' she would cry to one of the young maids in the kitchen. 'You mustn't leave Mr Hayward's shoes like that! You have to remember he likes the *welts* blackened too. Let me show you ...'

The Haywards had two inexpensive sixteen-year-olds from the orphanage to cook and clean. Merry girls who, at Pansy Hayward's suggestion, became keen Girl Guides. Pansy mothered her maids, chose their uniforms and carefully taught them to cook the nursery food Herbert preferred. He liked boiled fish and boiled mutton, steamed canary pudding and semolina. Anything unusual he called foreign muck.

Her father irritated Sophy, but she accepted him with philosophy. She was as accustomed to him as a woman who has lived all her life in a roomful of awkwardly shaped furniture and has learned to move about avoiding bruises.

As for the rest of the sex, men of every age reacted to Sophy in an identical way: young and old, clever or blimpish, they made it clear they admired her and wished to persuade her to stay wherever she – and they – happened to be. In a garden, in the village, in a room, leaving a cinema, outside a shop. 'Do stay, Sophy!' was in their eyes.

Pansy Hayward was plain and modest yet the house was hung with looking-glasses, not for feminine vanity but because it had been the fashion in the Edwardian days of her youth. From every one of these, mahogany or silver-framed, oval gilt or triple-mirrored, Sophy saw her own reflection: thick copper hair and the white skin which went with such colouring, a short nose, a handsome creamy neck. There was a radiance about her. The effect was lustrous, pearly, glowing; she enraptured men.

Sophy had never been vain and rarely thought about her looks; compliments dropped like lead weights on her toes. Her father's middle-aged friends liked to give her paternal pats and squeezes, Sophy was not annoyed; she smiled and somehow drifted out of reach.

Herbert Hayward was uninterested in his beautiful daughter and had no idea of the hot blood throbbing in the bodies of many of his friends. Lust. Love. Neither came into his life; his work as director of a London bank totally absorbed him. He had long since given up embracing his wife, who had never enjoyed sex in any case. The person in the family whom he admired was his son who was as reserved as he was, and went in for the same silences and omissions that were Herbert's speciality.

The realization that her daughter was a beauty came gradually to Pansy, for Sophy did not flower until she was well over fifteen: it was a sudden thing, almost as though one day she was a schoolgirl, a spider in black stockings or white socks, hanging upside down from chairs or sofas or performing dances on the kitchen floor. Then suddenly there was a tiger lily.

It was all the more strange because Sophy remained without vanity, an impulsive demanding hoyden who wanted her own way, quarrelled with her parents though not with her brother and often hid from the men who came knocking at her door.

Pansy saw that Sophy's gift was dangerous and worried over the girl's destiny until the evening when Sophy arrived back from London on an earlier train than usual, swung into

51

the drawing room where her parents were having tea and announced that she was engaged to be married.

'It's Bob Lingard,' added Sophy. She held out a white hand decorated with a sapphire.

Bob Lingard was popular with the Haywards. He was a sailor in the regular Navy, with money and manners in that order in Herbert's mind; fortunately, too, he never showed the least sign of sentimentality over the girl.

Sophy had expected reactions when she announced her engagement, not because her parents did not like her choice but because her father wished to make the decisions on everything she did, even to choosing a husband. She had had a three month battle before he allowed her to buy a car with her own money, put in the post office by her godmother. He had been very angry indeed when she walked out of the shorthand and typing college after failing her shorthand theory test eight times. She declared she preferred to stay at home. Her father eventually ruled that she might do so for three months, after which she must take up some other training. He had, he said, no intention of supporting her.

Sophy promptly found a fiancé.

Her brother worked as a lawyer in the Temple, and had been invited to the summer ball at Dartmouth.

'The Navy knows how to do these things well. Why not come along, and bring a partner?' said Jack's colleague, whose young brother was a midshipman.

Jack, aware of ructions between his father and sister, asked Sophy. She was flattered. Her brother was eight years older than she was, the only man who actually impressed her. He was clever and wise. Her parents treated their only son with respect and his mother adored him. Jack was a good son, concerned, attentive if somewhat sardonic, but Sophy was his heel of Achilles. As he grew to manhood and she to beauty, he loved her with the awe of an ugly man who has a sister lovely as the day.

He had been born with weak sight, and a cast in one eye so marked that at school he was nicknamed 'Chester Conklin' after the cross-eyed comedian of silent movies. 'Poor old

Chester' said the swift boys at school, 'too blind to hit a ball and too slow to run a yard.' From his youth, Jack was heavy, burly, inheriting his figure from a Dutch grandparent on his mother's side. He could not run fast, and in any case it was his nature to move at the same pace as his thoughts – they were slow and deep.

At eighteen, after a successful operation, his dark short-sighted eyes were straightened. He was no longer a comical Chester Conklin, although he saw things in a blur without thick-lensed glasses. He was a plain strong-looking man, blunt-featured, with a low attractive voice. He did not smile much and took refuge in facetious jokes.

Sophy's perceptions about her brother were almost as sharp as those of an identical twin and she knew very well that he had a series of love affairs; but when she daringly asked, 'Who's your current mistress?' he burst out laughing and said, 'No cheek from you, youngster.' Sophy realized that his work in Chambers, its connections, friendships, complications and patronage, provided the perfect alibi. After a while his father agreed to his taking a small flat in Beaufort Street, Chelsea. Nothing grand, a tube ride to the Temple and a view, if you craned your neck, of the river.

She visited his new home delightedly.

'Thomas More's garden used to be down there,' he said, pointing out of his window. 'Those bent-looking trees are reputed to be his. Mulberries. They're probably not old enough, but the porter's wife brought me a bowlful last night. Very tasty.'

Jack liked Sophy coming to stay a night in London with him when she went to a party or a dance. He enjoyed the tales of her conquests. He pushed aside the law books and briefs and listened while she told him about her admirers. Her scorn of any man who developed a crush on her made him grin.

'You'll have to take one of 'em. Can't put off the married state for ever.'

'Do you *want* me to marry?'

'Not particularly. Better for you, though.'

'I could marry late.'

'Bit of a mistake. The elderly bride.'

She made a horrible face at him.

'Shall you miss me?'

'Why should I have to do that? I'll come and sit on your doorstep.'

'Better still, I'll come here. Then I can get away from that horrible husband you've clobbered me with.'

'Why should he be that? There's Barry. A bit pompous, but steady. There's Dennis whatshisname. He isn't too bad. And the other chap, goodlooking, Geoffrey somebody? But didn't you say he's usually in debt?'

'He sold his gold watch to take me to the Savoy.'

'Don't swank. What about Dennis Whatshisname?'

'He buys enormous boxes of chocs and eats them himself at the pictures.'

It was a delight to Sophy when Jack invited her to drive to Devonshire for the Naval ball. He had bought a runabout, a little Morris Minor, and they left Sussex at six in the morning. He had taken rooms for Sophy and himself at the best hotel in Dartmouth and his lawyer friend was to meet them at the college before the ball.

'We get presented to the Admiral or someone. Wear your glad rags.'

'I certainly will.'

A new dress had been made in three days by the local dressmaker, it was very clinging and Sophy decided not to wear the breathlessly tight elastic roll-on her mother took for granted was essential to keep one's stomach flat as a board.

The drive to Devonshire was enjoyable: cautious Jack, well-known in the Temple for the judicious weighing of facts, was a different man behind the wheel. He drove very fast.

'It's Mr Toad!' cried Sophy with approval.

They arrived in Dartmouth in time for tea, Jack in his stolid way, Sophy in her lively one, fresh as daisies. They had baths, changed into evening dress, had a sherry and set off for the college. Sophy's new dress was long, Greek in cut and made of weighty silver lamé which clung and swung; it had a metallic scent about it.

'I smell like steel shavings,' she remarked.

'Then mind you don't behave like them. You be nice to the chaps. I can't have naval officers shooting themselves on the terrace.'

'That's only when they lose their all at Monte Carlo.'

'Well, won't they be losing you?'

It was at the ball in a huge building filled with thumping music, fresh-faced children in uniform, snobbish parents and tough officers that Sophy met Bob Lingard. To the disappointment of boys of fifteen and officers of forty she danced every dance with him. Bob was as English as the Devonshire countryside, his hair fairish, paleish, the colour of a teddy bear, his manner quick and humorous, he was obliging and attentive and danced better than any man Sophy had met in her life. She loved to dance and melted, all steel filings and flaming hair, in his arms to be whirled round and round the slippery floor. It was midsummer and when he finally took her back to the hotel at the end of the evening, there was an enormous moon over the sea making a path along the water. The dark, faintly lit, mysterious and disturbing night turned her into a figure made of silver. They travelled in an open horsedrawn cab and on the improbable journey, to the music of horse's hooves, they kissed. He put out a hand and traced her cheek.

'You have freckles.'

She did not know it was a declaration of love. She had never had an admirer wearing uniform before and when he kissed her she enjoyed it, in a way. She snuggled close, the star in her hair winking vivid blue, glad of his warmth and the muscly arm inside the velvet-feel of his naval jacket.

'You're a stunner,' he said.

They met on his leaves which were infrequent, he was serving in a C-class destroyer and was away for months. Sophy, out every evening with a different young man, bored by the languish in their eyes, positively flew to greet Bob when she met him at Victoria Station. They were going to a play and to supper and Bob had asked if he could drive her back to Sussex afterwards.

They kissed unselfconsciously on the platform; neither had planned to do that.

It was very late when he drove her home to Sussex – he had hired a car for the journey which pleased Sophy. She felt looked-after. And, stopping the car under a long avenue of beech trees in the empty roads of midnight, Bob asked her to be his wife. It was brave, because he knew a refusal would hurt him more than he could imagine. He was astounded when Sophy, nestling close, said yes.

Of course Bob will win, thought Sophy, appearing in the garden to watch the end of the match. He did, 6–2, 6–4. 'Game, set and match,' shouted her father, trying not to sound annoyed.

Cissy, one of the family's two maids, appeared, carrying a tray of tea and looking very smart in lace afternoon cap and apron.

Sophy liked Cissy. 'You look the tops.'

Cissy grinned shyly. 'I'm going to the Guides tonight, Miss Sophy. Folk dancing.'

'Mother says you are going to win a badge.'

'Mustn't count my chickens.'

Cissy had a face like a clown and a flop of brown hair and bad teeth but her smile was irresistible. The two girls, much of an age and belonging to different worlds, walked down the sloping lawns to where Pansy Hayward had begun to open a deck chair, which Bob gently took from her and set up so effortlessly he seemed to do it with one hand. He did everything better than other people, thought Sophy. He won at games, he drove well, he danced like Fred Astaire; and when he'd taken her to sail at Itchenor, it had been a revelation. Sophy admired him and was pleased with him, and with herself too. But although she enjoyed his kisses, she sometimes wondered if it was true that sex could make you faint.

After the tea had been served, Cissy vanished towards the house, walking quickly; Sophy could see she was hoping she wouldn't be asked to do anything more. In a few minutes she glimpsed the maid pedalling her bicycle fast, on her way to glory at the Guides.

There was an open-air silence. Herbert drank his tea. Nobody but his family would guess defeat had put him into a bad mood. Pansy cut the lemon sponge and Bob looked at his fiancée and gave her a slight wink. Birds were singing their particular evening song. It was very peaceful.

Like a swimmer who has climbed to the top board, and then hesitates as if measuring the drop to the water so far below, Sophy paused. The invisible birds went on conversing with each other in the trees, believing the long English afternoon was never going to end.

'I had a letter from Anne-Marie this morning,' began Sophy in her clear voice.

Pansy Hayward gave one of her indulgent smiles and remarked that she'd noticed the French stamp, and how was Sophy's friend?

The expected answer, of course, was a cliché. 'She's fine.' 'It's hot in the south of France.' Things like that. But Sophy did not reply, and Bob, glancing over at her, saw that something was up. Her face was concentrated. He'd seen that expression at sea on the faces of sailors when the weather was worsening and the destroyer beginning to shudder, roll and plunge.

Herbert Hayward fitted a cigarette into a tortoiseshell holder. His face in repose was rather noble, like one or other of the apostles in Michelangelo's cartoons. You could imagine him, an apostle, bent over the boat in the Sea of Galilee. He had never lived up to his looks. He was a spoilt man, disagreeable, not generous and vain. His virtues set off the vices; high moral principles, reliability; he would as soon jump from the roof of his house than lie. He was a loyal if careful friend and honest as the day. Probity was a halo round Herbert, he was respected by banking colleagues, enjoyed using his good judgement and never lacked moral courage. He also treated his wife badly, his manner to her never free from a certain contempt, and because he made her nervous she was inclined to talk in a disconnected way which

Sophy called 'Ma's stream of consciousness'. Pansy in her way was as good a judge and as fair a friend as he, but he gave her no chance to be. He treated Cissy better than he treated his wife.

Smoking, he did not bother to listen to his daughter and her mother: Pansy was asking Sophy if there was any chance of Anne-Marie Dufour coming to stay in Sussex. The French girl had been a success with Pansy in the past.

'She'd never be allowed to come over again, Ma. Surely you remember how her mother cut up rough when she was sent here to school? I told you about it. She didn't want her coming to England at all. Besides, we entertained Anne-Marie a lot, that stay in Worthing and all the weekends here at the house. Now she's written today to say it's her turn.'

'What does Anne-Marie mean by that?' enquired Pansy, smiling and unaware of trouble.

'She's asked me to stay in Cannes.'

Pansy gave a quick nervous glance at her husband. But Sophy was watching Bob. His good-looking face did not change, he didn't frown but merely looked at her with his usual open affection. Good, thought Sophy, taking things as she wanted them to be, I haven't hurt him. I knew I wouldn't.

'She's asked if I'd like to go to Cannes for a few weeks. I think it sounds fun,' said Sophy without emphasis, and turned charmingly to her fiancé.

'You don't mind, do you, Bob? *You're* going to be at sea and you'd like me to have a good time in Cannes, wouldn't you?'

He gave a slight laugh.

'What sort of good time?'

'Don't tease. Swimming. Seeing the sights. Do you realize,' turning to her mother, 'that I have *never* been abroad! Lots of girls went to Finishing School and learned French and had a tremendous time, while all I did was –'

She stopped before the shorthand school came up.

'Anyway, it will be my last chance to have a fling, as we're getting married in September.'

She looked at Bob again with a bright expression as if daring

58

him to object. He murmured that he trusted it would not be too much of a fling and she giggled.

Her mother continued to gaze at Herbert, who deliberately stubbed out his cigarette.

It was his habit to come late into family conversations and then demand to know what they were talking about. He would listen in an impatient, martyred way as if forced to hear so much poppycock. He gave an incredulous frown as his wife began to speak in her soft voice, with its trace of a Cornish accent.

Bob Lingard began to look at his shoes: there was a grass stain on one toe.

'You are suggesting the girl should go and stay in France?' said Herbert, when Pansy trailed to a stop. 'Quite out of the question.'

'Why?' said Sophy, very sharply.

Herbert lifted up his hand. 'No arguments, please. I repeat. It is out of the question.'

In Bob Lingard's book of rules anybody outside a family, even if he happened to be engaged to one of its members, had no place in a family quarrel. He stood up, murmured something about getting a letter off on the evening post, and walked away with easy strides across the grass to the open French windows.

'You see. You've hurt him,' said Pansy.

'Oh, Ma, don't be *stupid.*'

'Don't you dare speak to your mother like that!'

Sophy went pale instead of red, furious with her mother for implying that she was selfish to Bob and more with her father for his usual tyrannical behaviour. How true to form they ran. How boring it was to know exactly how they were going to react. There wasn't a single surprise in either of them.

'I might point out,' she said, staying on the point, 'that my dear fiancé happens to be leaving tomorrow to go waltzing round the Med with his ship. Why should he care tuppence where I am while he's away? In France or Timbuctoo. In fact,' she added, 'I know he'd prefer me to be in France having a good time rather than hanging around here.'

She looked at her father. She was not afraid of him.

'You are not going to France and there's an end of it.'

'*Why?*'

He gave a reply, which, in its absurdity, was guaranteed to make the girl more pigheaded and furious.

'Because I say so.'

'I will go. I will!' she shouted, and rushed towards the house.

Bob Lingard was in the drawing room, smoking and pretending to read when she came bursting in, flung herself into his arms and landed on his lap like an angry child. Her warm body, her smell, her soft silkiness affected him in a wave of sensual longing. He wrapped his arms round her and kissed her, rocking her to and fro, listening to her furious whispers; he embraced her and pressed his hard cheek against her velvet one. He would have promised her anything.

The trouble between Sophy and her father continued long after Bob had left Sussex and returned to his ship. It was the worst row between them so far and poor Pansy went about with a doleful face, shaking her head and giving her daughter looks of speaking reproach as if to say 'How can you upset him? How can you upset me?'

In a final set-to one evening of late May, Sophy declared war. She still had money in the post office after having paid for her car; she had withdrawn it all. She had booked her ticket to Cannes and sent Anne-Marie a telegram. She was leaving Victoria Station on the following Monday morning. She had also written to her brother, who was away.

'He won't be here to see me off, but if you both want to come, that's fine. If not, I'll see myself off,' said Sophy defiantly.

She had the cruelty of youth and the will of a girl who always won in the end. She thought her parents unreasonable; she was also strong in knowing that Bob agreed she should go to France. He was on her side. But he always was.

Adding sugar to his coffee, Herbert hesitated. He had come, for the second time, up against the fact of money, without which the parent of an adult child has no weapon except love, which was not part of Herbert's armoury.

60

He had to save his face.

'Very well, very well. In any case I've had second thoughts. I've decided to let you go.'

Pansy believed him and looked melting and grateful.

Sophy behaved rather well. She could be quite magnanimous to the old despot, as she'd privately nicknamed her father, and she gave him one of her radiant smiles and actually thanked him for agreeing to come to the station.

She was delighted with herself.

Herbert's first refusal to his daughter had been the automatic reaction of a man who preferred to say No. But when he thought over the idea of her going to France, he had been disturbed.

Anne-Marie Dufour's letter, replying to Sophy's telegram saying when she was going to arrive, had come swiftly. She wrote flowering descriptions of the delights of the Côte d'Azur during this early summer of 1939.

'We will show you life here in our dear country,' declared Anne-Marie, and listed race meetings, swimming championships, balls and fêtes. 'Cannes has never been gayer,' said the French girl at the end of the letter. When Sophy, in tearing good spirits, showed it to her father he was astonished at the picture of a country set on enjoyment.

He could not help feeling uneasy. Every time he opened his newspaper, while the press declared 'There will be no war!' the news seemed worse. A handful of months ago Hitler had invaded and dismembered what was left of Czechoslovakia. Mussolini had grabbed Albania. And now Hitler's greedy eyes were on Poland, demanding concessions which that country could never give him, and accusing the Poles of barbarous treatment of the German minority. Japan was now at war with Russia. Everywhere you looked, despite the newspapers' optimistic Leaders, there was the hideous word 'war'. The times were dangerous.

'I don't like it, Pansy,' he said to Sophy's mother. 'I'm not at all sure she should risk going abroad.'

Pansy's round face went red with alarm, not for warring nations but warring relatives.

'But she can always come home if you think things look bad, Herbert.'

'Yes. That's true,' he agreed.

Most of his friends, like the newspapers, were optimistic despite both the English and French declaring that they would stand by Poland if she was attacked.

Herbert, by nature pessimistic, did not share the general feeling that peace was going to last. But he had done his duty. He had tried to prevent Sophy from going abroad; and as Pansy pointed out he could always order the girl home in good time. In a rare gesture of paternal duty, he went with Pansy to see Sophy off.

His daughter was looking very smart in a suit the colour of toffee, and a tiny hat shot through with a turquoise feather. She and her parents stood by the open door of a first-class compartment. The platform bustled with travellers as smart as she was. 'A good bit of money about, anyway,' thought Herbert.

'Now, Sophy, don't forget,' said her mother, a refrain for the last hour, 'you have five pieces of luggage including your hatbox.'

'I'll remember, Ma.'

Excitement had given a glow to Sophy's petal-pale cheeks, her dark eyes shone. She even gave her father a smile but he looked away. Suddenly, glancing up and down the platform, Sophy gave a girlish shriek.

'It's Jack! It's Jack!'

Her brother had been in Newcastle-on-Tyne for the last two weeks engaged on some long legal tussle, and had telephoned to say he could not be in London in time to see her off. But he was up-to-date with her plans and had approved of them. Now here he was. Sophy was radiant. He wore a grey and battered trilby hat at an unsuitably rakish angle, a pale macintosh with the collar turned up; he resembled a New York reporter in a film. He greeted his parents and presented his sister with a wedge of glossy magazines and a box of Terry's Spartan chocolates.

Sophy hugged him tightly, Jack laughed, and Pansy beamed at the sight of family unity.

'Off to the Côte d'Azur, eh? What do you suppose you're going to find there?' asked Jack, releasing himself from being throttled.

'Oodles of fun.'

'Maybe. But mind your p's and q's and don't take wooden nickels.'

'What is the boy talking about?' wondered Pansy.

'Ma. It's American,' said Sophy, laughing.

There was a whistle, a slam of doors.

'Oh, it's time!' cried Sophy, scrambling into the compartment as if the train was going to move that instant.

Jack slammed the compartment door after her. She leaned out and took his hand. He gripped hers hard. Both parents waved as the train began to move. But Sophy, leaning further out until the platform disappeared and the train curved away, saw only Jack. There had been tears in his eyes.

She thought of him as the smoky journey began through the suburbs of London, passing districts like Sutton and Carshalton, where the summer gardens were sooty but washing hung on lines, and prams were pushed under the trees. She reflected briefly about what her father had said, only last night, about the crisis. That old crisis, she thought, had been going on since last year. She had grown used to headlines about Hitler marching into countries which didn't belong to him. But it was going to stop now, since Chamberlain had been to Germany and fixed things up. The Germans and the English had said they'd never go to war with each other again. 'It is peace in our time,' Chamberlain had said.

Sophy was not going to worry. Why should she?

Bob had written to her, the letter posted from Gibraltar, saying he missed her and loved her and thought about her and her letters were ripping, more please, and she must enjoy herself in France but never forget he was her loving Bob.

Without realizing it, Sophy, deep in thought, was looking across the carriage at a man facing her. He gave a knowing smile. Oh lor', he must be at least fifty, thought Sophy and hastily picked up one of Jack's glossy magazines. The pages were crammed with duchesses, actresses, men in tail coats, and girls and men on horses. She gazed indifferently at clutches of débutantes in their presentation dresses, those feather-things in their hair.

The journey, interesting, unfamiliar, took her across the mercifully calm Channel and into the train. When it arrived in Paris it crawled, taking what seemed hours to cross Paris and finally anchoring at the Gare du Nord where it waited for more hours before setting off again on a tedious journey across the city. But when it arrived at the Gare de Lyon she was too nervous to get off and go for a walk on the station, although a fellow passenger (another man) assured her there would be a wait of half an hour. She felt safe in her sleeper, reading the magazines which, thought Sophy, positively bowed and scraped to anybody with a title. At last the train left Paris, and feeling cheerful again, she stood at the window in the corridor, and waved to startled strangers in a suburban street.

She dined alone. The restaurant car was full of middle-aged couples, and once or twice Sophy was given an up-and-down look by some stout Frenchman; she pretended not to notice it. Retiring early to her sleeper, she climbed into the bed which had been made up for her by the attendant, turned out the light, lulled by the steady music of the train. Tomorrow, she thought as she slipped into sleep, I shall be on the Riviera.

When she switched on her bedside light and looked at her watch many hours later, she saw it was scarcely five o'clock. The train seemed to be going slowly and quietly. There was not the same loud thunder that had run through her dreams, it was a gentle sound, and she remembered Jack saying at the end of their long drive to Devonshire, 'Can you hear? The car's tired.'

How softly the train was going now. And then Sophy realized they must be in the south.

She pulled on her clothes and went into the corridor. The attendant had not raised the blinds, the long carpeted passage was empty, a line of closed doors. She half lifted a blind and looked out.

Scarcely lit by the beginning of dawn, still with colours dimmed and to the quiet song of the train, she had her first vision of the south. Everything was strange to her and had a kind of heart-rending quality she could not explain. Her English eyes did not recognize the trees, they were different from Sussex beeches and oaks, thin-leaved and silvery, looking like puffs of smoke. She watched the panorama outside the windows with a curious feeling. It made her sad. The train sighed its way through a tiny deserted station, and against the paling sky was the high roof of a church and the dark figure of a Virgin, holding a little child in her arms. The country stretched away into acres upon acres of vineyards in full leaf, giving Sophy the solemn knowledge that she was a thousand miles away from home. Then the vineyards melted, there was scrub, rock-strewn wildernesses and all the while at the edge of the horizon the mountains which kept back the day.

Cannes station was crowded with families all throwing themselves into each other's arms. Cries came from left and right.

'*Enfin!*'

'*Cher enfant!*'

On a platform six feet below her, the train attendant put out both hands to Sophy for her to jump down. The moment she landed she heard another cry, this time in English.

'Dear Sophy!'

Anne-Marie, running up to her, did something she'd never done in England – she kissed Sophy on both cheeks.

There was a great deal of counting luggage, enquiries about the journey which Anne-Marie treated as if Sophy had crossed Arabia, and signalling for a taxi. Sophy scarcely had time to take in the busy streets, the dazzling sunshine, the foreign smells of coffee? fish? garlic? There was a sandalwood scent too, it came from Anne-Marie who leaned forward, smiling and patting her hand with pleasure.

'I can't believe you are here at last. I never thought your parents would allow you to travel alone.'

Sophy gave the carefree laugh of a girl who had had no

opposition whatever, and Anne-Marie gave her the old familiar admiring look of a daughter whose own parents' word was law.

She kept repeating how much 'emotion' she felt at seeing Sophy again. Now and then she forgot her colloquial English and the effect was quaint. She said her family were looking forward to 'receive' Sophy, who had done Anne-Marie 'such service' by coming here to stay.

The taxi drove down narrow streets which reminded Sophy of paintings of the East, the shops filled with necklaces and bangles and cheap cotton clothes displayed on the pavement. There were bread shops, shops with bunches of sandals hanging outside on strings like bananas. There were antique shops, one had a penny-farthing bicycle at its door. Then they passed a market with fruit piled in crimson and yellow pyramids and baskets full of carnations and great masses of lilies. To make the journey perfect, the taxi finally turned a corner and there, a sparkling blue diamond, was the Mediterranean.

France. I'm in the south of France, thought Sophy blissfully. She would learn to speak good French with Anne-Marie, they would chatter all day long, and swim, and it would be the perfect holiday before marriage and real-life set in.

The two girls had been friends for nearly three years. It had been Monsieur Dufour's idea to send his only daughter to England to learn the language; her mother, no lover of foreigners, had fought against her husband's decision. But he had prevailed, and poor Anne-Marie, with scarcely a word of English, was packed off to Sussex. She had the good fortune to share a bedroom with Sophy.

The French girl was no beauty. Her face might have looked better on a young man, there was nothing feminine or delicate about it, she had lumpish features, thick lips, and her indeterminate brown hair was worn with a childish slide. She looked older than she was, partly because of her ugly figure and heavy face. Physically, she could have been a peasant born in the south, yet she had none of the Provençal vivacity,

66

easy rages, flashing eyes, the habit of embracing forgiven enemies. She was sentimental and solemn.

In England, from the first, she badly needed a champion. Girls cleverer than she was made a butt of her. They went in for chauvinistic teasing and vulgar imitations of her accent; she suffered from their sarcastic laughter, and more from their pretended pity. Within days, Sophy had weighed in. She had a nice turn of invective and enjoyed using it. She had soon worsted every school-uniformed enemy who hove into view.

Anne-Marie thought her new friend a marvel, did not envy her beauty and never stopped being grateful. She spoke of Sophy's kindness embarrassingly often; she was, she declared, eternally in her debt.

Unlike her cavalier attitude to male admiration and compliments from too many men, Sophy enjoyed her friend's appreciation. She loved Anne-Marie because she had been good to her. Now it looked as if the tables were turned – she already felt dependent on Anne-Marie and the sensation was unfamiliar. Newly arrived in Cannes, Sophy found it as strange as the plains of India and rather similar in temperature.

The taxi windows were open but she fanned herself with her hand.

'You must change into cooler clothes, Sophy,' said Anne-Marie, looking at her affectionately. 'Your travelling suit is very chic. But not suitable for the Midi.'

'It feels as if it weighs a ton,' said Sophy, envying her friend who wore cool gingham with no sleeves.

'We will swim this morning,' said Anne-Marie. 'Our house is just across the road from the sea. Look, we're almost there.'

They were driving along a broad rich-looking promenade lined with palms and bright with flower-beds. The beaches, even now at only half past eight in the morning, were scattered with sunbathers and there were swimmers in the calm sea. They passed the Carlton Hotel with its twin cupolas, other hotels as large and elegant, and many pink and white houses which looked, in style, like the Italian ice-cream cakes served at masonic dinners.

At the far end of the Croisette – the name of the promenade – the land reached out into the sea. The taxi slowed down, turning through open gates and drawing up at the steps of a large white house festive with yellow sunblinds. The garden was shady, with lanky palms by the gate, the grass, hectically and falsely green, watered three times a day.

'I won't take you up to your room just yet, Sophy. I must present you to my parents.'

Anne-Marie led her round the side of the house to a much larger garden, a chiaroscuro of brilliant light and welcoming shade. There were beds of yellow and orange flowers, riots of shrubs covered in white blossom, or resembling pale blue exotic jasmine. Seated under the trees at a garden table were a man and a woman.

Anne-Marie took Sophy's hand and hastened over to them, presenting Sophy rather as if the visitor was being received by a royal family. Sophy's hand was shaken, and she made a short speech in French, thanking her hosts for inviting her to stay.

Anne-Marie's mother said brightly, 'English. We must speak English, *n'est-ce-pas*? It is important for Anne-Marie not to lose your language, I think.'

She gave a little metallic laugh.

Sophy had seen many holiday snaps of Anne-Marie's parents, but in real life they were far older than she had expected. Anselme Dufour strongly resembled his daughter, he had the same heavy face, thick lips, lank hair and looked almost immoveable, sitting down. When he stood up to greet Sophy, he was impressive by sheer size.

Calling her 'Mademoiselle', he pressed her hand in an enormous paw, hospitably smiling at her. His smile had a trace of delighted optimism about it. It reflected the luck which had been his for years.

Anselme was not clever, and when he grew to manhood his family took it as a matter of course that he would work for his father, a wholesale fishmonger in Nice. Anselme had begun as a fisherman, as his father had done before setting up Dufour et Cie, a flourishing little business which sold fish at slightly lower prices than the competition.

The Dufours' elder son Louis was as smart as his father, and when the father died, he built the business up still more. Dufour et Cie, Poissons, Coquillages, had handsome offices and a large warehouse. Anselme lumbered along doing as his brother told him, a happy young man who spoke of the great fortune of having Louis as head of the business. It was an unbelievable shock when Louis caught pneumonia and died. Suddenly Anselme's life utterly changed. He became wealthy and important. Within a year, he married Yvonne, a pretty Parisienne who knew a good thing when she saw one.

In France in the 1930s business was bad, scandals rocked the governments which fell so quickly that government itself became a bad joke. Markets rose and collapsed. But as Yvonne Dufour said, people had to eat. Dufour et Cie prospered and it was she who became its motor. She advised, pored over accounts, never appeared in the office and made all the decisions. The firm was ruled from the house on the Croisette. Anselme retired early, glad to put a younger man, chosen by Yvonne, in his place.

Now Anselme, a man of leisure, had a life which suited him perfectly. He called in at the warehouse, liked to drive to the harbour sometimes and take a look at the dawn catch. Fish was in his bloodstream.

The Dufour son, Paul, now worked in the family business too. A year younger than Anne-Marie, a serious boy, he was busy learning the trade in Nice. The only member of the family not actually connected with Dufour et Cie was Anne-Marie. But she was proud of the family business and it was a shock when she arrived at an English school to learn that trade was despised and fish the subject of unkind jokes. She could not understand it. Why did they have to laugh? Fish were beautiful when they were in the sea and when caught were good food, good business and made her family's fortune.

'*Je ne comprends rien*' was Anne-Marie's helpless answer when time and again she met the sneers and jeers of girls who were supposed to be well bred. Once when she opened the lid of her desk she discovered a chalked drawing of a plaice to which the artist had added Anne-Marie's face and three exclamation marks on the fish's tail.

'What's a fish doing at Hillcrest?' was written below the sketch.

Anne-Marie, eyes brimming, took the sketch to Sophy.

'*Je ne comprends rien.*'

It was impossible for Sophy to explain that schoolgirls thought it vulgar to make money from selling fish, yet perfectly acceptable to be the third generation of a family who had flogged casks of beer to thirsty English labourers. Anything in trade, as they called it, was fine if it was far enough in the past. Sophy tried to make Anne-Marie grasp, at least, the idea. She never succeeded. To French logic it was utter nonsense.

Sophy saw her point. But took the trouble to lie on her friend's behalf. She confided in the school's worst gossip, ensuring the story would get about by swearing her to secrecy, that Anne-Marie's family owned a business they had inherited years ago. 'She doesn't like to boast, but they're rather wealthy – she has a sort of inverted snobbery, you know how it is,' said Sophy airily. She indicated that it was fifty years since a Dufour had actually handled those slippery moneymakers.

Now here was Sophy in a garden paid for by the harvest of the sea, near a handsome house bought by Mediterranean fish, meeting a benevolent elderly man, and a smart woman who was no such thing.

Yvonne Dufour looked as if she had lately come off the train from Paris; she was petite and neat, with dyed blonde hair fashionably cut, a white silk dress and large diamond rings. She had a matchingly neat Parisian voice and was as intimidating as Queen Mary.

How had the journey been? Had Sophy travelled first class? *Tiens*, second class was of better value, you had as much comfort and only a smaller basin in the sleeping compartment. She gave a laugh. Had Sophy remembered her bathing costume? Good. More than one? No? *Tiens*, Anne-Marie had four. Did she wish her coffee black – Yvonne Dufour raised the coffee pot – *Tiens*. She understood English people only drank it with tinned milk.

All this was said with a gracious manner and Sophy tried to tell herself that surely it was not possible for Madame to dislike her already.

As for Monsieur, after another kindly smile and apparently unconscious of his wife's behaviour, he picked up the local newspaper.

It was as much a relief as iced water to replace the scalding and bitter coffee when Anne-Marie, nervously darting into the conversation, asked if her mother would excuse them; she and Sophy would like to go for a swim. Sophy was very glad to go. She was unused to being interviewed as if by a detective.

Her friend took her up an imposing staircase to a bedroom with elaborate Provençal furniture the colour of pale brown satin, much carved and curlicued. The bed was large enough for two giants, and lofty French windows opened on to a balcony overlooking the garden at the side of the house. There was a table and chairs on the balcony. Anne-Marie smilingly said, 'We will have *petit déjeuner* together each morning, shall we? Now, I'll leave you to unpack.'

Sophy threw her clothes into huge empty drawers and hung them in immense empty cupboards. The morning, advancing stealthily, brought more light and heat. Not a breath stirred the red damask curtains at the windows or the greyish leaves of a mimosa tree outside. It was glorious to strip off her hot travelling clothes and pull on a skimpy white bathing suit. Barefoot, she came out of her room in search of her friend.

Anne-Marie appeared at the end of a passage, muffled in a scarlet and white towelling cape tied at the neck with ribbons. When she saw Sophy she stopped dead.

'You cannot walk about the house like that! Where is your cape?'

'I'm afraid I haven't got one,' said Sophy, surprised.

'No cape? Then how do you get to the beach? Never mind, I will lend you one of mine.'

Anne-Marie hurried away, returning with a cape similar to her own, except that it was blue and white instead of scarlet.

In summer heat-waves at home, Sophy lived in her bathing suit. Sometimes her mother sprayed her with the garden hose – Pansy enjoyed that and laughed like a girl. Now Sophy found herself enveloped in the towelling cape which covered her from her neck to the calves of her legs. It was very uncomfortable. Anne-Marie carefully tied the bow at the neck, and told Sophy to fetch her beach shoes.

Muffled and shod, the girls went out of the house through the garden and across the road.

On the beach, Anne-Marie thought it allowable to discard capes and shoes. The sand burned the soles of their feet as they ran down the shelving beach and fell into the water. The sea was flat calm, the waves nothing but inch-high ripples breaking with scarcely a sigh on the wet edges of the sand.

Sophy swam. She dived under Anne-Marie and bobbed up, water dripping from her hair. Anne-Marie wore a bathing cap decorated with a large rubber-petalled flower, but Sophy's hair was plastered to her cheeks. Away from home, Anne-Marie romped like a sheepdog, her clumsy body splashing about, bosoms wobbling.

'Tomorrow we must swim before breakfast, it is the very best time,' she said. 'So beautiful, with nobody else in the ocean. In the first hours of the day, I feel the Mediterranean belongs to me.'

A narrow fish beside her, Sophy swam lazily, remarking, 'I'll tell you somebody else who's in the Mediterranean. Well, *on* it to be exact. Bob. He's been sent on one of those long trips, his ship's stopping at places like Aden and Malta. They call it showing the flag.'

'In Cannes also,' said Anne-Marie, 'we have seen the English Navy. Sometimes they anchor facing the Carlton, and at night the ships are decorated with lights. It is very pretty. The town so crowded with English sailors handsome and pleasant.'

'Oh good! Perhaps you will marry one, and then we'll be two English Navy wives,' said Sophy, ducking under the water and bobbing up again.

Anne-Marie ignored the idiotic idea of marrying a foreigner.

Beyond them to the right along the Croisette at a distance were the beaches of the rich. Rows of coloured parasols, white, blue, each section with its lines of matching mattresses. There were small restaurants and bars built at the top of the beaches and little boats could be hired, and people played ball games on courts made in the burning sand and protected by high nets. The men and women who sunbathed on beaches called La Joliette, Le Carlton, La Grand Bleu, Chez Marcus, were as bronzed as Jamaicans and lived all day long in bathing dress, their skins shining with oil. They were the inhabitants of pleasure, denizens of the wealthy world. But opposite Anne-Marie's house there were no paid-for beaches, only scattered rocks with pines growing along a sandy path and here and there a parasol stuck into the sand.

Emerging at last from the water, the girls wandered, dripping, over to the flattest rock and lay down. They scarcely bothered to talk as they stretched on their backs, then on their stomachs, nailed by the sun. They swam again later on, to come out glistening with salt water, and return once more to the rocks ...

Sophy could have spent the entire day in and out of the sea. But the pleasure was too good to last and finally Anne-Marie, examining the wrist watch in her cape pocket, exclaimed that it was time to get back and change for luncheon. Modesty and the capes were resumed. The asphalt on the road was melting as they ran back into the garden.

'How beautiful the sea is –' said Sophy, looking back over her shoulder. 'And that island there in the haze.'

'That is why Maman called our house Les Hesperides.'

4

In Anne-Marie's letters to Sophy there had been elaborate descriptions of her life in Cannes. Sophy had scarcely believed them. When you wrote in French things took on an improbable importance and grandeur. They sounded stately. Or perhaps it wasn't only the formal language but the way Anne-Marie saw things? Sophy now looked forward with amusement and incredulity to the pleasures to come. There were the '*promenades en bâteau*', the '*fêtes des fleurs*', the '*soirée dansante*' and many expeditions to the country where the wild flowers appeared to send Anne-Marie into a state of speechless astonishment. So she wrote. She also mentioned her companions a good deal, as if the French girl were part of a group of beautiful young people of the kind Sophy found so tiresome in *The Tatler*. Sophy could not believe them either.

But Anne-Marie had written no more than the truth. Life at Les Hesperides was sociable and crowded, the house filled with friends who appeared, not occasionally, but every day. They arrived as early as ten in the morning and rarely left before midnight. Lively and sunburned, talkative and slightly formal, these were the young men Yvonne Dufour called 'the friends of my daughter'.

Sophy was accustomed to a certain inhospitality at home in Sussex. To her father's elegant 'is that damned woman coming to tea again?' and to the need for apologies when she invited a friend to dinner. But Yvonne Dufour enjoyed visitors; if there was one thing which put her in an excellent temper apart from well-cooked food it was the presence of young men. And all Anne-Marie's friends were male. There were two brothers, Serge and Stefan, dark and tall, excellent swimmers and tennis players. Although there was a gap of three years between them, they were so alike that Sophy found it hard to tell them apart.

Anne-Marie's brother Paul was one of the group. He worked at Dufours in Nice, but was always home early in the afternoon to join in the various expeditions. There was Alexis Lucas a tiny man, half-Dutch, who wore a beard like d'Artagnan and was very voluble and amusing. He was a painter and Anne-Marie's longest-serving friend. And finally there was Claudio Arrighi, by way of being a star.

Claudio, Italian, worked in the wine trade and never appeared at the house without a bottle of wine for Monsieur or one of liqueur for Madame. He was a powerful-looking man, as thick-set as Sophy's brother Jack, but there the resemblance ended. He was swarthy, dark as a raven, with a handsome aquiline nose and a manner of exaggerated gallantry. He paid too much attention to Sophy from the first day of her arrival; but he also flirted with Anne-Marie, who blushed. Sophy, accustomed to compliments, merely smiled and drifted away.

Until now Anne-Marie had been the only girl in the group, but the arrival of a redheaded foreign beauty made for sexual competition. Sophy's English admirers, sensing a rival, would have retreated into pride. But Stefan or Serge, Claudio or little Alexis chased after Sophy and were unembarrassed when she was not interested. The only man at Les Hesperides who did not eye her and make a fuss of her was Paul; she liked him the best.

Exactly as Anne-Marie had described and Sophy dis-believed, life was a round of pleasure. They swam, of course. They hired canoes and pédaloes. They lay on beaches, chatting and laughing. They drove in open cars along the high, dangerous Corniches to Monte Carlo. They gambled, but not for very much money, nobody could afford it. In the broiling heat they played tennis. The only social thing they did not do was to dine out – meals were at the house, and Yvonne Dufour thought nothing of entertaining ten or twelve people to luncheon or dinner. When Sophy mentioned to Anne-Marie that it would give her pleasure to take the Dufour family out to dine, Anne-Marie tut-tutted. A foolish waste of money. It would be more practical to buy Maman some roses in the market.

Within a week Sophy had settled down effortlessly to the new life, and began to dream in French.

Every Sunday the family went to midday Mass at the cathedral in Cannes; despite the heat, it was a day for dark suits, silk dresses, straw hats and suede gloves. During breakfast on the balcony, Anne-Marie said she was sure Sophy wouldn't want to attend Mass with them. 'After all, you are a Protestant.'

In reply to the note of pity, Sophy promptly said she would. She dressed in her most formal clothes; it was like getting ready for Ascot. The family assembled in the hall to drive to the church, their manner to Sophy very much as if they had converted her. Madame lent her a missal.

In the evening there was a particularly elaborate dinner party given to celebrate Claudio's thirtieth birthday. For the second time that day the Dufours were got up to the nines, Monsieur in a dinner jacket and Madame showing a good deal of bosom in a tight Parisian evening gown. Anne-Marie wore pink. There were place-names on the dining room table, and finger bowls in which yellow rosebuds floated. Sophy was seated between Paul Dufour, and a young man who was a newcomer to her: introduced as Daniel Vergé.

When the meal began Sophy talked to Paul who, slightly younger than she was, was very shy. He thawed a little during the soup, answering her remarks with a relieved eagerness, grateful for the attention of his sister's beautiful friend. When the second course, salmon and a fish called St Pierre, was served, it was time for Sophy to talk to the man on her left.

76

Daniel Vergé said easily, 'I must tell you I know all about you from Anne-Marie. She sings your praises.'

'Oh, you poor thing,' said Sophy, laughing.

'You think, when you are the subject of our conversation, people should be sorry for us? We are perhaps bored?'

'I'm sure of it.'

He was far and away the most attractive man in the room, his hair as black as Claudio's, his eyes reminding Sophy of shiny liquorice. There were blueish shadows under them; he looked tired. He had a longish face with an actor's high cheekbones and a smile full of malice.

'I believe I am at last hearing an example of the English hypocrisy,' he remarked.

Sophy assured him she had been speaking the truth. Wasn't it boring to hear stories about somebody when they contained nothing but praise?

'Anne-Marie is prejudiced. Kind and prejudiced.'

The more she protested, the more he teased. He teased her about her attitudes, her nationality and her country's reputation. Accustomed to her usual effect upon men, a mixture of flattery and innuendo, Sophy was on her mettle. She guessed Daniel Vergé thought she was expecting compliments and wasn't going to pay her any. But he was wrong. It was a pleasing change.

He told her he had been to London a couple of times.

'I do enjoy your fogs.'

'That corny old joke.'

'Is it a joke? Is it corny? I was staying at an hotel in the Cromwell Road and when the fog descended, it had been threatening all day, it was like a thick yellow blanket. I went out to buy a newspaper at the Métro station. In two minutes I was utterly lost. I could not find the Métro which was just across the road. I couldn't find my way back to the hotel, it was as if I'd been struck blind. I stumbled about in the smoky dark and when I finally more or less knocked over some man coming towards me and asked him the way, he replied in a language which was totally incomprehensible.'

'Bad luck. You collided with another foreigner.'

'No, Mademoiselle, we managed to make ourselves understood after a struggle. He was a Cockney, I think you call them.'

Sophy looked at him serenely.

'Are you being a little unkind about England, Monsieur Vergé?'

'Indeed no, I am telling you things I have seen. Or to be accurate things I could not see as I happened to be out in the fog. But say whatever you want about France. Criticize her as much as you like. I'll agree with you.'

'I've only been here a few days. I can scarcely start saying I don't like this or that. It would be rude.'

'And we French are so very very polite?'

'You seem so.'

'Polite. And stupid.'

Sophy raised her eyebrows, but he ignored the quizzical look.

'France and Britain are in trouble, Mademoiselle. We all know it. Belgium and Holland as well. We're in danger and pretending not to be.'

The voices were noisier, the good wines were having their effect. People's faces were flushed and many toasts were being drunk to Claudio at the other end of the table.

'Can one imagine,' said Daniel Vergé in a low tone, 'that at this very moment our frontiers could be invaded? And the tragedy of the last war happen all over again.'

He turned to look at her. What he saw made him say thoughtfully, 'May I ask how old you are?'

'The same age as Anne-Marie. We were born in the same month, as it happens.'

'As it happens,' he repeated. 'One wouldn't think so.'

'Why not?' asked Sophy provocatively without meaning it to be.

'Anne-Marie has a good deal more sense than you have.'

She was not put out. She knew her beauty affected him, whatever he said.

'She is, isn't she?' said Sophy, 'I believe in French she would be called "*une jeune fille serieuse*".'

'Exactly.'

78

Sophy, longing to say impolitely, 'So what?' gave him a deliberately melting smile.

'*Sérieuse*,' he said. 'And since it would be useless to have a *serious* conversation with you, perhaps we should have a silly one later?'

He turned back to Anne-Marie.

Sophy was amused. She rested on her good looks like the exquisite Tiepole saints painted upon ceilings who knelt on clouds or the Boucher goddesses on celestial thrones supported by cherubs. She wore their expression of laziness, a blissful confidence. Her beauty upheld her, she could float wherever she wished. This dark Frenchman had expected more of her than she'd given. It was perfectly true she was not interested in 'the crisis' talked about so much at home and now appearing at the Dufour dinner table. It was a subject she didn't want to think or worry over. She was twenty and lovely to look at, and the only time she'd shivered had been last year during the other crisis, that of Munich. It had been while she was making up her mind whether to accept Bob Lingard as her husband. She had been enjoying the luxury of a decision – should she? shouldn't she? Suddenly everything had changed, people went about with anxious faces, her father and mother listened to the wireless three or four times a day. Even Sophy, self-absorbed, lighthearted, frivolous and cheerful as a cricket, was alarmed. Chamberlain had three meetings with Hitler who was claiming the Sudetenland, the western frontier of Czechoslovakia, which, said the papers and the wireless, 'is largely populated by Germans'.

The discussions Sophy heard always hinged on that.

'One has to admit what Hitler wants is not unreasonable. After all they are *his* people,' a man in the train had said to his companion, putting down the newspaper. His friend, considerably older and grey-haired, agreed.

'*The Times* says the demand was inevitable. And when this is all settled, there will be no more trouble.' He sighed as if he didn't believe what he was saying.

Fear was in the air. Sophy did not catch it until Bob telephoned to say he wouldn't be coming to Sussex after all.

'So disappointed, darling. But I shall be at sea. Can't say more. I know you understand.' It was then for the first time that Sophy shivered.

But Chamberlain, wearing his half smile of modest satisfaction, came back to England. The headlines in the papers shouted welcome. The Sudetenland would be handed over to Hitler. And that meant peace.

Sophy, with millions of others, breathed again.

Sitting at dinner in an atmosphere of laughter and good humour, knowing her dress suited her and all the men in the room admired her, Sophy wished Daniel Vergé had not introduced a note of gloom. But she had noticed that when French men weren't flirting, they turned to politics.

Anne-Marie had mentioned it. 'It's a national disease, Sophy. How they talk! In cafés, restaurants, on the beach, at meals. Up until now the boys have been on their good behaviour with you, but when it wears off you'll see how they talk. They just go on and on, getting nowhere.'

'Why don't you join in?'

'Good gracious. They wouldn't listen to *me*.'

Dinner was over, the night had fallen and the warmth ebbed in through the open windows, wrapping itself round Sophy's bare shoulders. Monsieur and Madame went into the grand salon with two of their elderly friends, and Anne-Marie said 'we, young' would go into the garden. The two girls, the five young men, wandered out through the French windows. The garden was scented and hot and filled with shadows, the moon lighting the grass here and there, leaving pools of blackness under the thickest trees. They walked over to where the shade was darkest and lay on the grass still warm from hours of the sun. They propped themselves against the trunks of the palms or on their elbows, cigarettes the only points of light in the gloom, except where one bar of moonlight lit Anne-Marie's pale pink dress. To lie in the dark among a crowd of people of her own age was a new experience for Sophy. On rare English nights of high summer, at parties and dances when there were gardens beckoning outside some country house or other, people split into couples and disappeared into the dark. Here it was apparently expected that they should all stay together. It seemed almost a rule. And as she listened to the talk, which was blessedly not about politics but food, it slowly came to Sophy that they were together by design. This was the reason that Madame Dufour, as it were, allowed them to go out into the dark. There was safety in numbers. It was curious and old-fashioned and it was true. She and Anne-Marie were young girls who, in France, must be protected. She rather liked the idea.

Leaning against the ribbed trunk of a palm tree, she became vaguely conscious of a sensation as if there was an insect on her arm. She was about to flick it away when she realized that it was a man's fingers, caressing her arm, creeping gently down to encircle her wrist. The hand was large, muscled, its back was hairy when she touched it with her other hand. In the pitch dark she knew it was Daniel Vergé paying her this disturbing physical attention. He ran his fingers lightly up and down, tracing the shape of her arm, her elbow. He tucked his fingers into the leather strap of her tiny wrist watch. He slipped his hand under hers and pressed the palm with his forefinger. She wanted him to stop. She wanted him to go on. She felt slightly faint.

None of Anne-Marie's friends seemed to do much work that summer always excepting her brother Paul who went to Nice every morning before six. Sophy drowsily heard the putt-putt of his motor bike leaving the house. He worked hard, Anne-Marie said, learning the business of Dufour et Cie.

'He has a head for figures. He says they are interesting but difficult. Paul likes a challenge.'

'He seems a quiet person.'

'That is his strength,' said his sister proudly.

The rest of the young men seemed to be studying and not very seriously at that. Serge and Stefan were both at an engineering college, little Alexis Lucas was at the École des Beaux Arts. He told Sophy he wished to be a 'real artist. Painting pictures which the world will love.'

He spoke with a twinkle, which might have been an

ingenious way of hiding that he meant it. She often heard him arguing about painting with Daniel Vergé, the only one who appeared to do nothing. He was at Les Hesperides far more often than the rest.

'Is Daniel going to be an engineer, like Stefan and Serge?' Sophy asked Anne-Marie one morning during breakfast.

'An engineer! He is a brilliant photographer. Did he not tell you that's his *métier*?'

'He hasn't told me anything about himself,' said Sophy.

'He has great talent, everybody says so. And a great future. The best news photographers are much in demand, they go everywhere and can get high prices for their work. Daniel is attached to *Paris-soir* which pleases his father very much, I believe. Monsieur Vergé is in the *beau monde*.'

'What does that mean?' enquired Sophy, nettled.

'Well, he is wealthy and has a magnificent apartment in the best area of Paris and has a position of a sort in the government. He is proud of his son, particularly so last year when Daniel was sent to Algiers with the Legion.'

'The Foreign Legion?' repeated Sophy, with memories of *Beau Geste*.

'He said some of the soldiers are very violent and very unhappy,' said Anne-Marie, sighing, 'but he took brilliant pictures ... he has a career which spans the world.'

'Then what's he doing here? He only seems to be wasting his time.'

'He dislikes being idle. Poor Daniel, last month in Paris – a serious accident. He fell off his motor cycle.'

Sophy burst out laughing and Anne-Marie's face grew heavier. It was not a matter for mirth, she said, he could have been killed. A man in a large car had come suddenly out of a side turning near the Madeleine. Daniel had been sent spinning and fallen upon his right arm. He had been taken to hospital and a bone was badly bruised although, thank heavens, not broken. But it still pained him to use the arm and the doctors said he must rest. He could use his camera but he must not exhaust himself by travelling, which was why he had decided to spend a few weeks of the summer in the Midi.

'He is a real Parisian. He and Paul met last year when Paul was doing a summer course at the Sorbonne. Paul was so nervous to be going to Paris, he is the true Provençal, you know, he loves the Midi and he's only happy here. Sometimes at weekends he goes climbing in the mountains ... when he talks about the region, he is a poet.' Anne-Marie paused reverently. Sophy prompted.

'And when Paul was in Paris he met Daniel Vergé?'

Anne-Marie roused herself.

'At a dinner party given by my godmother, she has known Daniel and his father for years. Paul and Daniel took to each other at once. Real comrades. They have been friends since then, and Paul looks up to Daniel as an older man. That is good for him.'

'I think Paul's much nicer than Daniel Vergé.'

Anne-Marie was in a quandary. She dearly loved her brother, but Daniel was a close friend.

'You do *like* Daniel, though, don't you? I'm sure he likes you,' she said with simplicity. 'And he's somebody – you will find this when you know him better – worth listening to. Partly it is his mind. A good mind. Clear and realistic. And then, you know, to be a photographer is to reflect life.' She turned to Sophy with her heavy face grave as a judge.

'I suppose that's true,' said Sophy, bemused by her friend's sententiousness.

Instinct told Sophy not to betray to Anne-Marie or indeed to anyone including Daniel himself, that he interested her not as a photographer or a clever companion but as a man. She wasn't used to the feeling he gave her, a sort of unwilling fascination. She had never known this with Bob. When she saw Daniel at a distance on the beach, or saw him entering the house, or heard his voice from a nearby room, her stomach plunged as if she were jumping from a height. He excited her. He had a habit of watching her, waiting to find something he could tease her about. He never treated her seriously. But as Sophy swam well, dived neatly, danced lightly, and even spoke French with few, although charming, mistakes she was not an easy subject to turn to mockery.

He concentrated on her opinions.

'Now, Sophy, tell me your opinion of La Belle France.'

'*Belle.*'

'And . . .?'

'Bigger than England and it smells nicer and your language is prettier to listen to, well, *I* think so, and –'

'And our men are better looking.'

They were sitting on a rock at the far end of the Croisette under some trees. Daniel, walking round the point, had found Sophy by herself, sunbathing in a dream. He sat down beside her. The long pale beach curved away towards the port and the hummocky village of old Cannes on the hilltop. Across the water was the low uneven shape of the Île Ste Marguerite, thickly green with pine trees. The water was restless, the heat made the distances waver.

'Do French girls feel they *have* to flatter men?' asked Sophy, stretching out a lazy brown leg glistening with drying salt water. Her body was relaxed and soaked with sunshine.

He gave a laugh like a snort.

'Consistently. Their plan is very simple: to get us to church and the marriage bed.'

'And men fight every inch of the way.'

'Oh no, Mademoiselle Sophy. Some men are naturally uxorious: is that an English word also?'

'Yes. Hideous, isn't it?'

'The married state is not too pretty either.'

He was lying on the rocks close to her. He wore blue swimming trunks with a white belt: the rest of his body was so dark that it had the sheen of a black grape. To listen to him decrying marriage bored Sophy who turned to look at him, remarking that it must have taken many wasted hours for him to become so brown. She enquired mockingly about his arm.

'It is mending. You see? There's the scar,' he bent his right arm to show the long wavering still-red line running down it; it looked as if somebody had drawn a mark with red ink. It made her shiver slightly.

'So Anne-Marie told you about my stupid accident. I decided not to. I knew you would laugh.'

'How nasty of me.'

'Not at all. It is normal for somebody English,' he said, using the favourite French word for various kinds of behaviour; it was normal to be polite, to be punctual, to do somebody a good turn, to carry heavy packages for a girl, to listen politely to older people (when talking nonsense), and to treat women as if they were made of porcelain.

Sophy saw she must make amends for laughing at his accident.

'There are rather a lot of things *we* think funny and you don't,' she said. 'And it must be the same with you and us. Anne-Marie had quite a horrid time at school because the girls thought it funny that her father is a *poissonier*.'

'But you sprang to her defence.'

'That's a fancy way of putting it, but yes. I stuck up for her.'

'Gallantly, I heard.'

'Does Anne-Marie always confide in you?' asked Sophy curiously, after a little silence. She could not imagine herself telling this sardonic man a story in which she did not show up in a good light. Being jeered at because your father sold fish was distinctly unglamorous. It occurred to her that she had never asked Anne-Marie just how close a friend Daniel was. The idea of their possible affection for each other gave her pause.

Daniel appeared to guess what she was thinking.

'Anne-Marie and I have known each other since I met her brother in Paris,' he said. 'I often come to Cannes for my work and visit the Dufours. As a matter of fact Yvonne asked me to take Anne-Marie to her first dance. At the Palm-Beach Casino. Poor child. Terrified and trembled like a jelly fish.'

'It would be prettier if you said "shook like a leaf".'

'Jelly fish is more exact. I do not criticize her, Mademoiselle Sophy. How could one? She is like a little piece of bread.'

'What does that mean?'

'Wholesome. Good. Real. Necessary.'

Sophy envied the traits and let them go. She said after a while, staring not at Daniel but at the great flat stretch of blue, 'I'm glad I came to France. My family tried to stop me. But here I am.'

'Do you always get your own way?'

'Don't you?'

'Usually, but –'

'But you're a man which is different.'

'Very.'

'Pooh,' said Sophy. She made him laugh.

'It seems we both get our own way. That's going to be difficult.'

'Now what does that mean?' she said innocently.

'Guess,' was the annoying reply.

The sunny days went by one after the other. Stefan and Serge came to the house, shouting to the girls to come and play tennis – 'Don't think you're going to win!' Italian Claudio drove up with a boxful of wine and the sweet liqueurs, favourites of Madame Dufour. Paul returned on his motor cycle from Nice, hurrying to change from sober clothes into slacks and a tennis shirt. The house filled with masculine laughter, and later they all sat down to enjoy another elaborate meal, and talk politics. (Sophy gave Anne-Marie a speaking look and threw her eyes heavenward, but her friend liked such talk and pretended not to see.) Later they all crowded into the garden to smoke and argue. Sometimes they sang. '*Couché dans le foin avec le soleil pour témoins*' was a favourite; Paul sang the best.

If there was a scatter of rain, they danced to the gramophone, kicking aside Yvonne's Persian mats in the grand salon. Every window in the house was open, and the sweet smell of wet earth came in like scent.

Easily the best dancer, demanding Anne-Marie or Sophy in turns, was Claudio. Fattish and short and sweating more than the other men, he was so good-humoured and energetic, he held them so skilfully and swooped them round so swiftly, that it was a joy to be his partner.

But it was Daniel Sophy wanted to dance with. He said he preferred to sit and watch.

She didn't know why. Perhaps flirting with her had stopped interesting him. He seemed to her to be a man of impulses, moods. She didn't understand him and she certainly didn't understand herself.

Like a woman who pretends that the symptoms of a cold or influenza are her imagination, Sophy refused to admit that she was falling in love. The idea was absurd. Impossible. And not practical either, to use the favourite French word, since she was getting married in September to Bob. She had received a few letters from him since she'd arrived in Cannes. Short sailor-like letters which touched her, they were so like him and so dear; she replied eagerly, describing her holiday, biting her fountain pen to try and think of one or two jokes. Bob liked to laugh. She scarcely mentioned Daniel in the letters but she didn't leave him out either and that was as it should be. She was engaged. Settled. Content.

Why, then, did she think of Daniel the moment she woke each bright morning, why did her heart expand when she saw him walking up the sun-checkered drive towards the open doors of the house? He gave her no reason for this joy: he had not changed his manner. He wasn't tender or gallant, what he liked was to tease. But he was never far away. He sat with her on the rocks, swam when she did, joined her, stretching out long legs, in the cafés and beach restaurants. And always lay close in the dark garden.

Months ago when she first became engaged, Sophy had written to tell Anne-Marie the news. When she arrived in Cannes she showed her the sapphire engagement ring and they talked about Sophy's romance. Anne-Marie had shone with sympathetic pleasure, asking shy questions about love.

'I've never known the grand passion yet,' she confessed quite seriously.

'Your turn will come.'

'I hope so. Oh, I do hope so.'

One evening, when they had all spent hours in the garden and Daniel had not sat close to Sophy, he seemed to be avoiding her, she went to bed restless and disturbed. The air was hotter than ever as she climbed into a double bed made for a married couple a hundred years ago. The windows were open and the night so quiet she could hear the waves breaking with a sound like a repeated sigh. Now and again there was the sound of a car ... then silence again. And the sea.

She couldn't sleep. Her thoughts kept her wide-eyed and they were to no purpose. She couldn't, she simply could not be in love with Daniel. She was promised to dear Bob, she always thought of him like that, and in a few weeks' time she would take the train northward and cross the Channel and return home. Her mother would already be getting into a fuss about the wedding. There would be plans, clothes, invitations, wedding presents, bridesmaids to choose – all the arrangements which were expected and were so inexpressibly tiresome. She thought of her father's closed face when her mother chattered about wedding dresses; it was just the sort of talk he despised. For once Sophy agreed with him.

Then the idea of her certain future melted and dissolved. She lay awake but dreaming. Another part of her, her body and her imagination, murmured different and frightening truths. She wanted Daniel. She wanted to kiss him, be embraced by him, lie down with him, and let him do whatever he wanted with her. A virgin, she longed to give up her innocence. A girl promised in marriage, her eyes were on another man.

What Sophy had told Daniel was true, she did get her own way; when she wanted things, she wanted them badly and at once.

She would make plans, then act suddenly. She had wanted to drive to Brighton – her father refused to lend her his car. Sophy took her brother's without asking. Even Jack, usually indulgent, had been annoyed. She had wanted to go to a film when she had flu and had been ordered to stay in bed. She telephoned an admiring boy friend, crept out of the house and went, burning with fever, to the cinema. Idiotic. Fun. She borrowed money from Jack for a dress when her mother ruled it was too expensive. She stayed out until four in the morning when Herbert had ordered her to be home at midnight. When she finally returned he was in the hall, angry, in old-fashioned pyjamas like a figure in a farce. Those scrapes, in all of which Sophy had done exactly as she pleased, were nothing to the way she now felt. She wanted Daniel and could not have him. She must return to England to be married, and put Daniel out of her mind for always. It was only a run-of-the-mill holiday romance. Wasn't it?

Daniel liked to tease her about her engagement.

'And what is this English suitor like?'

His voice had an edge and she enjoyed describing Bob, such rank in the Royal Navy, such British virtues. But now her very engagement ring winking with a small blue fire in the moonlight on her dressing table was something she did not want to wear. What could come of this hunger of hers? Nothing.

How hot it was tonight. Hotter than ever. In the early morning the garden hoses poured rainbows on the thirsty grass, but in the great matrimonial bed, Sophy sweated. She lay with open eyes, listening to the sad sound of the breaking waves. Her thoughts, fed on Hollywood films, imagined Daniel appearing at her open window. He must have climbed (of course) up some thick-stemmed creeper or convenient tree, neither of which existed outside her window. In her fancy she saw him outlined against the night sky. He walked towards her, came closer, into her bed . . .

When she had been at school, a girl friend had lent her an old-fashioned romantic novel which often returned to Sophy's imagination. It was about a woman who during a violent love scene with a man tripped, hitting her head, and fell unconscious. When she recovered she *believed* she'd been raped and although she was in love with the man, she thought she was ruined as they used to call it. In deepest shame she married him. The romance had an unreal and happy end but it was the central idea which fascinated Sophy. Despite her daring ways, her contempt for social rules, her sexual charms, she was ignorant of the mechanics of sex. She imagined herself the heroine of the book, coming to her senses as Daniel left her bedroom. Horror. Bliss.

When she at last drifted to sleep, she had strange dreams.

In the morning, fantasy had blown away, another bright day waited outside. Daniel will be coming round, she thought, he always does. And Anne-Marie has planned for us all to go down to the port and see the preparations for the Fête de la Mer.

That 1939 summer there was a string of such entertainments, and Anne-Marie was determined for her visitor to see every one of them. She was eager for Sophy to appreciate the social glories of the south of France. She and Sophy and some or all of their companions drove to the country on feast-days, to visit ancient churches where there were processions and hymns, ceremonies dating back hundreds of years. They watched motor-boat races. They went to a dance where every girl, for a considerable sum of francs, was awarded a wreath of white roses.

Last week the big occasion had been the Fête de l'Air: fifty planes flying across the bay to the admiration of a transfixed crowd, heads moving in unison to right and left like corn blown by a frolic wind. The planes were small and daring, as they flew higher and higher they looked like insects. They turned and twisted, rose up, fell like stones, then up they zoomed again to the admiring gasps of the crowd.

Daniel had been with Sophy to watch the celebration; he told her that only the most reckless pilots were chosen for the event.

'A sense of safety is not amusing to watch. Although the audience pretend they're not hoping for an accident, of course they are. Do I shock you?'

'Not in the least.'

'What a disappointment.'

He explained the rules.

'You see the crowd of ladies in the marquee?' he said, pointing out a tent larger than that for the smartest wedding, where well-dressed women, all in ankle-length dresses and exquisite hats, were crowding together. 'They're the jury for today's Concours d'Élégance.'

Sophy did not understand. He meant the ladies were

competing? They certainly looked very chic. No, no, no! said Daniel, laughing, it was the elegance of the planes which was to be judged.

Sophy looked at him in total non-comprehension.

'But how can you decide whether an aeroplane is *elegant*? Some are big and some small, some go faster than others. There are the Ash's and the Magnifiques,' trotted out Sophy glibly. She'd learned the names this afternoon. In a Concours d'Élégance, didn't you decide who was the best-looking girl driving the smartest car? Or the prettiest girl parading with the best-bred poodle or Borzoi? But pilots in planes!

'The ladies will simply decide which pilot's the most attractive and which plane they like. We French enjoy competitions for style. Ships, cars —'

She waited for the inevitable 'and women'.

This time he didn't say it.

She and Daniel were always together and never alone. She grew accustomed to the fact that in France one moved in a crowd. Stefan and Serge were constant visitors, she could always tell when the brothers arrived at the house, they were so noisy. She had at last sorted out that Stefan was the one who danced better, Serge a special favourite of Yvonne Dufour's because he paid her so much attention. They were handsome boys, both, and an asset to every party. Alexis Lucas, the miniature d'Artagnan, came nearly every day — he was painting a screen for Yvonne. Claudio, of course, was essential to every gathering; his high spirits, jokes, ebullient strong personality made people laugh. Paul was there, quiet, retiring and shy. He sat and listened or was he thinking his own thoughts? Sophy was never sure. Surrounded by young men, courted — as the French called it — by them, for Sophy there was only Daniel. He never made any secret of his interest in her — walked straight over to sit beside her and tease her. He swam with her, talked to her; and hadn't kissed her once. Their love passages, if that was what they were, consisted of nothing but a feather touch traced up and down her arm when they sat in the dark garden at Les Hesperides.

Cannes was in a festive mood as the summer went gaily

onwards. A year ago there had been the Munich crisis and the universal call-up, the entire nation was alarmed. But war hadn't happened and now the Coast was prospering again. Tourists arrived in the Midi like summer birds, the expensive beaches filled with beauty and money. Anne-Marie was rather attracted to those beaches, and sometimes treated Sophy to visits to the Carlton beach where they hired expensive mattresses and lay under costly parasols.

While they sunbathed, she liked to whisper to Sophy if she recognized anybody well-known.

'That is the Marquis du Bourg. Don't look yet. And Baron and la Baronne de Rothschild, they have such a beautiful villa, truly magnificent, in Fréjus. That is a Rajah –' a thin young man with the face of a poet had walked by, 'I forget his name. And there are those rich Americans ...'

An avid reader of the social columns in the *Nice Matin*, Anne-Marie knew their names too.

'That's Henry Lovatt III,' she muttered, looking at a handsome blond man with brilliant blue eyes. 'And his friend, I think, the short one, is Donald Whittaker II.'

'They sound like yachts,' said Sophy.

In the sea-haunted sun-struck afternoons Daniel came to join them, taking a mattress next to Sophy, the drying salt making patterns on his olive-skinned back. He seemed perfectly content to waste his time on her. Once Sophy remarked on that.

'Anne-Marie says you hate not working. I'm not sure I believe her.'

'I don't like it much,' he spoke without emphasis. 'I miss using my camera, but my arm's still weak.'

'So you don't mind wasting your time,' said Sophy, half fishing.

He shrugged.

'It isn't a waste, swimming is making the arm stronger.'

She could scarcely be disappointed that he had not said something to touch her heart. He never did. But implicit in his words was the fact that time with her was time wasted.

On an afternoon some days after the Fête de l'Air Anne-

Marie again extravagantly took her friend to the Carlton beach; Claudio Arrighi joined them. He and Anne-Marie went down to the sea to swim and Sophy, with the familiar and uncomfortable thrill, saw Daniel lazily threading his way through the ranged mattresses to join her. All he said was 'Salut' as he lay down. He was silent. At first she scarcely noticed, only happy he was near her, but then the interval grew too long and she sat up, reaching for her sun oil, and said rather coolly, 'Daniel?'

'What is it?' He did not raise himself on one elbow but lay flat. She saw his profile, strong nose, thin cheeks.

'You're very dull this afternoon,' she said.

The tone, the expression of her face, were those of a girl aware of her beauty and using it.

'Perhaps I am thinking about you. You are, after all, a woman promised to another,' he replied in his usual manner.

'So I am.'

'Perhaps I do not wish you to be.'

A thrill went through her.

'What are you going to do about it?' she managed to say.

They were in the shade of parasols, their heads and shoulders in shadow, the rest of their bodies stretched in the sun.

'I can do nothing about it. I shall soon be gone.'

'Gone! Where?'

'To Paris. To the start of the war, I suppose.'

She went scarlet.

'There isn't going to be a war!'

He finally turned to look at her. He was not the Daniel of a moment ago.

'Some of us are sure that all this can't last,' he said. 'And isn't meant to. I haven't been able to work because of my arm, but I've been glad of the respite, in a way. At least I met you. But it's coming, Sophy, can't you feel it? There were reports yesterday of German troop movements on the Polish border. Invasion? The tensions are growing and growing. And what does Hitler say? In between conciliatory speeches we can't believe he shouts "I shall strike like lightning." No ...

don't say anything,' he said breaking off and looking at her with a curious expression, 'I know you're going to protest and what you say will be foolish.'

He spoke so kindly. She couldn't bear it.

Along the beaches, down to the sloping edges of the sand where the tiny waves broke, dragged back and broke again, were beautiful girls. They wore bathing suits in the colours of tropical fish, orange and black, emerald, a golden pink. As *Vogue* rightly said, what better accessory to show off a woman's beauty than a man? Every one of the girls had her masculine companion. Their voices were swallowed up in the open air, but there was a constant zing, like a musical instrument, for most of the couples were playing the new craze, ping-pong not with bats but with circular frames like tambourines, stretched with thin leather. Zing! went the ball, and zing! as it was returned. It was the music of the summer.

Daniel watched for a while.

'My poor country is a drunkard at the edge of a cliff. Weaving around and swigging from the bottle.'

Sophy burst out, to stop him, 'You don't believe that. You can't! Why only last night Monsieur Dufour was telling us about the Maginot Line. He said it was impregnable!'

'So he did. So they say. The Germans have a line too. The Siegfried Line. Both countries sit in their fortifications and look at each other, is that it? When have the German soldiers *sat* once since Hitler began to move across Europe? Before my accident I was working on a story with Henri, a reporter I know, and we tried to get some real information about the French air force. We were told nothing but lies. Henri believes that there aren't enough planes to make a couple of squadrons of eight planes apiece. Would they stop the Germans from coming into France?'

'But the Maginot —'

'Sophy. Such a thing will never be enough: 80 million Germans, only 40 million French? The Germans, I'm told, have 120 divisions. We're lucky if we have 90 . . .'

She wanted to block her ears. She hated the way men enjoyed talking about Doomsday. They seemed to relish it. It had been like that in England before Munich, she had heard it everywhere and become angry because it frightened her. Bob never talked in that way, never foretold disaster, he had had a comforting optimism. But she wasn't thinking of Bob now.

'Why are you so gloomy?' She sounded very cross.

'Dear Sophy.'

'There are treaties, aren't there?' she was again quoting Monsieur Dufour. 'France and Britain have signed one with Poland, and Germany agreed that things will stay as they are.' She did not know that she was comic: a girl with the face of an innocent, a halo of burning hair, a clinging bathing suit, spouting second-hand politics. He bit back a smile.

'Hitler signs anything people ask to shut them up and give him time to plan his next move. When he sees the time is right, he tears up the treaties.'

'You're just determined to take a black view.'

'I take a real view. I don't expect you to feel as I do, Sophy. England is an island. When were you last invaded? A thousand years ago. And there's something else. I don't think you despise your country the way many of us despise France right now.'

Sophy was not used to Daniel being serious, he made her indignant and miserable at the same time. Last night Monsieur Dufour, on the whole a quiet man, had had an argument with a friend of his. Both men had fought in the Great War, both felt strongly and Sophy had been present on the rare occasion when Monsieur Dufour grew loud and indignant. Of course it had all been on the subject of France and Germany and of course it had harked back to the last war although neither man had been in the front line. But it was Monsieur Dufour who was the patriot. He had positively shouted. His friend Monsieur Gomis, who was as small as Dufour was huge, as incisive as his friend was blustering, remained pale and calm. Monsieur Dufour went crimson and banged his fist on the table. The young people listened in silence, and later, trooping into the garden, whispered that it was Gomis who had won.

'Poor Papa feels too strongly,' said Anne-Marie.

'He is right. One must,' came, surprisingly, from Paul.

The whole noisy argument flooded back into Sophy's thoughts and she said passionately, 'What about the honour of France? What about *that*?'

Daniel gave her a strange look. He took a long time to reply and finally said, 'I won't swear in front of you, but I'd like to.' That was all.

When they returned to the house, he said he wasn't coming out with them this evening. He had to work.

Up in her room after a cold shower, Sophy tried to settle for a rest before dinner and the expedition planned by Anne-Marie. She lay down in her cotton petticoat, hot and uneasy. Daniel said he was leaving Cannes. She couldn't bear it. He talked of the coming war. She wouldn't believe it. Nobody did, except Daniel and the flat-voiced Monsieur Gomis last night. Why couldn't things stay as they were, she thought childishly, with Daniel beside her and sunny days and nights in the garden and whatever it was growing between them ...

She thought about this coming evening without Daniel. It lacked all flavour. Anne-Marie had said they would walk to the Quai St Pierre to look at the yachts and see the preparations for yet another Concours d'Élégance – tomorrow was the Fête de La Mer. All kinds of craft were competing for the elaborate silver cup; there would not only be yachts and pleasure craft but canoes, rowing boats and the Cannois fishing boats. 'A delight, Sophy!'

To Anne-Marie, a good many things were a delight. Sophy wondered if this went for people too and if so, which of Anne-Marie's friends was the one she probably loved? She treated them all in the same way. She was shy and easy with them and had known most of them for years.

There was a tap at the door and the girl herself looked in. Anne-Marie's lank hair was in curlers, she wore her enveloping floor-length dressing-gown. Until they had shared a bedroom at school, Sophy hadn't known it was possible to undress under a gown without showing an inch of flesh. Anne-Marie, here in Cannes, wore bathing costumes with longer legs and higher necks than any other girl on the beach. Sophy rather admired the modesty. It was rare.

'I'm afraid this has come,' said Anne-Marie. She was holding a small blue envelope as gingerly as if she had struck a match and wished to be rid of it before it burnt her fingers. 'It's a telegram.'

Sophy grinned.

'I expect it's from Jack. He loves telegrams and sends good ones. Jokes, mostly.' Tearing open the envelope, she expected one of her brother's prankish messages; he had sent her a birthday telegram last year, six lines in rhyme. She read the message.

'Prefer you return home soonest stop' ran the telegram. 'Letter follows stop Wire time of boat train Victoria stop Father stop'

'*Blast*,' said Sophy.

Anne-Marie watched her anxiously. Was it bad news? People did not swear when they received bad news, they went pale or began to weep. Anne-Marie had never received a telegram in her life, and her parents only sent or received them in case of illness. The idea of Sophy's brother wasting money on telegraphed jokes must be one of her English friend's inventions.

'Somebody is ill?' she said.

Sophy looked up from the words gummed on a pale ribbon across the telegram.

'Nobody's ill.' She passed Anne-Marie the telegram. 'My father wants me to come home.'

'By why?' Anne-Marie was aghast. 'Does he think you are homesick? Or does your fiancé wish you to go back?'

'Don't be silly. Bob's at sea and the parents know perfectly well you're giving me the best holiday I have ever had. I keep writing and telling them so. I don't know why Father's sent it, he's so boring. Anyway I shan't go.'

'But Sophy! Your father –'

'I shan't go. I shall write and say so. You won't mention the telegram to your mother, will you? Do you think she saw the man bringing it to the house?'

'No,' said Anne-Marie. Her mother was resting, and Clara, the maid, had brought it straight up just now.

'Won't *she* tell your mother?'

'I shall ask her not to,' said Anne-Marie courageously. She was afraid of Clara.

The evening passed pleasantly and Sophy, although she missed Daniel and had been upset by the telegram, tried to forget both her troubles and enjoy herself. By coincidence on the same evening that Daniel was absent, so were all the rest of their friends and the only companion for the girls was Paul. He walked with them along the Croisette to the port. Sophy liked Anne-Marie's brother very much, but felt she hardly knew him. They had scarcely talked to one another at all except if she sat next to him at dinner when, with her encouragement, he sometimes engaged in a kind of conversation. Although he was only a year younger than Anne-Marie and Sophy herself she thought of him as still a schoolboy. He had none of the French poise she admired – he was just shy and quiet.

Anne-Marie had told her that Paul had been brilliant at school and at the Lycée and was 'serious', her favourite word for her brother and one which in French or English suited him perfectly. He was nervous, she said, at the prospect of being the future head of Dufour et Cie one day.

'But it is inevitable. He is the only son.'

Sophy knew Paul was attracted to her. He had rather protuberant eyes of the usual dark brown of the Midi and when he looked at her she saw a shy admiration. He wore a tentative smile when she made silly English jokes. But when she returned the smile in friendly fashion he looked away.

Tonight he was pleased to be the only man in the group and walked between the two girls, giving his arm to each. He pressed Sophy's arm slightly against his side: she could feel his ribs. He was so thin.

Like an actress in her dressing-room preparing to play the leading role, the Quai St Pierre was putting on its beauty this evening. The harbour had become steadily more fashionable in recent years and now pleasure craft came here from all over the world. Beautiful yachts and cruisers, highly varnished, perfectly appointed, costing impossible-to-imagine-sums of francs or dollars, English pounds or the plentiful money from wealthy South American families who loved Europe. Tonight the craft rocked lightly in a breath of wind; they looked as if they had never known a rough wave.

Tomorrow was the 'Conteste Fleurie' and all the craft were to be dressed with flowers. The winner would be awarded a large and elaborate engraved silver cup, which would be his for a year. Already at half past eight this evening many yachts had been garlanded with ropes made from marguerites, with branches of flowering yellow broom, or the small-headed red and pink carnations grown on the mountains. And lavender. So many bouquets and wreaths and strings of lavender everywhere that the air of the quay was as scented as the streets of Grasse.

Some yachts had pompous silver vases arranged on their decks filled with gladioli. Canoes had sprays of roses tied to their oars. Flowers were everywhere, and at Sophy's feet was a poor rose which some enthusiast had dropped. She picked it up. A fat cabbage rose with a deep rich smell.

'I should have given you that,' said Paul as Sophy sniffed the flower. For some reason the unexpected remark gave her a pang. Nobody should look as vulnerable as Paul; she wished his cheeks weren't so hollow. 'Rosemary can be dried, can't it, Paul?' she said, wanting to please him. 'Why not give me a little branch from the garden and I'll take it back to England.'

She was rewarded with one of his deep looks, and Anne-Marie hearing the word 'rosemary' pointed at a sailor as craggy as a pirate, who was clambering along the deck of his fishing smack with his arms full of the flowering stuff.

It was amusing to walk along the quay, admiring and commenting, and Sophy was very surprised when Anne-Marie said it was getting late and they had to go home. Who retired early in this warm land? It was scarcely ten o'clock by the lighted face of the clock on the Le Suquet church tower. But Sophy could scarcely argue, after all she was a guest, and Paul was apparently unaware of how much she was enjoying herself; he turned round to accompany them home.

On the walk back along the Croisette the restaurants and bars were crowded and festive and from the windows of the great hotels music came flooding. Everybody, thought Sophy, is enjoying themselves. Les Hesperides had few lights shining, the music had faded, the only sound was a chorus of frogs.

There were the usual formal goodnights at the foot of the stairs. Anne-Marie asked if she could make Sophy a tisane?

'I am going to have one. It is so good for sleep.'

But Sophy politely refused the wishy-washy brew of lime flowers. Paul took her hand and pressed it, giving a little bow.

'I will remember the rosemary in the morning,' he said.

Sophy trailed up the stairs. Why did Paul make her feel uneasy? She had never encouraged him. Yet he seemd to reach her heart in a way her languishing and lascivious admirers never did. Swallowing a yawn, she opened her bedroom door.

And came to a stop.

Sitting calmly on a chair by the window, thin legs crossed, dress sweeping the floor, was Anne-Marie's mother.

Yvonne Dufour lifted up her hand, indicating that the door must be closed before they spoke. Sophy thought immediately of the telegram. Clara hadn't held her tongue after all — but why should she? And Madame was here to tell her it was high time to pack her bags.

When the door was safely shut, Yvonne Dufour smiled coolly and indicated the second chair in Sophy's room which she had drawn up facing her own as if for an interview between headmistress and pupil. Hell and damnation, thought Sophy, swearing at her absent father. Now I'll have to go.

'I came to speak to you in private and this seemed the most practical place,' began Yvonne. 'I requested my daughter to come home early tonight. I told her she was looking tired and needed sleep. Evidently she does not look tired, but she is a good child and very obedient. This gives me the chance to speak to you, Mademoiselle.'

She never called Sophy by her name.

The girl sat down in the velvet chair. She looked pretty and pale under her sunburn. She was alarmed and resentful but all her face showed was a certain blankness; her inquisitor put that down to the disliked English phlegm.

'What I say must be in strict confidence,' continued Yvonne Dufour.

'Madame?'

'You must not think me unreasonable.'

Here it comes, thought Sophy, she's making a few preliminary remarks before telling me to go to Cook's. How can I possibly refuse? Her thoughts rushed wildly about like a bee trapped under a glass, buzzing impotently.

'I want to speak to you about Anne-Marie,' said Madame.

Sophy was staggered. The sight of the Frenchwoman in her bedroom had been something of a shock but her words were totally unexpected. She was not going to be asked to go after all. Then what was coming?

Yvonne Dufour paused for a moment, playing with her rings, a fashionable platinum *alliance* as a wedding ring was called in French, and two hoops, one of diamonds, one of rubies.

'Nothing I am about to say is official yet,' she said. 'But of course I know my own child's feelings upon this subject. And my husband and I saw Monsieur Christian Vergé in Paris last year. The point, Mademoiselle, is this. It is hoped that my daughter and Daniel Vergé will marry next year. He already has a good career in journalism and is a young man of excellent family,' added Yvonne whose husband used to go to Nice market in a fishing apron. In fact, the lady continued, leaning her coiffeured head against the crimson back of the chair, in fact both she and her husband, and Monsieur Vergé (his wife, alas, was dead) hoped the engagement would be announced within the next few months.

'There is the Film Festival at Cannes in September. That might be a good opportunity.'

While she was speaking, Sophy had not moved. Yvonne Dufour looked steadily at her.

'So you see, Mademoiselle, how things will be ... I did not

101

think,' she added, one finger tracing the carving on the arm of the chair, 'it would be necessary to tell you this. But as things turned out ...'

The pause was expressive. Sophy found her voice.

'But *why?* Why hasn't Anne-Marie told me? What is so secret about it?'

She was still pale. Her freckles stood out.

Madame Dufour gave a little laugh.

'My dear Mademoiselle, my daughter does not know about it at present.'

Sophy's mouth fell open.

'Of course she is fond of Daniel, we all are, but there has been no talk of marriage to the child. We thought it best to wait. Daniel, of course, was consulted some time ago and agreed not to propose until we thought it was time. After all the child has scarcely left school.'

'So I mustn't mention it either?' Sophy managed to say.

'I'm afraid not. I expect you find this difficult but you must believe me, we do things a little differently in France. Young girls do not have the liberty you have in your country; that is not to say,' sweetly, 'we have not their happiness entirely in our minds when arrangements are made.'

Yvonne Dufour's voice was hard and rather flat; it now grew sentimental, like a woman putting icing sugar on a cake with a palette knife.

'Daniel Vergé will suit my little one. He is a good young man. Intelligent. I'm told he has great talent and is set for a worthwhile career. Yes, he will suit Anne-Marie. So, Mademoiselle,' still fixing Sophy steadily, 'you will keep my confidence?'

'Naturally, Madame.'

Yvonne Dufour studied her dispassionately.

'It is evident that you are *ravissante,*' the manner was now kindly. 'Perhaps you should seek the company of Serge or Stefan.'

'I don't need to "seek the company" of anybody in particular.' Sophy was very sharp. 'You have been good enough to give me a very happy holiday. But as you know,' she tried to shovel up her dignity, 'I am engaged to be married.'

'So I hear,' said Yvonne, standing up. She walked to the door and quietly opened it, turning to Sophy to wish her a good repose.

Sophy threw herself on the bed and hit the pillow with clenched fists. She wished it was Daniel's malicious face. How dare he hang round her when he was promised to Anne-Marie? Why hadn't he kept away from the start? Why had he indicated over and over again that he was attracted to her? That she was the one he wanted to be with? When in all the weeks she'd been here had he sought out Anne-Marie? And when for that matter had Anne-Marie betrayed jealousy of herself or even an interest in Daniel? She always looked her brightest with Claudio Arrighi. Daniel's face came into her thoughts: she mentally hit him with all her force. But phantom blows, like phantom embraces, were poor stuff. She was too angry and humiliated to undress and go to bed. Her body seethed with emotion. Unable to bear the light, she switched it off and lay in the dark – the heat a suffocating eiderdown. Everything's spoilt, she thought. How can I stay here when I have to avoid Daniel all the time? I shall keep watching him with Anne-Marie. I shall be so self-conscious, what I'm thinking about will be obvious to Yvonne and to him. She did not blame Anne-Marie's mother for warning her off. But it meant she must go home.

Lying in the dark airless room, full of hate and humiliation at being made to look such a fool, she never once remembered Bob.

And then, tossing and turning on the bed, she began to think how she was going to face Daniel. If I don't tell him what a bastard he is, I'll burst, she thought. How can I do it in public? How can I see him alone? The moment the second question came to her she realized what she had to do. Go and see him now. She knew where he lived, although she had never visited the flat. It was in a small newish block called Les Embruns, on the other side of the point of the Croisette. Anne-Marie had showed it to her on a walk the other week, saying Daniel had taken a small flat there. It was inexpensive and he liked the view of the Île Ste Marguerite.

Sophy sat up and listened. Les Hesperides had settled for the long hot night. Not a sound except the croaking of the frogs.

She climbed off the bed, pushed her fingers through her hair which was damp with sweat and bent to find her sandals. The mirror was a silver oval in the wardrobe door but she did not look into it. The moon, almost at the full, shone through the windows. The light was ghostly.

She crept across the parquet floor and gingerly opened her bedroom door. The passage was empty and shadowed. She gave a sudden jump when a clock struck eleven – how loud it sounded. She waited. But the house slept on.

Closing her door silently, Sophy set off, holding her breath when she went past the Dufours' bedroom. What could she possibly say if Madame suddenly appeared? I'll have to make up some rigmarole about needing air, thought Sophy. Anyway, she won't come out. Anne-Marie says her mother takes sleeping pills. Oh, there are the stairs. Do any of them creak, I wonder?

She began to make her way down, moving in slow motion. She tested each tread before stepping upon it and one gave an agonized creak as if the wood were in pain. Sophy stood frozen. But no light sprang up, no dressing-gowned figure called 'Sophy! What are you doing?'

At last she was safely downstairs, slipping through the marble hall as lightly as a dancer, unlocking the front door which – Clara was a good servant – had an oiled lock which turned like silk.

The garden smelled of herbs and the coconut fragrance of a great fig tree. Sophy walked across the grass, through the gate and at last was safely out in the road.

The ordeal of creeping from the house was over and she was free to hurry, to ignore the flap of her sandalled feet on the pavement. She quickened into a run and with speed her anger came back. She detested Daniel. He'd treated her like a cheap pick-up, like a sexy visitor you played the fool with, somebody of no account; and all the time he was promised to Anne-Marie. A quiet road towards the end of the point led to the other side where Les Embruns faced the sea, and Sophy swerved into it, running hard in spite of the heat. There were the flats in almost total darkness and there across the water was the island and the looming shape of the prison where the man in the iron mask had languished. Sophy hurried to the front door and pressed a bell marked 'Night Porter'.

An old man grumblingly let her in. He had been asleep and resented being woken up. But at least he had opened the door for her without the puritanical look of disapproval she would have been given in England. Probably night porters at home would not admit a girl to a house or a block of flats at night at all. They'd look at her as if she were a prostitute. Sophy slipped past him, muttering her thanks.

He grunted and returned to a glassed-in box in the corner of the entrance hall where he dozed on a chair until six the next morning.

Sophy darted up the stairs. She knew Daniel lived on the first floor and when she came to the landing saw there were only two doors, both of which had visiting cards pinned upon them. There it was. D.P. Vergé. And a Paris address.

She put her hand on the bell and kept it there.

She heard it buzzing and buzzing and almost immediately the door was thrown open and Daniel said in French,

'What in the name of –'

His voice was loud. So was the bell. Both stopped.

'Sophy!'

'May I come in?'

Surprise faded from his face. He stepped back with a mocking gesture of welcome.

The flat was hotter than Les Hesperides, smallish and poky and smelled of Gauloises. The doors to the balcony were open, and he had been sitting outside at a table covered with newspapers. Beyond was the peaceful sea.

She turned and faced him like a spitting cat.

'How *dared* you? How dared you make a pass at me?' the stale American euphemism came out unconsciously. 'Why didn't you tell me, *pig*, that you're going to marry Anne-Marie?'

'So that's why I'm being honoured with this visit.'

'Don't jeer at me, I won't have it! How *could* you behave like you did? How *could* you!' she repeated, longing to smash the malicious face.

'Yvonne Dufour told you, I suppose?'

'What the hell has that got to do with it?'

'A great deal.'

'You mean does your precious fiancée know. Well, she doesn't. Yes, it was Madame. Telling me to keep away from you. That'll be a pleasure from now on.'

'Sophy, Sophy, calm down. Control yourself. You're breathing so fast you'll choke.'

'*Shut up!*' she shouted, almost crying from temper, 'I hate you. Hate you. You –'

'Never made a pass, as you call it, now did I? I don't recall that we've even kissed, or, let me see, have we?'

She glared at the implication that he couldn't remember. She still breathed fast and stood at bay. Daniel sighed and looked around for a cigarette.

'There's nothing settled between Anne-Marie and myself, Sophy. I should have thought that was very obvious.'

'How do I know how you French behave? *We* don't have arranged marriages, thank God!'

'My dear child, neither do we ... Or very seldom. The idea was entirely Yvonne's.'

'And your father's.'

'*Dieu,*' he said, grinning in spite of himself. 'She gave you the full fairy tale, didn't she? Well, yes it seems that Yvonne and my father talked over the matter in Paris at one time. My father, I'll confess, liked it. Not surprisingly.'

'Because Anne-Marie is going to be –' began Sophy bitchily. She was going to speak of her poor friend's money, and indeed her lack of sexual attraction. She stopped from sheer shame.

'Because Anne-Marie will inherit. Is that what you're going to say? Now let us stop talking this nonsense. I have no idea whether I shall marry her or not. The thing isn't settled and it has certainly not been discussed seriously by me or my father.

I haven't thought about it. In any case I've already told you I shall soon be gone.'

He began to smoke, leaning against the wall, looking at her through the cigarette smoke, screwing up his eyes. What was that favourite word of Monsieur Dufour's for the Maginot Line? Impregnable. That was Daniel.

What had she thought would happen when she crept out of the house and came running here? That she would have the satisfaction of slapping his cruel face? That she would burst into sobs, and Daniel would grovel and deny everything? Did he look like a man who would apologize? He stared at her. She stared back.

'And now, Sophy, why are you really here?'

'To tell you to go to hell.'

'Why? For finding you beautiful?'

'Stop. I won't listen.'

Her voice died away and to her impotent rage she felt her eyes brimming. He came to her in a single step, she recoiled but he put his arms round her. He kissed her wet eyelids.

She began to cry from anger and despair and when he whispered to her in French she couldn't hear a word. She was still weeping when he picked her up and carried her into the bedroom.

'No, no, I didn't mean –'

'Nor did I, little one, nor did I.'

He began to kiss her gently, lips apart, the first kiss he had ever given her. He undid the buttons of her dress and kissed her breasts with their wild-rose coloured nipples. He undressed her tenderly, and made love to her, gently at first and then with passion. Sophy had been a virgin when she ran out into the hot dark that night but Daniel took away that treasure for always. She had been a free spirit, she had belonged only to herself when she had crept out of Les Hesperides, but when he walked back with her hours later and left her before they reached the gate and when Sophy climbed the stairs just before dawn, worn, melting, wet with sweat and lovemaking, Daniel had changed her.

She slept until broad day.

When she woke she lay for a long time. Thinking about sex.

5

The right true end of love was no end at all. Sophy and Daniel had spent hours in each other's arms and she had not known until it was over that the effect of love making was to make you weak. She'd believed, running through the night, that all she wanted was the satisfaction of telling him he was a swine. She would be revenged by insulting him, she would make him look as much of a fool as *she* was, then she would march off to Cook's and buy her ticket back to England.

Nothing like that happened. He'd never said he was sorry, never denied he might perhaps marry Anne-Marie – he had simply made love to Sophy as if that was why she was there. Had it been? Satisfied desire, awoken desire, the dreadful knowledge that this was love, lay heavy on Sophy.

Last night when they were naked together and love making was over for a while, she'd said, 'Why didn't you leave me alone? You belong to Anne-Marie.'

He raised himself up and leaned on his elbow.

'What a child you are, although your body is that of a glorious woman. Why am *I* not angry with *you* for promising yourself to some English stick in the English navy? We mustn't waste ourselves, Sophy, thou and I. You don't read the newspapers, foolish one, raging about arranged marriages when our two countries are on the edge of war. We'll soon be dead, Sophy. Let's enjoy our sex while we can.'

'You're saying that to frighten me.'

'I wish that were true.'

He ran his fingers up and down her arm, brushing the fine hairs, in the curious caress he had used when they were in the garden. He transferred his touch to her belly, slowly, slowly then further down ...

Later again, she couldn't stop herself from talking about Anne-Marie. Her body was sated and swimming, but her mind had begun to work.

'I never guessed she loved you,' said Sophy, looking at him with a heart-rending face.

He gave a slight laugh.

'She probably doesn't. Yvonne Dufour is the one pushing the affair. She wants Anne-Marie settled, which is normal,' he added, using the French word.

'Wants to get her off her hands, you mean. I can understand that.'

'Don't be cruel, Sophy. It does not suit you.'

She stared at the ceiling. They lay in the southern half-dark half-light, it was luminous, as their bodies were.

'She'll make you a wonderful wife,' Sophy remarked, after a silence.

'And you will be the spouse of an admiral. Must you play the fool?'

He looked at his wrist-watch.

'There is half an hour, Sophy, and then I must take you home. I must be sure you get safely indoors without being seen. Yvonne Dufour would have an ugly name for you if you were caught.'

'And what would she say about *you*?'

'Sophy. I am a man.'

Sophy's thoughts stopped there. At least, her thoughts of Daniel stopped. She faced instead a thought – a person – she had avoided until now. Bob. What had last night done to Bob? She'd betrayed him. She thought hazily about a husband who discovered on his wedding night that his bride had been possessed by another man. She tried to visualize a scene between Bob and herself when she would confess. She couldn't do it. Couldn't imagine herself as Bob's wife any more. Her yearning heart, her physical self, were with Daniel. Bob was yesterday and although for a moment she tried, she couldn't remember the tone of his voice.

She climbed out of bed and tugged the curtains open. The sun came in like a giant, its radiance blinding her. When she recovered her sight, everything in the room had paled, the carpet's flowers, the bed's carved head, her own crumpled dress, the cabbage rose she'd picked up from the pavement when she had been with Paul.

There was a tap on the door.

'I couldn't believe you could still be asleep, Sophy. You were over-tired,' said Anne-Marie, entering in blue and white stripes, fresh as a milkmaid. She was carrying a little sprig of rosemary.

'Paul picked it for you before he went to work this morning. Shall I put it in the tumbler with your rose?'

The sight of her friend, loving, calm, made Sophy feel truly wicked.

Anne-Marie rang for breakfast and sat companionably while Sophy drank coffee and ate a croissant with home-made black cherry jam.

'It is the Ball tonight. Of course you haven't forgotten?'

'Of course not. Are you excited?'

'It is a great event,' said Anne-Marie, as usual. 'We must try to look our best.'

Sophy had heard a good deal about tonight's ball. Although Anne-Marie invested everything festive in Cannes with glamour and importance, here was an event which even impressed Yvonne Dufour. It was the Bal des Petits Lits Blancs, given every year at the Palm Beach Casino, and the millions of francs raised by this dance for the rich, went to hospitals for children with tuberculosis.

Perhaps because it was on the Côte d'Azur, perhaps because it was for so good a cause, the ball had a certain glory attached to it. The grand world came to waltz and to give. Not only those already spending the summer in Cannes, but from Paris too. Millionaires, French duchesses, English dukes and old and new money from America.

'And of course the ball is good for our city,' Anne-Marie had said, 'for trade.'

She and Sophy had new dresses for the occasion. Sophy had saved one of hers, black satin bought in London with money given her by her brother. Anne-Marie's was virginal white organdie made by a local dressmaker. She was enchanted with it, but Sophy thought the girlish sash a mistake.

The Dufour family were all going to the ball – Monsieur and Madame, Paul, Anne-Marie and her guest. Serge and Stefan would be there and so would Claudio. But Alexis said he was too busy, which Anne-Marie later translated to Sophy as meaning he could not afford the ticket. She wasn't sure whether Daniel would be there or not.

'He has bought his ticket. But sometimes Daniel says he'll come to things and never turns up.'

'Does that annoy you?'

'No. Why should it?'

In the afternoon Anne-Marie suggested that 'to relax' they should go again to the Carlton beach. She wanted to pay but Sophy, flush with money recently sent by Jack, insisted. Anne-Marie looked complacent; she was generous but when Sophy impulsively bought her flowers or managed to get ahead of her to the beach bars and pay for the mattresses she was pleased. She liked to admire her friend.

They lay dozing on their mattresses after a swim, too hot to talk, while voices round them murmured or laughed. Swimmers wandered up from the sea, to buy drinks and return, glasses clinking with ice, to gossip and sunbathe. Sometimes when the talk was at its most serious Sophy noticed it was about food. In the Midi they discussed things to eat in the way people in England spoke about gardens.

She shut her eyes, pretending to sleep. When would she see Daniel? And what was going to happen next? She was in a fever of emotion, she did not know whether she could bear the grand ball tonight when she would spend every moment waiting for him to arrive – and then he would not come. Her thoughts tired her and opening her eyes she stole a look at the girl beside her. Anne-Marie really was asleep, her mouth half open, her eyelashes two crescents on the immobile olive-coloured face. Sophy looked away from Anne-Marie's plump body, trying not to imagine Daniel claiming it.

She put her arms above her head, and concentrated on the only embrace she felt at present: the sun.

Coming from nearby Sophy heard the sound of an unmistakable English voice. It was not unusual to hear English spoken on the Carlton beach but this girl's voice was louder than usual.

'Is it *really* on the posters, Dave? Your French isn't so marvellous. You must have got it wrong.'

'I sure didn't, ma'am.' replied an American voice. 'I saw it right outside the hotel just now. Pasted over those affiches for the film festival. There was some sort of heading, Calling to the Colours, I think it was. Reservists, categories 2, 3 and 4.'

'What on earth does that mean?'

'I asked the porter. He said every able-bodied man, from eighteen to forty-five.'

'Called up? In *uniform*?' The girl sounded incredulous.

'That's right, I'm sure sorry for France, and for England too. This is going to be sump'n we'll keep out of, I'm afraid.'

'But in the English paper it said only the youngest lot are being called up at home –' the voice still loud. 'Why the panic? I don't get it.'

Sophy turned, pretending to reach for her sun-oil. The girl, small-featured, conventionally pretty, bronzed from months of sunshine, was bolt upright beside a big rangy-looking man.

'I shall have to ring the parents. They'll be having kittens. Oh hell, Dave ... will you come with me? My father likes you and maybe ...'

The American stood up, putting out a strong arm to pull the girl to her feet. They walked away through the lines of mattresses, still talking.

Unable to go on lying at ease, Sophy sat up, biting her lips. With the obsessive selfishness of sex all she thought was – Daniel's going to be called up. And I'll be forced to go home.

She looked at Anne-Marie, deep in contented oblivion, and

wanted to shake her awake, snatch away her peace in the way Sophy's own had been wrenched from her. Anne-Marie didn't stir. Sophy went barefoot under striped awnings to get herself some iced lemonade. She removed the ice with her fingers – only fools left French ice in their drinks – and was throwing the melting squares into the sand when she saw Daniel standing at a distance, surveying the mattresses and supine brown bodies. He saw her at the moment she saw him and came towards her with the unhurried walk of the great heat.

It was strange to see his body again. He was hairy, his strong legs darkened with black hair, his chest too. Last night lying against him she had said it was like putting her cheek on a fur rug. Seeing him now, her legs felt weak.

'Sophy.'

He picked up her hand and gave her wrist a careless kiss. 'I hoped you'd be here. Where's Anne-Marie? Ah yes, I see her. Dead to the world.'

'Oh Daniel. I'm so glad you came. I had an awful idea you might be gone.'

'Not for a day or two, Sophy. Maybe longer.'

'But you're going to be called up!'

He looked pleased at her distress.

'You've seen the posters? Do you know this is the third time there's been a general call-up. It's growing monotonous. We had one last September, everybody in a great fuss. Then again this March. Now today. But this time it is real.'

She scarcely heard what he said because she couldn't bear it. She felt frantic and dared not blurt out her old song that surely war would be averted. She asked, putting her hand on his arm, 'Will you have to go into uniform, Daniel. *When?*'

It seemed incredible that he remained so cool. This was the man who had made wild love to her last night, yet now belonged utterly to himself; he explained that as a photographer he would be exempt from the call-up, his was a reserved occupation. His newspaper had rung this morning and told him to get as many pictures as he could of the call-up civilians arriving in Antibes at the Fort Carré.

'I'll drive over this afternoon. It's my guess it will be a big

113

fiasco, thousands of men arriving at the Fort Carré, nobody ready for them, and all hell breaking loose.' He laughed. 'Good pictures, though. The paper also wants me to see if I can get permission to go to the mountains along the Italian frontier. There's been optimistic talk about Mussolini turning into an ally. Imagine! But the Italians at present aren't showing signs of joining anybody.'

He walked with her to her mattress and sat down at her feet. At least, she thought, embracing him with her eyes, he wasn't in that peculiar uniform French soldiers wore. He was here, lighting a cigarette and smiling at her through the smoke.

His eyes turned to Anne-Marie.

'She looks like a saint on a tomb,' he said, 'she's too good, that girl.'

'Aren't *I* good?'

'Not in the way I mean when I look at her. You're a different book and one I have just begun to read.'

Selfishly happy at once, she gave a deep sigh and just then Anne-Marie slowly opened her eyes, saw Daniel and put out her hand to him in a gesture which gave Sophy a faint frisson. When Daniel told her about the call-up, Anne-Marie looked horrified. Then gloomy.

'Paul will have to go. And Serge and Stefan and Alexis. And then,' she added, looking at Daniel, 'what about poor Claudio?'

'But he is Italian,' said ignorant Sophy.

Daniel silenced her with a look.

Anne-Marie was not to be comforted. Everything alarmed her, most of all the future of her friends. There would be a call-up in Italy too, wouldn't there? Daniel agreed that it was very likely but comforted her with murmurs about reserved occupations, supply, Claudio's work and long association with France. His manner to her was very different from the way he treated Sophy. He was gentle.

No amount of remembering last night's embraces could stop Sophy from feeling jealous and when Daniel left them at the gates of the house and she and Anne-Marie went indoors,

114

she said impatiently, 'Oh do cheer up! Nothing awful's happened yet. What about tonight's ball? You said how much you'd been looking forward to it.'

'Perhaps Paul and the boys and Claudio will not be allowed to come. They'll have to go to the barracks —'

'Daniel said it could be today or tomorrow or even the day after,' said Sophy, rallying her. 'Otherwise there'll be a huge mass of men and it'll be completely unmanageable. Anyway,' she went on, determined to shake the girl from her depression, 'perhaps it isn't so serious. There have been two call-ups already and nothing happened.'

Anne-Marie was looking, not at Sophy, but at her words. She stood with her hand on the banisters, the picture of solemn thought.

'Yes,' she said at last, 'it could be our government's gesture. To show Hitler we are in earnest.'

'Exactly. Come on, Anne-Marie! We haven't much time if we are both going to have a bath.'

Sophy's ignorant predictions about the call-up proved correct. Paul, Stefan and his brother, and bustling Claudio all arrived for the little champagne party Yvonne was giving prior to the ball. None of the young men had received his papers and when Paul had gone to the Fort Carré that afternoon, the crowds were almost out of control. He climbed back on his motor cycle and drove home.

The talk was noisy, all about politics but somehow cheerful.

'Hitler doesn't want war!' exclaimed Claudio, 'I have a close friend, a banker in Paris, and he was telling me ...'

He went into long optimistic descriptions of how financiers would prevent a conflict, quoting a favourite phrase – 'money talks'.

'It's said the Soviet Union might even come in on the allies' side,' Paul said, speaking for the first time. Stefan and Serge, whose grandparents were White Russians, loudly denied that. Claudio returned to talk of bankers ...

The Palm-Beach casino was not far from Les Hesperides and as they walked towards it Anne-Marie, quite her old self, muttered 'incredible'. Long strings of lights hung across the roofs and outlined the Moorish balconies. There were lights threaded into the palm trees, and hidden among the shrubs. They shone on marble terraces, they ringed the fountains.

All the Côte d'Azur, probably most of 'tout Paris', London and New York, were sweeping towards the Casino's open doors. Footmen in blue and gold livery took the tickets. No guest was admitted who was not in evening dress, and all the men wore tails. The women were visions of high fashion, in the enormously full-skirted dresses, modern versions of the crinoline, which had made the headlines at the Paris collections. The women moved with the swish of stiffened silk petticoats.

This, thought Sophy, is the life. She put away her heartache and the agitations of this morning, she looked round at a ballroom filled to the brim with beauty and money, like a basket crammed with flowers. The dresses and the music, the sound of French, spoken so much faster and with more spirit than English, the resinous scents, the distinguished men and beautiful women, the positive mountains of roses in golden baskets, it was a scene from some fantastic film. She had been to charity balls in London and Brighton. Never like this.

Monsieur Dufour and their party were ushered by a waiter to a table at a slight distance from the ballroom floor and not too close to the band which was playing *Parlez-moi d'Amour*, as bands all over Europe were playing perhaps at the very same moment. With his guests settled, Monsieur Dufour ordered pink champagne; Anne-Marie was carried away at once to dance with Claudio. Stefan, the more serious of the brothers, leaned on his elbow talking to the Dufours, and Serge stood up and went over to ask a blonde girl to dance. This left Paul and Sophy. The young man drank his champagne in an embarrassed way.

'Are you going to ask your English guest to dance, Paul?' enquired his mother, breaking off her talk.

Her son stood up, eager and shy, and accompanied Sophy on to the floor. She smiled at him, wondering where Daniel could be.

They began to waltz. He had no sense of rhythm and Sophy had to concentrate to follow his not-very-expert steps.

'You are very beautiful,' he said after a while. 'But you are to be married to an Englishman. I cannot tell you how sad that makes me.' She was surprised at the declaration; he had been made brave by the music.

'But I like you very much, Paul. Shall we be friends?'

'Yes. Yes, please.'

'Thank you for my little sprig of rosemary. I will treasure it.'

He looked at her, his face full of expression. He was such a boy, with his romantic face like an actor's, thin and dark. She could never love a man so inexperienced and diffident.

'In English we say rosemary for remembrance,' she said. 'And we're to be good friends. Comrades.'

He pressed her close, but only for a moment. His dark face looked as if he had been hurt.

Daniel had assured her earlier that he would come to the ball, but would be driving first to Antibes to the Fort Carré; he had to see some army people.

'They will give me the necessary permissions for any pictures I'm allowed to take. Dealing with the army is always a great bore. They behave as if one were a spy,' he'd said, laughing. 'But I promise I will come.'

An hour, two hours, went by. The Dufour party had supper. More champagne was served and Sophy danced a number of times with Paul and then with Claudio who made her laugh with his comments about other women.

'Now that one,' he whispered, as they whirled by a lady in an elaborate black and gold Chinese dress, 'is no longer as you say in English a small hen?'

'Spring chicken, and it's very rude.'

'Forgive me,' said Claudio, flashing his smile and some wonderful gold teeth.

The music changed while the party were having coffee and liqueurs, the French band replaced by South American players in skin-tight satin trousers and frilled shirts with huge sleeves. Neither Claudio nor Paul could do the South American dances and Sophy who was good at them had to watch other women elegantly wriggling to the sound of the maracas. Quite suddenly as she was drinking her crème de menthe, there was Daniel.

'*Tiens.*' Yvonne Dufour did not look best pleased. He had not been one of the invited guests and she had not known he was coming. She coldly asked if he would like something to eat. 'We have finished,' she added.

'No, thank you, *aimable Madame*,' said Daniel, with more grace than she deserved, 'I dined with the adjutant at the Fort Carré.'

He looked about, found a spare gilt chair, and drew it up to the table, undisturbed by Yvonne's expression, and turned to her husband.

'Monsieur Dufour, you cannot imagine the chaos! Dozens, scores, of recruits pouring into the Fort in their best suits, poor unfortunates, all talking at once. The sergeants were totally unable to cope. One man looked as if he was going to have an apoplectic fit. I took some excellent photographs of the whole disorganized scramble. Excellent.' He chuckled. He was interested, amused, stimulated by the scenes; it had been clear to Daniel in the mêlée, hearing the shouts of commands, the arguments with well-dressed civilians, that the young men who had been called to the colours were still essentially free citizens. Still themselves.

He leaned forward, talking, laughing, drawing Yvonne, who never stayed cold with him for long, into the conversation. Sophy had a moment of naïve wonder. Was this her lover of last night? He was a vivacious stranger.

Anselme Dufour, always glad to recall the past, recounted what had happened when he had been called up in 1915. 'Of course I was a boy then, and at first alarmed at the prospect of being shouted at and turned into a slave.' He grinned. Apparently there had been almost a riot in the barracks on his first evening because the soldiers had not been given a hot meal. Oh, they'd been given a good dinner in the end, certainly they had. And an extra serving of red wine. The French army, he said, was made up of individuals with the true Gallic spirit. But nobody would dare to deny that when a

Frenchman was moulded into a soldier, he became part of an army which was, to put it simply, invincible.

'True. Very true,' agreed Yvonne, looking from Daniel to her husband and back. 'You, Daniel, are too young to remember how magnificent we are in action.'

You'd think she'd been fighting at Verdun, thought Sophy. Anne-Marie's mother got on her nerves. She had never liked her and the midnight warning-off still festered in Sophy's thoughts. Now Yvonne Dufour appeared to have turned into a patriot, a figure clutching the tricolour. Sophy didn't believe a word of it.

Daniel and the Dufours continued to talk about the possibility of war and Claudio, looking disinterested, took Anne-Marie back to the dance floor where they managed a passable imitation of the rumba. Sophy and Paul sat in silence while the conversation with those repeated names, Hitler, Mussolini, went on and on. Paul was smoking nervously, Sophy playing with her tiny liqueur glass, conscious of nothing but the man on the other side of the table. At last in a pause Daniel looked across at her.

'Shall we dance? I'm sure you'd like to show me how good you are at the South American gyrations.'

She jumped up with alacrity.

The floor had now become more crowded than ever, a mass of satins and taffetas and flying coat tails. Daniel put his hands on Sophy's hips and they moved in unison. She'd known he could do it. Daniel seemed able to do everything well. Sophy performed the curious movement, in which the upper half of the body remained static, while from the waist down the hips and legs moved and swayed. She fixed her eyes on his, letting the music have its way, thinking – did I exist before I met you? When the rumba ended he took her arm.

'Come and walk in the garden; there will be fireworks soon. We needn't go back to the Dufours yet.'

'But Madame will be expecting me, and when we do get back she'll give me one of her looks.'

'Like a cut-throat razor. I get them all the time. Come along, Beautiful.'

They left the ballroom and the music began to fade into the distance; Daniel pressed her to him. Sophy shut her eyes, abandoning herself to the half embrace, the sensation infinitely more frustrated than it would have been a day ago. He was her lover. Or had been.

How heavy the air was, it weighed on her bare shoulders as they walked through a dark which was not dark at all. Here and there a light shone down from the trees, on figures of girls crowned with flowers which would soon die in their warm hair. Or silhouettes of men, in sombre black like destiny. Sophy could hear low voices, and the sound of a fountain. Alone, by a spreading fig tree, Daniel kissed her. She put her arms round him, returning the kiss with passion, thinking – oh, if it would only last. And when he stopped the kiss, she crazily thought – now he will say something to me: something so beautiful that I'll remember it all my life.

Daniel looked up at the sky.

'The stars have gone. It must be clouding over.'

Before she could answer – and what was there to say? – she noticed the sudden dry rustle of the palm trees. A wind had begun to blow, a hot wind. She heard a voice nearby exclaiming, 'Zut! I'm sure I felt a drop of rain.'

It was almost time for the fireworks which were due to start at midnight, and the couples in the gardens had begun to drift back towards the terrace. The ballroom doors were open, and people flooded out – there was now an enormous crowd, all waiting for the delight of falling stars.

'Fireworks are our great national tour de force,' remarked Daniel. 'This year the officials in Cannes have brought some experts from Indo-China to give us the show. Enjoying oneself is a serious business.'

The crowd was getting thicker every moment, and everybody near Daniel and Sophy was discussing the weather – what infernal luck to have a Mistral tonight of all nights. The awnings were cracking with sounds like small pistol shots. A sudden fierce gust knocked over a garden parasol which narrowly missed a man nearby – the crowd laughed as they watched him chasing after the scattered contents of the garden table.

He retrieved a bottle of champagne, lifted it up and shouted:

'Good luck! Not broken!'

There was a burst of applause.

Hundreds of people were jostling and pressing along the terrace, and Sophy was wedged against Daniel, who put his arms round her, pushing her in front of him.

'I'm holding on to you. I don't want some enemy stealing you away!'

Up went the first rocket.

Higher and higher it climbed, bursting at last into a great chrysanthemum of yellow stars to be greeted by voices giving the long drawn-out sigh – 'Aaaah.'

Scores of rockets followed one after the other, or sometimes in glorious unison, bursting into huge flowers which shone their brief eerie light on the upturned faces, turning them blue or gold, crimson or pure white. One single floating star descended slowly . . . but the wind blew it away.

'The Mistral's taking over,' whispered Daniel in Sophy's ear. It was true; it was now blowing so hard that the diamond-threaded and curled hair of the girls was being messed up and disordered, and some women tried to get back indoors through the crush. Now the magnificent fireworks came faster in rainbow colours, circles, stars, and the crowds were bewitched and tried to ignore the battering of the wind. Then somebody screamed. A rocket bursting low and blown by a gust, came fiercely burning straight into the crowd. There were shouts, a surge of people, and another rocket, then another, spurted down on the crowds. At the same moment there was a blinding flash of lightning, a deep roar of thunder. And down came the rain.

Sudden and heavy, it was a cataclysm, beating down on pale dresses, drenching them and turning them dark with rain in seconds. The lightning flashed again, the thunder roared, this time sounding nearly overhead. Daniel, holding Sophy who would have been swept off her feet, began to push her ahead of him and by sheer strength, protecting her with his arms and forging forward, got them both into the ballroom. They were wet to the skin.

'My God, some storm,' he said, steering her as best he could behind a ballroom table. At that moment, after a further enormous flash of lightning and burst of thunder, the entire Casino went dark.

The air was full of shouts and the noise of upturned furniture as people blundered and stumbled in the dark, snapping cigarette lighters which were blown out by the wild wind rushing through the ballroom. There was the noise of smashing glass, and curses, and the screams of frightened girls.

Daniel shouted 'Hold on to me,' and picked Sophy up in his arms. He made his way a second time through the struggling crowds into a kind of blackened Hades and in what seemed an eternity but must scarcely have been a couple of minutes somehow arrived in the total obscurity at the foot of a staircase. A faint almost imperceptible light came from a glass roof on which the rain hammered; Daniel, still carrying her, ran up the stairs. The hellish din from below was fading into the distance.

'Where are we? Where are we going?'

'Up to the top floor, I've often been here to talk to the Patron and you might say I know my way blindfold,' he said. 'No, don't try to get down, Sophy, you'll only get lost in the dark. I don't want to spend my time groping for you. Yes. This will do.'

She heard him turn a handle. He carried her into a room faintly lit at a distance by a single pale square of window. He set her on her feet and led her over to look out. From their high vantage point they saw that it was not only the Casino, but the whole of Cannes which was in darkness. Every hotel, house, street, was obscured. The only lights were from cars driving away from the chaos of the Casino, their headlights bars in the lashing rain.

'There must have been a total power cut. Probably the storm,' said Daniel after a moment. And then, matter of factly, 'Shall we make love?'

'But Daniel –'

'What?' he said, caressing her.

'The others. Perhaps they are hurt. Shouldn't we —'

'Return to that hell downstairs? What an idea. Kiss me. That's right. That's right.'

Their second lovemaking was different from everything Sophy tremblingly remembered of Daniel's first possessing. It was more real. Yet it was strange to be in this lightless place with the muffled sounds of the escaping crowds and the hammering rain. But Daniel was in her arms, giving her such bliss, such pleasure, the sharpest pleasure. And the nightmare storm excited her, it was like a sensual dream. When the lovemaking was over they slept on the floor. The noise from the ruined ball had died and there was nothing now but the relentless beat of the rain.

Sophy was woken by grey daylight from the window. She saw it was still pouring. There was her satin balldress in a crumpled heap, her scattered underclothes and Daniel's too. The clothes looked as if they belonged to people killed in a disaster. A goose went over her grave.

She looked at the naked man sprawled beside her. She had never seen him asleep before. On mattresses on the beach he never slept. When *she* did, and woke and looked at him she always met dark eyes fixed on her, as if he were a kind of demon cursed never to lose consciousness.

Now at last the demon was asleep. She looked at his face, high-cheekboned, severe, and wondered why she was not swept with happiness. Her body's moisture told her she ought to be. Here he was and here she was and that was all there was to the mystery. Wasn't it? She lay back trying to sleep again. She couldn't.

It was broad day when he finally woke, giving a loud yawn and sitting up, rumpling his hair.

'How long have you been awake?' he asked, adding with a gleam, 'I should have thought I'd silenced you for hours yet.'

'Do I talk too much, then?'

'Like a sparrow. Twitter, twitter, twitter. Well, English girl, I suppose we must get you home and provide an alibi. Any ideas?'

'Oh God, I'd forgotten the Dufours.'

'Don't look alarmed. Yvonne can't eat you. Anyway, we suppose they ran off without looking for you, so they didn't show much concern, did they? How do they know one of the rockets hadn't incinerated you?'

'They couldn't find me in the dark.'

'And *you* couldn't find them.'

He stood up and walked over to the window. Sophy sat staring at his naked back. She noticed the long curved row of knobs of his spine, he was very thin, and his body which was a deep bronzed tan in sunlight had a greenish tinge in the room's rainy light.

'It's still pouring,' he said.

She stood up and began to pick up her clothes. The satin evening dress was as creased as a rag. She pulled on her stockings and fastened her suspenders. After she'd remembered the Dufours the thought of sex, the thought of love, evaporated. She was horribly nervous. She had no experience of having been out all night with a man, then forced to return home with some unbelievable story. She would be sent back to England in disgrace. She felt shamed already.

Daniel finished dressing, tying his white tie with more skill than Sophy managed when she fumbled with the delicate buckles of her sandals.

'The Carlton is expensive but very comfortable,' remarked Daniel. Seeing her expression he added pityingly, 'You're slow this morning. The storm was much too dangerous for us to get back to Les Hesperides. Somebody – a duke? – gave us a lift to the Carlton and we managed to get a room there. You telephoned the Dufours last night and again this morning without result.'

She said nothing. How could he look at the prospect ahead as if it were a comedy? He appeared to be accustomed to getting girls out of scrapes. The room where they had spent the night was an office. It was curious to think somebody would soon be coming in to sit at the desk, dictate letters, use the filing cabinet in the corner. Last night was as if it had never been.

Daniel opened the door, took her across a landing and back

down a broad staircase. He knew his way and they soon arrived in the Casino's entrance hall. The whole building was silent except for the noise of the rain.

Suddenly he exclaimed, 'Good God! Look at that!' He had walked to the open doors of the ballroom. It was a scene of utter devastation. The great golden curtains, tugged from their poles, hung flapping in the Mistral which blew in from slamming French windows. Tables which had held mountains of plates and hundreds of champagne glasses had been pushed over, the floor was inches deep in broken china and smashed glass. Chairs lay everywhere like so many unconscious guests. Daniel ventured into the room, his feet crunching on broken glass. Sophy, picking her way, following him. The elegantly planned decor, gilded screens, heaped baskets full of flowers, everything was smashed to pieces. The glass-topped table which had held a display of diamonds had been broken open and was empty. And through the lofty doors, slamming, rattling, slamming, came the cruel Master Wind.

'I wish I had my camera,' said Daniel.

His was the only car left parked on the rain-swept road lined by palm trees, their branches streaming like hair. Head downwards into the wind and rain, Daniel and Sophy struggled to the car and he pushed her inside. They drove down the Croisette. Not a car or a human was in sight and the Mediterranean was a grey mass of thundering waves.

'Somebody has torn down the mobilization posters, unless it was the Mistral. Now, Sophy, head up. Remember, the Carlton gave us an excellent breakfast.'

Not a light showed in Les Hesperides as Sophy and Daniel ran up the steps. The front door was unlocked and they went into a welcome dryness. Daniel nodded towards the petit salon. They could hear voices.

'It's Yvonne. Here goes. *Aux barricades.*'

He pinched her as they walked into the room together.

'Madame! You must have been so worried about poor Sophy,' exclaimed Daniel at once. 'We've telephoned a dozen times but the lines seem to be down. We were forced to spend the night at the Carlton, the Marquis of Choiseul drove us to

125

the hotel. The storm was still very bad, and he insisted we shouldn't try to get back here ...'

His explanation petered out. Yvonne Dufour was not listening. She was sitting at a table with a tray of untouched breakfast – bread, cherry jam, a pot of coffee, an unused porcelain cup. In front of her as if at an interrogation stood Guilietta, the fat old Italian cook, and the young kitchenmaid Maria. Both were mopping their eyes.

'Ah, Daniel and Sophy,' said Yvonne, scarcely turning round to look at them but adding, 'Sophy, what a mess you look. Have you not had a bath?'

'We managed to get two rooms at the Carlton but we hurried here in case you were anxious,' explained Daniel. Yvonne ceased to give them her attention. She was looking at her two servants.

'Guilietta and Maria have told me they are leaving for Italy this morning. Did you ever hear anything so absurd?'

'We must go home, Madame,' from the cook, eyes still brimming.

'I thought you told me Les Hesperides was your home,' said Yvonne very coldly indeed.

'But Madame, we are aliens. It is no longer safe in France.'

'What nonsense. Nothing has changed. And how long have you been working for us, pray?'

Sniffing, the cook said she had been at Les Hesperides for eight years.

'Eight years,' repeated Yvonne. 'Eight years. What can you possibly do when you get to Italy? Have you relatives there?'

'Some. I think.'

'You think!'

'We must go, Madame,' repeated the old woman, while the kitchenmaid listened, looking frightened, her poor nose red from crying.

Guilietta said loudly, as if gathering her courage, 'At least in Italy we will be alive.'

Yvonne gave a martyred sigh and turned to the only man in the room. Daniel, hands in the pockets of his evening trousers, was deeply interested. Sophy merely stood, relieved at being spared trouble but too conscious of her wrecked appearance to care about the departure of the Italians.

'Daniel. What do you think about all this?'

Guilietta appealed to Daniel before he could reply. She had always had a soft spot for the handsome young man who used to come into her kitchen and flirt with her and praise her cooking. She said in a trembling voice, 'Oh Monsieur Vergé, please, please explain to Madame that we dare not stay. It is Gérard ...'

Gérard was the gardener, a taciturn old man who usually worked whilst ignoring both the family and the staff and when spoken to, replied in monosyllables.

'He threatened us, Monsieur Vergé. He came into the kitchen and –'

A wail from Maria.

'And showed me a knife,' said Guiletta, with a violent shudder. 'He says he will cut the throat of every Italian who remains in this house.'

6

England declared war. France, a few hours later, did the same. All the talk now was of the gallantry of Poland and the infamy of Hitler. When Anne-Marie and a subdued Sophy went down the Croisette they saw a regiment of Senegalese troops marching smartly down the centre; they had come to replace the Chasseurs Alpins stationed in Villefranche. The girls waved to them and the soldiers grinned; one tall man, handsome as an ebony statue, winked.

It was extraordinary to see the Mediterranean scattered with yachts like a regatta, not for festivities but obeying the order that private yachts must leave Cannes harbour within 24 hours. Anne-Marie was agitated and kept talking about Claudio.

'Our dear friend will be interned!'

'Anne-Marie, don't bid the devil good morning before he's here,' said Sophy, repeating a cliché of her brother's which comforted Anne-Marie not at all.

Soon the lively Cannes harbour was deserted, the Croisette strangely empty. The young men, like the yachts, had begun to disappear, some of the cafés had almost no staff and when the girls passed the big dusty-looking stretch under the trees by the harbour, reserved for the popular game of boules, the only ones playing were either old men or lanky youths in their mid teens. The sight was curiously depressing. Yet where, after all, thought Sophy, exactly *was* the war?

When they returned home Paul was on the lookout for them.

'You've had a telegram, Sophy,' he said, handing it to her. Anne-Marie went into the salon to talk to her mother and Paul lingered. 'I imagine that's one of the last to come from abroad,' he said. 'All foreign telegrams, telephone calls too, have been forbidden. It must be from your family?' He stood beside her, sympathetic, concerned, as she opened the envelope.

'Return home at once, Father,' was the short message.

'Yes,' said Sophy, folding the telegram up small. 'They say I must go home.'

'Do you want to go?' asked the young man looking at her searchingly.

'Not one bit.'

'Then surely you could stay. I'm certain Anne-Marie will want you to. As for me –' he added, 'it would be a sadness to lose you, Sophy. Is that selfish of me?'

'Oh. It is kind!' It was always the same, that quality in Paul which reached her.

'You'll be quite safe here,' he said.

She impulsively touched his arm, then ran up to her room to push the telegram into the same drawer where the previous one lay. She knew she ought to leave France. She sat on her bed trying to invent reasons why she should stay. One barrier, at least, could keep her here for a while. She could not send a telegram in reply.

The thunder and lightning which had raged along the coast, extinguishing the lights and presaging the newly arrived blackout, had vanished. The drama abated. People settled down to a war which some said would last five weeks but far more declared would last five years.

The first restriction was the rationing of petrol, followed by a noticeable absence of cars in Cannes. People walked or cycled, yet despite the rationing there were still army cars driving to and fro, resented by the public who thought they could not possibly be essential, and the petrol must have been obtained illegally.

Petrol difficulties. A form of blackout. The vanishing of beautiful yachts. Yet Cannes looked as it had done a week – a month – ago and the sun still shone.

'Well, Sophy?' said Daniel. They'd arranged to meet at a bar at the Quai St Pierre, 'Are you going to try and get back to England? Yvonne's servants aren't the only ones rushing to get back to their own country as if France had caught fire. I was in Nice today and there's only one passenger train a day to Paris; you should see the crowds at the station! People squeezed on the platform like sardines, some of them have been camping for forty-eight hours waiting for a train, and the journey to Paris can take as long as thirty hours. No restaurant cars. The passengers were all loaded with food and water like mules. Everybody in a panic, I'm afraid.'

'It sounds horrible.'

'It wasn't exactly pleasant. Good pictures, though.'

'That's all you think about.'

'It's my *métier*,' he said dryly.

She stared down at the marble-topped table which was patterned on its dull pink surface with white wavy lines. She traced one of these carefully with her finger. How young she looks, he thought. Too young for all this mess – which was how he described the beginnings of the new war.

'Sophy?'

She looked up quickly.

'Isn't it time you used your head?'

It was evening, warm, gold, lazy, the very best hour of the day. Along the quay the yachts which a few days ago had been crowned with flowers had gone like swallows.

'I may not use my head. But I use my heart,' she said in a low voice.

'Perhaps that is not enough.'

'Daniel, do *you* think I should go?'

'Don't look so tragic, and don't ask me to make your decisions for you. How can I do that? But certainly you're in no danger. This is an odd sort of war at present. Where's the Apocalypse we've heard about? Hordes of enemy aircraft arriving like black locusts to destroy Paris and London?

What's happened since we've declared war? Not a thing. Petrol rationing. A bicycle or two. And the portholes of boats painted dark blue. In the *Petit Niçois* this morning they asked what sign a man falling out of the sky would see to make him guess we're at war? A few sandbags outside municipal buildings are scarcely evidence of a world conflict. It's a *drôle de guerre*.'

It was the first time Sophy heard the phrase. Daniel, like all journalists, was a magpie who picked up what was lying about. Within a few days the phrase was commonplace. A *drôle de guerre*.

He showed his teeth in a grin.

'After I left you at Les Hesperides the other day, I went back to the Casino and took some photographs. I sold the lot. Apparently the Mayor is furious. Cannes has decided to pretend there was no panic at the ball and when the lights failed everybody left calmly in perfect order. Not a glass broken. We believe what we want to believe, isn't that it?'

'I suppose so.'

'Poor Sophy. You don't care a fig about the Mayor and the Bal des Petits Lits Blancs, do you? Be comforted. There's no reason why you shouldn't stay. Write to your parents and tell them how peaceful it is during this *drôle de guerre*.'

To Sophy it certainly was droll. She did as Daniel suggested. She wrote to her parents, assuring them that everybody was 'okay', that the Dufours might want her to stay on for a while, Anne-Marie needed company and Sophy herself was 'quite a help'. It did seem unkind to pack up and leave immediately and in any case she would not be able to get a train for days. She used Daniel's description of the crowds on the station and the difficulties of any kind of transport, making things sound rather worse than he'd done.

Her desire to remain at Les Hesperides turned out to be easily achieved; it was true that Anne-Marie longed to keep her in Cannes and Yvonne Dufour seemed coolly pleased to agree. She was gracious to Sophy. Her manner had altered, it was less cold; Sophy had no idea why that should be. She was merely grateful and said so.

Anne-Marie decided that she and Sophy ought to join a Red Cross course being organized in the largest library in Cannes. They set off, full of patriotic fervour, one fine afternoon. The course was mostly attended by middle-aged Frenchwomen who argued with their teacher, a stout fierce Breton who argued back and won. Anne-Marie and Sophy, sitting at the furthest end of a long library table, made notes upon the subject of bandaging and applying splints.

When they returned home full of self-congratulations, Sophy said that she had another letter to write.

'It is to Jack,' she said. Anne-Marie looked sympathetic and said, 'Of course. Of course.'

Neither of the girls mentioned Sophy's fiancé. Sophy knew that until she had explained things to her brother, she could not possibly write to Bob. And – like being unable to send telegrams – that was a considerable relief.

Jack was the one she needed now. She needed his thoughts, his understanding, his good opinion. They were as necessary to her as the air she breathed. She picked up her pen.

'Darling Jack.'

He never called her anything but 'Sophy' or occasionally 'Sophe'. He was a man to whom endearments were a foreign language, he couldn't get his tongue round them. She didn't care. When he put his arm round her and hugged her that was better than a dozen 'darlings'.

She bent her head, her red hair fell across her face. She wrote out everything that had happened. She wrote 'I am in love', adding 'we are lovers now'. She confessed the tremendous thing that had happened.

'I know at first you'll think badly of me, but please don't. I realize how terribly I've let Bob down. I promise to tell him as soon as *you* tell me how I can put it to him. I feel so guilty ... yet I don't. You are so much sensibler' – was there such a word? – 'than me. Is it awful to behave – to feel – as crazily as I do? Jack, be your marvellous self and somehow get the parents to accept that I want to stay in France. I am actually being a help too! And patriotic!! Anne-Marie and I have joined a course for the Croix Rouge and we're learning all kinds of important things like bandaging and setting broken legs and I've been going round helping with the collection of *ferraille* – that's metal objects that aren't useful, fire irons, pokers – well, I suppose they are useful but heaps of people have two sets. Anyway, you'll be impressed with my French when I finally get home. It's really fluent. Madame Dufour has agreed that I can stay and the money you gave me for emergencies is tiding me over. I suppose when I run out there's some way you could send a little more? I'm very economical. Honestly.

'So your silly sister is in love, and she doesn't want *not* to see you but feels this is where she should be. Do, do understand.

'I haven't told you a thing about Daniel. I don't know what to say. He is a darling and I love him. He is a press photographer and works hard but as he's based for his newspaper down here at present it means we can see each other a lot. Never enough for me, though.

'With tons of love from your tiresome sister.' A row of kisses ended the letter.

She folded it and put it in a thin French envelope and addressed it in her flourishing hand and – I'm getting so French she thought – wrote her address on the back. Even after three months, she thought 'Cannes' looked chic on the back of the envelope.

She called to Anne-Marie to say she was going to walk to the post again. 'I'll feel happier when I know my letter is on its way.'

When Sophy left the house the sun was high over the Esterel mountains, it was softly warm. How glad she was to be staying in France. She was sure her parents wouldn't be worried after they received her letter ... the scenes about her were soothing. People still went down to swim in the calm sea, to lie on the beaches. And some of the smartest bars were still open and crowds sat talking and drinking together. True, there were few young men now except those in new uniforms. But it was unreal to think of Nice station and the crowds fighting to get on to a train.

Returning from the post office she walked slowly home, thinking about Daniel and longing to be made love to again. When would it happen? Didn't he want her? That was ridiculous, she had known by the way he touched her hand the other evening that he still did.

In the garden of Les Hesperides Anne-Marie was sitting in the shade, wearing a huge straw hat. She was a figure belonging to the Belle Époque. Sophy flopped down beside her on grass still green from being watered daily by cruel Gérard who had driven the Italians away.

'Did your letter go off safely?' asked Anne-Marie, who was sewing with the swift skill of a nun.

'Yes. I'm glad I went to the post myself. It's good to know Jack will get it quite soon. In a week, with luck. Anne-Marie . . .'

'Yes?'

'I'm so grateful. To be still with you.'

'I don't see why you shouldn't stay as long as you like,' was the gentle reply, 'Papa says it's a *drôle de guerre.*'

'So does Daniel.'

Why was it that when you were in love, you couldn't stop speaking about your beloved? She hadn't meant to talk of Daniel. Her conscience, which Sophy treated brutally most of the time, rose up from its prone position and swore at her. Hadn't she stolen this girl's future husband?

Anne-Marie carefully put down her sewing, after pushing in the needle so that it would not be lost. She studied her English friend for a moment and when she spoke it was in French instead of her customary accented English.

'Do you love Daniel Vergé?'

But like and love in French were the same word.

'Of course. He's a good companion,' said Sophy. She had rehearsed this.

The French girl nodded in agreement. Yes, he was a good comrade, she and Paul were very fond of him and so were her parents.

'I have something to tell you, dear Sophy.'

Oh God, here it comes. Why did I think I would get away with it?

A little wind of evening began to blow, weak sister of the mighty mistral. It set the checkered light and shade from the palms flickering. The cicadas, sounding like miniature sewing machines, whirred tirelessly overhead somewhere. Hadn't Paul once told her that was a mating noise? Anne-Marie was quiet for a moment which seemed to Sophy to last an entire year.

'I ask about Daniel because once or twice I have thought you had a penchant for him.'

A casual laugh from Sophy.

'Why, yes I have thought so. But now I must ask – what about the English sailor to whom you are betrothed?'

'I am still betrothed, Anne-Marie. How serious you look. What,' said Sophy, 'are you trying to say?'

Anne-Marie sighed. It was something she often did, punctuating their conversations, giving emphasis where perhaps she meant none, sighing when she reflected over some private thought or other, or when anybody told her a story which had the least echo of difficulty or problem. Sophy had once heard her sigh so loudly, when standing on the front doorstep, that it penetrated the door and reached her on the other side in the hall. Why did Anne-Marie sigh now? It couldn't be about Daniel, could it? Yvonne had been so definite that her daughter knew nothing of the proposed marriage. It's her nature, thought Sophy; such a dear solemn old owl.

She looked up at the sigh and waited.

'I want to tell you something, Sophy. You must swear you will not repeat it. It is in the greatest confidence.'

Sophy's heart turned over. I am wrong, Madame *has* told her. The appalling thought struck Sophy that Daniel would grin and agree to the marriage, merely looking his amused and amusing self.

'Claudio and I are in love,' said Anne-Marie with another louder sigh.

A joy so intoxicating went through Sophy that she felt giddy. The word '*amoureux*' sounded as weighty as a vow.

'But that's wonderful! I never dreamed – you have neither of you given the least sign!'

'No. We are very discreet. But we have been feeling something important for each other a long time. Since last year. We have not admitted it, but it has grown and grown. You know how it is with such things. We love each other.'

'I'm so glad for you! And Claudio is so nice.'

Sophy liked Claudio Arrighi. Who could help it? He flirted with every woman he met, including Yvonne Dufour who positively smirked if he sat beside her. When he came into a room he brought a vitality, a busyness, an enjoyment of life to be shared with whoever was around. It was true that a burly man shouldn't eat so heartily, he was putting on weight. And he used so much brilliantine on his hair that Sophy now wondered how Anne-Marie managed to put her hands through it. He smelled of a sweet Italian scent, sickly and flowery and very different from the tangy perfumes of France. But, fattish and effusive and brimming with energy, Claudio was sexually attractive. He was fun. No wonder Anne-Marie had fallen in love with him.

'You must be so happy,' said Sophy. She was mystified by her friend's expression. 'Surely what you have told me is a matter of the greatest joy?'

Oh dear, she thought, I wish we could talk English. I do sound pompous.

'There are very serious objections to our engagement, Sophy.'

'What could there possibly be against him?'

Anne-Marie looked at Sophy as if her English friend had taken leave of her senses.

'He is an Italian.'

Sophy tut-tutted. There was no question of Italy coming into the war, everybody said so. How foolish Guilietta and Maria had been, packing themselves off to Genoa. They could have stayed here with good jobs at Les Hesperides. Hadn't Guilietta often said that she appreciated life in France? Why, continued Sophy cheerfully, Claudio himself was almost a Frenchman. He'd lived here for years, he scarcely had an accent at all.

Anne-Marie listened to all this politely, but her expression showed that she was merely waiting until Sophy had finished, and wished to explain matters.

Sophy's words of comfort finally trailed to a stop, and Anne-Marie began. Her way of speaking was formal and sentimental, at times it had a quaint charm and cadences like poetry. She said that Claudio had great success with his business here on the Coast, he was one of the most notable wine shippers, and in the vineyards and cellars of the Var, the Bouchês du Rhône, even as far off as Burgundy, he was known and respected. He was happy here in France and he had fallen in love with Anne-Marie and had asked her to share his life. But he had never taken French nationality.

'He has a great emotion in his soul. He is an Italian.'

Anne-Marie launched into the tale.

Claudio's story was a romantic one. He had come over the border from Alassio when he was scarcely fourteen years old. With no money for the train or bus he had walked. He had first obtained work as a waiter. 'Oh, Sophy, the terrible hours which are so late, so late, and all the waiters gamble for they are tired and take risks to stimulate their exhausted thoughts. Claudio gambled with his friends and sometimes lost all his pay, and if it had not been for the kindness of the chef, my poor Claudio would have gone hungry.'

He was ambitious and by luck had met Anne-Marie's uncle, Anselme's clever brother who had inherited the business. Dufour had taken a fancy to him and given him a job. From there Claudio had moved to a restaurant where he had risen to be maître d'hôtel. At twenty he started work for a Nice wine shipper. From there – the steady climb to his present success.

'He is a serious man,' said Anne-Marie.

Sophy thought of Claudio's gold-toothed grin and awful jokes and innuendos.

'Yes,' she agreed quickly, fearing after the life story, a recitation of his virtues. 'So why is there any difficulty about you getting married?'

'Claudio thinks maybe Italy will become embroiled in this war. He loves his country.'

'He left it.'

'You also have left yours, Sophy. It does not mean you don't love England, I suppose?'

'I've never thought about it.'

Anne-Marie did not believe her. She continued in her grave voice, using formal phrases, to speak of what might happen if Italy turned against her old ally France. It was possible. It was terrible.

Some of her unease reached Sophy, who could only repeat the things she had heard, the comforting phrases. Mussolini, she declared, having rarely thought about the Italian dictator except to see him as more ridiculous than alarming, was working for peace. Anne-Marie paid no attention.

'Claudio could be locked up for years in a French prison. He could not return to his own land.'

'But he lives *here*.'

'He loves Italy,' was the flat reply. Anne-Marie added with one of the sighs, 'Poor Claudio. *Mon amour.*'

'Oh Anne-Marie, don't worry so! All this won't happen and what's important *now* is you getting engaged. Let us be practical. Surely your parents will be pleased?'

'I pray so.'

Wanting to give her a good shake, Sophy encouraged. 'When are you going to tell them?' She knew she should not be so disgustingly cheerful.

'It will not be for me to do that. Claudio will speak to them, of course.' Anne-Marie looked alarmed at the prospect.

They had arranged to go to a film that evening but before dinner Anne-Marie came to Sophy's room and, white as a sheet, said Claudio was calling this evening to see her parents. Sophy threw her arms round her. Anne-Marie looked emotional and embarrassed and hurriedly left the room. Sophy smiled to herself. She was happy and soon the silly girl would be happy too. The Dufours would certainly see that Claudio was a better match than Daniel would ever be.

Daniel had told Sophy he might meet them at the cinema but was not sure he could manage it. He was like that. He often made appointments which he could break without breaking his word: there was a quicksilver element in Daniel. You could not put your hand upon him, he seemed to slip away.

Sophy set off after dinner well before Claudio was due to arrive, leaving a pale, silent Anne-Marie in the grand salon with her mother. Monsieur came to the front door to see Sophy on her way in the blackout.

'I am not at all sure, my child, I should allow you to go out unaccompanied.'

'I promise not to speak to a soul,' said Sophy, laughing.

'No, no, I did not mean that. I mean you must not trip in the dark or walk into a lamp-post like Clara did last night. She has a purple bruise on her forehead.'

'I will take the greatest care,' said Sophy, shaking his hand in a goodnight greeting. That pleased him.

The blackout, much discussed, was already resented in the Midi. Most people hovered between not caring about the regulations or loudly objecting to them. There had been an alert in Nice a few days before, a trial and not a genuine alert; the only result had been huge curious crowds in the darkened street and a tangle of traffic which took two hours to set right. As for the blackout, should one, asked the newspaper, 'YES or NO', pick up one's real life again, one's economic life? If the answer was yes, then one must be allowed to live and work. It was perfectly useless, said the paper sternly, to keep the entire Côte d'Azur in darkness from five in the evening until dawn. How can we get the tourists back? How can our commerce work efficiently when we are staggering about in the dark?

Some people had taken the law into their own hands. Sophy passed a jeweller's shop which dully but daringly twinkled.

Daniel was standing in the dimness outside the cinema. She recognized the set of his shoulders and ran to him. Kissing her, he asked after Anne-Marie. Sophy had her story ready – she had no intention of springing the bombshell just yet. Anne-Marie had a little migraine, she lied.

'Then you can come back to the flat and we'll talk,' said Daniel.

Of course he meant – make love. They undressed and lay down naked to repeat the breathless joy, the exciting forgettable union of sex. They were still new to each other and for Sophy passion had a desperate quality. When it was over they lay immobile as if love had killed both of them.

Daniel recovered too soon.

Sophy, lying in a state of physical bliss, knew it was something in him she must accept. He switched from love to ordinary life with no effort at all, a man stepping from paradise through a door on to a pavement. She stirred, thinking she would tell her news of Anne-Marie. It was fascinating to see how he would react when told the girl to whom he was half promised was marrying another man. But before she spoke he said something which stunned her.

'I'm leaving Cannes tomorrow.'

'How long for?'

'Probably months.'

'*Months!* Where are you going?'

He sat at the end of the bed, one leg dangling. His thick hair fell in a crescent on his forehead, his face was enigmatic. This wasn't the man who had muttered sexy secrets in her ear a few moments ago before his climax came, when they'd joined their bodies and, she'd imagined, their souls.

'My dear girl, you surely didn't think I would stay on the Coast? My paper rang, they've managed to pull off something good. I've been given a permit to visit the Maginot Line. I might even be allowed to go up to the advanced posts, and no photographer has been there yet. The Army are rather hellish over pictures, I've had trouble with them even in peacetime so I don't know how it'll be now. Tough, I imagine. But the quality of their official photographs is pathetic. I think I can show them the way things ought to look. In fact I'm sure of it. I'm catching a train at six tomorrow morning. Well ...' smiling, 'let's say I'm fighting my way on to it. Foreigners like you, Sophy, are still crawling all over Nice station.'

He patted her foot.

'Come along, come along. Where's the vaunted English phlegm? You look *triste*. One of the things I've always liked

140

about you, yes, there are a good many but this particular quality is your difference from French girls. You don't make a song and dance. You don't expect to be courted day and night. You're very passionate and you don't mind showing it, that's what I like. And you have philosophy. So, *ma belle*, Malbrouk is off to the wars, to see how our brave soldiers are doing or not doing. I'm told they're bored and beginning to worry, poor brutes. About home, shops, their children and their wives' fidelity. You'll manage without me, yes? Staying utterly faithful to your French lover and working for the Croix Rouge.'

'I'll go back to England. I only stayed because of you.'

Had she imagined that would work?

He laughed.

'Somehow, I don't think you will go back.'

'Why not?' she said with a smouldering look, feeling her heart would split.

'Because, as you've proudly told me, you never do anything you don't want to do. I've often pitied your unfortunate parents.'

Sophy said nothing. Lovemaking was at an end. Love also. The life that stretched ahead, weeks, months of it, was an unending road going towards infinity and covered with flints on which she must drag herself barefoot. She never thought of going back to England.

After they had dressed, Daniel decided they must eat, and fetched bread, cheese and wine from his small kitchen. He took the food out on to the balcony. They had to put out all the lights before opening the curtains, and sat in the faint radiance from sky and sea. When the meal was over he made strong black coffee and sat smoking. Sophy knew he was taking little notice of her because sex was over. She was shattered that she was going to lose him, yet was not allowed to say so. She must use, it seemed, her non-existent English phlegm.

'I have some news too,' she said. 'It's about you.'

The crude ruse worked. He looked up.

'Your arranged marriage is off. Anne-Marie is in love with Claudio.'

'Of course she is. Has been for months.'

'Oh, you're *impossible*! Why did you let me think you might marry the beastly girl?'

'Are you speaking about your dear friend?'

'Shut up! Why did you lead me on, implying you and Anne-Marie might actually get married? And what was Madame Dufour doing marching into my room that night, telling me to keep away from you?'

Daniel chuckled. She truly amused him. Her reactions were flattering and plain silly. He stood up and came to her, pulling her to her feet and kissing her nose. She shied away but he held her more tightly. She could feel him laughing as he stood pressing against her.

'I was teasing you. I can't resist it, you're so wonderfully easy to tease. That stuff about the arranged marriage was only an idea of the Dufours and my father. Parents nowadays can't get it into their heads that they have to bow out. They still try to interfere. Pathetic, isn't it?'

Sophy laughed. Wishing she could cry because he looked so fascinating and felt so beautiful, standing against her, each bit of them touching from breast to knee.

'You must go,' he said, 'it's getting late. Don't forget, we saw the Jean Gabin film and it was so exciting, and you screamed when he nearly got caught by the gendarmes. Remember now.'

They walked back by the sea to Les Hesperides. Sophy knew she shouldn't say it, and couldn't stop herself.

'Daniel. Will you write to me?'

'I don't expect so. I'm no letter writer, never have been. And I shall be working at all hours, and on the move most of the time. I'll ring. If I'm able to.'

'*Of course* you'll be able to.'

'Not necessarily. You don't know the French bureacrats. They're more fatal than poison gas. But whether I ring or not, you'll know I'm thinking of you.'

Dreading his absence, the days turned into weeks and months. A French Christmas went by, with letters from home

142

which gave her, for a while, a pang of homesickness. In France the festival was not the holly-decorated, scarlet-packaged, cards-on-the-mantelpiece, sometimes snowy feast she had known since childhood. It was dull and the only big excitement was Mass in the church in Le Suquet, and a crib made of tiny clay figures called *santons* which – if you put in a ten-centime piece, moved to a music box. Shepherds and their sheep. Farmers and their oxen. Our Lady bending over a clay crib and a miniature baby in swaddling clothes.

The Dufours had readily agreed to Claudio's proposal for their daughter and Anne-Marie, still sighing, was very happy. She flashed a solitaire diamond ring, and spoke of the price of sheets. The girls attended the Croix Rouge, but bandaging each other's arms and legs, and lectures upon shock, tourniquets, and other dramas, had a certain unreality. Anne-Marie arranged for them to sell programmes at a charity concert at the Mairie. It was to raise money for 'Our Brave Soldiers'.

There were curious rumours about that first wartime winter. The Dufours were too discreet to speak about them in front of the two girls, who picked them up from voluble ladies at the Croix Rouge. Despite all the newspaper leaders, and the politicians' speeches about Magnificent France and Our Enormous War Effort, it seemed that what Daniel had mentioned to Sophy before he left was true. The vast majority of the men in uniform were miserable and worried. Idleness increased their fears, and one girl, newly married, whispered to Anne-Marie that she had had a letter from her husband and 'the trouble is' – lowering her voice still further – 'sex. He thinks *they* are up there in the North sitting in the trenches doing nothing, and *we* are having a good time. I keep telling him. I am faithful to the grave.' Another rumour which the two girls overheard when they were at their table studying instructions on 'fainting and unconsciousness' was that the wine, free of charge, served on station platforms every night by ladies as a government charity and poured into the soldiers' flasks, contained bromide. It explained why some wives were … well … not exactly happy after the soldiers came on leave.

The subject became a national joke. After they had heard it whispered at the Croix Rouge, Anne-Marie and Sophy recognized the references in newspapers or in the conversation at home. The soldiers felt their masculine pride had been insulted, there were leaders in the newspapers and an officer of high rank in the Army denounced the legend – stating categorically that 'bromide has never been introduced into the wine for our troops.' It had been invented by spies to make the Army look ridiculous.

For Sophy, the true image of this *drôle de guerre* was a photograph in the *Figaro*. A lonely French sentry, machine gun at his side, helmet on his head, sitting in an orchard 'somewhere in France', on guard. There was an article about the symbol of this war, 'the watcher. Do not laugh at him' said the writer, 'we need the watchers. There are two great armies face to face and his task is noble, he faces danger, he is guardian of a country which is getting on with its life as best it may. He watches in the icy night, attentive to the smallest gleam or sound. The dark, peopled by phantoms, deceives him in its distances, even the trees are menacing. It is only the dawn – and hope for France – which blows nightmares away.'

That is where Daniel is, among the watchers, thought Sophy. She had become accustomed to nothing happening, to the droll war. She was French in her thoughts. She had written a second letter to her parents strengthening her arguments about remaining in Cannes. Anne-Marie, she wrote (it happened to be true), had begged her to stay on until her wedding. Her mother's reply was not very warm, but she had accepted that 'for the present' her daughter was remaining in France. Her father hadn't written since he sent the telegram after war had been declared. But since Pansy mentioned him a good deal, 'your father is fire-watching', 'your father has become a member of the Savings For Victory campaign to raise money', she presumed he, too, had become used to her being in France.

Winter, a series of dull cold days, vanished suddenly, the mimosa began to bloom, and oranges hung like out-of-date Christmas globes on the trees. One evening there was a telephone call for Sophy. It was Daniel. His voice was diminished and scarcely recognizable – he sounded a million miles away.

'Daniel! Are you still in the Maginot Line?'

'We must not speak of where I am. I ought not to be using the telephone at all, but the Colonel here is a man of feeling.'

He paused for a moment.

'Sophy? I just wanted to hear your voice and know you still love me.'

'Oh! oh!'

Then she did recognize the laugh.

She had not had a word from Jack since she'd written to him about Daniel. His silence annoyed and worried her. She grew tired of running to the door when the letters came. He's furious with me. I can't help not loving Bob. Both were refrains she repeated in her mind and which gave her not a drop of comfort. But on a fine afternoon of early spring the post was brought out into the garden by Yvonne. Anne-Marie was wearing last year's gingham, mauve and white. Sophy was in last year's gingham too, green and white. The two girls made a charming picture, thought Yvonne, now content to have the English girl with them as company for her daughter. Besides, Sophy was paying a reasonable amount for her keep every week.

She gave Anne-Marie her letter from a girl-friend. Anne-Marie looked pleased and immediately became absorbed in six sheets of pink writing paper covered in flowing handwriting. Yvonne then graciously handed Sophy two letters. Sophy saw immediately that at last her brother had written to her. But strangely, the envelope was stamped 'HM Ambassador for the United Kingdom, Paris' remarked Yvonne; she had taken to calling her by her name.

Sophy, still bemused by the French stamp, had the grace to blush; she had not noticed the second letter marked HM Forces' Mail.

'I hope all is well with your fiancé. Is he safe on shore?' said Yvonne who was in a good mood.

Sophy smiled. But she opened her brother's letter first. It went straight to the point.

'*If* you get this, Sophy, and nowadays one can't be sure, don't put anything of what you have written to me in your letters to Bob. You will wonder how on earth my letter comes to you from France and the fact is I'm managing to get it put into the diplomatic bag. Through one of my chaps in the Temple. If I wrote by ordinary post what I have to tell you would be censored. It is about Bob and it's been a bit of a shock. His ship was on Atlantic convoy, has been for months, and it was hit 'somewhere in the Atlantic' as they say. I saw him last week and he looks pretty ropey. Had a dose of pneumonia, which won't surprise you when I tell you he was in the water nine hours and one of the poor lads with him, they were in lifebelts, went right off his head, so all the time Bob was with a poor beggar laughing and screaming and so on. They were finally picked up by a merchant ship. Bob was quite amusing about the rescue, he said they carried him straight down to the boiler room, opened the boiler doors, sat him in front of the blaze and filled him full of neat whisky. He was as drunk as a lord. But he doesn't look in good shape after pneumonia, although he can't wait to rejoin his ship. He's very thin. Please, repeat please, Sophy, write to him. More often. And at greater length. I know what an awful correspondent you are, having been at the receiving end of some pretty dire missives of yours, but Bob needs to hear from you. And under the circs, with you waltzing about the Côte d'Azur, it's the least you can do. Sorry to lecture but somebody's got to.

As for your brother, I'm at Aldershot and I've got my commission so you'll be glad to hear I no longer wear a forage cap over one ear, which made Ma wince. And kindly address me as second lieutenant in future, please. But I may be transferred to the War Office (and out of uniform). Will let you know. Meantime the parents send love and Ma needs letters too, so you go and buy a bottle of French ink. If I have further news you ought to hear, and which the censor would smear out, I'll try and get into the Dip Bag again. My friend said they'd do it for me.

Your affec. brother,
Jack.'

The letter also contained fifty pounds in francs. A fortune.

Aware that Yvonne Dufour was watching her, Sophy hastily opened her second letter. As she expected, there was not a word of what Jack had told her. Bob had suffered a terrible ordeal, had narrowly escaped being drowned. But his letter was what he would call 'merry and bright'. It was funny, reserved, endearing, and as English as Dartmouth College. He thought it fun, he wrote, that she was 'going the pace' in France, but she must remember that if it looked necessary, she must be sure to come home. He sent his love. He did look forward to hearing from her and was sure her letters had been held up somewhere.

She smiled again at Yvonne and said meaningless things about her fiancé being fine, and her brother's promotion. The sort of things Yvonne would approve.

'I think I ought to answer right away. They don't seem to have been receiving mine,' Sophy piously said. She had not written for weeks.

'That's right. Do it at once,' agreed Yvonne, glad of the opportunity to have a private word with her engaged daughter on such things as wedding dates and trousseaux and the difficulty of obtaining petrol to drive into Nice.

Sophy went up to her room and shut the door. The balcony windows were open, she could hear pigeons cooing on the roof, the mimosa had come and gone, it was now the flowering spring. She sat down at her desk and picked up her pen. What on earth could she write to Bob? Could she describe cookery lessons, the Red Cross, charity bazaars and French army gossip? It was footling to a man who was at sea, every moment risking his life with the submarines, the sharks under the water. She tried not to think of that. There were a good many things she tried not to think about, and now Jack's letter put an end to her easy escapes. It was hypocrisy to write to Bob as if she still loved him, but she knew her brother was right. She'd have to keep quiet until the time – something she could not imagine – when she saw Bob again.

Weeks ago she had confided in Anne-Marie about Daniel. Her friend had not been surprised, but when Sophy confessed that she must break off her engagement, Anne-Marie's advice had chimed exactly with Jack's words today.

'You will have to wait to tell him. You cannot wound a man serving his country. When you *do* break the news, he will understand that love is something one can't control. It is not a horse or a dog. It is a spirit.'

Anne-Marie had sighed.

'He will eventually understand.'

'Oh, I dunno,' Sophy said.

Her letter now came with difficulty, she was like a child forced to write an essay, she stopped at every sentence. But she put some affection into it and some jokes and added a row of kisses under her name. She was licking the envelope when Anne-Marie looked in.

'Telephone for you.'

'*Daniel!*'

'Yes. He says hurry, he has only a few moments.'

Sophy hurled herself down the stairs. The only telephone was in the hall on a table above which Yvonne had hung one of the enormous French looking-glasses she was so fond of. They were in almost every room in the house. As Sophy snatched up the receiver she saw her own face in the glass. A ghost.

'Oh Daniel!'

'*Ma belle?* I must be quick, I only rang to hear your voice. How is it with you?'

'Is that all? When am I to see you? Soon?'

'I don't think so. I'm in Paris to photograph the arrival of one of your British regiments. The Guards? They are to march down the Champs Elysées.' The prospect, it seemed, amused him.

'You're in Paris! Surely you could get on a train and –'

'No, Sophy, I couldn't. I have to remain here. And besides, things may happen.'

'What things?'

'Read the newspapers, Sophy. Ah, now I remember. That's something you never do.'

She was not listening.

'Daniel. *I'll come to you.*'

He chuckled, saying that would be delightful but scarcely possible.

'Why can't your father let me stay in his apartment?' cried Sophy. His voice was fading as he answered.

'*Ma belle*, I didn't telephone to argue. My father knows nothing about thee and me,' he used the French '*tu*'. 'We are fated to stay apart like Romeo and Juliet —'

She did not hear the rest of the sentence, only 'remember —'

'I shall see you in Paris,' shouted Sophy and the line went dead.

7

Like an animal throwing itself against the bars of a cage, Sophy's thoughts hurled themselves at the barriers against her getting to Paris. She had some money. Jack's fifty pounds. Little of that was owed to Madame Dufour – how much did it cost to stay in a hotel? Why couldn't she stay at Daniel's home? What had he meant, 'my father knows nothing about you'. That had upset her.

She went for a walk round the point of the Croisette and stood looking at Les Embruns. Longing and desire, impotence and the sound of his laughing voice were in her. She couldn't go on without him. All the time she had stayed in the Midi she had believed he would come back. And like Anne-Marie, Monsieur, Yvonne, Claudio, and the elderly friends who came to Les Hesperides, Sophy was convinced that the *drôle de guerre* would continue. The French to whom Sophy listened had good opinions of themselves and their country. And yet ... they felt uneasy. Which is why they talked so often about Italy as non-belligerent, Italy as the safety valve. 'We are not at war with Fascism, only with the Boche. That's proved by the fact that Italy is outside this war we are fighting.'

But the war was being fought by nobody and the belief remained – that was how it was going to stay. It was strange. It was phoney. It was a new kind of combat.

Of course it was a tragedy that Poland had fallen, but the Poles, Monsieur Dufour had said, 'did not fight hard enough' and in any case Poland, thousands of kilometres away, was nothing to do with France. Everybody Sophy talked and listened to said the same things. This wasn't a war of aggression and invasion, but a war of defence. Sophy read an article about life in the front line – she was interested in anything that was connected with Daniel in the Maginot. 'Provided the enemy's artillery lets us alone and there's a bit of sun, one can for a moment forget the war and think it's a picnic.'

The only one who did not join in the conversations about the possibilities of an armistice, the likelihood that the static war of waiting would last and last, was Paul. He was now in uniform, his regiment stationed in Nice. Sophy could not get used to seeing Paul in ill-fitting khaki, he made an untidy soldier who somehow couldn't look the part. He turned up at Les Hesperides for an afternoon or an evening. He talked about his comrades and shyly told jokes, his eyes crinkling with laughter. He always greeted Sophy as if he had been thinking about her – and said nothing to show that was true.

Sophy, walking home from Les Embruns with the wind blowing grit from the beach into her face, half closed her eyes. This is a phoney war, so why can't I be with Daniel. I *will* get to Paris.

She had told Anne-Marie of her desperate plan and her friend had been sympathetic but none too hopeful. Sophy refused to be cast down by that. Since when had Anne-Marie shown any real gumption? It was curious that when Sophy went into the house the first person she met was her excited friend.

'I want to tell you something. Come into the petit salon.'

Sophy followed, wondering what was up. Anne-Marie carefully shut the door like a conspirator, turned and said:

'Guess what! We can both go to Paris!'

'*What?*'

'Now you look happy again,' said Anne-Marie fondly. She explained that Claudio had called round to see her just now. He had come to tell her it was necessary for him to go to Italy; he would be away at least three weeks.

'Of course I'm desolate,' said Anne-Marie in the voice of a

girl describing a headache. But her words about love always sounded like that. Claudio was anxious about his business and had arranged important appointments in Genoa and Rome.

'Just as I was feeling very sad, Maman told me she has heard from my dear godmother in Paris. Tante Odile hasn't seen me since I've become betrothed, and she wishes us to have a little talk. So I am to go to Paris. Sophy, I'm certain she will welcome you too.'

Even before Anne-Marie approached her mother, Yvonne had decided that her visitor should accompany her daughter to Paris. Yvonne did not want the English girl hanging about Les Hesperides on her own. Anselme was doubtful about the idea of the girls going to Paris. Determinedly cheerful, looking on the bright side, pooh-poohing any of his friends who said things were more serious than they looked, he had a feeling it was safer for his daughter and her friend to remain at home. He was ashamed of the feeling. It persisted. But when he stumblingly told Yvonne about it she quoted a speech that the President had made recently at the Assembly. 'Normal life must go on. Nothing must interfere with the heartbeat of France!'

She repeated the second phrase. 'And the child is to be married, Anselme. She is not going to Paris to waste her time. Odile has a settlement in mind.'

Anselme agreed that his objections had no foundation, and Yvonne wrote to Paris asking whether Odile would be kind enough to receive 'our very charming English guest who has been with us now for many months and has become a member of the family. You will find her a well-bred young woman. Her parents have large estates in the region of Sussex.'

Waiting for Tante Odile's reply from Paris – and her fate – Sophy was on tenterhooks. She'd borne separation from Daniel for so long. Now a day was insupportable. She kept inventing reasons why Anne-Marie's godmother would not agree to invite her.

Was there enough room? Sophy desperately asked her friend, 'Perhaps it is inconvenient and she will not be able to fit me in.'

'My dear Sophy, her apartment has six large bedrooms.'

'Your godmother may not like strangers.'

Anne-Marie couldn't help smiling.

'She is a woman who welcomes the unusual.'

'But having *two* of us cluttering up her apartment ...'

'Tante Odile leads a life of great sociability.'

None of Sophy's 'wouldn't-it-be-awful-ifs' happened. From Paris came a cordial letter. The girls began to pack. Claudio had not yet written, but Anne-Marie was not worried and said piously that his business must always come first.

'I told him that, when he said loving things to me. "Remember, Claudio. Your future wife must be second in your thoughts and your work, though not in your heart".'

During the months since the outbreak of the war it was an odd fact that the girls had never been anywhere near the station. They'd heard about the crowds, of course. Heard about the troop trains. Seen regiments smartly marching through Cannes. But the evening of their departure was the first time they had actually entered the station at Cannes. Monsieur came to see them off. All three had been prepared for a mass of people but not for the scale of the scene which met their eyes when they arrived. There were soldiers squatting on the ground, women arguing with the ticket collector, couples laughing or crying, girls with babies and old men already worn out by the crowds. Monsieur Dufour did not explain to the girls how it had been done, but through one of his friends he'd managed to get two reserved places on the train. Sophy felt embarrassed when he shoved through the crowds, using their suitcases like small battering rams, and managed to make his way – and theirs – into the train the moment it drew in at the platform. 'Excuse me,' said Monsieur Dufour, charging ahead along the packed corridor until he found the right compartment. The very squares of paper marked 'Reserved', and fixed to two facing seats made Sophy uncomfortable; so did resentful looks from people pushing in from behind.

On the station the human drama went on. Boys as young as Paul, awkward in their clumsy uniforms, embraced sobbing girls whose babies cried too. To Sophy the air was deafening with goodbyes.

Crimson in the face, Anselme Dufour heaved the girls' luggage onto the rack, unceremoniously shoving aside other bags.

'Sit down, sit down,' he said. Aware of inimical looks, they obeyed. He regarded them critically.

'Put your feet on each other's laps when the light is lowered and everybody reposes themselves,' he said. 'And do not, either of you, go alone into the corridor. Keep together.'

Does he imagine one of the soldiers will rape whichever of us happens to be standing by the window? thought Sophy. She looked at the homely old man with affection; he was so comfortable, so ordinary. All Sophy's hopes, beliefs, the reason she was cheerful and sanguine she owed to Anselme Dufour. Over the months since the start of the *drôle de guerre* he had told story after story, patriotic, heartening. He described how the officers in the Maginot Line took pride in their fortress, one commander spoke of it as a vast battleship.

'If it is necessary, I can hold out in a siege against the enemy for six to eight months.' Monsieur Dufour often quoted that. It was he who liked to talk of Italy's non-belligerence, something listened to eagerly by Anne-Marie. 'Signor Mussolini continues to work for peace.'

Sophy was deeply fond of the elderly man and when he talked she was relieved and grateful to hear just what she and Anne-Marie and the whole of France wanted to hear ...

At last the whistle blew. He hurried out of the compartment, nearly tripping over the soldiers' rifles and kit bags and followed by the two girls. The soldiers made way for them and one sergeant gallantly wound down the window.

'Papa! Dear Papa, I shall miss you!' cried Anne-Marie, stretching out her hand. Sophy smiled and waved. Dear Monsieur Dufour, she was devoted to him. And delighted to be going away.

The soldiers standing in the corridors – there wasn't a train in Europe that was not filled with troops – talked and laughed when the journey started. The potential rapists drank wine from aluminium flasks and after a while began to sing. Sophy liked the song, they sang it two or three times, it had a cheerful tune and she soon learned the words.

Come on, Hitler, to the Maginot Line!
Our *poilus* are waiting for you.
And if that comes to pass
They will kick you in the ass,
Come on, Hitler, to our Line!

The hours went by, the song stopped and the men collapsed on to the floor or leaned against the corridor walls asleep standing up, like horses.

The long night began, and in the compartment the air was used-up and stuffy. It was after midnight when somebody decided to lower the lights. A ghostly blue radiance then shone down from the ceiling; the two girls opposite each other stretched out their legs as Monsieur Dufour had suggested, feet on each other's laps. The journey went on, it was noisy and monotonous and should have lulled them to sleep, but every time Sophy opened her eyes, she saw Anne-Marie was also awake, her eyes two pools of shadow in a blueish face.

Unwisely, Monsieur Dufour had been positive the train would arrive early in the morning, the girls had brought no food and nothing to drink. At dawn they crawled out into the corridor, pressing by the pale soldiers to queue for the filthy lavatory and wash their smut-smeared faces. The journey to Paris usually took less than fourteen hours and Monsieur Dufour had been assured the timetables had got back to peacetime standards, but by midday it was still in the centre of France. It stopped. It waited at empty stations. Once at the other end of nowhere an old woman wheeled a trolley containing an urn along the platform of a country station, ladling out hot wine for the soldiers. Sophy wondered about the bromide ... poor men, they looked as if it was the last thing they would need.

At last, a whole day since Anne-Marie's father had waved them goodbye, the train began to crawl through the grey

155

Paris suburbs. Anne-Marie came into the corridor to stand by Sophy as they watched endless streets and dull-looking houses under a rain-filled sky.

Anne-Marie had been astonished when Sophy once confessed that she'd never been to Paris, exclaiming it was unbelievable that her friend had never seen the pearl of the world!

Sophy was in no mood to admire the pearl. Both girls were dirty and exhausted and hadn't eaten for a day. When the train finally drew up at the Gare de Lyon and they were swept by the crowds outside the station they were faced with what looked like an endless queue for taxis.

'We'll just have to wait. We couldn't possibly walk, it's too far. And have you seen the buses?' said Anne-Marie deeply sighing.

They waited an hour and a half. At last it was their turn and they more or less fell inside the taxi. Sophy leaned back, shutting her eyes. But Anne-Marie was at the window, open-mouthed at the streets denuded of cars.

'Of course in Cannes we're used to having no petrol, but *here*!' she exclaimed. 'How strange to see Paris without them. Why – it might be Amsterdam!' Bicycles were everywhere, skimming down the broad boulevards, swerving round corners as if in a cycle race.

'We like it,' shouted the driver over his shoulder. 'We have more work, and everybody's glad to see us. It's good for the shoemakers too,' he added with a heartless laugh, pointing at crowds of pedestrians.

He set them down in a narrow cobbled street, the Rue des Ardissons. Anne-Marie pointed out, two double doors which opened into a kind of courtyard round which on three sides were old and handsome houses. Anne-Marie's godmother lived on the far side of the courtyard; they entered the building and stepped into an antique lift which juddered its way to the third floor.

'Tante Odile will be worried that we are so late,' said Anne-Marie rather anxiously. Like Sophy's, her face was white from sleeplessness and smeared with smuts: the wash in the train had made it rather worse. Arriving at a door marked with a smart recently cleaned brass plate announcing 'Madame Odile M-T Gombert,' Anne-Marie rang. An old woman with white hair plaited round her head, dressed in starched blue to her ankles, opened the door, saw Anne-Marie and threw open her arms.

There were kisses and exclamations.

'How we worried. So late you are, chicken,' she said, patting the girl's grubby face. She bowed and smiled to Sophy, took all four suitcases as if they were feathers and ushered the girls into a high-ceilinged room dimmed by lace curtains.

Odile Gombert, enjoying a tisane, did not rise when her goddaughter ran over to kiss her. She muttered the French '*Enfin*' and allowed herself to be embraced, she then presented Sophy with her hand and gave her a look more piercing than Sophy had ever received from Yvonne.

Anne-Marie's 'dear godmother', a distant relative of Anselme Dufour, had the same burly peasant build, broad face and hands and thick neck. She had married unusually well, her young husband – met during the Great War – was socially far above her and had money. He had been killed in 1918 and Odile grieved for a long time and still wore nothing but black. But she had inherited her husband's money and lived well, moving in far higher circles than she had known as a girl. With money behind her, and well-wishing relations of her dead husband, Odile developed a good deal of command, had influential friends and made a successful Parisian life for herself. If Yvonne Dufour was a mosquito who could sting, Tante Odile resembled some huge uncertain animal, perhaps a bison, who sensing an enemy would lower its mighty shoulders, charge and squash its enemy flat. Sophy was intimidated by her hostess and, being offered a chair, sat with unaccustomed meekness.

Tante Odile did not ask if the girls were hungry. They'd had nothing since yesterday but sips of hot wine given them by kind soldiers, and were almost faint with hunger. She offered them tisane and a slice of cherry cake which she pronounced 'kek'. Sophy stayed quiet but Anne-Marie chattered more than she did at home, describing the journey and playing down its discomforts. The girls were eventually told to go and change for dinner.

Francine, the old maid, took them to the room they were to share and ran a bath which it seemed they must also share.

'Alas, hot water has to go a long way.'

Refreshed by her bath and changed into clean clothes, Anne-Marie sat brushing her hair and smelling of Claudio's sickly scent when Sophy, whose turn had been second, returned from the bathroom. The girls had been given what Francine described as 'the room of marriage' which looked as if it was permanently kept for honeymooners. It was larger and loftier than any room at Les Hesperides and like Aladdin's cave, shone with gold. Gold twinkled on the furniture and gleamed in laurel leaves round a large looking glass. It glittered on a goddess and her cherub sitting on top of the clock. Even the bedcovers were fringed with gold, like church vestments.

'So here we are, Sophy,' said her friend, turning to give her a kindly smile. 'How surprised Daniel is going to be.'

'But I haven't his address,' said Sophy, producing new problems. 'I never asked him for it.'

'I'm afraid I didn't ask Maman. I thought you might not want her to know you hope to see him.'

'What shall I do?' asked Sophy, all set to be gloomy again. 'Will it be in the book? If so, could I get a taxi, and go round to see him tomorrow?'

'A taxi! You saw the queues and Francine says there are none except at the stations. I'll find his father's address. I think it's near the Avenue Montaigne. If it isn't raining we can walk there tomorrow morning, it won't take more than half an hour. We'll leave our cards.'

'What do you mean?'

'He may not be there, but at work. We'll leave our cards with Tante Odile's telephone number. Then he will telephone us.'

'I haven't got a card.'

'I have a walletful.'

Silence.

'Perhaps he'll have left Paris by now.'

The extremes of Sophy's moods made Anne-Marie smile. It was a comedy to see her successful friend so unreasonable and irritable. Quite stupid at times. Anne-Marie felt fond and superior.

The evening was rather dull, but at least the girls had a good dinner, veal stew, plenty of vegetables and a sticky pear tart. They were offered beer which Sophy, concealing a shudder, politely refused. The girls went to bed before ten and slept deeply.

Anne-Marie found the address easily enough and they set off the following morning. The day was greyish but dry and Tante Odile, when informed that they wished to call on a friend, agreed that they might lunch in a restaurant. 'I leave the choice to you, Anne-Marie,' she said in a tone implying Sophy would probably choose a brothel. Another of my failures, thought Sophy.

As they walked along broad boulevards under budding trees, Sophy was in a state of almost unbearable expectation, telling herself Daniel would be out and not believing it. Anne-Marie calmly talked, full of news she'd gathered from old Francine. Tante Odile was living a more social life than ever, she'd met some of the smartest people in Parisian circles and was on the committees of many war charities. She'd even been to luncheon with a duchess. Paris, said Anne-Marie as they passed a crowded café, had settled down. Look how smart the women are. There was an air of normality, the girls in bright colours, everybody wearing gas masks slung over their shoulders in elegant leather cases. The clothes, said Anne-Marie, impressed with anything Parisian, were quite different from Cannes. Ski pants and wide-skirted jersey dresses.

'It's so that the girls can ride their bicycles,' she said, admiringly watching a girl spinning by. They saw a real rickshaw, pulled by a hefty man in porter's uniform towing a little carriage in which a lady in an exaggerated hat looked from a tiny window at poor creatures doomed to walk.

'How amusing. How amusing,' said Anne-Marie. Sophy, who thought it extraordinary, managed an insincere smile.

Daniel's father, Christian Vergé, lived in a cul-de-sac, the Impasse Clérissy, a few streets away from the Avenue Montaigne. The girls arrived at the usual double doors like those in the Rue des Ardissons, leading into yet another courtyard surrounded by stylishly ancient houses. The lift was smaller and more shaky than that leading to Tante Odile's. Sophy couldn't say a word when Anne-Marie, saying 'Ah, here we are,' in cool tones, pushed open the gilt doors and crossed a landing to a ring a bell.

Sophy wanted to run away and stood at a distance.

The door was opened by an old woman, a less attractive version of Francine, to whom Anne-Marie spoke in a quiet voice which Sophy – still standing apart as if the visit was nothing to do with her – couldn't hear. Anne-Marie spun round.

'Sophy! He's here!'

A moment later Daniel came hurrying to the door.

Exclaiming, astonished, laughing, delighted, Daniel kissed them and welcomed them into the apartment. He kept saying '*Why* didn't you tell me?' as he led them into a salon where he'd been working at an old-fashioned desk covered with photographs. He was an unself-conscious as Sophy was tongue-tied while Anne-Marie explained that she was visiting her godmother.

Daniel said, 'You needn't tell me your journey to Paris was a nightmare. Poor girls. I expect you starved.'

Unlike Tante Odile, Daniel guessed exactly what it had been like. He was lively, brilliant-eyed and very amused, behaving to Sophy exactly the way he did to Anne-Marie, very warm and pleased to see them. Could he take them to luncheon? There was a passable restaurant nearby.

Unlike her old teasing companion in the Midi he did not remark on Sophy's unaccustomed quiet. When their eyes met he smiled and that was all. He seemed rather pleased that his beautiful companion was silent, and concentrated on Anne-

Marie who assumed the air of hostess she had worn last summer. But at one point he did reach over to Sophy, to take her hand and kiss her wrist.

Sophy still said nothing, but Anne-Marie looked gratified at the gesture to her friend. 'Tell us *your* news, Daniel,' she said. 'Are we allowed to hear? Were you at the Maginot and was it all very exciting and very secret?'

'Oh that,' he said, shrugging. 'It wasn't much of a success for me. The military authorities are half mad about security. I had a row with a captain in charge of the press the other day. It's quite obvious they prefer the public to know nothing at all, they're absurd. The army have almost no official photographers and those they do have spent all their time not doing their job but trying to hack through the censorship. When we do get good pictures and I managed — God knows how — to get three or four, they behave as if we're spies trying to help the enemy. The Germans, I may add, are a damned sight better at propaganda than we are.'

'Poor Daniel,' said Anne-Marie. But Sophy could tell by her tone of voice that Anne-Marie agreed with the authorities.

As for Sophy, she saw him. Heard him. His arm in a dark fashionable jacket brushed hers now and then. She unconsciously sighed, hearing the sound of French spoken round her, seeing the boulevard through the restaurant windows where the trees were budding. She was silent. Happy. Far gone. He'll find a way for us to make love, was all she thought.

'Our English friend isn't hearing a word I say,' said Daniel, lighting a cigarette. 'Now, Sophy, will you pay attention when I tell you you're still very beautiful. Isn't she?'

'Of course she is,' agreed Anne-Marie, taking pride in Sophy.

When the meal was over they went into the late afternoon and Daniel said he must leave them to go to his newspaper.

'More English troops arriving tomorrow, Sophy. I hope to photograph them on the march. Will you be watching them? To show a proper British patriotism?'

161

He left them at the corner and the girls walked home. The moment he was gone Sophy found her tongue.

For the next two days she did not see him. He telephoned to explain that work was being difficult.

'Didn't you and Anne-Marie see them marching down the Champs Elysées? How disgraceful,' he said in the familiar teasing voice. But then he remarked that some of the newspapers reporting on the British were very critical.

'Is there a song in England, about hanging the laundry on the Siegfried Line?'

Sophy couldn't help laughing.

'It isn't *laundry*, Daniel, it's *washing*.' Her brother had quoted the song to her in a recent letter.

'How is that different? The papers think it shows lightness of mind.'

'Do you?'

'I take pictures.'

After this conversation Sophy bought the *Figaro* and found a report about 'the dissatisfaction we feel with the troops of our allies'. The British, said *Figaro* severely, showed too much levity. What about the ridiculous 'Lambeth Walk' used as a march? There were also comments on the habit of chalking jokes on the sides of the troop trains.

'What is this British passion for jokes and games at a time when the destiny of the world is at stake?'

When she showed the newspaper to Anne-Marie, her friend hesitated for a moment and then said Francine had spoken about this. 'Dear old thing, she's worried because the British pay their soldiers much more than we pay our *poilus*.'

'Then the British are quite wrong!' exclaimed Sophy. 'Either we should lower our pay or you should raise yours. Otherwise there's hideously bad feeling between us.' Even as she indignantly spoke she saw Anne-Marie despised her fair-mindedness, which looked to the French girl like weakness.

Sophy was still waiting on a knife-edge to see Daniel alone, when the news burst across Paris: Hitler had invaded Norway and Denmark. Paris was aghast. 'Germany has occupied or conquered Czechoslovakia, part of Poland, all Denmark and

162

Norway' said *Figaro*. 'Her giant ally Russia clutches the other half of Poland as well as Finland, Estonia and Lithuania.' The news went across the city like a tidal wave.

Everybody talked about it. Old Francine looked crushed, as if her children and grandchildren were somewhere in those invaded countries. Tante Odile was up to the minute with the latest political views. When Sophy and Anne-Marie went to the café, they heard round them conversations about nothing but that one subject – Hitler's new invasion and the slowness of the allies. Sophy tried to remain cheerful, refused to be affected by the general unease. She still had only one idea in her head. Daniel and sex.

The decibels of talk which rose so high began to lower. Two days after the bad news, reasons had already been found why Hitler's latest move had been inevitable. 'Frankly, it changes nothing,' said Paris, calming down again. Yet somehow Sophy couldn't be as carefree as she had been in the Midi. Was it really still a *drôle de guerre?* When the wonderful day came and she was actually alone with Daniel, she would ask him. But she was a moral coward and knew she would not dare.

Daniel hadn't yet managed to see her alone, but he did pay a call on Tante Odile whom he had met in the past but 'not had the pleasure of seeing recently'.

The old woman liked him and smiled more in his company than with her own goddaughter; she pressed him to glasses of port. Sophy, sitting in the salon, had to listen to conversation about Norway, Sweden and Great Britain (of whom Tante Odile clearly didn't approve). Watching the old woman's expression when she talked to Daniel, an idea came into Sophy's head – had the match between Daniel and Anne-Marie been *her* idea?

The girls had been in Paris some days when they were invited to meet Daniel for luncheon in a smart restaurant in the Champs Elysées. The sun was shining and Anne-Marie left them for a few minutes to buy some flowers for Tante Odile; flowers were no longer sold from baskets on street corners and she would have to go to an expensive shop a little distance away.

163

The moment they were alone, Daniel said, 'Well? When is this quietness of yours going to end? But I know the answer, do I not?'

'Oh, Daniel.'

'I agree. Oh, Sophy too. My father's away and the servant is out today. You can come home with me if you want.'

'*If!*'

After luncheon Anne-Marie said she would return home to write to Claudio, and Daniel asked Sophy if she would like a walk – he wasn't due at his newspaper until half past four. Anne-Marie gave her friend a meaningful look which Sophy pretended not to see.

The apartment at the Impasse Clérissy was as deserted as any lover thirsty for sex could demand. He picked her up in his arms, carried her into his bedroom and undressed her. He kissed her throat, her shoulders, breasts, he laid her on his bed and at last they made love. It was more intense than before and at one moment while he possessed her he looked down at her upturned swimming face and said, 'How few times I have made love to you. I am mad.'

He gave her one final embrace, stood up and wandered naked about the room, looking for cigarettes. Sophy slowly came to her senses. The room which she had not even seen when he had carried her in had the stuffy antique look of a museum. The pictures were so dark she could not make out what they were supposed to be.

He squatted beside her, smoke curling in the still air.

'You're lovely.'

'So are you.'

He gave the smile of a man who knows how to please a woman. She lay on high square pillows, staring beyond him at a painting darker than the rest.

'*Ma belle.*'

'Yes, my darling?'

'I have something to say. You will not like it.'

'Whatever you say I shall adore.'

'Not this. You are wrapped up in love. It is very natural. Those silences speak for you. You are distracted from seeing what is actually happening, Sophy.'

She gave a movement, almost a recoil as if expecting a blow.

'I think you and Anne-Marie should go home.'

He had dragged her out of her trance.

'What do you mean? Of course we won't go home. My home,' she added, clutching at his naked foot, 'is you.'

He kissed her automatically and continued to smoke. It was as if he did not see her. He was like that after sex, she thought. Brooding about work perhaps. He eluded her and she had to learn to bear it. She began to caress his foot, thinking men's feet very ugly, the toes long and prehensile.

'Sophy,' he said, taking his foot away, 'I have to talk to you seriously. Yes, I know you don't want to, but I'm afraid this time you must. Are you listening? I've seen so much since I left Cannes. I've met many many people, journalists and politicians, soldiers, flyers, important people and little ones, and I tell you this static war isn't going to go on. *Anything* can happen. The British may fight Hitler at sea – suppose for a moment they actually do, and your country's fleet is destroyed. England would starve.'

Like a silly child, she put her hands over her ears.

He gently took them away, forcing her to listen. He was like a man watching a livid sky while his companion, back turned, lifts her face to the sun. He looked down at her naked beauty and told her what he had learned of his country's lethargy, of the 'perhaps Hitler is right' attitude of the wealthy, that most French people now 'scarcely believed in this war. And that can be fatal.'

He was patient, kind, grave, tender, holding both her hands. But he saw that he was up against Sophy's immoveable desire to have what she wanted. '*Venus à sa proie attachée*' thought Daniel. It was not the knowledge that he was the prey which darkened his eyes.

He stopped talking. Sophy had pulled away her hands and blocked her ears again.

What, thought Daniel, was the use?

Before they left his bedroom he remade the bed, plumping

up the pillows and rearranging the bedcover. It annoyed her. And as they went through the apartment she thought she'd never seen anywhere so stuffy and over-furnished.

Daniel suggested they should go to a café on the boulevard and have coffee and brandy.

'We need it after such a busy afternoon,' he said.

Gravity was gone.

But when Sophy was back at the Rue des Ardissons changing for dinner she began to think – not of sex – but of the long speech he'd made. She almost hated him for it. Paris was such a glamorous delectable place, she understood why it was called the pearl of the world. Even the shortages, oil or coffee or petrol, were somehow chic in this city; they created their world with a kind of dashing authority and Sophy now admired them as Anne-Marie did and wanted to share their attitudes. She felt French. In a way, she had made her life and her home in France. Her English thoughts had been replaced by obsessive love, by the violent desire to believe in good news so that she could be *here*, with Daniel, in love, in France. She absorbed every speech which promised this desire. It wasn't the Germans who'd declared war. The Germans still wanted peace. The two countries would 'come to an arrangement' – that favourite phrase at every dinner table.

Anne-Marie, painstakingly determined that her friend should enjoy her stay, took Sophy sight-seeing. They fell into the habit of meeting Daniel almost every day. When he wasn't working, he met them in cafés in Montmartre or in the Rue de Seine where Anne-Marie enjoyed showing Sophy shops selling paintings and statues and pieces of embroidery which belonged in churches. Sometimes on the thinnest of excuses Daniel took Sophy back to the Impasse Clérissy.

He didn't speak again about her return to Cannes. The matter apparently was closed. He was once again his sardonic, teasing, handsome self, the man she adored, wanted, dreamed about, hungered for. She shied away from the other Daniel who'd talked of Armageddon. It had been an attack of depression, thought Sophy. He looked gloomy sometimes.

One sunny afternoon when she was longing for love and had not been kissed for three entire days he took her to his father's apartment and they made love for a long passionate time. Afterwards, sitting up while he still lay flat she sighingly remarked on his male beauty and terrible vanity.

'You're a pasha,' said Sophy, tickling his nose.

He smiled lazily. Suddenly he sat up, looked at the clock by the bed, and swore.

'My father will be here in twenty minutes. He wants to meet you.'

'At last, at last.'

'We must get dressed at once. Do your hair, it's like a bird's nest.'

'Oh thanks,' from Sophy, rocketed from tenderness.

'God, I forgot the time. Do make yourself respectable, Sophy. I want you to look your best.'

'Am I being presented to the King?'

She pulled on her underclothes, found her dress, made up her face. Then marched out of the bedroom so that she need not watch Daniel at his humiliating task of removing every trace of herself. He took longer than usual, blowing face powder off his dressing table and opening the windows to get rid of her Worth scent. He's like a criminal wiping away the fingerprints, she thought. Why doesn't he wear gloves when we make love?

At Les Hesperides, at Tante Odile's and here in Daniel's father's apartment there were two sitting rooms, one for use and one, thought Sophy, for show. She was willing to bet she would be introduced to Monsieur Vergé in the one for show, and sure enough, Daniel joined her there, politely pulling up a horrible goddess-embroidered chaise longue for her and taking a ton-weight gilt chair for himself.

Sophy had never seen such an uncomfortable room – Louis something or other. The walls were panelled in gold and white, the carpet decorated with the Napoleonic 'N' and a great many laurel wreaths, the chairs covered in tapestry were deeply carved and so heavy you could scarcely budge them. White-wigged characters (how had they saved their

167

necks at the Revolution? Perhaps they hadn't) looked super-ciliously, not at Sophy but just over her shoulder. The room did not suit Daniel and it did not suit her, it was pompous and artificial and there wasn't a comfortable seat anywhere.

A clock on which a gold lion sat heavily chimed four.

'He will be early. He always is,' said Daniel.

Sophy frowned.

'You're nervous.'

'Of course I'm not.'

'Admit it. You're afraid of what he'll think of me. Afraid of your father.'

His easy manner was gone.

Sophy couldn't imagine feeling the way he did. Her own father was difficult and they never got on well but the idea of being frightened of him or his opinions simply didn't enter her head. She often disagreed with him, she always ignored his edicts. From a distance of time she remembered her bad behaviour with contrition, thinking – the French have more respect for their parents. But this was followed by the unsettling impression that at present she despised Daniel. Surely that couldn't be.

'Come on, Daniel,' she said like an encouraging schoolgirl, 'he won't eat you.'

He made no reply but lit another cigarette and Sophy, who now saw how very nervous he was, had the grace to leave him alone. There was the sound of a door opening somewhere then the voice of Margot, the Vergés' old servant, calling.

'Monsieur Daniel? Are you home?'

'Yes, yes, Margot. We are in the grand salon waiting for my father.'

'Ah. Good. I will get the tea when Monsieur arrives.'

She did not come into the room. The waiting dragged on, the silence was more marked. Sophy could even hear the quiet tick of the clock. This is getting stupid, she thought, how can I cheer him up and amuse him? She was about to speak when Daniel exclaimed, 'There he is!'

He sprang to his feet, as a man came swiftly into the room. Christian Vergé was as tall as his son but emaciated rather than thin. His grizzled wavy hair was worn as short as a soldier's on a well-shaped narrow head. His brow was high, his nose prominent, his chin deeply cleft, his face was cadaverous but still handsome. Above all, he had an air.

Daniel presented Sophy. His father kissed her hand rapidly, bowed and rang for 'English tea, perhaps?' He took one of the weighty chairs and crossed his elegant legs.

He began to talk to Sophy with a charming attention, asking her about herself, but not in the cross-questioning manner of Yvonne Defour or with the steady probing looks of Tante Odile.

When the subject of Sophy in France began to wear thin he mentioned that he had been in Versailles for a conference.

'I think I may say I've returned to Paris with good news. We have been assured –'

He did not say who 'we' could be but the word was weighted. 'We have been assured that Italy intends to remain neutral. That is enormously important – everybody feels this. Signor Mussolini may even agree to negotiate in some way with the Germans ...'

Sophy muttered something suitable. She thought of Anne-Marie's happy face.

Christian Vergé treated the girl with a pleasant smile, in some way indicating that she was, as it were, on his own level. 'You know, Mademoiselle, we are not at war with Fascism as such. Only with the Boche, who had the bad sense to invade us the last time and get soundly beaten.'

Sophy nodded, looking as if she'd never heard the sentiments before.

'My father's colleagues have never been against Germany,' said Daniel with a constrained smile.

He looked straight at Sophy. Love went flooding through her. She could not even question the alarming man facing her; it might hurt Daniel. And she was so ignorant about the war.

She fell back on the favourite French subject, the army.

'Yes, yes, they are magnificent,' agreed Christian Vergé. 'And our generals understand that their task is not to defeat an enemy, but to prevent invasion. All that is needed is to protect our beloved French soil.'

Margot had not been rung for, but magically appeared carrying a loaded tray which neither of the Vergés helped her to place on a gilt table.

Christian Vergé nodded without thanking her.

'Daniel, my son, give the young lady her cup. And she must try these macaroons, a Parisian speciality.'

While drinking the tea, which was weak as water, and nibbling a sticky macaroon, Sophy was treated as a minor visiting royalty. She was asked if she had watched the British regiment's march yesterday. Alas, said Sophy, she had not managed to be there.

'I photographed them in the Champs Elysées, Papa, I will show you the picture,' said Daniel. He didn't mention hanging out the washing on the Siegfried Line.

When Sophy finally said she must go, her host stood up, as light in movement as his son, and accompanied her to the entrance hall.

'What a pity you must leave so soon. Come and visit us again and dine,' he said, giving her hand the same casual swift salute. 'And Daniel must bring you to the little supper which Elise de Noailles is giving at her house in Versailles next week. There will be a compatriot of yours there. You will not be lonely.' He laughed, indicating a joke and she politely joined in.

'I think my father means the Duke of Windsor,' said Daniel.

Monsieur Vergé then instructed Daniel, as if he were fourteen, to see Mademoiselle safely home; and to return after that for there were some matters to discuss.

Leaving the apartment, and walking down the boulevard, Sophy and Daniel said nothing. She knew the handsome old man hadn't liked her. She knew *he* knew Daniel was her lover. She was resentful, but instinct told her not to make a scene. For once her head ruled her angry heart.

Daniel telephoned her the next day, but only to say with no emphasis that his father would be in Paris for a while. What he meant was that lovemaking was impossible. He came to see

Tante Odile again, this time bringing a set of uncensored pictures he'd taken of the Maginot Line.

Tante Odile welcomed him like a son, invited him cordially into the petit salon and poured him the customary glass of port, offering the two girls nothing.

Sophy thought Daniel looked tired and strained as he bent down to spread out the photographs.

'Of course I wasn't allowed near the stores of ammunition or the gun installations. But you'll see the lengths of the passages. Aren't they astonishing? These are the lifts which take the soldiers deep, deep underground. One thinks one is never going to reach the bottom.'

The three women looked in silence at the pictures. There were the men's quarters, beds very close together, row upon row. The soldiers lay on their beds reading, or sat at tables playing cards. Somehow they looked relaxed, despite the prison-like narrowness of their rooms.

'They all said how much better it is down there than up in the cold and mud,' Daniel said. 'It's been a tough winter.' He described life in the Maginot; the troops were well treated. They could buy cigarettes, beer, chocolate in the vast fortress, there was a canteen where they could sit and drink 'as if they were at home' and listen to the radio. There were unbelievably large stores of food, ammunition, armaments.

'Battleships underground,' Sophy murmured the worn-out phrase.

Tante Odile exclaimed over the quality of the photographs, noticing the finer details. Leaning forward with her elbows on her knees, she looked rather like Anselme Dufour. She asked Daniel if he'd sold many of the pictures.

No, was the reply. Newspapers didn't want photographs of the Maginot any more, the public knew them all by heart – or at least what official pictures the papers were allowed to publish. When he'd seen Daniel's photographs, his editor had said they could easily have been a series on the Paris Metro. Odile was horrified. Why, the Maginot Line was the greatest French masterpiece of engineering since De Lesseps had built the Suez Canal.

'Yes, it's very impressive. Superb,' he agreed. 'But it's impossible to hide from the public that army morale isn't good. The men are worried about their homes, not the war. If they're farmers, they receive letters telling them of failed crops, losses, mistakes made by inexperienced old men trying to replace them. Even crops not sown and fields untilled. How can women at home find worthwhile help when every man between eighteen and forty – except myself', he used an ironic tone when speaking of himself as a civilian, 'is in uniform. The shopkeepers are no better off. All they get in letters from home are complaints about bad stocks and rationing. There isn't a soldier I meet who isn't anxious. Even desperate. And there's German propaganda pumping out all the time, broadcasting that our army is at the front while –'

He suddenly stopped.

Tante Odile gave a downward smile.

'What you were going to say is that our soldiers are at the front and the British in the rear. What few have been sent to France, that is.'

Sophy went scarlet. Anne-Marie looked horrified. Daniel said quickly that the British Minister of War had been to Paris recently and given the number of British troops now on French soil.

'Yes,' said Odile. 'We were told 300,000. But it seems there are scarcely 150,000. What sort of share is that when you consider the size of *our* army?'

The touchpaper of Sophy's anger flared. Exclaiming that she wouldn't stay to hear her country insulted, she rushed out, slamming the door. In her room, she burst into tears. Where was her recent loyalty to France? She was in a foreign country where they sneered at the British who had come to help them. She did not know what the truth was; she had read that there were 400,000 British troops now in France. But any numbers seemed so vast and so unreal. All they meant to her were the soldiers kissing their girls on Cannes station, Daniel's pictures of men in their narrow beds in the Maginot Line, or slogging down the roads, looking cheerful and haphazard. She could not grasp the idea of huge armies or understand it. But the expression just now on Tante Odile's face, and the icy courtesy given her by Daniel's father, she understood those.

Anne-Marie came in quietly, sat down beside her and begged her not to upset herself. Her godmother was bitter. 'It is understandable. Her husband was killed on the Marne, one must remember that.'

Sophy mopped her face, thinking one could scarcely forget it. The apartment was full of photographs of the dead hero, with bands of black ribbon tied across the frames. And Tante Odile always wore mourning. She muttered that she was sorry for leaving the room.

'But it is normal,' was the reply, 'to love one's country.'

Anne-Marie thought it courageous of Sophy to return to the petit salon where Daniel was shuffling his photographs together. He looked up and gave her a smile filled with sympathy. As for Odile, having shot her anti-British bolt, she graciously suggested that the girls might have some tisane.

But Sophy was deeply offended. When she met Daniel for lunch – there were still no visits to the Impasse Clérissy – he annoyed her because he saw both sides of the argument. She quarrelled with him about it. They had begun to get on each other's nerves because they couldn't make love, and in any case she sensed Daniel's dark mood. He never repeated his advice that she and Anne-Marie should return to the Midi and he avoided talking of the war. But instinct as well as knowledge of him made her realize he was more worried than seemed either necessary or even sensible. He was out of tune with the people Sophy and Anne-Marie met every day. Tante Odile's friends were relaxed. They appeared to have lost interest in 'Nos braves' as the soldiers used to be called in Cannes; when the war did crop up one elderly man at dinner laughed.

'All the troops are doing is to sit. It will probably go on for years.'

Sophy, crumbling a bread roll, thought of the girls at Cannes station crying when they were kissed goodbye. I suppose it wasn't because their men were going into danger, she thought. Only because they were going.

Sophy had had the foresight to send her Paris address to Jack. She received another letter, again through the Diplomatic Bag. Jack wrote that Bob was at sea again, but before leaving had rung to say that Sophy's letter had arrived.

'He did sound chuffed. Good girl. As a matter of interest isn't your French jaunt just about played out? It won't be too easy to get you home, but I have one or two ideas and I think you should make the move soon. And I mean soon.'

Sophy grimaced at her brother repeating the advice she'd blocked her ears against when Daniel gave it. She was far more interested to find Jack had sent her a thick wedge of francs.

Tante Odile and Anne-Marie were impressed when Sophy told them she was probably going to a party at Versailles given by somebody called Noailles.

'She and her husband only happen to be among the wealthiest and most distinguished names in Paris,' said Tante Odile crushingly. 'Your own king of England was entertained by them last week. I saw it in *Figaro*.'

'I think you mean the ex-king,' said Sophy. The mixture of republicanism and snobbery in France often confused her.

Seeing that her friend was so intrigued at the coming party, Sophy said she would ask Daniel to get an extra invitation. Anne-Marie was genuinely shocked.

'You must do no such thing! Don't you realize it isn't an event for which you can ask to bring friends? I am sure Madame de Noailles prepared her list weeks ago. And Daniel is included because Monsieur Vergé has high government connections.'

Piqued by curiosity about Christian Vergé, and recalling his return from Versailles at which he had apparently been conferring with bigwigs, Sophy asked Daniel about the invitation when they met one afternoon near his newspaper office in the Champs Elysées.

'Madame Gombert and Anne-Marie are behaving as if I'd been asked to Buckingham Palace,' she said casually. 'Is your father a close friend of the de Noailles family?'

'Not exactly,' he said in a sour voice, 'Mathilde de Noailles and my father were lovers at one time.'

Sophy's eyes flashed.

'Oh. Really? So your father goes in for affairs, does he? Then what right has he to disapprove of me? And don't say he doesn't, because I'm not a fool. It was obvious that he'd guessed about us.'

'You imagine things.'

'Come off it, Daniel. I could feel it.'

'He was perfectly polite.'

'Don't be so maddening. We both know what he thought.'

Daniel lit a cigarette and proceeded to deny what she had said. Where did she get her crazy ideas? She was over-sensitive, it was all in her imagination. She was irritated by the indulgent way he spoke of his father, the dismissive way he referred to her. She blurted out that he was 'disgustingly deferential'.

His face changed to stone.

'You are very charming, Sophy.'

'It's true. You're so *impressed*. He might be the Duke of Windsor or something,' she said, unaware of bathos. 'Why? Is it —' she continued, the ground beneath her feet more dangerous every moment, cracks yawning, 'is it because if he takes against you he won't leave you his money?'

'My God!'

He sprang to his feet and walked off.

Returning to the apartment, Sophy told Anne-Marie what had happened and burst into angry tears.

'Now he won't take me to that stupid party after all.'

'Of course he will. You are on the list and it would be a serious breach of etiquette to leave you behind unless in a case of illness.'

Still half crying, Sophy couldn't help laughing at the same time.

Daniel made it up when a few days later they made love. They went to his father's empty apartment one afternoon and kissed, each taking the blame, each sorry and loving, each desperate to be in the other's arms. Beautiful sex, exchanged and rising and enjoyed, made all things right.

It was already well into May but the evening of the ball was chilly from the previous day's rain. Sophy took an hour to get ready. She had chosen her most formal evening gown of black taffeta with fashionably huge skirts and bouffant sleeves; she looked like a Sargent portrait. Anne-Marie helped her to dress, lent her a little diamanté bracelet and gave her a kiss.

Paris was dark and deserted at night. The only taxis came from the stations, but even those were beginning to grow fewer, there was so little petrol. There had been a number of air-raid alerts recently; Parisians had grown accustomed to bundling out of their apartments to go into basements or shelters. Not Tante Odile, who refused to move, exclaiming, 'I have the soul of a fatalist.' The girls had remained with her in the apartment – feeling brave – during the two alerts since they had come to Paris.

Ordinary people going out to dinner walked to their destination in the dark, but Daniel and his father arrived in an enormous limousine ten minutes early to collect Sophy. Daniel helped her into the car. She arranged the enormous skirts of the dress, its hem so stiffened with buckram that it billowed over all three of them.

Christian Vergé complimented her on the gown.

'I can just make out that it is very beautiful.'

He threw over her knees a soft fur-lined rug against the cold.

Sophy sat between the two men. It felt strange, until Daniel took her hand. He put his finger into the centre of her palm, pressing hard, the gesture of lovemaking.

That was the dreadful thing about sex, which she had discovered since the start of this love affair. You wanted it more and more. It seemed a lifetime since they had been together in the empty apartment.

The journey to Versailles took over half an hour. Her host, apart from enquiring in his perfect English if she were quite warm, said nothing. Daniel and Sophy were also silent, simply clasping hands; the curious light-less journey went on until at last the car slowed down and the dim shapes of other

176

cars could be seen crawling ahead and behind, monsters like the Vergé limousine, loaded with the petrol that ordinary mortals were refused. The long queue crawled past high wrought-iron gates towards the dim shape of a mansion under a chilly, starry sky.

Through the doors the guests advanced into a hallway also plunged into darkness, then under heavy curtains into a reception chamber lit by hundreds of candles. The ladies were taken into a kind of salon to leave their cloaks. Sophy looked at the other women under her eyelashes. There were three girls of about her own age, wonderfully dressed in gowns designed by master-hands – there was something instantly recognizable about Paris dresses of the haute couture. One girl was in floating net sewn with violets. All three girls clearly knew each other very well and whispered and chattered like birds. The rest of the women, elegant and enamelled, were rather old and reminded Sophy, in their faultless chic, of the Duchess of Windsor. Not a hair or a jewel out of place.

Daniel was waiting at the foot of a great staircase which curved up to a landing lit by chandeliers. The scene resembled a Hollywood film – women in ample or sheathlike dresses, men in uniform with the scarlet tabs of generals, the gold lace of admirals; beauty, rank, wealth, all climbing a stairway to paradise. There was no sign of Christian Vergé, and Daniel looked himself again.

'The women are so glamorous,' murmured Sophy, giving him a veiled look.

'And you the only beautiful one.'

'Oh good.' She smiled radiantly as they joined the souls making their way to heaven.

At the head of the stairs, the deity turned out to be a short grey man with a line of miniature medals across his coat and a lady beside him, taller than he was and powdered so thickly that her face was a mask. She wore a ribbon across her shoulders and a star on her bosom. When Sophy was presented – a major-domo intoned her name – they took Sophy's hand in turn and bowed indifferently. But they smiled at Daniel and enquired regally about his work.

177

Sophy enjoyed herself as the evening started; she was well aware that most of the men looked at her with admiration. She was used to that, she swam in such male consciousness, but she hoped it would impress Daniel and put him on his mettle. She sometimes thought he took her beauty for granted. They danced in a ballroom, the ceiling of which was symbolically painted with gods and goddesses. Afterwards Daniel took her to the supper room. More Hollywood grandeur, tapestries dim on candle-lit walls, scented white flowers, candles in silver candelabra. Daniel found them a small table where they enjoyed a delicate supper, while he watched with amusement the members of noble French houses loading food on their plates like workmen. She felt happy. She moved closer to him, at ease, knowing she looked lovely and that he saw it.

They finished supper and were walking slowly back to the ballroom when a young woman greeted Daniel. Her blonde hair, dyed almost white, was drawn back tightly from a haggard interesting face. Ignoring Sophy, she put a hand on Daniel's arm and pulled him away to whisper in his ear. Daniel, bending to listen, burst out laughing. His manners returned and he brought the girl over to Sophy, introducing her as Paulette Desvignes. Sophy smiled and waited for the girl to leave. She didn't. She hung around and Daniel, amused by her, paid her compliments and beckoned to a waiter to give her a glass of champagne. They were talking, of all things, photographic shop.

'Paulette isn't one of the grandees tonight,' said Daniel, as Sophy pretended to be interested, 'she's working for Madame de Noailles. Recording all the rooms of this house.'

'I happen to be a photographer too. And a better one than Daniel,' said Paulette. Just then, while Sophy, still managing a rapidly fading politeness, wondered just how long she must bear this young woman, a familiar figure came through the crowd.

'Mademoiselle Sophy. Will you do me the honour?'

It was Christian Vergé.

He danced even better than his son; his rhythm was

perfect, he was as light as Fred Astaire and steered Sophy with such skill through the dancers that she did not even brush against a skirt or sash. He complimented her.

'You are light as a feather. A pleasure to dance with,' he said leading her through the mêlée. The quickstep ended, followed by a waltz. 'Will you do me a second honour?' he said.

They spun round the floor as if they were flying. After the waltz, Christian Vergé accompanied her over to a group of his friends and she was claimed by a colonel in the Hussars. Then by an admiral with a red face and a good many medals of the Great War on his breast. There was a succession of partners never less than field rank, all of whom referred to her as 'the English beauty'.

Dancing with light-footed elderly men of consequence, talking in her charming English-French, accepting their fancy compliments, smiling up at them, Sophy was a success. She thought them rather exhausting with their gallantry and their self-confidence and for the first time since she'd come to France quite longed for a shy English boy who would be tongue-tied and never utter a word. She didn't catch a glimpse of Daniel and inside her breast a fire began to smoulder.

Among the dancers she caught sight of the worn bulldog face of the man who had been her king, the little Duke of Windsor. He was partnering the satin-clad figure of his Duchess, as loaded with jewels as a window of Aspreys. Sophy was whirled past the royal couple, decided she did not like the Duchess and that the Duke looked at his wife as if hypnotized. I hope I don't look like that when I am with Daniel. Damn Daniel. Why hasn't he come to rescue me?

The smile on her face was fixed, she was getting steadily angrier as partner after partner claimed her. In between waltzes, quicksteps, she was waited upon, given cold champagne, a tiny gold chair, a speech, a string of speeches on her 'lovely English looks'.

At last Sophy knew she must get away from this end-less procession of elderly Frenchmen. Her fixed smile was beginning to become as set as a grimace. At last some sort of interval gave her the chance to murmur an excuse and get free of her latest partner. She walked away through the crowds in search of Daniel.

Outside the ballroom to the left she entered a tapestry-hung room, and looked about; but there were only a few elderly guests drinking coffee and talking in low voices. The room was the first of a chain of elaborate rooms, one leading to another through open double doors. Sophy went through the first, the second, the third. Couples stood around, talking, flirting, smiling in the way of men and women engrossed in each other. She went through yet another open door into a smaller more dimly lit room ... and her heart turned over.

There was Daniel. He was standing at a distance, apparently studying a painting, his arm round the waist of Paulette Desvignes. They were laughing together. As Sophy dumbly watched, he pressed the girl close to his side and brushed a kiss on her hair.

With a shudder Sophy hurried out and made her way to the salon set aside for ladies. She collapsed on to a divan, her head throbbing with a sudden intense headache. How *could* Daniel still be with that blonde bitch? How could he desert her the entire evening? It was only too obvious that he did not care for her any more. All he had wanted was sex, and now that they had been to bed he was set on seducing somebody else.

She stood up and went out on to the landing, conscious of nothing but fury. Outside was a long table set back under the curve of the staircase; it was piled with an assortment of officers' caps, folded capes with gold chain fastenings, leather belts, even a dress sword. Stupid with misery she stood staring at the table – and then she saw it. Pushed to the back behind an officer's cap, was an Army dagger in a stamped leather scabbard, a uniform toy worn attached to a handsome belt.

The dagger hypnotized her. She looked over her shoulder. It was already late, nearly three in the morning. Many of the staff, pale with weariness, had slipped away into the kitchen to sit down and rest. There wasn't even the usual ladies' maid on duty.

Sophy looked round again. Not a soul. Putting out her hand, she slipped the dagger from its sheath, it was very small and very sharp. She put it gingerly into the gold mesh bag hanging by a chain on her wrist.

Strangely armed, she felt a vicious stab of satisfaction. She returned to the ballroom.

The evening was finally ending and the orchestra had begun to play the opening bars of the *Galope*, an Edwardian scramble enjoyed as the last dance at a ball. The fun began as the music speeded up. As Sophy stood at the edge of the floor and the *Galope* started, a hand touched her arm. It was Daniel.

'Come along, *ma belle*. We'll whirl the party to a close.'

'No.'

'Come on. We've scarcely danced at all, but I've been watching your success. You've had the time of your life and I should think every duchess in the room wants to scratch your eyes out.'

He laughed, showing his white teeth, put his arm round her waist, and swept her on to the ballroom floor. The music grew faster, the dancers threw themselves into it as if it was a race, couples rushed by, laughing as they scrambled and slipped. Daniel began to laugh too at the intoxicating rhythm and the speed it was played, grasping her, rushing her almost off her feet, sliding at the corners and sweeping her along as if they were flying. With a final crash of chords the *Galope* ended. Everybody was breathless and smiling. Then the dancers stood to attention and 'The Marseillaise' was played.

When it finished Daniel said, 'My father told me he is staying on for a while, there are some people to talk to, apparently. Get your cloak. He's fixed for us to take his car.'

Sophy didn't look at him or reply. She walked straight out of the ballroom, ran down the staircase, out through the entrance hall and into the garden.

She knew he would follow her.

Cloakless in the enveloping chill, she darted away into the dark, hearing his running step behind her and his laughter as he shouted, 'Crazy girl, what are you doing?'

She rushed across grass drenched from yesterday's rain and swerved into an enclosed garden walled with high hedges all black under the starry sky. Daniel had almost caught up with her, still laughing, and as she stopped he called out, 'Do you know, my love, you are quite mad. Rushing about like a bat in the middle of the night.'

She swung round to face him.

'*Beast!*'

At that moment the moon hidden behind a thin cloud floated free and shone down on Sophy, a ghost in black with a white face, as she lifted her hand and hit him across the mouth. She struck with all her force, so hard that his lip was split and poured with blood. He staggered back, astonished at the unexpected assault, his hand to his mouth.

'Bastard. Pig.'

She ran at him like a devil, pulling out the dagger which caught the moonlight in a glitter of silver, and raised it to strike. He dodged and she spun round to attack again. He hit out wildly, missing her by inches. Sobbing and breathless she ran at him, her face mad with rage, but this time he was ready and slapped her so hard across the face that she staggered. They closed in for the struggle of enemies. She scratched and kicked, hampered by her long skirts, while he tried to catch and twist the hand which held the wildly flailing knife. Finally with a cruel wrench of her wrist he got hold of the dagger by the handle, avoiding the dangerous blade, and with a sound of disgust threw it over the hedge.

'Bitch.'

He turned and charged at her, picked her up in his arms, lifted her high and hurled her as violently as he'd pitched the dagger, straight into the hedge. Before she could scream, he was gone.

Sophy was caught, skirts and hair skewered, arms almost impaled by stems which grazed and pierced as she fought to free herself. Every move was excruciating and she heard her dress tearing as she tried to disentangle her skirts from sharp thorn-like branches which continued to cling and wound. She sobbed from pain and vented fury. Pulling herself away from one thick branch, she heard the tearing sound of taffeta again. At last, dragging herself from the hedge, she fell to the grass. Moonlight was flooding down, it caught the gleam of her handbag at a distance away. She dragged herself over to pick it up. She tried to smooth her disordered hair and set her torn dress to rights. In the distance she could hear the slam of car doors, voices raised in farewell, then the noise of cars revving and driving slowly away down the dark drive. It was bitterly cold. Anger had gone out of her and shock and pain made her shiver violently. She had no idea where Daniel had gone. How could she get back to Paris? The only two people she knew were Daniel and his father. And she was a tattered wreck. She looked down in the moonlight at the edges of her torn dress and when she put a hand up to her hair, felt a long spiky twig. She must look like a mad woman. In the struggle Daniel had viciously tugged at her hair and her scalp still hurt.

Creeping towards the house, she saw a French window open on to the supper room. Risking discovery but desperate, she slipped indoors. The smell of alcohol and food was strong, the place deserted, piled with used plates and glasses and rows of gold chairs. She picked up a still-full glass of champagne and drained it. Then another.

Trembling, she went to the inner door and waited. She could hear voices, but most were coming from the outer candlelit room which opened on to the front door. Drawing a long breath like somebody about to plunge into icy water she went out of the room, head bent. A few people were in the hall, lingering and talking. She dared not look up in case she saw incredulous stares, even disgust. She fled to the ladies' salon. One or two late leavers were still there, gossiping and painting their faces to no purpose, since they were about to be driven home in total darkness.

Staring at the floor and looking at nobody, Sophy went through to the lavatories. On one wall there was a gigantic mirror with a shelf for combs and make-up; when Sophy saw herself she reeled. Her face was covered with blood and green stains, spatters of blood and scratches like those of a wild animal were across her cheek and down her neck, inflicted by the spiny hedge. She cleaned away as much as she could manage, the wounds were superficial and beginning to dry. She put on as much powder as she could manage. The late-leavers had gone and hers was the only cloak on the rail. She wrapped it round her ruined dress.

Out in an entrance hall still glowing with candles the host and hostess were bidding their last guests goodnight.

'Dear Mademoiselle!' exclaimed a man's voice. It was one of her dancing partners, a stout and facetious admiral.

'I thought Christian said you and Daniel were returning to Paris in his car. Yet I saw Daniel leaving ten minutes ago – and you still here!'

'He had to leave in a hurry,' managed Sophy.

'And left you unaccompanied? Disgraceful,' said the Admiral, looking pleased.

The candlelight was dimmed, the candles had burned down, Sophy slightly bent her head.

'May I have the honour of offering you a lift back to Paris?' he said. 'My wife is already in the car outside, we will take you safely back. Will you join us?'

Six hours later, as dawn crept over the city and Sophy, bruised and desperate, lay awake, the Germans invaded Belgium and Holland.

8

'Sophy. Wake up!'

Anne-Marie's voice reached Sophy from a distance, and as she came slowly to her senses she heard her friend's voice saying something she couldn't understand.

'Tante Odile says we must leave at once.'

Sophy still couldn't take in what Anne-Marie was talking about. She opened her eyes and looked towards her stupidly, then remembered her bruised face. But Anne-Marie was not standing near her, she was at the window looking out. She spoke in a strangled voice.

'Oh God, Sophy. At first my godmother thought it was some hysterical rumour from the porter who came this morning very early to tell Francine. But Francine went out and bought a newspaper and it's true! The Germans have invaded Belgium and Holland. Parachute regiments are landing even now. Isn't it terrible?'

Sophy listened in a daze while Anne-Marie walked up and down the bedroom, saying the Germans had already captured Belgian airfields, it looked as if the Belgian army was in retreat – Anne-Marie shuddered – 'And so close to France. Isn't it terrible? Tante Odile heard on the wireless just now that the Government says to keep calm but people must remain in their own homes. We have to get back to Cannes. Francine went to the station and queued for ages, and managed to get two tickets —'

She put a newspaper on Sophy's bed and as Sophy picked it up and looked at the enormous black headlines Anne-Marie suddenly cried out.

'My God! What's happened to you?'

Distraught, she had not once looked at Sophy until now. She couldn't believe her eyes.

'You were in car accident last night! My poor Sophy, why didn't you wake me? Your face – all that blood! And you crept in like that, wounded, why, you should have gone to the hospital – what did Daniel think he was doing allowing you to come home in such a state? Did he crash the car? He never spoke of this when he telephoned.'

'*Daniel telephoned*?'

'Oh yes,' Anne-Marie was still staring in disbelief at Sophy's bruised and grazed face. 'No, that's not right, it wasn't Daniel, it was his father who spoke to Tante Odile. She telephoned Daniel to ask if he knew anything more about the invasion – she even had an idea that Daniel would be going back to the Midi and could take us with him. His father told her Daniel has gone.'

Sophy felt she could take in nothing more.

'He has been sent to the front, Sophy. Or to where they expect there may be fighting,' Anne-Marie shuddered again. 'Monsieur Vergé told my godmother that Daniel was very excited at the chance of taking real wartime photographs. How can men think like that? Such courage! Daniel is joining our army somewhere, though of course we do not know exactly . . . but you haven't told me about the accident. I must get antiseptic and bandages.'

'I wasn't in an accident and I don't need anything, Anne-Marie,' said Sophy quickly, to stop the fuss. 'I tripped and fell last night straight into a stupid hedge in the pitch dark. I tore my dress too. It doesn't matter. I am perfectly all right, I washed my face at once. But what are you saying? Daniel sent to the front. *What front?* France is not actually fighting.'

Anne-Marie bent to show Sophy the newspaper map, to repeat with shudders that the enemy was so close and to declare that wherever Daniel had gone he had the courage of a lion.

She left Sophy to have a bath 'but be quick, we have little time!' Sophy climbed out of bed, drenched in a kind of hideous disbelief. Like every other man and woman in France, she could scarcely grasp that the *drôle de guerre* was over.

She dressed, shocked at her own face. She had a black eye of the kind Jack used to call a beauty. Did Daniel look as bad as she did? Her bruises were green and purple, her grazes jagged lines of dried blood, her arms marked as if she had been beaten. She tried to cover the worst signs on her face with cream and powder, thinking did I really go at Daniel with a knife? I might have killed him, how horrible I was. I was mad. And now I can't beg him to forgive me. I may never see him again.

She finished dressing and left the bedroom, thinking – nothing mattered now but Daniel. Not this new war. Not Anne-Marie saying they must leave at once for the south. Nothing but Daniel. If only I could see him. Somehow. Somehow.

In the salon Tante Odile and Anne-Marie were sitting at a table heaped with more newspapers. Anne-Marie was already dressed in her travelling coat, but Sophy only wore a summer dress chosen because the long sleeves hid her arms.

Odile Gombert glanced up. Anne-Marie had already explained Sophy's battered appearance and in any case it did not interest her.

'Go and get ready.'

Her manner was openly rude. Anne-Marie stared at the carpet.

'The train leaves in two hours,' continued Odile Gombert, addressing her goddaughter. 'If it goes at all. Anne-Marie, I have told Francine she is to wait with you until it leaves. It will do so eventually, one supposes. As for you,' turning her eyes on Sophy, 'I advise you not to speak a word of English. In fact, it would be better if you held your tongue altogether.'

'What do you mean?' asked Sophy, gaping.

She had given the woman the chance she was waiting for. Ignoring Anne-Marie's agonized expression, and the angry blush spreading across her guest's bruised face, Odile Gombert launched into an attack on the British. Soon the great French army would be facing the full strength of the Nazis. The enemy was on the move and it was up to 'our brave soldiers' to hold him back. France stood firm as she had always done. But who must take the responsibility for this new catastrophe? The British had got France into this war. France's so-called ally had forced the war on France and then sent less than half the number of British soldiers promised for defence. What was happening today had happened before. The British simply waited for the French to fight. They won wars by shedding French blood.

In the voice, in the hard eyes, Sophy faced for the first time in the long months that she had been in France, a woman who retained the deeply implanted never-dying ancient hatred of Britain as France's hereditary foe. The two nations had been enemies for hundreds of years. They still were. The Germans were cruel invaders, but it was Britain who was loathed.

'So do not speak English if you value your skin.'

In ordinary circumstances Sophy would have rushed into the quarrel but she said nothing. She was shocked at the words and the venom drenching them; but she had only one idea in her head, to get to Daniel. What did this woman matter now? Sophy would be gone in an hour.

'I won't deign to defend my country to you, you're contemptible,' she said, dredging up the word from some old-fashioned history book about the Great War.

She slammed out, ran to her room and began to throw her clothes in her brother's suitcase. She hunted for her handbag to be sure his money was safe. She was ineffectually adding more powder to the worst of the bruises when Anne-Marie came into the room.

'I am so sorry, my dear friend. She scarcely knows what she is saying. She is thinking of her husband. That other war is all coming back to her now.'

Sophy picked up her case in silence.

'Yes, yes, we must go,' agreed Anne-Marie, glad the subject

of her godmother's cruelty was to be dropped, 'It's a very long walk to the Gare de Lyon, I'm afraid.'

'Anne-Marie, I am not coming. I'm going to find Daniel.'

Her friend didn't believe it. What did Sophy mean? How could she find him? Hadn't Sophy taken in what she'd said, that Daniel had left Paris and was on his way to the war zone this minute where 'I pray to God he will be safe'.

A chill went through Sophy. Just then Francine, in cloak and old-fashioned bonnet, came in to say that it was time to leave.

'Sophy, will you say goodbye to my godmother?' began Anne-Marie timidly. But then she saw the look on her friend's face.

As the lift descended to the ground floor, Anne-Marie very fast, urgently, desperately, kept telling Sophy that she must, she must, return with her to Cannes. She was nearly crying as the passionate persuasion went on, and Francine frowned, looking from one girl to the other. The trio went out into the street, Francine carrying Anne-Marie's bag and Anne-Marie sharing the weight of Sophy's. The French girl came to a despairing stop as Sophy continued to do nothing but shake her head at everything she'd said to her.

'Oh Sophy. Oh, please, Sophy.'

'Don't cry, Anne-Marie. I'll be okay,' said Sophy, using the idiotic words people use when they choose danger.

Francine put a work-worn hand on Sophy's arm.

'You must travel with Mademoiselle. Only fools, forgive me, think of going towards the possibility of death.'

'I have to find the man I love,' said Sophy with simplicity, and suddenly kissed the old woman's sad face.

Then she embraced Anne-Marie. The eyes of all three women were wet and Anne-Marie gave a sob as Sophy, weighed down with her suitcase, began to run at a jog-trot away from them round the corner of the boulevard.

Out of sight, she hurried in the dusty shade under the trees. As she neared the newspaper offices in the Champs Elysées, she noticed many cars waiting outside large houses and blocks of apartments and more cars at the entrances of hotels.

People were hurrying out, servants and porters beside them, with trunks, suitcases, boxes, objects wrapped in sheets or newspapers; mattresses were being hoisted, secured by ropes, on to car roofs.

At first, Sophy thought the mattresses must be for sleeping by the roadside. Then with a thrill of fear the grotesque idea came to her that they were meant to be some kind of protection against bombardment, shrapnel, God knew what. The ordinary midday traffic of Paris, the bicycles and buses, had almost disappeared. The Champs Elysées cafés were crowded, but as Sophy passed she noticed the quietness. No clatter of talk. People sat reading the newspapers in silence, while down the great avenue of the pearl of the world, the first cars loaded with luggage were fleeing from the city.

As if on cue, the air raid warning began. Sophy and Anne-Marie had been in two or three alerts since they had come to Paris and at the wailing sound most people dashed to the safety of cellars or the Métro or to air raid shelters built at the corners of some of the main streets. Today nobody moved. They glanced up at the empty sky of a perfect day in May, lit cigarettes and drank their coffee. It was the same with the waiters. As the wailing went on they leaned against the bars without moving.

The offices of the newspaper were in an imposing building at the far end of the Champs Elysées. Sophy and Daniel had often passed it and Daniel once pointed up at a window and said, 'That's where they refuse my photographs'.

'Why do you pretend you are not a success? What about the huge picture they published the other week, the Brigade of Guards marching down the Champs Elysées and that little boy with the flag?'

'You only remember that because it was about the English,' he said, squeezing her arm. 'You should see how many pictures get thrown into the paper basket ...'

Sophy recalled the name of the picture editor, it was Jacques Ouastou; Daniel had said the name was Provençal.

'He's Parisian to his finger-ends but he often talks about his ancestors related to the Counts of Provence,' Daniel had said derisively. 'And speaks a little Provençal to prove it. A barbaric tongue, but if I said so to Jacques he'd light a match and burn my photographs on the spot.'

Sophy entered the building unobtrusively. Nobody was about and she left her suitcase in a dark corner at the back of the lift shaft, then took the lift which ascended, trembling slightly, to the second floor. Sophy did not tremble. She was keyed up, as full of excited optimism as last night she had been full of poisonous rage. She would succeed because she *must*. People did such things in wartime, didn't they? If you were steadfast, if you set your mind to it, if you had guts, couldn't you achieve the impossible? She would get to Daniel by hook or by crook. She imagined his face when she appeared somewhere or other and found him with the other journalists. How mad he'd think her. How brave. What happened next did not come into her thoughts. She was set on the one impossible, beautiful, violently desired objective. I *will* get to him, she said over and over in her mind.

She had never been inside a newspaper office, and when she pushed open a door marked 'News Room' she expected to be stopped and challenged. But nobody took the least notice of her. The long room was furnished with tables and desks, the floor was scattered with discarded newspapers and long galley proofs, a handful of men, none of them young, were working in their shirt sleeves. A boy scarcely more than a child was running in and out of a far door, carrying armfuls of newsprint. Sophy was not sure who to ask, who to disturb. She was hesitating by the door when a young man in uniform entered, with the usual polite 'Excuse me, Mademoiselle,' and an admiring glance at the visitor. Heartened by masculine interest, she asked tentatively where she might find Monsieur Ouastou.

'Jacques is over there,' he said, indicating a glassed-in office at the end of the room. 'Just barge in. I always do.'

'But ought I not to wait until Monsieur Ouastou is alone?' She could see through the glass wall that there was somebody standing by the desk, apparently in conversation with a man sitting facing him.

'There's always somebody with Jacques. If you wait to get him by himself, you wait till doomsday. Just go in and say what is necessary and he'll listen. He's good at that. Are you a journalist?' asked the young officer giving her a friendly look. He reminded her of Paul.

'I am the fiancée of one of your photographers.' Sophy had thought of that in the lift.

'Ah. I understand.' He looked sympathetic. 'Jacques isn't so bad, you know, you just have to get him to pay attention and then he's helpful. Good luck.'

Sophy's lie was what she needed. It heartened her and gave the reason for her being here. She walked across the room, ignored by men telephoning or typing, conferring or merely staring at their typewriters, smoking and concentrated in thought. They were accustomed to strangers. But there was a tenseness and an urgency in the noisy room which even Sophy, excited and set on her own mission, could feel all round her. The door of the glassed-in office was open. A big man standing by the desk was talking almost at a shout.

'I tell you, I saw the orders. Huntzier is in command of the Second Army, is he not? Well, *he* is the one who gave orders for the destruction of every concrete anti-tank obstacle and what is more –'

He stopped talking when he saw a girl in the doorway. He was smoking furiously, his waistcoat covered with ash. Brushing it ineffectually away he gave Sophy an annoyed look. But Daniel's editor had a faint light of interest at the sight of her. He was small, with a youthful face and white hair. He looked exhausted. But gave her a faint smile.

'Mademoiselle?'

'I am sorry to disturb you. I wondered if – if you could tell me where Daniel Vergé has been sent.'

The interest deepened for a moment. He took in the sexy figure, the red hair escaping from a girlish straw hat. The bruised face.

'Whom – have I the honour?'

The big man impatiently picked up a newspaper, turned to its front page and interrupted rudely, 'The anti-tank obstacles were built in March for the express purpose of blocking any advance on Sedan –' he said, but Jacques Ouastou held up his hand.

'I won't be a moment, Frédéric, this young lady wants something. You are enquiring after Daniel?'

'I am his fiancée,' said Sophy. The lie sounded emptier the second time she spoke it. 'His family say he has left – I was not told –'

'And you want to bid him farewell? I'm afraid you are too late, Mademoiselle, Daniel left four hours ago. On his way to the Ardennes. He should be there soon if our luck holds,' he added, looking at his watch.

'I have to see him. It is a matter of urgency.'

'I'm sure it is,' said Ouastou quite kindly, looking at the young rather desperate face. 'But you will have to be patient. You must know that Daniel's work as a photographer can take him anywhere – and now with what has happened … I'm afraid I can't tell you when he will be back. If you will excuse me?'

He turned his attention to the man by him, who began to talk again, ignoring Sophy, and repeating his story about the general and his orders for the destruction of Sedan's defences. Sophy muttered her thanks to Ouastou and left the office. She walked down the long room. Set on her own purpose, she was still conscious of the atmosphere which, hurried and tense, reverberated round her like the ringing of a bell. In the distance the young officer, sitting by a man who was violently gesticulating as he talked, lifted a hand to wave her goodbye.

She took the lift to the ground floor. The Ardennes. Daniel was in the Ardennes – that could mean anywhere in the region of forests in the eastern part of France. How could she get to him? She knew the name of the city the man in Ouastou's office had been discussing so loudly – a cloudy piece of history she had learned at school came back into her mind. There had been a battle of Sedan; though who had won, the French or the Germans, she had no idea. That's where Daniel will be, she thought. That's where I'll go.

The small station of the Gare de L'Est was as crammed

with troops as a barracks. Soldiers squatted on their packs, others milled round an old woman who ladled red wine into their metal cups, others were in the station buffet and many more sat on the platform beside the only train in sight.

Dodging and pushing, Sophy managed to get to the ticket office. It was locked. A scrawled notice on a piece of board said '*Pas de Billets*'.

As she turned away she tripped over a rifle and fell into the arms of a French officer. He caught her and laughed.

'Have you been attempting to buy a ticket?' he said, releasing her and grinning. He had teeth like a rabbit and a heavy moustache and beard; there was an old-fashioned look about him. He seemed part of another, earlier war.

'How can they *close* a ticket office?' asked Sophy, dismayed.

'Evidently because there are no trains. The only travellers are here, Mademoiselle, and all bound for the same place. The zone of danger, one might call it, which you will certainly wish to avoid.'

'I am going to the Ardennes,' said Sophy boldly. But realized as she spoke, with a thrill of dismay, that she had no papers. If she was an accredited journalist allowed on a troop train, sooner or later they would ask for her official pass. She had nothing but her British passport.

The officer appeared to have taken a liking to the girl who should not be here at the station at all. He said quizzically, 'Let me guess. Can you be a journalist?'

'A keen one,' declared Sophy, and gave him the smile which had made Bob Lingard fall in love with her. 'I represent *Le Jour*,' she added. One might as well tell large lies as small ones.

'A good journal. I read it occasionally. Shall we see whether a little influence, a little rank, can help a brave young foreigner to report on our Army at this dangerous time?'

The band of journalists bound for the Ardennes had left hours ago; the train at the platform, it was only the third that day, had not a civilian on board. There was nothing to be seen anywhere but French khaki, with the occasional flash of scarlet on an officer's shoulders, the squares of colour on the breasts of officers or men who had fought in other campaigns. Shepherding her through the crowd Sophy's new friend introduced himself as Colonel Tassigny. He spoke first to a harassed transport officer, then to an efficient sergeant. To her relief and secret triumph, Sophy then found herself installed in a first-class carriage with the Colonel. The atmosphere of urgency reminded Sophy of the News Room of *Le Jour*, there was something desperate and disorganized in the shouts, the commands, the seeming muddle as groups of soldiers were herded on to the train. The only civilian was a young girl accompanying a colonel; people were too busy to pay any attention to her except for soldiers who winked as they made their way down the corridors.

It was dusk when the train puffed out of Paris, hours and hours since Sophy had kissed Anne-Marie and Francine. She wondered where her friend was now. Like a child, she amused herself, imagining Anne-Marie's expression if she knew Sophy's success at present ...

The men in the corridor began to sing, as the soldiers had done in the train from Cannes. Perhaps, thought Sophy, soldiers always sing. But this was no ditty about beating Hitler; the song was haunting and sad, the voices in unison sweet. The soldiers knew verse after verse; Sophy never heard the song again and the only phrase she understood was 'It cannot be. No. It cannot be.'

Colonel Tassigny talked to Sophy for a while about the life of journalists, shrugged when she mentioned the German advance, smoked thoughtfully and then fell asleep. He looked even more old-fashioned, a caricature of an officer in some French farce, when he slept, head back, eyes closed. France is asleep, thought Sophy, and asked herself about this stranger who had been kind to her. There hadn't been a sign of sexual interest, a gleam of flirtation; he had been fatherly. Approving. He thought her courageous, a worker off to the war.

It was dawn when the train halted in what seemed to be the middle of a wood. Through the window Sophy saw there was a thin fog.

Colonel Tessigny woke, looked at his watch, and opened the window; the air smelled of trees and was sharply cold. There were voices calling out commands, and an officer ran up to speak to him. The Colonel nodded, then returned to Sophy.

'We are de-training here, Mademoiselle. I shall try to get you a lift. Apparently there is one lorry remaining from a convoy going through the forest. We are marching and will take a shorter route.'

Sophy spoke at a venture. 'To Sedan?'

'Evidently. The news is that the Panzers are over the Meuse near Dinant.' He spoke matter of factly, with none of the desperation she had sensed elsewhere. He turned kind eyes on her.

'You will be able to report on the French defences. Be confident we will keep the Boche from putting his foot on our soil; but take the greatest care, Mademoiselle. You are young for such a daring métier. Will you be joining your colleagues?'

Sophy said firmly that that had all been arranged and she was working with a 'brilliant war photographer'.

The Colonel looked relieved. He took her hand and bent with the age-old gesture to kiss it. He wished her luck and Sophy thanked him.

'I wish,' she said impulsively, 'I could do something for *you*.'

'Write about us. Write of our army. Tell our allies what you see,' he said, smiling.

The sergeant in charge of transport took Sophy over to an army lorry drawn up by the side of the station. A soldier jumped down to give her a hand and she was told to sit at the back among piles of wooden boxes.

She stared across the station at the train she had just left, trying to catch a last glimpse of Colonel Tassigny. But all she could see were the soldiers, a mass of khaki, gathering like flocks of birds, before setting off into the fog.

The lorry started up and drove away into the cold dawn. The pine trees seemed to go into infinity and fog hung on their branches like cobwebs. The road was rough, stony, potholed and Sophy's teeth rattled in her head. She looked down and saw that the boxes she was sitting on, and more piled up all round her, were painted with the skull and cross-bones and a large DANGER! lettered across each lid. She realized that they contained ammunition. She had no sense of danger, she thought travelling with explosives exciting, she felt she was in the centre of the conflict already. She began to think about Daniel now, with real plans. There must be an hotel at Sedan where the journalists stayed. Daniel had told her something about his work, and had once said that the authorities insisted on journalists staying in the same place, if it was possible. 'So that they can keep an eye on us. And my God, Sophy, the rules and regulations. French bureaucracy gone mad.'

It was getting lighter and the lorry was making good progress. The sun had begun to slant through the forest dispersing the veils of fog and lighting a seemingly endless vista of green armies of trees.

At last the lorry drew to a stop. The driver and his companion, a big moon-faced soldier with a curling moustache, his képi on the back of his head, climbed out. The big man put out his hands and jumped Sophy down.

'We are going to eat. In Sedan, we may not get the chance.'

The trio, crossing the road, went into the edges of the forest and set down on mossy fallen logs which seemed impregnated with days of rain. The soldiers gave Sophy a hunk of stale bread and a lump of cheese, and offered her a swig of red wine from the bottle. She thanked them and managed to swallow the food; but felt that wine at this time of the morning would choke her. She thought of Francine's fragrant coffee.

Having done their hospitable best for the stranger, the soldiers sat and talked. They were dissimilar in every way but their uniform, and even in this the driver wore a corporal's stripe, the big round-faced man was a mere *poilu*. The corporal, small and wiry, stubbed his cigarette out in the wet pine needles and picked up the bottle again. The big soldier, mouth full, looked over at Sophy.

'Sure you want to go to Sedan?'

'I have to. I am a journalist.'

'Shouldn't be travelling on your own should you?' He pushed his képi further back on thick curling black hair. Did the young lady know the Boche were already over the Albert canal and 'beating the hell out of the Belgians'?

'So we *heard*. But the army's nothing but a saucepan of rumours,' said the corporal.

The big soldier, with an exaggerated expression of incredulity, continued to talk to Sophy.

'Did your newspaper hear the tank traps outside Sedan have been destroyed?'

Sophy hoped she looked professional as she nodded, and repeated what she'd heard in Jacques Ouastou's office.

'What a scandal, eh?' said the big man. 'I was there when we built them, I saw them with these eyes. Great lumps of concrete poured into moulds and set hard like that,' smacking his enormous hands together. 'Why, a tank could not advance a millimetre on a road covered with those things! How could it have happened? The order to remove them came from the general himself. Huntzier.' He spat.

The corporal regarded his companion as if such reactions were usual, and smiled slightly.

'You know the old saying in the army. Don't try to understand. Do as you're told.'

'And don't ask questions because the answer will stink,' said the big man. 'The townspeople in Sedan asked them all right. They shouted them at the top of their lungs. If my guess is right, the poor sods won't be shouting now. They'll be dead.'

'You're a depressing beggar,' said the driver. 'The Nazis won't get to Sedan.'

'Won't they, just?' said the big man, playing with his moustache. He turned to Sophy.

'If I was you, Mademoiselle, I'd **** off back to Paris pretty damned quick. Forget your job. Look out for yourself. Get back while there's time.'

Sophy managed a weak smile and a shake of the head. Half

of her believed even now that the lorry would drive into Sedan and somehow without much difficulty she would find the hotel where the journalists were staying – and there among his colleagues would be Daniel. She tried to imagine that moment, tried to see his face when they met. Such amazement and joy. But there was another part of Sophy's mind that was beginning to tell her this was all a fantasy. What the hell was she doing here in the middle of a forest, refusing to listen to warnings from a soldier who could scent danger?

They returned to the lorry and drove on. Sophy, on the ammunition boxes, stared at the endless procession of trees. Then she began to notice that the big soldier was leaning out of the lorry looking ahead. He did it again. Then again. He shouted to the corporal to drive more slowly, raising his hand for the speed to reduce even further. Suddenly he shouted. The driver put his foot on the brakes, swerved straight off the road bumping across pine needles and bracken and somehow skidded to a halt behind an enormous stack of logs the size of a house.

The men sprang down, dragged Sophy from the lorry and set off, running through the trees. 'Down! Down!'

They lay flat on their stomachs. At first she was tense with fear, lying in the wet bracken. But nothing happened and after a few minutes she attempted to sit up. The big soldier put his hand on her back and forced her to lie down again ... and then she heard it. It was low at first, a noise like uninterrupted far-distant thunder. It grew steadily louder until it seemed to fill the whole forest. They appeared at last, a line of tanks advancing down the road on which a few moments ago the lorry had driven. Sophy counted them – there were thirty-five. They were brand new, painted a dull khaki colour, the Nazi swastika on their sides, guns pointing ahead, making their inexorable way ahead, a procession of juggernauts. The two soldiers and Sophy lay immobile, just lifting their chins from the wet ground to watch the enemy go by.

It took Sophy days to get back to Paris. All her crazy hopes of finding Daniel were crushed by the Nazi tanks which thundered towards Sedan. The Germans were already in France. Where had they come from? She did not ask, did not think. Given a lump of bread by the two soldiers, she fled into the forest. She walked miles, hiding whenever she heard a noise which could be tanks, lorries, even marching feet. The troops she hid from were sometimes French; she was too frightened to find out.

People befriended the foreign girl when she emerged, lost, out of the forest. She was given a lift in a farm cart; she was allowed to sleep in the barn of a broken-down farm where she was given food and kindness. The farmer helped her to find a lorry whose driver was going in the direction of Paris. 'My destination is Neuilly. If I get there ...' He would be glad, he said, of somebody to talk to.

As they drove, he told her that Hitler's troops, supported by Stuka dive-bombers, were moving so fast that the French seemed unable to stop them. Sophy listened in a despairing silence. She was alone in a country which seemed to have gone mad. She had no idea what to do next, and was only trying to get back to Paris because Odile Gombert would surely give her a bed and a chance to recover before Sophy somehow got herself back to England.

She had lost her luggage, she had only her handbag still containing Jack's money. She was dirty and exhausted. She remembered Daniel counselling her to go back to Cannes with Anne-Marie. Jack telling her to come home. Why hadn't she listened? At last the driver arrived in Neuilly. When Sophy thanked him he refused to allow her to pay a sou. Her eyes filled with tears.

With shoes scratched to ribbons, and painful blisters, she walked the rest of the way to Paris.

It was strange when she reached the boulevards. The lively avenues were deserted, a dreadful kind of silence reigned. There were almost no people to be seen, only one or two cars, topped with mattresses, were filled with passengers driving by in the direction of the Porte d'Italie.

After hours of painful walking, Sophy finally turned into

the Rue des Ardissons and went through the street doors into the familiar courtyard. When she saw the apartments where Tante Odile lived she almost cried with relief. She knew that she had behaved like a lunatic when she set off to find Daniel. The kindness shown to her by Colonel Tassigny, by the two soldiers in the forest, by the farmers, by all the French people grey with anxiety, made her ashamed. I know Tante Odile dislikes the British, she thought, but she will be kind. Everybody is now. And I am her goddaughter's friend.

There was no electricity in the city, the lift did not work, and she toiled up to the third floor. She had left many of her clothes behind when she'd packed the bag lost in the Ardennes. She would take some clean clothes with her when she set off to get – somehow – to Boulogne or Calais.

She rang Tante Odile's bell. Too tired to stand, she leaned against the wall. There was no answer and she rang again. At last the door opened a crack. Francine.

'Francine! It's me!'

The old woman's face puckered into alarm, she pushed the door nearly shut again, whispering, 'Wait please, Mademoiselle.' Surprised at the lack of welcome, Sophy ignored the half-closed door and walked into the hall.

There was a step on the tiled floor. Odile Gombert came out of the salon.

'Oh Tante Odile! I'm so glad to see you, forgive me appearing like this –' burst out the girl. 'I've had such a dreadful time, it's so good to be back and –'

'Leave my house.'

'But –'

'Get out. Leave. What are you doing here?' Odile Gombert's voice was savage.

'I went to the Ardennes –'

'Oh yes, Francine told me all about your plans.'

'I only went to try and find –' stammered Sophy and, seeing the hatred in the woman's face, began again, 'I only want –'

'I do not care what you want. I will not have you here. You are English –'

Sophy began to shout her down, 'Is Anne-Marie still here? Did she get a train to Cannes? If not I demand to see her —'

'She's gone, praise God, and won't be exposed to the danger of being with *you*, treacherous English hussy,' Odile Gombert had worked herself up into a fury. 'How do I know who you are? You may be a Nazi agent. What were you doing, going to the Ardennes? To do such a thing would be impossible without help. Whose help? How do I know where you've been and what you're planning in our beloved city. You are spying for the enemy. Get out. Get out.'

'You've got my clothes,' yelled Sophy, beside herself with answering rage, 'I will have my clothes.'

Using all her strength, she gave Odile Gombert's stout figure a violent push and ran into the bedroom she had shared with Anne-Marie. All her belongings had been thrown in a heap on the floor, some dangling out of a paper basket. Swearing in English, she grabbed them together and tied them into a blouse, knotting the sleeves. Turning round, she saw Francine in the doorway. The old woman's face was pitiful, she was holding a pile of Sophy's underclothes and handkerchiefs washed and ironed. She bent down, gently unknotted the blouse and pushed the clean clothes into the bundle.

For the first time since Daniel had left her, Sophy really cried. She put her arms round Francine's neck and hugged and hugged, the tears streaming. A moment later she had run from the apartment, down the stairs and out into the street. Then she came to a stop, trying to collect her thoughts. She must go to the British Consulate — it was *their* job to help now; they would tell her how she could get home. She'd passed the Consulate two or three times in her many walks through the smart parts of Paris with Anne-Marie: it was near the Étoile. She had to walk very slowly, her blisters painful at every step, and as she passed a newspaper kiosk she saw big headlines on the placards, 'The Government will not leave Paris!'

Everybody was hurrying. The effect was strange, they did not seem conscious of each other, they pushed by with set faces, like people escaping from a plague. The boulevards had been empty when she'd arrived in Paris but now trucks went by filled with soldiers, and Sophy saw troops busy constructing something which looked like a sort of barricade. She thought of the big soldier in the forest. How he would scoff.

Clutching her bundle like a gypsy she finally reached the Consulate. There were people everywhere – on the steps, in the entrance hall. They talked together in low voices, looking as if their nerves were stretched to breaking point. At first, seeing the numbers, Sophy thought it useless even to wait. But what else was there to do? She queued behind a thin irritable man who talked angrily to his wife, who was pretty in a subdued doleful way. He kept repeating 'Didn't I *tell* you? I told you, didn't I?' Sophy wondered how the poor woman could bear him.

At last, after nearly three hours, it was her turn to go into an office. A harassed Englishman who looked like a weedy schoolmaster was trying to answer questions from half a dozen Britishers at the same time. He held up a desperate hand.

'Ladies and gentlemen. You want to know our intentions with regard to British subjects now in France. We can give you this advice. Unless you have very good reasons to stay, you should leave as soon as possible.'

'But how?' demanded a chorus of voices.

'I'm afraid we cannot help. You must make your way as best you can.'

There was an angry noise of protest. One indignant voice demanded, 'What are the duties of a Consul, pray?' Sophy did not bother to wait for the reply. She remembered her brother saying to her once, 'In trouble, what you need is money.'

Edging her way through the hall and out into the street, she began to walk towards Lloyds Bank. Fortunately for Sophy, worn out, footsore and driven only by desperation, the bank was not far. There was yet another crowd milling in and out; as she joined them a man went by, gave her a horrible look, shouted '*Anglaise*' and spat at her. Sophy looked after him in amazement. She couldn't understand. Everywhere in her frightened wanderings in the Ardennes she'd met kindness. What had happened to make this awful change?

She realized with apprehension that she knew nothing of the possibly terrible things now happening in France. During all the time she had been out of Paris, she had been set only on surviving, on returning, she'd been too hurried and frightened to ask questions of the people who had helped her. And they had said nothing to the foreigner they temporarily befriended.

There was a middle-aged couple ahead of her in the queue. She did not need to ask them a single question. The man, grey-haired and elderly, with a military look, was saying, 'Of course our troops may have to evacuate if the situation gets any worse. But they'll land again. Sure to.'

In the well-bred voice she heard a subdued hysteria; it shook slightly. Sophy herself had started to tremble when she got to the counter and asked the clerk to cash her travelling cheques. The man looked at her for a moment. He was quite old, everybody out of uniform was old, and more like a vicar than a clerk. He counted out her money carefully and handed it to her in a thick wedge of notes. Then leaning across the counter, whispered, 'Don't show your money to anybody, Miss. And only spend the notes one at a time.'

'Thank you. I understand. Do you think I may be able to get a train?' she said, knowing the stupidity of the question. Somebody behind her sighed loudly, almost a groan of impatience.

'I don't think so, Miss. I've heard there are no trains now. Trying to get back to England, are you? Then I'm afraid your only hope is to get a lift from a friend. Not easy, I know. And there's already fighting in the north. But remember. Hide your money. And try not to speak English.'

Leaving the bank, Sophy simply did not know what to do next. It was too late, oh much too late, for her brother's string-pulling to get her home. How could she get a lift to the coast? She knew nobody but Tante Odile, who had treated her as an enemy. Lost as she was, she thought with a pang of love about Daniel, wanting him, longing to have him with her, weeping in her heart for the way they had parted. It was then, standing alone in the city, that she remembered his father.

Sophy threw her bundle over one shoulder like Dick Whittington and set off to walk through the frightened streets. Once she stopped at a café, and remembering the warning, only just muttered 'coffee and bread', trying to conceal her accent. An old waiter served her, but did not look at her.

It was eerie to walk down the beautiful sweep of the Champ Elysées, tree-decorated, with the distant Arc de Triomphe glittering in the sunshine, and see only cars roofed with mattresses, or people hurrying by with set faces. In one car she saw a little dark woman beside the driver, clutching a cage in which a canary hopped to and fro. The poor woman looked dazed.

Sophy finally reached the Impasse Clérissy, and when she went into the courtyard, she had a sudden senseless moment of hope. Suppose Daniel was actually there. She had no idea what to expect, and when the Vergés' servant opened the door, dressed in a fresh blue overall and starched apron and said 'Mademoiselle?' the very normality was a kind of shock. Sophy, aware of her appearance for the first time in days, asked for Monsieur. Would the young lady have the aimiability to wait, said the old woman, and showed Sophy into the grand salon.

Seated on one of the embroidered chairs, the sun streaming in upon her as if she were lit upon a stage, was a small elegant young woman in the most fashionable Paris clothes. Her fair hair curled from under a little straw hat tied with velvet ribbons. Her legs were faultless, her heels very high. She was older than Sophy, perhaps thirty and exquisitely made-up; the look she gave Sophy was one of unabashed French curiosity.

'Good morning,' she said, when the servant had left them. 'Have you come for Christian's help, by any chance? I most certainly have.'

With good breeding, she appeared totally unconscious of

Sophy's dirty face, gypsy bundle and pauper's air.

'Yes, I have something I want to ask him,' said Sophy, unnerved.

'Most people do,' said the young woman, smiling. 'I must introduce myself. Violette Duplessis.'

'Sophy Hayward.'

Violette Duplessis looked thoughfully at her, saying surely she had seen her at Versailles last week. 'My God, imagine, a ball! How could we have believed ... and the news now so awful.'

Sophy nodded sombrely but repeated what she had heard the soldiers say in the Ardennes, 'The Germans will never cross the Seine.'

'They have already crossed the Meuse,' said her companion. She offered Sophy an Egyptian cigarette which Sophy refused. Violette Duplessis then lit one and smoked in silence. Scarcely two minutes had gone by when the door opened and Christian Vergé came quickly into the salon.

He smiled at Violette, went across to her and kissed her hand. Then, turning to Sophy, repeated the gesture, but it was subtly different. He let go of her hand too quickly and it was to Violette Duplessis that he addressed his entire conversation, only once turning to Sophy and then looking straight back at the other girl. He spoke rapidly, repeating that there was 'so little time'. He had done what she asked, he said to Violette Duplessis, he had arranged for her to have 'as much petrol as your car will take. The tank is now full, and I calculate you should get as far as Saulieu. I also attempted, my dear, to telephone the hotel for you but without success.'

'You are so kind, Christian.'

'Nothing. It is nothing. But at least you have some transport. And you will let me know, when you can, how it goes with you?'

'Of course.'

She thanked him and spoke about the stream of cars leaving Paris, adding with a smile that she had seen 'two hearses brimming with the undertakers' relatives, one supposes, looking quite festive! As for bicycles, I am told one can sell them today for a small fortune.'

She spoke coolly and Christian Vergé was also composed. But what they said frightened Sophy. It took all her nerve to break into the conversation and claim the attention of the man ignoring her.

'I came to ask, Monsieur Vergé, if you knew anyone who is trying to get to – to Calais or Boulogne. Or another of the Channel ports. Somebody who might be good enough to give me a lift.'

He turned to her.

'I'm afraid not. A good many English and American people are already on their way, to Biarritz apparently. Including your Duke and Duchess of Windsor. Alas,' there had never been so meaningless a phrase, 'I cannot be of service to you. I do not think, without your own friends, you will get back.'

Sophy went red in alarm. Perhaps from compunction he added, 'You would be safer if you went south.'

'I'm driving to the south,' put in Violette Duplessis, 'but it is a very long way from your own country, Mademoiselle.'

'She has friends there,' said Christian Vergé, as if anxious for the chance of getting rid of Sophy.

'Well? Would you consider coming with me? At least you would be joining your friends, and perhaps from the Midi ...'

She left possibilities encouragingly open.

Sophy, the blush dying, said hurriedly that she would be grateful to accept. She knew as she spoke that it was crazy to travel *away* from England, but she could think of no other solution. Infected with fear, she was like the people streaming out of Paris, her only instinct was to flee.

'I'm glad you will come with me,' said Violette, slightly smiling. 'I've an idea it will be safer. Two instead of one. So that is settled. Well, Christian, we must say goodbye. Again my gratitude. What would one do without you?'

He made deprecating noises, not looking at Sophy again. It was her last chance. Speaking with an effort she said, 'Monsieur Vergé. Have you news of Daniel?'

'He was sent to the Ardennes,' was the cold reply.

'Yes, yes, I know. But have you heard since then?'

'I fear not.'

He walked with Violette out of the salon, kissed her hand, merely bowed to Sophy, and just as the girls went to the head of the stairs called, 'Violette?' He added something futile about her taking the greatest care.

He did not say goodbye to Sophy.

The two girls went out into the street. There was the wail of an air raid siren and Violette looked up at the empty blue sky.

'Much defence *we* have when they come,' she said. 'Do you know how many barrage balloons there are in Paris? Six.'

'It isn't possible!'

'Oh but it is. And where are our anti-aircraft guns? I suspect there are none. I have a feeling,' she added, looking up and down the boulevard, 'that we ought to hurry.'

Violette's car had been in a garage belonging to the Vergé apartments, she had already packed, and Sophy saw two mattresses fixed to its roof with ropes. There were a number of suitcases, books and blankets in the back; Sophy's gypsy bundle was easily stowed away in a corner. Before they set off, Violette insisted on going to a bar at the corner of the Impasse Clérissy to buy rolls and have her two flasks filled with what now passed for coffee. As they came out Violette put her hand to her eyes and swore. Sophy, too, felt her eyes beginning to sting. There was a peculiar acrid smoke in the air, and when Violette removed her hand her finger had left a long sooty smudge on one cheek, which Sophy helped to wipe away. The day was bright, but it began to get strangely dark. Even as they stood at the door the mist blotted out the sun.

'What on earth is it?' exclaimed Violette, looking with distaste at her gloves – like Sophy's bare hands they were streaked with black.

A woman who had been leaning across a table in the bar looked up; she was purpled-faced and dirty and very drunk and turned bloodshot eyes towards them. She was like a witch.

'It's been sent by God. A fog to protect Paris from the Boche planes. Yes, they'll get lost in it and they'll crash. Crash in flames and burn ...'

Her head fell on the table again and she lay inert.

'It smells like burning wood,' said Violette, sniffing the air.

A waiter standing nearby began uselessly polishing a table.

'The priests are taking statues of Ste Geneviève through the streets,' he said, 'She's our patron saint, isn't she? She can't save us. What you can smell is the funeral pyre of Paris.'

Violette gave him a strange hard look, very bright and dangerous. She said to Sophy, 'Let's go.'

They went out into the thickening fog.

Violette knew her way through a maze of narrow back streets and steep roads, climbing the hills, descending into tiny squares. For a time she avoided the traffic, but as they neared the Porte d'Italie which led out of Paris to the south they were forced to join a solid mass of crawling cars. It was the exodus.

The sight was so horrifying, so impressive, that neither of the girls said a word. There were cars of every kind. Rolls Royces glittering with the care of chauffeurs, battered old roadsters which looked as if they were about to break down, family cars, bicycles, even farm carts drawn by huge horses. Violette and Sophy had become part of the great slow moving mass. They drove behind a shabby Fiat crammed with people and were followed by a rich two-seater sports car driven by a man in goggles like a pilot in the Great War. He had no passengers. The seat beside him was piled with crocodile leather luggage.

As the time went by on a journey of starting, stopping, crawling, stopping again, Violette and Sophy scarcely spoke to each other. They saw that it was not only the road which was massed with traffic. The pavement, too, was thick with people, everybody moving like a river in the same direction; women carried babies in their arms, men carried bigger children on their backs. People wheeled bicycles strapped with bundles, some pulled loaded handcarts. The sight struck a terrible chill into the heart. It was so extraordinary, the number so huge, the movement away from Paris so universal and in every face but those of the very young was the same set look. Now and again the vehicles moved faster; once they passed an Army lorry on its side on the edge of the road. There was a group of soldiers attempting to push it back upright again.

Later Violette pointed to a tank. It was upended in a ditch, and its occupants, two soldiers, were sitting on the grass beside it, smoking.

'Look at them,' she said contemptuously, 'one tank and already it is useless. No doubt it is the only one to defend Paris.'

The filthy fog smeared the windscreen and penetrated the inside of the car, it masked the walking and driving crowds, it filled the air and continued like a miasma until they reached Fontainebleau, when it finally dissolved and the sun reappeared.

Sophy was worn out. She simply sat by the French girl and stared at the roads. Once Violette said, 'You look exhausted. Try and sleep.' Sophy couldn't. What was happening was too strange and too fearful.

The mass of people behaving like a herd of animals instinctively on the move kept the two girls silent. Invading armies always drove refugees ahead of them. The Jews had fled, a whole nation, out of Egypt. Now it was the turn of the French.

Often the huge cavalcade halted when a car somewhere broke down and had to be towed to the side of the road and abandoned. After another long silence on the agonizingly slow drive, Sophy said, 'Do you really think the Germans will take Paris?'

'God knows.'

'I had a feeling Monsieur Vergé thinks they will.'

'So did I. Sometimes I suspect Christian ... there goes another unfortunate,' added Violette. A car a little ahead stopped; smoke poured from its radiator.

It was evening when the mass of cars reached the city of Cosne on the Loire. Violette seemed to know the place, managed to back out of the traffic stream and parked in a stableyard.

'We'll try to and get a bed at the Lion d'Or.'

210

'Surely that will be impossible?'

'Maybe so. Maybe not,' said Violette.

Sophy realized the car was parked at the back of one of those very old posting houses turned into hotels on the great roads leading from Paris to the south.

It was to be expected that there should be a milling mass of travellers in the entrance hall, but Violette barged through in a very French manner, not hesitating to use her elbows and calling over her shoulder to Sophy, 'Come on!'

A woman at the desk, fending off the loud demands of refugees, looked in a state of shock. Her face altered when she caught sight of Violette. She reached out to shake her hand and say, 'How good to see you!' Violette whispered something, the woman nodded and gestured to a porter. Then, with a harassed patience she returned to the babel of voices shouting for rooms and food.

The porter took the girls to the back of the hotel, up three winding flights of stairs to the attics. Violette saw that they'd been given a tiny bedroom; she smiled and tipped the old man. He bowed politely, muttering something incongruous about it being a pleasure to serve Mademoiselle.

When they were alone Violette looked at Sophy and said dryly, 'I often come here.'

'So I gathered.'

'I drive to the south every month. Madame Pin is quite a friend of mine. Lucky, wasn't it? Otherwise we'd have slept in the car.'

Sophy said that what Violette had accomplished was a small – no, a large – miracle.

'Perhaps it is,' agreed Violette. 'Now the next miracle is to get something to eat.'

The dining room was as crammed as the entrance hall, but Violette's presence was again noticed, the waiter shook hands, and they were given a table marked 'Reserved'.

When she had been on the train at Cannes, Sophy had felt self-conscious that Monsieur Dufour had managed to get them reserved seats. Such niceties were in the past. Now, when they sat down, she and Violette scarcely looked at the

211

queues waiting at the door. They were given a passable meal of some kind of stew and drank an exquisite wine chosen by Violette.

'We may as well enjoy something good,' she said and gave Sophy a tired smile.

There was no electricity at Cosne, the dining room was lit by rows of candles and Madame Pin at the desk gave the girls two to light them to their room. The girls undressed in a wavering golden light which sent gigantic shadows on the walls and inward sloping ceiling. Far below in the street, lorries thundered by on the cobbles. Once there were shouts and Violette, remembering to blow out both candles, ran to the window. She leaned out and waved. She was answered by more shouts and men's laughter. She called down to whoever was below and stayed for quite a while, before pulling the blackout curtain back into place and relighting the candles.

'There were a great many,' she said. 'Did you hear what they were calling? It was what the soldiers used to shout at Verdun. "*On les aura* – we will get them." Poor things. Poor things.'

With her elegance laid aside, weary and white-faced, Violette looked changed. She had taken off her Parisian air with her satin blouse. She brushed her hair in silence, creamed her face. She was wrapped in thought.

Sophy climbed into the bed, which was as hard as a board. She lay quietly, too tired to think. Her companion said suddenly, 'I think we should call each other by our first names. Do you agree? We may be together for a long time yet.'

'I'd like to,' said Sophy politely.

Violette also climbed into bed plumping up the pillow and arranging her watch, a handkerchief, her car keys and some loose change on a chair by her bed. She seemed in the mood to give a little information about herself.

'I am trying to get to Menton,' she said, 'I have friends there. To tell you the truth, I'm worried about them. Particularly now the Italian situation looks so dangerous. And you want to go to Cannes?'

212

'That is where I've been living with my friends, the Dufours. But I must get back to England. Somehow.'

'The first thing was to get out of Paris. There may be all kinds of ways of getting to your own country once you're safe from what's happening in the north,' said Violette. 'We have to thank Christian Vergé for our petrol. That has given us a start. Let us tell each other more of ourselves on the journey. It will pass the time.'

She blew out the candles.

When Sophy woke she did not know where she was. Then saw the outline of a cheap wardrobe, the sloping ceiling, the extinguished candles; she sniffed the scent of Worth's *Je Reviens* floating in the poverty-stricken room. A shaft of fear went through her when she saw that Violette's bed was pulled together and her clothes – watch – keys – had disappeared. The French girl had gone; she'd decided it was easier to travel alone.

Sophy went to the window and pulled open the curtains to look down at a medieval street whose houses had been old in Elizabethan times. They pressed together as if to support each other from falling down. She was trembling. What am I to do? What the hell am I to do? She went to the basin, poured out some stone-cold water and washed her face. She was hurriedly dressing when the door opened. Violette, neat, made-up, and rather triumphantly smiling, came in.

'What luck. I managed to get some more petrol. I know the garagiste here, I always go to the same place. The Thermos is filled and Madame at reception gave me some bread. You can eat in the car.'

'But the bill —'

'I've paid. I'll tell you how much you owe later. I've divided it into two and added the price of coffee last night. The wine wasn't expensive, I chose a local one.'

Sophy, over her shock, did not tell her companion of her unjustified fears. She hastily finished dressing. As they went down the stairs Violette whispered, 'Don't talk English. Your troops are leaving France.'

'It can't be true.'

213

'I'm afraid it is. Belgium has capitulated, there's no cover on the northern front for our army or the British. They say Lille has fallen after a brave, useless resistance. People are bitter against you, Sophy,' using her name for the first time, 'so don't speak. You don't look very English' she added, regarding her critically. 'There are redheaded Frenchwomen in the Loire region. Much admired.'

The little Renault set off out of Cosne into the same mass and mess of cars and lorries, carts, bicycles and foot passengers. As they drove, they passed crowds still sleeping under the trees or feeding babies, or stealing the green apples from the trees or simply shouting to each other to wait! they were coming! as they shovelled blankets and bundles together and dragged their children by the hand.

There was no question of Sophy and Violette telling each other about themselves to 'pass the time'. The refugees were the only reality. When the girls stopped in a village, there were always the crowds foraging for food and trying to get shelter, and sometimes Violette and Sophy slept in the car, hungry, having obtained only a drink of water from a village fountain. In every village they drove through, they saw crowds sitting in the cafés huddled round the wireless. It had become the only way people could learn what was happening. Day after day the news was blacker. The broadcasts stopped talking of strategic retreats to prepared positions. Orders and counter-orders came over the air addressed to '*Le Peuple Français*' always prefaced by the sound of 'The Marseillaise'. '*Aux armes, citoyens!*' sang a voice.

The days went by. Violette's gallant little car had almost reached Lyon when one afternoon Violette said, after a long interval, 'Look over there.' There was a crowd of cars not very thick but growing, on the other side of the road. Streaming in the direction of Paris.

'But what's happened? Surely the Germans aren't *in the south*?' said Sophy, appalled.

'All the car number plates are BA. Basse Alpes. My guess is they want to get away from the Italians.'

'The Italians!'

214

'Yesterday the talk was all about Italy being next to declare war. Didn't you hear it? Now the Germans are advancing so fast, Italy wants to join.' She looked out of the car window at the cars driving to the city they had abandoned.

'We are all running away,' Violette said.

When they stopped at cafés, or by the roadside, Sophy dared not open her mouth. Villagers, straggling soldiers, hotel keepers, men in garages, spoke of the British. 'They have deserted us,' said an old woman, slamming bread down in front of Violette and Sophy, together with glasses of watered wine. 'We have defended them, manned the port where they escaped. Dunkirk! We let them go because they betrayed us. Left us in the lurch. My God, if I had an Englishman here in my café, I'd –' she made a practised gesture of wringing a chicken's neck.

When they were alone at night under the stars Violette consoled Sophy. She had listened greedily every time they stopped, getting any scraps of news she could glean and she assured Sophy – and herself – 'the Maginot Line is intact. There will be a magnificent counter-strike. Just you see.'

They both wanted to believe it.

On the road two pretty young women, even though worn and whitefaced, found help now and then: from soldiers who gave them swigs of brandy and teased Sophy for her silence. 'Why is your friend dumb? and such a mignonne.'

'She is the timid one,' it was Violette's stock reply.

'She's deep. She has her secrets,' said the soldiers.

It was men who helped them. Not a single woman in a single town or village offered succour to the girls. It was true that charity flowed for the mothers with small children and for the old and the lame and the frightened. But not for two girls who wore, despite their pallor, the wonderful cloak of youth.

On a night in June somewhere outside Lyon, they slept on the side of the road, sheltered by the car parked on the grass in front of them. There were refugees everywhere, on the sloping rocky ground, in the woods, by the dry bed of a small river. There were no lights but the occasional spurt from a match or a lighter. A low constant sound of voices came out of the dark. Violette made their coats and blankets into makeshift beds. Her elegance was long gone, she and Sophy were twins, both in none-too-clean skirts and blouses with the sleeves rolled up, both bare-legged and wearing cheap sandals Violette had bought at a shoemaker's in Pont de Vaux. They never took off their clothes at night. They did not dare.

Lying on the ground they looked up at millions upon millions of stars and a rising moon. The June night was warm, smelling of green things. The girls lay awake thinking of the day gone by. That afternoon for the first time the refugees had been bombed. Planes had appeared out of the sky, people screamed, rushing all over the place, scattering like terrified ants. It had been horrible. But there had been a storm earlier, a strong wind was blowing; it literally blew away the bombs which fell harmlessly in a nearby valley. The ground quaked and the running·crowds threw themselves face downwards. During those few minutes in the car tightly holding each other's hands and not moving, Sophy and Violette thought they were about to die.

When the panic was over and the planes disappeared towards Lyon, Violette drove on for a while, and then managed to draw out of the column into a tiny side road and reach a village. They left the car on a verge by the river, and went to look for a café: they were dreadfully hungry. There, as always, was the mass of villagers huddled round a wireless. Sophy had to stay mute but Violette asked the patron quietly if there was anything to eat.

'We have a little bread. And Marcel will sell you his peaches.'

The girls sat down at a table near the wireless, devouring bread which was like a stone. Marcel, who looked like a bedraggled bird, a crow perhaps, came up with a basket crammed with peaches. He was glad to sell as many as they wanted. 'There are no markets. I watch my fruit go bad,' he said. The fruit was delicious, scented, full of juice, the best thing they'd eaten for many days. It was while they ate the peaches that they heard the news on the wireless. It looked as if Paris was about to fall.

Now Sophy lay staring at the night sky. What about Daniel? Was he dead somewhere in the forests where she had hidden? Was he alive with an army fighting for its life? Violette said thoughtfully, 'Christian must have left Paris with the rest of them. Did you hear the man talking in the bar?'

'No. I was listening to the wireless.'

'You were lucky. I couldn't bear them. Defeatists. They made me sick. Now I keep wondering about Christian.'

'Is he a close friend of yours?' asked Sophy after a moment.

'Didn't you guess? We were lovers when I worked for him. It was like that in the department. Most of the girls went to bed with their bosses. Christian was very attentive, you know. And generous. He used to take me to expensive places to dine – the best. He kept offering to pay my rent.' Violette laughed a little. 'He is so old-fashioned.'

There was a pause while she groped for her packet of cigarettes, finally saying, '*Merde*. I shouldn't smoke. I'll be spotted from the air.'

'The Germans won't see one cigarette burning! They'd spot that camp fire over there, why don't they put the damned thing out?' As if the people along the road had heard, the fire was suddenly extinguished.

'And did you love Monsieur Vergé?' asked Sophy; it was the nearest she could get to talking about Daniel. Violette gave a little snort.

'Who could *love* Christian? He is so antique. Formal. He talks about his ancestors – the boredom of it. And he is distinguished even in bed. He was a good lover, I admit that, but then he's proud of doing everything well, including that.' She stopped talking for a moment and then remarked, 'He used to give me salary increases. That was nice.'

'I thought you refused to let him pay your rent.'

'Don't be logical. That's a French trait. There's a difference anyway. I was worth the extra salary, I am very efficient. As for the rent, if one goes to bed without true love one cannot accept ... you know how it is.'

'I've only been to bed with one man, I'm afraid.'

'Afraid?'

'I keep thinking he may be dead. I do – I did – adore him. You know who I mean.'

What did it matter if she told Violette? What did anything matter on this journey to nowhere? Perhaps the planes would come again and this time would bring death. Daniel, dark stranger, was receding so fast from her now. Hope was leaving too. She clutched at the chance to talk about Daniel.

'Of course you mean Daniel Vergé,' said Violette. 'When you asked Christian about him and he was unpleasant to you, I supposed Daniel was your lover. And Christian had decided you weren't a suitable young woman to join the so-aristocratic family. How long have you and Daniel known each other?'

Sophy's story poured out. She described meeting Daniel in Cannes and the night when Yvonne Dufour had told her he was to marry Anne-Marie and how she'd gone to confront him and they had made love.

'Your first time, Sophy? That is surprising.' Violette was deeply interested.

Sophy's voice was level when she talked of all that had happened – until she got to the fight at Versailles. She expected horrified interruptions. All Violette said was, 'Bravo.'

'But I might have killed him!'

'Not you. I'm sure you *wanted* to kill him. I have felt the same. And you happened to discover that impressive weapon. But subconsciously you knew all the time he could twist your wrist and knock the knife away and probably knock you down as well.'

'He threw me into a hedge. And I had a black eye.'

'Yes. I saw the remains of one when you came to the Impasse Clérissy. What do you suppose Christian made of your somewhat odd appearance? Wouldn't it have shaken him out from behind that façade if he'd known he was talking to his son's armed opponent?'

She giggled.

But Sophy did not think the subject funny.

'So you love Daniel,' said Violette thoughtfully. 'He's

certainly attractive. He was staying with his father, when Christian and I were having our affair. He didn't seem to realize what was going on; of course Christian was very suave when I turned up sometimes for a glass of champagne, or if we were going out to dine. Daniel was nice. He made me laugh. But –' she sighed. 'But then he came home unexpectedly one afternoon and caught us.'

'That's impossible – he didn't burst into his father's bedroom!'

'Oh no. I'm afraid we were in the grand salon. On the Aubusson.'

She paused.

'All that scrambling to one's feet and pulling on underclothes. One feels such a fool. Daniel only opened the door, saw us on the floor and slammed out, but poor Christian was very discomposed. I'd never seen him like that before. He looked angry and foolish. After that, I'm afraid Daniel couldn't bear me. You know, Sophy, it was a pity. I was sorry. It isn't fun, is it? being disliked. I always think – why doesn't he or she like me? I am rather nice. *Sympathique.* Not a fool. Not bad looking either.'

'I would say you are beautiful.'

'You are kind, Sophy. I shall try to believe you.'

Speaking of Daniel, Violette told Sophy things she'd never known; he had loved his mother devotedly and she had died of tuberculosis when he was just fourteen. The disease was infectious, and the family for all its grandeur hadn't take proper precautions. Daniel developed a patch on his lung. 'Which is why he hadn't been called up, you see.'

The sad truth was that Daniel had adored his mother and when he'd seen his father with Violette, 'writhing around on the Aubusson,' it was not something any of them could pretend had not happened.

'Afterwards he refused to speak to me.'

Violette stubbed out her cigarette and scrabbled in the dry earth to bury it.

'The affair with Christian ended two years ago. I felt guilty asking him for help when you and I met, I have scarcely seen him for months. But I knew he'd do what he could. Have you noticed vain men are the ones to ask for help? They'll do anything to prove themselves to you. Dear Christian ... I still have a fondness.'

'Would you have married him?'

Violette gave a belly laugh, oddly coarse and amusing from a sophisticated Parisienne.

'Would I take on the duty of a nurse? He's over sixty! And in any case, supposing I had been crazy about him and he about me, I was born in the suburbs, Sophy. What a terrible thought. He was so like himself when I told him we must part. He gave me a valuable locket of rubies, diamonds and tiny pearls. "Pearls mean tears, and they are mine", he said.'

'I think that's lovely.'

'I daresay he'd used the phrase before.'

'Violette!'

'Now you're being English,' Violette smiled in the dark. 'And while we talk of Daniel, you must not upset yourself over him. He has not been killed. He's quick and resourceful, he won't expose himself to unnecessary danger. He is not that sort. Well, Sophy, shall we sleep? We never know what tomorrow will bring.'

Day followed day as the exodus continued to trail down the roads of France; it was growing slightly less as people began to scatter to the east and west, taking roads over the mountains towards Switzerland or across the hills to Roanne and the many tiny villages among the forests. But Violette drove due south.

The progress was slow, the days long, as they took the road by the side of the swift-flowing Rhône. Above, high as heaven, on mountain-tops were churches built a thousand years ago and bringing no blessing now. The country was very beautiful, with acre upon acre of vineyards spread like carpets on the sides of the hills, many of the vines sadly untended.

During the stops, at midday, in the evening, the girls somehow managed to get something, anything, to eat, and sat at café tables under the plane trees. Violette talked to old men who had fought in the other war once called Great. The men shared their loaves sometimes, or sold them cherries. And the refrain like music that everybody repeated and never tired to hear and sing, was always, 'There will be the moment of history. The counter-stroke. The Maginot Line still holds.'

But the news grew worse, the advance of the German armies so rapid it was difficult to know what was happening from hour to hour. After Arras and Amiens fell, the enemy took the whole valley of the Oise and there were no more broadcasts from Paris. Yet the Maginot was still intact. Sophy and Violette passionately hung on to that. So did the refugees in their cars and farms carts or on their aching feet. All were accompanied by an angel called Hope.

The sun was hot, summer had come. Above the chaos of the road arched the pure sky.

'*À Valence commence Provence*', quoted Violette as they drove, stop and start, into the town. 'Georges is a Provençal. It is to Georges I'm going, Sophy; every day a little nearer.'

There were no beds at hotels or lodgings now. The girls slept in the open. In Valence, Violette remembered a big park and when they drove through its open gates, they saw in the dim starlight the scores of people already camped there, many muffled like corpses under the trees.

Violette parked the car in an avenue and they took coats and cushions to a patch of deserted grass in the gloom.

'Are you sleepy, Sophy?'

Sophy said she wasn't, and Violette remarked that was because she was hungry. 'Shall we talk instead? Shall I tell you about Georges?'

'I would like that.' Sophy had asked herself questions about Violette's lover since the now-distant day when they'd first met; she was glad to listen. And more glad to try and take her mind off her empty stomach.

Violette settled down, her back against a tree. She described Georges in a matter-of-fact voice with no romance in it. He had a good body, strong, with big shoulders and a fine back. But his legs weren't good, he walked badly and was offended if she teased him about it. He had beautiful hair, soft and floppy. He was very generous, even more than

Christian Vergé, a quality rare in Provence. 'I have found generous women there, but never men. The men are careful, Sophy, and that's another word for mean.'

Georges was well-known in Menton. His family were wealthy, he'd inherited money and he was also a successful civil servant. Married, of course.

'He is only just thirty-five but there are two children, twelve and ten, and his wife. I've never seen any of them. His wife is older than he is and has the nervous depression rather often. He does not say why.'

Violette had met him when she was on holiday in Menton. He had been sailing and had brought his yacht up to anchor near the rocks where she was sunbathing. He called out to ask if she'd like to sail across the bay to the other side. 'You can dive better there, it is very deep.'

She had been attracted to him. 'Physically, you know? Later it has become much more.'

The affair began that first evening, his family was in the country and Georges took her out to dine and then they had made love. Since then, they were together whenever it was possible. Georges managed to get to Paris sometimes. Or Violette drove south and spent time in Menton where Georges had taken a flat for her. When she wasn't living in the flat, he still paid the rent and it was kept empty.

'I find that touching. So like him. So extravagant.'

She said the flat was very discreet, Georges had chosen it because there was no concierge and it faced the sea. Sophy thought the combination of discretion and a good view somewhat comic, but to Violette it was practical.

'Isn't it odd, Sophy? I was contemptuous when Christian offered to pay my rent as if I were a *poule de luxe*. But with Georges everything seems right. And I so long to be with him, now that we are all in danger. I couldn't bear to remain in Paris. Whatever happens, whatever unbelievable things this new kind of war brings, I must be near him. Even if I only see him for five minutes in a week.'

'That's love,' said Sophy.

'I know. And it is ridiculous.'

It was hot the following day on the road. Violette remarked that the 'great heat' had started. She stopped at a village fountain to fill their water bottles. By the afternoon other fountains in other villages were almost dry.

In the dusk they halted in a small town and sat under an awning of cannis through which the first stars winked. There were the usual crowds. The usual mass of cars. The usual wireless bleating from inside a fly-blown bar. The news was announced by the cracked record playing 'The Marseillaise', and when the tune began to wheeze everybody stopped talking.

The first item of the news was brief.

Mussolini had declared war.

Violette's eyes grew enormous. She leaned over - and gripped Sophy's hand, whispering that Menton was on the Italian border. The news went on. The French army was now 'divided into groups'. The Government, having left Paris, was 'operating from Tours'.

When they left the café and returned to the car, Sophy took Violette's arm and squeezed it tightly.

'You told me not to imagine bad things about Daniel. Try and feel like that about Georges.'

'Yes. I will,' said Violette and Sophy heard in her voice the hard bright quality she'd heard in Paris.

It seemed to Sophy as the days continued, that in spite of the news which grew daily more dark, people still believed all was not lost. She knew *she* must not speak – since Dunkirk an English accent was a positive danger – but Violette talked to anybody and everybody. To refugees like themselves. To men in bars. To old men working in the fields from whom she bought basketfuls of apricots and nectarines. Hope had not quite abandoned the poor travellers. The counter-stroke would come. Weygand would make a stand on the Seine ... on the Loire ... anywhere.

And then on a morning hotter than the rest Violette's luck ran out. The girls had slept later than usual on the roadside and were at the tail of the cavalcade when Violette stopped the car, muttered '*Merde*' and stared fixedly at the petrol gauge.

It was miraculous that they'd managed to get so far. It had been Violette's ingenuity, patience, her many acquaintances on the road, her practical charm, her money, which had kept the car with enough petrol from day to day. Now she and Sophy climbed out and shook the last quarter of a litre out of the tin they had so often surreptitiously filled. They pushed the car off the road and sat down on tinder-dry grass.

'Poor old car,' said Violette. 'She's done her best.'

'So have you.'

Violette looked at Sophy, and gave a shrug.

'We may have just enough to crawl into Orange, and that will be that.'

'Mightn't we get even a little in Orange?'

'No, Sophy. Remember the garagiste swearing at us yesterday? I'm afraid from now on we will have to use our feet.'

Sophy did not reply. The sun beat down, it was unbearable just then. Not a scrap of shade. Violette sat, one arm clasping her knee, cigarette smoke going straight up into the still air. A farm cart went by, a child was crying. The cavalcade was thickening again.

'You're not well, are you, Sophy?' she said, after a while.

'It's nothing. I expect I'm hungry.'

'I expect it is something else. My poor friend. You are pregnant, aren't you?'

Sophy swallowed.

'How did you guess?' she said in a low voice.

'I've known for quite a few days. I saw it in your face. There was a girl in Paris, a friend of mine, it was the same with her. As if the face was blurred somehow. Out of focus. How far gone are you?'

'Over two months.'

'Careless of Daniel.'

'*Shut up.*'

Sophy was at the end of her tether. Everything made her want to vomit. The smell of the Gauloise. The heat of the sun on her head and neck. The sight of the trudging people. The cries of the children. Her dirty clothes. Something else had begun to frighten her and she knew it was also alarming Violette. That crowd on the other side of the road which had lessened for a few days was now growing thicker and thicker. People were going north, escaping from the very places which she and Violette strained to reach. The refugees fleeing from the Italian border upset Violette, but she scarcely mentioned them. Yet Sophy had no spirit to comfort her valiant friend. She felt hauntingly sad. Where was the girl she used to be, the Sophy whose temper had flamed like her hair?

'My friend in Paris tried neat gin,' remarked Violette, drawing on her cigarette. 'And she jumped from the kitchen table a number of times. Neither attempts worked, but she told me the neat gin cheered her up for a while.' She looked at the end of her cigarette. 'You could try jumping from the car. Climb on the seat and jump down. It might do the trick.'

'I couldn't.'

'I didn't think you would. Let's see if we can make it to Orange.'

The Renault, in a last expiring effort, did get them to the town and Violette free-wheeled on a slight incline, landing up by the enormous dusty walls of the Roman theatre. It was breathlessly hot, but the trees gave some shade. Sitting on the edge of a fountain, Violette said she had an idea.

'I know a couple who live in Orange. I've called in occasionally. She used to work for Georges before they moved here. Perhaps we could ask to stay a couple of days. We could wash our clothes and our dirty selves, don't you think? And try to plan what to do next. I'm sure Thérèse would be glad to see us.'

Sophy agreed, scarcely taking it in. She had begun to feel ill, and hoped Violette would not notice. They made their way through the town which, like every other town, had been invaded by hordes. Trailing behind Violette, Sophy was now sure she was really ill. Supposing Violette, intent on getting to Georges, decided she must make her own way alone? The idea terrified Sophy.

They were weaving through jostling people, avoiding queues at little crammed shops; they stopped at a crossing in a narrow side street. Orange was very ancient and here the houses on either side of what was almost an alley seemed almost to meet; it was dark away from the sun. As Violette halted Sophy mumbled.

'I'm sorry, I –'

The edge of her vision began to grow grey. A mist was all round her. It joined. She collapsed.

Violette told her later that, landed with her unconscious friend, she'd found two men who offered to carry Sophy to the cul-de-sac where Violette's friends the Gautrys lived. Thérèse Gautry, as was her habit, was sitting at her open door watching the world go by. She shouted a welcome and without any questions bustled Sophy straight to bed. When Sophy recovered she found Violette and a middle-aged woman standing by the bed looking down at her.

'I'm sorry, stupid of me –' began Sophy nervously in French. Violette said, 'Thérèse doesn't mind you being English.'

'Thérèse minds you having a fever,' said the woman, who had a vivacious lined face and hair dyed almost the colour of Sophy's own. 'Lie still. Thérèse will take care of you. And you, Violette, also need repose. Heavens! You are so fatigued.'

Thérèse Gautry was a woman born to be needed. She had been a children's nurse, a housemaid, she had run a small hotel, she had been a concierge, and had owned a fruit shop. Now she looked after her stout husband and did good deeds when they were necessary in her part of the town. The curé knew her well. Sophy and Violette stayed with the Gautrys for some days. Whatever germ Sophy had caught on the road also infected Violette in a milder form and Thérèse nursed her patients with tender bullying which extended to her husband Jacques, who was sent off daily to look for food, wine, buckets full of water and anything he could buy or borrow. Violette was generous with her money, which Thérèse loudly refused. As for Sophy, for the first few days she was too ill to do more than sleep and sweat, drink water thirstily, and sleep again. As she began to recover and Thérèse forced her to take bowlfuls of vegetable soup – a standby in the house – Sophy was more aware of the conversations coming from the next room, the door of which was always open so that Thérèse 'could hear if her patient wants anything'.

Thérèse and her husband sat talking, talking, about the war. It was then that Sophy realized the French Army was broken. And that the famous defences, the great Maginot Line, had been completely turned and the defenders surrounded. Huge stores, which had been amassed to last France's defenders for seven years, had fallen into the hands of the enemy.

But Thérèse and Violette were calm when they came in to be with the invalid. Seeing the deliberate reserve in both women, Sophy did not dare to speak of what she had heard.

At last the girls, their health restored, their clothes washed, were well enough to take to the road again. Thérèse embraced them hard, hugging them to her, kissing them impartially as if they were her daughters. Her husband wrung their hands. As they left the little house, Thérèse stood at her doorway, shouting her final good advice after them. 'Keep to yourselves! Don't drink the water if it says "*non potable*". Good fortune. God bless you!' She was still waving as they reached the street corner. When they were out of sight, Violette asked anxiously how Sophy was.

'You didn't pretend you were better? It would be like you.'

'No. Truly. I feel quite different. Quite strong.'

'Thank God,' said Violette, pious for once.

They began to slog, slowly and in unison, out of Orange. At the edge of the town there was a big corner café and Violette suggested they should try to get a coffee before they continued on what might be a long day's trek.

The café was very full and the moment they went inside, where there were the usual crowds of old men and women and a few soldiers, both girls noticed the atmosphere. It reminded Sophy of the café in Paris the day she had left; it was hideously quiet. And the people sitting or leaning on the bar or hanging round the wireless all seemed to have the same taut expression.

A burly soldier with cropped hair sitting with a companion as large as he was, pushed a chair with his foot in Violette's direction.

'And here's another,' said his friend, who had bright blue eyes. He dragged a chair from a nearby table.

'Brandy, mesdemoiselles?'

'You are *aimable*,' said Violette. Her enamelled chic, her beautiful cared-for hair, her Parisian style and poise were gone. She was a traveller in a world of travellers. But she was young and had a relaxed charm even now. Both men reacted, scarcely paying attention to the silent redhead beside her.

The first soldier, whom his companion called Jacques, shouldered his way through the mass of tables, returning with four glasses.

'No coffee. No beer. No bread. The Patron gave me these from a bottle he keeps hidden. He said it would be good for our livers. Death to the Boche.'

The soldiers gulped back the brandy as Russians drank vodka, in one swallow. Violette sipped hers. So did Sophy. The raw brandy tasted like fire.

The familiar anthem struck up, 'The Marseillaise' repeated three times. The ancient record, constantly used on the air, announced a broadcasting station somewhere in the chaos which was France.

'*Aux armes, citoyens*' sang a voice, sounding at a great distance.

The soldier called Jacques made a noise of disgust. 'What's the use of calling the citizens to arms when most of 'em are running for their lives, and so is the **** government?' he said. He picked up his glass, saw it still contained a little brandy and drained it, 'Death to the Boche.'

The anthem ended. A voice, louder than usual, announced: 'Citizens. Friends. Frenchmen. The Marshal Pétain will now address our nation.'

The café froze.

A little child started to wail. His mother literally put her hand across his mouth.

Then Pétain began to speak.

It was the voice of a very old man, it was reedy and thin and slightly high. It shook. He spoke of honour. Of the honour between the soldiers of 'our two great nations'. He spoke of the future of France, 'our country, beloved, respected, incomparable'. It was his duty to tell his countrymen that today he was asking for an armistice. His appeal was already with Herr Hitler.

The speech ended with the repetition of the ancient record. The once-magnificent Marseillaise.

But nobody was listening now. People had begun to weep. Tears came into the big soldier's eyes as he picked up the empty glass and put it down again; the man at his side unashamedly wept, exclaiming, 'Betrayed, we are betrayed.' At a nearby table a woman hid her face in her hands, crying with shaking, heart-rending sobs.

Sophy turned to Violette, and the girls put their arms round one another in a convulsive, hard embrace. They wept too. For the defeated country. For lost honour. For the unbelievable, the terrible; the French girl put her head on Sophy's shoulder and cried as if her heart would break.

When Violette, drying her eyes, told the soldiers about their abandoned car and impossible journey, the two men offered them a lift in their tank.

'We're going as far as Salon where the army is supposed to be mustering, God help us.' The rest of the tanks seemed to have disappeared, Jacques said, so much for the officer in charge. He used a good many obscenities in a quiet voice, making poor Violette smile. Sophy did not understand them.

The tank moved as slowly as some prehistoric animal, 'something wrong with the engine' whispered Violette, putting her lips to Sophy's ear. The noise was deafening, the smell of oil asphyxiating. The girls sat watching the roads. They had not seen much of the army until now, only the streaming refugees, but suddenly as if some invisible dam had cracked, there were soldiers everywhere. They had become refugees too, some in small groups, some alone simply straggling along the road. People in the villages ran out to give them wine or – often there was no wine – their hoarded water.

When it grew dark the four made camp among the rocks in a countryside where the exodus had begun to melt away. People had taken side roads, some had stopped in the towns, there were fewer vehicles now rumbling towards the south. Jacques, the older of the two soldiers, tried to get some food in a shop in the last village they passed before it was dark, but returned to say dispiritedly, 'No coffee, no oil, no bread. Not even a cigarette.'

His companion, who had blue eyes, he was called Pépi, declared that there was nothing to look gloomy about.

'Have you forgotten this is my country? Wait until it's dark as pitch, then I'll just take a little trip up the mountain.'

Jacques and the girls settled down among the rocks, rolling themselves in their coats. The girls huddled together. Pépi, saying '*À bientôt*', disappeared into the night. Sophy was asleep and dreaming when she was shaken awake by Violette.

'Pépi is back. He's brought a chicken!'

Sophy saw that the soldiers had lit a small fire ringed with stones. 'Food!' announced Pépi.

The quartet squatted on the ground round the fire, eating lumps of chicken skewered on the soldiers' bayonets and cooked over the fire. They drank sticky brandy floating with cherries. 'My aunt bottled them specially for me,' said Pépi. 'She's an old bird like this chicken, but a game one.'

Next morning the tank took the girls as far as Privas, where the soldiers had to leave the main road to get to Salon. Jacques and Pépi climbed from the tank to jump the girls down and Jacques enveloped Violette in a hug like a bear. Pépi advanced towards Sophy. 'My choice is the mute,' he said. 'The way to use the mouth, Beautiful, is like this.' He gave her a long wet kiss.

There was a final shout of 'Death to the Boche' as the tank shuddered away along the dusty road in the blazing sun. Violette stood watching until there was nothing but a cloud of raised dust. She turned to Sophy and rubbed her chin.

'Did it occur to you that we might be raped by our friends

last night? I was worried when you went off with Pépi to see if there was any water in the river bed. You wouldn't have had a chance. Nor would I with Jacques.'

'I suggested going,' said Sophy. 'I wanted a word alone.'

'*Alone?*'

'Yes. I told him I was a war widow, English of course, and I was married to a French officer in Paris and that I was pregnant. I said your husband was in Menton fighting the bloody Italians.'

For the first time since they had joined forces, Sophy had taken the initiative. Violette was impressed.

'What made you think your fairy tale would work?'

'Because they are sad, Violette. Like us. Like them,' said Sophy as two women with the faces of mourners passed them in the road.

The last days of their journey were the worst. Without the car they had no independence and Violette had lost her cool head. Sophy, with the energy and single-mindedness of a pregnant woman, flagged cars or waved to farm carts. Violette still had to do the talking and all Sophy could do was smile and say '*Merci*'. They travelled how and where they could. Once Sophy stood in the road, arms stretched out, and literally danced up and down as a motor cycle approached. The rider was forced to stop in a cloud of dust.

They did over thirty kilometres, clinging on – Sophy to Violette, Violette to the boy who, affected by two female passengers, began to swerve and roar and make more dust than before. Where did he get petrol? was the obsessive question in both their minds.

He finally left them under a long avenue of trees, grinning when Violette thanked him, and setting off up a steep rocky lane, waving with one hand backwards until he vanished. The girls walked in silence in the grateful shade. How long ago, in so different a France, some landowner, some mayor, some benefactor or group of villagers had planted the plane trees of the south. The long approaches to a village, after hours on the burning plains, were a cool blessing. They walked. They trudged. At one time they bought two ancient bicycles, but one developed a puncture and they finally abandoned them in a dry river bed. They actually caught a bus for a few kilometres. It did not take them far. And now the girls began to be affected by the people they met. There was defeat in the air, a dullness. When Violette spoke to men in the villages, they were interested in nothing but how to sell their cherries and peaches.

'France is finished,' said a farmer, filling the scarf held out for him by Violette with yellow peaches – the price he asked was exorbitant but she paid it without a word. 'She's finished and she deserved it.'

The girls journeyed on. Without car or clothes, without friends. But there was something they both had and were conscious of its protection and that was money. Violette had provided them both with money-belts she'd bought in Paris, cotton contraptions with press-stud pockets like soldiers' belts used for ammunition. The girls wore their money always, never taking it out in public but only in the stinking lavatories of cafés or before they reached a village, hiding behind trees or rocks. The kilometres began to lessen. Violette studied the map she had brought from the car, it was torn and had to be carefully fitted together before she could read it. They had come to a village, more than a village, called Brignoles.

They sat in a square under the plane trees by a fountain covered with moss which had dried in the heat; it looked like some centuries-old brown carpet. The fountain basin was empty. Perhaps it had not worked since the beginning of the war.

The square was almost deserted, the dust at their feet did not blow or move, it was soft, dove-coloured like the silent buildings. An old woman went by, her sandals making a flapping sound; two pigeons rose with the curious sound of wings, like stringed instruments. It was already evening.

Sophy, finishing the last peach of their store, dried her sticky hands on a filthy handkerchief.

'Look! A hotel,' she said, pointing. 'And no crowds either. Shall we try and get a room? It's called Le Sauvage which seems rather suitable.'

She looked at Violette in a feeble attempt to rally her. Violette was too quiet. Sophy touched her hand.

'*Now* what is it?' she said. Inured to disaster she half expected Violette to say she had lost all her money.

'I saw a woman reading a newspaper in the shop over there. The headlines said Menton is occupied by the Italians.'

'Violette, that's impossible, there's an armistice.'

'Yes. But they've occupied the town. I'm going to ask if I can read the paper. Don't speak to anybody, for God's sake. Just stay here.'

Sophy obeyed and watched her friend cross the square and go into a small shop. Outside on a stone seat fixed to the wall, an old woman in black was sitting, staring at the ground.

Violette emerged from the shop after what seemed a long time. Sophy knew by the way she walked what the news was.

'It's true. Menton is occupied, the Italians are still there. According to the man in the shop there was tremendous fighting everywhere along the frontiers and our troops did wonderfully. Wonderfully. Not like those bastards in the north he said.'

'Poor Bastards in the north,' murmured Sophy.

Violette said nothing. Her face was robbed of its calm and strength, she looked bereft. Sophy tried to find words of comfort. Hadn't Violette said Georges was a man of importance in the town? He would have foreseen what was going to happen and got away. He was sure to be safe – perhaps in Monte Carlo or Nice.

'Then I will never find him.'

Violette began to smoke the butt end of a cigarette she had saved, as soldiers do, keeping it in an old packet. A moment of selfish fear went through Sophy.

'Do you still want to go on?'

Violette looked at her blankly.

'Don't be a fool. I've got to. He may still be in Menton. He may be dead. I must know –' She stopped talking.

Later they went wearily into Le Sauvage; the hotel was scarcely an hotel at all but a poky old house on the corner, an inn which had long since lost its pride.

A girl who could not have been more than fifteen with black hair in crescents on either side of her cheeks – she looked as if she should still be at school – gave them a narrow-eyed look too practised for her years. She reminded Sophy of an animal. A ferret with sharp teeth.

'Got to pay in advance,' was all she said.

Violette, who never produced money in public, had a note folded in her hand and slammed it on the counter. She said in a hard voice, 'A receipt. One night only, for two.'

The ferret snapped. 'And am I not to be trusted?'

'A receipt, please.'

The girl, with a sound of contempt, scrawled something on a scrap of paper.

After a meal of sorts, a little stringy meat and tough parsnips, the girls trailed up a narrow stair to a bedroom which was stiflingly hot. They lay down in beds for the first time in weeks. Violette turned on her side away from Sophy and slept.

But Sophy lay awake in the heat and the half light, the curtains were thin, thinking about the future. It was curious. She supposed Daniel was still in her heart, but the agonies of sexual love, the sweets and bitters were gone. He scarcely seemed real and the memory of that time, so recent, such hundreds of years ago, when they had swept in the *Galope* round a ballroom and she had carried a knife to revenge her furious pride, was utterly gone. It no longer interested her and she thought of it occasionally with contempt. The armour of pregnancy, the defence of nature, had come to cover her with its thick cloak. She no longer felt she would die without her lover. She scarcely worried about anything, not what she and Violette would eat, not how tired they were or how sick she felt; all that occupied her, that stood in her thoughts like a guardian, was that she must get back to England. This body of hers did not belong to her any more, and the place to take it was the place of safety. England. Her brother.

She knew that the only people who would help her in a France where the English had become the enemy now that the whole nature of the war had changed, were the Dufours.

She thought with affection and guilt of Anne-Marie who loved her. She would help, or try to. So would Monsieur Dufour, although Yvonne would not do much. Apart from the girl sleeping beside her she had no friends in France but the Dufours. She must get to Cannes and throw herself on their mercy.

She looked again at Violette who had moved in her sleep and lay on her back, sleeping as quietly as a fallen leaf. She saw her in profile, fine-drawn, so tired and pale, still so pretty, her hair like a baby's, her eyelashes long, lying on thin cheeks. What will happen to Violette and me? If we survive, will we see each other again? Perhaps never.

Very early in the morning, she had slept little, Sophy climbed quietly out of bed, washed her face in a basin, and crept downstairs. She was hungry and thirsty and longed for coffee. She was absorbed in her own thoughts, tired and indifferent, when she noticed the ferret girl at the desk, flirting with a man in blue overalls. Sophy completely forgot her own necessary dumbness; she asked if there was any coffee to be had.

The man spun round. The girl's sharp face altered from smiles to a glare. She almost spat.

'*English!* You're filthy English. If I'd known that, you would not have been permitted to sleep in this house.'

'You're right, Minouche,' said the man. They stood staring at Sophy, and the man said, 'You English fought your way through the French lines with revolvers. What are *you* doing in our country?' He used an obscenity.

Sophy was not even angry. She said contemptuously, 'I am married to a Frenchman.'

'Lies. Filthy English!' said the ferret girl, baring her teeth.

The night the girls came at last to La Napoule near Cannes there was a full moon. It was July and the great heat of the Midi was in full flood. Long after sunset the walls of gardens and houses, the stone seats in the squares, the very trunks of the trees retained the hot embrace of the sun. Sophy and Violette walked the final kilometres, they had found no tanks

235

or army lorries to show them a kindness. They walked doggedly, grateful because it was cool.

At the seaside village of La Napoule it was Sophy who suggested they might swim.

'Wouldn't it refresh us, Violette? I do long for the sea.'

'If you want,' was the indifferent answer. They went down a road which led to the beach.

There it was. The dark, calm expanse of the Mediterranean. Even Violette gave what sounded like a sigh of pleasure as they pulled off their clothes, keeping on their knickers from modesty, and ran across the empty beach into the water.

They swam into the long wavering line of moonlight. Sophy noticed that as she lifted her arms, showers of greenish fire seemed to fall in the drops of water. She splashed with the flat of her hand. It glowed with dull fire.

'The sea is phosphorescent!'

'Yes. I've seen it before. With Georges once.'

Leaving the water at last, seeing the waves break in dull greenish fire, they dried themselves on their spare clothes. Sophy was invigorated, even excited to be here at last. She suggested they should walk the rest of the way on the beach.

Violette agreed and they made their way, ankle deep sometimes.

'I don't feel I ought to impose myself on your friends,' said Violette, as they continued to walk now on the damp flatness of the sand. The effect of the swim had worn off. She was so weary that her voice slurred. 'Perhaps I could find an hotel.'

'You'll do no such thing. The Dufours will be so glad to see you. And they'll have up-to-date news about Menton. Think of it, Violette! How many hundreds of kilometres we've covered; all the people, all the adventures, Thérèse looking after us when we were ill. It's a kind of miracle.'

Violette gave a faint smile.

'You've changed, Sophy,' she said. 'You sound strong.'

So the girls, ghostly figures in the moonlight, reached the promenades of a town actually bright with lights. The flags did not hang at half mast as they had done in other towns.

236

The great hotels looked cheerful and shining, the Croisette's long palm-lined stretches were edged with lamps. But there were no people about. Just the lights and the palms and the sea.

'Les Hesperides is at the end of the Croisette. Oh Violette! We've done it. The end of the journey.'

'Yours. I still have to get to Menton.'

'Yes, yes, and I shall help.'

As they crossed the road and went through the open gates, Sophy felt that she was home. There was the garden where she used to lie in the dark with Anne-Marie and Daniel and all their friends. There were the palms, great branches like feathers against the starry sky. And there the comfortable square shape of the house. Her heart swelled.

They went up the steps and she rang the bell.

9

Looking back, Sophy often wondered what would have happened to her if when she appeared at Les Hesperides she hadn't been with a French girl.

Yvonne Dufour's behaviour was grotesque. She came running down the staircase and shouted – just like Odile Gombert – '*Allez-vous en!*'

It was Violette who emerged from her own misery and shouted back.

'Are you telling us to sleep in the gutter?'

Violette harangued her. She described everything they had seen. The bombs which had fallen on the refugees outside Lyon. The sufferings of people half starved. The soldiers who swore they had been betrayed.

'What have *you* seen here in the Midi? Do you call yourself a Frenchwoman and tell us to sleep in the gutter?' Violette succeeded with Yvonne where friendship and conscience miserably failed. The two girls were told they could stay.

Standing beside his wife during the scene was Monsieur who did not utter a word or look in Sophy's direction; hearing raised voices Anne-Marie came running down the stairs, saw Sophy and gave a sob. She started towards her but Yvonne prevented her from embracing Sophy, putting out a hand and grabbing her daughter's arm.

Grudgingly Yvonne finally told Anne-Marie to show the visitors to a bedroom. Anne-Marie obeyed in silence, only giving Sophy a speaking look before leaving them.

When the door of Sophy's old room was safely shut, Violette whispered, 'Sophy. My poor friend.'

'I'll manage somehow,' said Sophy between her teeth. 'I'll get Anne-Marie to help.'

'Don't rely on her. She's weak as water. At least we've a roof over our heads,' said Violette.

She didn't tell Sophy that the Dufours' behaviour was exactly what she'd expected. She had felt tenderly towards her friend and had not had the heart to disillusion her too soon about poor Sophy's so-called friends.

Violette left early the next morning. She and Sophy put their arms round each other and kissed. Neither of them cried and both had tears in their hearts. In their embrace was all that they had suffered, seen, the forged link of all they had shared. Sophy walked with her to the corner of the Croisette where Violette, looking slightly recovered and wearing a fresh dress borrowed from those Sophy had left at Les Hesperides, turned and gave her a final hug. Then she set off briskly. Sophy stood in the sun and waved until Violette, with one final turn and one final gesture of farewell, was already a good way off.

From the moment Violette had disappeared, Sophy felt a pain as intense as heartbreak. Daniel no longer hurt her thoughts. Violette did. She missed her and thought of her constantly. Violette had become Sophy's second self. Their friendship resembled the vows given by the Vikings, who cut their wrists and tied the wounds together with leather thongs, mingling their blood. In imagination Sophy travelled on with Violette as far as the occupied city of Menton. She thought of her alone, self-possessed, on her own journey towards destiny. Sophy had promised to help her. She'd done nothing.

From the very first day she spent at Les Hesperides, Sophy had the insane idea that it would have been better to have left Paris and gone towards the fighting in the north than to be here among people who hated her. Yvonne Dufour and the old servant Clara, neither of whom disguised their feelings, behaved to the newly arrived foreigner as if she were a leper who would infect them if they got too close. Yvonne had never liked Sophy except for a few months after war was declared when she had softened towards her; now her manner was a cruel and exaggerated version of what it used to be. Clara imitated her mistress. The person who had changed out of recognition was Anselme Dufour. When she and Violette had appeared on that first night he had actually embraced Sophy, she had heard him mutter 'dear child'. It must have been an automatic reaction, as if for a moment he and she were still in the *drôle de guerre*. Now, his country defeated, *her* country still at war – and in a way with his own – the old Frenchman did not know how to treat her. He could not love the young English girl any more, her presence upset him. When she entered a room he looked away. If she spoke to him, he fidgeted and could scarcely reply. His fat face was dolorous as if he were silently begging her to go.

In the days that followed her appearance, so unexpected, so unwanted, Sophy knew it was essential to keep out of Yvonne Dufour's way. Anne-Marie, when her mother was not about, was kind but nervous. 'Maman is deeply affected by the tragedy of what has happened to our country,' she said to Sophy after Yvonne had been particularly rude during a meal. Poor Anne-Marie looked at her friend helplessly; Sophy recalled that she had had the same task in Paris, to be spokeswoman and diplomat for another elderly inimical Frenchwoman.

Sophy never heard Anne-Marie, when they were alone, say a word in defence of England. Once she drew Sophy into her bedroom to whisper that she must tell her something terrible. Did Sophy know the British had bombarded French ships at Oran? 'We are treated as your enemies, Sophy. And some of our greatest warships have been sunk.'

Sophy sat staring in bewilderment, thinking how much she didn't know, how much she and Violette, intent on keeping body and soul together, had missed of the tragedy enacted all round them. And the Midi was under the rule of the new Vichy government.

'Of course that means that *we* are still free,' Anne-Marie had said.

In the family, at the sparse meals getting steadily worse, Marshal Pétain figured in the conversation. A hero in the Great War, he was now head of the Government and one evening, a week after Sophy's arrival, Anne-Marie said gravely that the Marshal was going to address the nation and the family were meeting in the grand salon to listen to the wireless.

Everybody trooped in. Yvonne and Monsieur, Anne-Marie, the old servant, and Paul, who had been released from the army after the armistice to work again for Dufour et Cie. Anne-Marie told Sophy that her brother was doing 'work of national importance'.

The grand salon was stuffy, it was never used now; they all sat down except Clara, respectfully standing, who shot a look of contempt in Sophy's direction.

'The Marseillaise' wheezed out as usual, the Marshal's ancient voice began to speak.

He addressed 'our dear and beloved people,' and talked of a defeat which was due to the nation's sad lack of moral fibre. In the recent past the people had fallen into grave error, they had 'demanded', they had never 'served'. He called for unity. The Dufours sat listening in silence, Monsieur with his head bent, Yvonne brightly attentive, Anne-Marie with the expression Sophy had seen at Mass, a concentrated reverence. Sophy thought the old general was mouthing platitudes. Why did he blame France with shaking reproach as if he were addressing a sinner? As if he were a priest? He spoke as if defeat was a crime. 'Our country deserved what has happened,' he said; then, raising his voice with an effort, declared now was the time of re-birth, the door of hope; Frenchmen would turn to the two great saviours, Work and The Family. His 'dear France' would rise stronger than before.

Sophy stopped listening to the feeble voice declaiming a false-heroic speech. In the familiar salon where they used to dance to the gramophone, she imagined the teasing laughter of the past. Daniel sat, legs outstretched, on the divan where now Monsieur was sunk in attentive sorrow. She remembered how deliberately Daniel used to avoid her eye, because when the young people crowded out into the garden he would lie beside her on the grass. With a wrench of the heart she thought how this family had turned against her. She remembered Violette's whispered, 'Don't speak English, Sophy, for God's sake!' The French hated her country and the Dufours hated her.

At dinner after the broadcast, at a meal which was barely edible, Yvonne spoke of the Marshal's nobility.

'Yes. We have been betrayed,' she said.

Nobody spoke just then. Betrayed, thought Sophy. How often she had heard and seen that word. On the road to the south. In the mouths of the soldiers. Scrawled on their tanks. Betrayed by whom? The suffering and angry people did not know, they felt it dumbly, instinctively. Sophy recalled the distant danger of the Ardennes and the tank traps destroyed on the roads outside Sedan. And Violette had one pointed to a lorry on which was chalked 'Betrayed. Sold. Not conquered.'

Sophy guessed Yvonne Dufour meant that France had been betrayed by England. She did not say it aloud, but her face spoke.

The days were miserably long and only lightened at first by Anne-Marie's surreptitious kindness when her parents were out of the way. Once Anne-Marie nervously kissed her. Like poor France itself, Les Hesperides was cleaved down the middle into two separate pieces – on one side Yvonne and old Clara and poor confused Monsieur. On the other, a secret ally in Anne-Marie. I suppose it's only because she is my friend that they allow me to stay, thought Sophy. But more and more she began to see that the reason she had not been turned out was Paul. It was Paul who had welcomed her most warmly, who, ignoring his mother, had embraced her. Paul often came to Sophy's room when he returned from Nice, he wanted to hear the saga of her journey and marvelled at what she and Violette had done and had escaped. He was his old self, more than his old self, stronger, kinder. When Anne-

Marie was with her brother, she took her colour from him. Sophy saw that when Paul was present, Yvonne tempered her manner to her, was at least civilized and bit back sneering remarks. When he was alone with Sophy Paul talked of the war very differently from the old Marshal or his parents. He had served in the southern mountains of the Alps where, he said, the French defences had been strong.

'We were garrisoned in small platoons with magnificent guns, Sophy. When the Italians attacked, pouf!, they made no progress at all. On the coast they advanced, if you can call it an advance, two kilometres. They had four or five thousand casualties and do you know how many men we lost? Eight killed, less than forty wounded and thirty missing.' His black eyes shone. He seemed older, tougher. 'The French army against the Italians kept its pride.'

The soldiers were beginning to trickle home now. Sophy often saw them, one by one or in groups traipsing down the Croisette on their way to their homes. They came from the north where the battles had been lost so horrifyingly fast; from the south where, Paul said, 'our tails were up, not down'.

One evening Sophy, glad to escape from the atmosphere of the house, went to sit alone on the beach and Paul, returning on his motor bike, came across the road to join her.

He sat down by her side, scooping up the sand and letting it run through his fingers. He scrawled 'S' in the sand and looked up at her and grinned.

He likes me still, she thought, more than Anne-Marie who is frightened of being my friend.

'I'm glad of the chance to talk to you,' he said.

'About the fact that I've got to go.'

'You want to, surely?'

'Oh, Paul.'

'Poor Sophy. I apologize for them. I feel for you.'

'How kind you are.'

'No, Sophy, not kind. Fair. You must pardon them. When people are afraid they are not themselves. Later they will wish to forget how they are now. Perhaps they will pretend it never happened. But at present they are frightened and are cruel to you as a result of their fear.'

They were silent for a while. In the distance, wavering from the day's heat, was the Île of Sainte Marguerite thick with its dark pines and its thousand-year-old history. The very sea breaking gently on the sand was the ocean on which French ships had sailed to glory. And rising from the coast's uneven shores were huge mountains with names like legends, Mercantour, Lubéron; the people had once sung there, and begun an extraordinary march towards liberty.

'Yes, you must leave us, Sophy,' he said at last. 'You cannot stay and be happy.'

'I know. I know. When I came back I truly thought –'

'That it would be the way it was? Of course you did. But nothing is.'

He continued to draw on the sand. An S. A P. 'Sophy. Will you promise not to repeat what I am going to say to you? Will you solemnly swear?'

'On my word of honour.'

She put out her hand and he gripped it. For a moment the boy he used to be looked out of his eyes. Then he dropped her hand.

'Something must be arranged for you, Sophy. Say nothing. Trust me. Yes?'

'*Oh yes!*'

He nodded and his tone became practical.

'As it happens, I didn't come to talk about getting you away from Les Hesperides, although I promise it is never out of my thoughts. I want to speak about my sister.'

Sophy gave him her full-eyed attention, leaning towards him. She had regained her looks, her hair shone, she looked pretty in a loose clean cotton dress, green and white. She was brown from the long days on the road. But fatter.

'Anne-Marie told me that Claudio is soon due back,' she said, 'she sounded so happy.'

'That is what I want to talk to you about. Claudio was in Rome; he didn't join the Italian army.'

'Would he have fought against *us*?' She forgot for a moment that she wasn't French.

244

'Fortunately he did not have to: he was given some sort of government post. He is now of high standing with the German authorities and because of his business connections it looks as if he will get an important position in Cannes. In charge of supplies.'

'Isn't that good news?'

'Not for the French. All our goods are sent to Italy now. I myself have seen trains taking our Provençal fruit and vegetables to the frontier. Our fish at Dufours, also. The fish comes in at dawn, Sophy, and is packed in ice and taken away in lorries. It is never sold here. The feeling of the people is getting bitter.'

'You mean, they may hate Claudio?'

'I don't know. Some people will admire him. But there will be others ...' He was silent for a time. Eventually he gave a sigh not unlike his sister's. 'As I told you, Sophy, they never beat us. When I was near Vésubie they attacked over and over again, the Blackshirt battalions; we drove them back with ease. The soldiers and their families, anybody connected with the Italian campaign feels exonerated. They despise the Italians. It won't be easy for Anne-Marie.'

'What about your parents?'

'Oh, they will be glad Claudio is now important. I don't talk of the campaign to them – not ever – because of my sister. She knows and does not know what happened in the fighting ... and she will be married soon. That will settle things. Women,' he added almost to himself, 'are very adaptable.'

Sophy gave an involuntary laugh.

'I suppose we should thank God for that,' she said.

There were almost no English people left on the coast. They had escaped during the fall of France by ship, by car over the Pyrenees, by bribing officials for permits and arriving in Spain, a country in a different kind of turmoil. They had shaken the golden dust of the south from their British shoes and somehow managed to get back to embattled England. Those who remained were too old and set to face the shock of

245

giving up their homes and the lives they had made in the Midi. The French were openly hostile to their previous friends.

There were many Yvonne Dufours. On the walls of the English church in Nice, in huge letters, was the chalked word 'LÂCHE!' Sophy was in a bus when an elderly English lady was pushed off by the driver who leaned out and sent her spinning. Sophy, swearing, jumped out after her. The old lady was unhurt and stood up brushing away the dirt from her respectable English skirt. She tried to smile.

'Thank you for helping me, it was good of you. But you have missed the bus and will have to wait another half hour,' she said in the unmistakable tones of an English vicarage. Her mouth trembled.

'I shall walk. Good for me,' said Sophy. The lady put out a thin ringed hand and pressed hers and Sophy thought, but might have been mistaken, that she heard 'God bless you.'

In Unoccupied France, in a France which the invading Germans assured the authorities would be 'allowed to live and flourish' the restrictions multiplied every day, food grew scarcer, the faces of the people more drawn. They openly loathed the British, who were execrated in conversations in bars and cafés and at dinner tables where the fare was little but turnips and swedes. Rationed bread was made of bran and the worst quality rye, there was occasionally some skimmed milk, there was no butter. Women queued for six hours and returned home with baskets empty. Yet it was not the thing to vilify the Germans. England took the brunt of the shortages, the misery. Every man and woman – except, it seemed, Paul Dufour – believed England had deserted France in her worst hour and was responsible for the army's collapse.

Pregnant, helpless, Sophy could scarcely rush to her own country's defence. Not a soul in the house knew about her condition and as the dangerous days went by and she nervously watched her figure subtly changing, she wondered how soon, oh how soon, Paul could help her to get away. Suppose Yvonne Dufour found out she was pregnant? She would order her out of the house, calling her a whore.

Her condition made Sophy very hungry, she found it impossible not to think of food the entire time. But there were curious advantages to her dangerous situation. She had not known that pregnancy was a kind of armour. It made a woman strong; gave her philosophy and a hardy attitude, almost a form of indifference. She often thought that perhaps in Yvonne Dufour's place, she would detest the English; she began to see that the woman had a certain right on her side. Her husband had fought in one hideous war which France had won; the once-proud country was now in the dust. Sophy could not hate Yvonne or Anselme, she looked at them sometimes with a dispassionate curiosity. That was when she felt safe. At other times, conscious that she would no longer be able to walk long distances or hide in ditches without endangering the stranger occupying her body, she half believed Yvonne would get rid of her somehow. The only person who could stop such a thing was Paul. She needed his good opinion.

The person Sophy thought of most often was not Daniel, not her family – who seemed as if they were at the other end of the world – but Violette. She remembered her every day. Their shared danger was a glue of friendship, she missed Violette and often dreamed of her tired gallant face; and dreamed they were again in the Renault driving along under the stars, hungry but together, on the long roads of France.

Anne-Marie had begun to count the days before her fiancé's return: it gave her a glow and cheered her up. She had been cast down by the presence and the problem of her English friend and had no courage to stand against her parents; in any case she secretly agreed with them. At last the day she looked forward to so eagerly arrived and Claudio was due. Anne-Marie, pale with excitement, put on her best last-year's silk dress. He did not come to Les Hesperides but telephoned his fiancée and arranged to meet her at the Carlton.

She returned, rather early, driven to the gate in a large car which Sophy glimpsed from the windows of the petit salon. It was black and glittering, like a gangster's car in a 1930s movie.

Sophy saw Claudio getting out, one could not mistake the burly ape-like figure. He put his arms round Anne-Marie and kissed her; he did not accompany her to the door. He drove away.

Anne-Marie came into the house looking radiant, but before Sophy could run out to ask friendly questions, Yvonne suddenly appeared, took her daughter into the grand salon and shut the door. Sophy heard voices talking for a long time.

When Sophy had the chance to ask if she had enjoyed herself, it was next day after breakfast, Anne-Marie was non-committal and embarrassed, but certainly happy. Sophy heard her singing in the bathroom. Her description of the evening was vague. Yes, they had dined at the Carlton. 'It was very elegant, and imagine! We had roast lamb à la Provençale.' She seemed undisturbed by the fact that her mother and father had sat down to a feast of stewed crow.

'Oh, there is one thing,' Anne-Marie was casual, 'Maman asked me to enquire from Claudio if it was possible for you to get a travel permit. Claudio said the queues at the Mairie are very bad, people are so stupid. And it would be wise for you, a foreigner, to keep quiet for a while. Not to draw attention to yourself. You understand?'

'Yes. I understand.'

So Paul became Sophy's only confidant. He fell into the habit of joining her when she went alone to the beach. A wind had been blowing for days and it blew the sand into their faces, but they did not mind. He sat down and touched her hand and said, on the afternoon following Anne-Marie's evening with her future husband, 'Well, Sophy? How is it with you?'

'The same.'

'With me also. The entire catch of fish this morning removed as if it had not existed. I couldn't even smuggle a piece of hake for Clara to cook. Do you know where our fish is going now? Not to Italy but to Occupied France. To feed the Germans. Here in so-called Vichy France they plan to starve us. Pigs.'

'Don't say things like that, even to me.'

248

'Oh, I can trust thee.' When they were alone he always used the intimate 'tu'. He turned round to look at her. He reminded Sophy of a bird. His big nose was like a beak, his face so thin, his black hair glossy feathers.

'I trust you because you are the enemy.'

'That's a big word.'

'Isn't it?'

They watched the water. The waves were noisy.

'Paul.'

'Yes?'

'I have something important to tell you.'

'I know it already.'

'You can't. You don't.'

'Yes I do. You are pregnant. Daniel Vergé, I take it?'

'But how could you possibly –'

'How big your eyes are when you are surprised. They are so green. I like that colour. Don't be anxious, nobody else knows, even Maman who is so sharp. It was Clara who told me. I've always been her pet, you know she calls me Pol-Pol, isn't it absurd? It was what I called myself when I was four years old. Clara told me the morning after you had arrived. She warned me against you. "That foreigner who is here is carrying a child out of wedlock."'

'But if Clara knows –'

'No, no, she won't tell my parents or my sister. She is one of the Provençal women who shut their mouths like a trap. Knowing something secret gives her satisfaction; she hoards it like money. Anyway, she said "that girl is *enceinte*, so keep away and don't sniff round her; you always wanted her, well, now it is useless." She looked very pleased when she said that.'

'What else did she say about me?'

'"She is not virtuous. She is no good,"' quoted Paul.

'I suppose you agree with her?' A pregnant refugee, she had her sexual vanity.

'Oh, I accept that I can't win you, Sophy. You are still the most beautiful girl I have met in my life, and the most fascinating. You are so –' he considered, shrugged. 'Would it be

249

foolish to say mysterious? I do not really know you, and that bewitches me. From the time we first met, a year ago, I have desired you and in spite of your condition, I still do. But I am wonderfully unselfish,' he added, 'a canonized saint, who intends to get you back to your own country somehow.'

'Dear friend.'

He looked older again. He had that curious quality, sometimes a boy, sometimes a considerable man.

'What about Vergé?' he said. 'Did you happen to marry him in Paris, by any chance? And have decided not to tell us?'

'Of course I didn't marry him.'

'But you wish you had.'

'Not one bit. He does not – did not – love me. Even if I knew where he was now I wouldn't tell him about the baby. Oh Paul! How I long to go home.'

'Ah,' he said, 'I understand that.'

They sat for a while, and then decided to swim. The sea refreshed them. And when Sophy dived and inadvertently got salt water into her eyes she was glad, because it was better than tears.

They went back to the rocks and lay in the sun until they were dry, then modestly dressed under the two towels Sophy had brought with her, hoping Paul would join her: he almost always did. Neither wanted to return to the house. But the shadow of the umbrella pine leaning over them grew long. And it was late. Time to return to a meal of soggy bread and swedes and the seaweed Clara had learned to cook.

'Be content, *mignonne*,' Paul said as they walked through the garden. 'I will get you home.'

Things deteriorated. In Cannes. In Les Hesperides. Anne-Marie never brought Claudio to the house and vanished in the evenings, to be returned by the large black car and be closeted with her mother and secretive with her friend afterwards. But one morning in the street when she and Sophy had gone to try and buy some fruit, Sophy inadvertently said a word in English to her and a woman passing turned and lifted her hand to slap her across the face. Anne-Marie seized Sophy by the arm and ran.

The next morning at breakfast, of ersatz coffee and stone-hard bread, Yvonne Dufour put down the coffee pot and said, 'Claudio has informed my daughter that you will be allowed a permit to travel to Spain.'

'Maman, there are still such crowds,' said Anne-Marie timidly.

'The Mairie is closed until Monday,' put in Monsieur heavily. He did not look at Sophy but at his wife. 'After that it would be wise if she rose and got to the Mairie before six in the morning, I'm told. Then you are given a number and will get your turn in good time.'

'Before six!' echoed Anne-Marie in dismay. 'But –'

'I'll do exactly that,' snapped Sophy, and pushed back her chair. She couldn't wait to get out of the room.

She fetched her straw hat and walked away from the house along the southern point of the Croisette. This time Yvonne, and poor hangdog Monsieur, had succeeded in upsetting her. She was to be despatched, to stand in the street for perhaps four hours. She was to be got rid of and a good thing too.

She walked on, past the Moorish buildings of the casino. And suddenly in a mind which had been seething with resentment, she actually saw the place. She recalled fireworks blown down on the crowds, and Daniel carrying her up the stairs, and making love in an empty office. How they had loved. Such bliss, such sharp joy, yet now she could scarcely remember what it had felt like, only the fact itself. She looked up at the line of windows wondering which one had brought the light of dawn in upon them as they lay on the floor. The windows stared back, fixed and blind.

She rounded the point of the Croisette and walked faster to get away from her thoughts. But she still couldn't escape Daniel. A few yards further on where the Île de Sainte Marguerite seemed at its closest across a stretch of water, and now shone pink in the early sun, was Les Embruns. She stopped again and stared up at the balcony of what had been his apartment.

'Oh Daniel. I did love you. I did. I did,' she said aloud.

She hadn't meant to speak and the sound of her own words

seemed to reverberate, as a harp does set in an open window. His name made her cry. She walked on, trying to stop, putting as much quick distance as she could between the past and now, but still the tears ran down her face. For she was at the heart of it. She did not love Daniel now. She remembered him, but not with her body. She was as deserted as when he'd thrown her into the hedge, and the spikes had impaled her like instruments of torture. She forgot she'd attacked him with a naked knife, and only remembered the blood streaming from her lacerated arms, and her face in a huge mirror, scratched and bruised. He must have hated her to treat her so. She wiped the tears away with the back of her hand.

The road ran along the border of the sea, then curved inwards to follow the railway, eventually returning to the sea again and the small port of Golfe Juan. She knew it well. She and Anne-Marie, Daniel, Paul and the others used to drive here to swim or dance. Through the little town she walked on, scarcely noticing the closed bars and dreary deserted look of the place. She reached Juan les Pins, more deserted than Cannes, and climbed the rocky headland to where a great hotel, like a Loire château, hid in its gardens and pinewoods. Down a dusty road, and then a narrow lane winding between olive groves and broken glass-houses, Sophy walked. She did not know why she walked so far, she was getting exhausted, yet she did not stop, and during the long long hours, she scarcely passed a living soul.

At last she went down a slope shaded with olive trees, and reached the bay. The beach was thick with dark seaweed and brushwood from last winter, the sand from a scarcely retreating tide was wet but drying fast. Tired out, she sat down on a rock. Once, in days as unreal as those in fever-dreams, she and Daniel used to come here. How busy this place used to be, the swimmers bright as tropical fish. Now there was only Sophy. The pine trees which flourished in sandy places grew thickly in a walled garden which belonged to an old empty stone house. Pushed by the prevailing Mistral which was fierce in spring and autumn, they were bent and threw circles of shade. So did thorny bushes covered with creamy flowers.

Sophy sat down and leaned against the rocks. She did not even bother to look at the sea on this beach called the Garoupe, floored with white sand and coloured a glassy emerald shading into darkest blue. She was thinking about Paul. She had a feeling he was afraid for her. Why should that be, here in Unoccupied France? It was true she'd seen one or two German officers in Cannes. But no more than that, and they had been a rarity.

As she stared at the water sparkling in the brilliant light, Sophy's eyes suddenly focussed – she saw a strange thing. Round the corner of the bay where the rocks were highest a very small boat was approaching. At first she vaguely thought it must be a fishing boat, then she made it out as a kind of rubber dinghy which lay very low in the water. The man was paddling fast and soundlessly; as he came closer to the shore she saw how carefully he took the paddle from the water, how silently he pushed it back. He was now within earshot, but Sophy could not hear a splash.

Instinct told her to pretend to be asleep. She half closed her eyes, watching through her lashes. He climbed out into shallow water, looked from left to right, then bent down and began to fill the boat with rocks. It disappeared almost at once. He did the same with his rubber boots – curious things nobody wore in the Mediterranean, filling them with stones and watching them sink. At one moment he straightened up and looked in her direction. Sophy lay as still as death. She knew he had seen her – a girl stretched out in the sun fast asleep.

He waded to the shore, crossed the beach and stripped off his shirt, then dug a hole in the sand and buried it, brushing the sand flat and scattering it with pebbles. He took a thin package, it must have been wrapped in oil-skin, from his pocket, and unfolded a shirt of the French '*bleu de travail*' which he put on swiftly, adding a beret pulled on at the right workman's angle. Walking casually away from the beach he disappeared into the olive grove.

Sophy waited for some minutes before she felt it safe to sit up. She was fascinated. Who was he? An Englishman? A Frenchman working against the Germans? A smuggler? A criminal? How she wished she could have spoken to him and how was it that she was sure he was her countryman? Something in the way he walked reminded her of Bob Lingard.

She lingered at the Garoupe, postponing the long hot walk back to Les Hesperides, puzzling over the man from the sea. Alone, in the buzzing midday filled with the sound of small waves, and cicadas in the pines, she went to sleep.

It was hours later, well into the afternoon, when she was roughly woken by somebody shaking her arm. Two gendarmes were standing over her. They demanded rudely that she show them her papers.

'I've walked here from Cannes where I live. I have nothing with me,' Sophy said, frowning and yawning.

The men were both very young and very smart, with nothing of the look of returning soldiers. They both spoke at the same time.

'A foreigner!' They began to question her, scarcely listened to her replies and finally shouted at her, forbidding her to stand up.

'If that's what you want,' said Sophy, raising her eyebrows.

'It is an order,' said the older gendarme, a man in his late twenties, pale and sullen-looking. Threatening her if she so much as moved, they left her and went down to the beach, conferring together. Sophy watched them as they began to search, crossing and re-crossing the sand, heads bent. They left deep footprints at the edge of the sea; even those had an ominous look. This has turned into a country of spying, she thought. Will they find that man's clothes? At last the older gendarme shouted out, bent and began to dig, finally dragging the shirt from the cache where it had been buried. His companion joined him. They were excited, shaking out the garment and examining it, throwing angry looks towards Sophy and behaving, she thought, like characters in a melodrama. They marched over, the shirt clutched in the older man's hand and barked at her that she must come with them to the police van.

There was nothing for it but to obey. At the station she was pushed into a room so airless and hot that she began to feel faint.

During the next four hours until it was dark, Sophy learned what it meant to be grilled. Everything she said was rudely disbelieved. She was battered with questions, first by the two gendarmes and later by their superior officer with a long nose and a good many gold teeth. At first she was quite calm and tried to answer the endless questions reasonably. But when at every turn the inspector contradicted her and tried to trap her, she began to lose her temper. She knew he must realize, unless he was a complete fool, that whatever plot they were after, their antagonists would scarcely leave an accomplice fast asleep on the very beach where the spy had hidden his clothes, so that she would be picked up by the first inquisitive gendarme. They had arrested her, if that was what they had done, because she'd been on the spot and had perhaps seen something she wasn't telling. They had arrested her because they had nobody else to shout at after they had triumphantly unearthed buried evidence. In the van Sophy had seen that the shirt was bone dry. Thank heaven for that; it could have been hidden for days.

Replying to the battering questions, repeating in her English-accented voice that she did not know what they were talking about, had seen no-one, had been asleep, she said over and over again that she wished to telephone the Dufours. She was refused.

The grilling continued, and by eight in the evening Sophy longed to pick up her chair and smash it in the inspector's face. The man lit his tenth cigarette. The smell in the dungeon-like room made her want to be sick. She tried to use her brains, looking for a stronger weapon than a chair. And thought of it.

'Monsieur.'

'Yes?' He expelled some smoke. There was no question of addressing her or behaving in the usual courteous fashion.

'Do you think it will be well-received when Signor Arrighi gets to hear I have been detained for no reason?'

The inspector said nothing. But she could see she had scored a hit.

'The family with whom I am living, Monsieur and Madame Dufour, have a daughter, Mademoiselle Anne-Marie. She is the future wife of Signore Arrighi who has recently been elected – have you heard? – to be in charge of supply in this district. Monsieur Arrighi is also a close friend of mine.'

The man ground his cigarette out on the floor under his heel and said rudely, 'Such claims have to be verified.' He walked out.

Twenty minutes later Paul arrived to collect her in the fish van. At the station neither of them said a word, Paul kissed her on both cheeks, spoke to the gendarme on duty, and having signed some paper or other took Sophy's arm and hurried her away.

They continued to be silent as he drove home. But when they were almost at the casino she burst out, 'Paul! Of course I didn't tell them anything and I don't even understand what is going on, but there was a man who landed on the Garoupe. I pretended to be asleep and I watched him come ashore in a rubber dinghy. He sank it with stones and then –'

Paul put out his left hand and squeezed hers so tightly that it hurt. 'No, Sophy, you did not see that. Forget what you *thought* you saw. It is very dangerous.' He stopped the van by the casino. 'Shall we walk a little?'

The air was balmy and to Sophy, liberated from the foul cigarette smoke in the cell-like room, it felt as if she were breathing the air of paradise. It was filled with the scent of night-flowering lilies from a tree in the casino gardens. An enormous moon hung over the sea. They walked to the beach and sat down.

'You must go, *mignonne.*'

'Oh, I know, I have to queue at the Mairie at six in the morning the day after tomorrow –'

'I do not mean to get a permit. When I was waiting for you just now I overheard the gendarmes. Claudio's name helped

256

for tonight, they are not easy about that, but when they have consulted with headquarters they intend to come and get you again tomorrow. They are very suspicious, Sophy. Because of what I told you that you did not see.'

'You sound as if you know who that man was and —'

'Sh.' He put a finger on her lips. 'We must not talk about it. But I can tell you one thing. We are not all collaborators. Not all the creatures of Vichy and the Germans. But you must leave France now, Sophy. For both our sakes.' He leaned close and said, with a break in his voice, 'Ah, *mignonne*,' and gave her a violent kiss.

Sophy never said goodbye to the Dufours. She had no chance to embrace Anne-Marie. Paul went into the house by the back staircase to fetch her money belt and passport and a thick coat. An hour later she was in a small fishing boat, part of the fleet which worked with Dufour et Cie. Paul introduced her to a haggard sailor with a sardonic grin who wrung her hand, had a private word with Paul and took her into a cabin no bigger than a cupboard. She had to stay there until the boat was well out to sea, after Paul, giving her a final hug, vanished into the dark.

Sophy travelled by many boats. The first few were owned by sailors who knew Paul, but later in a motor boat beyond Marseilles, his name was no longer mentioned among the sailors who looked after her. She had become a temporary piece of contraband to be smuggled out of France. She was aware through the long night journeys at sea that the taciturn sailors were already in some kind of secret war. And that Paul, her dear rescuer, was a part of it.

She did what she was told, was given food and drink, stayed concealed in daylight, and was allowed on deck at night. For two days there was a storm and Sophy was very sick. At last, the sun returned, the heat returned, she was set down on a beach at La Escale over the Spanish frontier. And soon in a sweltering Spanish train.

England was a shock. She'd left a country in the rich days of peace, she returned to a place already shabby and sandbagged to its eyebrows. On the train to London she knew that she looked even worse but she did not care. Her travels had made her immune to her appearance when there was nothing to be done about it. What she had was her hard philosophy and the cloak of pregnancy. She'd even managed to keep some of her money.

It was with a wave of real excitement at Victoria station that she telephoned the War Office. It took a long time to get through to the right department, she had to hang on, almost crazy with impatience. But at last she spoke to a girl whom she did not know, apparently Jack's secretary. The girl said incredulously, '*Who* is speaking?'

'His sister,' repeated Sophy, good manners running out with her loose change. 'Tell him it's his sister Sophy and my money won't last, I'm at a box at the station.'

A moment later there was the voice she had not heard for a year.

'Is that really you?'

'Oh Jack. Oh Jack.'

And then she did begin to cry.

10

'High time,' was all he said. He told her to take a taxi to Halsey Street.

'Have you any money?'

Sophy, still half crying, said yes, she had lots, 'Nearly all the money you sent me months ago.'

'Well done,' said Jack. 'Now. Mrs Powell will let you in. I'll be with you in quarter of an hour.'

Sophy knew her brother's lodgings near Sloane Square; in peacetime she used to stay with him after she had been to parties or dances. Jack was never particularly hospitable, he often forgot to ask the housekeeper to provide her breakfast, but she enjoyed being there. He would give her a drink before she left for the Dorchester or the Savoy and admire her ball dress. 'Quite something,' was his highest praise.

When the taxi drew up at the house, Sophy climbed out and began to unfasten one of the pouches of her now-filthy money belt. She produced a much-creased five pound note as dirty as the belt. Jack had given it to her years ago, 'for luck', he'd said. It had become a kind of talisman. Now was the moment to use it. The taxi driver, an elderly Cockney, was much amused. 'Cor, Mate! You know how to do things, don't you, Miss?'

Halsey Street was terraced, the houses smallish and plain, built in early Victorian times for clerks and dressmakers. Jack liked the district, it was unpretentious and he knew the man at the newspaper shop and the landlord of the corner pub.

Mrs Powell, his housekeeper for years, was devoted to him but had been reserved with Sophy who had worn, in peace-time, the dubious adjective glamorous.

When Sophy rang the bell, Mrs Powell opened the door. She was dressed in a smart unfamiliar green uniform with orange pipings. She gave the travel-worn visitor a look of astonishment.

'If it isn't Miss Hayward after all this time! Come to see your brother, Miss? He left a good two hours ago.'

'I know, Mrs Powell, I just spoke to him. He said would you let me into his rooms and he's coming round to see me.'

'Is he?' said the woman not bothering to hide her surprise at Sophy's bedraggled appearance. She took her up to the first floor and unlocked Jack's door, said she must go to the WVS meeting and clattered back down the stairs, slamming the front door.

Looking at herself in a mirror in Jack's sitting room Sophy understood Mrs Powell's expression. She had only seen herself in lavatory mirrors and the reflections of dirty train windows. She had no idea just how awful she looked until she saw herself in a looking glass which used to reflect a pre-war girl in taffeta crowned with flowers. She wondered if it was worth while trying to clean herself up. Scarcely. She had nothing to change into and at least her face and hands had been washed at the station. She was tired.

She flopped down in an armchair by the empty grate and shut her eyes ...

'Wake up!'

The voice came from a distance and for a moment Sophy thought Paul was calling her. Or the captain of the fishing boat. Or the guard in the Spanish train. She stared up myopically and then her eyes focussed and she was looking at a pale face with thick spectacles, at a round head with dark hair brilliantined and brushed back, and a pair of very dark eyes.

'*Oh Jack!*'

She sprang up, he put out his arms and they hugged. They

stayed for a moment wrapped in each other's arms.

'Let me see you,' he said at last with a slight laugh, releasing her and holding her at arm's length. 'My God, Sophy, you look like something the cat's dragged in. Now, now, don't start to cry, where's the red-headed fire-eater we learned to know and dread, mm? Sit down, sit down, sorry I woke you.' He walked out into the kitchen and returned with a large whisky, neat.

'Drink that down. It'll make you feel better.'

'I mustn't drink, I'm afraid.'

'You haven't been ill, have you?' he exclaimed.

Before he had time to ask anything else Sophy had to get it over and said, 'I'm having a baby.'

It had never been easy to know what Jack was thinking and Sophy didn't now. He regarded her with detachment, taking in the creased dusty clothes, bare legs, those extraordinary sandals one of which had been mended with string, the broken fingernails. The glamorous sister was gone.

'I think,' he said, taking it, 'I'm the one who needs the whisky.'

He telephoned the War Office while Sophy was having her first bath for two weeks. She heard his voice, low, cold, now and then enlivened by one of his jokes. The voice gave her extraordinary comfort. I'm here, she thought. With Jack. I've made it. She felt proud of herself as she wallowed in the bath, dried herself on his towel and put on his silk dressing gown. She emerged barefoot, smelling of Russian Leather. She had washed her hair which still dripped on to the shoulders of the dressing gown.

'You need another towel, my dressing-gown's soaked,' he said. Fetching one, he insisted on drying her hair himself in the way he used to do on the beach at Brighton. He tugged the towel to and fro, he was very rough and made her laugh. When he released her, her cheeks were pink, her russet hair in spikes.

'Now I'll make some tea and you'd better tell me all about it.'

'The story's long.'

'With you looking like that I didn't imagine it was going to be short.'

They sat in the old-fashioned room in wartime London, on a day of summer like other days. Sophy put her feet up on the sofa and hugged her knees, modestly covering her bare legs; Jack was fussy about things like that. She told him all that had happened, leaving out nothing, not even the fight at Versailles.

He smoked his pipe and listened in silence except, occasionally, to chuckle if she made a joke. Wanting a reaction she exaggerated adventures which had been alarming enough anyway, the bombing outside Lyon, her illness in Orange, the hours at the police station at Cap d'Antibes. She finished with her terror of being caught during the many boat journeys to the coast of Spain.

'Well,' she finished at last, 'what do you say?'

'That you've been damned lucky.'

Sophy was regaining, inch by inch, the self which had been laid aside for months. She was with the man who loved her more than anybody else. More than Daniel. More than Bob Lingard. More than Paul. The man who, disapproving and criticizing, was her true conquest.

'Admit that your sister has guts.'

'Not sure about that. Your friend Violette sounds to me as if she has more.'

'That's monstrous.'

He took no notice of her scowls, but felt the teapot. It had gone cold.

'Now we know where we are,' he remarked, standing up and glancing at his watch. 'The first thing we'll do is to get you some clothes. There are some of your old things still in my wardrobe. Pop those on, and then go round to Peter Jones and buy yourself something suitable. Here are my coupons.'

'*Coupons?*'

He laughed. 'Of course, you don't know anything about those yet. Well, well. Get as many clothes as the coupons allow, and we can talk about anything else you need later. Here's something to be going on with.' He put some pound notes on the tray.

'You are sweet, darling.' Sophy was delighted at the thought of shopping. 'But I have loads of clothes at home, I can get them tomorrow.'

A pause.

'Hm,' he said. 'Well. I'd prefer you not to ring the parents until you and I have talked again. Understand?'

She knew the tone and agreed with rare meekness.

'Good. Seven, then.'

He might, thought Sophy, when he had padded off with a kind of slow determination, he might at least have looked shocked when I told him I'd been seduced.

By the time he returned from the War Office, she was transformed, having spent an interesting afternoon. The London she hadn't seen for fourteen months astounded her. It was another world. It was not deserted like the Midi, defeated and poor but still breathtakingly beautiful. This world buzzed with activity, the streets were filled, not with troops dragging home in defeat but with smartly uniformed men in RAF blue or khaki or dark Navy blue, every one of them cheerful. The city itself was shabby. Not its people.

Sophy decided to buy herself a cheap wedding ring, exclaiming gaily to the assistant, 'Isn't it a tragedy, mine fell off and we can't find it anywhere!' She also chose a tan-coloured dress with a broad white collar designed for the mother-to-be. It magically expanded, its double skirt fixed with a sash which could be loosened as one grew fatter. She bought low-heeled shoes and white socks. She noticed a lot of girls out of uniform were wearing those.

In Jack's wardrobe she found – how one forgot everything – some clothes she had left behind to change into after parties. In the pocket of a jacket was a ball of silver paper. She smiled, smoothing it out, when she saw traced across it the word 'Terry's'. Bob Lingard used to buy her Terry's chocolates; they both feasted on them while watching Fred Astaire and Ginger Rogers.

Bob, she thought with a slight, only a slight pang. She had not thought of her fiancé for weeks. Months. He had been part of the forgotten England she'd thrown aside when Daniel first embraced her; she had been at the mercy of sex, of Daniel, distanced from Bob in a way which had been both convenient and terrible. Now he was a fact again. She wondered uncomfortably what Jack was going to say about Bob.

She was sitting on the sofa, after painting her lips with her last stub of French lipstick, when Jack let himself in to the flat. He saw his sister, russet-haired, russet-dressed, fresh as a tea rose. And self-possessed.

'That's more like it.'

Sophy gave a satisfied grin.

'You did look a bit shattered at seeing me this morning. To tell you the truth, I was rather shattered at seeing me too. In the mirror. A wreck.'

'All over now.' He made for the drinks cupboard and poured himself a whisky. 'Sure you wouldn't like a snifter?'

'Wish I could. I can't stand drink any more. The same with coffee. I nearly throw up.'

He did not reply. Unlike the French people she was accustomed to, he did not answer from temporary interest or sheer formality. If he had nothing to say he was silent. He sat down facing her and the evening sun came through the open window and shone down on him. He looked tired, and so familiar that her heart swelled.

'Oh Jack. I'm so glad to be home.'

'Do you mean it?' he said, sipping his drink. 'I should have thought –'

The sentence died the death.

'That I'd rather be with my seducer? Well, I wouldn't. I'm over him. Finito. End of chapter.'

'Scarcely.'

'You're looking at my bump,' said the girl, regarding her stomach, 'it's getting quite big, isn't it? They quicken at four and a half months, you know. Start to jump about. It's almost that now, so any day –'

'I think we could cut out the gynaecological talk for the present and concentrate, not on your health which looks to me as if it is fine, but on your future. This Daniel Vergé you've been talking about.'

'Sleeping with, you mean.'

She didn't know why she felt impelled to show off.

'What a child you are, pregnant or not pregnant. Stick to the point.'

'You don't seem very annoyed that your sister was seduced,' she said pettishly, repeating her earlier thought.

'Don't be stupider than you can help, Sophy. In any case how do I know who seduced whom? You probably asked for it.'

'*How disgusting.*'

'No, it isn't, it may be the truth. I am not interested in your seduction, as you dramatically call it. That's history. You have miraculously and, it seems to me, entirely due to that brave young chap Paul Dufour, managed to get back home. For which I'm more grateful than you seem to be. The point is you're here. In good health and carrying the child of a stranger I've never set eyes on. So what are we going to do about you?'

'What is there to do?' She was annoyed again. 'You know perfectly well the answer's nothing. I don't know where Daniel is except that he was in Occupied France, in the Maginot. There's no way of finding out anything about him.'

'Vergé. Daniel. I could make enquiries.'

'What do you mean?'

'The War Office has different departments; some may have information from enemy sources.'

'Oh, you mean spies,' said Sophy, scoffing.

He knew he must be patient with her. He rarely showed what he was thinking but he could not help an expression of amusement and irritation as he regarded his sister. The girl had suffered, escaped danger and even death, was expecting the child of a man who had disappeared, was heavy not only with pregnancy but with unsolved problems. She behaved like a pre-war butterfly. She had no sense of proportion, even of reality.

'What I'm trying to tell you is that it might be possible for me to find out whether anything is known of Daniel Vergé. He was an accredited photographer for *Le Jour*, you said.'

265

Sophy paused. She half believed her brother could do it. Could actually find out what had happened to Daniel. There was something in Jack, an authority, a lack of drama, a quiet assurance which impressed. She once said to him, 'If I got in a scrape, I know who I'd come rushing to. You're the lawyer who'd get me out of trouble.' 'It would depend whose side I was on.' 'Pooh. You're always on mine!'

Now she sat hugging her knees and reflecting on what he had said. Suppose he really did find out whether Daniel was alive. Jack never said he could do things which were impossible. Suppose it turned out that Daniel was alive, did her brother imagine she still clung to the idea of the man? Loved him with all her heart, and, carrying his child, was willing to wait. Then the day would come when – as at the end of most Hollywood films – they would be blissfully united, Daniel gallant in uniform, Sophy in a cottage with a pram at the gate?

'You're very silent for such a chatterbox,' remarked Jack quizzically.

'I was thinking of what you said about finding Daniel.'

'I never said I could do that.'

'I know! I wish you wouldn't keep treating me like a fluffy blonde –'

'With fluffy complexion like plums on the wall, and fluffy opinions and no brains at all,' quoted Jack. It was a poem they used to laugh about.

'Exactly. I am quite capable of grasping the fact that it's a thousand, no, a million to one chance you'd find out nothing.'

'Wouldn't say the odds are as great as that.'

'A million to one. You forget,' crushingly, 'I'm the one who's been in France, not you. I *know* how things are. But ... I was thinking whether I wanted you even to try. The answer is No. I'm in this on my own, and I have been for nearly four months. I'm on my own except for you.' She leaned across and took his hand.

He dutifully squeezed it. But physical gestures, apart from an occasional hug or brief kiss on the cheek, were not in his style.

266

'Very well,' he said, he accepted she did not want to see Vergé again. He did not ask if she still loved him. That wasn't Jack's style either; he never used the world 'loved'. He said 'fond of' if he was cornered, or 'quite liked'. Now he sat, rubbing his nose, and told her what seemed a solution to what he charitably called her little problem.

The first point was that she couldn't go home.

'Why not!'

'Have a bit of sense, girl. You can't turn up in your condition unless you're willing to go through an elaborate farce with the story that you were married in France and Vergé has been killed or is missing.'

'Oh.'

'You don't fancy the idea?'

'I don't fancy pretending to be Daniel's widow. I did that once in the Midi, but it was only to make sure I didn't get raped.'

'For pity's sake, Sophy, stop showing off. Talk like that is something you'd best forget. So shut up about your so-called dramas. Very well, you don't want to pose as a war widow, so you can't go home to our parents in your condition. We can spare them that. Thought about Bob Lingard at all?'

Sophy was silent. She hated Jack to think badly of her.

He gave a snort which turned into a laugh.

'Well, we can't tell him either, can we? The problem of Bob will also have to wait. There's another little matter,' he went on, 'this baby of yours. Do you plan to keep it?'

The matter-of-fact voice, the lawyer's detachment, the active lack of emotion which simply laid facts upon the table in front of her, was Sophy's first shock; except for sandbags in the London streets.

'*Keep* him? I haven't thought about it.'

'Like Bob Lingard. Out of sight for the present, out of mind. You've got to decide on that one pretty smartly, Sophy. If you do want to keep the infant, you're stuck with the alibi of being a war widow, however much you dislike it. If you don't, I must make some enquiries and find out about adoption agencies. There are far too many illegitimate kids born at

267

present and I imagine getting one adopted isn't easy. So we must get a move on.'

Sophy had gone pale. Her sallow face, without colour, showed up her freckles like scatters of brown confetti.

'Do I have to decide right away?'

'Give it to the end of the week. Now we've talked enough. We'll go out for a bite. Food's awful, but the pub's only down the road.'

Lying in the pokey spare bedroom with the sounds of London coming through the blackout curtains, Sophy could not sleep. It was funny. No, it was not, it was disgraceful, a sort of sin, that she hadn't made a single plan about the child inside her who grew a little more each day. She had accepted her pregnancy and concentrated on saving herself, and the baby as a part of that self. She'd needed her wits and used them. Huddled in a cargo boat, half fainting in a stifling Spanish train, certain she'd never get on to the cargo boat which eventually brought her to England. Even this morning at Victoria, waiting to speak to her brother, she had never thought – all this is going to end in January. I shall have a baby then. Until now she had simply forged ahead, made plans for the next emergency, changed them at a second's notice. She had become like Violette.

Now she lay awake, sure her phlegmatic brother was snoring, and thought about what he had asked. Was she willing to take on the role of widow, live a boring permanent lie, rear a little child whom she and Daniel had accidentally made one long sexy Paris afternoon?

She thought of Daniel with the same remembered pain she had felt walking past Les Embruns. Had she truly loved him? Was there enough love left to keep her going? She did not think so. She was not sure she believed you could love somebody after they had gone; she had always thought it unnatural that women could mourn all their lives – why, Madame Gombert had worn black for a man who had been killed twenty years ago! She recreated Daniel in her thoughts, his weariness, his thin challenging face, his body thrust exquisitely into hers, his mind so often absent from her. She deliberately remembered how it had been at Versailles when he had walked away with another woman and left her. He slept around, she was sure of it; that night he had gone off with the first silly bitch who made eyes at him. Was this the man for whom she must now make up noble romances, lie to her sympathetic mother, face the world and herself? She and Daniel had quarrelled often and it had always been Sophy who capitulated. Once she had rushed into his bedroom in the apartment and locked the door against him, convinced that he would hammer and beg her to come out. He did not. She waited, aching, sobbing, but Daniel never called to her. Not he. Who had given in? She had, unlocking the door to come running to him. Remembering it, she despised herself.

The next morning Sophy and her brother had breakfast in the sitting room. The meal, well-laid with a clean tablecloth, was the first hot breakfast Sophy had eaten since she had left England in peacetime. It was brought in by Mrs Powell who placed it in front of them with a slight flourish.

'Thanks. What a sight for sore eyes,' said Jack.

Sophy was not sure if he meant Mrs Powell or his bacon ration, grilled and divided fairly into two, plus bread the colour of brown paper, very weak tea and a dab of margarine. Jack thanked the housekeeper; he had a flirtatious manner with elderly women, all of whom were devoted to him. He never used the same manner with the young and pretty. Sophy hungrily ate her own share of the bacon and then, encouraged by Jack, his as well, plus most of the bread and margarine.

'I'm taking you to the Ritz tonight,' he said, pouring more tea.

'You're kidding.'

'No. I hear they sometimes have a chop. You need building up.'

That evening, wearing a pre-war navy blue silk dress she could just squeeze into, fortunately it had always been loose round the waise, Sophy sparkled with pleasure. Her brother took her into the still-stylish hotel, and before the meal they had drinks in a pretty lounge where a fountain still played, and the tables were marble topped and edged with gilt. It was all rather like Paris.

Jack, a glass in his hand, looked relaxed.

'How's work?' she dutifully enquired.

'Dull. Not for long, I'm afraid.'

'What does that mean?'

'Let's hope, nothing,' said Jack. He turned to look at the insouciant young woman at his side.

'Sophy. I have things to say.'

'Which is why you're spending a fortune on me tonight.'

He chuckled. She obviously did not know, he said, that the government had passed a handy law, forbidding restaurants to charge more than five shillings for a meal. 'However – I brought you here because it's nice and cheerful. Better than talking at Halsey Street. Besides, Mrs Powell sometimes pops in unexpectedly – and she might listen at the door.'

'Jack! You don't mean she –'

'No, I don't, but one can never tell. The most unexpected people turn out to be busybodies, and curiosity killed the cat. Mrs P knows nobody you and I know but I take no chances. Suppose Mother took it into her head for the first time since I've lived in Halsey Street to come up and pay me a call. It is Mother I want to talk about.'

He had been reflecting a great deal since his sister's dramatic return, not about their father who needed nobody's concern, in Jack's phrase he was his own man, but about their mother whom Jack liked to call by her first name, Pansy. Pansy had been deeply worried about her daughter ever since war broke out. It was only to be expected. Jack tried to calm her down, not very successfully, and Pansy continued to fret. Now here was Sophy, safe and well, and he could not allow her to return home.

'Poor old Pansy,' he said, 'she's been pulled down over you. Can't stop worrying. Father isn't much help when she starts up. Gets a bit tetchy.'

'He doesn't want to be inconvenienced by Ma being miserable.'

Jack raised his eyebrows with an expression of disapproval

which Sophy, who was looking at some RAF officers, missed.

'You do see things in black and white,' he remarked. 'You haven't been worrying about Pansy, have you?'

'Not much.'

'Don't sound pleased with yourself. It is never a good trait, even in your condition.'

'You'll admit, I suppose, that I've had other things to think about apart from the parents. Staying alive, for instance.' She waited for the effect. There was none. It's like letting off fireworks while Jack deliberately stands with his back to them, she thought.

He gestured to a passing waiter for a menu, studied it, remarked 'Not very inspired' and continued.

'I've been thinking you over. And I've worked out a way of setting Pansy's mind at rest. Bob Lingard's too, come to that. You must write to them both and I'll get the letters put through the Diplomatic Bag. It will look as if you're still in France. Now, Sophy, just listen and don't interrupt' – seeing her bursting with questions. 'Here's what to do. Write really good letters, but give no details whatsoever. Use that friend Violette. Say you're staying with her, I'll give you an address both Ma and Bob can write to. Their letters won't get to you, but that doesn't matter. Write affectionately, for the love of Mike. And take that look off your face. Did those Frenchmen you've been with all this time never stop flattering you?'

He suggested, during the dull but hot dinner served with a Ritzean flourish, that Sophy should go to North Devon.

'But that's miles away!'

'Yes, yes, isn't that the point?' he said patiently. She could stay there for the five months until the child was born. A colleague of his in the War Office, a really good chap, had a second cousin with a farm near Barnstaple. He had promised Jack he would write at once to the cousin, and was sure the family would put Sophy up. 'I shall pay on the generous side. Farmers like money,' added Jack. He and his friend Lawrence would cook up a good corny story about Sophy's widowhood; she must learn it and get the details right.

Listening to Jack's careful plans, Sophy was impressed. She

often felt like that about her brother. He had the talent for hacking his way through thickets of difficulties.

After they had talked over the Barnstaple idea and Sophy, who had no alternative, was forced to agree, Jack added that during the few days she would be staying in London before leaving, she had better not go about. There was always the chance, far-fetched and thus inevitable, that a friend might happen to see her.

'That's why I decided on the Ritz. We scarcely know people who frequent the place,' he remarked. Sophy poured some more coffee and looked around, and for a moment a little stab went through her. An officer went by. The flash on his shoulder, which she could read at a distance, said 'Free French'.

'So I'm to stay a prisoner in your poky flat?' she said.

'Go to the cinema in the King's Road. That'll pass the time,' was the unsympathetic reply.

Three days later, facing the prospect of separation from her brother with depression, Sophy was on Paddington Station. Jack steered her through the mass of soldiers and civilians and got her on to a train as crowded as any in France or Spain. She stood by the window trying to see him through the inch of space allowed by a big woman waving goodbye to her husband.

'I'll miss you,' called Sophy.

He nodded and smiled. She looked drawn, he thought, pregnancy did not suit her; he had known young women who positively burgeoned. Not his sister, though.

'Take care of yourself,' he shouted as the whistle blew. 'They won't have any books. I'll post some.'

Doors slammed. The train, loudly puffing, began to move.

Sophy had not realized just how tired she was. Lulled by the noise and movement of the train, knowing the journey was long, she fell asleep. Travellers arrived or left the compartment, stepping over her legs and muttering 'sorry'. Vaguely, half asleep, she wondered why they spoke in English. Soldiers stumbled into the carriage. When she was awake for a short time one of them gave her a doorstep sand-

272

wich of slippery stuff with a faint taste of ham. She smiled a
thank you, ate it and went back to sleep again. She dreamed
of Violette at the wheel of the Renault, of Daniel's malicious
smile, she woke at last to realize that the sun was setting. The
train window was masked with dust, but through it she saw
the turned earth. It was deep crimson.

'Devon,' said the soldier who had given her the sandwich.
He had seen her wake up. He had a rough, snub-nosed,
impudent face like a comedian.

'It's so red!' said Sophy, intrigued.

'Devon, glorious Devon. They say there's thick cream to be
had but I don't believe it, do you, Miss?'

Jack's friend Lawrence had written to the farmer whose
name was Sam Pearmain, and asked him to meet Sophy at
the station. There had been a reply saying he would be there.

'Pearmain is a distant relative of Lawrence's,' Jack had
said. 'I think Lawrence is rather ashamed of him; Pearmain's
a tenant farmer and Lawrence went to Eton. A good chap,
though. When he wrote to Pearmain he sent your photograph.'

'Which one?' said Sophy, not deserted by vanity.

It was dusk when the train drew up at a tiny country
station. Sophy, with a case-full of new clothes paid for by her
brother, was the only passenger to alight. Most of the soldiers
had left at Exeter and various middle-aged people, leaving
dirty wartime London, had descended at other stations along
the line. Weeds were flowering on the edge of the platform,
purple and white, and out of the twilight a man came towards
her. He was short and wore leggings and looked like an ostler.
His face was weatherbeaten from forty years of wind and sun,
it was reddish with broken veins, it resembled the faces of old
sailors she'd seen as a child in Worthing. His hair was short-
ish, fairish and he had a yellow and brown checked waistcoat.

'You're Sophy, aren't you?' he said with a Devon burr so
pronounced that it was almost a foreign language. He took
the suitcase. His teeth were terrible but his smile was as warm
as the day gone by. Sophy was helped into a horse-drawn
trap. Sam made a chirruping noise and the horse conde-
scended to amble down the road, through a village of not

more than six thatched houses, up a hill and into country as deep and lost as the end of the world.

Sam Pearmain was married to a worn overworked kindly woman called Elsie, they had a son, Arthur, of fourteen. Arthur's accent, Sophy found, was more impenetrable than that of his parents. Jack's friend, Lawrence, had told them all about Sophy; it was clear that they were very sorry for her. A widow, husband killed in France, poor thing, and a baby on the way. Besides, as Sam had told Elsie, the weekly money would come in handy.

'My cousin Lawrence said they're mortal afraid of bombs falling on London,' said Sam, on Sophy's first evening. They were all sitting at a long kitchen table having supper. 'No bombs in these parts,' he added, laughing and showing his dreadful teeth. His son joined in. Elsie, buttering yeast cakes, was not listening.

Jack had told Sophy that from what he gathered she would 'at least eat well and have the chance to put her feet up.' During the next four and a half months of her pregnancy, Sophy ate better than ever in her life. She was a Home Counties girl who had by chance spent a year in the most glamorous coast in Europe before war had ended all that. She had seen the best and worst of times in France and had grown accustomed first to French luxury and later to being half starved. It was not surprising that when she stepped off the train into the soft Devonshire twilight, she looked haggard.

Now she was thrown, willy nilly, into a life which was as extraordinary as anything that had happened to her during the fall of France. Not a violent dangerous life, but one which had not changed its pattern for nearly five hundred years. And she ate. Elsie cooked like an angel, the farm hands, there were four, crowded in for a hot dinner at midday every day except Sunday – and when Elsie was not working beside them in the fields or washing and ironing her husband's and son's clothes, or scrubbing the long table which could have accommodated twenty, she was cooking.

Sophy had never known anything like Elsie's Devonshire food. For breakfast there were slices of home-cured bacon as thick as her fingers, and home-made bread and as much farm butter as anybody could want, and home-made plum jam sharp and fresh, a positive beach of plum stones. For the hot midday meal with the farm hands, who might be only four but were all so enormous they seemed a regiment, there was rabbit stew or lamb stew. Or roast pork with thick brown crackling. The apple sauce was as sour as quarrels, thought Sophy, helping herself to more. There were canary puddings and chocolate puddings made with cocoa, and things which Elsie called syllabubs. There was no evening meal but a huge five o'clock tea – also with the farm hands – with plates and plates of yeast cakes which Elsie made by the hundred on Tuesday, her baking day. She had a long cool larder, a room, not a cupboard, and along its marble-topped shelves were yeast cakes, loaves, treacle tarts and apple pies all made on Tuesdays. Sophy had never seen such plenty.

The attitude of the Pearmains to their visitor was rather embarrassed, not warm; they talked more to each other than they addressed any chat to Sophy, who felt cut off from human society as if she found herself in the jungle or at the South Pole. When she tried to start a conversation, Sam was the only one who replied and he often looked as if he had no idea what she was talking about. Sophy knew she bothered Elsie, who looked askance at Sophy's pregnancy dresses – only two but very pretty and smart, and at her shoes and her lipstick.

'You'll get mucky,' was Elsie's invariable reply when Sophy offered to help; in the end Sophy understood that what Elsie meant was that she had never asked for or wanted help, that her work was her affair and she wished the London visitor would shut up.

It was a curious existence, an exile, to which Jack doomed his sister. The farmhouse was so old that nobody knew its dates, perhaps it was Tudor, perhaps earlier; there were strange carvings on the walls and indecipherable curved, carved lettering which nobody could read. The floors were of stone with a curious silky surface from age and use, and were almost lilac-coloured. All the life of the farmhouse was in the kitchen. On her first morning in the house Sophy went for an exploratory wander and found a sitting room, with the most elaborate of the stone carvings on the wall, and the hardest and most hideous stuffed furniture ranged in a kind of circle.

'That's our winter room,' said Elsie, appearing in an apron sprinkled with flour. She looked like a woman who'd been in a snow storm. 'In November we have a nice fire and I knit and we read a bit.'

I wonder, thought Sophy, politely admiring the stuffy ugly room, what on earth they read.

She had been given a large bedroom with a brass bed and a mattress so bouncy that it almost threw her out on to the floor when she sat down on it. The china was patterned with violets. The lavatory – alas – was a hideous little lean-to at the end of the garden and Sophy dreaded visiting it. What happened when it rained? But apart from that one disadvantage life was well-fed, idle, empty of any kind of work, beautiful because of the Devon countryside and as lonely as it was possible to be for a pretty young stranger in a houseful of people.

She thought perhaps she could make friends with Arthur who was only five years younger than herself. Arthur was a hardy, wiry, plain, energetic boy; it took Sophy two or three days to interpret the accent. When she said, 'Do you think this'll be too heavy?' indicating a basket of early apples she had picked up for Elsie in the orchard, Arthur – who knew all about pregnant women not carrying weights – replied, 'You'm know you'm got 'um'. Meaning, Sophy mentally translated, 'you'll know you've got it', or in English, it's too heavy and you oughtn't to pick it up. But Arthur was not ill at ease as Elsie was, or invisible as Sam was except at meals. It was the end of August, hot, sweet-smelling, feathery with long grasses, ripe with red and emerald apples, and Arthur was willing to take the stranger for a walk now and then. Her pregnancy, she was getting suddenly fatter, did not bother him. He looked at her belly and grinned.

'*She's* swellin' up nice,' he said once. Sophy, now accustomed to his language, knew he meant her stomach and not a future daughter.

Arthur took her on one wonderful walk across the fields. Some were under grass, with sheep grazing; later they skirted great stretches of barley, shivering in the slight wind. Arthur said it would soon be harvested. In one field in the distance Sophy spied a magnificent and alarming bull.

'*He's* a caution,' from Arthur, surveying the giant beast as if it were a kitten, 'I calls him Turnip. His rump's just like 'n, inn't?'

Down fields which began to slope steeply they came to a river brimming after rains earlier the previous month. A rushing river, it threw itself across white stones, deep, shallow, with the noise of somebody laughing.

'Oh, it's beautiful!'

'She'm not bad,' agreed Arthur, throwing a stone. On the way home, walking beside her and whistling between his teeth, he suddenly made a rush forward and began to hack at something in the road with a stick. 'An adder,' he said, throwing whatever it was into the hedge.

'Why didn't you leave it alone?' Sophy had gone pale.

'They likes your ankles.'

Jack was as good as his word and a heavy parcel arrived for her, full of books. Classics. Light stuff. Poetry, even. 'These will keep you out of mischief,' Jack had scrawled on a piece of War Office memorandum paper.

'Hope 'ee doesn't get another of these too soon-like,' said the postman, presenting Sam Pearmain with the package. The postman only called once a week, walked four miles across the fields where she and Arthur had walked to the river. The nearest town, fifteen miles away, was Barnstaple.

'We go there to market, you oughta come. Rare fun,' said Arthur, winking as if at a rude joke. Sophy had a garish vision of country orgies. She did have to go to the market one Friday, mounted with Elsie and baskets full of apples, in the pony trap. Sophy had toothache and needed to see the dentist. The market was disappointing; the most wicked thing she spotted was a man selling bottles of pink medicine and shouting through a megaphone 'for women's diseases, every one of 'em.'

Soon after Sophy's arrival in Devonshire, the Battle of Britain started. And by the time the baby was born in a cottage hospital in Barnstaple, the battle was in the past, fought and won. Her son was a stout little fellow, weighing over nine pounds.

Sophy had been put into a side ward, the name for a small room shared with only one other patient, a young woman called Joan, who was sociable and happy as a lark. She had been an actress before she married. 'It was a thrill, you know, but it's all over now!' She retained the actor's liveliness and generosity and Sophy knew she was lucky to have Joan as her companion.

The day after the baby's birth Jack was due to arrive. He sent her a telegram of congratulation and the time of his train.

Joan, who knew when Sophy's brother was expected, tactfully decided to go and call on the girl who had had her baby, also a daughter, on the same day as herself. 'We'll compare notes. Always fascinating,' said Joan, now allowed up and tying the belt of her dressing gown. Sophy lay and watched the clock. When at last the door opened and Jack came into the room, broad-shouldered and dark-suited and as familiar as her reflection in the glass, she started to cry. He came over and put a large bunch of red roses on her bed. They were out of season, scentless, and very expensive. It was unlike Jack to produce a bouquet. He stood beside her and took her hand.

'A son, eh?'

'Yes,' sniffed Sophy.

'Over there, is he?' He glanced towards a basket cot placed on Sophy's side of the little room.

'Yes. He's fat. Have a look.'

Jack went over to peer briefly at a scrap muffled in a shawl. A minute face the colour of a white rose faintly flushed with pink, appeared at the top of the bundle. Jack was relieved the child was asleep. He had expected wails.

'Nice little chap. Looks like me.'

'I thought so too.'

He sat down on a hospital chair pulled close to her bed. He took off his glasses, polished and replaced them. He looked very slightly embarrassed.

'How was it?'

Sophy mopped her eyes. Everything at present made her laugh or cry. She felt undefended. Where was the cloak which had kept her safe? Joan said the tears were par for the course. 'Everybody *howls*.' – She already had two children – 'The hospital people expect it. "Ah" they say, "it's her crying day".'

It was Sophy's crying week.

'It wasn't bad,' she said. 'he only took six hours to come, and when he did, it was quite quick.'

He nodded, without the interest of a father or a lover. He was thinking, instead, that the radiance had returned to his sister. It was a marvel. Her skin looked as if it were lit from beneath; she glowed. Her eyelids were the colour of pale violets, her dark red hair rich as a mop of coloured silk.

'And I suppose,' he said carefully, 'you feel all maternal.'

'Ought I to?' said Sophy.

11

Jack returned to London and Sophy remained in hospital for a full two weeks. The hospital was small but competent, there were a number of young nurses and Sophy was popular. The nurses spoiled her and so did Joan, who finally went home, kissing Sophy an actressy goodbye and bearing away a handsome baby girl called Caroline. 'My springtime Caroline,' crooned Joan to her husband. No new patient came to sleep in Joan's bed or talk about children, the theatre, the war, husbands (Sophy had found herself talking about Daniel) or the awfulness of hospital food. It was boring when Sophy was alone and she was pleased, on her final afternoon at the hospital, when the doctor came in to speak to her. He was tall, and as redheaded as she was: there was a sort of bond there.

He sat familiarly on her bed, eating one of the grapes Jack had arranged to be sent from the only expensive fruit shop in Barnstaple.

'And how are you today, Mrs Vergé?'

It was still very odd to Sophy to hear the name that she and Jack had decided upon. 'After all, you're a *French* widow, so why not?' Jack had said. The Pearmains had never used it. They had called her 'Missus'.

Sophy muttered to the doctor that she was fine and he said good, good, and this grape was delicious.

'I must be eating half a crown,' he said. 'That bunch cost all of five quid.' She pushed the white grapes towards him, smiling and saying, 'Then have five shillings.'

'No, I mustn't steal any more from my patient.'

He dropped his facetious manner. His freckled face became serious. 'There is something I want to say to you, Mrs Vergé. About David.'

She had given the thriving little boy a first name which was the nearest she could get to 'Daniel'.

Sophy fidgeted. She was aware that there was something lacking in her attitude towards the baby. Of course he was a dear little thing, good as gold, the nurses said. He did have a faint look of her brother, something in the shape of his round head. But his nose and the dark unwinking eyes looking up at her sometimes were Daniel's. When Joan had shared her room, Sophy found it hard to behave as she realized a young woman would do with a new baby. Somehow she did not want to try.

'Your brother telephoned the other evening. He was enquiring about the procedures for adoption,' said the doctor. 'I must confess, I was surprised.'

Jack had spoken to her about that when he had been with her. Sophy had nodded and said nothing. She found, since then, that she could not make up her mind about the fate of the little scrap rolled like a parcel in a knitted shawl. But she had a curious premonition, like a warning bell, that the decision had been made. Her brother had not forced the issue by the weight of a feather; he had only spoken of it in a practical what-do-you-think way. But she knew he wanted it for her. What he hadn't said, what they both knew, was that a girl with a baby and no husband was a girl chained by the leg.

'Yes?' said Sophy, breaking the profound silence between herself and the doctor. It was cold and grey that afternoon. The room had a gas fire which he bent down to light. It popped and began to roar. He returned to the bed.

'So it is not only Mr Hayward's idea. I had thought perhaps –'

'My brother only wants what's best for me,' said Sophy, unaware of the barbarous simplicity. She did not add 'and so do I.'

The doctor said nothing. He had come into the room to persuade the enigmatic young woman to keep her child. There were mysteries about her. Unlike the nurses, sentimental one and all, he did not accept young Mrs Vergé as the sad brave widow of a dead soldier. He thought her beautiful and odd and nothing else. When the brother in London telephoned to ask his advice on what Doctor Scotney thought the appalling question of finding somebody to adopt the baby, he'd been genuinely shocked.

'I know your circumstances, Mrs Vergé, and they are tragic. As are those of many young women in wartime. But isn't that the very reason you will want to keep your little boy? He is your inheritance. Your husband's son. A reason to live for,' he added, aware of the unsuitable phrase. He'd never seen a woman look more alive.

Sophy said nothing. She looked down at her hands on which the cheap ring shone. Suddenly she longed to be free. Free of the baby who wanted milk, and attention, and milk, and anxiety, every hour of the day. Free of Daniel whose face was reflected in miniature in the tiny child crossly screwing his cheeks into a grimace, or howling, or sleeping with heart-rending quiet like a rosebud, like a baby. She wanted to be twenty again. Not riven with jealousy or screaming with anger. Not rushing at a man who has made her look a fool and grappling with him in a deserted garden and thrown into a hedge of thorns. Not hungry and dirty on a road of nightmares. Not an enemy where you'd been a friend. And not, oh most of all not, a crooning mother with a small being totally dependent upon her. The nine pound weight of the child seemed a ton.

'I don't think I shall keep him, Doctor,' she said with a bright dark look. 'My brother and I both think adoption would be best.'

Doctor Scotney did not get up and walk out. He sat looking pensively towards the basket cot. The baby snuffled.

'You will regret it one day. Women always do.'

'Not this one,' said Sophy with the same smile.

Jack fetched her from the hospital and they stayed one

final night at the farm. Elsie and Sam Pearmain were less than their usual selves with Jack. The young woman who had been living with them was Londonish, with her smart clothes and drawling voice but they were used to her. She'd been like some unusual animal, a white antelope, say, who had strayed among their flocks and become tame, eating from their hands. She had sat at their table and enjoyed Elsie's food and been nice to Arthur who'd had the cheek to tease her. She was all right. And paid well.

The brother was another matter; an impressive stranger whose city clothes were as unfamiliar and bothering as his polished shoes. Sam asked about the blitz.

'Oh. Nothing much. A few bangs here and there,' said Jack.

The Pearmains stared at him in silence. Sam made a second effort at conversation and this time succeeded; the two men began to talk politics and Sam looked less awkward during the meal of yeast cakes and cocoa and cold apple tart. He laughed loudly over one of Jack's jokes as he would have done with the farm hands. Constraint had disappeared. But not with Elsie, who looked at Jack sidelong. Sophy was sure she would be glad when he had gone.

It had been very different when Sophy had arrived this evening with the baby; Elsie had run out of the kitchen the moment she heard the taxi drawing up in the yard, wiping her hands on her apron. Smiling, eager, she took the snowy bundle from Sophy's awkward arms.

'Isn't he just the treasure? Isn't he just the jewel?' Her tones were just like the ones Joan had used for her Caroline.

Farmers kept early hours, and after supper Jack smoked a pipe and then Elsie showed him up to a bedroom much like his sister's, with a double brass bed and china patterned with violets.

'Very comfortable. Many thanks,' said Jack. His embarrassed hostess hurried away.

The baby was in Sophy's room in an old cot which had once contained the infant Arthur. At two in the morning he woke with piercing screams. Sophy got up and stood looking down helplessly at the angry scrap of humanity. The nurses had impressed on her that the baby must never, never be fed except at strict times: six in the morning, ten, two in the afternoon, six, and again ten. Every four hours by the clock. 'If you feed him at extra times you'll make a misery for yourself. He has got to learn,' they said.

Sophy changed his nappy. He went on screaming. It was an awful noise, not loud but penetrating and she sat by candlelight, there was no electricity in the farm, wondering what the hell to do now, when the door opened. Elsie, in white cambric nightdress buttoned to the neck, her hair in a plait and carrying a candlestick, appeared. She looked like a Victorian ghost. Placing the candle on the dressing table she picked up the child who stopped for one blessed moment, moving his small head to and fro searching for milk in the buttoned bosom.

'Feed him, the lambkin,' said Elsie, handing the angry scrap to his mother.

'But the nurses said I mustn't.'

'They know nothing about it. Feed the lamb, he's hungry. Can't you hear it? He's a big boy, the jewel, he needs lots of food. He's telling us so.'

Sophy pushed the lace and satin nightgown from her shoulders and put the child to suck. He was greedy, making golloping noises and pressing her swollen breast with tiny hands. Elsie stood watching, a smile purely beautiful on her worn face.

In London, Jack took his sister to stay at the Hyde Park Hotel where she was waited on hand and foot and so much done for the baby that, apart from feeding him, Sophy did not lift a finger. The next morning she and her brother, the baby was on her lap, had coffee in the lounge.

'Well? All set?' said Jack. 'Feel okay, do you?'

'I suppose so.'

'Right, then let's go.'

They walked down Sloane Street and into Belgrave Square, to an imposing house which was the office of the Royal Marlborough Adoption Society (established 1879) as it announced in gold letters over the fanlight. Sophy and Jack were shown into an office made dark by the usual criss-cross strips of brown paper on the windows. Shelves climbed to the ceiling crammed with box files. A man with a lined face and sleek grey hair stood up as they entered, shook hands, nodded to Jack whom he had already met and asked them to be seated.

'This is the child?' he said, scarcely glancing at the baby who was snuffling, preparatory to a howl or two.

'My sister's son,' said Jack. He did not indicate that the question was pretty stupid.

'Sixteen days old,' said Sophy in a thin voice.

She had begun to tremble.

The man introduced himself as John Strickland, wrote down David's age and Sophy's details and then asked, in a colourless voice, if Sophy had carefully considered the step she intended to take.

'You understand you are giving up any legal claim to the little boy?'

He explained that for the next three months it was possible for her to change her mind. But that would be regrettable; there were already putative parents lined up.

The enormity of what she was about to do came over her, as it hadn't done earlier today or in the hospital or at any time until this actual moment. Now it was real. She looked at the small creature in her arms. He was making a grimace, his minute brow frowning. Daniel. Daniel in miniature, a bud which would grow and flower and repeat her lover's beauty and perhaps his malice too. If she kept this little thing she retained a physical part of Daniel. All he'd given her. So much. And nothing. She stared fixedly at the baby. Jack rubbed his chin. Strickland clasped his hands. The two men waited.

'Why not take a week or two –' began Strickland as the pause was lengthened.

'No, oh no!' exclaimed Sophy with sudden vehemence. 'I've decided. He'll be best with people who want him.'

She did not notice what she'd said.

'Very well. If you are quite certain.'

Strickland stood up and put out his arms and took the baby with a neat practised gesture. He was unperturbed when David began to cry.

'I fed him just now –' began Sophy.

'Oh, it's wind. We have bottles of gripe water,' said Stickland, frostily smiling.

Jack didn't say a word when they walked out into the grey wartime street of a February morning. Sophy felt extraordinary. She had walked into the building with her baby and came out with empty arms. It was a sin.

'We'll go back to the hotel and collect our bags,' said Jack, padding beside her. He sounded perfectly relaxed.

'Are you sure he'll be all right? Do you know *anything* about the people he is going to? I just – just handed him over like a bundle of rubbish!'

She was shaken, distraught, she felt like a murderer.

The radiance which followed childbirth had deserted her, throwing her contemptuously aside as if deciding she had no right to its after-beauty.

Her brother stopped walking, turned to her and said with no emphasis, 'Not too late to go back.' She didn't seem to hear him.

'He told me nothing about them, what will happen to him, *who are they*?'

Jack had been expecting the storm and here it was. His instinct was to take her in his arms but what was more dangerous than sympathy? It would weaken her, cloud her judgement, throw her to the mercy of unfeeling Nature. The only course was cruel practicality.

'Sophy. The Marlborough is one of the most respected adoption societies in England. The committee are all distinguished people and the adoption rules are very tough. You should just see the official stuff that has to be gone through before people are allowed to adopt. It's taken very very seriously. That's not what we're talking about, is it? What I'm saying is that it's not too late for us to go back.'

He meant it.

She stood stock still. He looked at her with compassion and a chill at the heart.

'No, I don't want to go back. I hate myself, but I can't keep him.'

How pinched her face was.

He said nothing as they began to walk again. After a time he tucked her arm into his.

'Cheer up,' he said rallying her, 'think of the people who will be allowed to have the little chap. They're going to be happy.'

'I shan't be.'

She couldn't have it both ways. But all he said was, 'What you need is a glass of something.' It was Jack's panacea; before the war it had been champagne.

He gave her three days, a short enough time for recovery before he said she must be in touch with their parents. He treated her gingerly but not tenderly. Reflecting over what had been done, Jack realized he could know nothing about its results, neither on the child whose destiny had been taken over by experts, nor on the mother. Had it been an amputation? Would his sister, so to speak, walk with a limp or wear an empty sleeve for the rest of her life? Was it a wound which healing healthily, would leave an interesting silvery scar, or would it fester? He loved her deeply and thought her a burden he would be glad to take off his back. He wanted her to be the way she used to be, radiant and frivolous and scintillating and utterly different from himself. He set himself to coax back into her drawn face the youth which must still exist there.

They dined in underground restaurants whose entrances were concealed between mountains of sandbags. They met for drinks at posh officer-filled hotels. They visited expensive shops where Jack, who seemed to have supplies of coupons, bought her new clothes. They enjoyed themselves. Or that was what he hoped.

Jack did not dance, he never had, and a number of times at Hatchettes or the Mirabelle, a young man in uniform would come to the table and ask Sophy tentatively if she would dance. When she hesitated, Jack said encouragingly, 'Go along. Tread the light fantastic. Show me how it's done.'

The young man, whoever he might be, looked delighted at winning such a prize even for one short dance. When they danced on the small crowded floor, he asked if she would see him again, perhaps next day – his first – his last – on leave? Would she meet him for a drink, for lunch, for dinner, for a theatre? She had six such invitations, and in the eyes of her partners was that look, of men who thought Sophy the dream they'd never hoped to find during their short soon-finished leaves spent in a strange wartime city.

Sophy told them she was going to the country. She was sorry they could not meet again. She smiled at them. Their admiration suited her just then: it was like putting on diamonds.

On the final evening, when brother and sister were dining at a restaurant in Knightsbridge, a small dark woman crossed the room to speak to Jack.

'There you are at last, I keep ringing. Where have you hidden yourself lately? I have been,' said the woman with a smile at Jack and a look like a stab-wound at Sophy, 'desperate.'

Jack stood up and introduced her.

'Hélène, this is my sister Sophy who is staying with me for a day or two. I'm sorry I haven't been in touch. I will ring tomorrow and we'll make a date.'

Hélène, dressed in severe black and surrounded by a heavy exotic perfume, then concentrated entirely on Jack, her manner positively sexy. So was his. Sophy was sure they were in the middle of an affair. In the taxi on the way home, Sophy asked him if she was right. He gave a chuckle.

'Enough said.'

'Oh, am I not to be allowed –'

'No, you are not and you're too clever by half.'

The sirens were wailing as they walked home in the dark but there was no sound of gunfire, no scream of bombs, and they went into the house in Halsey Street in silence. The night was cold and Jack lit the gas fire. He heated Sophy a little powdered milk mixed with water and poured himself a Scotch. They sat down.

'Tomorrow's your big day. You'll telephone Pansy in the morning,' he said. 'Got the story pat?'

'Do you want me to say it over to you?'

'Not really. As long as you have it straight.'

'Escaped from Paris to the Midi. Awful journey. Met Violette. Dufours wanted to get rid of me so Violette put me up in her apartment in Beaulieu,' gabbled Sophy. 'There for months, filthy food and had to lie low. Violette finally managed to find a boat going round the coast (which is what happened, only it was Paul). Eventually got to Spain and so on, then the cargo boat to Southampton and I was seasick. True. That bit's easy. Then I was at Victoria and couldn't get through to the parents on the telephone ... incidentally, why couldn't I?'

'Telephone lines down.'

'Were they?'

'Shouldn't think so. Go on.'

'So I couldn't get them and rang you.'

'That'll fill the bill. Don't bother with details. Pansy won't take them in and Father won't ask.'

'I'll remember.'

Sophy was sitting on the carpet by the gas fire. She was steadily losing weight and tonight had managed to squeeze herself into a pre-war evening dress of vivid blue taffeta with an enormous skirt which fell in a circle all round her. She was quiet.

Jack was thinking about Hélène. There was something alluring about her. Hungarian? Rumanian? He always forgot which. Very passionate, foreign women. Surprising in bed too.

He turned his thoughts and his eyes on his sister. He noticed that her bloom had returned, her hair was a kind of aureole round the pale radiant face. He marvelled, not for the first time, at the resilience of the very young.

'There's one name we haven't mentioned much since you hove into view, Sophy. Apart from a letter I asked you to write which I popped into the Diplomatic Bag.'

'Bob Lingard.'

'Why the surname? Is he a stranger now?'

'I'm sure I am to him. Have you told him I'm back?'

'Don't be sillier than you can help. What would I do that for? Tomorrow morning when you telephone Pansy —'

He gave a deliberate pause. Then, 'Why don't you ring Bob as well?'

'*Bob!* But where is he?'

'Happens to be on leave in London. Rang me a day or two ago. Putting up at the In and Out Club.'

She looked at her brother with mixed feelings. He might understand her, she certainly did not fathom him.

'You don't half play God,' she said.

He looked bland; his round swarthy face gave nothing away, he reminded her of Strickland at the adoption society. Men don't show their feelings, she thought. No, that is not right. Some men don't. She remembered Daniel blazing with rage, heavy with sex, comic, teasing, attentive, unkind.

'Yes, you play the Almighty,' she said, as if he had spoken to deny it. 'You sent me money in France, and if you hadn't what would have happened to me? Father didn't help. You found the Pearmains where I could hide until the baby came. You took me to the Marlborough —' She gave an involuntary shudder which he did not miss. 'And now,' she added a little wildly, 'you're throwing me at Bob.'

'Who said anything about throwing anybody? All I said was why not have a word with the chap.' He repeated a favourite phrase with all its undertow. 'Don't have to make up your mind yet, do you?'

That night Sophy slept as she had not done since the baby was born, deeply and without dreams. No wails woke her. No tiny creature angrily needed her, mystifying her with its anguished fury, its small mottled face. She slept on until after eight in the morning, when her brother, black hair in spikes and silk dressing gown in a thousand creases, came in with a cup of strong tea.

'Get it over, Pansy's always up with the lark. She'll have finished breakfast by now.'

Sophy swallowed the tea, shook herself like a dog and went barefoot and chilled in her thin nightdress to the sitting room telephone.

Hearing her daughter's voice, Pansy Hayward sounded hoarse. Oh, was it really Sophy? Was she actually in England? How she had worried, how her father had worried (Sophy discounted that). Pansy stammered and now and again her words were jumbled: she sounded as if she found it difficult to talk. Sophy parried the questions, was bright and steady and explained that Jack was bringing her to Sussex and she was so longing to see them!

Jack, who had been running his bath, came into the room as she put down the telephone. He had heard every word.

'Not bad. Crikey, woman, you'll catch your death. Have my bath, I'll have one tonight at home. And smarten yourself up. Then you can ring Bob.'

'I haven't decided if I want –'

'Give the guy a chance, Sophy. You treated him damned badly. You owe him a bit of good behaviour.'

Sophy, in no frame of mind for home truths, flounced into the bathroom to have a lukewarm bath which made her colder. The discomfort caused her to hurry, and by the time she had dressed in a new turquoise sweater bought for her by Jack who had produced yet more ill-gotten coupons, she felt better. Jack was late. He finished his breakfast standing up and was pulling on an ancient Savile Row overcoat made for him ten years ago.

'You're the sort of man who should have a valet,' Sophy said, fetching a clothes brush from a hook in the hall. She brushed him vigorously; he stood like a dog, liking it.

'I'll be back by four. Plenty of time for the train. Well?'

'Well?' she countered.

'What about Bob?'

'I suppose I could ring. After you've gone.'

'Mind you do.'

Taking his South African walking stick, a kind of knob-kerrie with a weighted handle, he left the house. Sophy sat down by the telephone, crossed her arms and hugged herself

291

with cold. Jack was gone and with him his electric charge, his concern which was not only from affection but from the rule book of doing the decent thing. Without his presence she looked her destiny in the face.

What a mess I've made of my life, she thought. Is that why I feel so sad? She looked back to the spoilt girl of less than two years ago, flirting and playing in Cannes and further back still to the girl who had accepted Bob Lingard because he adored her, the reason she had given to herself and once in a fit of honesty to her brother.

I'm second hand now. Made love to by Daniel. Made pregnant by Daniel. No, I'm fifth hand if you count that awful journey across France, and turning into a bedraggled refugee practically thrown into the gutter by the Dufours. Now what? I had a baby and gave it away. What sort of woman does that? She knew it had been practical; paradoxically there might even be a certain rightness in giving her baby to people who would adore him; guiltily, realistically, she knew that *she* did not. She had been afraid, she hadn't faced up to anything, she had hidden behind Jack whose shoulders were broad enough. But somehow, although he had accepted her terror, the very facts would not allow him to take it on himself. She had been afraid of what would happen to her, afraid of the impossible position of a girl with a bastard child. Apart from Jack, who cared a farthing what happened to her? That was not true now but it would have been. If her parents had known she'd borne a child out of wedlock they would have been so disgusted they would never see her again. That was how people were who had been born in the 1880s. Adamant. She knew how her father would have behaved, how her mother would have capitulated. Her mother was like Anne-Marie.

And then her thoughts went not to Daniel who haunted her like a malevolent ghost but to Bob Lingard. She had scarcely been conscious of Bob for months, apart from the duty letter Jack had forced her to write. She had treated his love disgracefully, she had been hideously selfish and irresponsible and had not given her own heartlessness a glance. She had only thought affectionately of Bob and been concerned for him once in all the time she was in France; that had been when Jack wrote to tell her Bob had been nearly drowned at sea. Yet Sophy did not see Bob in her mind in wartime but in peace. She remembered an English time of tennis parties and long shadows on the grass and blackbirds whistling and deck chairs in which they sat talking about a game when Bob beat her father, 'but only' added her father, joining them, '6–4 and 6–3'. She remembered the Sussex moonlight and the beech trees, and the empty roads and holding hands in cinemas. Once they had walked on the shingle at Brighton and listened to the sea and he had called her Funny Face.

'Am I funny, then?'

'Of course. And I worship you.'

She went to the telephone, dialled the number of the club and asked for Lieutenant Robert Lingard.

'We have a Commander Robert Lingard, Madam,' said a polite porter.

'Oh. That's him. Yes, I'm sure it is.'

Bob had risen higher and she hadn't known.

The porter said he would see if the commander was in the club at present. Sophy fiddled with a pencil, making her mind blank. This is something I am not going to rehearse, she thought.

'Hello,' said a man's voice, 'Lingard speaking.'

'It's Sophy.'

There was a pause like a thunderclap.

'*Who?*'

'Sophy. Have you forgotten me? I wouldn't blame you if you had ...'

'*Where are you?*'

'In Jack's lodgings. Halsey Street, off Sloane Street.'

'But –'

'I can't tell you the whole rigmarole. I only just got back to England and we're going home to Sussex this afternoon ... I just wondered ...'

'Can I see you?' he interrupted. 'Now?'

She refused to let him 'come in a cab at once' to Halsey

Street but said she would be with him in half an hour. He was insistent that she should make it less and Sophy's heart, bruised, confused, lifted a little.

When he had rung off, after saying twice 'Sophy!', she spent some time dressing, choosing the things she liked best, a heathery-coloured suit, a lilac-coloured blouse. She put on some scent, looked at herself dubiously, pinched her pale cheeks and went out to look for a taxi.

There was little traffic that morning except buses looming up out of the mist. She was at the In and Out Club sooner than she wanted to be. It was absurd, but she was painfully nervous.

She was getting out of the cab at the club entrance and opening her purse when a voice said, 'I'll do that.'

Bob had been watching and waiting. He came out with money already in his hand, paid the taxi and put an arm round her shoulders. He looked handsome in the dark uniform, rings on his sleeve. Taking her indoors, he turned her round and held her at arm's length.

'Sophy,' he said, as if her name were a kind of spell.

'Bob.'

He was so thin. He looked older. Tougher. But he had the same smile, as if they shared a secret joke.

'I can't believe it,' he said in a voice as practical as Jack's. 'I simply can't believe it. Come inside. Your teeth are chattering with cold.' He laughed as if it was very funny.

They went into a big old-fashioned pompous room with a Turkish carpet and leather-covered chairs and tables for drinks. He led her to a corner at its far end where there wasn't a soul. They sat down and continued to stare at each other.

'Well,' he finally said, 'you've given us all a high old time. Not a word for months and months until that letter which came in the Diplomatic Bag – how did you manage that? And it told me nothing. I used to ring Jack now and then. Even he began to think you had bought it.'

'Did you go into mourning?' There was a note of teasing in her voice. His manner, appearance, the uniform even, gave her a feeling of safety.

'I suppose you wish I had,' he said in her own tone, waving to a waiter and ordering coffee. He muttered 'It's pretty foul but at least it is hot.'

He continued to take her in, looking her up and down. Once he picked up the hand on which his engagement ring shone. Sophy had put it on this morning. It had been in her money belt for a year.

Coffee came, and Sophy told him, as briefly as she could, the story Jack had prepared for her parents. The exodus from Paris. Violette. Her sojourn at Beaulieu. The getting to Spain and thence to England. She gave details when they were true, and when they were invented went at them without anything but a few facts, adding her feelings. 'I was so bored.' 'We had almost no food, it all went to the Germans.' 'I wasn't frightened to start with but later, yes, I was scared.'

He listened, now and again narrowing his eyes.

When she stopped talking he said, as Jack had done, 'You've had some luck, Sophy.'

'So have you. Picked up from the sea.'

'That was ages ago.'

'And now?'

She had noticed a ribbon on the breast of his tunic and touched it with one finger.

'Is it the DSC?'

Bob laughed slightly, 'They have to give it to somebody.'

A pause.

He picked up the coffee pot and poured out. His short fair hair fell in a brief lock across his forehead. Daniel's hair used to do the same thing but it was longer, and black as ink.

'Sophy ... is it ...' He stopped as if it was impossible to go on. She did not help him out. He reached for her hand.

'Is it still on with us?'

'Yes, please,' said Sophy, and, feeling her hand trembling, he shut his eyes.

PART THREE

12

The last entry ended halfway down the page, followed by a long series of loops of the kind Roz had seen under the signature of the first Queen Elizabeth. It was as if the writer had decided that was that. No more to be said.

Roz turned back, looking through the handwritten pages, examining newspaper cuttings so old that they had turned yellow as if they had been burned. Pictures of tanks; of carts full of refugees, of people wheeling loaded bicycles. Earlier there had been theatre ticket stubs and once a picture cut from a glossy magazine. Underneath it in Sophy's bold writing were the words, 'Me in the *Tatler*!' Roz saw a girl, faintly recognizable as Sophy, sitting on a flight of stairs in film-starrish white satin, with flowers in her hair. She was with a good-looking young man in evening dress. Other couples sat nearby; the curious thing to Roz was how alike everybody looked. Perhaps it was their clothes. Or was it the bland smiles?

Fuchsia Cottage was quiet. The sun came in through a window Roz had forgotten to open, the room was getting hot and it was dusty. She must have been sitting here for hours. She stood up and stretched, half grinning to herself. She felt like a detective who, by chance not by skill, discovers the perfect clue: a footprint in the soil which shows the ribs of a shoe, a finger-print of which police-dust reveals every curve and circle. How satisfactory to know so much about her grandmother. And wouldn't she see her now in a completely different light?

If I manage to see her at all, thought Roz.

Her neck ached from bending over the diaries. She yawned and blinked, collected the books together and replaced them in date order. Then she went downstairs. Her great uncle would be home soon. How was she going to persuade him to tell here where Sophy had gone? Christ, thought Roz, he's a secret man.

Thinking over all she'd learned this afternoon she realized how important Sophy's brother had been to her. He was the one she'd turned to in the past – and it was clear she'd done the same thing recently. Roz was appalled at the fact that Sophy had actually given up her child; it was the first time she had known her grandmother do anything that truly shocked her. What was so difficult about keeping a baby? The child only needed food and a bit of love. Her great uncle had always been there to help his sister. He would have helped if she'd kept the little boy, he would have found some way of working things out, thought Roz vaguely. It was terrible to hand a child over to strangers. I love Gran but she had no conscience, thought Roz.

She herself knew at least three girls who were so-called one-parent families. There were allowances and things and the girls managed to get jobs and look after their babies as well; they were proud of them. That last war, about which Roz had been reading for hours, was ancient history, but surely heaps of women had kept their illegitimate children. Roz felt little pity for her grandmother. She judged Sophy to have been gravely, almost unforgiveably wrong.

She went into the garden and sat down under a crab-apple tree, thinking – why shouldn't I tell him all I found out this afternoon? That'll shake him. Then he'll have to spill the beans now I know so much.

She felt optimistic again. Losing her grandmother had made a jagged hole in her life. She hadn't known until Sophy was gone how much she needed her.

The afternoon was waning when she finally heard her great

uncle's car turning into the drive. She darted along the terrace calling cheerfully, 'Hi there.'

Jack was busy locking the car against the impossible event of anybody walking by and deciding to steal it. Roz couldn't imagine a thief giving it a second look: it was at least ten or twelve years old. He turned when he heard her and blinked through thick spectacles.

'You still here?'

'I thought I would make you some tea.'

'Just had some.' He did not bother to conceal that he'd hoped she would be gone. He walked into the house without saying anything more and Roz followed him into the kitchen where she ostentatiously filled the electric kettle. He went to find a biscuit tin, took out a digestive biscuit, did not offer her one, and began to chew it. He left the kitchen, went into the sitting room and shut the door.

Roz made herself some tea. She did not make an extra cup for the disagreeable old man who wanted to get rid of her. She helped herself to some of the biscuits and carried the tray into the sitting room. Installed in his high-backed chair he looked over the top of *The Times* at her and then continued to read.

She drank her tea in silence. She was thinking about Sophy whose photograph, taken years ago, sitting on the grass in Jack's garden, was in an elaborate silver frame on a side table. There were no other photographs in the room. Is he one of those men who has a thing about his sister? thought Roz. It happens. In the diaries Gran said he'd had affairs, but that could have been wishful thinking. Perhaps he always had a crush on Sophy and didn't even know it himself. People in those days weren't as sex conscious as we are, thought Roz. Of course they must have been sexy ... though it's difficult to imagine. She stole a look at her great uncle, who had apparently ceased to fear she was going to talk and had lowered his newspaper. It's difficult to imagine him in bed with anybody.

Was he ever attractive? I'm sure Sophy was. I keep thinking of her now as Sophy.

She compared the girl in the diaries to the woman she knew, matching the voice of the past, passionate or angry, lighthearted or self-justifying, with her grandmother's mixture of sophistication and a kind of girlish enthusiasm. Yes. It was the same person, although the years had blurred her and chalked her with grey. It was difficult, even now, to take in the fact that Sophy had borne an illegitimate child. He would be Roz's own uncle, wouldn't he? Roz wondered what happened to that baby left at the adoption society years ago. Now he must be quite old! Did Sophy think about him sometimes? How peculiar it must be to know that somewhere there was a grown man who was your own flesh and blood.

Roz twisted her hair round her finger, missing Sophy more than ever now that she saw her against the painted background of the past. She wanted to talk to her, hug her, accuse her, hungrily demand why she had gone. And why wouldn't Uncle Jack tell her? It was infuriating. He reminded her of an old tortoise disappearing into its shell.

'Finished your tea? What about a sherry to brighten you up?' he suddenly said, as if remembering a host's duties.

Roz disliked sherry but accepted with what she hoped was a delighted smile. He nodded, faintly pleased, and went to a curved wall cupboard set in a corner, opened it and plunged his head inside, pouring out two drinks. The back of Jack, his heavy shoulders and old-fashioned grey hair worn in the same style as when he was young, straight back and oiled, touched her. She did not want to be moved by the sight of that stolid back, by the effect of that stolid silence, but she was. How can I blurt out what I discovered from being plain nosey? she thought. If I was him, I wouldn't want my great niece to know any of it. I'll only offend him. Damn it, I can't do it. She could just imagine the expression on that unforgiving face if she crudely told him she had been upstairs all the afternoon poking about and had 'just happened to find Gran's diaries'.

'Oh?' he'd say.

'Well. They weren't locked up, were they?'

There would be a silence.

'I didn't imagine anybody would read private papers,' he'd say. 'What are you? A private eye?'

Jack never liked me, she thought, and this would put the kibosh on it. He'll get his knife into me. And any chance in the world of finding Gran will be out of the window. Anger and hurt came flooding back. How could Gran leave me? How could she?

Putting out a pale twenty-year-old hand for the drink which was given to her by a thick paw freckled with age, she thanked him. She noticed his watch for the first time. It was gold, with Roman numerals, and very old-fashioned. She vaguely remembered Sophy had said it had belonged to his father who had worn it all through the Great War.

'Great Uncle –'

For the first time he smiled. He looked different when that happened. The dark eyes behind thick glasses twinkled.

'Be damned to that for a name. Sounds silly, doesn't it?'

'Is Uncle Jack any better?'

'A bit. Drink your drink. You look white in the face. What've you been doing with yourself all afternoon? Thought you were hurrying back to London?'

She took time to sip the sherry which was as dry as a Bath Oliver. He drank his whisky with relish, and returned to the drinks cupboard to prepare himself a second one. Roz watched him walking back to his chair; he was pigeon-toed, she'd never noticed it before. He fell more than sat down again.

'Don't expect you've hung about for the sake of my beautiful eyes,' he remarked. Roz had no idea what he meant and her face showed her thoughts like a mirror. He smiled a second time.

'Don't expect,' he translated, 'you stayed for my company, mm?'

'I'm glad to be here,' she said politely. Then in a rush. 'Uncle Jack, I do wish you'd change your mind!'

'What about?'

'You know very well.'

'No, I don't,' he said, the smile vanishing as if he'd taken a duster and wiped it away. He drank up and set down the empty glass.

'I mean I wish you'd change your mind over whatever reason you've got for keeping Gran's whereabouts a secret. Honestly, it is a bit hard. I really do want to know.'

'So I gather.'

She leaned forward, fixing him with her appealing eyes and looking, he thought with a spasm of the heart, too like Sophy. She had his sister's trick of clasping her hands, Sophy's turn of the head, tone of voice. But nothing like his sister's charm, that was for sure.

'Uncle Jack,' repeated Roz, wondering if she had found a crack in his armour, 'please tell me what happened. Gran isn't ill, is she? I mean, some people hate it when they find that they are ill, and they crawl away –'

'I never heard such bosh,' he interrupted impatiently. 'I told you last night. Sophy is not ill. She is a very silly girl and she's gone off on her own and there is nothing to worry about. You understand?' he repeated, treating her as if she were a fool, both in his voice and expression. 'Nothing to make a song and dance about. The subject's closed.'

'But that's ludicrous!' she burst out, angry at the flat refusal, the unreason, even the look he now gave her which had in it both his strength and her helplessness. 'It was disgusting of Gran to disappear without telling me, and you're as bad as she is, refusing to help when you know how upset I am. What sort of people are you both? God! I wish I'd never come here.'

She jumped up. The old man gave her a look of interest as if to say, well now, will that make you go?

'Hell!' shouted Roz and rushed out, slamming the door.

He waited, rubbing his chin, until he heard the rev of her car engine. It backed out of the drive and a moment later drove noisily away up the hill.

He poured himself another drink.

Roz drove home fast and scarcely to the public safety. She was in a vile temper. Worse, she was frustrated; like her absent grandmother she was not used to being refused, she

302

had only a thin veneer of philosophy, and not getting her own way over something as important as this was a blow straight to the stomach. She was angry and she was miserable so she drove at eighty miles an hour. Her car would not oblige her by going any faster and it was lucky that there was a dearth of police cars that evening on the M4.

Back in Chiswick she parked in a side street and walked back to Bowling House, letting herself in and slamming the door as loudly as she had slammed her great uncle's. It was an evening to dream about. The daffodils were faded but there were daisies all over the lawn, just beginning to close. The river brimmed and sparkled. She went out into the garden and threw herself down on the grass, sitting hunched and looking at the old benevolent house.

I suppose, she thought with a bitterness rare in the young, Gran thought I'd be delighted to camp here in this big place and be able to run up accounts at the shops, and I'd fill the house with guys from University, and have the time of my life. Rock music day and night and not a penny to pay. Even the drink free. Is that what she thought? I bet she didn't think at all. She just buggered off and left me to it.

Reading Sophy's diaries had affected her. It had taken her into a life she'd scarcely imagined, told her things she never guessed; yet nothing she had learned made her want to forgive Sophy. She was cut to the heart because she was certain she was no longer loved. She had taken her grand-mother for granted as she took her own beauty and good health for granted. Try as she would she couldn't get used to her loss.

When she heard the telephone ringing through the open kitchen door, she sprang up in relief at getting away from her miserable thoughts. It will be Mary DuCann, asking if I managed to get any news. She'll guess I failed. She knows Uncle Jack better than I do.

The telephone was in the hall and she sat down on a huge old chest where the croquet mallets and balls were kept, and old broken tennis racquets which Sophy had not bothered to throw away.

303

'Hello?' said Roz, a query in her voice.

'Roz? It's Mike. I keep ringing. I thought you were supposed to be back this morning.'

'I'm here now.'

'And with no news. I can hear that in your voice.'

'Nothing.'

'You sound low. Can I come round?'

'I am and I wish you would.'

'I'm on my way.'

Apparently somebody did give a damn after all. Roz went to open the front door. She left it wide and returned to the garden.

Michael arrived sooner than she expected. He saw her from the kitchen door, came to her quickly, knelt down and touched her shoulder.

'Poor Roz. So you found out nothing from him.'

'I tried everything. I was polite and later I was rude. It didn't make a blind bit of difference. He's like a tortoise. He poked out his head and looked at me and then disappeared into his shell. It was all a waste of time. The thing is he *knows* where she is and for some reason she's asked him not to tell me. Or anybody else. Frankly, Mike, I think it is bloody of Gran. I asked and asked and he turned me down flat. He thinks that's the end of it and I'll shut up.'

'Isn't it? Won't you?'

'I don't mean to let it go.' She had no idea what she meant.

He had bought a bottle of wine, went to find a corkscrew and returned to the girl who did not stir from her refuge under the trees. She was wrapped in a kind of desolation. He poured two tea-cups of wine and handed her one.

'Gran would have a fit,' she said, 'I shouldn't imagine she's drunk wine from a tea cup in her life.'

'One of the old school.'

'I suppose she is, but somehow that doesn't sound like her, she isn't of any school. She does have a few corny old rules out of the Ark, of course. Like I mustn't have the milk bottle on the breakfast table. And she uses hankies, not tissues.'

They both laughed. She felt slightly better. She did like the

304

man beside her and he was certainly attractive, with his thick curling hair and expressive face. She was drawn to him because, in a way, he did not seem to give a damn about anything much – except perhaps herself. I suppose, as usual, it's sex with him, she thought. When isn't it? I'm not sure about me though. I don't want to think of sex just now, it is too difficult and too easy.

'I'd like to tell you something,' she said. 'The trouble is it's long, the story I mean. I'm sure it would bore you to listen.'

'Latin conjunction requiring the answer No. "No, of course it wouldn't bore me". "No, you never bore me". That sort of thing. Don't scowl. Of course I want to hear the tale, long or short. Tell on.'

Carelessly, the words which tumbled out retained much of Roz's own curiosity and surprise. She described the south of France before the war and during the phoney war, and how Sophy had fallen in love with Daniel Vergé 'who sounds a right bastard to me', and how her grandmother had landed up in Paris and had to escape. Once Michael said 'Christ!' when Roz described the refugees being bombed. Another time he exclaimed 'Oh, poor girl,' as if Sophy were somebody of their own age. Roz finally came to what she considered the disreputable part of the story, when Sophy had the child adopted.

He did not agree when she spoke contemptuously of that. All he said was 'Mm. You seem to have opened a good many cupboards and seen a lot of grinning skeletons. How many diaries were there?'

'Five, or was it six? I wish I'd nicked them. My great uncle would never have known, I don't expect he's been up to that back bedroom for yonks. There were all kinds of things I'd like to have shown you. Old photographs and yellowed newspaper cuttings, even an enormous bus ticket marked One Penny. She kept the diaries when she was in France too. I don't see how she managed, trekking down south, do you? I mean, wouldn't one ditch everything but a pair of shoes and clean pants and some cash?'

'Not sure. People hang on to their diaries like they hang on to their lives.'

They drank some more wine. A blackbird gave a rather heartless solo in one of the cherry trees.

'So now we know your grandmother's grisly secrets,' said Michael after a while.

'Not where she is, though. I've been thinking. Mightn't she have gone to France?'

'Why should she go there? You've got France on the brain. That guy's probably dead anyway. He'd be as old as God by now.'

Roz fell silent again and Michael leaned against the tree behind him, looking up at the layers and layers of thin spring leaves, the branches criss-crossed like people's fates, this one touching and interlacing, that one bending away to avoid contact with other branches. The blackbird started up again.

'You said you don't mean to let it go, Roz,' he prompted. The silence had been too long. Looking round he saw she had fallen asleep. She was collapsed on the grass, her head against her arm, half curled. She slept without a sound. It was getting late and he pulled off his sweater and laid it across her. Then returned to his place against the tree.

When she woke with a start it was quite dark, except for a band of light from the distant towpath.

'What's happened?' she stammered, scarcely conscious. She sat up and saw with intense relief that he was still there.

'Michael! How long have I been asleep?'

'Over two hours.'

'You're crazy, why didn't you wake me, what's the time?'

'Nearly nine. I hadn't the heart. You did look peaceful.'

'Was I dreaming? I don't remember. I'm so sorry, it must have been boring – why did you stay –'

She stretched out her hand, it was cold, and took his gratefully. He moved over and began to kiss her. She was still sleepy and a little sad, and his kisses were tender and she found she needed them. They comforted her in this lonely place where she used to be happy. He twined his arms round her and they lay back on the grass and in a little while, with growing passion, they began to make love.

Roz did not fall in love with Michael Chance as he believed she would. She indicated, rather than explained, the reason for this failure. She was exciting, passionate and she wanted him as much as he wanted her. But her mind was not connected to a love affair.

It should have been an idyll, their time together in the old and friendly house with the burgeoning spring outside, the Thames flooding and retreating, the total solitude. They woke in bed naked and relaxed. They had gypsy meals and walked down the towpath enjoying the whole river bit, as Michael called it. Roz took him into her life, her sadness. She flung her heartache into his lap generously enough, and he knew that to give another person your worries could be as good as offering them your joys. But to his dismay after the very first lovemaking he discovered *he* had fallen in love.

It disturbed him deeply to find himself at the mercy of this beautiful anxious girl. He wanted her too often, too hungrily; it was true she responded and their sex was as satisfying as either of them could wish. But he was in love and wanted more.

He was not fool enough to tell his love, but not sure that he was clever enough to hide it. Characteristically, he played for time. When he came downstairs in search of breakfast he found Sophy already up and wearing an old woman's cardigan over her nakedness. He told her she looked like a naughty postcard.

'Do I? Oh good. I've been going through Gran's cupboards again and found the cardi. But not a single clue.'

'One doesn't strike oil twice.'

He came up behind her and bent to kiss the nape of her neck where the fine hair spiralled in reddish tendrils. She leaned back against him, not like a lover, but with the animal pleasure of being touched, as a cat leans against your legs. She almost purred.

He helped himself to instant coffee, poured her a cup, made her some toast and buttered it. He behaved as if she were a child. Roz flickered into life.

'I suppose the trouble is I've had a shock,' she said in an invalid's voice.

'So you have.'

'I can't get over it.'

'Of course you can, when you make up your mind to accept there's nothing to be done,' he said sturdily. 'And nowhere to go from here.'

He wondered how she was going to take that. Not well. He said it just the same.

'It's not true that there's nothing to be done,' said Roz, eating the marmalade out of the pot with a spoon.

He looked at her suspiciously. She sounded quite optimistic.

'I've had a really good idea, Michael. I think –' a pause for effect. Yes, she did look bright. 'I think we ought to hire a detective.'

All he managed was a feeble, 'Do you?'

'Surely you see it's the answer, why didn't we think of it before? I am not going to sit down under this, I refuse to. Why should I have to go on being riven with worry about stupid old Gran? I only need to know where she is and we can find that out by spending a few quid. You do agree it's a brain-wave?'

She spoke in the voice of someone who demands approval.

He muttered that it might be a good idea. Roz looked happy for the first time since she had discovered that Bowling House was deserted. She was her funny sunny self for the rest of the morning.

By the time they had bathed and dressed the sun was high and the tide was out, showing yards of gleaming mud. In the diminished Thames a few ducks quacked and gobbled. They went for a walk along the towpath and after a while he reached for her hand. She held it warmly enough.

He was shocked at his own emotions. He felt as if she'd thrown him, not into that gentle shrunken river but into the tide at full rip. He wanted this girl. He wanted her sexually, imaginatively, completely, to own, to share, to blend, to blur, to be. He could think of nothing but her. Roz noticed that he was quiet, looked at him rather teasingly and said nothing.

When they came back to the house, they brought some bread and cheese with them and picnicked in the garden.

308

Then, saying nothing, they went indoors and Roz opened the windows of the sitting room to let in the soft spring air. He sat on the sofa watching her. He held out his arms and she came towards him quickly and lay down and nestled close. At first she only let him cuddle her. But later she was roused and as passionate and hungry as he was. They made love three times, sleeping at last, sated with sex. In the evening, in a giggling mood, they fetched the yellow book to see, declared Roz, 'if we can find a brilliant private detective'. She read out the first entry.

'"Private and Essentially Discreet. Staff of great experience. Service 24 hours." Cripes, aren't they allowed to go home? Poor things, at it day and night.'

'What about this one?' said Michael, leaning over. 'The drawing looks like Humphrey Bogart. Dark glasses too. Rates on Request. That means they decide how much they can take you for. One peek at Bowling House and they'll charge double.'

'We could meet them at a secret rendezvous.'

'Good idea. Here's another.'

They turned the pages, now and again bursting into peals of laughter. 'Oh do look!' exclaimed Roz, 'What about the No Stone Unturned International Investigators. Missing person traced. Utmost discretion. Surveillance. De-bugging. Matrimonial. I feel sorry for straying husbands and wives, don't you. With No Stone Unturned outside clinging to the drain-pipes.'

'Sounds thorough,' said Michael.

They finally chose an agency with a small, less sinister entry, an address in Kensington and all the usual promises. Who would telephone? Roz said it should be Michael.

'They'll think they're on an easy option if they hear a woman's voice. Male chauvinism still reigns. I don't want to pay through the nose.'

He dialled the number and Roz sat on the arm of his chair, changed and cheerful. The woman who answered sounded as brisk as a nurse. Michael was transferred to 'our Mr Sydney Russell'.

'What can I do for you, Sir?'

Michael said that he and his fiancée (he mouthed 'sorry' to Roz, who gave him a cruel pinch) would like to consult him. Where could they meet? It was not convenient, added Michael elliptically, for Mr Russell to come to the house.

'Live locally, do you, Sir?'

'Chiswick.'

'First rate, first rate. Know the Hogarth in Edwardes Square? Nice old place and we can sit outside if it doesn't rain. Less likely to be overheard,' added Russell, with a sort of ghastly matiness.

Michael arranged that they should meet in two days' time. When he rang off Roz threw her arms round him and hugged him.

'What was that for?'

'Taking on my troubles.'

'Any time,' he said with a queer look.

Next morning when she was wandering round the house, unsettled and with some of her worry returned, Roz felt a sudden desire to talk to Mary DuCann. She had lived for years with somebody much older than herself and people of another generation gave her a sense of comfort sometimes; a solidity. She telephoned Mary who was pleased. 'I've been thinking about you so much, Roz. Did you manage to track Jack down?'

'Yes, but – can I come for a drink?'

Michael was in the garden reading. Roz said she was going out to see Mary for a while. She did not invite him to come too; she wanted a free hand.

The DuCanns lived a comfortable walk away from Bowling House, off St Peter's Square. Roz was always glad to visit them, she felt at home there. Mary's husband was a painter who was rather successful with people 'who want portraits of themselves they can recognize'. Roz, modern in almost everything else, admired his paintings very much and once declared to his amusement, 'You have real flourish.'

Mary was on the lookout, and opened the door before Roz had reached the top of the steps.

She kissed Roz affectionately. She was small and neat, with pretty eyes and curling grey hair, fascinated and sometimes apprehensive about life but brave. She took Roz indoors, saying, 'I can have you to myself today. Harry's up in the studio and won't emerge until suppertime. He's sorting out his engravings. He has portfolios bursting with them and an American buyer turned up yesterday, I'm happy to say. Come and have a drink. I can't wait to hear what happened.'

They went into a pretty room which had folding doors, opened today to make a long vista and a view of the garden with a plum tree in blossom. A newspaper lay all over the floor. Mary began to pick up the sheets, looking guilty.

'The only other person I know who treats a newspaper as badly as I do, is Jack. Harry has a fit after I've been at his paper, I practically have to iron the thing before returning it to him. Sit down, Roz. White wine? That's your favourite, isn't it?'

She bustled about waiting on the visitor. Roz had the lulled feeling, the spreading of the spirit, which her grandmother called '*mise à l'aise*', from being with somebody older – not Jack, of course. This kind, relaxed woman made her feel very young. She liked that just now.

She described the visit to her great uncle. It was the second time she had told the story and the effect it produced was identical. A turning-over of the tale. A frown of thought, of puzzlement, perhaps.

'So he didn't tell you anything. I can't say I'm surprised.'

'He infuriates me.'

'Poor Roz,' said Mary, with a half smile. 'He can be very annoying. He does it on purpose. But I do like him. Who could help it?'

'I could.'

Mary smiled more broadly.

'Sophy says the men fall like ninepins for you. Jack has been a failure and it's annoyed you. He's only running true to form. He's always been as silent as the tomb and never tells one anything. The only person he loosens up with is Sophy.'

311

Roz said curiously, 'Do you think he fancies her? Or did when he was young?'

The crudeness of the young still took Mary DuCann aback. She had lively grown-up children, two daughters, a son. Their conversation could make her jaw drop. 'You don't have to be sex-mad to be totally devoted to your sister, Roz.'

'But he's the sort, isn't he?'

Mary lowered her eyelids which, despite being sixty, she had painted a forget-me-not blue.

'I think I can tell you without giving away secrets that Jack used to be a great one for the ladies.'

'Really? Hard to believe now. Were you one, then?'

Mary laughed outright and said that would be telling.

If Roz could not, by the strongest stretch of the imagination, see Jack Hayward as having been attractive she could see Mary DuCann used to be. Might still be to the older man. But Roz's interest in sex-in-the past flagged. She hadn't yet told Mary about the diaries. She described them in her sort of shorthand, ending with, 'You're such a mate of Gran's, I'm sure it's all stale news to you.'

Mary looked fixedly at the girl.

'No. She didn't tell me. How strange to hear it now. I never knew about – what was his name – Daniel. Nothing. As for the baby, oh poor Sophy! Imagine having to give the baby up.'

'She didn't have to. She couldn't face bringing up a bastard. She just hadn't the guts.'

'Sophy has a good deal of guts.'

'Not then she didn't.'

Mary did not bother to argue.

'And the diaries ended after the baby had been adopted?'

'More or less. She was going to see Bob Lingard. My ghost of a grandfather. Even the idea of him's unreal. Gran does have those old wartime photographs, but everybody looks bleached out.'

'None of us knew him very well,' Mary said. 'I once had a drink with them after she was engaged, I remember. At the Berkeley. Bob Lingard had a terrific career in the Navy, he got to be captain. He died when your mother was about two. Apparently he was in Liverpool when there was a terrible fire in one of the ships and Bob went aboard and rescued four or five seamen. They awarded him a George Medal. He died in Lancashire, the following year.'

'Yes,' said Roz, 'I know.' She grinned.

The attitude of the young towards the German war was something of a pill to swallow but Mary was used to it.

'So,' said Roz, finishing her wine, 'you're up to the minute with the news except for my latest brainwave. Uncle Jack told me two or three times that Gran isn't ill so we don't have to worry about that. My next move is tomorrow morning. I'm hiring a detective.'

Mary didn't like to show that the idea shocked her. But she indicated surprise.

'Are you sure that's a good idea?'

'Positive. It's brilliant. Gran will look a big fool when I do find her.'

'My dear child —'

'It's no good, Mary,' interrupted Roz, looking stubborn. 'My mind's made up. You can come to the interview if you like.'

'Good heavens, I wouldn't think of it.'

'Okay. Then Michael and I will go it alone. He's a guy I know at Oxford. Not bad. Very helpful about the Gran thing. When the detective tracks her down I promise I'll ring you.'

'Sophy won't like all this, Roz.'

'Perhaps that's why I'm doing it. Wait and see!'

'I shan't want to see Sophy if she gets in a rage. I am surprised that you do.'

'My fuse is as short as hers. Probably shorter; hadn't you noticed?' said Roz coolly.

The young bored Mary when they boasted and although she was fond of Roz, she'd had enough of the girl. Roz had a certain brutality. Where were the delicacies of the past? Mary forgot, perhaps had never known, Sophy's brutalities. Mary was a delicate creature, who felt intensely. Her touch was so light. Her husband once said that the only reason she often dropped things was because she did not hold them tightly enough. She did not hold Roz at all and walked with her to the door with doubtful relief.

At Bowling House Roz found that Michael had bought a Chinese meal, and some wine, and was watching a TV programme about Occupied France. He came to the door the moment he heard her key.

'You've got to come and watch this! Your grandmother's very scene . . .'

They squatted on the floor, arms entwined, watching images of a time so far from them that it might have been Ancient Egypt. They knew little of the details of the Hitler war; it was not their subject. Michael was reading Modern History, but it was a famous joke at Oxford that Modern History started in 476 with the Fall of the Roman Empire. In Michael's case, it went as far as Napoleon. Roz was deep in Economics. Finals were uncomfortably close, there was much work to be done. But information about the Second World War was definitely of no use to their studies.

On the screen were pictures of advancing tanks, of long roads edged with poplars, those French roads made immortal in the blissful paintings of the Impressionists, but in the film strangely crowded with soldiers or hurrying crowds. They watched old newsreels of the dictators, and wild scenes of the Americans driving into Paris necklaced with flowers and waving bottles of wine. Everybody looked so happy.

'In the bit about Dunkirk they didn't say how unpopular the Brits were in France,' remarked Roz, knowledgeable on the point, 'Gran's diaries said we were loathed.'

'We'd have loathed them if they'd left us flat.'

'True. It's just who you happen to be.'

They watched television until the programme ended and a sit-com began which was too domestic for their taste. They ate their ready-cooked Chinese supper and went to bed to make love not – this time – for very long but still to their breathless delight. They slept in each other's arms; if Michael had a sense of sadness at her closeness and distance, he did not speak about it.

The next morning after a good many jokes they set off for Edwardes Square in the pouring rain. Neither had a raincoat and they were drenched by the time they ran into the pub. Roz shook her hair, spraying water drops on the stone floor.

'Roz, we should have brought an umbrella —'

'What's a little rain? Good for the skin.'

Michael swallowed the words he wanted to say — that her skin was so beautiful it did not need the rain. He tried not to pay her compliments.

They went into a bar in which a series of Hogarth's engravings hung on the walls — the Mariage à la Mode. Roz had never liked them. She pressed Michael's arm and indicated a man sitting alone at the bar counter; she told Michael later that she guessed it must be the detective by his shoes.

'Worn right down at the heels.'

The man saw them and stood up.

'Mr Chance? Miss Pearson? Sydney Russell at your service.'

He shook hands energetically and offered them a drink, but Roz said she would get them. The detective looked a little shy at a pretty young woman buying the drinks; he was about fifty. He exchanged remarks with Michael about the nasty weather until Roz, red hair glued to her head and a grin on her face, returned from the bar.

'Handsome of you, Miss. You shouldn't have,' said Russell grabbing his second pint.

The interview was not at all what Roz and Michael had imagined, and nor was the detective. They had thought of some leading character in a TV series, ironic, experienced, middle class, rather clever. Sydney Russell was facetious. He had a bulbous nose on a smallish face, brown hair which sprang up from his forehead, an expression of expectancy, waiting for a joke. He laughed heartily at almost anything. Sophy caught Michael's eye at a moment when Russell had bent down to pick up the newspaper he had been carrying. She made a doubtful 'what do you think?' grimace.

'Now to business,' said Michael, when it looked as if Russell

315

was about to tell another unfunny story; Roz thought he fancied himself as a stand-up comedian.

She and Michael had decided beforehand that they would give Russell the facts and nothing else. There was a photograph of her grandmother in Roz's room at Bowling House, taken only six months ago and a good likeness. She gave this to Russell together with a sheet of paper on which she'd written Sophy's name and London address and the date she and Michael had come back from Oxford to find that she'd disappeared.

'She left me a letter but it said nothing.' Roz had no intention of showing it to the detective and he did not ask for it.

He listened attentively to what Roz had told him.

'Did your granny ever indicate she wanted to escape?'

'Of course not. That's why we want your help.'

'Yes, yes,' he said patiently, 'but do you remember an occasion, for instance, when she was watching a telly programme about foreign parts and said she wished *she* could see more of the world. That kind of thing.'

'Mr Russell, Mrs Lingard could afford to visit any part of the world she liked,' said Michael pleasantly. He did not want to offend him and thought Roz very abrupt.

'Ah, but did she say she wanted to?'

'Never,' said Roz.

Russell looked at the scrap of paper.

'What about the old lady's past?'

'She was married in the last war. Widowed very young. She had a daughter, my mother, who was killed with my father ten years ago in a plane crash. My grandmother took me in and brought me up.'

'Did she? Very commendable,' said Russell, making a few notes. They scarcely ran to half a page in his shorthand book.

During a short silence Roz heard the rain whipping against the window panes. There was nobody else in the bar.

'It is extraordinary that my grandmother has gone like this,' said Roz. 'She said nothing beforehand. Nothing in her letter to me, only that she'd gone. I simply can't understand it.'

The detective gave a nod. Michael thought – how often has he heard that before?

'Well, you know, Miss Pearson, they do it,' said Russell. 'Just make up their minds and vanish as if they'd dug a hole in the globe. Know how many are never traced?'

'Thousands, and I'm afraid that does not interest me,' said Roz sharply.

He gave a guffaw.

'Why should it, why should it? I didn't mean that I won't find her. I've taken on far more tricky cases than this one. Last month I traced one elderly gent who had been hiding round the corner, if you please. Just round the corner in digs and his wife couldn't discover hide nor hair of him. He'd been there living the life of Riley for two years. Used to go out for his constitutional when it was dark.'

He laughed again.

'This shouldn't be too difficult. The great thing, Sir and Madam, is not to worry. Put Mrs Lingard into my hands and forget the problem. Remember I'll be ferreting away on your behalf.'

'Which reminds me,' said Roz, cheered by the active verb to ferret, 'we must pay your advance.'

13

When Roz parked outside Erith Road, she thought the house looked much smaller than when she had left it. That was the trouble with messing about with the past. It put your eye out. You had been living in your imagination in French salons or the Ritz and here was a poky little Oxford house with a patch of unweeded garden and a wicket gate with bars missing since the year dot. Ally had already arrived, unpacked, bought some flowers and was in her bedroom, combing her mass of nearly uncontrollable hair. Elizabeth Siddall returned to life, even to the ankle-length turquoise dress.

She turned round to smile a welcome as Roz peered in.

'There you are. Huw was worrying.'

'Not you, then?'

'I try not to. Things always work out in the end.'

Did Ally really believe that, thought Roz, and went to her own room, throwing bags about and thinking it would be boring to tell her friend the saga. Not that Ally wasn't the soul of sympathy. Perhaps that was the trouble.

It was a week since she and Michael had met Sydney Russell and they had not received a word from him. Eventually Michael telephoned. Russell was out and he was put through to the brisk woman who answered him with a somewhat pitying surprise. A report would be 'forthcoming' but it was 'not our practice' to send in more than one a month. In

318

the meantime things must be 'allowed to progress naturally', whatever that might mean.

Roz tried to follow Russell's advice and leave the problem with him. She knew the coming Oxford weeks were vital for her. She had far too much work to do to sit worrying uselessly over her grandmother. Yet when she sat down to work, a sort of pain hampered her as if – the moment she opened a book – an invisible hand swung a severe blow and knocked it out of her hand.

Michael Chance also interrupted her thoughts. She was attracted but still had not fallen in love. She had a curious feeling that this new man who claimed her time, whom she liked, who made love to her, was dangerous to her liberty. They had upsetting quarrels sometimes and when she thought about them afterwards, the reasons seemed ridiculous. He was touchy about being short of money. Once she had thoughtlessly said, 'I suppose I'm lucky. No problems. Gran's allowance is just fine.' Michael had given her a strange cold look, made an obvious excuse and left her. On another occasion when they were still in Chiswick she had flirted with a man, a friend she knew locally. When she and Michael returned to Bowling House he called her a bitch and in the ensuing fracas she burst into tears. Oh, those quarrels! Roz had never cried, never lost, in sexual prizefights until now.

But then work came and stood beside her like a gaoler. It threatened her, pointed a finger at the calendar and if she went to bed early to have a good night, jogged her cruelly awake. When she, Ally and Huw met in the kitchen for a meal, work came in like a spectre, sat at the table with them and gibbered.

They had been back in Oxford for a week, and one not-warm evening when Huw was with his tutor and Michael dining in Hall, Roz and Ally worked for five hours in their separate cells. At last Roz went out on to the landing and gave a loud groan for sympathy.

Ally's tall pre-Raphaelite figure appeared at the door of her room.

'Shall we have coffee and chocolate cake?'

'Oh please. Very black coffee to keep us going.'

The two girls went down to the sitting room and Ally, with difficulty, opened a rickety window. Dust and a smell of flowering privet came in. They feasted on bitter coffee and slices of sticky chocolate cake. It was only then, late and tired, that Roz blurted out about her grandmother's disappearance. She had kept the bad news to herself until then.

Ally was deeply sympathetic and determinedly cheerful. How sensible of Roz to get a detective: he'd be certain to find Mrs Lingard.

'The happy end?' said Roz. She loved Ally but found the starry optimism hard to take.

'Oh Roz, of course you'll find her. And the explanation will turn out to be perfectly simple. Your Gran is such a fine person, she'd never do anything to hurt you.'

'Ally, you are too good to be true.'

For once her friend noticed the satiric tone and looked hurt. Roz had a slight pang of contrition.

'I know, I know, you only take the bright view because it's what you want *me* to think. Sorry.'

She bit her pencil. She carried one about like a talisman. 'I found out a lot about Gran's past – we can talk about that later. What I want to hear now is how it went in Wales and what Huw's parents were like.'

'Welsh,' said Ally darkly.

Roz couldn't help laughing.

'You didn't expect them to be Spanish, did you?'

'I mean they're dedicated and intellectual and clever and musical and mad about one passing exams. If Huw doesn't get a first they simply won't understand. They both got double firsts, think of that! They'll say it's all my fault if he gets a second. Oh Roz. He loves them too much.'

'You like your parents too, don't you?'

'Sure, but I don't hang about thirsting for their approval.'

'And did the Welsh lot approve of *you*?'

'I'm too tall.'

'Ally, what can you mean?'

320

'His mum and dad are both about five foot high and when I was with them I loomed. Awful. I hadn't brought my flat heels, either, and I got a crick in the neck from stooping.'

'Poor Ally,' said Roz, laughing.

Longing to sleep, the girls returned to their poky bedrooms and to their books. Facts danced in front of their eyes. Helped by coffee, they managed to stay awake until three in the morning.

The days before the finals – Roz had ten papers spread over a period of a week – began to hurry by alarmingly, and soon there was scarcely a month left to revise in.

One of Roz's tutors, a white-faced Irishwoman called Mary Anthony, gave her specific advice.

'You've got a quarter of an hour for each question. If you can't finish one in that time, go straight on to the next. But show you know your stuff. Show off.'

Roz sighed.

'Now, Rosalind, what you've got to do is forage about in there,' said the tutor, pointing at Roz's head. 'Fish out what is certainly lodged in that skull of yours.'

Roz thought for a moment and then said, 'You must be used to all of us. Sitting here worrying.'

'Of course you worry. I'd blame myself if you didn't. You might try my trick. When anything bothers me, I divide it into sections. Here's the problem. What are the possible solutions? One, or two, or maybe three. If I don't do that, I lie awake and fret.'

Looking at her tutor, Roz doubted it. She thought Mary Anthony would wrestle with a problem and throw it over one shoulder where it would land on its back.

Roz walked home through an Oxford brimming with undergraduates. They rode by on bicycles, calling to each other. They walked hand in hand. They were recognizable by their youth and careless clothes, just as the summer tourists could be spotted because they had jackets or cardigans, cameras and maps, and stood awestruck at college entrances. Roz turned over her tutor's advice. Problem? Her grandmother was gone. Solutions? She could get on with her own life – but just now that seemed impossible. She could see her great uncle again. But he would only repeat his refusals and that would upset her. Or, she could rely on Sydney Russell. That detective had better come up with something soon, thought Roz. He's expensive.

Back came another present problem, Michael Chance. Roz was a girl who did not go in for casual sex, few of her friends did. She'd turned to Michael at first because he'd happened to be with her in Chiswick, and she was unhappy. Later she had been moved by the fact that he'd fallen in love with her. Rejected by the person she loved best in the world, she found Michael's love was a solace. But was he really the loving spoiling man she had imagined? Those rows, for instance, which always finished up in bed. They bothered her. What she needed was to be spoiled, petted, thought wonderful, as she shamelessly put it to herself.

A good many men had told her that was what they thought, but it had only been sex. I suppose I want real love, thought Roz, there was sex and to spare in Oxford. She had seen little evidence of love except with Ally and Huw. Yet now Michael had come into her life, she was afraid. She stood on the brink, not daring to jump.

Without Sophy she felt bereft – another reason for resisting the solace of falling in love. She envied Ally. Her friend had a mother and father who were proud of her; they telephoned her, wrote to her, appeared in Oxford to take her to the Randolph for lunch. And at Erith Road Ally had Huw. Often when Roz came into the sitting room in the evenings there was Ally, looking beautiful and absurd, all five foot eleven of her draped over Huw's lap.

When she wasn't poring over her work Roz met Michael for coffee or supper at Erith Road. On Sundays they punted on the Cherwell, taking armfuls of books and mooring under the willows. They sat for hours, with the water slapping against the sides of the punt while they worked. When it began to get dark Michael punted them back to the jetty and they walked home. In Roz's stuffy little room they shoved yet more heavy books off the bed and made love.

322

Michael was critical and sharp-tongued, but he'd begun not to talk about Roz's grandmother. Was that a desire not to upset her? Or did he hope she was getting over it? As if you get over being abandoned, thought Roz.

Three weeks after term began, Roz left College after a morning tutorial at which Mary Anthony had been harder than usual; she felt as if the tutor had been hitting her with facts like punches to the jaw. Along the High she saw Michael, walking with his light rapid step, the sun on his crinkly hair. Pleased to see him, she ran the last few steps.

'I came looking for you,' he said, 'I guessed you'd be through by now. I've had a letter from Sydney Russell.'

'No!'

'Don't expect too much, it's only three lines. But he asked if he can come to Oxford to see us today.'

'Then he must have news.'

'Or feels it's time to report or he won't get any more cash.'

'Oh you! You're deliberately downbeat. I'm sure the news is good, I can feel it. Did you ring and tell him to come?'

'Yes, he was out as usual but he'd left a message. If I said it was okay, he would catch a midday train. He was ringing in later to check. I've fixed for us to see him at The Marquis of Cardigan. It's almost time, shall we go?'

Arm in arm, they walked down the street and turned into a narrow passage which ran between two colleges. Late laburnum and lilac bent over a high wall. The air smelled of flowers.

'I hope he doesn't charge us a first-class rail fare,' said Michael.

'I don't care if he takes the Orient Express.'

They were early for the appointment and as they weaved their way through a mass of students, talking, drinking, smoking, alternating jokes and desperation, Roz heard somebody call her name. There was Ally with Huw beside her, tenderly regarding his goddess three and a half inches taller than he.

'Just the people!' cried Ally. 'Guess what. You never will, so I shall tell you. We've been and gone and done it.'

'She means we are getting married,' translated Huw, a certain nervousness in his grin.

Roz and Michael chorused congratulations and the girls hugged. Ally was in a state of euphoria.

'Isn't it extraordinary, I still can't believe it. I said to Huw this morning when we decided "I suppose this is *it*. I mean, life – what everything's about – I mean, is there any more? –"'

'Ally, you're burbling,' said her future husband.

'We're mad, of course,' said Ally with content.

Huw muttered something about the marriage not being yet awhile and Ally fondly picked him up on the point, did he mean by that he didn't positively *long* ... the sort of conversation followed to which Roz could scarcely listen ... Michael did not even pretend to do so.

To the disappointment of the newly engaged girl, Roz explained that they were meeting somebody.

'Okay, if you must go,' said Ally, calling after them with her radiant smile, 'but isn't it *amazing?*'

Safely into the crowd Michael muttered, 'Cor.'

'Don't be a beast. She's so happy.'

'Don't I know it? Ah, there he is –'

The detective had just come into the pub, he was standing by the door looking about. At that moment both Michael and Roz saw the working face of the man, not the jokes. He regarded the mass of noisy undergraduates with a probing curiosity, yet managed to be the most unnoticeable person in the place. You wouldn't, thought Michael, look at him twice.

'There you both are, good, good, what do you say to a shandy?' His face immediately changed to a grin.

'I'll get the drinks,' said Michael. 'Do you prefer draught lager, Mr Russell?'

He was giving Roz the chance to hear the news, if there was any, first. It was like Michael and her heart told her so.

'You have something to tell me, I believe,' said Roz the moment Michael had gone.

Russell remarked what a jolly crowd of folk and he hoped his son would go to 'Uni' as they called it in Australia. He did not appear to have heard what Roz said.

324

'I daresay you and Mr Chance have a high old time.'

'Oh yes, we do indeed,' said Roz with irony, thinking of the sleepless nights. Then, getting to the point, 'Mr Russell, what have you found out?'

He looked surprised. 'Afraid we'll have to wait until the gentleman gets back. Don't want to say it all over twice, do I?'

'Mr Russell,' Roz controlled herself with difficulty, '*have you found Mrs Lingard?*'

'You do jump to the gun,' said Russell reproachfully and then, with relief, 'ah, here's Mr Chance. That's very good of you, Squire.' He took the tankard which was damp from the cold beer. Michael handed Roz a glass and raised his eyebrows questioningly.

'Mr Russell hasn't told me. He said we had to wait for you.'

'Must deal with both at once,' remarked Russell, emerging from the tankard and wiping his lips daintily with his fingers. 'Well now. Anywhere we can sit down?'

'The wall outside,' suggested Michael.

Outside in the courtyard set about with rustic tables, was a long low brick wall which had once been part of some stables. It was a favourite perching place for students, who sat lined along it like swallows on telephone wires.

Sitting in a row, Russell in the middle, Roz and Michael on either side leaning towards him, Sydney Russell looked in charge. He took a long pull at his beer.

'Here we go. Case of Mrs Lingard missing since March from her residence at Bowling House in the area of Chiswick,' he read from a shorthand notebook.

'So?' said Roz.

'My enquiries have not yet progressed as far as ascertaining where Mrs Lingard is residing at present, Miss. These things take time. Wait a bit –' Roz, very white, was about to burst out when Michael leaned across Russell and took her hand, saying, 'Give him a chance.'

She subsided.

Russell droned out the prepared narrative of the work since they had employed him, the previous month. He was exact.

He described every step he had taken, in date order. Michael was rather impressed and considered him thorough and ingenious. Russell had started by combing the district. He'd interviewed the Indian woman who ran the corner shop on the towpath, he had spoken to Mrs Lingard's doctor, and had a meeting with the vicar at St Luke's church, where he learned that Mrs Lingard often called in for a chat. He had driven to see her dressmaker in Richmond, the man who delivered the milk to Bowling House, he'd even talked to the police – 'much good they are, they don't even patrol the towpath at that point, God help us'. He had visited the three houses adjoining Sophy Lingard's home.

All this had taken time.

'Not many outgoings,' said Russell. 'Mostly shoe leather.'

It was one of his non-jokes and Michael, who knew the value of encouragement, politely laughed. Roz did not.

'Now I come to something more interesting,' said Russell.

'Another beer before you begin?' interrupted Michael and Roz gave him a look of pure hatred.

'Wouldn't say no, Mr Chance.'

'You, Roz?' asked Michael, ignoring her expression. She shook her head, staring at the ground. But when Michael got up to go to the bar, she left Russell and followed him through the chattering crowd. Raising her voice above the noise she yelled, 'What the hell are you playing at? I don't believe he knows a bloody thing. Christ, what a waste of money.'

'Stop being stupid.'

'*I am not stupid.* My God, you have no imagination at all!'

'And don't turn on me. Let's keep calm and hear what he has to say,' said Michael, handing money and taking the filled tankard and a glass for himself.

Roz could have killed him, he looked so fireproof and uncaring.

'F*** off if you'd rather have nothing more to do with my *boring* problems,' she hissed in his ear like a stage villain.

'Roz, do shut up. Do you really think you'll get the best out of a guy by working yourself into a rage? Leave it to me.' Michael was not rising, for once. 'Keep your cool for pity's sake. It can't be as difficult as all that.'

He didn't swear back at her, although it was tempting to do so.

As white as only redheads go, freckles prominent, mouth a thin line and eyes glaring, she followed him out into the sunlight.

Russell accepted the beer with pleasure and drank thirstily. Then said yes, he was glad to tell them he had discovered something. Michael gave a sardonic look at Roz – but she was staring at the detective so tensely that he had a pang of love and pity. There were times when she looked as if her heart would break.

'From all I ascertained, and putting two and twelve together, ha ha, Mrs Lingard went to London Airport. This is her timetable. Her neighbour Mrs Bowes – know her, Miss Pearson? – saw your grandmother leave at ten in the morning. Our subject was accompanied by the Spanish maid Carmen –' he consulted his notes – 'Guerrero. They were carrying two suitcases. Mrs Bowes, talkative and a good pair of eyes in her head, saw Mrs Lingard get into a taxi just as ten was pipped on Radio Four, a black London taxi of the kind you hire at London Taxicabs Limited. I've been in touch and their records show the fare was ordered on your grandmother's account, Miss Pearson, and driven to London Airport at that time. We can presume, though it is not proved by witnesses seeing the lady board the plane, that our quarry is abroad.'

'*But where?*'

'That's one of the reasons I wanted to see you both. What connections has our subject got with foreign parts? Relatives abroad? Spain? Greece? Or is she one of those adventurous souls who enjoy going abroad and trotting all over the place. Perhaps she has a preference for one particular country? Our agency has good contacts with Interpol.'

'My grandmother never goes abroad. She has friends in Scotland and goes to them sometimes.'

'The lady might have flown to Glasgow or Edinburgh?' said Russell, nodding, pencil poised.

Roz dictated the address of some friends of Sophy's who lived in Kyle of Localsh.

'You've contacted them yourself recently, Miss?'

Roz confessed that she hadn't thought of it. She did not tell the detective, who seemed pleased at a new lead and made jokes about bagpipes, that she did not believe for an instant Sophy was in Scotland. Russell snapped his book shut, drained the tankard and promised to be in touch again soon. Michael walked with him into the street and when they were out of earshot asked if he might pay a further advance.

'Well, now, Mr Chance, I take that very kindly. Clients often put off the moment of truth – and what can we do about it? Our agency attempts to avoid litigation.'

Russell looked gratified when Michael gave him the cheque he had already written – it was for fifty pounds and all he could afford. Russell scrawled a receipt and they parted, the detective setting off briskly to walk to the station.

In the courtyard, Roz had not moved. He had a wave of tenderness not created by desire, seeing her so pale and still, and put his arms round her shoulders. She leaned her head against him.

'Oh Michael, Michael. He's found out nothing.'

'London Airport.'

'But how many millions of people go there every day? What is the use of me going on looking for Gran? Must I forget her, then? It hurts,' she added. And it hurt to see her.

'Of course you mustn't forget her. We must let him go on digging for a bit.'

He kissed the poor white face.

The talk at Oxford as Finals loomed, was of keep-calm pills, keep-awake pills, vitamins for the brain and coffee in which you could stand up your spoon, 'you don't sleep *at all*!' An air of hectic anxiety had begun to spread through the colleges and houses, flats, lodgings, cafés and bars across the ancient city. Undergraduates with one or two more years to go before the fatal week were affected by the miasma of gloom and tried to look agonized as well; but it was difficult to be desperate about anything as remote as their own eventual Finals.

Ally and Roz had different ways of approaching the crossing of their particular Rubicon. For all her romantic appearance and melting manner, Ally was steady. She worked in an organized way, morning, afternoon, evening. She and Huw only spent time together at supper, usually fast food hot and filling. Ally banned drink; she and Huw allowed themselves a few glasses of cheap wine on Sundays. Despite her untidiness, the ethereal look of the pre-Raphaelite pictures in which the man died of love and the girl, alas, of tuberculosis, Ally's beautiful eyes were on the main chance. She was clever and she worked.

But Roz was an extremist. She worked all night and gave herself a migraine. She tried the classic dodges to keep awake, from coffee the colour of marking ink to pills borrowed from crazier friends; the pills had the curious effect of keeping her awake for two entire days. She looked like death and Michael was furious with her. She worked like a car which can go like the wind or splutter to a stop.

Mary Anthony was severe and lectured Roz, not on future questions in examination papers but on a sense of proportion.

'It is,' said Miss Anthony, fixing her with green, at times bloodshot eyes, 'one of the more advantageous of the virtues.'

Roz's migraine came back inconveniently after one of her sleepless nights and she was lying down in her room with a wet flannel uselessly and pathetically on her forehead when Michael called in. He sat on her bed, took her hand and kissed it.

'I came to ask you what are the plans after the dreaded Finals.'

'I can't think further than that. Ow. My head.'

'Poor you.' He allowed a short interval, wrung out the flannel to make it cool again and returned to his point.

'I need something to look forward to afterwards. I want to take you to Italy. I've got it all worked out. Well? Will you come, Roz?'

'I don't know. It sounds so lovely. Unreal. How long would we go for?'

'Three weeks. A month. Until our money runs out. We'll

go to Assisi. We'll walk all over those Tuscan hills among the cypresses. Eat black olives. Make love . . .'

'I think I'd like that.'

Suddenly the Finals were upon them.

Roz was prepared for her ten papers to be spread over a week, some of her friends had papers spread over two weeks or even longer. She was half glad, half terrified at the intensity of her own ordeal. She had two papers each on Wednesday, Thursday and Friday. A nightmare weekend, then the last four ending on Tuesday. Every paper lasted three hours and it was very hard and very concentrated work.

And then it was over. For Roz and Michael. For Ally and Huw. The weight and misery of the last few months were lifted, as if Oxford herself had stretched out a hand, and taken a huge lid of iron from the groaning heads of her children.

The June weather was flawless, the evening streets were filled with people, not one of whom was over twenty-three. Everywhere there were undergraduates, frolicking and embracing and running to meet each other, standing outside colleges while they opened bottles of champagne, gowns over summer dresses or dark suits.

Michael, Huw, Ally and Roz were outside Michael's college sharing the half dozen bottles of champagne they had bought in advance and packed in the basket of Ally's bicycle. They sang drunkenly, swigged from foil-topped bottles and toasted each other. They shared a belief, a wondrous euphoria, that for tonight they utterly believed. The future was filled with delights. They saw themselves famous or happy or both. They saw their friendships eternal. Everything was glorious and funny and there was nowhere in the world to be but drinking champagne from the bottle in a street in Oxford.

They wandered to University College where the students had laid on an enormous party, still nothing but champagne and everybody in their gowns and mortar boards. They played something called champagne cricket with empty bottles for bats and wickets and a cork for the ball – which got lost at once, a reason for popping yet another bottle. They tried unsuccessfully to fire corks over the high college walls. Later scores of joyous couples went to punt on the Cherwell taking a wind-up gramophone. The party went on the entire night. The city was used to that.

It was dawn when Roz, her gown over her arm like a dead crow, and supported by Michael – she was limping and had broken the heel off her shoe – crept into Erith Road. Ally and Huw had left the party earlier in the evening, both yawning and dropping with sleep; they must have been in bed ages ago. The boy in the attic bedroom, Stephen, who had another year to go at Oxford, kept religiously early hours. The little house, soon to be emptied of youth and anxiety, was quiet. In the narrow hall where Ally's bicycle took up most of the space, they embraced. Their faces swam. They wanted to make love. Tonight was the end of a sort of lifetime, God alone knew what would happen next. Never before had they felt the wing-tip of time across their faces. Never before had they known real goodbyes.

They went slowly up the steep staircase and stripping off their clothes, fell on to Roz's bed. They began to make love with a tired passion more intense because somehow it was sad. Practised lovers now, they knew how to excite and to enjoy, they were so close they became one person, not two, and when the love was finished stayed together, Michael lying on top of his thin lover, looking down into her face.

'You're so lovely.'

'So are you,' she said drowsily.

'I must get off you; I'm crushing the breath out of your body.'

'Stay. I like it.'

He did stay for a while but then rolled off her and as they fell asleep it was already day.

They slept on when the house woke and Stephen packed his bags and threw them over the bannisters. They slept on while Ally and Huw, more fresh than seemed possible, went off for a grand lunch at the Randolph with Ally's parents.

Michael stirred at last, Roz was still deep asleep; it was half past two, the light was an afternoon light and the sounds from Erith Road were few. Most people had driven away.

He climbed out of bed and looked into Ally's room. Bags and cases neatly packed and piled by the door. Flower vases empty. Pictures and posters gone. He looked into Huw's room. The same. Plus squash racquets and a pack of Huw's research folders. Huw's posters, too, were gone from the walls leaving only a few drawing pins. On the floor were two screwed-up tickets for a concert Huw and Ally had gone to weeks ago.

Michael went down into the kitchen and made two mugs of instant coffee. The place was an army of empty champagne bottles but Ally, typically, had washed the glasses. On the way back to Roz's bedroom he nearly fell over a heap of books tied with rope.

He opened the bedroom door, deliberately making a noise, and the naked girl on the bed stirred and slowly opened her eyes.

'Hello. What time is it?'

'Nearly three.'

'Impossible. How we slept. Crikey. My head.'

'Yeah. Mine too. Cheap champagne, I'm afraid.'

Roz put out a shaking hand.

'Coffee.'

They drank in silence. Michael had a moment of tired happiness. This life was over and he did not know how he'd done in the Finals. But he had been given many things at Oxford. Much curious knowledge. Fun. Friends like Ally and Huw. A good many hopes. And most of all this beautiful girl. His heart swelled as he thought of Roz in his future, Roz as his fate if he put it in a fanciful way. He imagined doing things for her, making her happy, rescuing her from the trouble her grandmother had left behind. He felt protective and capable and kind and clever. He wanted Roz that moment, but it was too late and too soon to begin sex all over again.

Reaching for the mug he had put on to the chest he noticed an envelope and then remembered he had found it on the floor by the front door when they came home in the dawn.

Through champagne-blurred eyes he had seen Roz's name and brought the letter up to the bedroom. He remembered nothing more except sex.

'Roz. This came,' he said.

She was yawning and pushing her hair out of her eyes; when she saw the envelope she sat upright.

'*Where did you find this?*'

'It was on the mat when we got home – why?'

'*You forgot to give it to me, how could you?*'

His tenderness and lust evaporated like shining drops exposed to a burning sun.

'Roz, what are you on about?'

'It's from my great uncle.' She tore open the letter, read it in seconds and said, 'Oh God.'

She handed it to him. He recognized the handwriting.

'Roz darling,

I know you'll have been upset at my leaving the way I did. I've felt so guilty about you, but truly there was nothing I could do. I had to go – and go fast. I wish I could explain what has happened, dearest girl, but I can't.

You'll just have to forgive me and try to think lovingly of me in spite of everything. I think of *you* a lot. Be happy at Bowling House. Take care. I only wish – but no, it's impossible.

Your stupid but loving,
Gran.'

He said tentatively, 'I suppose your great uncle forwarded it. She sounds okay, anyway.'

Roz snatched back the letter.

'Of course she doesn't. What does she mean – "I had to go, and go fast"? She's in trouble. She may even be running away from the police. How do I know what Gran's been up to?' she went on wildly. 'Drugs. Anything.'

'Why in hell should your respectable old grandmother –'

'How do we know she's respectable?' demanded Roz, unaware of comedy. 'What do we know about anybody? It's true that Gran's rich. My grandfather left her a lot of money.

That doesn't mean she doesn't want more. Rich people are like that. It's perfectly possible,' she continued, looking at him with sarcasm, 'for somebody *old* to get into criminal hands as much as somebody young. She'd be a good front.'

'Far-fetched.'

'And possible.'

He shrugged. But what she said had a ghastly kind of truth. Enormous sums of money were made by totally unexpected people who became involved in crime. The scandals in the press often exposed characters of the highest reputation. It had always been like that, but traffic of drugs had made it worse ... since the long ago and filthier traffic of slaves.

Roz, unconscious that she was naked, as if the act of love was long forgotten, stared at her grandmother's letter.

'Are you going to pay off Russell?' Michael said.

She looked up.

'In case he digs up something? Yeah. We'd better get rid of him. Not that he'd have found her anyway. She makes it clear that she's covered her tracks.'

'She didn't say that.'

'Any fool can see that's what she means,' said Roz, still with sarcasm as if somehow all this were his responsibility. 'She doesn't want to be found.'

She climbed out of bed and went to the bathroom where he heard her having an ineffectual shower; the taps at Erith Road had minds of their own. She returned with wet hair she scarcely bothered to dry, dressed in silence, zipped up her jeans and pulled on an old university T-shirt.

He watched her. Where was the wild lover of last night, where indeed? He sat back on the bed which was narrow. There had never been room for them both unless they lay locked. Roz put a comb through her damp hair and picked up her shoulder bag. Without looking at him she said, 'I can't come to Italy.'

'*What?*'

'It's obvious, isn't it? She's in trouble. I've got to find her. Sorry.'

There was a dreadful indifference in that last word. She turned her back on him, hunting through a drawer. Such a slender back, the long neck faintly covered with reddish down; the damp hair in a duck's tail.

'Where are you going as a matter of interest?' he said.

She was counting her money, and looked round, the wallet in her hand. His voice was cold, but something in his face reached her and she came across and sat on the bed, landing painfully on his feet, muttered 'hell' and moved off. She clasped his feet with both hands for reassurance. She was herself again, anxious and upset, but herself. She was looking at him and not at the damned letter.

'I am sorry, Mike. I was so looking forward to Italy. It would have been lovely. But I must help Gran.'

'My dear love. How can you?'

Her grip on his feet tightened.

'I'm going to see Uncle Jack again. I won't be put off this time. I'll sit on the ground and yell until he tells me where I can find her.'

Michael took the hand that was holding his feet and kissed the palm. He shut his eyes.

'I'm coming with you,' he said.

14

She began to pack. Ally and Huw did not return from their
family lunch at the Randolph. The afternoon was far
advanced when Michael walked to his own digs and threw his
possessions into two bags. He came back to Erith Road and
looked at the little house, seeing it for the last time.

During his absence Roz, like Ally, had removed all her
possessions and packed them or thrown them away. The room
where they had made love so often, poky little room with a
view of a cabbage patch, was quite bare. It had turned into a
room waiting for lodgers again. Roz had stripped the bed,
packed her own sheets, folded the blankets; the very bed
denied love. She had torn down the posters, scrumpled them
up and thrown them in the dustbin at the back of the house.
Nothing remained in her room but the tang of her scent. That
would soon blow away, for she had opened the window; it had
a broken sash cord and was propped open with a wedge
Michael had made for her.

She carried her luggage down into the hall, and piled it
round Ally's bicycle.

Michael went up to her room to check, but she had
forgotten nothing. He clattered back downstairs. Roz was
going through the bookshelves. Erith Road had a shelf of
books left by students and Ally and Huw had already
bequeathed a number of detective stories and science fiction.
Roz did the same, but she discovered a paperback Michael

had given her, a jokey book but it had made them laugh.

He stood in the doorway.

'Ally and Huw didn't ring, then?'

'No. They must have gone off somewhere with her parents. We'd better leave them a note. And my London telephone number.'

She hunted out a piece of paper and scrawled a brief goodbye. Michael added his name after hers. She didn't seem upset at not getting the chance to see her friends in their home for the last time.

'Pity they aren't back,' he said.

Roz said oddly, 'I have to get to my uncle's before it is dark.'

The remark was absurd. It sounded as if she were a girl in some movie about vampires. He thought of making a joke, but the poor girl's humour had deserted her. She looked so serious, earnest; as if driving to see Jack Hayward was the only thing in the world that mattered to her. She couldn't even spare a thought for her friends.

He helped her to pack the car with their luggage and she drove away.

Oxford, as if doing it on purpose, was at its loveliest on the day they left her. The gardens were so green they seemed to overflow into the streets. All the lilac was in flower and as they drove down the Banbury Road Michael heard the sound of bells. He felt melancholy. Roz was beside him but she was miles away. And when he'd returned to his digs he had telephoned his parents in South Carolina, an extravagance he certainly couldn't afford; but he had put in a call which the Americans called 'collect'. Both his mother and his stepfather sounded more distant than the thousands of miles of ocean separating him from them. It was always the same when he rang them; he felt hollow afterwards.

He did not ask if she wanted him to drive. She had times of being very much in charge of her own life just as at other times she collapsed into his arms. He liked both moods but the second more than the first. Roz did not drive well. Before the journey had started she'd pitched the luggage anyhow into the back of the open car. Michael had taken it all out again, to her irritation, and repacked it, wedging it close. When she jammed on her brakes for the fourth time he was glad he had, or their bags would certainly have been all over the place.

He knew going to see her great uncle again was a last-ditch move of hers; it was the only thing she could think of, the only hope. He doubted if it would succeed. From the description she'd given him of the old man, he could exactly imagine what Jack Hayard was like: a great immoveable rock which had been there since the beginning of the world. Trying to get a guy like that to change his mind could drive you out of your wits. But it was useless to try and dissuade her. She was not unlike her ancient relative, come to that.

The drive was less than forty miles and her desire to get there before dark was nonsense. There were hours of daylight left on the long long June day which followed the finals and the champagne, the wild cricket and the wilder laughter and all the lovemaking in the beautiful city lost to them for ever.

Roz had said they would try and get rooms in the local pub. This, rather typically, thought Michael, turned out to be the Linden Arms, a smart hotel on the edge of a river. When they went into a reception hall filled with rich summer flowers, the man at the desk – Mr Sinclair-Grove, who was in fact the owner of the hotel, greeted her cordially.

'Why, Miss Pearson, two visits in such a short time! What a pleasure. And it isn't even Christmas.'

Roz, deliberately bright, introduced Michael. She chatted about past Christmases, admired the improvements, an annexe, a swimming pool. And asked if by any luck there were two rooms for tonight.

'Not staying with your great uncle, of course?' said Mr Sinclair-Grove who knew about the family. She dutifully laughed. They were shown up to two bedrooms, gentrified with flowery pink curtains and bedcovers, and pink bathrooms to match.

When the owner had left them in Roz's room, she put her arms round Michael's neck.

'I know,' he said, 'you're breaking the bad news. You're off to see him right away.'

'I want to get it over. Do you mind?'

'It would have been nice to have a drink in the garden first.'

'I know,' she said, meaning no such thing. 'But I can't settle until I've seen him.'

'Will he be there?'

'If he isn't, I don't know what I'll do.'

Michael walked with her to the car, and took out two bags, one for her, one for him, and rearranged the rest of the luggage with capable hands. Roz stood watching and wanting to scream. What did it matter if the luggage collapsed all over the car? She waited until he had finished, then said, 'Bye for now,' and drove away.

The day was in no hurry to end. It floated along, only slightly deepening and lengthening the shadows. When she drew up at the house, every rose Jack had planted was flowering at the same time and the birds were positively shouting, Roz thought. She went to the front door and lifted her hand to ring the bell but the door was open. She went inside.

'Yoo-hoo.'

There was no answer. The house, ordered, smelling of something like lavender, clean, empty, did not welcome her. It was as indifferent as its owner. She looked into the sitting room. The only sign that Jack was in residence was *The Times* strewn all over the carpet. She went into the kitchen and looked out of the window which ran the whole length of the wall facing the garden. And there he was.

But not gardening. He had taken out a deck chair and set it on the terrace and was merely sitting quite still, apparently looking towards the little orchard. He wore a white short-sleeved shirt and the same old baggy trousers. Roz called from the open window, 'Yoo hoo'. Then went out through the kitchen door.

He had started when he heard her voice. Now he got to his feet, holding out his hand to shade his eyes; the sun had begun to sink and its rays were low. The shadows on the lawns were long.

'Me again,' she said. 'The bad penny.'

'You do turn up without being asked. Well, well. Haven't touched the garden today, and now you've appeared —'

'Can't I help? Still time to do a little weeding.'

'You be careful. I might say yes.'

He gave a chuckle at his own joke. Roz thought he looked older. He was very old anyway, anybody over forty was ancient to Roz, but tonight somehow he looked shrunk. From the distance of the kitchen he had looked his burly self, but closer he seemed changed. His face was very pasty and there were blackish shadows under his eyes, like those an actor paints on his face for a tragic performance. It seemed impossible that they could be real shadows, they were too dark.

'How have you been?' asked Roz, falling into his slow step as they went back to the house. He regarded his finger-nails which were encrusted with earth.

'Not too full of the joys of spring. A bit of indigestion. Mrs Matthews' cooking isn't the greatest and I live on bicarbonate.' She was very surprised at being told anything so detailed about himself and made a noise of sympathy.

In the kitchen he washed his hands under the tap and made an ineffectual dab at his nails with an ancient nail brush.

'A drink?' he said with a faint gleam as if the prospect was a pleasant one. They went together into the sitting room. The morning sun came there but in the evening it was in shadow. Such a tidy, empty room except for the photograph of Sophy, and the gardening books with their tattered dust jackets.

He shambled over to the drinks cupboard and went through his routine of pouring martinis while Roz bent down and picked up the newspaper, carefully putting it in page order. He did not ask why she was here. He handed her the glass.

'I put a bit of lemon peel in it. Brightens it up.'

He sat down heavily.

'Must be near the end of term,' he remarked, after sipping his drink.

'Finals were over yesterday. The term's ended. University too, for me.'

'Is it?' He spoke with indifference.

'I suppose you know why I'm here to plague you, Uncle?'

He looked into space, patted his jacket and pulled out his pipe. When he lit it it went out twice. Cursing softly, he tried again and at last managed to make it draw. A cloud of fragrant smoke filled the room. He went on smoking steadily. Roz wondered if he said nothing because that would force her to speak. Or perhaps he was just tired and wished she hadn't come. She gave in, after a long two minutes.

'Uncle. I'm sure you know why I've come to see you.'

'No. Why did you? Not for the pleasure of my company, I suppose.'

'I *am* glad to see you,' she said, surprising herself because this time it was true.

He took the pipe from his teeth, gave her a sardonic look, and said, blinking, 'Indeed. Glad to see me, eh? You still haven't said why you're here.'

'Oh, come on, Uncle Jack. Because you forwarded that letter from Gran, of course.'

'So I did. And?'

'And now I'm positive she's in trouble, so you've got to tell me where she's gone. Then I shall go to her. She needs me. You don't plan to go, I suppose?' she added, with a sudden clear vision of her opponent.

'Me chase after the silly girl? I should damned well think not.'

'The more reason for me to go.'

He rubbed his chin with his hand like a man who was undecided if he needed a shave.

'What did she say in her letter?'

She was astounded.

'Didn't you read it?'

'Good lord, girl, I don't steam open other people's letters, what potty ideas you do get into your head.' He gave a bark of laughter.

Roz took the letter from her shoulder bag and passed it to

341

him. He read it and returned it.

'Don't see what you're fussing about. She thought you'd like to hear from her so she sent a word or two. That's all there is to it.'

'I don't believe you.'

He began to smoke his pipe again seeing, with a pain which was real and breathless, how like Sophy this girl was – the Sophy he had been thinking about all day. All his life.

'Why,' he said, speaking quietly and even with a certain care not to hurt the girl looking almost beseechingly at him. 'Why do you imagine it's a good idea to go rushing to help somebody who doesn't want you?'

She longed to explain that she was not like him, surely he could see that? Not only because of the unimaginable countries of the years which separated them, with all the perilous mountains and chasms, deserts and flowering wildernesses that were his past and her future, but in their very natures. He had been active towards his sister because she had demanded it. She had needed him and Roz, knowing Sophy, was sure she had loudly said so. Jack was a man who only helped somebody if she yelled. Otherwise his philosophy was to let things be. Roz couldn't do that – oh most desperately she couldn't.

The old man, true to her judgement, looked yearningly towards the newspaper she had folded and put out of reach on the other side of the room.

'You think I only see Gran as she is now. But I don't. She isn't the worldly woman who knows all the answers. I suppose that's what she wants us all to believe but she isn't like that at all.'

'What does all that mean?' he asked patiently. He still longed for his newspaper.

'She did things you thought were crazy,' said Roz, and then recklessly, 'I know about what happened to Gran, all the stuff she never told me. Her going to France and the affair with that French guy and having his baby. And the way you helped her to get it adopted. I read her diaries. I read every word.'

She hadn't bargained on quite so extraordinary an effect. She'd never even seen him disconcerted. Now he simply gaped.

'Gran's diaries are upstairs in the maid's bedroom, I suppose you shoved them there. Did she ask you to look after them or what? Anyway the last time I came to see you I poked about and found them.' She put on her best, bold face.

She expected ructions but none came. She was like a girl defending herself from a coming blow, who bent away, arm raised and finally lowered it to find her opponent had put his hands in his pockets.

He shut his eyes for a moment and instead of the opponent she saw an old man who grimaced; a kind of wince went across his face. She thought – I've hurt him. How can I have done that?

Opening his eyes, he glanced about for his pipe which he had put nearby in a big pottery dish. He picked it up and looked at it.

'So you dug up our past, did you?' he said without resentment, his voice as dry as dry. 'Why didn't you tell me at the time?'

'I thought you'd be furious.'

'I might have been.'

She did not understand that and left it unresolved.

'Uncle Jack. I beg you. Now I know so much why not tell me the rest? I do love Gran, you know. That isn't the sort of thing you'd ever say but I believe you love her even more than I do. Why not tell me? Please.'

He received her tender attack with his returned impassivity and sure enough, it was easy to guess what he would do, he stood up and went to the drinks cupboard, busying himself with filling their two glasses.

Roz waited. She knew she had had an effect.

He turned round, sighing slightly, and shambled over to her. How badly he walks, she thought, he is almost lame. He brought her out of her own selfish absorption; she watched him with compassion and an uneasy feeling which couldn't be affection, could it?

343

Sitting down he lifted his glass.

'Slainte Mhath.'

'What does that mean, Uncle Jack?'

'It's the Highland toast for good health. The Gaelic. I've always liked the Scots. They're rogues.'

'I think you are too.'

For a moment he looked pleased.

'Do you? Bless my soul,' he said and laughed.

A small silence fell.

Something had altered between them. It had happened at the moment she'd expected he would be angry. Did he feel a kind of relief, a sharing, something Jack did not do with other people, as far as Roz could tell.

'So you read Sophy's diaries?' he remarked. 'Not cricket, was it?'

'I suppose not.' She resisted her usual desire to put herself in the right. His laws were his own, and she unexpectedly found herself understanding them.

'I never read 'em, you know. Sophy said go ahead if you want to. She brought 'em here years ago. I did glance at them once but they were womanish.'

'*Uncle Jack!*'

'But they were,' he repeated. 'So is Sophy. Sometimes I feel she's the only out and out woman I've had the bad luck to cope with.'

'Have you coped with a lot, then?'

He squinted at her.

'One or two. One or two. Very pretty they were. I have dinner with an ex-mistress of mine now and then. She lives in America but she's been known to pop over. Dyed hair now.'

She felt a triumph, an expanding of her heart. She liked the old man, and was on his side, whatever that might mean.

'So you still want to know where that potty sister of mine has got to, do you?' he said. He did look tired. He stared at her for a moment through his thick glasses and added, 'Want to stay the night?'

Roz tried not to laugh at the reluctant hospitality.

'No, thanks, Uncle, I'm at the Linden Arms. Look, I'm

sorry to barge in and start nagging. Would you prefer it if I came round in the morning? I mean —' she added, rare for Roz, 'if you can put up with me at all.'

'Daresay I could.'

There was a pause.

'Mrs Matthews is off to some shindig at Chipping Norton. Yes, the morning would be better. You could make me a cup of coffee, mm? About eleven would suit. Then you can hear the whole damned tale, as that's what you're so keen about.'

'Oh, thank you, thank you!'

'Don't look like that,' he said very suddenly, as if the radiant face turned towards him gave him intense pain. 'Never look like that. Nothing's worth looking like that.'

She scarcely took it in but sprang up and went over and kissed him. His cheek was cold and flabby and he smelled of eau de cologne and tobacco smoke. When she smiled down after the kiss, she thought he looked shy.

Roz found Michael in the hotel garden on an evening still warm after the long day. They sat under the trees and she told him what had happened. She repeated her great uncle's remark that to read somebody's diaries 'wasn't cricket' and when Michael laughed, she wished she hadn't told him. She felt protective about Jack.

'Was he shocked, then?' Michael asked, still smiling.

Roz said no. Staggered, really. It was obvious he had forgotten all about the diaries and there she was blurting out the grisly secrets.

'He was rather nice, actually,' said Roz, who found no words to describe how she saw the old man now. 'He's such a loner. So tough and solitary and he was so very good to Gran . . .'

'I'd like to meet him,' said Michael, hearing the changed voice.

'Would you? Perhaps I could fix it. I'm to go and see him around eleven in the morning. I could ask then. Why don't you hang around somewhere, there's a lane down the road

345

which leads to a wood? If he says okay after he's spilled the beans, I can come and get you.'

'That sounds fine.'

The next day was fresh and sunny, matching Roz's mood. She positively sparkled, and Michael was amused, impressed even, by how affected she was by good news at last. Her desperation at losing her grandmother had impressed him. It showed a loving heart; he wanted her to care for him like that; no, much much more.

They made a simple plan. Before Roz went to her great uncle's house, she would drop Michael, having shown him the lane and the wood.

'It's the best bluebell wood in Oxfordshire, but of course they're over. Take a book,' she added. The Oxford refrain. 'After I've asked him, and I may be some time, I am pretty sure he'll say yes to meeting you. So then I'll come and collect you.'

Punctually, Roz's shabby car approached the house, which turned out not to be half as grand as Michael had imagined. It was just a building of Cotswold stone, rather square and unremarkable except for the climbing roses. Roz put on the brakes.

'There's a signpost down there on the left, it leads to the farm. You'll see the gate to the wood on the right, only a few steps along the lane. Okay?'

'Fine. See you when I see you.'

She watched him walking down the road, then turned in at the gates of Fuchsia Cottage and parked her car near Jack's. At last, at last, she thought, going to the front door. She rang the bell.

There was no reply.

'He'll be in the garden, of course,' she said aloud, and walked round the house and along the terrace. In the garden the lawn sparkled with the remains of last night's dew. The raspberry nets were slightly awry and a blackbird had managed to get inside, he was clucking and stealing. The sky was deep cloudless blue. The morning hummed with country sounds, all small but combining into a low steady thrumming, from bees, from insects. It smelled like paradise. Every rose Jack had ever planted was blooming this morning. Pink, white, salmon, dark dark red.

There was no sign of him.

Confidently she went to the kitchen door and turned the handle. It was locked.

'Damn, what goes on?' said Roz, speaking aloud again. 'Uncle Jack, you are a real bore.'

She returned to the front of the house. He must be in. He'd never tell her to come and simply go off to see friends; in any case his car was parked in the drive near her own. She tried the handle of the front door. Also locked. She rattled it and rang the bell again. She felt so frustrated she could have screamed. He can't hear the bell, she thought, his hearing isn't all that good. She went on ringing.

The morning round her continued to hum and whirr with the sweet noise of high summer; there was a flutter of wings as a robin came by, vanishing into tall pink mallows at the gate.

'It's ridiculous, I *know* he's in!' said Roz, vexed and frustrated. She gave the front door a kick.

She stood trying to decide if she should fetch Michael. No, that wouldn't do at all. Jack must have taken a sleeping pill, old people who slept badly did that. He'd be snoring away upstairs and if she and Michael managed to get into the house, how would Jack feel, woken up and unshaven, with a perfect stranger around? He had locked the front and back door last night before he went to bed and now she couldn't even get in to shake him awake.

Returning to the back of the house, Roz looked up at the windows, peered through into the kitchen, pushing aside the thorny stems of a climbing rose. In the end, saying loudly, 'To hell with it!' she took off one of her shoes and broke a small pane of glass in the kitchen door with her heel. Gingerly putting her hand through the hole, avoiding the sharp broken slivers, she unlocked the door.

'He won't be pleased, but I don't care. He can't sleep all day,' she thought.

She stepped over crunching fragments of glass and entered the kitchen. A tray of breakfast things had been laid, violet-wreathed cup and saucer and matching teapot. The marmalade had been transferred to a glass jar with a silver lid. What an old bachelor he is, she thought, as she went quietly up the stairs to the first floor.

His bedroom door was closed.

She took a deep breath and knocked.

'Uncle Jack! It's me! You've overslept,' she shouted gaily.

No grunting noise, no grumbling voice replied. No sound came through the door.

'Uncle Jack?'

She opened the door slowly from a kind of politeness and peered in.

The old man was lying in bed, turned on his side facing her. His hair, sprayed out on the pillow, was like grey seaweed. One of his arms was out, the hand half open. His dark brown eyes were open too. They looked fixedly at her.

She knew he was dead.

'Oh no. No, no,' she cried out and tears came rushing into her eyes and the strange solemn presence of the dead stood by her like a great dark figure and she was afraid. The figure in the bed was as still as waxwork. Somehow it wasn't Jack any more. It was a husk. A shell. Something and nothing. But she was afraid and she fled down the stairs as if pursued by the dark figure and with trembling hands unlocked the front door and ran out into the blazing morning. She did not stop running until she came to the bluebell wood where Michael, perched on a gate, was reading a paperback. Looking up, he saw the wild figure running towards him and jumped down and caught her as she flung herself at him.

'He's dead. Dead. I found him – I –' She couldn't stop sobbing.

He sheltered her in his arms, petted and soothed her and at last she managed to tell him.

'I'll come with you,' he said.

'Isn't it awful, Michael, oh isn't it awful? He died with nobody there. He was all alone and I only saw him last night and you and I might have saved him and how did it happen, isn't it awful —'

'Stop, my darling. Stop. He probably died of heart failure, it can happen like that, it was a stroke or something. Isn't it really a good way to go? Don't be so upset. Please don't be so upset.'

But Roz, shivering and sobbing, was not to be comforted. They went into the quiet house and up the stairs and there was the figure who would never move again, lying with outstretched hand and open eyes. So dark, those eyes were, thought Michael as he gently closed them. The lids were stone cold.

'Don't cover him up! He'd hate it!' said Roz, trembling at the door and Michael, who had been drawing up the sheet, did as she asked.

She ran down the stairs into the sitting room, and sat down in the old man's chair and leaning back, not bothering to hide her distorted face, she sobbed as if her heart would break. Why wasn't I kinder? Why was I so rude and stupid? I never liked him and supposing I had, he would have liked me and been fond of me as he was of Gran. Uncle Jack, Uncle Jack, why did you go away like that and never even say goodbye? The awful, foolish questions, the awful sense of loss, the solemn presence of death standing in the room at the top of the stairs rent her heart.

Michael let her cry for a while, then came over and knelt on the floor beside her and gave her his handkerchief. With a sob and a sniff, she wiped her face.

'Do you know who his doctor is?' Michael asked.

'It's too late to get one,' she said, not understanding.

'I think we should try to find him, Roz. Dear love, don't cry so.'

'He had nobody. He was by himself. I never even knew he was ill.'

'You said you kissed him last night.'

'Yes, I did do that.'

She was comforted but only for a moment.

He began to look round the house for an address book; by

the telephone, in the bookcase, the kitchen. There was nothing.

'Perhaps it is by his bed,' said Michael. She caught at his arm.

'You can't go up there. He doesn't want us. I can feel it.'

She was rolling the handkerchief up in a ball, smoothing it out and rolling it up again.

'If that's what you want, Roz. Who do we know who might tell us the doctor's name?'

'Nobody. Nobody. He's got friends but I don't know their names or where they live. It's not my fault,' she wailed like a child.

'Didn't you tell me there's a woman who comes in to clean?'

'Mrs Matthews. I don't know where she lives – in one of the villages – anywhere.'

He reflected for a moment.

'Okay. Nothing to be done about the doctor. So we'd better go to the police right away.'

'The police!'

That brought her out of her grief with a jolt.

'Roz, look. One can't discover a dead body and not report it. We don't know any of his neighbours and this house is a mile from anywhere. We don't know his friends. No doctor. No neighbour. Come on, we must find a police station.'

He shepherded her out of the house, carefully locking the door with the key he'd left on a windowsill. Odd to lock the door, he thought; against whom? The angel of death was there already.

Chipping Norton was busy, there was a good deal of traffic. The shoppers jostled and hurried about with bulging plastic bags or children in buggies, waving windmills. To Roz everybody seemed somehow to look doubly alive: the red faces of country women, suntanned faces of country children, struck her like a garish painting. How pale he'd been. I should have known he was ill last night, why didn't I realize it? He was such a funny colour, not like he used to be, and then he made that face as if he was in pain. The unanswerable questions,

350

the self-reproaches, rushed back like a plague of stinging insects.

'Wait here, I'll find out where it is,' Michael said as she pulled the car into a space near the town hall. He got out of the car and strode away. For the first time since she had entered Jack's bedroom, she suddenly remembered her grandmother. Sophy's brother was dead. For an idiotic moment she thought – I'll ring her.

Michael returned almost at once, saying the station was nearby. Roz locked the car. He led her as if she were a child or perhaps a dog, down some streets to the police station. A sergeant at the desk was dealing with a woman who had lost her watch.

'It fell off in the supermarket. Are you sure it hasn't been brought in yet?'

Michael muttered, 'Let's sit. This may go on some time.'

Roz followed him to a bench and they waited. The woman kept repeating herself, the sergeant was not very patient, it was minutes before she finally left. He turned his attention to them.

'Can I help, Sir?'

Self-possessed, Michael walked over to the counter and said they had come to report a death. This was Miss Pearson his fiancée and they had discovered —

'Wait a bit, wait a bit, please, Sir,' said the sergeant, a lantern-jawed man with an Oxfordshire accent. 'You can't just come in and report a death, as you call it. What are you talking about? An accident? Why haven't you rung for an ambulance? Who said the victim was dead?'

He looked fussed, and shouted for a colleague.

Michael, tart but still cool, said there had been no accident, the death – of this lady's great uncle – was of natural causes.

'Are you a doctor, Sir,' said the policeman rudely.

'I am not a doctor, I am a student, and – if you will let me tell the story –'

'Oh yes. We'll do that. You'd better come into our interview room if you please. You too, Miss. Didn't the gentleman say it was you who –'

'Yes. I found him,' said Roz.

In a small stuffy room smelling of disinfectant they were given two hard chairs. They were asked for the facts, please. Grief and shock began to leave Roz, she kept thinking about Jack alone in his house, alone in his room, with nobody to take care of him.

The sergeant had begun slowly writing down their names and addresses. She burst out, 'Send for a doctor *at once*! My great uncle is dead, he is stone cold and alone and a doctor should go – and it's horrible of you to keep us here!'

'You need a cup of tea, Miss.'

For the following hour Michael and Roz were rained with questions, made to give 'statements', and – particularly when Roz said she'd broken into the house – treated with rising suspicion. Michael sensed that the broken back door was the worst possible part of the tragedy as far as the police were concerned. From the moment they heard she'd entered the house 'illegally' as they called it, their manner, at first quite bullying, changed and was rude. The fact that Roz was a relative of Jack, already called 'the deceased', cut no ice. Michael saw their point. Just because you were related to somebody who had died did not mean you weren't up to something. On the contrary it could mean that you were. The police could think Roz, and indeed he himself, had something to do with Jack Hayward's death. Their innocence could be proved easily enough, there were no signs of violence, the house had been as neat as a pin and all the doors locked. The poor old guy had simply died. But that didn't mean Roz and he hadn't broken into the place, perhaps to steal.

A point occurred to him and he said suddenly to Lantern Jaws, 'If you are thinking we've been up to no good, why do you suppose we came here to report the death? We could be in London by now.'

'That's as maybe, Sir.'

'That's as it *is*,' said Michael. He was getting as angry as Roz, who had only held her tongue because Michael had gripped her arm until she almost screamed.

The day dragged on. A doctor was sent for, drove out to

Fuchsia Cottage and later, very much later, handed in a report. Roz and Michael were offered more tea. The sergeant who left them for a while returned to inform them that 'the deceased died of natural causes.'

'I told you that three hours ago,' said Michael.

'Yes. Well. Couldn't take your word for it, could we? There's the matter of breaking and entering.'

'Sergeant,' shouted Michael, at the end of his tether, 'this lady was fond of her great uncle. She had an appointment to see him, as I have told you fourteen times. We came here of our own free will and unless you intend to charge us – and God help you, you'll look a proper fool if you do – my fiancée and I propose to leave right now. Here is my address. Here – Roz, give it to him – is hers. Here is my Barclaycard, bank card, driving licence and Roz – give him yours – here are hers. A photograph of us both at Oxford, see? That's my fiancée's college, Somerville. Her Access. American Express. Anything else you need? Fingerprints?'

His temper was as hot as the girl's when roused and he was furious. He was also within his rights and the sergeant knew it. With a look which was as good as a punch in the stomach Michael glared at the man, took Roz by the arm, shovelled up the plastic cards lying like a rainbow on the table and marched out of the station.

'I will telephone you tonight. We wish to go to the funeral,' he shouted over his shoulder.

He dragged her to the car.

'Come on. Let's get back to London. I feel like murdering the entire police force.'

They returned to the Linden Arms, paid and collected their luggage and although they'd eaten nothing set off for Bowling House. They scarcely spoke a word until Roz said, 'Michael. Are you hungry?'

'No. Anger is my meat.'

'Mine too.'

'Don't let's talk until we get home.'

They left Oxfordshire at the time when streams of cars were driving from the capital all set for long Cotswold weekends, drinks in the garden, country pleasures. It seemed a lifetime, it was somebody's lifetime, since Roz and Michael had left Oxford.

Michael had asked if she preferred him to drive, and this time she was glad to say yes. During part of the journey she fell asleep. He was sorry when she woke very suddenly and he knew memory had come back to hurt her. He felt her shiver.

It was dark when they arrived at Chiswick; the lamps on the towpath were a line of orange moons and a pub down the road was noisy, somebody was singing – it sounded like an Irish voice, it was melancholy. People like to celebrate the good weather, Michael thought, and if you're Irish you sing sad songs.

The sitting room at Bowling House was dusty and airless and when Roz opened the windows, the song came into the room.

He sat down and patted the cushion next to him. He was glad when she came close. He didn't know why but he had half expected her to put a distance between them. But when he put his arm round her, his heart dropped. She did not respond.

'Well, Roz?'

'Yes?' she said vaguely.

'I think it's time we decided about the summer. Losing your poor old great uncle has been a hideous blow, but now you must try to get better and get over it. The best thing is for us to go to Italy the way we planned. Do you agree?' She didn't answer. He went on talking. 'Roz, you must see that everything's changed now. Your only lead was your great uncle and he's gone, and with him all the answers. We must just pick up where we left off before your Gran's letter came.'

Her listless silence made him exasperated and sorry.

'She doesn't know he's dead,' she said.

'I realize that.'

He didn't add – and if anything happened to you she wouldn't bloody well know about that either. From the very beginning he'd had his own ideas about Sophy Lingard. The old had no right to be unfeeling egotists. He'd been with Roz from the start of all this, had seen its effect on her. And now this sudden death. She was in a bad way.

The night was hot, and sex was in his thoughts and he knew it was miles from hers. He went out to make some sandwiches with the food that he, not Roz, had thought to buy in a garage shop on the drive back to London. Coming back, he found her hunched in the corner of the sofa. He switched on the television. It was an old black and white movie made in the 1950s at the time when Hollywood had fallen in love with Italy; a sentimental tale of an American virgin loving, and resisting, Italy's ancient toils. There was a good deal of film on location: fountains spurting water from the conch shells of river gods, exquisite churches approached by enormous flights of steps freckled with age. There were the towers of the old, old churches and the sound of their pealing, tumbling bells. Michael was pleased at the fortuitous appearance of the country which was in his thoughts. He had been to Italy two or three times and loved the unchanged green hills, the dark exclamation marks of the cypresses, the rivers and bridges and pure skies unchanged from those glimpsed over the shoulders of saints in medieval paintings. It was a country for happiness. But Roz on the other side of the room was in shadow; the single table lamp turned her hair into a halo but left her face in the dark. She did not bother to look at the pleasant nonsense on the screen. She was as immobile as the poor body lying in the cold double bed in the empty house.

He stood up, saying he wanted some water and went out into the kitchen; frustration made him thirsty. He poured a glass of Malvern water which he had remembered to put in the refrigerator – Roz had not even switched it on, or the hot water either. She seemed to have given up. He stopped feeling tender and wanted to shake her and tell her to pull herself together. Much good that would do.

On the kitchen table was her bag, the usual out-sized leather satchel-affair, open because she had thrown it down without fixing the clasp. The contents had half spilled out. What a mess girls carry around, he thought, remembering how often he had watched almost any girl he knew burrow

355

into the disorder to hunt for her keys.

He picked up the bag which was heavy and began to put its contents back as methodically as he could manage; a paperback, a wallet, letters, lipsticks, a broken comb and her examination papers. He shuffled the papers together as best he could, and then noticed familiar handwriting. It was the letter her great uncle had forwarded to Oxford – the second from her grandmother.

He sat on the kitchen table and re-read it to see if it contained anything they had missed. He saw why Roz had been worried: what *did* 'I had to go – and go fast' mean? Or 'I wish I could explain what has happened, dearest girl, but I can't'?

How infuriating women could be. With a pleasing sense of male chauvinism after days of hiding it from his lover, Michael thought that a man would be incapable of writing such a letter, because he'd realize its effect. No, I don't like Sophy Lingard, he thought. I'm surprised Roz is so attached to her.

He read the letter over carefully a third time. The fanciful handwriting matched his idea of the woman whose photograph Roz had pinned on her board at Erith Road: a woman whose lined vivacious face had traces of past beauty, whose smile was open, carefree. I still don't like her, he thought. He studied the sentences as if he were researching: one by one. He looked at the postmark. Then from curiosity and thoroughness he held the letter up to the light in case there was a watermark.

Then he saw it. The profiled head with coarse nose and strong chin – the face from the Delacroix paintings. The heroine who held flags over dying heroes, whom they called Marianne and who wore the cap of Liberty.

'*Roz!*'

There was no reply. Still shouting, he ran into the sitting room. She scarcely bothered to look up, although he had yelled at the top of his voice.

He switched off the television.

'Your grandmother's in France,' he said.

15

Four days later they returned to the Cotswolds for Jack Hayward's funeral.

It had been a time of telephone calls. Michael had spoken twice to the lantern-jawed sergeant and been given the information that there was now a complete doctor's report and that Mr Hayward had died from a massive heart attack: death had been 'instantaneous' droned the sergeant and would he and Miss Pearson, please, sign 'certain documents'. Michael agreed, giving the date of the funeral which had been arranged by some of Jack's many friends, not one of whom, on that fatal day, he and Roz had been able to find.

After her first passionate grief Roz did not talk about her great uncle, but often when Michael looked at her, her face was sorrowful. She was closer to Michael now, they made love every day, giving and exchanging a sweet temporary joy. He wondered if her shock and sadness made her such a wild lover. He put away the thought because it hurt.

'I've never been to a funeral,' Roz said on the morning they were due to leave for the Cotswolds. Hunting through her cupboard for something black, she dubiously produced a woollen dress which had seen better days.

'Will this do? It looks awful.'

'You're not obliged to put on the trappings and the suits of woe. Most people don't nowadays.'

She struggled into the dress which clung round her narrow waist and fell with long skirts below her calves.

'*He'd* like it if I did.'

'Are you sure?'

'Positive. Uncle Jack kept all the corny rules and regs.'

'I expect he did. An act of respect,' he said smiling. 'And you do look good in black. Nervous?'

'Yeah. Do they really play piped music of "Nearer My God to Thee?"'

'Of course they don't. That was the *Titanic*.'

'You've been to a cremation, have you?'

'A friend of my father's ages ago. The music was treacly. Wouldn't it be?'

'Does the coffin disappear behind little curtains like in that old James Bond movie?'

'Stop worrying, Roz! It's very quick and not at all impressive and as for James Bond, didn't he manage to escape?' he said, laughing. Then could have bitten out his tongue because she looked as if she was going to cry. She gave a long sigh.

When they arrived at the crematorium, some miles from the town, they were surprised to see the large number of cars already drawn up outside the chapel. What a lot of friends he had, thought Roz; the thought comforted her. Most of the cars were clearly belonging to people with money and every woman waiting, in the sort of gathering that only happens at weddings and funerals, was in deep black. Coats. Dresses. Even hats. The men wore black ties.

'I told you,' whispered Roz. 'Rules and regs.'

The chapel was ugly and a large garden surrounding it was so well kept that the roses looked as if they were made of crimson plastic and the beds as if somebody had dusted them. There was no sign of the hearse. To Roz's dismay everybody seemed to know who she was.

'You're dear Jack's grand-niece. We've heard so much about you.'

That could not be true.

'You must be Sophy's granddaughter, you look so like her! It is so sad, my dear, that poor Sophy is abroad. She will be dreadfully shocked at Jack going like this. Will she be back soon?'

Michael said firmly that they hoped to see Sophy very soon.

People whom Roz had never met came over to take her hands and even, moved by loss from their customary reserve, to kiss her. Roz introduced Michael. He was correctly dressed in his only dark suit and had found a black tie from somewhere. He had subtly joined the elderly people, keeping their rules and regs. His hand was shaken, he was smiled at by strangers with sad faces. Do they think I am Roz's fiancé or even her husband? he thought. Or does it occur to them that I'm only her lover?

The hearse drove up and the crowd moved into the chapel, an empty meaningless place which did not feel like a church. The coffin looked small when it was carried in and placed in front of the altar. Is Jack really in there? she thought. But it is only his shell. That was what I saw lying in his bed. Not Jack. He had gone. Where is the old man who made such bad jokes and dived into the drinks cupboard and smoked that pipe which kept going out? It was less than a week since she had kissed him and he had looked shy.

The wreaths and bouquets were magnificent, tiger lilies, sweet-scented freesias, and most of all the multi-coloured exquisite English roses of summer. When Roz saw them she blushed – she had forgotten you send flowers to the dead. Syrupy music came out of the air. Could it possibly be a hymn? Surely not.

The vicar who took the service had a swathe of white hair and a lined face like an actor's. He said a few words about the dead man and Roz and Michael heard – it was a morning for shocks – that he had been 'a true believer'. 'Many's the time he took Holy Communion. And on some Sundays, we met at his house, such a pleasant welcome I was given. We talked,' added the vicar, smiling, 'about eternity.'

Just as in the James Bond film, after a blessing over the coffin the music changed and swelled to a climax and sure enough the coffin began to move slowly towards a small pair of red velvet curtains which pulled aside to let it through and then closed again. Roz wanted to giggle. Half from miserable nerves, half from mirth. It was so contrived, it had no solemnity, she thought. Can't we do better than that?

A little lady with diamonds came over to them after the service and invited them both back to her house 'just to drink to Jack'. Roz was instructed to follow her car. For a seventy-year-old, the lady drove like a competitor in the Grand Prix, landing up in front of a big country house some miles away where many of the other people at the funeral were soon assembled.

Roz and Michael spent three hours talking to total strangers and listening to eulogies about 'dear Jack' who had been a great local favourite. His jokes were repeated: that would have pleased him. After drinks, a cold luncheon, coffee, cakes, and the strain of behaving perfectly among people forty years older than they were, Roz and Michael finally managed to leave.

They were worn out.

The next morning while they were still asleep they were woken to the resented sound of the telephone. Roz tottered down the staircase to answer it. She felt she had done her duty. She felt she had had enough. She and Michael had decided to go to France and look for Sophy. She set her mind on only that. But was tired and cross.

'Yes?'

'Miss Pearson,' the voice was familiar, but she could not place it. 'Mr Russell speaking.'

Two days before, Roz had received a bill from the detective on which he had scrawled the receipt for the further fifty pounds paid without her knowledge by Michael. The bill was for a further hundred pound advance.

'I know you'll want to hear my report and some interesting plans for the future,' he cheerily said.

'No, Mr Russell, I'm afraid I don't. We have paid you what we owe you and I have now received a letter from my grandmother.'

'Oh, excellent! But does she give –'

Roz interrupted.

'Thanks for all you've done, Mr Russell, but I'm sure you'll understand that we don't need you any more.'

The silence was full of disappointment.

'If that's your decision, Miss Pearson. As a matter of interest, did your grandmother tell you where she actually is?'

She had a strong feeling that he knew Sophy had done no such thing.

'I don't see –' she was caught out and mislaid her good manners.

'Why I should ask? Only a natural pride in my work.'

The man was hurt. 'I telephoned to say that one of my London Airport contacts is pretty sure he spotted her. She checked in on a flight to Nice. Of course, that plane does go on to Italy, but he's positive he heard her say "Nice" at the checkout desk; he recognized her from the photo you gave me. So did your granny, beg your pardon, did Mrs Lingard write from the south of France?'

'Yes,' lied Roz.

Aware of her own gracelessness, she thanked him again and Russell breezily wished her 'all the luck in the world', which made her feel worse.

She was still annoyed with herself when she went into the hall to collect the post. There was nothing but junk mail and one typewritten letter for her. She looked at it indifferently and went up to her bedroom to do her hair. Michael came in, looking fresh, with his just-bathed look. He gave her a grin.

'I've been thinking, Roz. We'd better get a move on. Planes at this time of the year are packed, we'll have to take whatever reservation we can get. We'd better go to the bank this morning and get some travellers' cheques.'

Roz did not answer, she was opening her letter.

She suddenly shouted, 'Damn. Hell. Bloody, bloody hell.'

He looked alarmed. '*Now* what is it?'

'Only that I haven't a bloody penny.'

The letter was from a firm of solicitors in the Strand. It stated in ponderous language that for the present it was not possible for any of the banker's orders 'arranged by the deceased, Mr John Melville Hayward' to be met. No monies for the time being could be paid into Roz's account. And Probate, of course, had to be settled.

'Probate can take about two years,' Michael said. 'Stupid, isn't it? Will you inherit from your great uncle?'

'I don't know. I suppose so. Gran once said she and Jack were both leaving me their money. I told her to shut up, it sounded ghoulish. I suppose the cash will come to me eventually. But the point is – when?'

'Tricky. With your grandmother not here. You'll probably be quite rich in the end. That's never bad news,' he said, without much expression.

'But it's now that matters,' said Roz, biting her lip. A pause. Then she brightened suddenly.

'Of course. What a fool I am. I can use my plastics.'

Michael said nothing for a moment. Then, 'Better not.'

'What do you mean? Of course I can pay for everything with my account cards, that's what they're for. I wish you'd take that holy look off your face.'

The quarrel which followed was unexpected. Roz insisted that she could run up bills, why not? They were going to France and she needed some money. Her allowance had been stopped, and until Probate, whatever that was, how could she possibly manage?

'I simply don't see what you're objecting to.'

But Michael flatly refused to 'allow' her, his word, to run herself into debt. Perhaps some long-ago peasant among his forebears, some frugal ancestor's blood in his veins, had given him a horror of debt.

'We can live on my money,' he said. 'We'll get to France on standby. It'll probably mean flying in the middle of the night, but who cares. If we're careful we'll have enough to last a week or two in the south. Debt is like an octopus. It can wind round your neck and throttle you.'

She looked at him mutinously, then blurted out, 'I won't live on you.'

That was when the row began. His manner, which had been responsible and practical, altered. He said coldly, 'I see.'

362

She knew she had said the wrong thing and began, 'I didn't mean –'

'To hell with what you mean. Why do I bother with your affairs? Why do I? Go on, get into debt. Run up bills. Throw money around like shit, what do I care?'

'Don't shout at me, why are you so beastly, you know what a horrible time I've had –'

'That's right, now cry. It's the great way to win, isn't it?'

'Leave me alone, leave me alone.'

'That's what I intend to do.'

He slammed out.

It was Roz who gave in. She had to spend a good deal of time getting him out of an icy displeasure. At first when she approached him all he said was, 'Just leave it, Roz. I'll get over it later. But I can't come out of it like you do. I'm best by myself.'

She always recovered from her bad temper like a woman emerging from a muddy pond, good humour and a sense of balance being a shower of clean water. But it looked as if he would never come back to his normal self. When he spoke to her he looked at her as if he did not even like her any more. A doubtful voice in her head said – is that possible?

They embraced at last and passion was more intense because they had been separated, it gave an almost cruel excitement. They lay and loved and slept in each other's arms. And within a day they had left Bowling House and were in a plane circling in the night sky, swooping like a bird down on to the airstrip of Nice.

The flight was hours late, it was nearly five in the morning when they arrived, hollow-eyed. They could not afford the extravagance of a taxi. Michael said reasonably, 'We'd better stay here, then get a bus to Nice. They told me at Cooks that there's another bus, quite cheap, to Cannes at seven. Let's have a coffee.'

Roz agreed with an ill grace. Her head ached, there had been some kind of strike at London Airport where they had waited for hours, she felt dirty and exhausted. Here she was in the south of France, the place where Sophy had lived as a girl, here was the great adventure. And all she and Michael could do was drag through the hours until they caught a workman's bus.

'I hate having no money.'

'And I hate you having no philosophy,' was the reply.

Time crawled. But at last, in an early morning so exquisite that it was like a basketful of opals, they climbed on to a bus which trundled along the huge curved promenade towards the town. The sea, blue as a cornflower, stretched to a horizon edged with orange and red. On empty beaches of white pebbles, two people were going down to bathe.

Cannes was awake and buzzing when their bus drew up at the square near the port. Michael took over. His French was good and so it should be, thought Roz, considering he had only taken his Finals a few days ago. He had studied a guide of inexpensive hotels and had booked a room which suited his very limited resources. No taxi again. They walked, stopping for Michael to study his street map. Roz knew she could not complain again: it was Michael who was paying for everything.

The hotel, called Le Jardin Fleuri, was a curiously shaped house at the end of a triangular stretch of garden covered with trellis and a thickly growing vine. A few orange cannas were blooming in one narrow patch but apart from these, the hotel scarcely lived up to its name, for the vine leaves kept off the sun, and flowers didn't manage to grow under it. The entrance hall was piled with luggage, there was much coming and going, telephones were ringing, and English tourists in short-sleeved shirts, stomachs bulging, were paying their bills and making jokes in bad French to the pretty girl at the desk. The place, worryingly hot, smelled of cooking.

Michael asked for their room. Another young girl, there appeared to be no men working in the place, took their bags expertly and laughingly refused to allow Michael to help.

'With bath,' said the girl, unlocking the nastiest room Roz had seen in her life. It was as bare as a prison cell and had an unmistakable look of concealed dirt. The floor of plastic tiles was not clean. The windowsills were thick with dust, the bed sagged and the sheets of some coarse material were not exactly white. She was sure they were slightly dirty as well. The bath was behind a plastic curtain and screwed into the wall.

The girl flashed them a smile and clattered away.

Roz sat on the bed. It sagged further.

'Don't look so glum,' snapped Michael, unzipping his bag and pulling out his washing things, electric razor and a clean T-shirt. 'I can't help it if we haven't much money.'

'*I* can't pretend the place isn't awful, Michael. I was trying to decide what we can do about it.'

'Move, you mean?' He went to the basin and ran the hot tap. It was cold.

'Yeah. Move.'

He did not answer but began to wash and shave.

Roz sat on the bed, running her fingers across the scratchy sheets. When Michael had made the fascinating discovery of the French watermark on her grandmother's letter, when they had decided to come to Cannes.to the place where Sophy had spent a vital part of her youth, Roz had made up stories to herself. Gran must have come to France to meet her lover again. They might even marry; oldies did marry sometimes, it was rather funny and touching. The idea of her grandmother as elderly heroine fixed itself in Roz's mind. She had never imagined that her noble search would bring her to a smelly hotel with a bath screwed into the wall, in the company of a man whose manner was a reproach because she 'lacked philosophy'. She was behaving badly. She knew it.

Michael's withdrawal into disapproving self-righteousness got on her nerves. Sitting in a heap, not bothering to wash and change, she thought of Sophy feeling the same about Daniel Vergé. He'd got on Sophy's nerves. We're bad pickers, Gran and I. We need men who spoil and pet us; we don't get that kind. Well ... Sophy did with Bob Lingard, he had been the spoiler and Sophy had not loved him.

'I'm going downstairs. That will give you some space,' said Michael coldly. He was fresh as a daisy, washed, shaved, in clean clothes, his hair done with a wet comb. 'See you in the garden.'

He left the room. Without anybody to sulk at, Roz cheered up and examined the awful bedroom – she had been right about the dust under the bed, it was half an inch thick. She unpacked and put her clothes into a chest of drawers: she had to kick it to get the drawers open. She then ran a cold bath in the tub behind the plastic curtain. By the time she had bathed and changed, and splashed on some scent – 'when shall I be able to afford this any more?' she said aloud, she felt better. She put on a white cotton dress, and laced her espadrilles up her legs which were still suntanned from hours on the Oxford river.

In the garden which was not *fleuri*, Michael was sitting under the vine, drinking coffee and reading a French newspaper. He stood up as she came towards him, and the gesture, his expression – his very self – affected her.

'Mike, I'm so sorry.'

'So am I, and you look very beautiful. Why do I say that? You are, all the time. Now, shall we plan a campaign?'

People arrived and left while they sat under the vine. Roz and Michael scarcely noticed them. They were intent on what they must do next, unconscious of the sound of English voices or the traffic in the road outside.

'The first thing, Roz, is to remember some names from the diaries. The people we must try and contact.'

She banged her forehead.

'Oh Christ, I'm not sure I can remember ... except that the girl she travelled with was called Violette.'

'Concentrate,' Michael said and gripped both her hands. She sat racking her brains, as if reading again those bulging faded diaries. 'Yes. I remember. Sophy's lover was called Daniel something. Merger? Now, that's not right. Berger? Not right either. It was the French for something to do with apples. Got it. Vergé.'

'Good. Go on.'

Roz searched her mind like a woman searching through a shelf for a book into which she foolishly put a ten pound note. Slowly, slowly, she began to remember names and places. Anne-Marie Dufour and her parents. The house whose name

Sophy had derided — she had called it 'a bit much' — was called Les Hesperides. There was Anne-Marie's fiancé, Claudio Arrighi. Her brother Paul.

'That's my lot.'

'Not bad. Not bad at all.'

'Something else. The wholesale fish business. Dufour and Co in Nice. Telephone book?'

'Why didn't I think of that?'

They talked, and lazed, tired after the journey, and had some lunch which was inferior, but they were too interested in their plans to worry that the lettuce was limp and the ham hard at the edges. They drank Evian because it was cheap. 'The Brits,' remarked Michael, hearing a bellow of laughter from an adjoining table, 'are calling for madder music and stronger wine. They'll pass out later in the hot sun if they drink at lunchtime.'

'We don't care, do we?' said Roz, smiling at him.

The first stop was to find the Dufours. When they fetched the telephone book from the hotel, and opened it on the table under the vines they found over twenty Dufours. Over a dozen Vergés. Not an Arrighi to be seen.

Michael whistled.

'I can see us living on the telephone.'

'What about first names? Monsieur's was Anselme.'

'They only give initials in the book. When we telephone, if it's not the right family they won't know who we're asking for.'

'But isn't that what the police do when they're trying to trace somebody? They sit at their desks with telephone directories and toil through name after name until they find the right one.'

'How do you know that, Roz?'

'I've seen them doing it in TV serials.'

He thought over the idea and finally said, 'Okay, I suppose that's best. We'll try and do six every day. Early in the morning is the time to catch people. And when we've done our stint, we'll go to the beach.'

'Twelve would be better than six.'

'You *are* an eager beaver. Shall we say eight?'

They went to an enormous post office winking with computers and crowded with local people queueing or paying bills, arguing with girls at the counter or sitting at tables filling in forms. Sophy and Michael began the long task of standing in a telephone box.

'Like the policemen,' said Michael.

The days took on a pattern. Breakfast in the dusty garden. Then a walk, before the great heat started, to the post office. They began to know the streets and sometimes halted to look in ravishing shops, until Roz decided that she would rather not. It made being poor worse.

Michael did the telephoning. Roz thought his accent superb, although he assured her it was 'undiluted Brit'. Each time he put the plastic card into the machine, and asked if he could speak to Monsieur or Madame Dufour, she noticed that his manner had the intensity of an actor's. He concentrated. Then now and again, waiting for a reply, he took her hand and kissed it. She loved him. She stood thinking – we're here. In the very town where Gran was young and fell in love. Her heart expanded because Michael shared her search, understood her. Gratefulness made her tender, sex melted her, morning after morning when they telephoned perfect strangers.

They found nobody. They completed the list of the Dufours and not one of the polite people who answered had heard of Anselme or Yvonne or the daughter Anne-Marie, or the son Paul.

'I am afraid they are not of our family, Monsieur. I am so sorry.'

'I regret.'

'My excuses.'

'Unfortunately. No.'

None of the people to whom Michael spoke thought it a nuisance to be bothered by an English voice asking for somebody they had never heard of; they were sympathetic, as if it were a kind of compliment that a foreigner should enquire for a family of their own name. With a chuckle a man or woman would say, 'Our name is common enough in France.'

It took three days to get through all the Dufours. Early each morning Michael ploughed through his eight calls but they were rarely straightforward. Sometimes Monsieur, Madame or Mademoiselle Dufour was out and he arranged to call the next day. There were numbers that didn't reply, they had to be tried again. He had adventures. One woman who answered in a low and thrilling voice was a call girl.

'Why not come and see me, Monsieur? We can talk about the Family Dufour. Or other things ... my name is Colette. Don't forget. Colette. A little apartment in the Rue Colonel du Lys.'

Michael had conversations with a doctor, an engineer, a priest, a busy young woman who worked for a builder and an old lady who was deaf, so that he had to shout. Roz, standing beside him, was impressed with his French and more with his patience. He was fluent, and as polite as the people to whom he spoke. Sometimes when he was talking he made little jokes and listened and laughed at the replies.

In the afternoons they went to the beach, having found a Plage Libre at some distance from the rich pay-beaches, where even a coffee could be the price of three telephone calls. The beach was at the far end of the old port round the corner by the harbour. It was sandy and rocky, merry with children and families who brought their own sun umbrellas. Taking the point, Michael bought two raffia mats and a very cheap second-hand umbrella (split here and there), in a street as vivid as an Indian bazaar. Everything was sold there, from battered furniture to orchids, from mountain lavender honey to freshly-caught sardines. On the beach he dug the umbrella into the sand, and Roz, who burned easily, had a circle of cool shade. He also bought some sun oil smelling of coconut which Roz's freckled shoulders needed and Michael's olive ones did not.

At last the morning came when Michael screwed up the paper containing the list of Dufours and threw it into a bin by the telephone box.

'So,' he said, 'that's done, I'm afraid. We need a drink.'

'Can we afford one?'

'No.'

Roz wanted to say – do let's start on the Vergés. Her optimism was the wick of a candle which had become covered with grease, she had to clean it daily, hourly, to make it burn. This was proving to be the maddest of her attempts to find Sophy. Its very unlikelihood meant that it must succeed. But Michael divided time into segments. Work. Then fun. She knew he wasn't going to swelter any more in the post office today; he looked at her and raised his eyebrows.

'I know what you're thinking, my love, and the answer's no. We'll begin the Vergés tomorrow.'

They walked arm in arm down the street. Secretly he was not surprised the campaign so far had failed. He was more and more convinced they would never find Sophy Lingard. But he honoured Roz for the love which had brought them both here and in any case, like many men, he enjoyed the challenge. But one to be met in the mornings and not in the afternoons.

They had a scrappy lunch at the hotel, some vin rosé as a reward for all those Dufours, and set off on their third afternoon for the beach. It was hotter than ever, the sand burned the soles of their feet. The air was full of the shouts of little children, voices half swallowed by the sound of the waves. It was relaxing to lie in the shade, wet with salt water. Roz's shoulders were slightly burned and Michael insisted that until the red had faded she must stay out of the direct sun. Curled safely out of the glare she said, 'You're not asleep, are you?'

He was on his face, like a man felled in the boxing ring. His skin looked a darker brown every day.

'Of course I'm asleep. If you talk quietly you won't wake me up.'

'Idiot. I've had an idea. Shall we walk down the Croisette after supper and have a look at the house?'

'No Dufours there. No Hesperides address in the book.'

'I realize that. But if you call at a house and talk to the people living there now, don't they sometimes know where the previous owners have gone? Or even have a forwarding address?'

She was so enthusiastic. He couldn't bear to discourage that hopeful face. And she looked sexy in her swimsuit cut high to show her naked thighs.

'Good notion. That's what we'll do.'

He reached out his hand; it was clasped by a small damp paw.

Supper at the Jardin Fleuri was worse than usual. Michael suspected the meat in the Boeuf Bourgignon was horse: it had a sweetish sickly flavour. The service was very slow, the entire hotel appeared to be run by girls of sixteen, obliging and inept. He comforted Roz and himself by paying more than usual for the wine, but it turned out no better than the cheap carafes of plonk swigged down by the latest troop of package dealers. All the new arrivals were Brits, noisy and pleased with everything. Michael felt critical and fussy.

They decided to forget coffee and set off, crossing the rich rue d'Antibes where shops blazed and tempted. Outside a cinema a queue of Cannes youth, all in jeans and T-shirts waited to see an American film called *Gun of Death*.

Absorbed by the quest which took up every morning, by sun and sea in the afternoon, by lovemaking which took them early to bed, they had not once walked along one of the most famous promenades of the world. They had seen it only at a distance. Now with the heat round their shoulders like a counterpane they walked under the palms and the pines. Here was the azure coast which had sung like a siren to the English and the Russians, to princes, rajahs, dukes and whores, to the romantic Americans and the genius-painters for over a hundred years. They passed the Carlton with its twin towers, the restaurants and cafés where people sat, easy, idle, talking and talking; how vivacious they are, thought Michael. We only shout or mutter. They walked by many rich hotels and great rearing blocks of marble-faced apartments, balconies bright with scalloped awnings, yellow and white. All along the Croisette were carpets of flowers at the feet of the palms, spreading their colours in bands and crescents, thousands upon thousands of flowers, white and crimson, purple and pure dark red, watered every morning and night, so that despite the heat they burgeoned as if they grew in the jungle. There were fountains, lawns, and the small French roundabouts on which children, awake and bright at ten o'clock at night, circled slowly astride painted wooden pigs.

'Now, Roz. Put yourself into a trance again. Where exactly is Les Hesperides?'

They stopped walking and looked ahead at the long curve of land.

'I think – no, I'm sure – Sophy said the house was almost at the end of the point. Before you go round the corner past the Palm Beach Casino. She used to cross the road and go down to the beach to swim with Anne-Marie or Daniel.'

'Then on we go.'

They went slowly, gazing at the buildings facing the road and the beach. There were no houses at all; block after handsome block, well set up, large or smallish, were apartments. Many had gardens fronting them, some nothing but a drive, a bed of flowers and a palm or two. Crossing the road and leaving the promenade, Michael and Roz walked in silence as each apartment block succeeded its neighbour. Large cars were parked in driveways and water sprinklers were at work, spraying the grass to an almost unearthly green. The air was filled with the smell of wet earth.

'Michael!'

She clutched his arm.

There in large slanting letters along an awning at the entrance of an apartment block were the words Les Hesperides.

The block was high, white, newish, square as a box.

'How funny,' Roz said. Neither of them smiled. 'It doesn't have to be where the house was,' she added, after a moment, 'It could be a coincidence.'

'Shall I go in and ask?'

'Would you?'

She had no heart to go with him, but sat down on a white-painted rock which served as a marker at the driveway's entrance. Even that had the name painted upon it. She looked up at the unfeeling façade of the meaningless building, a honeycomb of people living in square-shaped rooms built one on top of the other. She thought with hazy memory of her idea of the house where Sophy had lived. Old-fashioned. With a French pretentiousness, a look, an echo, of a château about it. Indoors there would have been mirrors and marble floors and gilt-topped bannisters and old curly furniture. Was this patch of ground where Gran had fallen in love? Perhaps the house is further on, she thought, and knew there was no house any more. It had disappeared as Gran had done. As perhaps love does, she thought.

Minutes went by. The scent floated from a fig tree by the gate, sweet, intoxicating. She sat bathed in it, glad of the distraction when Michael reappeared, walking lightly.

'I'm afraid it *is* the same place. I met an old porter on night duty. He actually remembered the house that was here before. Don't jump up, Roz, he'd no idea who lived in it, the name Dufour didn't mean a blind thing. But he said there was a house called Les Hesperides, "*très chic*", which was pulled down in the 1960s, it used to be let furnished, but then somebody sold the land to a property company who built all the blocks as far as the corner.'

'But the name?'

'He was surprised that I should ask. He said in France they always keep the name of a house when they demolish it. He said if you see a petrol station called Les Iris it means there used to be a house called that, and if you see a block called The Garden of Eden – he laughed and said there actually was an apartment block called that – they'd merely used the name of the house which was there before. He said there is scarcely one real house, as he called it, left along the Croisette. And he told me what Croisette means: little cross. There used to be one standing on the spit of land where the casino is now.'

'I suppose,' said Roz, looking at the white building, 'it was crazy to think that fifty years later ...'

'Not crazy. Hopeful. Like you.'

'Not any more.'

'Come on. We've got the Vergés tomorrow, remember?'

They walked back to the hotel. A moon was shining and its pathway on the sea looked solid, as if you could run along it. The pleasure-seekers along the shore, people wandering, embracing, the hotels shimmering with light, the sound of voices from swimmers in the dark water meant nothing to Roz. The apartment blocks were like a rape. Cruel and mindless; she did not care that many people now lived where few had done, that things had to change and that nothing could stop them. The ghost of the house was somewhere there in her imagination.

Both Michael and Roz had begun to think separately that the cause was lost. He was somewhat falsely cheerful when the next morning they went to the post office to begin at the top of a fresh list, this time of families or businesses with the name of Vergé.

Michael wanted to make her happy, and unselfishly suggested they should lengthen the list by the addition of any Dufours who lived in Nice. He telephoned the wholesale fish business; it had been sold twenty-five years ago to a large company based in Paris.

'So,' said Michael, 'perhaps the Dufours made a bomb and settled in Nice. Maybe Paul did anyway.' Roz was too quiet and it was now Michael who was – or seemed – deliberately optimistic.

The calls went on. Michael was very practised now, using a courtly formula and identical words, in a pleasant enquiring tone; every time in more or less similar phrases the answer was the same.

'Ah no. No, nobody of this name here, Monsieur. I am desolated that I cannot help you.'

'Perhaps you might try the Town Hall?' suggested one kindly lady.

It was a new lead and they grasped it. The Town Hall was in a fine last-century building set among lawns and palms and looked rich and efficient. But the city, it seemed, had the same idea as the Jardin Fleuri: it hired girls who were no more than sixteen. The young woman in the entrance hall sat at a large antique desk on which there was nothing but a scarlet telephone. The marble-floored and marble walled chamber was hung with posters exclaiming:

'Cannes! The Croisette! The Festivals!'

'Yes?' she said to Michael, without the customary 'Monsieur'.

The weather was hot and heavy, but she was dressed as a caricature of an American businesswoman: navy blue and white striped suit, white blouse of dazzling freshness, a watch on a gold chain round her neck, navy blue stockings in a world of bare brown legs and very high-heeled leather shoes.

Michael began his enquiries in French – 'I speak English,' interrupted the girl. He explained that they were trying to trace the Dufour family and a Monsieur Daniel Vergé: none of the people they were seeking had been heard of since the 1940s. The girl did not show the faintest pique of interest in an English couple searching for French people who were probably dead and buried. Such requests might have been made daily, boring her out of her mind. Scarcely bothering to look at Michael she said, 'Have you consulted the telephone book?' Admirably, he remained polite. He said that they had. She shrugged. 'Then what can I do? I cannot find them for you.'

Before he could reply – his eyes narrowed slightly – her face altered. It became bright and human. A stout man with heavy eyebrows and the features of a clown appeared from an inner office. He addressed her as 'Anny-Flor'. She giggled and turned towards him with her back to the visitors.

'Let's go,' muttered Roz. 'She doesn't know a thing and what's more doesn't give a bugger.'

The girl's English was better than Roz guessed; she swivelled back and gave them a glare of dislike.

Outside the Town Hall Michael and Roz looked at each other, and groaned.

He continued doggedly with the burden of the morning telephone calls and finally completed the list of Vergés in the district of Cannes. There was no hint of Daniel Vergé and nobody who could help him. Afterwards, according to their established pattern, they walked to the rue Menadier, the

Cannes version of a street market, to buy their picnic and go to the beach. They swam and sunbathed. Drugged with sea and the fresh hot air, they finally wandered slowly back to their hotel.

Despite poor food and an excruciatingly uncomfortable bed, despite sheets which scratched Roz's delicate skin, they forgot everything when they lay down to make love. They found delight, breathless delight, in the poky bedroom. They slept in each other's arms.

Now and then Roz did not fall asleep at once. She kept thinking of the question she knew was in his mind as it was in hers. The question she dare not and he did not ask aloud. 'What do we do next?'

Sophy was still missing. Nothing was resolved. And Roz was entirely dependent on him. It was a strange sensation to her. She'd been growingly proud of her independence from the time she had left school. There had been a year of waiting before she could go to Oxford. She had got herself a job in a supermarket and later worked for a firm which packed books. She was determined to earn enough to supplement the allowance given her by her grandmother. Roz had an impression, no more, that Sophy was a little sad at her first steps into freedom. But Roz was delighted, as she told Ally later at Oxford, to be more or less in charge of her own life. Ally laughed. It was scarcely independence, she said, if you had an allowance. Ally had none. Roz was not put out. She continued to feel that she had taken her first steps into the real world.

Now, her grandmother and great uncle gone, she seemed to have lost more than family money. Where was her freedom? She needed Michael very much, not only because she was penniless.

She knew very well she could live at present on her plastic money. But if she did that, how would he feel about her? It would look so ungrateful, in exchange for his love and care. As the precious time in Cannes dripped by, day after day, she was more troubled and more involved than ever.

Michael had not quite given up the search. He tried Nice for the Dufours, spending what seemed hours of the growingly hot morning in telephone enquiries – never taking the first 'I regret, Monsieur' without more painstaking questions. But at the end of each session he shook his head and said to Roz 'no luck again'. The breathless summer heat went on.

That night, their lovemaking was more intense after the daytime sun. Slippery with sweat, they lay together, the heat on them like a great heavy blanket. Their window was always wide. They could hear music, but only faintly, for the Jardin Fleuri was away from the main streets and restaurants of the town. It was very late after they had finished making love. She lay for a long time facing Michael who lay on his back, but grasped her hand. She traced his profile with her eyes, wondering where the youthfully ironic features had come from, what other member of his family had his particular crinkly dark hair or cleft chin.

'You put up with me going on about Gran,' she said, lifting his hand and kissing it, 'I don't know a thing about your parents. It's awful that I've never asked. I remember you once said they were divorced and your mother married again and lives in the States. But you never said about your father. Where is he?'

'A good question.'

'What do you mean?' said Roz, startled, 'he is alive, surely?'

'Very much so. Somewhere or other.'

The answer had the effect of causing her to lift herself on her elbow.

'Michael. Tell me. I truly want to know, I should have asked weeks ago. How selfish I am.'

He had turned to look at her and she saw the effect of what she had said without understanding his expression.

'I suppose my situation isn't much better than yours,' he said. 'Well, both parents are in the land of the living but that's the only difference. My mother left my father five years ago. I'm surprised it wasn't sooner. He's a mining engineer and he was never with us – never. In the last fifteen years he's worked in, among other countries, Argentina, Honduras,

Turkey, Peru and Venezuela. He simply travels from job to job and earns a good deal, apparently. He's never been too anxious to part with his money, but that's another story. Don't think I don't like him. I'm sure everybody does. He's very tough and he can make you laugh. He's always sunburned and he gives you the impression of a man who enjoys life. He drops by to see me every two and a half years and spends a couple of days with me. We go out to a meal together and have some laughs. Occasionally he buys me something. Then again maybe he doesn't. You can scarcely call that having a father, can you? As for my mother, she married an American, a Southerner, who made a lot of money in his forties and fifties. He was a big name in New York property at one time. Now he's settled in his own country, South Carolina, and taken up painting water colours. Gets them exhibited, too, and sells most of them. My mother is very fond of him. But under his thumb. Big business men seem to have that effect on their women. She sort of jumps to attention when he wants anything ... I can understand that, he's impressive. Their home is rather extraordinary – I went to stay for a month last year.'

'It sounds romantic.'

'Does it? Well, alligators aren't, and they crawl out into the gardens sometimes. All that water. And the drippy trees. The entire population where Mother and Stuart live seem to be in their sixties and given to strong martinis. Did you know South Carolina is the only province in the States before the Civil War which wanted to be *English*?'

'What's that got to do with anything?' she said, laughing.

'Not much. Stuart told me. He sounded shocked.'

It came to her as she lay, her body touching his, that she should have known all these things. He had known about her from the first. She felt guilty and tender.

'Does it depress you?' she asked with her sometimes-childlike bluntness.

Michael laughed and pulled a lock of her hair. He said, with a look which was unconsciously beautiful, 'No, my dear one. It does not.'

The morning came when they finished the last telephone call. Michael said, 'Thank you. I am sorry to have bothered you, Monsieur. Thank you again,' and rang off. He turned to Roz and gave a kind of shrug and then, smiling involuntarily, 'Don't look so tragic! Let's go to the beach.'

They spent hours as usual by the sea, but the sky had begun to change. It was no longer blue but white and dazzling. The sun was there somewhere, the air was hot, but the light came through a glittering white haze and when evening came, there was no sunset.

That night when they were asleep, Michael woke suddenly to hear the heavy noise of rain. It did not patter down like English rain with an unceasing gentle sound, but poured fiercely, bouncing on the roof outside and beating through the open window. He hurried over to slam the window shut, and walked straight into a lake on the floor.

Roz woke and asked him sleepily what had happened. He climbed back into bed and put his arms round her. She was warm and dazed and sexy and soft and he made love to her accompanied by the tumult of the pelting rain.

Next morning when they woke there was scarcely any daylight. Outside it still poured. The air was strangely cold.

'We haven't a raincoat between us,' said Michael at the window, watching the rods of rain. 'And what about all those unfortunate Brits who arrived last night, poor things? They expected to spend a day on the beach.'

'They'll survive.'

Something in her voice made him say, 'You do sound unsympathetic sometimes.'

She sat up, sunburned shoulders flushed, the rest of her washed out by the grey half light. She gave a sharp little laugh.

'Why should I bother to pretend? I don't care. It would be hypocritical to say I mind if they get drenched. We're going to be, I suppose, so why not them?'

'Very unattractive.'

'What?'

Michael grimaced. There were times when her voice was

379

like a knife thrown in a circus. And not just to make an outline round his figure.

'Being hard doesn't suit you. Or me either.'

She gave a contemptuous noise.

'You always behave in that holier-than-thou manner whenever I tell you the plain truth. I am tired of pretending everything's "just fine" as they say in American films. It is not just fine, it is awful. It's quite true, I don't give a fig for those tourists downstairs, and we've failed to find Gran, and I've had it up to here racking my brains as to what we can do next.'

Ah, he thought.

'And besides,' continued Roz still in the same tone, 'if I can't think of something, why don't *you*?'

She took his breath away. He had come to France with her, shared time and money with her, taken on her worries and become, as it were, a part of her. He loved her, God damn it. But forgetting for the moment the treasure of her body, which made him strong to love her, weak to adore her – at times – the plain fact was that he'd saddled himself with a selfish creature obsessed with finding a relative who clearly wasn't going to be found. He was appalled at the way Roz sunk her teeth in her loss, gripped it, shook it to and fro. At the impotent anger when things went wrong. At the sheer egoism which she would say sprang from love, but was in his opinion nothing but a stubborn refusal to give in with a little grace. He said in a level voice, 'Roz. Face up to it. We must go home.' Her dark eyes looked black, her mouth tender as a child's fell open. She said again, 'What?' and this time the knife struck home.

'It is no good,' he said, watching the small furious face, the body leaning threateningly forward. 'It simply isn't any good, Roz. It was worth doing, of course it was, and I understand why you were so determined to come here but we've failed. I suppose it was doomed from the start, a wild goose chase. Yes, yes,' seeing her incredulous expression, 'I know I agreed that we'd try, and I might also point out I was the one who found the French watermark on your grandmother's letter, you didn't. But we have been here over a week, we have done every single thing we can. We have telephoned God knows how many people and we have not had one, no, not one single clue. We're as ignorant of where she is as we were when we landed at Nice airport. What's more, the money's nearly finished.'

'So you're throwing in your hand.'

'Yes. And so must you.'

'Must? I'll do no such thing.'

Exasperated, positively stuttering, the word he spoke was the wrong one – 'Darling!' – he actually sat down on the bed and reached for her, scarcely knowing what he was doing, only that he was angry and sorry. She scrambled away to put a space between them. Even then he tried to be patient.

'Roz. Use your nut. What good are we doing here ringing up strangers? They don't know any Dufours. They don't know any Vergés. The house went thirty years ago. It's all finished. It's dead.'

'Including Uncle Jack and probably Gran. Is that what you think?'

'Oh, stop pulling out the organ stops.'

She had succeeded. His kindness was gone. 'I do not think she is dead, as you know perfectly well. But I do think she does not want you. She's covered her tracks too thoroughly.'

It was what her great uncle had said. She stared at him, hearing the old man's voice.

'It was crazy of us to think this would work,' Michael said and added, when she continued to say nothing, 'since you didn't take it in just now, I'm afraid I shall repeat it. It's to the point. My money's practically run out.'

'Then go.'

'What do you mean?'

'Go. Go. Go. Get out. Leave me alone. Pack and bugger off, Michael Chance, and the sooner the better.'

She turned to face the wall, showing him only her beautiful freckled naked back and burned shoulders.

'Roz –'

'Go away. I hate you.'

'Okay, if that's what you want.'

He bathed, shaved, changed, packed. It was surprising how fast he moved in the silence filled with the hammering noise of the rain, the silence which had fallen heavily between them. Roz lay on the bed behaving like a child; she pulled a pillow over her head. The sheets smelled of sex and scent.

He finished packing, put his wallet into his breast pocket, then took it out again and laid his French money on the dressing table by her hairbrush.

'Roz.'

No reply.

'Do you really mean it? Do you intend to stay?'

'Yes.'

'What are you going to use for money?'

'I shall get a job in a bar. That English girl I was talking to at the port the other night says it's easy.'

He stood for what seemed a very long time to the listening girl. At last he said, 'I see.' But still did not move. She spoke in a voice muffled by the pillow. 'I really do hate you, you know. You don't understand anything. I wish I'd never met you.'

Then he walked out. But he did not slam the door, he only closed it.

Roz lay crying in the bed they had shared. She wept from anger and misery, from a heart which ached, from wanting Michael and telling herself he was a bastard and did not care for her, from guilt, and from a longing to see her grandmother and the unhealed wound of being deserted. At last she stopped, had a bath, looked at her swollen eyes with disgust, made up her face and put on some jeans and a sweater. It was very cold. She trailed down to the dining room. The poor tourists pitied by Michael were trying to make their breakfasts last a little longer; one of the young waitresses was running in and out with fresh pots of coffee.

I wonder if he paid the bill, thought Roz, with a pang. Damn. I'll use my Barclaycard now he's gone. I'll get myself into debt and to hell with it.

The croissant was more rubbery than usual but she was too

382

miserable to be hungry and ate because she knew it would be stupid to go out into the wet morning on an empty stomach.

She was drinking her coffee, fortunately hot, holding the cup in both hands to warm them when a man came into the dining room. He was not in the usual run of package dealers, he was distinctly French. His jacket was cut in the stylish Continental way, he wore his clothes with a sort of swagger and there was also something both swaggering and ironic in his face, which was long and attractively lined. He appeared to find the tourists, the child waitresses, the awful weather, the very world itself rather comic. Roz resented his expression. Who was he, to stand there looking superior? She swallowed another mouthful of bread and turned her eyes away from him.

'Miss Pearson?'

He had walked over to her table. Hearing her name Roz went crimson with surprise.

'I am sorry to disturb you,' he said with a French accent which was pleasant and not very pronounced. 'May I sit down? As the weather is so inclement' – (where did he learn such a word? In English classes?) – 'I imagined I might find you still in the hotel.'

'How do you know my name?'

'I was sent your address, Mademoiselle.'

'I don't understand,' said Roz hoarsely.

Oh, she wanted Michael.

'I have come from your grandmother,' said the stranger.

16

The first thing she thought on hearing the incredible words was – *has Michael gone?* She started to her feet, gabbled in bad French that she must fetch her companion – she scarcely knew what she said. The stranger took it more calmly than she did and said he would be glad to wait.

Roz fled. She ran out into the reception hall and asked the girl at the desk if Michael had left. The girl, busy with her papers, said she did not think so.

'Perhaps Monsieur is in the dining room?'

Shaking her head and saying he wasn't, Roz hurried up the staircase, rushed down the corridor and burst open the door of their bedroom. He wasn't there. How could she have imagined he would be? She returned in haste down the stairs. The girl in reception had just relinquished her post to a colleague with whom Roz had once or twice had little chats. A dark girl, friendly and perhaps a little older than the rest of the young staff.

'You are asking after Monsieur Chance, Mademoiselle? He left half an hour ago.'

'But are you sure –'

'Yes, Mademoiselle, I was on duty when he paid the bill. For you both,' said the girl tactfully. 'He went a little later. He did not,' she added, looking out at the rain, 'ask me to ring for a taxi.'

Roz stood. A wave of misery came over her. Michael had paid the bill, he really had left her; he was gone and this extraordinary thing had happened and he wasn't there to be part of it. She felt quite distraught with loss and disappointment as she returned to the dining room where her visitor was unconcernedly sitting, elbows on the table. He stood up as she came across to him.

'I'm sorry,' she said in English, 'I was here with a friend and I hoped to find him. But he's already gone.'

'Ah.'

The stranger asked no questions, ordered fresh coffee and continued to smoke, remarking on the weather and how disappointed the visitors must be to see Cannes at its worst. Roz replied automatically. She wanted to shout, 'Where is my grandmother?' But somehow this man was the one who held the reins, the winning cards, the initiative, the secret. She knew she could do nothing but wait, crazy with frustration.

At last coffee arrived, he told the waitress who served them that he preferred 'very little milk; the khaki colour I prefer, yes, that will do, excellent.'

Roz dug her nails into her hand.

The youthful waitress, more careful and respectful than with foreign tourists, left them. He drank his coffee, saying, 'As I thought, not good.' He gave her a middle-aged smile.

'You are asking yourself how I know you were here. And why I don't come to the point.'

'Yes.'

'I'm afraid my appearance is a little too sudden. The best way to prepare a person for the unexpected is by letter. Your grandmother would have none of that. She is so English. She said she did not trust the French post and that hotels are notoriously careless with correspondence. Letters of her own, important ones, had been lost at the desks of hotels. There was nothing for it but for me to come here in person. Of course, I could have telephoned. She would not have that either.'

He added humorously that Madame was a lady with a mind of her own.

'I know that,' exclaimed Roz, patience gone, '*but where is she?*'

'That is why I've come, Mademoiselle. She wants to see you.'

Here it was at last. The moment she had imagined and longed for, the fantasy that somehow in this country where Sophy had been young, Roz would find her at last. Roz had so longed for it, clung to it, disbelieved it, thirsted for it. Her break with Michael had been all for nothing. If only she – oh more than that if only Michael – had waited.

The man introduced himself, his name was Thierry. He explained that he was a friend of Madame's, she had been here in the Midi for some weeks living quietly in a village thirty kilometres away. She had written – had Mademoiselle received the letter? – about a month ago.

'Yes, I got it.'

'Good. That's good.'

'It wasn't good at all. It worried me more.'

'She will be sorry to hear that. She only meant to set your mind at rest.'

Roz said bitterly, 'Oh great.'

'What I tell you upsets you?' he said gently. The girl looked tense. Rather ill.

'My grandmother's letter upset me. The fact that she imagined it would do some good makes it worse. "Didn't mean to hurt me",' Roz repeated savagely. 'Well, she did and she does. I want to see her and I'm furious with her. And there's another thing, much much worse. She doesn't even know her brother is dead.'

'Yes. She does know.'

'How? How? How could she possibly know my great uncle died when *he* was the only person in England who knew where she was!'

'Whatever we do in life, Mademoiselle, banks have to be informed.

'Yes,' he continued, the cigarette smoke veiling his face, 'she heard the news last week. It was a terrible shock. That was why –'

He stubbed out the cigarette and took another from a packet. Roz was not used to a man smoking, none of her friends did; it made the conversation strange, as if smoke fogged the words.

'When she heard her brother was dead she knew she must see you. She asked the bank to telephone to London. She was told that you had left England and a friend of yours, Monsieur Chance? had given this hotel as a forwarding address. You see, it was not difficult to find you.'

She said nothing. She swallowed.

'When would it suit you to see her?'

'*Now,*' said Roz.

His car was parked in the drive and they had to run through the rain, they were drenched in a matter of seconds, Roz's jeans were splashed with mud from the drive, her espadrilles waterlogged. The gutters in the road were overflowing, the sky hung over the town as if somebody had erected a giant grey tarpaulin. Safe in the car, dabbing at her wet face, she said, 'Where are we going?'

'Into the hills. I know you're impatient, but I'm afraid we won't be able to go fast.'

More and more nervous, Roz actually began to look at the people passing in the street in the mad hope of seeing Michael. Cannes was crowded with cars and shoppers under black umbrellas, the progress up the Boulevard Carnot was stop and start. At last they left the town behind. Neither of them spoke except now and again when her companion made a remark about the awfulness of the weather. 'We need the rain and complain about it.'

They drove into a country with all its colour gone, along roads where the olive groves planted a hundred years ago stood along terraces edged with crumbling stones. They went through villages where the shops were lit against the dark morning, and fountains beside which the women used to gossip, ran uselessly into worn stone basins. Then they began to drive into the hills. It was the Provence which Roz had seen in films set in the past; but today no blinding sun shone down, no sunburned peasants worked under the trees, no boy with a reed instrument or girl wearing a striped skirt watched the sheep. The snaking road began to rise steadily; after a while they seemed to be on the side of a mountain. On the right was a drop filled with mist which later turned into cloud.

'When the rain is heavy, this road is practically invisible,' said Thierry, switching on his headlights and leaning forward to follow the white line in the centre of the road. The mist lapped and floated. On the right the valley was filled up with cloud like a saucepan brimming with milk. He was driving at a walking pace, peering into the obscurity; later he apologized and opened the window to hang out and watch the verge – 'they are supposed to be repainting the white lines but when?' he said sarcastically. Rain blew in. At last the road rose higher and the car emerged into a stretch without fog.

'There is the village,' Thierry said.

Appearing out of the mist, an illustration from a children's book, was a small castle, a medieval toy, turreted, bastioned, with arrow slits and even a motionless flag hanging on a flag-staff. Clustered round the castle were stone houses, big and small, high and low, their walls part of the side of a valley which must be hundreds of feet below.

'That's the gorge of the river Loup,' Thierry said. 'Well-named in bad winters. Well, Mademoiselle, we've arrived. I'm afraid our journey was not of the best.'

'You're a brilliant driver,' she said. He smiled slightly. It was obvious that he rather agreed with her.

Where among the jumble of houses, thought Roz, was her grandmother? She swallowed a naïve gasp when he slowed at the castle entrance, drove across a tiny stone bridge and through doors into a courtyard. He parked in the lee of battlemented walls. A door in the castle opened.

A woman in an apron came hurrying out, sheltered under a big umbrella and ran to Roz, leaving Thierry to shift for himself. She bustled Roz indoors. The castle was warm after the penetrating chill outside, Thierry had not put on the car heater and in her thin jeans Roz was shivering.

'Good morning, Mademoiselle, you're as wet as a duck,' said the woman, mopping Roz with her apron and giving her a look of brilliant curiosity. She was quite old, with black eyes fanned by laughter-lines. In motherly fashion she dried Roz's arms and shoulders, exclaiming about the weather, her word was 'diabolical'.

'Is Madame in the turret room?' asked Thierry, joining them and dripping on the stone floor.

'Where else would she be on such a morning?' said the woman laughing.

Thierry took Roz down a stone corridor, up a spiral stair carved into a tower and down another corridor. She was shaking now. Not with cold.

The room he led her into was completely circular. Through turret windows was a view of the misty countryside. A log fire burned.

'Here she is,' said Thierry and left them.

Starting to her feet, arms outstretched, was Sophy.

'Oh Gran. Oh Gran,' sobbed Roz, and ran to her and Sophy hugged and hugged.

It was the girl who finally drew away. Emotion had made the moment – only a moment – beautiful. Now she burst out, '*How could you?* No, Gran. It's no good using that voice and that soppy face, it was unforgiveable of you. Horrible. How could you go off like that and leave me flat? I suppose it simply means you don't give a f—' Habit came back. She swallowed the word.

Sophy stood looking at the rainswept accusing figure of her granddaughter. It was Sophy, not Roz, who had gone pale. The rouge stood out on her cheeks.

'I am so sorry, I didn't think –'

'You don't, do you? That's what your brother implied.'

'You saw him. You saw darling Jack?'

'What the hell did you think? Of course I went to see him. Gran, I'm very very glad to see you but I shouldn't be, because I'm still furious at what you did to me. It was cruel and heartless and if I'd had any sense I'd never have looked for you at all, but taken the hint that you obviously don't care about me. Perhaps you never did.'

'Darling, don't be silly.'

'Silly? I know I'm right.'

But Roz looked and looked at her. Her grandmother was a

389

reality, living, breathing, within arm's reach. She realized now that she had nearly believed, nearly accepted she would never see her again. She'd set her face against that thought, had driven herself and poor Michael mad, she had been haunted by the terrible truth that the old woman she loved had left her for good. Now she was so angry that she wanted to scream. She restrained herself, knowing if she was too extreme it would weaken her case. What was this 'case' she wanted to hang on to, this ascendancy she was determined to establish? It was a fierce clinging, a fury, an iron resolve never to let Sophy escape again. I need her, I love her, if she doesn't love me back I'll force her to stay from shame.

'I simply couldn't believe you could just walk out. Uncle Jack didn't think too much of it either.'

'He told me not to go,' said Sophy, twisting her rings. And then, 'Oh Roz, I can't believe he is dead.'

'I am not going to be sorry for you, Gran. You might have been with him if you hadn't disappeared.'

The merciless attack had, for a moment, the opposite effect of what Roz had intended. Roz had come at her more savagely than Sophy had expected, but she hadn't yet asked for any explanation. Whatever you do, thought Sophy, isn't in a vacuum. She had thought over her decision before she'd left for France. Not for long, it was true, but she *had* considered it and tried to see it from every angle. She still believed what she had done was right, despite Roz's accusing eyes and cruel tongue.

'Well?' said Roz, after a pause while Sophy stirred the logs in the fire. 'What are you going to say? What earthly reason had you for going?'

'Yes, I'll explain. Of course I'll explain,' said Sophy. She walked over to look out of the castle window and when she turned, her face was bright and almost humorous. Roz had no idea what it was that had taken her own power away. Sophy smiled and sat down.

'Thierry gathered when we tracked you to Cannes that you were with a young man. Did you leave him behind at the hotel?'

'He's gone back to England.'

'Why didn't he stay?'

'He just didn't.'

'I see,' said Sophy, who did. 'A boyfriend.'

'Boyfriend. Yuk. What an expression. But yeah, we were together.'

'How passionately you lot do talk,' remarked Sophy, quite back to her old self. 'Together. I suppose that means a big affair. Do you love him?'

'For pity's sake.'

'Put it another way. Does he love you?'

'He did.'

'In the past tense now.'

'We had a row. I don't want to talk about it.'

Serious and smiling, Sophy examined the girl for a moment. Roz stared back, flushed but not annoyed. Sophy said casually, 'Tell me, darling, how do you happen to be in France? I bet Jack never let on.'

'He was going to. He promised, the night before he died. But when I went back to the house next morning –'

She couldn't finish the sentence and then went on determinedly, 'So I still had no idea where you were. Then Michael Chance, that's his name, had a brainwave. He discovered where you were.'

'*How?*'

'There was a French watermark on the letter you sent,' said Roz, and went straight on, seeing Sophy's fascinated expression. 'That was an awful letter, Gran. Anyway, we decided to come to France and see if we could find you. Michael, I might add, paid for everything. Because now Uncle Jack is dead, I haven't a bloody penny.'

'My poor child!'

Roz triumphed at the sight of her grandmother's stricken face and pressed the point home.

'Didn't you realize that? Your family lawyers wrote and said my allowance had to be stopped because of Probate, and in the meantime they wouldn't – well, the bank wouldn't, meet my cheques.'

Still on a winning streak she could not resist adding, 'Michael asked me not to use my plastic money.'

'Why not? Surely the obvious solution,' murmured Sophy, recovering from concern.

'He said Probate can take forever and I bet that's true. He didn't want me getting into debt. *He*,' continued Roz, 'worried about me. He paid for everything. The tickets, standby, and we had to get a bus into Cannes at seven in the morning, we'd had no sleep and the travel agency had found us a cheap hotel which was fearful. The food was totally disgusting. Michael said the meat at dinner was horse.'

She had overplayed her hand, and Sophy threw back her head with a laugh like a schoolgirl. Still giggling she went to the door and called, 'Thierry. You can come in now.'

The Frenchman must have been waiting somewhere nearby, he entered the room almost immediately, glancing from the elderly woman to the girl. Roz had a gloomy resentful face but there was a change in her. She looked younger.

Sophy went back to her seat by the fire and Thierry piled on more logs. He remarked, 'Yes, Sophy, she is like you. Two flowers from the same stem.'

'Oh good,' said Sophy vaguely. 'Darling –' to her grand-daughter.

'Yes?'

'Come on, Roz,' said Sophy, unperturbed, 'You want to know what all the mystery's about, don't you? Now you're going to hear: I asked Thierry not to say anything. I wanted to be sure the story was fairly told.'

'Did you think I would misrepresent you?' he asked.

'Probably. Or miss bits. Anyway, my dear child, it all started in France when I was here, as I may vaguely have told you, as long ago as 1939. What I didn't tell you was –'

'Don't bother. I read your diaries.'

If Roz wanted to throw a thunderbolt she succeeded.

'My diaries? I haven't any.'

'Oh yes you have. Booksful. 1939 to 1941.'

Sophy was astounded. Thierry amused.

'Good God, Jack never burned them! Were they page a day, with newspapers cuttings and –'

'Theatre tickets and photographs. They were in the maid's bedroom at the top of the house. I found them when I was nosing about.'

'After Jack died?'

'I didn't look at *anything* after he died,' said Roz in a thin voice. 'It was when I went to see him. He was going to lunch with some people, and made it obvious that he hoped I'd go off to London and leave him in peace. I'd been nagging about you and getting nowhere.'

'Jack keeps – Jack kept his promises,' said Sophy sentimentally.

'You don't get it, do you?' said Roz, now speaking with a kind of scalding disdain. 'You'd gone and I wanted, I longed to find you. I was worried about you. I thought you were ill – no, don't interrupt, I don't want to hear – I thought you were mortally ill and then later I was sure it was not illness but some other kind of terrible trouble. Uncle Jack wouldn't help. Yes, yes, I know all about the promise he made to you but to hell with that. Wasn't what I felt important? Anyway, I stayed behind deliberately when he was out and did some detecting. I went through his desk but some of the drawers were locked. Then I searched all through the house and I finally found the diaries and read them' – her mood swung back again – 'I know about you going to France and what happened. I told Michael.'

'Tell her the rest,' said Thierry slowly. 'Tell her that I am your son.'

PART FOUR

17

The morning she met Bob Lingard again was hard for Sophy. It was like putting on fancy dress. In the year before the war Jack had taken her to the Chelsea Arts Ball; they had enjoyed hiring their costumes, Jack in a cutaway coat and silk cravat, Sophy with sausage curls and a hooped crinoline. The clothes had been unfamiliar and heavy, difficult to wear and very amusing. She had the same sensation now, she was in disguise. But it was not a game.

She was overwhelmed by the way Bob welcomed her. He was gentle and concerned, grateful, moved by her accepting him all over again. His gallantry was so old-fashioned. She was awed by such extravagant gifts of the heart.

He kept looking at her, smiling not from amusement but from pure joy. The sun slanted through windows latticed with brown paper strips, every man who entered or left the huge club was in uniform; and there was Bob in his dark blue, handsome and terrifyingly happy. And Sophy in fancy dress.

For what Bob saw and what she was were no longer the same. He saw a virgin and she was not. He saw an English girl from the home counties and she had France in her very blood. He saw a girl who truly loved him and she, alas, did not. He saw — to Sophy this was the most alarming because of its approaching physical difficulties — a girl with an untouched body who had never had a lover or a child. But Sophy had given birth to a sweet-smelling black-haired scrap who had sucked her milk and whom she had rejected. Her body was no longer the thing Bob would promise to worship in the marriage vow.

During lunch he was thoughtful and Sophy, in a moment of cruel relief, thought he might be going to break the news to her that his leave was over tonight. It would be a respite at least. Instead he said doubtfully, 'Sophy ... I wonder ...' a hesitation, 'might I buy you something?'

She beamed with a resolute brightness.

'I would love that.'

'Would you? It's just that it's been so long and ...'

His sentence trailed and she knew he was offering more than just a gift. They began to discuss what it should be, a bracelet, a brooch. Sophy felt nervous and tender, filled with the guilty affection of the cheat who has not been found out. And it was so very obvious how much he loved her.

There was a telephone call from his adjutant while they were sitting over their coffee. Saying 'Don't stir or I shall believe you're going to vanish again,' Bob left her, and crossed the crowded room to go out through the swing doors.

Sophy sat playing with a coffee spoon, oblivious of men who glanced at her with covert admiration. Why was it that there were times every day when she wanted to lay her head on her arms and cry her eyes out? Her physical hardiness had brought her through France with Violette, given her the courage to face the cruelty of the Dufours, kept her going on terrifying journeys in little boats on an enemy sea. It had remained with her throughout her pregnancy. She had leaned on it. Spent it. It had magically renewed itself. Her sexual passion for Daniel had faded and she had been set on single goals – getting to England, bearing the child, surviving, living. Every scrap of that was gone. Nature had no further use for her.

Lulled by the voices of strangers Sophy knew how empty she was. Yes, empty. Hollow, void, drained. At school the teachers used to speak of qualities which would keep the self strong in future life: self-respect and self-command, self-denial, self-discipline. She did not believe she had one of them; she had come face to face with a Sophy she could not bear.

She pulled herself together when she saw Bob coming back. He sat down and pressed her hand.

'I don't have to be at Pompey –' he meant Portsmouth, 'until tomorrow night. You said you were going home, my darling —'

'I can put it off.'

'Sophy, you don't mean it? You haven't seen your parents yet, you must be counting the hours –' he was torn between his love for her and his reverence of her parents.

'But I'll be home with them for ages, weeks, months, perhaps.'

'Until you're called up.'

'Exactly,' said Sophy to whom the idea hadn't yet occurred, but who immediately assumed an invisible Wren uniform. 'The point is *we* only have until tomorrow.'

'Oh my darling. Thank you.'

In the afternoon in dusty London they went to the Burlington Arcade where he bought her a gold bracelet, the bright links and chains of her future marriage.

The telephone call to her mother was not easy but soon over and Sophy spent the rest of the day with Bob. They went to a film, then to dine and dance, and finally to kiss on the doorstep of Halsey Street in the deep blackout.

'You're so wonderful. Sophy. Sophy.'

He would not come into the house to see Jack that night.

'I don't want to talk. Only to think about you.'

He pressed his cheek against hers, then waited until she disappeared into the black square through the doorway.

Jack was not in bed, although it was after midnight. He was sitting with a file of papers on his lap, a pad of paper and a pen. He had been at work but looked up, pleased, as his sister in long pre-war finery floated into the room.

Using one of his phrases loaded with meaning he said, 'Any good?'

She sank on the floor, her skirts frothing around her. She

had not seen Jack since this morning when he had urged her to telephone Bob. She launched into an account of what had happened. She told him how happy Bob had been to see her, how glad, almost overcome, and how he had bought this – holding up an arm emblematically hanging with golden links. She spoke of dates.

'For the wedding?'

'Sure. I said Christmas.'

'Why not earlier?'

'You mean why aren't I going to be off your hands at once; like tomorrow.'

He didn't bother to contradict her. His affection was strong and thick, an oak tree of brother's love older than either of them, hundreds of years old if you counted the rings.

'It's cruel to keep a chap waiting.'

Sophy was pleating and unpleating the hem of her skirt. She was searching for the least crude way of explaining what was on her mind. She picked her words.

'Jack. There's something I want to say to you. I expect you've thought it yourself, but were too tactful to say.'

He took her up on that.

'What's on your mind?'

'Isn't it obvious? Bob is going to find out about me. I mean, find out that he isn't the first man in my bed.'

She did not say 'the first man in me,' which she rather wanted to. After the day's pretence it would be a relief to talk like that.

Jack lit his pipe. The scented tobacco gave them both a vague sense of comfort. It seemed to blur the worst of the difficulty with homeliness.

But he could not help being slightly amused at the quandary. Up until now he had dealt with a girl who had lost a child not from death but from choice. He knew it to be a heavy, possibly a terrible experience for a woman; but he did not believe his frivolous sister hankered for the little chap. She was often bright and her looks had come back. Yet she had certain times of darkness, of inward grief; he had heard of those from one of his mistresses, a passionate Swedish girl

398

with whom he'd slept before the war — a gymnast in sex. She'd had an illegitimate baby and given up the child and talked about it too much until he successfully silenced her by taking her to bed. Now Sophy wanted his help again — how was she going to get round the fact that she had had another man? The puzzle interested him.

'Bob's potty about you, isn't he?' he said in his vernacular.

'Oh yes.'

'Then that's your trump card.'

'You're a lot of help.' She sensed his apparent unconcern and was heartened. She tried to be fair to her brother and herself by thinking aloud.

'I do love Bob in my own way. I mean I'm very fond of him, and he is lovely and I want to have a go at being a good wife and all that. But I keep thinking of the wedding night. Those scenes in old-fashioned novels — they're in Shakespeare too. A man is disgusted at finding his wife isn't a virgin and he refuses to have anything to do with her. He throws her out. She's been ruined. I don't *feel* ruined,' Sophy continued flippantly, averting her eyes from the sorrow which often waited patiently to destroy her. 'What can I do about all that, Jack? What can I possibly say to him? And don't suggest that I should tell Bob the truth.'

'I wasn't going to.'

He puffed at his pipe. His silence seemed to imply that he had no ideas and he startled her when he suddenly asked, 'How's your stomach looking?'

She couldn't help laughing.

'Not bad. Flat. Look.' She gave a slap at her belly covered in white taffeta. 'Well, it is still bit flabby but I'm doing the exercises they gave me at the hospital and I'm wearing a roll-on. And it does seem to be getting more like itself.'

'I thought women got stretch marks after giving birth.'

'What strange things you do know, Jack. Yes, I've got one. But only one. The midwife said that was because it was my first. She said when a girl has a lot of kids her stomach gets to look like an old elastic corset. Mine doesn't.'

'That's not such bad news.'

'I suppose it isn't.' She sounded doubtful.

He took the pipe out of his mouth.

'Tell you what. I'll bet Bob's the sort who only makes love in the dark.'

Sophy met Bob the following morning and they spent the day together. She liked him very much. She was affected by his handsome looks, his rank, the casual way he wore his uniform, his medals, his mystery. He had almost lost his life and never spoke of that. He asked her many questions and listened absorbedly and marvelled at her adventures. While she talked and he sat watching her, she remembered that Paul had done exactly that. For a moment she thought of Paul with a kind of longing, she did not know why.

Bob said her return to England was nothing short of a miracle. He took her hand, and thanked her as if she'd given him a gift of limitless value, for putting off her return to her parents so that she could be with him.

When the time came for them to part he refused to let her come to see him to the train at Waterloo. 'You don't want to break my heart, do you?'

'You'll break mine if you don't kiss me again,' she heard herself say.

When she was in bed that night in Halsey Street and began to think about Bob, a passionate gratitude filled her. She loved him because he loved her. His kisses, his way of looking at her, his strong hand holding her, his half-choked declarations, were so many necklaces of flowers. She was sure of him as a queen might be who stood looking at the courtier kneeling at her feet. To be with Bob was to be safe at last. It did not come to Sophy that nothing was safe any more. She was sure of her future, sure of Bob, and began to compare him with Daniel. There was not an echo, a look, a trait, a single attribute of resemblance. Daniel was selfish, as she'd noticed was the case with a good many Frenchmen. He was vain, proud of his masculinity, his authority over her. He had never allowed her to get away with anything. Courting her, as they called it in France, he firmly kept the ascendance. On the fatal night when mad with jealousy she had attacked him, Daniel had hit her across the face, thrown her into a hedge and left her. She imagined Bob's horror at the idea of a man lifting his hand against a woman. Not a single thing about Bob resembled Daniel: not his appearance, his voice, his kisses, his nature.

The ordeal of going home to her parents which Sophy had been dreading because of the necessary lies, was not as difficult as she had thought – entirely because of her brother. When they arrived at the house, he went into the hall, pushing Sophy ahead of him and shouted, 'Pansy? Ready to kill the fatted calf?'

Sophy's mother came literally running out of the kitchen, to laugh and kiss her daughter and – while Jack stood making jokes – mop her eyes.

Their father heard voices and appeared out of his study. This time Jack said, 'Look what I found hanging about in London!' His father's grunt was nearly a welcome.

Pansy, smiling, not-quite-crying, went straight back to the kitchen to make some tea and Sophy's father agreed to come and sit with 'the women' as he called his wife and daughter.

Prompted now and again by Jack, Sophy told the parents her story. 'Don't forget about how awful the food was,' put in Jack. 'Ma, you won't believe it, your child ate roasted crow!'

All evening there was Jack, strong and solid and ordinary. A blessing.

Sophy was very conscious that the difficulty was transposing six months in Devon to the same period of time spent in France and Spain. But Jack was undismayed by the needed somersaults. Before they arrived at the house he said, 'Don't bother about it. People never want much detail, even parents. They ask questions and don't listen to the replies. Unless they're the police, of course.'

'What do you know about the police?'

'Nothing much,' was the bland answer.

Sophy, only temporarily distracted from her worries, said, 'Surely Mother will listen and take it all in and probably see the holes?'

'Pansy listens less than most. Haven't you noticed?'

Gazing at Jack, Sophy realized that she hadn't. She was slightly offended at his certainties about their mother.

'Didn't she miss me *at all*?'

'You don't go in for much daughterly feeling, do you? You seem to expect a lot of the maternal kind.'

His voice had a touch of asperity.

Her return to Sussex, as Jack had suggested, proved a short-lived wonder. Her mother became accustomed to Sophy's presence in less than a day. Most of Sophy's local friends were gone – they were in uniform overseas or scattered across the British Isles; they were driving tractors as Land Girls or working in hospitals. The few she did meet looked at her with curiosity. They could scarcely credit that she had actually lived in France after the defeat.

'Why didn't the Germans put you in prison?'

Sophy explained that 'her' part of France was under the Vichy Government. But nobody appeared to see the difference.

'What was the food like?'

'People queued for six hours and came home with nothing. We had no potatoes, no milk, almost no meat. The cheese went bad,' said Sophy who liked giving some slightly supercilious old friend a jolt.

The friends disappeared, their leave over. Soon Sophy's presence was taken for granted and local people no longer wanted to hear about her time in Vichy France. The middle-aged women who met her with her mother in the town were cordial enough. Pansy did not tell her daughter that they'd begun to ask when Sophy was going to be called up.

Before they parted, Bob asked Sophy if they could be married on his next leave, whenever that might be. She agreed fervently. She wanted very much to marry him and an idea had taken hold of her – that she could become pregnant as soon as possible. Wouldn't having a baby fill her empty self? In the meantime she kicked her heels at home, bored, and decided she must join the Forces.

When she told Jack this he said it was 'a bit soon, don't you think?'

'Why? I might just as well.'

He rubbed his chin in the way he had.

'Not sure. You need to rest up. Why not leave things for a few weeks? The chaps who send out call-up papers won't catch you yet awhile.'

'There's my ration book and all that.'

'The Ministries aren't as efficient as you might think. The mills of God ...' said Jack comfortably.

The days as a returned daughter, days with nothing to do but knit or go shopping with her mother or listen to the wireless, irked and depressed Sophy. She was pleased and relieved when her future mother-in-law telephoned.

The Lingards had met Sophy a number of times during her pre-war engagement to their son. They liked her and were all set to welcome her as a daughter. In return Sophy was fond of them. Bob's father, a retired admiral, was a caricature of a naval officer, short and gruff and bandy legged with a weatherbeaten face and a sudden laugh. His blue eyes were red-veined, his short wavy hair thin on top, as if wearing a naval cap for years had worn it out. Sophy had once thought he should have gold buttons on his pyjamas; they would suit him.

Bob's mother Denise was as short as her husband – they were a small dumpy couple, poised and worldly, with the ease of private money. Denise Lingard was sweet-natured and spoiled. Her husband spoiled her and so did her son and her ageing servants. She had a happy disposition, accepted the spoiling kindnesses of the world and liked to return the compliment. Her generosity was not confined to her family, herself, any staff she managed to keep since the war, to godchildren, assiduous vicars and rheumaticky gardeners. It spread to charities. Everybody knew Mrs Lingard was a soft touch. She wept easily, and when she heard of a hospital short of funds or a woman whose husband had been killed at Dunkirk, little Mrs Lingard, eyes brimming, soon extracted a cheque from the admiral, as she called her husband when speaking of him.

She had been puzzled and upset when Sophy left England in the summer of 1939. She said nothing of her feelings to

Bob who apparently took his fiancée's whim calmly enough. But when Sophy was stranded in France, Denise asked her son far too often what was happening to the girl. When Sophy finally reappeared and Bob telephoned his mother with the news, Denise had such a shock she needed strong sweet tea.

She wrote warmly to Sophy, her letter covered with exclamation marks in the place of happy tears. When she telephoned, her voice was warm.

'I'm coming to town for a day or two. (Such a joy to see you.) We must get you a few little things. Shall we meet at Harrods? How is your luggage, darling? I've been thinking about your honeymoon.'

Inspired by the very word, Sophy said laughingly that she'd lost it all in France.

'Oh, my poor dear. I keep forgetting the dreadful things that happened to you.'

Denise Lingard did indeed manage to forget dreadful things, and those included her son's shipwreck and her painful anxiety when he was at sea. She was blessed with a happy disposition. People smiled when they saw her.

'So new luggage is on the cards.' She sounded delighted. 'We must have leather, of course, but some of it is quite light nowadays. Shall we say Harrods Bank tomorrow morning? At half past ten?'

Denise began her serious shopping early.

The next day Sophy caught the London train which was packed with businessmen who went to work every morning from the country, and shared cars from the station to get home at night. The compartment was smoky and warm. Outside the train window she watched a countryside touched with autumn.

From Victoria, she cut through Belgravia and walked up Sloane Street. There was a tang of smoke in the air, they were burning leaves in the gardens. The ordered procession of the seasons went on, as if bombs never whistled down to make gaping holes in the grass where lovers had lain, or houses where families had been happy. As Sophy walked, a small boy passed by. He was hanging on to his mother's hand. He had a rosy face under a white knitted hat, and talked in a high sweet voice. 'Mummy, may I ask you something? I don't want to *disturve* you.' At the voice, at the child's face, Sophy felt a momentary pain so sharp that it took her breath away.

Harrods was wartime-smart. The windows were reduced for safety to small squares, the rest filled in with elegant painted boards depicting cheerful men and girls in uniform walking under autumn trees. Sophy was early for her appointment, but it was a waste of time to look at clothes; she had no more coupons. Hats, however, were not rationed. She had a weakness for hats. Once Jack had counted the hats in her millinery cupboard – twenty-six.

The department was empty and the hats, made in soft felts, stiffened silks, velvets, were arranged on stands with stems like the stalks of tulips. She took off her own dull felt and picked up a hat of rich plum-coloured velvet. It was small, like a tam o' shanter, but had a great bunch of pale net fluffing out on one side. Sophy recognized that it was patriotically based on the caps worn by the famous white-kilted Greek regiments, the Euzones. She was studying her own reflection when a figure appeared behind her. The woman was in uniform and standing quite still. Sophy ignored her. She must be waiting, an annoying habit of some customers, for Sophy to relinquish the hat so that she could grab it in her turn and try it on. Just because I look good in it doesn't mean she will, thought Sophy, admiring her own freckled face under the velvet.

And then she saw the woman smile.

For the second time an extraordinary pang went through her. She gasped –

'*It's you!*'

'*And you!*'

They did not touch. Did not kiss. They simply stood with enlarged eyes taking each other in.

Sophy managed to stutter, 'I thought –'

'So did I –'

'That you might be –'

At last they spoke each other's names.

'Violette. It's impossible. How – *how* – are you here in London?'

'And you safe, Sophy. How is that?'

They couldn't take their eyes off each other until Sophy suddenly remembered the time.

'Oh damn, damn, I'm meeting somebody. I have to go. Violette, where can I find you?'

'At the Free French HQ. In Kensington. I work there. I'm a driver.'

'That sounds wonderful.'

'Don't be silly,' said Violette, amused, 'it is not wonderful at all but dull. And rather nasty when there is a fog. Where can I find *you*?'

'I'm at home with the parents in Sussex but I can come up. Can we meet? Where? When?' Sophy could scarcely believe she was actually speaking to her lost friend, now standing beside her slender and stylish in khaki with the Free France flash on her thin shoulders.

They exchanged addresses. Violette was far less emotional than Sophy, who begged her to say 'just something about what happened to you!' No, said Violette, it should be saved until they met for a longer time.

'If you really can come to London, meet me at our HQ and I'll give you a meal. We manage French food, even here. It is not so bad.'

'Oh, I'd *love* to. Can we do it soon?'

The old eagerness, the way of speaking, the light in the English girl's face, the familiarity, the unexpectedness, touched Violette.

'Of course we must. I will ring you. Don't try to telephone, it is impossible to get through. Give me your number.'

Sophy scribbled wildly, she was already late but couldn't bear to let Violette go. She forgot to take off the Greek soldier's cap.

'You really will telephone?'

'How could I forget, Sophy?'

Violette walked out of the department, turning at the door to wave. Sophy was then approached by a saleswoman. She explained that she wished to buy the hat, 'keep it, please!' and promised to come back.

Her meeting with Denise Lingard was an anti-climax after Violette. Her future mother-in-law, wet-eyed, gave her hugs and kisses smelling of Chanel 22, talked non-stop during coffee, during luncheon, spent a fortune on luggage for Sophy and busily arranged for 'my dear girl' to come to stay in Wimbledon. Now and again, putting a plump chin on a plump hand during luncheon at the Ritz, Denise gave a wavering smile.

'You're here. At last. How happy Bob is now.' And Sophy felt herself turned into the untouched girl of this woman's imagining. She slipped into her part and played it so well that for hours she forgot it was not the truth.

On the train home she kept thinking of Violette. Her French friend dressed in uniform, knowing she had a purpose and what she had to do, paradoxically epitomized the England to which Sophy had returned. It was a place where every single human being was absorbed and involved in war. She was like an unbeliever on the steps of a church with wide-open doors. Inside was the huge congregation on its knees in prayer, while all she did was stand and stare. She wanted to be part of them, to be absorbed, dedicated, swallowed up. Her energy was beginning to come back.

Four days later Violette telephoned.

'*C'est moi.*'

'I thought I'd imagined you.'

'Oh, I am only too real. Now, Sophy, what about coming to London one day next week? I can offer you a meal in the canteen at lunchtime. And you could get your train back home before it gets dark.'

Sophy's mother was very impressed when she learned that her daughter was going to meet a member of the Free French forces.

'Your brother always says they're first rate.'

'What about the Poles and the Norwegians? And the Czechs and South Africans and Dutch?' reeled off Sophy. She had amused herself counting the different nationalities of the troops filling London, and she liked contradicting Pansy when Jack's opinions were given as Holy Writ.

'Yes,' Pansy was unruffled. 'But Jack says the French have General de Gaulle.'

Jack arrived in Sussex for the weekend, to his mother's joy and his father's 'so there you are'. When he came to look for his sister he found her on the floor by the fire. She jumped up, hugged him and then carefully shut the door.

He raised his eyebrows enquiringly.

'Guess what! I met a girl the other day and I'm seeing her on Tuesday in London. She's with the Free French.'

He got the point.

'The one who drove you south from Paris.'

'That's her.'

He thought for a moment or two. They had no need to spell it out.

'Did she know you were pregnant when you were together all that time?'

'She guessed, because I looked ropey.'

'You want to know how much to tell her of the rest of it?'

Sophy was looking straight at him; there it was again, the shadow on the pretty face.

He thought for a moment or two more.

'Might as well. It's no good faking up that you had a miscarriage. I don't want to sound coarse, Sophy, sorry to mention these things. But I'm sure you prefer not to start up a whole new set of inventions. Tell her the lot.'

'Are you sure?'

'What's she like?'

'French.'

He chuckled.

'Then she'll keep her own counsel, if you ask her to. She'll see that it's "practical" as they call most things. When did you say? Tuesday. Sorry I can't take you out for a drink that day. I'm meeting Hélène.'

'And she doesn't like other women.'

'How did you guess?' he said with another chuckle. He looked rather glad that his girlfriend was difficult.

The French forces had taken over a number of large London houses, including one not far from the Albert Memorial. It was an enormous mansion with dirty white pillars and a flight of marble steps which had not been washed since war was declared. The lofty windows were inconveniently large for the usual protective brown paper strips, the windowsills which in peacetime had flowered with red geraniums were cracked and dirty and there were lumps of stucco missing.

Men and women in uniform passed in and out of the open door and when Sophy entered the house she was conscious of the nostalgic, immediately recognizable scent of Gauloise cigarettes. She went into a room marked 'Reception', with an accent over the first e.

A girl wearing pancake make-up, she was very dark and handsome, looked Sophy up and down. Sophy explained she had an appointment with Mademoiselle Duplessis.

'Corporal Duplessis,' corrected the girl. 'I will see if I can find 'er.' She had the kind of French accent used by naughty chambermaids in 1930s' farces.

She asked on the telephone in French for Violette, turned to Sophy and said, 'She will be 'ere shortly. You can sit down.'

Sophy took a chair and gazed about. The room had four desks pushed together and loaded with wire baskets of papers and dirty coffee cups. Ash-trays brimmed. How the French do smoke, thought Sophy. I wonder where they get their Gauloises? Dropped by parachute?

Soldiers came and went, eyeing Sophy in the sexy way Frenchmen had and Englishmen did not. One or two gave her a smile and when she smiled back the dark girl at the desk was not pleased.

At last Violette arrived, as trim and poised as she'd been at that strange moment when Sophy caught sight of her in a Harrods' mirror. But now Sophy looked at her more carefully and thought her friend seemed older. I didn't notice it last time, it was all such a shock, she thought. And I'm older too.

'It was so good of you to come all the way from the

country,' said Violette, kissing her on either cheek. The girl at the desk frowned slightly as if a foreigner had no right, on French territory, to a warm welcome.

The canteen was in what had once been either a very grand drawing room or even a ballroom. It had elaborate ceilings and wallpaper patterned with Chinese trees and birds. The floors, sadly splintered, were of parquet. A number of houses nearby had been destroyed in the blitz and the glass in every high window of the canteen blown out, with the result that the windows were filled with matchboard and the room had no daylight. Bare bulbs hung rather festively from the ceiling. The crowds of men and women in uniform queued for their lunch or were eating at little tables; there was the pleasant buzz of talk over a hot meal.

'We'll get our food first. I asked the sergeant to keep me a table. I said we had important matters to discuss and that you worked at the War Office,' said Violette without a wink. She placed her gas mask on the small corner table as a sign of occupancy.

They were served soup-plates of *pot au feu* from an enormous steel container, glasses of wine, bread and even some kind of salad. How did the French make such delicious food from the same ingredients which the British ruined? thought Sophy. The bread was war-time grey but it had been baked that morning. The salad was dressed with something which tasted like oil.

'The General insists that his army eats well,' said Violette, lifting her glass of coarse red wine.

'To the General,' said Sophy, toasting the absent hero.

It was not until the meal was over that Violette looked at Sophy with her tired eyes and said, 'We have much to tell, haven't we?'

'You begin.'

'I would rather hear yours first, Sophy. Mine is not good, and I think perhaps yours may be. You got safely away from those Dufours, at any rate.'

'Thanks to Paul. He helped me.'

'Yes ... I thought it would be that young man. And you

410

came home to England. What about the baby?' Violette sounded interested but cool.

Sympathy, sentiment, would have opened the floodgates. Sophy was glad of the tone and said in the same kind of voice, 'My brother and I thought about it a lot, and decided to have him adopted.'

Violette leaned her elbow on the table. She smoked and considered.

'I think I would have done the same.'

'Are you sure?'

'Yes. You and the little child will both have a better life without each other. Did you meet the people he went to?'

'Oh no! No.'

'That was practical,' said Violette, as if she hadn't heard or noticed. Then with a smile, 'I see you are wearing your engagement ring again.'

It was neatly done. Sophy found herself telling the story as Violette seemed to want it told. The French girl smoked and listened, blue eyes fixed on Sophy sometimes with amusement. She was intrigued by the months in Devonshire. Round them the canteen continued to hum with French conversation, the cigarette smoke a strong-smelling mist. Gradually the noise became less, figures in uniform began to leave and the room grew emptier. The girls sat on.

Sophy's story ended and Violette said, 'It is good, as I thought. You are to be married and all is well. I'm so glad for you.'

She put out her cigarette and looked about vaguely, remarking that coffee was still being served. She would get some more.

'Are you going to tell me what happened to *you*?' Sophy said eagerly.

'Do you want to hear?'

'So much!'

'It is not a nice story,' the French girl said.

18

Violette had another sixty kilometres to travel when she left Les Hesperides very early in the morning. But after weeks on the road with Sophy the last lap to Menton seemed easy. She set off in the first cool of the day. She did not go along the beach road – she had consulted Sophy about distances – but took the N7 which was shorter and straighter. She walked briskly for about an hour, rested and refreshed from a night in a real bed, a bath and food. Sometimes she met soldiers making their straggling way homewards, and lorries went by filled with more French troops. But they were never travelling in Violette's direction, always away from the Italian frontier. Some of the soldiers grinned and waved, others, heads bent, were dispirited and silent.

By luck, just when her feet had begun to ache again she spotted a bus at a stop under the trees. It was already crowded, but there was room for one slender young woman, and she climbed gratefully on board. The destination was Beaulieu.

Standing among the passengers, shaken by the ruts of the ill-kept road, Violette thought of Georges. Every minute, every corner, led her closer to him. In the past weeks she had thought he might be gone from Menton, that she had lost him, but pessimism evaporated now. She thought longingly, passionately, about Georges. He was a wonderful lover. Physically he was rangy, broad-shouldered, handsome in a conventional way, easily smiling and easily roused. Violette was hot-blooded, and her sex with Georges was all she wanted and needed and must have. For a while, as she held on to the central metal pole in the bus and it rocked on its slow way and the lorries and soldiers passed them, all she thought about was being in Georges's arms again.

But then the doubts which she'd denied when she set off this morning in the dawn began to crowd back. What made her so sure now that he was alive? He had been in the only town on the Mediterranean coast taken over by the enemy. There had been a good deal of fighting there, and although she knew the Italians had done badly, they had still *fought*. Georges might have been killed. Or maybe when the Italians occupied Menton, he was thrown into prison and transported to Occupied France. He was forty-three and not in uniform, a civil servant with responsibilities in the town. It was a dangerous position. Anything might have happened if he'd defied the Italian authorities.

Violette looked blindly at the road ahead. Suppose when I get to Menton I am told he is dead. No, I won't look that far. I must concentrate on getting there.

The bus set down its poor-looking passengers in the main street. Beaulieu was desolate, as if the golden days when it shimmered with wealth and foreigners in great open cars like yachts had never been.

Violette looked wearily up and down the road. A noisy old Citroën was approaching, driven by a fat old man with small features squeezed into the middle of a great big peasant's face. He stopped the car and leaned out of the window.

'Where are you going, Mademoiselle?'

Violette wryly guessed that he was sorry for her. Always aware of her appearance, and in spite of clean clothes borrowed from Sophy, she knew that she looked a wreck. She was thin as a skeleton, exhausted, with black rings under her eyes; even the clothes didn't fit. She was being offered a lift from charity.

The old man was so kind that had she been a girl given to tears she would have cried now. His name was Cuittier. Jean

Cuittier. He was going 'almost' to Menton – in actual fact to a village on the hills outside the town. He settled Violette in the front seat next to him. The back of the car was packed with straw baskets containing fruit; cherries and peaches and early apricots: the scent was overpowering. He explained that he had been ordered to take all his produce to the jam factory, the *Usine de Confiture.*

'I am a coward to obey, but we lose our courage when we are old. I have the papers, I do as I am told,' he said. 'I am a fruit farmer, as you will guess, Mademoiselle. Do you think I am allowed to sell my goods to our own people? I can scarcely keep two eggs and a leek and some of my good peaches for my wife and daughter. All is for the enemy. The confiture, the fresh produce. All.'

'But the Germans are not here,' said Violette.

'They are at the other end of the railway. And must be fed.'

He spoke of the defeat. He talked like a man reciting a lament. France was the lover of his heart who had died. The pity of it.

Two or three times on the road he turned his old eyes on to the girl. Finally he said, 'Are you sure you wish to go to Menton?'

'Yes. I have a friend there.'

'How do you know he is still ...'

'Alive? I pray so.'

'I also.'

When he set her down just outside the town, he leaned out, patted her hand and said, 'God be with you.'

Violette walked the last half kilometre of her enormous journey, thinking of that blessing. How can He be with me? she thought. Even supposing Georges is alive, our affair is a sin. I don't think God is with me at all.

The roads leading to the town had a comforting normality. She actually saw a woman at a window, picking off the dead heads of some pink geraniums. On the outskirts of Menton there were many rich villas built in the last fifty years. They looked occupied, they looked undamaged. The gardens shaded by tall palms were full of roses.

The road swung to the right, and finally reached the promenade and the sea.

It was only then that Violette saw Italian soldiers.

It was an extraordinary sensation to be looking at men who had been her country's enemies until a handful of weeks ago. They wore khaki of a different, more greenish hue; they were much decorated with ribbons on the breasts of their tunics. Most were short and olive-skinned, not physically dissimilar from the men of Provence. But lack of height, black hair and khaki were all they shared with Frenchmen. In a single stark moment of vision she saw what victory and occupation meant. The soldiers were loud, a little drunk and staggered along the street more or less shoving passers-by into the gutter. When they caught sight of Violette they whistled and hooted and one soldier came up and tried to kiss her. She shoved him roughly away. His companions with noisy laughter shouted encouragement to him. Violette, mustering her last energy, waited until he was right up close and then hit him in the face. Livid, he raised his arm to strike viciously back when his friends yelled some kind of warning. An officer appeared round a corner from the promenade. Violette's tormentor cursed in Italian and returned to his friends. For the moment, she was safe.

She walked through a town unrecognizably changed. Part of Menton had been bombed and the ruins were roped off with 'Entry Forbidden' signs chalked on pieces of wood. Part was still the little town she knew. But here every shop was shut except one baker's, where long queues of women grey with tiredness squatted on the pavement or leaned against the shop windows. Along the beautiful promenade which in the Belle Epoque had been laid with coloured marble patterned, like a pink, yellow and black carpet, were huge rolls of rusting barbed wire. A funeral pyre of burnt chairs stood by the steps of a hotel – once the haunt of elegance and now closed and shuttered. A wrecked Army car had been left in the centre of the promenade. Not a living soul walked on the beach where the sea shone like a sapphire.

The town brimmed with Italian soldiers. They crowded the few cafés which were still open and Violette saw with a weariness of the spirit that many pretty girls were with them, flirting and giggling and drinking from the soldiers' glasses. One blonde girl sat on an Italian corporal's knee. Somebody began to play an accordion. And just then, as if given a signal, all the troops in the café started to sing as sweetly as a chorus in an operetta.

She walked on, summoning the dogged exhausted determination which had brought her down the roads of France. She went into alleyways to avoid the roped-off streets. She hurried, eyes downcast, as fast as she could manage until at last she arrived at the block of flats where she had her apartment. It was still standing. But as she approached the swing doors an Italian officer passed her.

'*Bellissima!*' he said, making a grab. Violette swerved, she heard him laugh as she fled indoors.

Her flat was on the top floor. The lift had 'Out of Order' on a piece of paper which hung lopsidedly from the gate. She took the staircase thick with dust, which scraped under her feet like sand. The whole building smelled of dust. When she arrived at the top landing she looked with dread at her own door. But no troops had kicked it in, it was unmarked, closed. She put her key in the lock and went into the apartment, not knowing what to expect. It was uncanny to find her home just as she had left it. In her bedroom the wardrobe was closed, the bottle of Chanel on the dressing table together with the photograph of Georges in a leather frame. The double bed was creaseless. When she pulled back the bedcover and lifted a pillow she found his folded pyjamas. Violette picked them up and buried her face in them. They still smelled of Georges.

She hurried to the telephone. It was dead.

Unlocking the balcony windows, Violette lit a cigarette and went out to stare at the calm sea, where not a ship sailed and the horizon blindingly shone. Was Georges alive? If so, was he here? Or had he left before the fighting and managed to get to the mountains with his family? She knew none of his friends. She had been kept in the old-fashioned situation which had

416

suited him and had not upset her – she was a sexual secret. From the start of the affair Georges had developed a neurotic fear that his wife would find out about it. For him a peaceful life was essential. Marital scenes would be a disturbance. They would get in the way of work – and that was everything to him. More than his wife's happiness and much, much more than the pleasures he enjoyed with his young mistress.

There was only one man whom Violette had met and who was a friend of her lover's – his doctor Marc Bonnerat. Once when she and Georges had spent a day in the country she had suffered a nasty insect bite on her arm; Georges, alarmed, telephoned Bonnerat who came late at night to the apartment and treated the bite swiftly and successfully. Surely he would have news of Georges, thought Violette. And there was nobody else she could ask ...

When she arrived at the house she saw at once that Doctor Bonnerat was in residence. The corridor and waiting room were crammed; people sat on the benches as if they had been there for hours – young and old, prosperous and poor, babies sleeping in their mothers' arms and an elderly woman sleeping in a wheelchair. Violette was struck by their faces, which all had the same drawn attention, the same sad patience she had seen in the cafés during the defeat.

She waited for two hours before the nurse showed her into the consulting room.

Marc Bonnerat gave a slight start when he saw her; he stood up and came over to shake her hand. Violette remembered a handsome man; she thought he looked smaller.

'What can I do for you, Mademoiselle?'

'I am not ill, Doctor. I've come for a different kind of help,' she said and then, in a rush, 'have you – have you any news of Georges?'

He looked very surprised.

'He is here, of course. In Menton.'

'Oh. Thank God.'

He gave her an odd look and Violette said nervously, 'Is he all right? He hasn't been wounded or anything?'

Marc Bonnerat replied that Georges had managed 'wisely'

to take his family to the mountains some time ago but had himself returned. He'd been perfectly in health when the doctor had seen him last, and working hard.

She was too relieved, too wrapped up in her emotion to notice something which much later she remembered – the careful tone of Bonnerat's voice. She explained that she had only today come to Menton, she had travelled from Paris and 'it had been difficult'.

He murmured 'Indeed?' and looked at the papers on the desk. All day long patients came into this room and told him stories of despair. Often he could not help them. Always he strove to try. He had to decide. To judge. He had literally no energy or desire to be interested in this girl. She was not ill or hungry. He was more exhausted than she.

Violette saw some of this and said she had come to him because she could not telephone Georges and needed news.

'Private telephones are cut off. If you want to see your friend, Mademoiselle, you must go to his Bureau.'

She thanked him and stood up. He shook her hand again, and before she went to the door the next patient was ushered in.

It was late afternoon when she set off again. There was no avoiding the Italian troops and after her bottom had been pinched half a dozen times by grinning men, Violette walked in the gutter.

Georges's offices were in a large and elaborate house which had once belonged to a Russian prince; the government had bought it cheaply in the 1920s. It was not a surprise when she entered the marble-floored and spacious hall to see the same sort of crowds she had left at the doctor's; worried people who had waited for hours, perhaps all day long. The door of one of the offices opened and she heard a French voice shouting with laughter. 'You have no money? You will have to go to an internment camp!' A fair haired man with the unmistakable look of an Englishman, came out. His face was set. He went over to whisper to a girl waiting for him.

Violette asked the official at a desk if she could speak to Monsieur.

'You have an appointment?'

'Yes,' said Violette coolly. She expected an insolent demand for some piece of paper to prove her statement. But luck was with her. The door of another office opened. And she saw Georges.

He saw her at the same moment, stood still – then lifted his hand and beckoned. She had to stop herself from running as she went towards him.

He took her into his office and carefully shut the door, put his arms round her and kissed her. Violette closed her eyes. Here at last was the end of the long, long journey. When the kiss finished he looked her up and down.

'You're a witch. A sorceress. How in the name of Confucius did you get to Menton?'

'Oh Georges. Georges. I will tell you everything. When can we meet? Tonight? I know I shouldn't be here –'

'Certainly you shouldn't, you must go at once. Are you back in the apartment? Good. I'll be there –' he looked at his wrist watch, 'by nine.'

'Not before?'

How she loved and wanted him. He was so handsome and easy, so loose-limbed and boyish. His figure made her ache with love and desire. When she touched his hair and put her hand to his face it smelled of the same scented brilliantine.

'Not a minute before nine,' he said, grinning. 'Even later. But I'll be there.'

He did caress her cheek for a moment. Then his face took on a religious fervour.

'There is a very great deal of work,' he said.

Violette even forgave the bottom-pinching soldiers when she walked home. She bathed and changed into a dress which had been in her wardrobe all the time she'd been away. She poured scent over her neck and hair. As women had done since the world began she sat waiting for her lover. And when he came into the bedroom – she heard his key but could not move – at last they made love. It was as exciting, as violent, as dazingly beautiful, as hungry and as satisfying as it had always been.

★

419

The days that followed were a marriage, a honeymoon. Georges was overjoyed to see her, wanted her, made love to her, surrounded her with his particular smiling indulgence. He listened to the saga of her escape and, unlike the doctor, questioned and marvelled. 'I am proud of you,' he said. The very idea that she'd been in danger roused him sexually. In exchange Violette heard of his own journey with his family, of difficulties overcome, of early bombardments of Menton. But she did notice from the first night his absence of any feeling against the Italians. He did not call them 'the enemy'. When she exclaimed at the loathsome presence of the invading soldiers he placed his finger on her lips.

'No, Violette. We don't talk like that any more. Let us talk about ourselves. About tomorrow. I'll bring something home for supper. Shall we have it here? Just like the old days.'

Food was delivered to the apartment every night; packages and boxes were carried up the stairs – the lift remained broken – by a driver. Georges had a large official car at his disposal, it often waited for him outside the apartment when he visited her for short periods and needed to return to his Bureau afterwards. In the evenings he lay in bed after love-making, smoking and talking about himself. Violette waited upon him. She made omelettes and coffee, she cut smoked salmon sandwiches very thinly just the way he liked them. She sat watching his handsome face, filled with content.

His look was classic, his profile almost Greek, with a nose of dramatic straightness, a rounded firm chin and curved lips. His thick hair with a natural wave sprang up, falling on his forehead in a crescent and constantly pushed back. The gesture was that of a famous pianist, perhaps. Certainly not of a civil servant no longer young.

Lulled by sex, at times she closed her eyes from a sheer dreamlike joy, she sat beside him, watching, admiring him, wanting him, loving him. Here was the end of the journey. She would do anything for him. She was his.

At first they made love, made jokes and played a game of domesticity; Georges came to the apartment every night and

Violette prepared him a meal from the 'delicious surprises' delivered earlier in the day. They scarcely talked, after he stopped her the first time, of the Italians occupying Menton. They never once mentioned the defeat and the armistice. Violette was too happy to notice for a while. She began to encourage him to talk of his work. He looked pleased. She held his large pale hand and listened and in the way Georges had, he looked to her for reaction now and then, waiting – as it were – for applause. What he said at first surprised her and then began to jar.

There was great work to be done, he said, and it was his duty to help. People must be made to see exactly what had happened to France and why the country had become weak. Did Violette remember how things had been in the past? Dishonest. Decadent. The morality of the people had been at its lowest, it must be raised, their eyes raised to high ideals again. The great work was of reconstruction.

'You understand we must all play our part in the task and it will be magnificent.' He was in full flood. 'My job is to tell the people what lies ahead. They must be re-educated, taught to unite and collaborate and work for our common aims. We have promises to make, we must gather round the Marshal.'

He looked about for a cigarette and Violette handed him his silver case. He lit one and drew hard, then continued, 'The Marshal is our head, our symbol. Against anarchy and for discipline. Against the old false liberty, for a real united freedom. Against the bourgeois value and for human solidarity.' Violette could tell he was quoting, but whether it was a speech of his own used at another time, or somebody else's, she couldn't guess.

'Marshal Pétain is to give us new and noble words to epitomize the new spirit, Violette. They will be on the new money. No longer Liberty, Equality, Fraternity. Those three represent the dead past. Our new words are beautiful. Work. Family. Country.'

He smiled at her and Violette smiled back. Her heart was cold. When he left the next morning after their night together and she was alone, she knew that sex and its release, love – of a sort – and the huge burden of fearing that he was dead had made her stupid. She did love him. But she saw that he was working closely with the Italians and with the Vichy government. It was in every word he said. The expensive booty brought to the apartment showed the same thing. It was not only the speeches, his almost fanatic way of talking of the 'great work of reconstruction'. It was because Georges now lived like a prince. He had risen higher than he could have dreamed. He was the head of a key department in the city, he could have anything he wanted – a car, food, brandy – and money too, of course.

She was troubled. She tried to believe that he must be working for the common good, for the people as well as for himself. Georges was alive, in her arms, in her bed, in herself. Should she not be as loving, passionate, grateful and downright encouraging as he wanted?

But the next night and the next, as he grew totally relaxed with her, he did not watch his words. He talked of 'the battle against vain liberty'. He spoke with contempt of 'the invention of democracy'. He was a leader in a new organization, the Légion des Combattants formed by the Vichy Government for returned sailors, soldiers and airmen. A huge rally in the Arena at Cimiez was planned.

'It will be a magnificent opportunity to give the lie to that impostor who fled to England – de Gaulle.'

During the day Violette went for walks through a Menton half ruined and hungry. Yet Georges brought her rich food, explaining that for those in 'essential situations of work' there must, rightly, be provision. He told her of dinners and soirées for people of consequence. A German trade commission had arrived in Menton; there was to be a formal dinner and a ball.

'You are going to enjoy yourself,' Georges said, smiling. 'You must put on your prettiest dress. You'll meet the people who play vital roles, not only here in Menton but in the creation of a new France.'

With his family still away in the mountains, Georges was no longer nervous at being seen in public with her. They went out to dine. Violette, in the smart clothes she had left in the apartment before the defeat, felt self-conscious. They drove in his large official black car through streets in which there were, perhaps, four bicycles.

He was happy with her. Passionate with her. She was treated to more speeches about the rebirth of France. He looked Greek and godlike as he declared, 'Our country must find her soul again.'

The day of the reception for the Trade Commission, Georges left the apartment very early to be at his Bureau by 8.30 in the morning. Violette, still in her dressing gown, sat on. In her ears she could still hear those speeches – they bored and disturbed her – on the theme of French decadence before the war, the governments which had fallen, corruption in high places, families ruined by millionaire financiers 'of the Jewish persuasion'. France had suffered because she deserved it. Now was the time for obedience and purity.

Is he right, thought Violette, does France need to find her soul? Or is she in the dirt and are they treading on her? She remembered the people at Doctor Bonnerat's, the timid crowds waiting in the office corridors, the men sobbing when Pétain's ancient voice announced that war was over.

She had nothing to do all day. No queues to join, no hungry child to anguish over. Putting on her oldest clothes, the only ones in which she felt comfortable, she went for a walk. The same Italian troops tried to pinch her, muttering their ludicrous '*Bellissima*'. The same shops were shuttered, the same long queues stood waiting for bread. Crossing the square by the hotel where the Trade reception was to be held that night, she saw a couple of French military policemen, noticeable for their smartness among the shabby crowds. Three or four French soldiers went by with that walk Violette found so heart-breaking, the shambling walk of defeat. The policemen shouted at them to stop, called them to attention and berated them loudly for undone buttons. There was a roar of laughter from the hotel window. Leaning on the windowsill were some men in German uniform: they must be members of the Trade Commission. They were laughing as if at a farcical play. The police continued to show off, and began to stop not only any soldiers passing them but also some civilians.

It was then that Violette, with a prickling of her scalp, saw an old man trying unobtrusively to cross the square and avoid the police. He was Jewish. His face was very thin, Eastern in cast, once handsome, infinitely sad. One of the policemen ran over to him, swore at him and knocked him down.

Violette stopped and turned to Sophy.

'It was then, when I saw the poor old man on the ground, that I knew. I had been fooling myself. Telling myself that nothing mattered but Georges. He mattered all right. To all the poor wretches at his mercy.'

'What did you do?'

'Oh, I didn't dare say anything to him. I began to realize how dangerous he was. He had thrown away any idea of loving his country, perhaps he'd never had any. What Georges loves is Georges. For all I know there are thousands of men in France like him. I just stood in the street, and it was like pulling out a plug and feeling my love drain out. I went home. I had already decided what to do. I packed and hid my bag. Then I dolled myself up and went to the party with him, which was pretty horrible. It ended late and we went home and made love, but I didn't want him any more. That felt strange too. I waited until he was asleep, Georges sleeps like the dead after sex. Then I crawled out of bed and went through his wallet.'

'Violette!'

The French girl smiled slightly.

'I had a plan worked out, based on something I once saw in a gangster movie. In the afternoon I cut up small pieces of newspaper, measuring them to exactly the size of a thousand franc note. Georges is the sort who carries stacks of cash around. He likes the feel of a lot of money. He used to peel notes off the wad when he paid for anything and look at me and smile. So. I found the wallet in his jacket pocket and took out all the money except two notes. Then I put the newspaper

424

squares inside and the two notes on the outside. It looked just like the same thick bundle of francs which I slipped back in the wallet and replaced it.'

'Weren't you *terrified* he'd wake up?'

'Sophy, I slept with Georges during four years. You could practically shout in his ear and he'd only mutter and go back to sleep. Then I took his gold wrist watch —'

'Violette!'

'I do wish you wouldn't keep saying my name in that scandalized voice. You sound like Monsieur le Curé at home. Yes, it was a good watch, heavy and solid. Twenty-two carat is worth something. I sold it in Paris. Not that I needed more money, I was loaded with the stuff.'

'Did you leave him a note, explaining why you'd gone?' asked Sophy, eyes like saucers.

Violette looked surprised.

'A *note*? What on earth for?'

The canteen was empty. The two girls stood up and went slowly down the corridor. Violette lingered before they arrived at Reception.

'When I got to Nice I bribed a man to get me on the Paris train. In Paris — well — I have good friends there. Brave friends. But my God! I'd never imagined what it would be like to see the city full of Germans. So smart too, riding horses down the Champs Elysées or arm in arm with girls who were painted like whores. I shall never forget it. Then I bribed somebody else — the money from Georges did a lot of good work — to get me to the coast. That was a hair-raising journey. Finally I landed up in a rowing boat, of all things. It stank. Those herrings. I thought I'd smell of fish for the rest of my life.'

Violette grinned.

'You look a little stunned.'

'You're so cool.'

'Perhaps I am learning to use some English phlegm,' said Violette.

Her voice was rather flat. But at the front door she said, 'Don't disappear again.' And she kissed her.

*

425

Sophy admired and envied Violette for recovering so completely from the past. From faces peering from rich cars or poor overloaded farmcarts, from the sight of ashen-cheeked children, old women with rosaries twined round their wrists, the cracked and fatal sound of 'The Marseillaise' giving worse and worse news. And from love. Violette's journey like her own had been for nothing. Both had ended with empty arms. There had been a moment when she had sat with her in the canteen and had tried to say that. But Violette leaned forward, picked up Sophy's left hand and said, looking at the ring, 'Everything is good for you now.'

Before she had gone to France, Jack once told Sophy she must not expect anything in common between 'them and us'. 'The French,' he said, 'make clever dinner guests and I'm told,' he added vaguely, 'imaginative lovers. They are magnificent farmers and their courage in the Great War is beyond question. But they make god-awful poets.'

'I'm not going to France to listen to poetry.'

Sophy had felt the foreign-ness between Daniel and herself when they had been in love. She had been conscious of the same thing in Violette. The French girl in her smart uniform, telling her matter-of-factly about the death of her love, was matter-of-fact about Sophy as well. All she saw when she met her again, was that a girl who'd been homeless and pregnant with a bastard child was now a well-dressed young woman about to be married, and repossessed of her good looks. Curiously enough, Sophy was glad Violette saw no more than that.

A week after Sophy visited the French army she was in the garden one morning, cutting cabbages at her mother's demand. 'There may be one which hasn't been eaten by slugs, dear.' Looking up she saw her brother padding across the frosty grass with his pigeon-toed walk. He wore the collar of his tweed overcoat up in the rakish style of Humphrey Bogart.

'Jack, you never rang to say you were coming!'

'Didn't know I could get away.'

She planted a kiss on his swarthy cheek.

'I've been longing to see you.'

'Have you indeed. What are you doing out in the cold when there's a good fire going in the drawing room? Your nose is red.'

She put up her hand and touched it.

'Yes, it's freezing. Like a dog's. Ma sent me out to look for this —' holding up an icy cabbage. 'Don't let's go indoors. We can talk much better here. Ma won't be faffing in and out.'

'Secrets?'

He thought she looked well in spite of the nose.

They began to walk down the brick path with the diminished vegetable beds, frostbitten and iron-hard, on either side. The beds used to be planted with pink phlox.

'Why do you want to talk out here? I don't expect it's sisterly affection. Any news from the King's Navy?'

'Not a word. His parents haven't heard either. Denise Lingard rings and we moan about Bob not writing.'

'You like your future ma-in-law, do you?'

'One couldn't *not* like Denise,' said the recipient of costly presents.

Poor Mother, thought Jack, she can't compete. Pansy was fonder of her daughter since her return, but Sophy was too wrapped up in herself to notice. Or perhaps, since the mother-love like thick cream had only poured over *him* until now, she wasn't in the habit of it.

'What's the problem?' he asked.

'Father keeps saying my call-up papers will come any day now. I just wanted to ask you — I bet Bob would like it if I was a Wren.'

They strolled towards the orchard. The bark of the trees glittered with frost, the air was bitter. Jack plunged gloveless hands into the pockets of his coat — how many pairs of gloves had he lost? Well, not pairs. One glove at a time. Hélène had recently given him a new pair — where had they got to?

Sophy looked down at the curled stout leaves of the cabbage and then up at her brother.

'A Wren, then?'

'There isn't a girl in England who doesn't want to join the Wrens. They're all dotty about the uniform. So are the men, come to that.'

'Okay. So I'll join the Wrens. But do you think I should?'

The voice was Sophy's, rather cheerful, too cheerful. Beneath it he sensed something else. He did not look at her because he felt a surge of pity. Sophy was proud. She was never sorry for herself, only sad; how she would detest to see herself a poor thing in the eyes of her brother. He kicked at a stone, wearing the frown of a man considering what was best. He hid the pain he felt. She was so young. What had the last year done to her? There were scars across her nature, how could he make them heal fast and thickly? He dreaded that Sophy might suddenly and unexpectedly collapse. It was not impossible. Obscurely suffering, she might find that she could not be happy with Bob Lingard, could not begin a new and different life. She might remember too often what was in the past. For all Jack knew she might still care for the Frenchman who had made her pregnant. And he was probably dead.

It was scarcely two months since that child had been born, and less than four weeks since, trembling, she had handed the little chap over to strangers.

He thought of the lives of young women thrown into one or other of the services. Camaraderie and hard work, sex, discipline, self-discipline. Was she ready for those things?

'You're jolly quiet,' said Sophy, pinching him with a hand encased in a red and brown knitted glove. She did not lose hers. 'What are you thinking about, old owl? Which of the services I'd like the best. Of course I may not be allowed to choose . . .'

'No, you probably won't. I'm not thinking about that. It seems to me we might find some way of putting the thing off.'

'That's impossible. Father keeps saying –'

'Our sainted parent,' he interrupted, 'enjoys the bad news. He's teasing you about the call-up. He often tells me the War Office will be destroyed for certain, sooner or later, in a raid. He's quite disappointed after a hit and run raid when I turn up and tell him London has not been flattened.'

'I've noticed.'

'So don't let's bother about that. The point is I happen to know a doctor in London, nice old character, discreet as the grave, who would give you a check-up and the requisite certificate. That'll let you off the hook for the time being.'

'I don't want to be let off any hook. I ought to be in uniform like everybody else.'

Her brother's face lost its somewhat enigmatic bonhomie. He looked tough, even rather alarming.

'Do as somebody else tells you for once.'

'I did as you said when –' she began and then broke off and said, 'bloody hell.'

He dared not show a flicker of sympathy.

'Just listen sensibly, and put off rushing into uniform or tying your hair up in a rag in a munitions factory or any other damned thing. Go and see my doctor pal. I'll whisper in Pansy's shell-like ear that your time in France and Spain pulled you down and you'd never pass a medical. She'll tell Father and she'll wrap you in cotton wool for a while, nice and cosy. She'll also tell her friends. So if you're getting beady looks from some of them you won't any more. Your state of health will explain why you're still at home. Now –' he cocked an eye at her – 'that doesn't sound too difficult, does it?'

'I still don't see why I can't join up like everybody else.'

She avoided his eyes and looked across the orchard to where her old swing used to hang. She had loved to swing very high, then drag her feet through the thick grass as she descended. She could just make out at a distance the dangling end of a rotted rope.

He took her arm and turned her to face him.

'How do you feel at present?'

'Fine.'

'Don't think I believe you. How do you sleep?'

She didn't answer.

'Wake up a lot?'

'Most people do.'

'When you're old, yes. Not at twenty. Sophy, answer me

429

this. Do you feel in yourself that you're over it?'

'Of course. It wasn't the end of the world. And now Bob and I are getting married –' she began in a bright hollow voice.

But something searching and compassionate, though he tried to hide it, was in his face. It pierced her through. She was still carrying the cabbage and she dropped it. It fell like a stone on the hard ground. She began to weep.

'Oh Jack. Oh Jack. It was such an awful thing I did. I keep remembering the baby and thinking and thinking and I do wake up and I see his face and how I used to wrap him so tightly in that shawl. I never thought ...'

All the sorrow she had kept back, the sea hurling itself against a slowly breaking wall, washed over her. He gave a long sigh and put his arms round her and let her go on crying.

Her call-up papers, a fat envelope-full that would make even the coolest young woman blanch, arrived on a morning in early April. Sophy's father watched while she opened the envelope; he had seen the OHMS on the outside.

She looked through the papers in silence. Herbert Hayward spread thin margarine on his wartime toast.

'Jack tells us you're somewhat below par after all your travels. Call-up papers have come, though, haven't they?'

A catty note was in his voice.

'Yes, and I shall join up. I'm perfectly okay,' she was nervous and offended.

'That'd be damned silly if you are not A1. You'll take yourself into a recruiting centre, be given a medical, waste their time and be sent home again.'

'People get by, whatever the doctors say.'

'Your mother's brother did. Sydney. Had a patch on the lung but joined up in '14 in the Royal Flying Corps,' Sophy's father remarked. It was a story she had heard from her mother. There was a badly painted portrait in the downstairs cloakroom of Sydney looking about fifteen and wearing an old-fashioned uniform.

'Know what happened?' said Herbert. It was a rhetorical

question. 'He was killed in a flying accident at Hendon aerodrome.'

Sophy did not follow her father's reasoning; he appeared to think her uncle's fate was connected with pretending to be healthy when he wasn't. Well. It could have been so.

'Don't worry, Pa, they'll scarcely want me to be a pilot in the RAF,' she said, knowing he disliked being teased.

Jack telephoned the same day that the call-up papers arrived. She was used to his intuitions, or perhaps he had a way of finding out such things. He'd always been rather mysterious. 'Ah,' he said, unsurprised, he had believed they might come in about now. He'd fixed for Sophy to see his friend Doctor Renshawe tomorrow.

He added that he would give her lunch first; he suggested meeting at the Westbury.

Sophy felt a country bumpkin when she walked into the Curzon Street hotel, which was very glamorous and very wartime, with attractive men and girls in uniform drinking in the bar. She found Jack exchanging a joke with the barman. Whenever Sophy saw her brother at a distance he was chatting to somebody: a taxi driver, a porter, a soldier, a farmer in Sussex. She had never seen him talking to women, except once, to the resentful Hélène. And whoever he was with, thought Sophy, he seemed to be enjoying himself. Yet when she arrived all she heard was the tail-end of stupid jokes.

They had a good lunch with Jack as usual remarking on the pleasure of the controlled price. 'I enjoy it more when I think it's only five bob.'

He saw her into a taxi. She leaned from the window to stretch out her hand in an unconscious gesture as if for reassurance.

'Good luck,' he said, giving the hand a hard squeeze.

'Am I going to need it?'

'Get along with you.'

The house in Montpelier Square had been handsome once. But pieces of plaster, some as big as dinner plates, had been knocked off during the blitz, which gave the place a mottled look, like measles. An ancient maid took Sophy into the waiting room, where she read a six-month-old *Vogue*. It was very severe.

'We must not turn into a nation of frights. *Care* for your looks! Baby yourself with a tiny speck of precious skinfood. Exercise as rigorously as they do in the Services. If you are at home learn to cook, sew, knit. Above all, stay beautiful! You owe it to your men as well as to yourself.'

'Miss Hayward?'

An elderly woman, sturdy and square, with bobbed hair and a pair of bright hazel eyes, was standing in the doorway.

'Come into the consulting room, please.'

The doctor's room was plain. There was a desk, two chairs, a couch behind white starched curtains, and one painting of misty hills and lakes, at which Sophy looked with longing. She wished she was there and not here.

She had had no idea the doctor was going to be a woman. It was like Jack not to tell her.

Doctor Renshawe asked the usual questions, name, date of birth, any infectious diseases as a child, any serious illnesses? Sophy did not mention the baby and her answers were all in the negative. The doctor remarked, 'You appear to have been a healthy young thing. Now we'll take a general look, shall we?'

Sophy was asked to take off her clothes. The doctor prodded about, took her blood pressure, even banged her knee with a tiny silver hammer to see it jump.

'Good. Good. Dress and come back to the desk, please.'

Well, that wasn't so bad, thought Sophy. The doctor had not commented on the tell-tale stretch mark. I suppose now she'll give me the certificate and that settles that for a while. She was surprised to find that she was pleased, after all, that her call-up would be deferred.

Doctor Renshawe waited until Sophy was seated facing her. The doctor was old, perhaps seventy, perhaps more, but there were traces of a prettiness long ago. Her nose was well modelled, her mouth turned up at the edges, her eyes were absurdly bright, sparkling. In her voice there was a faint flavour – could it be a brogue?

'Did your brother mention that he is by way of being a friend of mine?' she said with a slight emphasis on the word friend.

'Yes. He said he'd known you some time.'

'Five years. I like Jack. A remarkable man in some ways. He told me all about it. About your baby.'

Sophy ought to have expected it. But she flinched.

'He didn't say he . . .' The words faltered.

Doctor Renshawe looked straight at her.

'Isn't that what this visit is about? Now, Miss Hayward, I'm going to tell you some home truths which you won't like, but they have to be said. To begin with I do not approve of what you did. Don't make excuses, I know all about the reasons for your decisions. I talked them over with Jack for hours. I tried to dissuade him from helping you and I begged him to dissuade *you* from the whole idea. I don't approve of women giving up their children. I understand perfectly why you and your brother went ahead with the adoption. I realize, only too well, all the difficulties. You doubtless think I am unsympathetic, but that is not true. As far as your baby is concerned I have no doubt that he'll be well and happy. I know the Marlborough. It's not the little boy who is going to suffer, it is you. That is what I am bound to tell you. You mustn't imagine and nor must Jack that this thing can be put out of mind simply because you want it to be. That the slate can be wiped clean. You'll probably go on being unhappy for as long as a year. More. It is a kind of mourning. You have done yourself a terrible injury, I'm afraid. I am sorry to be the one to tell you, but there it is. So,' finished the doctor with a straight glance, 'one thing I do agree with Jack about is that you need time to recuperate. Say three months. You want to rush off and forget it happened. But your body has not forgotten. I'd like to make the time longer, but I'm afraid that's not possible. Three months at any rate will do some good.'

The girl said nothing. You came to a doctor to be cured and all that happened was that she made the ache worse.

'There is also the matter of your getting married soon,' said

433

the old woman. 'Your brother told me you don't intend to tell your future husband about the baby.'

Sophy blushed a miserable red.

The doctor took off her glasses.

'Don't worry, I am not going to say that what you want to do is impossible. Physically, of course it is. Your virginity is gone. Your body has changed. But when a man is in love he can make himself believe a good many things. You *may*, it is possible that you may, get away with it. Well, now. Here's the certificate which gives no games away. Off with you. You've had a sad time of it,' she added, looking at the girl with bright eyes that did not take account of the beauty or the youth, but of something dark-winged and invisible, hovering perhaps for a while, perhaps for always over Sophy's head.

19

The three months' respite given her by Doctor Renshawe were odd for Sophy. She was now again the Hayward daughter, the virgin fiancée to a naval officer serving his country. Her life was dull and her adventures were stale. The long months she had spent in Devonshire had been less dull because, although she was often lonely, there was a reason for her to be there, for her to be nowhere else.

Sophy was more a prisoner in Sussex. The women who were still at home, too old to go into factories or uniform, seemed to knit the days away. They also listened to the wireless, cooked messes suggested by the Ministry of Food and met at the Women's Institute to make old clothes look respectable by turning the fabrics inside out. It was scarcely a life for a girl as young as Sophy, but she put up with it because somewhere in her heart she admitted she was too miserable at present to face anything harder.

She *was* beginning to sleep better.

To her real pleasure she had a letter from Violette, written in a slanting near-indecipherable European hand to ask if there was the chance of seeing Sophy in the country. She would not dream of bothering Sophy and her family by asking to stay, she'd find a YWCA somewhere nearby. 'I hear they are comfortable and clean.'

After the undiluted company of the middle-aged, Sophy was eager to see her French friend; she asked her mother if

Violette could stay the night. Pansy, a hospitable woman who rarely had the chance to be so – her husband described everybody but relatives as 'strangers' – was as delighted as her daughter. She knew Herbert would not dare to complain about a girl in uniform, let alone one who had befriended his own child in France.

It was cold for mid-April and raining steadily when Sophy went to the station. The waiting room steamed. Soldiers in enormous greatcoats, burdened with kit-bags nearly as big as themselves, filled the place like a group of giants. The waiting room was unheated and they stamped their mighty feet to keep warm.

At last the train drew in and Violette in khaki came towards her, bending her head against the rain.

'Sophy, it is so kind of you to let me stay.'

'As if we'd allow you to stop at a YWCA!'

During the bus journey through the wet countryside, Violette amused her with stories of the bureaucracy at Queen's Gate. 'Why is it that pieces of paper are what matters? We pore over them as if they're the Bible. We French are mad.' She made Sophy laugh, yet Violette was not completely at ease. The frank manner didn't quite ring true; the charming worn face seemed to hide secrets. Perhaps that's me, thought Sophy, I don't often see things or people as they really are. Perhaps she was always like that. I didn't really *see* Daniel, did I? Or the Dufours until after the fall of France when they were pathetic. I never understood Paul until we said goodbye.

The rain beat down on Sophy's umbrella as she guided her friend through the gate between yew hedges clipped into the shape of peacocks. Dripping, the girls ran to the front door.

'My poor dears, you are drenched!' Pansy appeared from the kitchen with a large towel, was introduced to the visitor, and helped them to peel off wet coats and mop their faces. She was all kindly welcome. There was a good fire in the drawing room and she would make them some tea. No, no, of course Violette would not be allowed to help! The girls could have the place to themselves; she herself had to go out and

Herbert was in his study. 'It is very good of you to come all this way, my dear,' she said as if Violette had travelled hundreds of miles.

Sophy took her friend into the drawing room which was comfortably 1930s, comfortably pre-war. It was the kind of room Violette had never seen before: so English. The flowery chintzes, the pale carpets, the army of framéd photographs, the shelves of Victorian pink and white china, the chiming clock on the mantelpiece.

'Let's sit on the floor by the fire and you can tell me the gossip,' said Sophy pulling a cushion from the sofa.

Violette sat smiling beside her. She was collected, approachable, poised, elegant, above all she was kind. Sophy told herself she'd imagined the change in her. Violette chatted about London which was, she said, 'gaily going on its way'. It appeared that she was having a very good time. London now fascinated Sophy, it was so crowded, almost hectic; she often thought of her brother and the scented Hélène and nights when there were raids and a city filled with men in uniform and love affairs, and danger. The idea was sexy.

When Pansy returned with a tray, Violette sprang up to take it from her; her manner was respectful and markedly different from Sophy's and that of other girls of the same age. Pansy looked flattered and asked her guest the question every member of the Free French forces heard within sixty seconds of being introduced.

'And how did you manage to get to England?'

Violette enlarged on the story she'd told Sophy in London. She explained that she had managed to make her way to Honfleur, which was a fishing port in peacetime, small but busy with many boats.

'And the Germans have need of fish.'

Pansy nodded solemnly. Sophy wondered if her mother imagined the Nazis sitting down to feasts of cod from MacFisheries. Violette's tale certainly had a fishy flavour. The girl had been hidden in a fishing smack for an entire day and when the boat went out at night she was taken a good way across the Channel.

'But not right to our coast?' cried Pansy.

'Not exactly. I swam a little. Then a motor torpedo boat came along. I was pleased. And the officer pulled me out with a kind of net just as if I were a turbot. I smelled like one too. So ... I landed up at Folkestone.'

'But what happens when French people ...?'

'Oh, they clean us up. And if we've brought things with us like food or brandy they take them away for a while. Then we're sent to Kensington and – what is the English word like cooking? – we are grilled.'

Pansy was mystified, she never went to films and knew no current slang. Sophy explained that anybody rescued or managing to get to England in a boat might be a spy. Pansy looked deeply embarrassed.

She left the girls soon after that and they exchanged glances and burst into muffled giggles.

The rain continued to veil the drenched garden and the burgeoning orchard. They could not go out of doors and when Sophy's father, duly introduced, came to sit by the fire, Sophy soon made an excuse and took her friend up to her room. They sat on the bed. The gas fire burned like an officious well-meaning friend.

'You must join the services, Sophy,' Violette gave her a pensive look. 'You'll enjoy it. Hard work and so many men.'

'Do they pay court to you?' asked Sophy flippantly, using the French phrase.

'All the time. Of course one has to remember that some are married and have two wives.'

'Nobody has two wives,' said Sophy laughing.

'In France they do. One in Paris, the other in Nemours. Sophy, I am afraid I have something to tell you.'

A goose went over Sophy's grave.

'Courage,' said Violette just as she used to do when they threw themselves down flat in the dust.

'Is it bad?' said Sophy, struck and afraid.

'I cannot tell you that. Only what you have to know. I've seen Daniel.'

Sophy threw both her hands up to her face. Through her

438

fingers as if through prison bars she stared.

'You thought he must be still in France, didn't you? So did I. Or possibly dead. He could have been dead. You remember he was sent to the Maginot Line.'

Still Sophy did not speak.

Violette asked if she might smoke. She received no reply. She lit a Gauloise and looked at the fiery point at its tip. The smoke went straight up, the air was quite still.

'I wonder if you know that the Maginot never surrendered. The English newspapers don't say so; how little they tell us of the débâcle. The Germans attacked the *ouvrages* of the Maginot over and over again without success. Daniel was there in the defences. He said the blockhouses were dive-bombed day after day, night after night and at the armistice the commanders in the Maginot refused to surrender.'

'He was *there*?'

'Oh, yes. He told me everything. He said the enemy got hold of a French colonel – bastard, bastard – who agreed to go to one *ouvrage* after the other literally ordering the garrisons to come out. They refused until there was a promise that they would go free. The promise was given. And—'

She paused.

'And they were made prisoners,' said Sophy with a dry mouth.

'Yes. But not all. There were hundreds, Daniel said, who didn't believe the German promise and escaped into the woods and tried to reach friends, and some of them, the lucky or the brave, got to England. Daniel was one. It was very strange to see him, Sophy. At Queen's Gate. Suddenly, there he was. I wept. Both of us wept. It is like that, isn't it? When you see somebody from that other life.'

She fixed her eyes on Sophy.

'He asked me how I'd got out of Paris and I'm afraid I told him that *you* had been my companion. No, no, Sophy! As if I would betray your poor secret. Only that we'd been together all that time, and that by wonderful chance we had met again in London. He asked for your address. He was so pleased, Sophy. He said he was going to write to you.'

'I don't want him to.'

'You do not need to answer, do you?'

And then, while Sophy was still shattered, the ridiculous dinner bell began to ring.

Downstairs Herbert Hayward had decided to be hospitable, an unheard-of metamorphosis. He spoke to the French visitor with warmth, poured her a sherry and jovially asked the usual questions. Violette was charming. Nobody would have guessed how often she had told her story, how exhausting it must be to react to identical English exclamations. Her manners to Herbert, as to Pansy, were impeccable.

The family stayed in the sitting room by the fire after dinner, talking and later listening to a play on the wireless. Violette seemed perfectly content to fall in with the family's evening pattern. Sophy, at a distance from fire and lamplight, felt ill.

Her head was bursting with questions, her heart with sorrow and what she feared was the last flare of love. There wasn't the chance to say a word. Pansy accompanied her guest upstairs to her room at the far end of the corridor away from Sophy's, and asked the French girl all kinds of friendly things. Was she quite comfortable? Did she need another blanket? Did she like morning tea, Pansy always had some and could bring her a cup? Sophy waited for what seemed an hour. When she opened her door a crack, there was her mother still talking.

Later when the house slept, Sophy felt she couldn't go and wake Violette. It was over-dramatic.

The next morning at breakfast Sophy said she would take the bus to the station with her. Violette, looking as fresh and springlike as her name, said regretfully, 'Oh, I forgot to tell you, I'm not going back to London by train. The officer I am driving has to come to Lewes to see a captain stationed in the town. He said he would pick me up here in the car.'

Both Sophy's parents came into the drive to see the visitor off, she had been the biggest success with them since Bob Lingard. Violette shook their hands with French politeness and then kissed Sophy in the old way, on both cheeks. She murmured, 'You will soon receive a letter, I am sure.'

To be passive after a shock which made you stagger, to sit with folded hands when your nature is for running forward, had always been difficult for Sophy. She'd chafed against the decision made by Doctor Renshawe and Jack that she must wait at home until she was strong. But *this* news left her gasping. Did it mean she and Daniel would become lovers again, reunited in the passion and sexual hunger they'd shared and which had blessedly left her? Did it mean she and Daniel would rush into each other's arms? She could not believe it. She went to her room after Violette had gone, to look at Bob's photograph. He was real. Daniel wasn't. He was tomorrow. Daniel was not even yesterday.

But she didn't seem to know what to do with her own body since Violette's revelation. She felt like a child who throws himself on the ground refusing to get up and wailing that he wants nothing. She hardly slept, made plans and threw them away. No, she was not a child but a monkey with the skins of eaten fruit. She didn't know how to get through the hours. She remembered Daniel's dangerous, often unkind smile. If he does write, what must I do? Shall I ask Jack? She knew this time her brother would say, 'What do you want to do, Sophy? Don't you know?'

That evening a telegram came and when she saw the boy standing in the doorway, she was filled with superstitious fear. It was God's judgement. Bob had been killed. She could scarcely bear to open the envelope. The telegram said: '48 hours leave, good news, darling, can you get to the parents, Wimbledon, tomorrow Wednesday. Can't wait. Bob.'

He was at the station when, hours late and in pitch dark, her train arrived. He clasped her in his arms and kissed and kissed her, and when he talked she noticed again that he laughed because he was happy.

'I'm sure you look gorgeous, my darling, it is hell not being able to see you in the blackout. Kiss me again. Dear, beloved girl.'

Wrapping her round with his love Bob took her into his family's darkened house and into the panelled room where his

441

mother and father were waiting with welcomes and kisses.

Like an actress who stands in the wings grumbling that her costume is too tight and too scratchy, yet when her cue comes walks on to the stage and into the flood of light to pick up her role and play it with grace and feeling, Sophy became the girl they waited for. She was affected by their admiration, by the love in Bob's handsome ordinary face. The Lingards were concerned and protective.

'You look a little better now, darling,' said Denise, studying her fondly, 'you're not so pale. It was such a terrible ordeal.' She spoke as if she had not already met Sophy a number of times and as if Sophy had but recently escaped from enemy country.

'I wasn't left in the sea for ten hours,' said Sophy gravely, touching Bob's hand.

'Oh, that's history,' said Bob.

During the evening he and the Admiral talked about the Northern convoy from which Bob had just returned. There had been great storms. Mountainous seas.

'I know those Northern waters,' Bob's father said. 'One's permanently drenched to the skin. The odd thing is one never catches cold.'

'Must be Navy rum,' said Bob and both men laughed.

He said the seas were so high they washed all over the decks.

'Do people go overboard?' said Sophy, before she realised what she'd said. There was the frisson of a pause.

'There are lines along the decks for the sailors to hang on to,' said the Admiral easily.

'That's right, sir. But we do lose men occasionally. We lost two this trip, poor devils.'

'No time to grieve over messmates on convoy, is there?' His father's voice was matter of fact. But it was not heartless.

When the parents had gone to bed, Bob and Sophy stayed by the fire. He kissed her a great deal and told her in a low almost inaudible voice muffled in her hair that he worshipped her. She clung to him, rubbing her face against the uniform of his jacket which felt like velvet. She wound her arms round

442

his neck, and for a little, roused by his nearness and her own sad state which she had kept at arm's length all the evening, she wished he'd make love to her. Their bodies were only separated by a few stupid clothes. She imagined what he would be like, she wanted him just then. But as he pressed her down into the cushions he said, 'My darling, I must stop.' His hands did not touch any part of her but her breasts through her silk dress. He pressed his cheek to hers. He stroked her hair and said it was a beautiful colour, and when he stared down at her, Sophy thought he looked young and strong and innocent.

'I do worship you, darling,' he said, as if knowing no other word.

His leave went too fast. The Lingards gave a small party for the engaged couple, so that Sophy could be introduced to relatives and family friends. One sharp-faced aunt who doted on Bob said, with a touch of sarcasm, 'So you're the famous Sophy,' and a small boy with hair slicked by a wet comb pumped Sophy's hand up and down and exclaimed, 'Golly, you're the girl who escaped with General de Gaulle.'

She found herself loving Bob more than she'd ever done. She did not know why this was so. Did the fact that Daniel was in England affect her? She didn't care just then. When she was at the station – his train left half an hour before hers – she put her arms round his neck and gave him a long, long kiss.

'Darling Bob. Keep safe. Swear?'

'Swear.'

She waved wildly as the train drew out, and it was only when she was walking along down the deserted platform that she thought how people in this war promised to do the impossible.

The carriage of her own train seemed full of tired eyes, and Sophy closed hers, fixing her mind on Bob and loving him. But soon on the horizon of her thoughts came the dark cloud of Daniel's presence in England, like a storm.

She arrived home dreading a letter. When her mother heard her coming into the house and called from the kitchen

'Sophy? A letter in the hall for you, dear. From that nice French girl,' she could scarcely go over to the salver on the table and pick it up. She had never received a letter from Daniel before. Yet she recognized the handwriting. He used to keep the score when they played word games at Les Hesperides.

Up in her bedroom she sat looking at the envelope for a minute. Two minutes. Five. It was no use. How did people manage to be so strong that they could destroy a letter unread? The very sight of it was a torment of curiosity, a kind of sexual temptation. She tore it open.

It was in French.

He had been so glad and surprised, he wrote, to meet Violette Duplessis in London. He and she had not exactly been good friends in the past but much had changed and their reunion was warm. Old differences were buried after all that had happened, wrote Daniel ponderously.

'As for me, I was emotional at learning that you are in England. Evidently I have thought about you. And you of me? I have asked myself very often what happened to you during La Défaite and whether you came safely to your own country or had become trapped in some way in mine. It is good that we can meet as friends. I want to see you very much. Violette told me you live in the country but sometimes come to London. Alas it is scarcely possible for me to visit you, our leaves are short, sometimes we have none. Our Army is more rigid than yours! So will you come to see me? And when? Write to me, ma chère Sophy, and give me the happiness of knowing I will see you again. Daniel.'

Rereading the letter she thought it a poor thing. There was not a word of anything but a correct friendliness, it might have been a letter from a middle-aged Frenchman in the summer before the war. It only just missed the set phrases which finish most letters in French. 'Be good enough to accept my sincere respects.' Is that all there was? thought Sophy. Did I get nothing right? I must have imagined that our delight and passion were what people call love at its worst and best, its lowest and highest. Oh, but I did love him once.

She would tear the letter up and forget she'd ever received it. He did not care for her now, and probably never did. How could she tell? Loving somebody was visiting the island of another human being; you took your canoe and paddled across the deep separating water between your island and his. You were allowed to land on that other, rock-strewn, forested undiscovered piece of land. For a while. But in the end you were fated to climb back into your own little boat and paddle back across the water to your island and to solitude.

Yes, I'll tear it up, thought Sophy. And sat down to answer it.

20

'Can't say I'm surprised,' was Jack's reaction when Sophy rang, using a telephone box in the town. She had expected astonishment.

'What do you mean? You can't have thought Daniel was still alive! You don't know anything about him.'

'I know this is a time when the most unlikely things happen and turn out to be perfectly natural. I've seen chaps back from the dead. The one I'm thinking about had been missing nearly a year and there he was in the office, bright as a button. My secretary looked a bit green round the gills, but she often does. Indigestion.'

'*Why* did you think Daniel was okay?' demanded Sophy, refusing to be sidetracked.

'Probably because it would be bloody inconvenient.' He paused. 'I suppose now you're going to tell me you want to see the fellow.'

'I can't very well help it.'

Jack knew this was untrue. Knew his sister's hot head. He remarked soothingly that if she was a wee bit worried –

'What do you mean?' she repeated, 'I'm out of my wits.'

'Very well, very well, out of your wits. I take it you're ringing to ask if you can meet him in Halsey Street?'

'Yes.'

'Want me to be there?'

446

'Yes.'

'Going to tell him about the baby?'

It was a clean cut. And it bled.

'Why should I? Why should I?'

'That's a moral question,' he answered deeply, 'I'm not sure I know the answer. But yes, ask him to Halsey Street and I'll be there. To keep you company.'

Sophy's reply to Daniel was as formal as his own. She wrote in English but when she read the letter over it seemed to have been translated from French and had a kind of meaningless formality. She posted the letter in a hurry, afraid she would change her mind.

After that she kept starting when the telephone rang. But a week went by and she heard nothing.

Then Violette telephoned her.

'Sophy? I'm glad to speak to you, but this time I'm somebody's messenger. Daniel asked me to ring. He's up to his neck in a case, defending some crazy corporal who went absent without leave.'

'I don't understand.' Sophy's voice was bleak. 'Daniel isn't a lawyer.'

'No, of course not, but in our Army the accused man can choose whoever he likes and this one trusts Daniel. Poor Daniel's as nervous as a cat. If one happens to be given the job as the defence, one just has to learn up as much Army law as one can. He'll be in court for at least another four days. He's so sorry not to be able to speak to you himself. He said it'll be settled by Thursday – oh, how he hopes he'll get the corporal off but he doubts it. Daniel said could you and he meet at the French club at Knightsbridge that night for dinner?'

Sophy said quickly that her brother had suggested Halsey Street. 'Jack would very much like to meet him.' She added suddenly, 'Violette, why not come too? Jack often talks about you, and all you did for me in France.'

'But Sophy, surely since you and Daniel haven't seen each other for so long –'

'It's better like this,' said Sophy. 'Truly, it is.'

447

Violette doubtfully accepted.

Pansy Hayward was accustomed to her daughter going to London to see Jack. She liked brother and sister to get on well, and when she saw them together wore a particular look of satisfaction which said 'that's how things should be'.

When she kissed Sophy goodbye, she thought the girl had never looked better. What had been Jack's song and dance about Sophy being unwell since coming home from those extraordinary adventures? One only had to look at her to see she was in perfect health, her hair and eyes bright and she'd always had a beautiful skin. But Pansy did wish, when Sophy left the house, that she would return tomorrow with the news that she was going into uniform. Daughters at home were an anachronism. There was not a woman among Pansy's large circle whose daughter had not been transformed into a driver or a firewatcher, a Land girl, a girl working on a balloon station, even on gun emplacements. Sophy was too young and strong and now too hearty to be dawdling about listening to the wireless or going for depressed country walks.

Spring was spreading over Sussex, bringing flowers to guilty gardens planted with onions. In London the plane trees were putting out tiny pale leaves. The daylight was strong and bright, there was a sparkle in it somewhere. It was out of tune with the war news. In North Africa, Rommel was besieging Tobruk. Every day the headlines said in different words 'Tobruk holds on', every day things looked worse.

As Sophy walked to Halsey Street, she was only thinking about Daniel. She did not know why she felt frightened. Did she think actually seeing Daniel again would upset her, weaken her? They had nothing in common any more. Their sacred bond, their baby, was in the arms of strangers. He was gone for ever. She knew she would never tell Daniel that she'd had his son. What would be the point, the cruel point? The last grotesque time that she had seen Daniel, they had fought like wild beasts in the dark. She remembered with vague surprise how she had bled. She could not wound Daniel now in savage return. She owed him neither duty nor revenge. It was better that their baby should stay a secret.

Hers and her brother's. And Violette's and Doctor Renshawe's. Good God, thought Sophy, they say a secret is only safe if no more than one person knows it. What about four?

An army lorry trundled by as she turned into the road leading to Halsey Street. And then she was alone except for a thrush giving an evening solo on the branch of a London tree. I wish I felt like that, thought Sophy. And I wish I was anywhere but here.

Halsey Street. She glanced at her watch and realized she was slightly late.

In the distance, standing outside Jack's lodgings, she saw two figures in khaki. Conscious, self-conscious, she began to run. Violette came to her, laughing at Sophy's hurry, to greet her and kiss her and as the girls embraced, Sophy looked beyond her shoulder at Daniel.

His appearance was a double shock. He was taller than she remembered and darker, the uniform gave him a different stance, less casual, more erect. But the second shock was how thin he had become, a gaunt apparition, a haggard version of the man she'd known. He was smiling, as Violette was, and like her, kissed Sophy on both cheeks.

'Hello, Daniel,' was all she lamely said. She busied herself finding the key while the two waited, remarking on the pleasant house and the quiet district. As they went into the hall Mrs Powell came down the stairs.

'Mr Hayward said you might be popping in,' she said, speaking in a gabble. 'Will you take yourselves up, Miss Hayward? Might be a raid tonight and Powell does like me safely back home. I'll be in in the morning, all being well that is. Goodnight.'

She scurried out fast, slamming the door behind her. Violette caught Sophy's eye and smiled.

In Jack's sitting room Sophy poured drinks and there were choruses of 'Santé' and 'Cheers'. Then the expected pause.

'So here you are in London,' said Daniel, setting down his glass and leaning back looking at Sophy with unembarrassed interest. 'You look very beautiful.'

'She does, doesn't she?' from Violette.

'Our friend admires you too,' said Daniel with his devil's grin.

'I've never given her any reason to, whereas I admire *her* very much. She's as brave as a lion,' said Sophy in the right casual tone.

Both her French friends laughed.

'If it's to be a contest, we're all heroic,' said Daniel, 'and where are our medals? At HQ there are noisy arguments from those who came over with the British at Dunkirk and those, like Violette, who hid among the herrings.'

'I forgot to ask Violette how long you've been in England,' said Sophy, still light. She felt as heavy as lead.

'I cadged a lift at Bordeaux. Well, before the Battle of Britain actually,' said Daniel. The English word sounded odd in the French voice. 'I am sure you don't want any more stories of escapes and beaches and Stukas. They're told by every man Jack at HQ –' Another English word – during the evening his conversation was peppered with them – 'The only interesting thing is what men bring with them when they come over. One of our soldiers brought a live chicken. He thought we were all starving. I couldn't understand why it didn't squawk when the Germans were searching for him the night he escaped. He told me he was a farmer and knew a way of silencing the poor creature. I didn't ask what he meant.'

'Was it alive when he arrived?'

'Loudly so.'

'What did he do with it? Give it to a farm?'

'Sophy, you are speaking of a Frenchman. He had it roasted.'

The conversation, most of it between Violette and Daniel, turned to the sins and omissions at French HQ. Their attitudes were caustic – jeers and sardonic jokes. Neither Daniel nor Violette had a sliver of respect for authority. Sophy contrasted it to the men and girls in uniform she met in Sussex. And, more than that and with wonder, to Bob.

At last Jack appeared, unconcerned and hospitable, shaking hands with his visitors and producing cliché jokes like a conjuror who impartially gives paper flowers to each guest in turn. Sophy thought he looked at Violette very approvingly; she had a moment of wondering if her friend was going to replace Hélène.

'So you're the gal who saved my sister's life,' he said to Violette.

'We saved each other.'

'I wish that were true,' said Sophy, 'Violette did it all. She wouldn't let me speak a word of English all the time we were going south.'

Daniel distinctly winced. Violette looked at him hard and said, 'It wasn't safe to speak English in France then. And isn't now.'

'I didn't see all that,' he said. 'It must have been hideous.'

'I was a deaf mute,' interposed Sophy to lighten the thing and Jack said, 'Ah well,' and changed the subject.

The quartet went to dinner at the French Club in Knightsbridge, chosen and paid for by Daniel. The meal was better than most London meals, but Daniel and Violette criticized it and Daniel actually sent back the fish, apologizing to his guests and fixing the unfortunate waiter with an indignant stare. The dish which appeared in place of the doubtful fish was delicious. Jack congratulated Daniel on his daring.

'English people haven't the heart to complain.'

'I've noticed,' Daniel said smiling and showing his teeth. Now he was so thin, thought Sophy, he looked like a wolf.

During the evening somebody played the piano and sang French songs. The favourite was '*Vous, qui passez sans me voir, sans même me de dire bonsoir, passez vous sans me voir?*' It had been sung all summer long in the Midi during the *drôle de guerre*.

The party broke up early. Jack was due to return to Curzon Street for firewatching.

'Bloody cold and boring, but I take a bottle of Scotch.'

'How fortunate you are to get one,' from Violette.

'I try not to feel guilty.'

Violette also had to get back, she was on duty next morning at six to drive her officer to the coast.

'I will walk your sister to Halsey Street before I go back to Queen's Gate,' Daniel said.

Jack thanked him. The four, leaving the warmth and lights and music, emerged into a pitch-dark street. There wasn't a star. During the goodnights Sophy thought she heard her brother ask Violette if he could take her out for a drink one evening. Perhaps somebody had got something out of this pointless evening.

Daniel took Sophy's arm to guide her across the road into Sloane Street, shining a pencil of torchlight on to the pavement so that she wouldn't trip. It was so black that at first they might have been walking under the earth. But their eyes grew accustomed to the darkness and they could make out the faint and starless sky.

'Tonight was a mistake,' Daniel said after a long walking pause. A bus went by, a dim glow.

'I'm sorry you don't like Jack.'

'Don't be absurd. He's a very good chap.'

The English slang grated.

'And very fond of you,' added Daniel.

'Yes. He is.'

Daniel took her arm again as they crossed Basil Street but dropped it when they were safely on to the pavement.

'The reason I think the evening was a mistake is that I haven't been able to talk to you. It might as well have been one of those dinners at Yvonne Dufour's. Stuck at the table and wanting to go into the garden.'

She refused to understand what he meant.

'Is there something you particularly want to say, as a matter of interest?' she said.

'Aha. I'm not sure I want to tell you now.'

How well she knew the half swallowed laugh, the implied catch-me-if-you-can. When she looked round she could make out his bony profile against what there was of the luminous half light. She thought – oh God, I love him still. Why, why did I see him again?

'You're still very beautiful,' he remarked dispassionately as they continued the Stygian walk.

452

'Well, *you* aren't.'

'I look a scarecrow.'

'You're much too thin. Was it because —'

'Because what, Sophy?'

'You had such a horrible time then,' she managed, allowing a little feeling into her voice.

'You mustn't waste your sympathy on me. As I told you, I came over from Bordeaux, there were a good many small evacuations along the Atlantic Coast and we were picked up by your Navy. I've no idea,' he added dryly, 'why I've become so thin and ugly. But from what Violette told me, you two girls had a nightmare journey.'

'Your father helped her. He gave her a lot of petrol.'

'So he did. Don't let's talk about him, he is not interesting. I wish we could talk quietly, thou and I,' he said, in French. And took her hand at last.

She felt her stomach drop when he touched her. Yes, she thought, if only we could. I would tell you how sorry I am for that time in Versailles. I was disgusting and I can't forgive myself. All the fault seemed to be hers, there was nothing against him any more, she only ached to be kissed.

They were walking by the railings of the Sloane Street gardens and Sophy noticed, or thought she noticed, that one of the gates was ajar. She knew the gardens well. Years ago Jack had obtained a key from some mutual friend, he still paid rent for it and used the gardens now and then. Once he and Sophy had picnicked there.

When she pushed the gate it creaked open.

'Somebody must have forgotten to lock it,' she said. 'I've often been in these gardens, Jack has a key and we go for walks sometimes. Shall we go in?'

'Oh yes,' he said, and she heard a laugh in his voice.

The paths were as she remembered. Sophy and Daniel emerged on to a sweep of grass ghostly grey in the starless light. The air smelled fresh, earthy.

'How like London,' he said, looking about.

'You have private gardens in Paris.'

'For the houses, not the street.'

453

The grass was wet and their heels sank in it as if they were walking on seaweed.

'There is a seat by the sundial.'

'Okay,' said Daniel in his new slang.

They sat down, neither close nor apart and Sophy turned her face up to the sky.

She said, half meaning it, 'Mrs Powell expected air raids. A plane may come droning over and drop a bomb and finish us off.'

'Unlikely. The barrage is very good now and the enemy's getting shy of the aircraft guns as well.'

'There are hit and run raids.'

'Small ones. The real blitz was over long ago. Were you in London then?'

'I was in the country,' was all she said to that.

'I'm glad.'

His empty concern, his physical nearness like a magnetic field, the very fact of Daniel beside her, made her say loudly, 'Why? Why are you glad? You sound as if we were at a dinner party making conversation. What rubbish we keep talking. I don't know why I brought you here. Take me back to Halsey Street, please, I'm tired.'

'We came here so that I could do this.' He kissed her. She responded, embraced him, answered kiss for kiss. And dragged herself away. 'No. Oh no.'

'Yes, Sophy. Yes.'

He pushed her down on the hard slats of the seat and pulled up her dress, forcing open her legs and embracing the part of her he knew and wanted, kissing her there so that she shivered with pleasure. They made love spreadeagled on the seat. It did not last, it couldn't, they had not made love for so long, and they were panting and hurried, greedy and wanting to come. When it was over they fastened their clothes. They sat apart in a deep silence.

'I wish you hadn't,' she said at last.

'You wanted me to.'

'Only part of me did.'

'The part that matters.'

'Stop it. Stop it. How I hate that.'

'Hate what?' he said, surprised out of the lull of satisfied desire.

'You. So pleased with yourself. So conceited. Self-satisfied. It's disgusting.'

'You're very extreme, Sophy. As you charmingly showed me just now, I don't disgust you at all. It is better than the last time, isn't it? Perhaps you remember you tried to cut my throat.' There was the laugh in his voice again. 'Where in heaven's name did you get hold of a bayonet?'

'I found it among a lot of Army caps.'

He laughed more.

'You were a madwoman. I've never fought a girl before, let alone one flourishing a dagger.'

'I'm sorry for what I did,' she managed.

'No you're not. You'd do it again.'

For the second time she was shocked by his confidence. She forgot remorse.

'You mean the next time you decide to flirt with another woman I'll become insane with jealousy and try to kill you.'

'If there's a dagger handy. But I can't imagine you'd find another so easily.'

In contrast to his teasing confidence Sophy said slowly and calmly, 'Daniel. You must believe this. I would never do such a thing again – or feel like that about you, either.'

He was silent for quite a long time. The girl whose body he had tasted scarcely five minutes ago was trying to escape him. She had not put on her coat, her arm was bare and very cold and in a long-ago gesture he ran his fingers up and down the arm, slightly raising the fine hairs which lay flat against her skin. Caressing her, he turned his haggard face to her; there were black holes where her eyes were but he saw the dim radiance of her haloed hair.

'You are lovely. More, much more than when we were in France. You've changed beautifully and that makes me want you more. We must have a real affair this time. An *affaire du cœur*. We will make love and I shall adore you and never give you a reason to look for a knife again ...'

455

As he continued to stroke her arm, emotion rushed at Sophy like the wall of water which sweeps up some rivers in flood, drowning, sinking anything in its way. The caress brought back, as his body in hers had done, her desire and bitterness and an awful sense of grief.

'No, Daniel. We won't meet again.'

Up and down her arm went the stroking hand.

'Don't talk nonsense.'

'Please don't touch me. *Stop it.* I shall not see you again. I am getting married soon and I had no right to –'

'To what?'

The caress stopped.

'To let you make love to me.'

'Making love is a verb that goes both ways. You made love to me.'

'Then I was wrong too, Daniel. Walk back with me to Halsey Street. Jack doesn't like me in the blackout alone. And we will say goodbye and forget this meeting.' She sprang to her feet and picked up her coat.

He said nothing. They walked across the grass. But then he stopped.

'Of course we will see each other. You always talked of getting married when we were in Cannes. Did it stop us then? Or in Paris? Of course not. I will walk home with you and we'll talk about when we can meet again. Lovely Sophy. Calm down. How angry you get ...' he said and laughed because when he tried to touch her, she flung away from him.

She hated both of them. Daniel for taking her, herself for opening her body to him. She felt degraded. She had lost whatever honour towards Bob she had cobbled together until now. She felt dirty.

'Sophy,' he said, trying again to reach her as she backed away, 'don't you know that you and I love each other? What is this old excuse about getting married? Nothing can keep us apart.'

'Yes it can!' she almost shrieked, weakening every moment, 'I won't see you. I won't! I won't! I had your baby, Daniel Vergé, and I had to give him up because I couldn't go through

456

life the mother of a bastard. And if you don't leave me alone I shall die!'

She rushed through the thickets and down the path taking a small alley which led to a further gate. She wrenched at it but it was locked and then, fearful as she heard his voice calling from a distance, she doubled back until she found the open gate and fled through it until in the deserted blackness of the street, his voice died away. She crept back to Halsey Street, half expecting a tall figure to be waiting for her.

But Daniel had vanished into the London dark.

21

Dusk had begun to fall, the peacocks at the gate were black against the sunset when Sophy went through the front door. Pansy, wearing a sleeveless blue and white apron she had made herself, came round the corner from the kitchen.

'I thought that was you, dear. Your brother telephoned.'

'Ma, I'm filthy. I've been packing Red Cross boxes all day. Can't I have a bath?'

'Yes, if you're mean with the water. But ring Jack first. He is going out, and wants to talk to you.'

'So,' said her brother the moment he heard her voice, 'we've been and gone and done it now.'

She was grateful at least for the 'we'.

'I suppose he's been on to you.'

'Turned up here while I was having breakfast. Mad as a mad bull.'

'What did you tell him?' she asked, afraid.

'What do you take me for?'

'Sorry. Sorry. Then what has *he* to be angry about?'

'He suspects what you said is true. I played total ignorance, pooh-poohed it, said it was a lot of hysterical nonsense. He listened, but I could see he was boiling all the time. I never saw a chap so furious. Reminded me of you at your worst. Is that what you've got in common?'

'We have nothing in common.'

'I wouldn't say that.'

The meaning reached her. Without realizing it she put her hand against her stomach. But at least Daniel going to her brother meant danger averted.

'What happened when you talked to him?' she asked, still apprehensive.

'As I said, he listened. Very white in the face he was and angry, very, but quite polite. All he said when I finished was that he demanded – his word – to see you.'

'I won't.'

'Good grief, Sophy, that's a bit hard. And not right either. You walked home with him last night after dinner and for some reason or other, I suppose he got your goat, you blurted out the truth. Any man would be shocked, and he seems to me a straight sort of chap. I don't blame him for being furious. I shall certainly blame *you* if you refuse to see him.'

She was pale as death.

'You think I'm a coward?'

'Not yet I don't. I will if you don't agree to see him. This time, Sophy, you can't hide behind anybody.'

'Meaning you.'

There was a pause.

'I suppose that's what I do mean. There are times when everybody, man or woman, has to stand and face whatever it is. Stand and fight if necessary. Lies and weakness and running are no damned good. Look what happened to France.'

'I don't want to. I saw.'

'Well, then. He's coming round here to see me tonight. Says he will have your address or he'll sit on the doorstep until I cough it up. I don't mind him on the doorstep, but the fellow would get court-martialled. Doesn't seem very fair.'

Sophy burst out – 'Hell.'

'Ah. I thought you'd come round.'

He talked then in a different way, the brotherly way. He pointed out that all she had to do was to tell Daniel 'how it had been and how it was'. That was the end of it. She was going to be married soon so Daniel and she would certainly not see each other again. But it was only honourable to talk to him now, poor chap. Jack was pleased when she drearily agreed.

Nothing happened. Jack did not ring again and although she tensed in miserable expectancy, nor did Daniel. She worked at her Red Cross packing and wrote to Bob and telephoned her future mother-in-law who asked her to come and stay. She picked up the threads of her daily life and decided that next week she would go to a recruiting centre in Brighton and try to get into the Wrens. Bob would be pleased.

Returning from the town one evening after her usual stint of packing she felt tired, but more satisfied with herself. She was walking down the lane leading to the house, hands in her pockets, listening to the loud evening song of the birds when she saw a figure by the peacock hedges.

Daniel. She had the craven desire to turn and run. To dive into the hedge, climb the stile, run as foxes and hares do for their lives. She slowed her walk almost to a standstill. Daniel came towards her.

'Your mother said I would meet you about now.'

'You went to the house!'

'Why not?' he said coldly. She had never heard that voice before. The French képi on his thick hair was worn at a rakish actorish angle. Beneath it was a stony face.

'We must talk.'

'No, Daniel, there's –'

'Don't dare to say there's nothing to talk about, I have a right to know. If you spoke the truth the other night, that is. Women are such liars.'

Now she saw the chance. The perfect painless way out. After all, she stood firm in the protection of her brother and her friend. Jack and Violette would never betray her. It would make an end to this drama which was of her own making. She looked beyond his shoulder at the long narrow prospect of the lane, as if at her own future. Weeds were in flower there. A man went by, clip-clopping on his horse towards the farm. He tipped his cap to them.

Daniel did not move. He let her have her silence and wondered, her lovely face was so blank, whether she was determining on a lie. My God, he thought, where *à la fin,* are you when you deal with a woman? It's like grasping an eel.

'Perhaps I did lie,' said Sophy, taking her first step to freeing herself from him. She waited for him to flare.

'Sophy,' he said. Astonishingly, the ice was gone from his voice. 'Are you saying there never was a child? Your brother told me nothing. I understand his loyalty to you, and I know he could see what I felt. He could not put me out of my misery and he pitied me.'

She could never have imagined Daniel saying such a thing.

'So here I am. He told me it was best to come. He believes, I think, that you'll tell me what I must know.'

'Why "must"?' she said with a strange look.

It was the question women had asked their lovers and seducers, their masters and tormentors, their partners and their enemies since the ancient days. How little Daniel had done, made, shared, suffered, over that lost baby. Love-making was his only part of the child.

But he did not look a master or a betrayer.

'Sophy.' Repeating her name, he used a mildness as if to somebody very young or very old. 'We can't just stand here in the road. Where can we go?'

For a moment she had the wild idea that he meant where can we make love? But they were both as far from wanting sex as it was possible to be. It had been her body's thought not her mind's. She still had the hare's instinct to run.

'We have to finish this conversation,' he said gently. 'You must see that.'

'We could say goodbye now.'

'That's what you want, but it is not what I want. And must have. I had to ask for compassionate leave to be here. And here I shall stay until you tell me all the truth.'

Still set on the enormous lie, she agreed to do as he wanted. Besides – someone might come by while she was talking to him. She was extraordinarily nervous.

'There's a wood at the end of the lane,' she said. 'There is never anybody there. It's all overgrown. I used to play there when I was little.'

461

If she imagined mentioning her own childhood would have a softening effect, she was wrong. He merely agreed and they walked away from the house, almost strolling, both occupied with their thoughts.

The lane wound past the cottage where one of Sophy's admirers had lived, Peter Silver. He was in Africa in the Army now, her mother said. Further on, they came to the muddy approaches to a farm. All farms turned the roads leading to them into quagmires and Sophy had to step gingerly, she was wearing her only pair of good shoes. The ground was covered in slippery stuff and once she almost fell. He put out a hand to steady her, and remarked that the road ought to be cleaned.

'Farmers can't waste time now on things like that,' disagreed Sophy, still picking her way.

'You could have broken your neck.'

'More fool me for walking across it. Anyway only the farm-hands usually come here. In boots.'

They negotiated masses of slurry and cowpats sprinkled with fallen straw. The road turned to the right and petered out, ending with a stretch of lumpy grass and a sort of stile. Beyond lay thick woods. She climbed the stile which was nearly rotten, and jumped down, sinking into dead leaves. Daniel jumped clear on to some grass. They went into the woods. Around them was a strong scent, indescribably fresh and clean, and a lack of light and low whippy branches. Under the hazel trees huge clumps of primroses were in flower, their petals so pale they were almost white.

'Is there a clearing anywhere?' said Daniel, stooping as he walked behind her.

'Further on, there's a pond.'

Sophy walked ahead. The flowers glimmered. If you put your face into them they had a sweet faint scent. When she was a child she would pick trugfuls of primroses for her mother, bring them home in triumph for Pansy to put in bowls on the piano. The walk through the woods now did not seem quite real; nor did the figure in uniform impatiently following her and catching at branches.

They bent their heads and ploughed on through the scented gloom until finally they emerged into a clear place. The pond was almost entirely covered with rotted black leaves but here and there the wind had blown them apart, and the water reflected white clouds and sky. A number of trees lay on the ground, felled or fallen years ago. Sophy sat on the nearest and he did the same. She stretched out her legs and studied her caked and splashed shoes.

'Now,' he said quietly. His face was set. 'Let us get this over. Was what you said the truth? Did you have a child? Mine.'

'Of course not.'

He was very still.

'You mean you made the story up?'

'You infuriated me. Yes. I made it up.'

'And thought I would be fool enough to believe it.'

'I didn't know what you'd believe.'

'Of course you did. You thought I'd feel –'

'I didn't know how you'd feel,' she burst out. 'All I know is that I wanted to hit back. You always used to make me angry and you still do.'

He took it in. He lit a cigarette. Sophy stole a look at him from under her lashes. His eyebrows were twisted, in the grimace of a man avoiding the smoke which rose in a thin line into the air. He was quite calm.

'You think I behaved badly to you in France, is that it? We made love the other night, but you still wanted revenge. Women usually do.'

'Stop it!' exclaimed Sophy, getting to her feet; her heels sank into the leaves and the mud beneath them and she had the sensation of becoming two inches shorter. 'I didn't agree to come here for you to tell me about "women". Or hear you compare your other mistresses to me. I didn't say it from revenge,' she cried, forgetting that was exactly what she had done. All she knew was that she must finish this now, get away, recapture the ghostly freedom which beckoned her like a vision from the other side of the wood. 'I should never have said that about having your baby, it was horrible of me. I'm sorry. I do beastly things,' she went on, 'and hate myself and can't take them back. Forgive me. Please.'

He threw the cigarette to the ground and pushed it with his foot into the dead leaves. He looked different. Relaxed. He gave a slight smile, but she could not smile back. Why did she feel literally wicked? As if she had committed some unlisted sin?

'You haven't changed. You're the same girl who used to rush headlong at her enemies. How did I happen to be one of them?'

She was harrassed and guilty and sad.

'Oh, you're not! I keep saying I'm sorry. Forgive me, please. Look, Daniel, I have to get back. My parents are expecting me.'

He stood up and for a moment as they looked at each other, she saw the man who had stood with her by warm seas, and danced with her to foreign music and lain in her arms on the long hot nights of the Midi. She saw him against a shimmering background of places ruined and betrayed. She held out both hands.

He gave them the briefest pressure and let them go.

They made their way back through the wood into the lane, across the mess of farm mud, and once more approached the house. They had almost reached the hedges topped with peacocks.

'Wait a moment, Sophy.'

She turned an enquiring face.

He spoke as if what he was saying mattered very much. He said it carefully, looking for the right words – something the old Daniel had never done.

'I expect you thought it was stupid, insisting on going somewhere private to talk when we could very easily have had a few words here. But I didn't know, you see. Suppose it had been the truth. That you had had my child – a baby –' his voice changed. 'We could scarcely stand in the road discussing anything as important as that. I did begin to believe it, I'm afraid. I can still be very naïve. So. Shall we say goodbye, *petite copine?*'

464

It was the only French word he used.

'Goodbye, Daniel,' said Sophy. And again she felt the sense of sin.

She did not, after all, go into uniform. Paradoxically it was Bob of all people who asked her in a letter if she could 'get some war work, darling, which means *I can see you* when I am on leave. And we can be married soon. I feel very selfish asking you to make this sacrifice and I wouldn't do it if I didn't know how many many jobs there are to be filled by clever girls like you ...'

Sophy did as he asked. She went to Brighton, and was given work at the Ministry of Supply in the old Corn Exchange. The time won for her by Jack and Doctor Renshawe was over, she was thrown into real life with a vengeance. Every morning she had to catch a train at the unearthly hour of ten to seven, every evening she returned after a day of pressure and boredom, typing documents in a huge echoing room with forty other women older than she was.

Pansy was delighted that Sophy was part of the war effort at last. Even her father grunted his approval, although he immediately asked her to contribute something out of her salary towards the housekeeping.

'I was going to do that in any case, I wish you hadn't asked,' said Sophy, blushing with annoyance.

'Why? Since you were going to do so, I've merely cleared up the matter. Give the money to your mother,' he added when she produced a brown envelope and pulled out a pound note.

Busy throughout the week, approved of by her mother, with enough money of her own and the prospect of a weekend with the Lingards, Sophy could not rid herself of a recurring idea which festered like a thorn in her right hand. Sitting in the train in the morning and evening as it made its noisy way through the Sussex fields, she told herself, repeated to herself, that she'd done what was best. Where was the sense, where the charity, in telling a man you'd had his baby and it had been adopted? She tried to justify what she'd done to him. Her thoughts became a permanent scream. No. No. No. The lie had been the only merciful thing. Why, then, did she feel so unhappy? Damn Daniel, thought Sophy, watching the spring advancing into pale beauty. Damn Daniel for appearing in London and Violette for discovering him.

Her brother, as his fond mother said two or three times, was 'noticeable by his absence'. It was nearly a month before Jack turned up for a short weekend. He arrived with presents. A bottle of Scotch for his father, 'Black market and none the worse for that'. Honey for his mother, 'A friend of mine works in Selfridge's food department'. Ten clothing coupons for Sophy, 'Don't ask where I got those', with a wink. Jack went off to the pub with his father, listened to one of Pansy's stories about her youth – she loved to talk about her girlhood, schooldays, little innocent tales to which only her son listened with attention and chuckled over. She never spoke of her parents without the prefix 'dear'.

Jack kissed Sophy, told her she looked glamorous and said he was glad to hear she was working for a living.

'Cash coming in instead of going out, mm?'

He said he would take her for a drink next morning, Sunday, at the Crown. It was a favourite pub and a haunt of the military. Sophy, who liked going there, looked complacent.

When she dressed next morning, and heard her mother and father leaving to go to church, Sophy was glad she would be alone with Jack. She had missed him badly. Everything was normal now. Her daily work. Her letters from Bob which sometimes arrived in batches of three. Telephone calls from her future in-laws. Conversations with her mother on the tedious subject of her future trousseau. Yes, things were normal and she had started to sleep badly again. Should she confide in Jack once again? She treated him as a Catholic does the priest from whom she seeks absolution. This time she decided she would not tell her brother what was haunting her. Oh, she didn't want to be serious any more, she was sick of it. She wanted to be approved of, teased, amused, admired.

Looking at herself in the glass she was surprised that her wakeful nights appeared to have little effect. Didn't a bad conscience, like an illness, begin to show?

To take her mind off herself, she decided she would ask Jack about Violette. She had noticed the previous evening that he'd said he had 'seen your French girlfriend once or twice'. Sophy turned this over in her mind, imagining Violette in her brother's arms in the narrow bed in Halsey Street. Even if they had made love, she thought, he'd never tell.

It was a fine soft day as gentle as June when brother and sister set off for the village, walking through the high-hedged lanes in a comfortable silence. Jack broke it by saying, as if in the middle of a pleasant thought, 'When this war's over, I might buy a cottage. Do some gardening. Always fancied growing my own vegetables.'

'But you'll get married and she'll prefer London, whoever she is.'

He looked tickled, but said nothing. He was carrying his knobkerrie; it had been sent to him on his twenty-first birthday by his godmother in Cape Town. He marched along flourishing the stick, and humming a tune.

Sophy was content. Nobody but Jack gave her the sensation of how it used to feel when she was a child. She felt safe, just as, when whining with tiredness at the end of a long walk, Jack gave her a piggy-back home.

They came in sight of the village and the church spire rising out of fresh trees. Her parents were at the service, she thought. Then selfishly, do they pray for me? In the old days on Sundays the bells used to ring, sweet tumbling peals across the fields. They would not ring again unless the German hordes, as Churchill called them, landed on English beaches. The very idea of Germans in England was unreal this spring morning. Safety was in the air with Sophy, if not with the statesmen in their bunkers in Whitehall.

The landlord of the Crown hailed Jack like a long-lost cousin.

'Mr Hayward, as I live and breathe. We've missed you. How is it going in gallant old London?'

He bustled away to get the drinks and Jack suggested they should go outside on to the terrace. 'Make the best of the sun while it lasts,' he said, handing Sophy his cliché and her glass.

A lime tree grew out of the paving stones in the terraces, it was yellowish green, its leaves sticky and small. Soon the leaves would grow large and broad and there would be shade under the tree. How quickly things grow, she thought, and then, jolted as if her teeth grated in her head, remembered.

'So,' said Jack, setting down his tankard on the rustic table, 'how are you liking the job?'

'Boring, boring, but I like going by train. I can read. And some of the women who work in the Exchange are rather fun; nobody else is young but they're friendly and they make me laugh. And it's good being in Brighton. I go down to what's left of the front sometimes. Barbed wire and tank blocks, but you can see the sea between them and it smells so good.'

He agreed. He'd like to see the sea too, it was odd how one missed it. Sophy waited for him to add that they were an island people, but this time he didn't. She looked at him – a comfort in trouble. How burly he was. Perhaps his physical solidity was one of the things that made her safe; his arms were so thick, and like iron. His whole figure was chunky. He sipped his beer, then remarked that the parents looked well enough and had Sophy noticed the honey he had brought for Pansy?

'It's the real stuff. Might feed her up a bit. She looks as if she needs it, so don't you go hogging it. You let her have the big spoonfuls. Pansy's the sort who gives her rations away.'

If it was a reproach she did not see it. She chattered away for a while, and then according to plan mentioned Violette. Had he seen much of her? How did they get on? Didn't Jack agree with her that Violette was pretty marvellous?

'A young woman with a mind of her own,' was all she was given in reply. 'Yes, we've been out now and then.'

'And –?'

'And you could say she and I talk the same language.'

'French?'

'Funny, Sophy, very funny.'

She gave him a sparkling look, expectant, friendly and then – with a startling suddenness – saw just how obtuse she had been. Why had she not realized that he'd brought her here for a purpose? There he sat, easy and relaxed, clever old Jack, casual and brotherly and cooking up something. She was immediately on her guard. It did not come as a shock when, emerging from the rim of the tankard, he said, 'Saw Daniel Vergé the other evening.'

'Oh.'

'Yes, Sophy. Oh. He turned up at my lodgings and asked me if I'd like to sample the cooking at Queen's Gate.'

'So you went.'

She wondered if she looked as pale as she felt.

'You couldn't say No to an offer as good as that, could you? Chap I know in the War Office had told me what wonders the French can do with our rations. When I went along I found he was right. Know what we had to eat?'

Sophy clutched at the side issue.

'I lunched with Violette at Queen's Gate and it was certainly pretty good. I think we had a sort of stew and some red wine. Violette criticized everything, but I thought it delicious.'

He said vaguely, 'Fish. We had fish. Why is it the French can produce a decent slice of fish and when the English serve it to you, it's already gone off? Beats me. It takes us to be willing to eat fish when it's started to smell ... the French cooked it with sauce and there was a salad, and pudding. Thoroughly good show.'

'You enjoyed yourself,' said Sophy, too bright, too tensed.

'Not really. But it was a pleasant meal and I like the man. He has interesting things to say. Told me about war photography. He said a real photograph must make people feel, have emotion in it and he thinks our photographers are too reticent. Or censored. Told me about the Maginot Line ... a tragedy, that. He introduced me to his colonel too. We had quite a chat. One of those little snappy Frenchmen, not a man to tangle with, I should judge.'

She listened: nervous, jealous. When had Daniel taken her into his friendship in such a way?

'Vergé told me later, when the colonel had gone, that French discipline in the army is much worse than ours. It bothers him. And so, Sophy —' changing the subject so suddenly that this time she wasn't ready, 'what did you tell that unfortunate man when he came here to see you?'

She met it bravely.

'A thumping lie.'

'So I gathered.'

'He *told* you?'

'Of course he told me, woman. He invited me to Queen's Gate to thank me for giving him your address. Spoke of you nicely, apologized for having been so extreme, as he put it, when he came to Halsey Street that morning. I have a notion he is more fond of you than he admits to himself. I'm not sure you aren't in the same boat. I am not enquiring about your love affairs,' he went on flatly, 'they're none of my business, thank God. What I want to know is — why didn't you tell him the truth when he came expressly for just that?'

'I couldn't.'

'What harm would it have done? It's over now.'

'For Christ's sake,' she said in a low trembling voice, 'you don't understand anything. I thought you did, but you're just like all other men. You don't understand a thing.'

She produced in him a deeper effect than he had expected.

'Have we been misjudging each other?' he said, with a short laugh. He was fascinated by women. They were enigmas, even this little sister. 'I need an explanation, Sophy, of what I don't understand.'

Sophy took some time before she spoke again. Her inescapable sense that she had done something terribly wrong, the haunting sense of sin which had pursued her after she gave up the baby, had become worse. Since she had lied to Daniel she couldn't get it out of her mind. Until recently she'd had a feminine, passionate, useful, essential capacity to persuade herself that what she did was right; self-doubt, self-dislike were new emotions. But just as she had been terrified of telling Daniel the truth, feeling too weak to bear what he would do, so now she began to fear she was losing her brother's love. It could happen, it wasn't impossible. She'd taken that love for granted like a plant takes the rains of spring. Looking at the hard, reserved profile she thought, am I going to be doomed for the rest of my life to try and get back his heart? Her thoughts made her flounder. She couldn't bring herself to speak.

He folded his lips prissily together, and the clear look he then turned on her said 'Well? I am still waiting.'

'You'll despise me.'

'Don't be a child, Sophy. Spit it out.'

'I should have thought you'd guess.'

'No. I did not guess. I am not a mind reader,' he said with cold patience.

She didn't want to speak and knew she couldn't keep silent. She twisted her hands.

'I lied because I was a coward. I was afraid to tell him the truth. The other night in London I got angry with him, there's always been something in Daniel that drives me mad, the way he treats me, I don't know, whatever it is I go crazy. He did it again then and I just shouted at him. I told him about the baby to hurt him. I threw the words in his face and hoped to shock him and then I just ran. Our affair was such a mess. Such an awful mess. I did love him, Jack, yes I did. But now I don't know and then the other day when I saw him waiting outside the house in the lane I was really frightened. How can I explain it to you? I could tell he wasn't a man who'd be sympathetic or see how it had been or how unhappy I was or how awful to have a baby when you aren't married. If it hadn't been for you ...'

He was listening intently and at the reference to himself made a gesture as if to say 'forget that'.

'You see,' she went on carefully, thinking aloud and telling herself the truth at last, 'there are two sides to him. I was in love with the fascinating seductive side, I shied away from the other part which I know, I always knew, was dark. I never understood him and I don't now, but I do know that if I'd told him about our baby it would have had an awful effect. He'd have been shattered and out of his mind and would have

471

accused me, and oh, I couldn't bear it. I couldn't bear it. So I said there had never been a child. And he took that very well. And said goodbye.'

She looked at him pitifully.

'You think I'm weak and you're right.'

'Don't wallow. Another drink?'

'No, thank you. I've tried to tell you how I feel. I'm sorry,' she was very bitter, 'you think it's wallowing.'

'I think your remarks about yourself are. Not your reasons. Okay, you hadn't the guts to tell him because you were afraid of the result. But I've been thinking about the chap himself. You owe it to him, you know. Isn't it his right?'

He sounded reasonable. She knew he wasn't.

'I don't accept Daniel has any rights at all.'

With the remark that if she didn't want another drink, he did, he went to the bar where the landlord, polishing glasses, began to talk to him. Two soldiers joined them and the four men laughed. One of the soldiers, a thin boy with a long face like a clown, laughed so much he had to mop his eyes.

Jack came back, carrying his tankard carefully so as not to spill it. He said 'Cheers' and drank with relish, saying that cool beer warmed the cockles of the heart.

She knew, as if he had shouted it aloud, what he was mutely saying to her. He expected her to go to London, meet Daniel and confess.

'I can't,' she said in answer to the words he hadn't spoken.

'I don't see why not. What can he do when he hears? Nothing, poor sod – I beg your pardon. There isn't a damned thing he can do except suffer. Will he, do you think?'

'*You* tell *me*.'

The distraught question had no effect upon him. He was faced with the person he loved best in the world. His love affairs, enjoyable forays – to his surprise women were attracted to him – were nothing to Jack compared to the protective and pitiful love he had for this stricken little creature.

She'd made a proper mess of things. He had pulled her out as best he could, throwing her the rope and dragging her, inch

472

by dangerous inch out of the quicksands. Here he was now, in a sense, chucking her back again. He hardened his heart. The moral issue was clear. Vergé had impressed him and roused in him a true respect. He had, in the two hours or so they had been together, liked him and thought he understood him. Of course one heterosexual man could scarcely be sure if another was attractive to women, but he was pretty sure that Vergé was. He could see the man could be fascinating. Yet, using a French word, Vergé was serious and Sophy for all her misery was not. She owed her lover the dubious gift of truth. It probably won't do any good, but it is wrong for him to be deceived, thought Jack.

'I've got to see him, then, have I?'

She did not expect him to let her off.

'Good,' he said as if the question were a statement of intention. 'Now you're being brave again.'

He thought her eyes filled, but perhaps it was a trick of the light.

He patted her hand vaguely. He felt the awful responsibility of love just then.

He stood up and said she must have another drink, they'd talk about the business later, there was no hurry. 'In the meantime I want you to tell me again all about how you met Violette and what happened?'

'Surely you don't want a repetition of that old story!' said Sophy, taking her cue.

'I think I do. I hadn't met Violette when you came back from France. It's different now. She's an interesting young woman. Quite a girl. Quite a girl.'

There was a slight, very slight, satisfaction to Sophy in telling her brother once again the saga of her adventures with Violette. Colour began to come back to her cheeks. She could not help enjoying the chance to retell the dramatic moments and the story was more detailed, more exciting, at times more tragic than when she'd burst into talk at Halsey Street on that first day.

She could see he was much taken with Violette and that as well as finding her particularly attractive, the French girl impressed him. He liked to hear how Violette had persuaded strangers to help them, how the girls had hidden in ditches or slept by the road, the very sound of the bombardment over Lyon absorbed him; yes, he said, it was like that during the blitz.

Before they left the Crown, Sophy said she would do what he wanted.

'But how? Where?' she asked. She sounded condemned.

He rallied her.

'Why not have a drink with him at Halsey Street? I'll get in touch with Vergé and suggest it, I could be there for a spell and then leave you to it. Or if you think that's a bit much, I needn't be there at all.'

Sophy thought it over. It seemed to her marginally worse for her brother to be pouring drinks and behaving as if it were a party and then going off to leave her to her fate.

'I'll see him alone,' Sophy said. She paused. 'You think I'm making a big drama.'

'On the contrary, I think what you're going to do will take guts. But it's fair, Sophy. It's only fair.'

Like all alarming or painful things that block the future she wanted to get the interview over. Her brother returned to London, having said he would ring when something was arranged. Sophy boarded her train to Brighton each morning and came home each evening and he did not telephone. The thought of seeing Daniel again hung over her like a darkness. She could not settle.

Her future mother-in-law telephoned, very affectionate, kindly, and certain that Bob would soon be back from sea.

'Do you count the days, Sophy, just as I do?' said Denise, sharing their love.

If only the meeting with Daniel was fixed. As the strain grew worse, Sophy asked herself why she'd agreed to it. But she knew exactly why. If she had said No she might have lost Jack.

The war news, commented on morning and night by her father, was both better and worse. The German paratrooper forces had attacked Crete where the British forces were fighting a bitter rearguard action. But the Italians had surrendered in Abyssinia, which gave the newspapers and the wireless the rare chance to celebrate. Sophy brooded over the news, nervously wondering if it could affect Bob's return.

At last, one dull-skyed evening, her brother telephoned.

'How about this Saturday evening?' said Jack without preliminary, the moment he got through.

'You saw him.'

'No, telephoned. I fought my way through French red tape. Cor lumme, they're infinitely worse than we are. Vergé sounded quite chuffed when I spoke to him, poor chap. Asked him for a drink but didn't say you were going to be there. Okay for Saturday, then?'

Silence on the other end of the line.

'Have you taken in Saturday? You turn up at Halsey Street, meet him and say your piece. I'll appear later on and take you out to supper.'

Still no reply.

'Are you all right?'

'Fine.'

'Come on, Sophy.'

She was early at Halsey Street and Mrs Powell opened the door with a far from welcoming smile. Sophy said a depressed good evening which Mrs Powell returned coldly and showed her up into Jack's sitting room.

Sophy sat down like a victim.

She was so nervous that every footstep outside in the street made her jump. At last the front door bell rang. She heard a man's voice and Mrs Powell's answer. Steps ascended the stairs and the door opened.

'Visitor for your brother, Miss Hayward.'

Daniel looked very taken aback when he saw her. Why was his dark thinness a shock? thought Sophy. In her mind he still looked as he used to do.

'Your brother asked me for a drink, he didn't say –'

'That I'd be here. He'll be along later. How are you, Daniel?'

He recovered, as she watched, his worldly attractive self. He said how pleasant it was to see her and why hadn't her

475

brother said she was expected, and was she working in London now?

This was the voice of his forgiveness when he had said goodbye to her in Sussex, and it struck Sophy with a sharpened sense of misery because it was almost tender and utterly undeserved. Outside the back window was a flat tarred roof where a woman who had lived here once upon a time used to grow geraniums. There were empty pots in the corners. It had started to rain. The soft sweet sound began and in through the half open window came the soft sweet smell.

'It is very nice to see you, Sophy. Wizard,' he said. That slang. It rent her heart, it was so boyish and unsuitable.

He offered her a cigarette. He did not remember, he never had, that she didn't smoke.

Daniel noticed that she wore a dark clinging dress this evening, purplish, blackish, it made her look frail. Whatever glow he'd seen on her so often, a radiance of skin and hair, was gone. She stood up and went to a table to pour him a drink, then sat down, arranging her skirts. The noise of the rain filled the pause.

'Daniel.' Oh, she had rehearsed the opening of the speech. 'Jack's not here because I asked him to come later. I have something to say to you.'

He drew on his cigarette and looked across at her with an almost serene curiosity.

When she saw his expression, Sophy was filled with sheer astonishment. How extraordinary of him not to *guess*. He had no intuition, not a thread of it or he would have known the moment he'd entered the room. He would have felt it, she thought, when we made love that night in the garden. We weren't naked, but my body has changed. And he'd have known I was lying when we went into the wood. He would have smelt it in the air. She had a strange moment of despising him for lacking the sixth sense that women took for granted.

She spoke steadily.

'I told you a lie the other day. First the truth. Then the lie. You'll hate me for both. Yes, Daniel, I did have a baby, your baby. And my brother helped me to get him adopted.'

476

22

It was worse, much worse than she had imagined. Like a swimmer entering a rough sea, she had been prepared to be knocked down, half stunned, half drowned, in danger of being sucked into the undertow. Nothing happened. A spasm went over his face, he seemed to breathe faster. That was all.

She sat like a prisoner in the dock, like a woman facing a murder charge. She could not take her eyes off her judge.

When he spoke at last, it was quietly. He asked her one or two questions and Sophy had a desire which she suppressed to exaggerate her own plight and elicit at least a pretence of sympathy. He did not ask about herself. The worst thing he said was, 'What did we have?' Such unison in that 'we'.

'A boy.'

'A son. Was he – is he – quite healthy?'

'Yes,' she said in a low voice, 'a fine baby, and large. He weighed nine pounds.'

She began to talk about the birth. She had not spoken of it since the morning Jack came to see her in Devonshire. Now it seemed necessary to tell Daniel. There were men, she supposed, who would shrug off all that – thinking what was it to do with them? Not Daniel with his grave face. He listened and lit another cigarette and when she finished he fell into a deep silence.

Sophy had looked straight at him all the time she was talking – it seemed essential to see. He took it hard. Very hard. It was more painful because his face, drawn and dark and desolate, was almost beautiful.

'Daniel. Are you very upset?'

What a question.

'What do *you* think?'

His voice was as cold as his eyes. Good God, she thought, with a welcome hot surge of indignation, you'd think he was the one who had carried the child and been sick on the road to Avignon and later alone and afraid. You'd think he was the one forced to make the decision, the one who still grieved. Well. He grieved now.

The silence oppressed her and although she felt bitter against him because of her own guilt she heard herself making excuses.

'I was too much of a coward to tell you when you came to Sussex. I thought you'd make a scene. I didn't think I could bear any more.'

'I am not angry,' he said indifferently. He smoked for a moment or two. Then said something which made her aghast, 'Would it be possible to see him?'

'See him? How could you? We don't even know where he is. They told us at that place –'

'The adoption society, is that what you mean?'

'That place. They said the mothers don't see their children again after they've signed the papers. The people who adopt don't want to meet the real mothers. They want to feel the baby is theirs . . .' Her voice expired.

Daniel reflected for a while.

'I still don't think it would be impossible to see him.'

Like someone with a cut scarcely healed, who sees a knife poised to cut again in exactly the same place she moaned, 'Please – oh please!'

Her voice this time apparently reached him. He put out his cigarette and stood up, saying with a kind of rally of politeness, 'I think you would rather I went.'

She sprang up and ran to him, clutching his arm.

'You won't do anything? I couldn't bear it if you tried!'

Daniel looked down at her with a strange expression.

'Tried what?'

'I don't know,' she faltered, knowing very well.

'I will write to you, Sophy. That would be best. Now I ought to go. Will you make my excuses to your brother please?'

He left the room and she heard fast steps down the stairs and the slam of a door.

Returning to Halsey Street after what he considered a 'decent interval', Jack asked himself what he was going to find. Trouble. Like all thoughtful men he knew the searing pain or indeed the slow poison of truth. He wasn't exactly sure why he had pressed his sister so strongly to tell Vergé about his son. It was a paradox that he felt he owed it to Sophy. Hadn't she borne the burden of the whole damned thing? The unwanted pregnancy when she was in danger of her life. Loneliness and fear. Banishment to the country. Worst of all their walk to the Adoption Society, with her carrying the little chap. Why should Vergé get off scot-free? Yet Jack liked the fellow. He entered the house doubtfully.

Instead of the murmur of voices all he heard was a silence. He found his sister huddled by the window watching the rain. She turned, tried to smile and quite failed.

'Well?' he demanded uneasily.

'It was awful.'

'He was very angry.'

'No. That was what made it so bad. He just looked ill. Cold and ill. Oh Jack, I am so unhappy.'

She put her arms round him. She didn't cry. He patted her back and muttered something and went for Jack's anodyne, some drinks. His burly presence, even his silence made her feel slightly better. She didn't know he was cursing himself.

He took her to dinner at a fashionable restaurant, a Belgravia folly built by some rich man in the 1920s to look like a church or a French town hall. The windows were stone-edged and fretted with Gothic curves and in the long dining room the tables could have been those of a monastery. So could the benches, their arms carved with acanthus leaves. Up by the ceiling gargoyles made faces at the men and girls in uniform eating dinner and flirting by candlelight. There was

479

no ballroom floor, so people could not dance, but there was wartime piano music. It was full of promises and goodbyes.

Jack had never been more gentle to his sister than during the long meal after she had seen Vergé. He set out to coax her spirits back and in some way succeeded in making her smile a little. Once she giggled in the old way. She did long to be herself again. She occasionally leaned forward to hold his hand. Hers was damp. Pressing it and releasing it, his heart swelled with guilt and pity. What hells we make for ourselves with our sense of what is right or wrong, he thought. Who am I to have made her look like that?

When the evening ended they returned to Halsey Street in a taxi. It was still raining. They entered the house and walked up the dark stairs and Sophy went to the spare bedroom, switching on the light.

He lingered by her open door, rubbing his chin as he did when thinking something over. She unbuttoned her coat and threw it on to a chair. He said, 'Are you sorry you told him?'

'Of course not. It was right.'

'Doing what's right can sometimes be completely wrong.'

Sophy laughed a little. She was standing with her back to the lamp and the light shone behind her, turning her hair into a reddish halo. He could not see her expression.

'Daniel had to be told,' she said slowly. 'I tried not to. But the way he took it proves he had to know. Poor Daniel. He minds terribly.'

She paused and added as if to herself:

'I did love him once.'

He raised his eyebrows.

'It's in the past, then, is it?'

She gave him a weary look.

'I seem to have worn out my feelings. I can't go on loving a man who isn't in my life any more. Daniel's over for me. I've never believed in people who go on loving a memory for years and years, I don't see how they can. We forget because we've got to.'

And then she said to him, 'I shall be happy with Bob.' She spoke as if she were the comforter.

*

Jack left for work early the next morning and Sophy stayed in bed. It was Sunday, her only day off from work and she lay with her arms above her head, trying to think objectively. She couldn't get it out of her mind that Daniel had wanted to see the baby. She didn't. She didn't. She was full of the selfish fear of being hurt again. But she pitied Daniel and she knew now, absolutely and appallingly, that he would have loved the little boy.

The telephone rang when she was having a meagre breakfast. She thought it was her mother and answered without misgivings.

'Sophy? It is Daniel.' Her heart began to thump. She heard her own weak voice, 'Yes?'

'I'm on duty until midday, then I can get away for an hour. No longer. Can you meet me?'

'I'm going home this morning – my train –'

'I beg you.'

Her heart went on thumping. He was perfectly practical, said the De Vere hotel opposite Kensington Gardens was close to Queen's Gate and he could walk there in five minutes.

'I'm sorry to make such a point of time but it's impossible to have more than an hour. That is why I suggest we meet at the hotel. Will you come?'

When Sophy agreed, all he said was 'Good'. He rang off.

As she walked to Kensington, Sophy knew fearfully why he wished to meet her. He was still determined somehow to see their baby. It made her tremble to think of it; suppose Daniel marched into the Adoption Society and demanded to see his son? What would happen? She did not know, but all her pity for Daniel dried up in pity for herself. He was making everything worse, making her feel wicked. He hurt her. I should have refused this morning, she thought. But when had she refused Daniel anything?

The De Vere hotel was showing signs of eighteen months of war. It was crowded with people who had fled from London during the blitz, and returned when danger was over with sighs of relief. Living in a hotel was a blessing for the elderly with a little money and no desire to have a home. It meant freedom from food queues and ration books, from shortages and 'making do'. It meant a certain amount of comfort.

When Sophy walked into the hotel a good many elderly couples were roosting in the lounge, reading the newspapers or – in the case of the women – knitting. A waitress older than the guests went by, with a tray of coffee which looked too heavy for her.

The only young faces in the large room filled with sofas, chairs and tables were those of two girls in a window seat, a beautiful blonde in dark red velvet and her plainer girlfriend in WAAF uniform. They were whispering confidences and giggling.

Daniel was at a table in the far corner. He stood up when he saw her and gave a sketchy salute. When she came over he took her hand and for a crazy moment Sophy thought he was going to kiss it. He drew up a chair for her.

Their table was too close to that of an elderly woman sitting nearby. She had a very made-up face and pop eyes; she looked amusing and catty. She was quite old but apparently still sex-conscious for she gave Daniel a veiled look.

He said to Sophy in a low voice which was not low enough, 'I must thank you for coming. I have something important to say to you.'

The woman was now unashamedly listening, and Sophy turned and gave her a cold stare.

'I don't think,' said Sophy loudly, 'this is a good place to talk.'

Daniel glanced at the lady, ostentatiously reading a magazine, and got the point.

'The meal is due to be served soon. Then we'll have the room to ourselves.'

Sophy raised her eyebrows at his words which were anything but flattering to the hotel residents.

'You seem to know the hotel well.'

'Yes. We use it when we can afford it. But French soldiers are very badly paid.'

They both glanced at the woman. She pretended she was not taking in every word.

Daniel began a conversation as empty as that of a stranger on a train. Sophy wondered just how long this was going on and how long she could stand it, when there was the tinkle of a bell at the lounge door. The effect was instantaneous. Every single man and woman, including their inquisitive neighbour and the two girls, stood up and surged out. In less than a minute the place was as deserted as if a bomb had dropped.

It was farcical, but neither Daniel nor Sophy smiled.

'Good,' he said. 'Now we will talk. First — I want you to listen and hear me out. Will you do that?'

He's afraid I'm going to make some kind of a fuss. Why? What is there left to discuss?

'Very well.'

'I have thought about what I am going to say very carefully,' he began, as if he were at that court martial Violette had spoken about. 'This is not said on the spur of the moment. I am very serious. And you must treat what I am going to say seriously.'

'Daniel. The decision's made.'

He shook his head.

'Listen. Just listen. I want you to marry me.'

She was thunderstruck.

'*Marry you!* Why on earth should I do that?'

A sarcastic smile crossed his face.

'I thought perhaps we loved each other.' He saw her flinch. He spoke then with a whole change of tone.

'I'm sorry. I don't mean to hurt you. Why am I always driven to try? Probably because you're so good at hurting me first. And more than that —' he was not watching his words, 'we have a son. We owe it to him and to ourselves to get him back and make a home for him. Give him a name. Mine. Marriage is the only way.'

He spoke so kindly.

'It's impossible,' she said.

'Of course it isn't. The fact that we have —'

'I'm marrying Bob Lingard.'

His eyes sharpened.

'The man you used to say you were engaged to? That ring?'

483

he pointed at her hand. 'You can't expect me to treat that seriously.'

She blushed to her ears and all down her neck.

'Bob Lingard loves me. And we are getting married.'

He did not vow his own love. He looked at her as if he'd never seen her before. Then repeated the appeal she'd never thought to hear him say.

'Sophy, I beg you.'

'No, no, never!' She gave a dry sob, 'It's too late, much too late, it was always too late.'

She sprang to her feet and ran as she'd run into the dark street the other night, as it seemed to her later that she always ran from Daniel in the end. All the way to Victoria, still half-running because she could not take a bus when she was in tears, she continued to sob.

She did not need to tell Jack what had happened. With his instinct he telephoned almost as soon as she was back in Sussex. There was no undercurrent in his voice, it was – to use the favourite French word – practical.

'Vergé rang. He told me he asked you to marry him and you turned him down.'

'Yes.'

She heard a smothered sigh.

'Look, Sophy, are you quite sure? Shouldn't you think it over a bit. Violette is here, why don't you have a word with her.'

Violette's voice came over the line as bright as new money and as useful. Jack had told her what had happened and she'd also caught sight of Daniel in the canteen. He looked *souffrant*.

'You must forgive me but I do feel a little part of your life, Sophy. And sometimes it is necessary to be frank,' said Violette who was never anything else. 'Jack has telephoned the agency. It appears your baby is not yet adopted. He's being fostered.'

'What do you mean?'

'Some good people are caring for him while the papers go through. Apparently it often happens. They make all the enquiries, you know, and check the home the baby is going to. And nothing is settled yet. Jack thinks, and I agree, that surely the baby's best home of all –'

'I'm sorry. I can't talk about this any more.'

'Can't you? I think I understand. I will put you back to your brother.'

Sophy wanted to ring off. She stood waiting to do just that. When Jack said, 'Don't make a decision in the heat', she burst out, 'I can't. I won't. I won't marry him.'

'Take your time. Vergé says he is going to write to you.'

'Ask him not to.'

'How do you know what will be in the letter? It might change your mind.'

'But you approved of Bob and me!' she cried, like a lament.

'Before all this came up, Sophy,' he said calmly. 'Things are altered. Your entire future will be settled in the next few days and this time nobody can do it for you. Perhaps I should never have interfered.'

'I asked you to. I wanted you to.' She was afraid to cry again. Her mother was in the kitchen.

'Just take your time,' he repeated, speaking as gently as Daniel had done.

Daniel did write. It was not the short note he had sent the first time, but at length. He wrote in French and because he used his own tongue the letter was strong. It made him suffer to think how *she* had suffered. She had been pregnant and had faced such dangers and he had not been there to protect her. She had been in his country when she had not even dared to speak because she was English ... he had shared nothing of all that had happened. All the risks, the weight, the sorrow had been hers.

But now they had something to share. They would make a real life together. Their son would be with them. He begged her to espouse him, as the French would say.

The letter was so filled with feeling, so anxious and in a way so sad, so passionately persuasive, so responsible and responsive, that Sophy carried it about for three days, reading it over and over.

But all the time that he must be waiting, and Jack too, Sophy knew she would never say yes. It was not the prospect of a scandal, of inflicting a shock on her parents who would not accept her any more because they were Victorian in their souls. She scarcely thought of that. What possessed her was that she saw the difference in Daniel's nature and her own. She remembered the quarrels which had separated them, she scarcely remembered the sex. Its delights had been terrifyingly brief, seeming to leave burns on the bodies which had enjoyed them. Staring in the mirror at night long after her parents were asleep, she saw how much she was changed. The bright angry girl in France had left her the night her baby was born. If I married Daniel, she thought, I'd never be free again. I am not what I was, but he is. He is more so. What happened to him, and to France, has made him stronger, just as it has made me weak. He'd find that out soon enough. He would always be the victor. I can't take him on. Or go and find my baby either.

She wanted to be cossetted, free, safe and have the delusion of being innocent. She wanted Bob.

At the end of three days she wrote to Daniel. She wouldn't, she said, see him again. She had made up her mind. He must believe her. She had thought with all her heart, she quaintly wrote, about what he asked and the answer was No. Their baby's fate had been decided, she knew that. (How could she? But she wrote it just the same). The baby would be loved and cared for, she had done what was best for the little boy. Daniel must accept it as she did. Make a new life and marry somebody who suited him and forget her and the baby and the past which for them both had been sad.

'I did – perhaps I do – love you, Daniel. But I don't want to see you again ever and this is goodbye.'

She signed her name and ran all the way down the lane to put the letter in the post box as if, by getting rid of it, she shook off everything but the future she'd chosen, the future she deserved.

The next morning, at the unearthly hour of five, Bob Lingard rang from Portsmouth.

INTERLUDE

Denise Lingard had the art of surmounting peacetime difficulties. She gave her solutions the stamp of style, she somehow made them fashionable.

The only way to get a ticket, she assured Sophy, was to arrive at Cook's in Berkeley Street at half past seven in the morning.

'Denise! Surely that's an exaggeration?'

'I'm afraid not, darling. Half past seven on the dot, and you must be well wrapped up, it's still freezing. The Cook's doors open at one minute past nine,' she was very exact, 'so you'll simply have to be patient. But think of the fun of being at the head of the queue. And when at last the door of Cook's opens —' Denise gestured with her plump hands and laughed, 'and you're lucky enough to get to the counter, well ... well, you might *just* manage to get a ticket for France!'

The war had been over for a year and a half and Sophy had been living in Wimbledon with the Lingards for longer than that: since Bob had been killed in the *Lancashire*. From the first, the stricken Lingards wanted her and her baby daughter Polly to stay. For a day. For a week. For a year. The Admiral knew that the company of Sophy and the little child would help his wife recover from a sorrow which he feared at first might be fatal to her.

Bob's ship had been acting as escort to a convoy which had been close to the West African coast. The convoy had been scattered by a storm, and Bob's destroyer had stayed to protect an oil tanker which had been hit and to take the crew of the tanker off to safety. The destroyer had been sunk by a U-boat with all hands lost.

The affection between Bob's mother and Sophy had always been warm, but after the tragedy it deepened. It was Denise, brave as her own son, who set out to comfort Sophy.

The winter of 1946/7 was bitterly cold, and reaction after the long war had set in with a vengeance. It was in a January of snow and freezing fog that Denise suddenly declared Sophy needed a short holiday and 'why not the south of France?'

'I think it's an inspiration,' declared Denise one evening when she, Sophy and the Admiral were having dinner. She continued to expand the idea in her tinkling voice. The flu had been beastly, hadn't it? And Sophy had taken weeks to recover and was still too thin, and as for the weather – snow all over the common and ice in the gutters; suppose she caught the flu a second time?

'You'd have to keep away from Polly, think how you'd hate that.'

The Admiral muttered that it wasn't such a bad notion, Sophy knew France well, didn't she? Spoke French too. Hadn't she made some friends there before the war? Sophy's version of her past had been censored, but its rough outline was true and both the Lingards looked on her, in a way, as a war heroine.

'You could go to the south and look up some of your old friends, you'd enjoy that. Mrs Adams was talking to me yesterday, she told me she is going to Cannes. That's what put the idea into my head (and her tip about queueing in Berkeley Street). Nancy Adams has a villa in Cannes. She doesn't even know if it still exists. May have been blown to pieces. Anyway, Sophy darling, if Nancy can get there, you can pull it off too. The great thing is the queue.'

It is never difficult to persuade somebody young to go and enjoy themselves and Sophy, widowed, the mother of a little fatherless girl, dependent on her in-laws as many young women were now that peace had come, was still young.

Twenty-six. Denise thought the southern sun was just what she needed, poor thing, so pale after the long winter. Bob would have wanted her to go, thought Denise, who had pearled over in her mind the worst of her sorrow.

Sophy exclaimed over her in-law's generosity. She had none of the pride that detests to accept a favour and thinks independence is a candle which can easily be blown out. She accepted Denise's generosity with the same untiring pleasure her mother-in-law felt at giving her things.

Those two women make a good couple, Jack often thought. It amused him to see his sister showered with gold. It was also a relief to know that her future and that of her little daughter was safe. The brother in him was glad, just as the lawyer in him was satisfied.

Listening to Denise's encouraging plans, Sophy admitted that she did long to see the sun. She had pangs about leaving Polly, but Denise declared that she 'couldn't wait to have my granddaughter to myself'. To Sophy, the very idea of going abroad was almost unimaginable. She spoke as the inhabitant of an island whose people had not set foot in Europe for more than six years. They had stayed in embattled England. The troops had crossed the Channel, flooded into France, dying on the beaches or necklaced with roses as they trundled through villages, cheered by people who wept with joy. The troops had sailed through dangerous seas, and seen dawns and sunsets over India and Ceylon. They had died in jungles or swum on the long beaches by Mount Lavinia. Now they were coming home, loaded with American nylons, French scent, ivory statues and peacock saris. But for Sophy and Denise there was nobody to come home, throwing his bag down with a thump in the hall and shouting for them as he stretched open his arms.

Denise had bought her granddaughter a book called *Carmello*, the story of a child living in Italy. When Sophy read it to Polly at night, with its descriptions of lemon groves and vineyards, the moon shining on the warm sea, the fireflies, the mule-carts, she felt like a woman hearing a forgotten song.

Sophy was excited when she arrived on an icy cold still-dark morning to join the queue already forming outside Cook's in Berkeley Street. She had borrowed Denise's fur coat and a cashmere scarf to tie under her chin. She wore boots, and thick hand-knitted socks inside them, she was kitted out to climb mountains. Breathless with cold, she stamped her booted feet while she stood ten places behind the head of the queue soon growing behind her, one arrival after another, until it snaked halfway down the street.

Huddling herself into the furs, Sophy felt jealous of anybody who had arrived before her. She tried to control the excitement sweeping through her like mouthfuls of brandy. Was it actually possible that she would get a ticket to France. *France!* At the Admiral's suggestion she had brought a medical certificate with her. The local doctor had stated that she had been ill and needed 'sunshine for a quicker recuperation'. She also had a bundle of the Admiral's virginal five-pound notes. He had the habit of walking to his bank in Wimbledon to change grubby notes for new ones.

Sophy stamped her feet again and looked at her wrist watch.

Twenty minutes to go.

In the wayward trick of time which crawls and then takes it into its head to fly in the air, just as Sophy was watching a girl walking down the street and asking herself where she'd managed to find those exquisite black nylons, the double doors were thrown open. The queue didn't move. It stampeded. People tumbled down the stairs into the booking hall and literally ran to the desks where a row of travel clerks awaited the attack.

The huge booking hall reverberated with noise, it sounded like the Tower of Babel, voices rising, asking, complaining. Sophy was wedged behind a woman and two men all demanding places on a train to Paris. She had not imagined there would be such chaos. She'd had the foolish idea that once one managed to get into the building, the reservations would be written out as they used to be in peacetime, stamped and then paid for by happy travellers-to-be. Her bright hopes sank to the ground. She was never going to get abroad.

The trio in front of her were dealt with at last, after much discussions and argument. Sophy waited to be told there were no reservations left. Ah well, she thought, at least I tried. She found herself facing the clerk. He looked across at her and said or rather grunted, 'Yes, Madam?'

He was boyish and good-looking and, odd in the bitter January, sunburned. She realized he must have returned from overseas and had recently been demobilized. This must be his first job. She put both arms on the polished counter and smiled radiantly at him.

He looked quite stunned.

'I want to get to Cannes. I mean, I suppose it's impossible, is it?' she said in all her friendly beauty. 'I've got a medical certificate as I've been rather ill. Does one need such a thing? I had this hideous flu. You don't look as if *you* have,' she added.

Life for the Cook's clerk suddenly took on a different colour. The prospect of an entire day spent fending off angry would-be travellers, of paperwork worse than anything in the Army, of long hours before he could go home to his family, brightened. The customer was really very pretty.

An hour later, snuggling back into Denise's voluminous furs, Sophy took the Underground train back to Wimbledon. Her tickets positively shone with foreign sunshine through her leather handbag.

It was two long years since Sophy had actually been happy – since the morning the telegram had come to say that Bob was dead.

Sophy had been stunned. She had never been in love with her husband, never felt her heart would break when his leaves ended, never sweated when she had no news or woken from sexy dreams in tears. But she loved him dearly and was proud of him. She glowed when she saw him. As for Bob he adored her and never stopped being surprised that she was his. She moved in the halo of his adoration. A goddess. She resembled a woman who lived permanently on champagne and packed her refrigerator with bottles of the stuff in case she needed a glass for breakfast. Bob's adoration was necessary to Sophy, and in return she welcomed him into her heart and into her bed. He was an uncomplicated energetic lover; sometimes she did not have a climax when he made love to her but she forgot about that. She lay in his arms, adored, and pleased by his joy.

She was the fortunate, the shallow? – the girl with a wondrous capacity for recovery. It had showed in her beauty and gaiety, her delight in their daughter, her laugh when she and Bob, sprawling in his parents' drawing room, watched the baby playing on the floor.

Bob vanished. It was so extraordinary to think she would never see him again. She could not accept it. One moment he was home on leave, fair and adoring, talking about his new command in the *Lancashire*. Then the telegram. Then nothing.

It was sad and human that in the two years after the peace, the gap Bob had left in her life and that of his parents should close up. It closed over his handsome head as water does when some large object is thrown into the deep. Sophy recovered. She was perhaps a little harder. She was still very pretty, although the first apricot bloom was gone. Thanks to Denise she wore beautiful clothes, her coppery hair done in a new fashionable style. She wore dresses of dull yellow and peacock blue and when the first New Look dresses copied from Paris arrived, Denise bought her one the colour of a tea rose.

Herbert Hayward had died the year Sophy was widowed. Both his children were saddened, Jack because he missed his taciturn father, Sophy because she knew she had not been a good daughter. To both the brother's and sister's great surprise, Pansy took her loss courageously and did not collapse. After the funeral, at which Pansy, in deep black, behaved with a dignity that was new to them, she refused offers of their company, kissed them and said she 'wanted to think'. A week later she asked them to come to Sussex for a weekend. She announced that she had decided to sell the house and go to live in a cottage she had inherited months ago from an old aunt in Cornwall.

It was a totally unexpected decision and left her children gaping. Pansy had gone through a metamorphosis. In the past she had twittered. She had found it almost impossible to make up her mind and had consulted Herbert about the smallest things. He made her nervous and even while he had irritably told her what to do, she would interrupt, missing the point. Later she did exactly what he'd said. She was an accepter, she made nothing happen.

All this was gone. She told Jack and Sophy that she was looking forward to living in 'dear Aunty Florry's cottage' and they must come and stay sometime – she clearly did not expect them yet awhile. She had been all through the house, she added, and pinned a note on each piece of furniture, stating whether it was destined for herself, for Jack, or – if she wanted it (which Pansy doubted) for Sophy. Like a small unfortified country which had been annexed for years and suddenly, not through its own struggles, becomes free, Pansy began to enjoy liberty.

She settled in Cornwall as if she had never been anywhere else in her life. She developed a talent for real gardening: in Sussex Herbert had hired a crotchety man who had kept her away from the flower beds. Now her patch edged with a low flint wall was so full of flowers that they elbowed each other out of the way. Below, far below, thundered the Atlantic. The cottage was built on a promontory and when Jack went to see her during the freezing 1947 winter there had been huge storms.

'I came to see if you're okay, Pansy,' he said, hugging her hard.

'I am perfectly well, my dear boy,' she smiled as if the question were slightly silly. And, as a thunderous roar came from the rocks below, 'I do like that noise.'

Sophy thought about her mother when she travelled back to Wimbledon in the Underground with her trophy of tickets. Pansy had married for love, turned into a doormat and now flowered like a late autumn crocus. Sophy had not married for love and – still young – felt she would never flower again. And wondered why, after all, she had wanted to go to France.

I must talk to Violette, she thought.

She had not seen her French friend for many months and was sorry. She supposed it was her fault, it was never difficult to pick up a telephone, was it? But everyday life filled up with small unimportant things which together formed a great edifice, castle, mansion, with a thousand rooms so comfortable and fascinating that it seemed to Sophy one simply never bothered to go out of the front door. There had been her marriage first with all its dramas of honeymoon-leave cut short, letters and sudden reunions. There had been her new position as the young Mrs Lingard taken into Bob's family, taken over by them. Her parents unflatteringly had not seemed to mind that, and Jack had approved. Later when she was pregnant, it had been Denise who bought baby clothes and pregnancy smocks like voluminous rainbows. Then Polly had come. And later after Bob had been killed, shared sorrow had glued her ever more closely to his parents.

Sophy had rather lost Violette and had lived for the day, the week, the year, with the people who had loved Bob.

Her brother was also little in her life now. It was a measure of his love for her that he did not resent it. In the Jewish phrase, he wished her happy. Besides, Sophy knew that he and Violette were together much of the time; when she telephoned Jack, it was always Violette who answered. When they met it was a trio.

Now she felt a need of them both. She wanted to break the news about her visit to France, to ask their advice, even to ask Violette if she, too, were thinking of visiting her country now. Sophy found herself wondering if Jack, at last, was going to be married. She liked the idea of Violette as her sister.

The day after she'd managed to get her French tickets, Sophy was going to the theatre with her parents-in-law; she decided to set off early to Chelsea and call at Halsey Street. Expeditions of any kind with the Lingards were dressed-up affairs and Sophy wore a new short silk dress, black shot with green taffeta, and her mother-in-law's emerald earrings.

Mrs Powell still worked at Halsey Street. She always seemed to be leaving to go home when Sophy called. She was buttoned into a thick winter coat, a scarf round her neck, when she opened the door. She gave Sophy the old familiar look made worse this evening by the girl's emeralds.

'Yes, your brother is home, Madam. Mind if you show yourself up?'

Sophy tripped up the stairs and opened her brother's door.

'Me! It's me!'

Jack was at his desk. The gas fire was burning but the part of the room where he worked was cold and he wore an old camel-hair dressing gown over his suit. Sophy couldn't help laughing when she went over to kiss him.

'Do you know what you look like? Somebody's worn-out teddy bear.'

'Hello, stranger.' He took off his glasses to polish them and put them on again to look at her. 'And where are you off to in those glad rags?'

'The in-laws are taking me to a play. A murder mystery. Bodies in the library. The Admiral loves those. I do too.'

'I remember.'

'Why the dressing-gown?' enquired Sophy, taking off her mink jacket and sitting in her favourite place on the floor by the fire. 'Did you have the flu? You never told me. Well, I didn't tell you either, did I? I was in bed a whole week and Polly wasn't allowed to come near me and the doctor said he'd never seen anything like my throat,' she added with a certain pride.

'No, haven't had the bug yet, luckily.'

'So why the fancy dress?' enquired his sister, still amused at his appearance.

'My version of central heating. I can't drag the desk near the fire. I tried once. Takes up too much room. This is very effective. When it's really cold I also tie a rug round my waist. Keeps out the draughts.'

'Jack! Violette can't approve of you turning into an old gentleman! What on earth does she say when she sees you looking like that? Old rugs and dressing-gowns are not Violette's thing at all.'

He gave a noise like a sniff, abandoned his desk and stood

up to pour them both a drink. He pulled a chair to the fire beside her. The belt of the dressing gown dragged alongside him. She giggled.

'I really believe you have no vanity at all, Jack Hayward. Don't you care what you look like? It's a miracle Violette's so attracted to you.'

'Not any more she isn't.'

Alarm went through her.

'What does that mean?'

'Violette's gone back to Paris.'

'When? For how long? Why?'

He sipped his Scotch, remarking that it wasn't strong enough, stood up again, with the belt now hanging behind him like the tail of some furry animal, and went to pour himself a little more. He returned to the fire. Looking up at him, Sophy could not see a sign of difference, of emotion.

'Taking your questions in order,' said Jack, 'Violette went a week ago. For how long? For good. Why? Because she wanted to. Very much,' he added to himself.

'But she was so fond of you,' was Sophy's helpless reply.

She had a dreadful sense that he was in pain. She hated herself for not knowing. Not sharing. She hated herself because he didn't need her.

'Yes,' agreed Jack in his dispassionate looking-at-it-from-all-angles voice, 'I think we can say she was fond of me. Of course she's not one to throw her bonnet over the windmill. Not like some girls we know.'

'Oh, I'm just a silly fool.'

He gave her a real look just then.

'No you're not. You're not. Violette thinks things out.'

'But one can't –' began Sophy and stopped.

He smiled then, the laughter lines creasing at the side of his eyes. His spectacles appeared to shine with a certain amusement at a kid sister.

'You're going to say one can't think out emotions, Sophy, but of course one can. Violette does. She's a girl of feeling. Sensible in the French way. Feeling. But practical.'

'She always was.'

'Which is why she saved your skin, eh? Do you know something, Sophy. I asked her to marry me. Imagine that. First time I've ever popped the question, have to admit one or two women have indicated ... however, Violette is the only one I've ever asked to take me on. She wouldn't have it. Can't say I blame her.'

She wanted to jump up and hug him, kiss him, say all the empty words of comfort, she wanted to decry her friend who had been cruel or mad or wise enough to turn him down. Hadn't Violette loved him after all? Yet many times Sophy had seen the two together and the French girl's manner had been fond and humorous and relaxed and sexy. She had looked, above all, content.

'Oh poor Jack. She's mad.'

'Not to have me?' he said. 'On the contrary it was probably the wisest decision she made in her life.'

'Oh poor Jack,' she helplessly repeated.

'Now, now, none of that. We can't have a scene from Heartbreak House. I admit I was a bit disappointed. Surprised too, really. Taking one thing with another,' he finished elliptically.

'Well, *I* think she's mad not to accept you. I'm sure she was in love with you.'

'Yes,' he said after a moment, 'I was too. We've been together, sounds like My Old Dutch, close on five years. We got on well. She's a delightful girl,' he added, rather grudgingly. 'Attractive. Very. I would have sworn we suited each other down to the ground. I thought she'd settled. For me. For England, come to that. But then I asked her – I said what about us getting hitched and I'd buy a house in the country, Oxfordshire, perhaps. She refused. She had been wanting to tell me for some time, she said. She felt it was time for her to go home. She'd put it off, the decision, for a long time. Since the peace. But there it was. She wanted to go home. To France. She missed her own country more and more. I understood that, you know. Violette is French in her bones. She came over here and that took tremendous guts, to serve France and follow the General. Of course she could have gone months ago, like most of the Free French who were still here on the staff. She had stayed because of me. There it is. She was homesick . . .'

He was absently unravelling the belt of the dressing-gown, turning it into a fistful of floss silk.

'I said – surely you could reconsider. You've been happy here.'

'Happy with *you*.'

'Yes. Yes, she was. People marry foreigners all the time, I said. We could visit France. She needn't lose the place, I'd see that she didn't.'

He considered and Sophy waited.

He pulled at the silk, which shone.

'Yes, she agreed with me. Lots of people marry characters from other countries and a proper mess they make of it. It wouldn't do, she said. Wouldn't do at all.'

Sophy drew an indignant breath.

'But *she* wanted *me* to marry Daniel Vergé!'

He looked up from his task of ruining the belt.

'So she did. That was for the child's sake. The French are very serious about the family.'

Sophy could see she was right, her brother was suffering. She felt helpless. The debt she owed him was impossible to pay. There had never been any way to do so until now, when she wanted to throw her arms round the unlikely figure, and kiss his swarthy cheek and say there were scores of girls he would fall in love with and hundreds who would fall in love with *him* in the future. She wanted to burn with sisterly indignation against Violette for being her practical self.

She couldn't.

She stayed a little and they talked of other things and Jack made a few of his jokes. Then she looked at the clock on the mantelpiece and sighed because she had to go.

She did kiss him then. And held him tightly for a moment.

'Don't be sad, darling darling Jack.'

He gave a dry chuckle.

'Least said soonest mended.'

'One does get over love. I have.'

He made a sound of indulgent mockery.

'What a sentimental girl you are.'

'Aren't I? Will you promise me something?'

'Shouldn't think so.'

'Don't wear that dressing-gown if anybody else comes to see you.'

Fondly embraced by her parents-in-law, giving her small daughter an emotional hug, relieved that Denise had typically bought the little girl a surprise present to take her mind off her mother in travelling clothes, Sophy left London. She read a magazine all the way to Dover. She felt strange. The Channel was heaving and showing its teeth; to a girl who had not set foot on a ship for nearly seven years, it augured dismay. The boat was crammed with travellers, she had been prepared for that, but not for the rough crossing. She spent the two hours at sea, before they finally docked at Calais, staring at the horizon. It was a sailor's trick for seasickness that Bob had once described to her, and it worked. As she walked down the gangplank she was almost the only passenger not green in the face.

It felt extraordinary to be in France; to hear the language again, see wrecked buildings, a devastation of half burnt walls, acres of fallen bricks, great holes in the ground, all from bombardments not by 'the enemy' but by the RAF. She was dragging her suitcase along the platform when a porter strung round with baggage and wearing a cap like a French soldier, took it from her.

'Number 44,' he said, pointing to his cap.

He shouldered his way ahead.

Sophy's experience of trains was now exclusively British. Whatever the journey, long or short, the floors were gritty with coal dust, the upholstery split from years without repair; British trains were dirty, crammed with passengers and always, always, late. She was shown into a train already waiting at the station. It was like a pre-war advertisement for travel by Wagons-Lits. Indeed, the train had been built in the mid 1930s, but was as smart and spotless as if it had just emerged from the factory.

In something of a dream, Sophy walked up the platform. A man in dark red Wagon-Lits uniform took her ticket and handed her up the steep steps. Still in the dream she followed him down a carpeted corridor to her own solitary first-class compartment. He would, he said, make up her bed after she had dined.

She sat down very suddenly. She couldn't take it in. The luxury. The impression that there never had been a war. And yet in the distance the ruined walls and heaps of rubble were just like London. How strange the French are, she thought. Are they right? Are we wrong? Her journey was occupied by the two questions.

The attendant appeared, to ask if there was anything he could do for her. Would she like him to reserve a ticket for the first sitting of dinner? Sophy, thinking of other journeys, gratefully accepted.

'The menu is larger and the cuisine better at the first sitting, Madame,' said the attendant who had noticed her wedding ring and addressed her correctly. She smiled and overtipped him. It was the turn of somebody French to be astonished: he was accustomed to tips a quarter the size.

As the train left Calais she sat at the window looking at the ruins, the familiar pattern of destruction which matched the huge city she had left behind. But it grew to dusk, and the train began to make its way through darkening country as flat as Holland, and soon she could see nothing but a few dully-shining lights from houses here and there.

She leaned back against the cushioned seat, a young woman alone travelling towards yesterday.

Sooner than she had expected her friend the attendant put his head round the door. The dinner bell was now ringing, Madame, and here was her numbered ticket. Sophy tipped him again: she felt profligate.

Nothing could have been livelier than the first French dining car Sophy entered in peacetime. Every table was occupied and everybody appeared to be talking at once. Pink-shaded lamps on the tables lit vivacious faces, the gold buttons of uniforms, the waiters' starched white jackets, the silver of a large dish of shiny brown circles of pastry which a waiter was tenderly serving to a woman in an exaggerated hat. Another waiter skidded up to Sophy and asked her if he could show her to a table. He looked round at the crowded restaurant, then took her up to a table at which a number of men in uniform were seated. One was particularly resplendent with much gold braid.

'Mon Générale,' said the waiter, and gave a respectful gesture both to the man and to Sophy, 'would you permit?' It seemed that the General, who bowed to Sophy affably, was willing to permit and Sophy was given a seat next to him – a junior officer moved immediately to make a place for her.

Sophy liked the General, who had grey wavy hair, many medals and a good deal of style. She was sure his beautiful moustache was waxed, and he had humorous eyelids. He introduced his fellow officers who greeted Sophy with great politeness. The meal began with a discussion about the wine. On each table, in a small basket, was a sort of bouquet of half bottles. Red and white, vintage and not, expensive and – possibly – cheap. There were even bright-coloured miniature liqueurs. The General, as if selecting a weapon for a duel, examined each bottle in turn, and turned to Sophy.

'The Saint Véran is a disaster. I have experience of it, alas. Now the Aligote . . .'

He waved at the waiter and ordered two bottles – four of the little halves were rushed to their table. With an officer of field rank next to her Sophy had never been given so much deference or attention. The meal ran for six delicious courses and Sophy spent it in the lively company of the French Army.

'For you, mon Générale,' said the waiter, lowering his voice at the end of the meal, 'a little *real* coffee.'

The General nodded affably. That would be acceptable. He smiled at Sophy, and said he supposed such a rarity was seen more often in England.

'We French have developed the taste, what other choice have we? for chicory and ground acorns. Disgusting.'

All five men stood up when their English companion left them, taking her hand, clicking their heels. Sophy felt she was playing the leading role in an operetta ... perhaps *The Daughter of the Regiment.* When she returned to her compartment she wondered who her charming companions had been. Were they part of de Gaulle's army returned to France? Somehow she did not think so. Where had been their Crosses of Lorraine? It was a puzzle.

The war was over. The subject was threadbare, everybody, everything, was to be changed, remade, rebuilt, made to shine like this train. The meal, the talkative free-spirited Frenchmen, the flavour of gallantry she had not met for so long that it seemed new, the very smell of Gauloise cigarettes, gave her a solace, half sad and half happy. She slept.

When she woke she saw by her wrist-watch that it must be dawn. The train was going very quietly now, although during the night it had roared and shaken its way down the map of France. She climbed from her bunk and lifted the blind. Yes, the sky was beginning to pale. And then she saw the countryside whose very colours made her heart ache: the dim dull rose, the smoky silver of Provence.

The luxurious train and the good dinner, the spirited company of French officers, a general air of style and, even more, of normal life had half persuaded Sophy that the worst of war had vanished. It had been made to disappear by sheer French determination. When she arrived at the Hotel Méditerranée she saw that it was not quite like that. Her friend at Cook's had warned her that only two floors of the hotel were – as yet – open. But she wasn't prepared to be taken to her bedroom across a network of builders' planks or helped by the porter to jump over great boulders of concrete. The final few yards were like picking her way on stepping stones.

Her enormous bedroom had a certain gloomy magnificence. The bathroom was equally huge. Feeling in need of a bath she turned on an outsized brassy tap marked Hot. A small trickle of rusty lukewarm water came out, accompanied by a great deal of steam.

She unpacked and went to open the windows leading on to a balcony. The morning sun was out, the air balmy. She smelled a scent, just then, which was so evocative that she had to shut her eyes. Beneath the window, covered in fluffy blossom, were great branches of soft yellow globes and long greyish leaves. A tree of mimosa.

When Denise first suggested this journey to yesterday, Sophy had been very excited. She was so grateful to Denise, surprised at the very idea of seeing France again. They talked about the south. Denise had often visited the Riviera before the war, when the Admiral's ship had been 'showing the flag' as it was called at Cannes or Nice. Preparing for her holiday Sophy thought about the Dufours. She would, of course, visit them. It was a slightly disturbing idea.

She remembered – dulled by distance but still remembered – the way the family had treated her. Her only friend had been Paul, who had literally rescued her and she often thought probably saved her life. Sophy argued with herself as she looked out at the bright sea, that she must forget that old history. She must think and feel as France now did. Things were new, the bad old days forgotten. It was seven whole years since she had been here and it seemed to Sophy that she had lived a whole lifetime since then. She had been married, she'd had a little daughter, she had lost her beloved Bob. She had now become settled, healed, yes, that was true. And Daniel long ago had been driven out of her heart.

Outside the window the Mediterranean sparkled. The day was so beautiful it took her breath away. She was here. No longer the enemy who must not speak French because of her hated English accent. She was welcomed, free of many burdens, and in one of the loveliest places in the world.

She lingered over her lunch and – rare for Sophy – went up to her room afterwards to read and look at the top of the mimosa tree. She was badly missing her little daughter and wished Polly were here, to climb up on the bed and snuggle and chatter. To rid herself of the pangs, Sophy decided to go and see Cannes again. Making her way through the builders' rubble along the corridor, she went out into the afternoon sun.

To her English eyes everything was startling and colourful. She had come from London, a study in grey and black. There, fog waited at the street corners and hung like cobwebs at the top of curtains. When you opened the door of a taxi the fog was there too. London was dun-coloured, a city of ruins and grubby faces. The ice had not melted, nor the old snow ribbed and stained with dirt along the edges of pavements and in the gutters. Here all was bright colour and the benediction of the clear air.

There were fishermen along the quay, their woven baskets filled with sea urchins like spiky horse chestnuts in beds of seaweed. 'Mademoiselle! Taste one! Try one!' shouted a fisherman laughing at her and stretching out a hand with a sea urchin in his palm. Sophy laughed and shook her head.

She went instead up the rue d'Antibes and stopped at a pâtissier. La Bonbonnière. It was as unchanged as when she and Anne-Marie used to drink chocolate and gossip here. When she went into the shop there were the same spindly marble-topped tables, gold chairs, mounds of crystallized fruit like glass globes, ruby, yellow, shiny green and dull orange. There were boxes of chocolates topped with crystallized violets, and oval-shaped almond sweets called callissons. How smart everything is, thought Sophy, and wished Denise was with her to enjoy the hot chocolate and petits fours.

She left the shop and turned into a side street which led to the Croisette. It was time to be brave. She must walk to Les Hesperides.

She tried to visualize how it was going to be. Clara, of course, would open the door. It did not enter Sophy's head that in seven years the old servant might have stopped working or even stopped living. Such old Provençal women, bulky and slow and tough as olive wood, were immortal. Clara would show her into the petit salon – the grand salon was only used after dinner. There would be a pause, and finally in would come Yvonne. She would be older, of course. But Sophy was sure her hair would still be dyed the blonde colour which had been its hue when she was young. Her figure would still be Parisienne and trim. Would the years of war, though, show on Yvonne's rather blank face? Sophy was willing to bet there wouldn't be a mark. She would shake Sophy's hand and say in the old way, '*Tiens*'.

Was it possible to revive a friendship which had been chopped to pieces, and make it live again? The Dufours had been cruel to her, even dangerous. But now everything was forgiven and forgotten. That was what people were doing now in France. In a way, they pretended the war and the defeat had never happened. The man singing in the restaurant was Italian, and so was his evocative song. You must clasp hands with the present, thought Sophy, and forget who used to be an enemy. The Dufours wanted to be rid of me because they were afraid. How do I know if I would have behaved any better?

And then she remembered Paul.

The sun undid the knots of melancholy as she walked by the sea in the mid afternoon. And it was not only the sun; it was the way people at the hotel were treating her. She felt welcomed. When she came, at last, within sight of the Dufour house, a little thrill of excitement went through her.

There it was, the very house where she had fallen in love, where she had been happy, the gardens through which she had crept one night to run to Les Embruns and Daniel's arms. The imitation château-façade was not its dazzling white self but she had not expected it to be. From her distant view, Sophy noticed that the palms in the garden were hung with dried dead leaves. In the rich past those were always chopped off in the autumn. A man had climbed up the trunks of the trees with a rope; Sophy and Anne-Marie used to stand and watch him. He lopped off the dead leaves very neatly with a long curved knife and they floated down on to the grass, great brownish fans.

The house spoke to her. Drew her. She could make out Anne-Marie's balcony window and half expected her friend's ungainly figure to appear, perhaps with Claudio.

She gave a sudden exclamation and said the name aloud.

'Claudio!'

How could she have forgotten him? Memory did alarming things, it enhanced and changed or totally blanked out. Claudio hadn't come into her thoughts for years. If she was honest with herself the Dufours themselves had been pushed into the back of her mind for a long, long time. Claudio, who had meant little to her, had vanished through a trap door into oblivion. Now she clearly remembered him. Not the facetious and ingratiating Claudio whom everybody had liked in peacetime, but the owner of a black official car which used to draw up at the gate to deliver Anne-Marie back home. Sophy had never met him when she returned to the family after the defeat, but she had seen his burly fattish figure embracing her friend. What difference had it made to Anne-Marie when she married an enemy-turned-ally? And what now, when the very word Italy again meant music and a light heart?

Sophy knew, everybody knew, about the French Resistance. They were the freedom fighters who'd taken their name, *maquis*, from the thorn bushes growing in the mountains where they hid, to attack, and hide again. Thousands of brave men had been killed by the Nazis. Now they were idolized in France: the country's heroes.

Her knowledge of the complexities of the war was scanty. She had followed the great victories of the Allies as they had fought their way through France. She had read the newspapers, but rarely looked at the maps or grasped the campaigns. Sophy was the typical Englishwoman, who believed what she read and heard, cheered at victory and expected, when peace came, the millennium.

France was General de Gaulle, who epitomized and symbolized his country as he marched at the head of his troops down the Champs Élysées, a noble humourless stork. Sophy was certain Daniel must have been among the soldiers marching behind their general and sharing the moment of triumph. Daniel, too, had done his share in saving France. That was the sum total of Sophy's grasp of what had happened to the country with which she had been violently in love.

She hesitated for a while, staring at the house and thinking about Claudio. But the Italian singer came again into her mind: Italians were friends to France now. Lifting her chin, strong enough to face all kinds of difficulties and suddenly longing to see Anne-Marie, she crossed the road.

She had been right about the garden, it was full of last summer's dried weeds. The palm trees, when she gazed up at them, were worse than they looked at a distance. Sophy went up the steps and rang the bell.

Facing the closed door through which her girlhood had passed, inwards, outwards, she tensed. She stood in the pose of a tennis player facing an adversary; she fixed her attention on exactly where she judged the ball would hurtle towards her, the adversary her own lost self.

The door opened very slowly to reveal, not the dark-eyed dour-faced Clara, but an old woman whose gentle face was as wrinkled as crushed tissue paper. She was respectably but shabbily dressed and looked at the elegant visitor with courtesy.

'Mademoiselle?'

Sophy supposed her to be an elderly relative of the family. Yvonne had scores of aunts and cousins. She asked respectfully if any of the family happened to be at home. She apologized for the unexpected call.

The old woman, whose face was a series of half-arcs, mouth, cheekbones, little thin circle of hair, repeated, 'The family, Mademoiselle?'

The single title surprised Sophy, who then realized she was wearing gloves and her wedding ring was hidden.

'Why yes, Madame,' she said pleasantly, 'the family Dufour.'

There was a very slight pause. The woman then invited her to come in.

Sophy stepped into an entrance hall which was totally unrecognizable. She could scarcely believe she was in Les Hesperides. Where was the white and gold clock in its glass case, the rough-cast pot of pampas grass which Yvonne had arranged in the empty fireplace and which Clara dusted every week? The bow-fronted chest of drawers was gone and so were the engravings of the palace of Fontainebleau. The hall, almost empty of furniture, echoed.

'I regret very much, Mademoiselle,' said the old woman, shutting the front door and turning to Sophy, 'but the family you are asking for does not live in this house. I'm told that they did, for many years.'

'You mean they have moved?'

'Yes, we must suppose they have moved,' was the dry answer. The old woman added, as if talking to a child, 'The trouble is that I cannot tell you where.'

Sophy was puzzled. It must be a misunderstanding, she thought, or it's my awful rusty French. She explained with careful politeness that she was very anxious to find the Dufours. Had Madame a forwarding address?

The old woman said as politely that she hadn't.

Is she really the owner of Les Hesperides? thought Sophy. This conversation is mad. Apparently reading her visitor's thoughts the old woman gave an explanation.

'I am a native of Lyon, Mademoiselle. I was born and bred there and lived there until last year, when the doctor advised me to come south for the climate. I purchased Les Hesperides through my lawyers, evidently, but before that when I came to look it over it was empty. During the war it was requisitioned and afterwards it became government property, so my lawyers informed me. That is all I can tell you.'

She studied her visitor for a moment.

'You were a friend of this family of whom we speak?'

'Yes, yes. The daughter, Anne-Marie Dufour, was at school with me. We were close friends. I used to live here.'

'Indeed? Forgive me but you are not French?'

'English. I am English.'

'Ah. I thought perhaps Dutch.'

She gazed at Sophy's fixed face with the elderly concern she might give to a stray cat found in her gardens. She gave the impression of somebody whose charity, like the sun, was uninvolved and universal.

'Letters do come sometimes addressed to Monsieur or

Madame Dufour. I return them to the post office.'

'And then they are forwarded?' prompted Sophy. Hope was still somewhere in her voice.

The old woman shook her head.

'That is what I had understood when I returned the letters. They will get to the family eventually, I thought. Then two letters came, one quite soon after the other, and both in the same handwriting. On the second of them was written, 'Urgent. Please forward if away'. Well, you see, Mademoiselle, it made me think that perhaps the family were not receiving their mail after all. I was worried. I went in person to the post office and talked to the gentleman in charge. He was most helpful. It is the rule, he told me, to keep letters which have no known address for forwarding. They are kept for two years. Then destroyed. The two year interval is a long one, is it not? That is because there is always a possibility in these uncertain times that people may return to the district. In which case they will, of course, collect their mail. I was glad to speak to him. At least I know the post office are doing their best. My mind is now easy.'

Sophy imagined yet another letter coming here from some lost friend. The old woman would pick it up and carefully send it to the post office where it would wait for people who were also lost.

'I wish I might have been of help to you,' said the old woman giving Sophy a thoughtful look and speaking in her passionless charitable voice. 'It is good to find one's friends again, particularly now. We need our friends. Would you –' she gave one of her smiles of peculiar sweetness, 'like to take a little look at my salon? Since you lived here it may interest you to see the room again?'

Sophy, oppressed by the strangeness of the house, could scarcely refuse. She followed her hostess into what had been the grand salon. Here Yvonne had queened it among the young men she invited to dine. Here Anne-Marie had played the piano, and Daniel and Claudio, Alexis Lucas, Stefan, Serge, had talked and laughed loudly and disputed more loudly still. Sophy had never heard a French discussion when anybody had agreed with anybody; the only person who never joined in was Paul. She herself had sat here scarcely listening to the talk, while she wondered and wondered when they would go out into the dark garden.

There was not a whisper of what the room had been. No Parisian elegance, no fringed curtains, no porcelain, no flowers, no piano. The walls had been repainted from soft ivory to a glaring white. Shabby furniture covered with dark red damask was pushed round the walls. If you sat here and wanted to speak to somebody, thought Sophy, you would have to shout.

The only remarkable things in the ugly room – and their effect was shattering – were the paintings. There were five. The style was bold and amateurish, the colours garish; scarlet and black, strong yellow, a harsh dark blue. The figures, particularly those of the women, had a look of Delacroix – of what a student might produce when trying to copy the painter. They depicted men marching in groups, arms raised and heads thrown nobly back. The women held enormous Tricolours which they brandished against a dark sky. The flags and the women's black hair streamed in a wind which had also blown the clouds into banners.

What was extraordinary was that the paintings were damaged. There were holes or rents right across every one of the canvases. No attempt had been made to repair them.

'You are looking at my pictures,' said Sophy's companion. 'I did those during the war when I was at Lyon.'

'You are an artist, Madame?'

The old woman gave a sarcastic laugh. Heavenly charity deserted her for a moment.

'Of course I am not. I painted them for myself and hung them in my apartment for pleasure. One night the German soldiers came. They were looking for some unfortunate, there was much hunting down then, and they suspected I had hidden him.'

'Had you?' Sophy asked, hushed, and still.

'Perhaps. They questioned me a great deal. They also saw my pictures. They did not like the subjects and put their

bayonets through them. I brought them with me from Lyon,'
she added. She stood regarding the ruined canvases with the
half arc of a smile.

Sophy stayed on for a while because of the old woman's
cool concern. When they left the grand salon she asked if
Sophy would like to see the rest of the house and again Sophy
was unable to refuse; the gesture was clearly the old woman's
way of hospitality. Sophy dreaded it but was shown into her
own room. It was as bare as the cell of a nun. Outside the
window was the tree she used to look at; now in wintertime it
was hung with oranges. One holy picture of a Madonna and
child was on the wall. Sophy was taken into other rooms just
as bare. She wondered if they were ever used. She thought
they were not.

They went back down the staircase. She longed to leave.
There were still a few exchanges to be made, of thanks from
Sophy for being received so kindly, of regrets from the old
woman who gave her one more arc-shaped smile in which
goodness seemed to Sophy to have little feeling.

'Are you staying in Cannes for a time?' she enquired,
accompanying Sophy to the door, 'with other French friends,
perhaps?'

No, explained Sophy, she was alone at the Méditerranée
Hotel and would be there for another ten days or so.

'Ah. Yes. A little winter holiday and some sunshine. Good,'
said her hostess.

She put out a hand as thin as a leaf and Sophy shook it,
trying not to squash its frailness.

When she looked back, the woman was standing on the
steps waiting to wave to her.

Sophy had not realized the full effect of the news – the
non-news – given her at Les Hesperides until she was back at
the hotel. The total disappearance of her friends was a let-
down. An anti-climax. She would never have come to Cannes
if she had known they were gone. It was laughable to
remember that only this morning she'd postponed walking to
call on the family, and had felt she needed energy to face
them after all this time. Now it seemed she was never going to

see them again. It was perfectly possible. People did disappear when a country was in turmoil. It began to occur to her, in all ignorance she had not considered it before, that the Dufours might have preferred to vanish after having been hand in glove with the collaborator Claudio Arrighi. Maybe the forgiving and forgetting Sophy had thought was everywhere in France had not existed two years ago or more. If Yvonne and Anselme had been afraid of her, might they not have been even more afraid, in 1944 and 1945, of reprisals against themselves? There were no answers to any of her questions. When she woke the next morning to the clear February sun, she looked ahead at the next two weeks and asked herself how she could get through the time in this paradise. Could she go back to England earlier? Would it hurt Denise's feelings?

When the telephone by Sophy's bed rang she gave a start. Nobody knew she was here. The voice which spoke was not French but lazy American.

'Sophy? Ah, I've tracked you down. Denise said why didn't I locate you at your hotel but you were out this afternoon and I wondered if you were visiting with friends.'

'Oh no. Just walking.'

'I'm glad to hear that, because I'm sitting here in an empty villa with no company but a pigeon on the window-sill. Did you in your life see anything as stupid as a pigeon? No wonder they say bird-brain. Such a fool that one is. Well, now ... how about coming around?'

Sophy eagerly agreed. In her determination to face the Dufours she had forgotten her mother-in-law's American friend, Nancy Adams.

She was glad of the distraction and took a taxi later that morning to Mrs Adams' address.

'Where is the villa, do you know?' she asked the driver.

The man said it was round the corner of the Croisette beyond Palm Beach Casino.

Sophy's volatile spirits gave a dive again. She would have to drive past Les Hesperides, and the apartments where Daniel used to live as well. She did not even want to look again at Anne-Marie's old home; she turned her head and

512

stared at the sea. But when they rounded the corner by the casino she couldn't resist Les Embruns. The small block of flats was dilapidated and rain-streaked. As in the Dufours' garden, nobody had chopped the dead leaves off the palms, they hung like broken arms. On the balcony of Daniel's flat a towel was drying in the sun.

More unpruned palms stood in the weedy garden of the villa where the taxi stopped; a broken shutter banged in the brisk southern wind. But there was Nancy Adams standing in the doorway, smiling and stretching out both hands in welcome. Sophy ran towards her and was given a kiss.

'You're a sight for sore eyes,' said Nancy. 'How did I ever manage to make myself understood in this country? Come along in. It's sure a pleasure to see a friend.'

Nancy Adams was slender from religious dieting, with a fine-boned handsome face and dark hair cleverly touched with grey. Her voice was lazy and she was not. She exclaimed, taking Sophy into the villa, that she'd been struggling since her arrival with her non-existent French.

'I'm here to tell you I have been in despair.'

The salon into which she took Sophy was large and spacious and in a mess. Enormous sofas, which would seat eight, stained white linen covers. The marble floor was speckled, cracked and dirty, and one glowing Persian rug of crimson and grey made it look worse.

'Isn't it all just terrible?' wailed Nancy cheerfully. 'Do sit down. You can trust the cushions, I just vacuumed them. But isn't everything just terrible? Anyway, the coffee's hot,' she added pouring out, 'and I bought some of these little almond things.'

As they sat together, drinking excellent coffee and eating calissons, Nancy continued to wail. The villa had been requisitioned by the American army during the landings on the coast in 1945. When the great Operation Anvil as it was called, the attack of American and French troops on the south had happened, she'd followed the campaign 'breathlessly'. Wasn't it exciting? All those thousands of troops including the French Resistance, and hundreds of ships ... but I did keep thinking, you know, about my poor little villa. Had it been blown to bits? After the armistice, what could I find out? Nix. I literally didn't know if it would be *standing* when I arrived three days ago. But here it is. A wreck.'

She looked round.

'I can't begin to tell you the state of the bathtubs,' she added, shutting her eyes, then opening them to look helplessly at Sophy. Nancy's eyes were charming. She wore a good deal of mascara, her lashes were long and the effect was of two clever stars.

The older and younger women were scarcely more than acquaintances but each, for the other, represented home. They were drawn together because they were in a foreign country. Sophy did not know Nancy well but had always liked the hard handsome woman whose manner was deceptively lazy. Nancy and Denise Lingard had been friends for years before the war. The Admiral had originally met one of Nancy's husbands at an Embassy Reception. In all, Nancy had been married four times. She took her present state of single-ness lightly; it appeared to suit her.

She poured more coffee and nibbled an almond cake.

'Do you like the new rug? I bought it in Monte Carlo yesterday; cute, isn't it? A Shiraz. And I've cleaned this table but as for the rest, don't look around, Sophy. Isn't it all just terrible?' It was Nancy's theme song.

Sophy thought the villa, in spite of the grime, spacious and splendid and asked how long Nancy had owned it.

'Jock, he was my husband in 1935,' said Nancy in the vague manner she used when speaking of any of the quartet, 'built the place. Before that we used to stay at the Eden Roc. Jock was a mean tennis player. I had a little dog then, Pompom, who was killed by a car. The hotel let us bury her in their dogs' cemetery.'

Sophy murmured suitable noises. Nancy spoke in the mournful tone of a widow.

'So, as we kept coming here to the Coast, Jock thought why not build and we planned this little place –' looking round the expanses of the villa with the same mournful expression. She then turned starry eyes on Sophy and remarked that she

514

wished she'd known Sophy had been here too.

'We did have such a swell time, you know? Denise told me you used to live a step away on the Croisette – is that right? Imagine, Jock and I here, house parties, all those things. Why, you could have visited with us.'

The voice echoed as if with endless American parties, music floating through open windows, girls in beach pyjamas, cocktails. There was a Twentyish flavour about Nancy. She wondered aloud if she and Sophy had had mutual friends on the Coast before the war.

'Did you know the van Lenneps? They're dears. Or the Whittakers, maybe? Their boy joined the Marines, I believe he was killed in the Far East, poor lad. I was fond of Rod Whittaker. Did you happen to meet one or two Americans when you were in Cannes?'

Sophy shook her head. She explained that she'd lived with a French family, their name was Dufour. She mentioned the young men who used to come to the house. Casually, she added Daniel.

Nancy lit a cigarette and crossed her long legs while she turned over the names. No, she couldn't recall any of those people. What a pity.

'We could have exchanged friends,' she said, giving Sophy one of her amusing looks which said more than her words. She resembled the second lead in many American movies, the wisecracking worldly girl who has an adoring beau whom she ill-treats and who sees through all men, 'it's too easy to understand them, pathetic!' and vainly attempts to bring the heroine to her lovelorn senses.

'Isn't it shameful, we didn't know many French people at all. Such a mistake. Friends came over from the States to stay. It was great fun, of course, but one should become part of the country and we never did ... Denise says that *you* speak French like a native,' she added casually.

Sophy did not know her well enough to see a trap.

'Awful English accent,' she said.

'Nobody minds a foreign accent now. Specially an Allied one. I suppose....'

And Nancy, using a 1930s style with its slangy exaggerations, its 'awfullys' and 'terriblys', its potent charm, said it would be just marvellous, it would be wonderful, how eternally grateful she would be ... the starry eyes shone ... if Sophy could help.

'The trouble is I need a mason. And an electrician. Of course a plumber too for the poor bath-tubs which the GIs ruined. And then a guy who knows how to lay tiles.'

She had at her finger-ends the entire cast she wished to assemble; it amused Sophy to see herself as director of the show and leading lady at the same time.

Drawling, Nancy indicated that things must move fast. She gazed again in despair at the dirty spacious room.

'I know I'm asking too much but it seems you have been sent by heaven ...'

Sophy agreed to help.

Here was a welcome distraction, something difficult and challenging to take on during the expensive days given to her by Denise. She had come to Cannes for fun, curiosity, sunshine – and although she hadn't exactly admitted it – to find Anne-Marie again. But the Dufours were gone heaven knew where; Nancy's presence was a balm. It also piqued Sophy's vanity to think that she would be forced to use her best French. She was glad to stay in Cannes until the allotted time was run. She liked the half-ruined hotel, the Provençal voices, the smell of mimosa, the fishermen shouting, the dry rustle of the palms. Yes, she was glad to stay.

She promised to spend a good part of every day at the villa. Nobody could be more grateful than Nancy, who, exclaiming at her goodness, and repeating 'I just can't believe it!' went off to find the telephone book.

Nancy's word for the following days was 'amusing'. Costly chaos, long discussions with Sophy as interpreter, workmen who did not appear, others who turned up an hour early, expeditions to the back streets for furniture, wooden poles for curtains, screws, brass handles, interviews in ancient houses with women who swore to give messages and didn't, were all amusing. And at times Sophy did manage to laugh.

A magician with stars pouring from the wand which she waved to and fro, Nancy waved money. Sophy saw the effect of the shimmering stuff on the people they tracked down. Workmen divided into two categories. Those of staggering reliability ('Why in the States, Sophy, *nobody* arrives early!'). And those who promised with all their southern charm, agreed a price with serious faces, arranged to appear at a given hour, and vanished.

Before the week was out Sophy had found a mason, Monsieur Chaméron, whose price and manner seemed acceptable. He was taken into the villa, shown round, made notes in a book which he closed with a snapping elastic band. There was a back wall in which Nancy wanted a window, it would overlook part of a neighbouring orange grove.

Monsieur Chaméron, feet apart, studied the wall.

'For this we will need permission from the Mayor.'

'But that'll take so *long*,' wailed Nancy, after Sophy had translated.

'But,' continued Chaméron without a blink, 'my son works in the Mairie.' Every morning at half past seven Monsieur Chaméron arrived and within minutes was covered from head to foot in white dust. Making the window fascinated Nancy and Sophy who stood watching from the safe position of the doorway. When a hole had been knocked out, Chaméron asked if they would get him a wrought-iron balustrade.

They toured the countryside in an expensive taxi, calling at iron foundries, and Nancy finally chose a design from a man who was as black as Vulcan. He said he would make it for her in three days.

Work began to happen at the villa. An electrician was found. A young man started to retile the bathrooms of which, like Nancy's husbands, there were four. The house reverberated with noise and was lit by Nancy's satisfaction. It grew dirty, not because it had been left deserted after being relentlessly used by the army, but with fresh builders' dust, pale and gritty, and wood shavings, and enormous piles of packing paper which had encased the tiles.

Sophy's first days went by filled to the brim with work. At

night Nancy took her to dine at different restaurants; she had the American nose for new and expensive places.

'It's the least I can do,' she said, refusing to allow Sophy to pay for anything.

Sophy rose early every morning prior to more work at the villa. On a day which looked as if it would be as warm as an English May, she was having breakfast in the dining room at her hotel when the waiter came to her table. A lady was asking for her.

'She did not know your name, Madame. She said an English lady who has been here four days. You are our only English lady.'

He presented Sophy with an old-fashioned visiting card on which was engraved: 'Madame Isabelle Cazou.'

The address in Lyon was crossed out and 'Les Hesperides, Boulevard de la Croisette, Cannes' written in ink above it.

'She is in the entrance hall, Madame.'

Sophy started to her feet and almost ran out of the dining room.

Madame Cazou was sitting in the hall, dressed in respectable black and looking, in the cruel sunshine, as if like the character in Rider Haggard she was about to crumple into dust. She had seemed a little more solid in her own house. But when she saw Sophy, her face took on its strange serene smile.

'Madame, how kind! May I offer you some coffee?' stammered Sophy, quite alarmed by the appearance of her visitor.

The old woman looked surprised, but accepted her offer and Sophy took her, almost steering her, to the window seat at her table where she had left her own unfinished breakfast. Madame Cazou exclaimed at having called too early and interrupted the repast. The exchange of meaningless compliments, like a dance of two birds, followed. Sophy was almost too curious to speak her own expected lines but managed to do so.

'I was indeed glad to know you were staying in this hotel,' said Madame Cazou, at last getting to the point. 'Memory, when you are old, is not of the best. It was not until the evening after you had gone that I remembered.'

'Yes?' breathed Sophy, her large eyes large.

'That I had a visitor some months ago. Last autumn it was. A gentleman came to see me. He was asking for the family Dufour and was, as you are, a friend. He was overcome to learn that I could not help him. Poor man, a great distress. He gave me his name and address in case I had any news. Well, naturally, I had none and do not expect any. Except that you have visited me. Perhaps you are acquainted with the gentleman?' She fished in her black handbag and produced a small very neat piece of cardboard, cut with scissors – Sophy could make out the pencil mark which made the square. In the centre in black ink, and in writing with a look of medieval script about it:

> Alexis Lucas
> 27 rue des Anges de Notre Dame,
> Le Cannet.

'I asked him if he had a telephone but he said he had not,' said Madame Cazou. 'So if you wish to see him ... but perhaps you are not acquainted with the gentleman?'

'I knew him well,' said Sophy, more struck by the card than she could say.

'Then I am glad I came to see you, Madame,' said Madame Cazou with her smile.

That evening after working at the villa all day, Sophy decided to go to Le Cannet.

Of all her friends at Les Hesperides, even Stefan and Serge, the man she'd known least was Alexis Lucas. He was very small, scarcely five foot one, a miniature of a man, and Sophy had been aware that he was attracted to her. But he had done nothing about it, apparently realizing from the first that her eyes were on Daniel. Alexis was half Dutch, had lived since he was a child in the south and was a painter; when she knew him at Les Hesperides he had recently left art school. Some of the lively arguments at the house had been on the subject of painting, about which he was such an expert that he invited arguments so that he could demolish them.

519

Anne-Marie was very fond of him, always calling him 'that dear Alexis'. He had been gallant to Yvonne. Sophy could not remember if he'd lived then in Le Cannet – surely not? It was too far for him to be so constant a visitor in the old days. Most of Anne-Marie's men friends lived a few roads away ...

Sophy knew Cannes well from her years of living in the town; she also knew the coast roads and the beaches from Palm Beach to the fatal Garoupe where she'd been arrested; she had never visited Le Cannet. It was a village more or less attached to Cannes but 'straight up the Carnot' said the porter who ordered her a taxi. 'Très chic, Le Cannet. The Begum lives there.'

'The Begum,' shouted the taxi driver over his shoulder as they shot up a boulevard lined with plane trees and with a Parisian look about it, 'has a palace. One must see the gardens. They are unbelievable.'

When Sophy gave him the address, the driver screwed up his face and shook his head. He explained that Vieux Cannet was a place of streets 'narrow as haricot beans' and he would be forced to stop in the square. He regretted, but the rest of the way Mademoiselle would have to walk. He set her down in a sandy space where in daytime men played boules under the plane trees. Before driving away he gave her detailed instructions, but Sophy lost her concentration before he finished speaking.

She set off up the steep streets of the ancient hill village. It huddled round her, surrounded by high walls built to protect the inhabitants from the Saracens. The houses were of stone, they were very old and solid, there were few lights in the windows. Washing hung on lines across the little streets and a statue of the Virgin in a niche in the wall had a jam-pot filled with twigs of mimosa. Two women in a corner stopped to stare at the stranger. When Sophy enquired the way they answered in accents of almost incomprehensible Provençal.

She found the rue des Anges de Notre Dame at last. Certainly the taxi would never have managed it, it was approached by a steep flight of steps. She followed the numbers on the doors and finally came to No. 27. Entering a dark hallway she made out a line of shabby post boxes on which names were pinned on scraps of paper. Alexis's name, on a card exactly like the one he'd given Madame Cazou, was pinned to one box. He had added in his elegant script 'Troisième'.

The staircase was in darkness. Sophy located a switch and began to ascend. Sixty seconds later out went the light. Somebody was saving money. As she went further up the stairs she felt like a ghost. She was the Spirit of Things Past. She turned up at strange houses and asked for vanished people. Ah, there was another switch. She just had time to get to the third floor when the light went out again.

But she had seen the door and knocked with her knuckles – where was the bell?

'Alexis?'

'*C'est qui?*' called a man's voice. Sophy recognized it with a lift of the heart and shouted back, '*It's me! Sophy!*'

The door burst open. A small figure stood outlined against the light. Seeing her, he did not hesitate – he threw open his arms.

She ran into them.

'Alexis. Alexis.'

'Sophy, by all that's wonderful. When I heard that English voice!'

They went on laughing and embracing.

When they drew apart she saw that here at last was somebody unchanged. He hadn't put on an ounce of flesh, he still wore his d'Artagnan moustache and beard, his figure was slim. The only thing which surprised her was that she'd forgotten just how small he was. Scarcely five foot high and everything to match, small hands, a dancer's small feet.

'Dear, dear Sophy. Old friend,' he said, leading her into his studio. It smelled of paint and turpentine. Canvases were lined up with their faces to the walls, propped on shelves or piled in corners. The most recent was on an easel by the window. The chair he hospitably pulled up for her was unsteady and dirty, he carefully draped it in a yellowing silk shawl.

521

'Sit down and let me look at you. What a miracle to see you. Where have you sprung from? I can't believe my eyes. And how did you manage to find me? You are a genius.'

Alexis pulled up a high stool encrusted with paint and perched on it, looking like a dwarf in a fairy story.

Sophy explained that she'd come from London for a very short stay. She was spending a few days at the Méditerranée.

He studied her. 'Sophy. Alive. Still beautiful. I have thought of you so often. And was afraid you might be dead.'

'I thought of you. Not dead, though.'

'As for that, I could have been. Fifty times. But didn't somebody tell me you got back to England, or at any rate escaped the filthy Vichy government. You come from London? Why weren't you blown to pieces?'

'Because during the blitz I was in the country,' she said, laughing.

He allowed himself a smile but continued to look at her with a raking glance, running his eyes up and down her face.

'You're indeed a miracle coming here to see me. What has your life been during all the years, Sophy? In the English countryside? Why I do believe —' he leaned over and picked up her hand, 'you are married. An *alliance*,' he added, using the French word for a wedding ring.

'Yes, I was married. But he was lost at sea. Nearly three years ago.'

'Ah. My poor girl. What can I say?'

The break, a moment of silence, was a brief de profundis.

'Poor child,' he said. Then in a practical voice, 'Pastis. You must have a glass of pastis. It is smuggled from Italy, impossible to buy in this land of shortages. How long is it since you drank this?' He fetched a bottle and poured out, adding water to make the drink turn a clouded green. Sophy remembered, faintly, the aniseed taste.

She decided not to ask him yet about the Dufours or Daniel – supposing by chance he had news of them. There was something crude about appearing here and showing at once that she had not come only from friendship. Instead she told him briefly how she had got back to England, how she had married a man in the Navy. She didn't say a word about anyone else, and nor did he. Sophy wanted to hear about his war and he told her he had fought on the Northern front and been taken prisoner, together with scores of his comrades. 'They captured us because they were a hundred kilometres beyond the Oise. Nobody could credit they'd advanced so swiftly.' He had been sent to Germany. He had imagined horrors but it had not been too bad. After all, the Boches, said Alexis, are practical. Sophy heard echoes of Violette.

'They did not want the prisoners eating German food and doing nothing to earn it. They taught me a trade.'

'To paint houses like Hitler?'

'No, no,' said Alexis, laughing. 'They taught me to be a hairdresser. I was hairdresser for the entire camp.' He laughed when he told the story, his black eyes filled with tears of mirth. He'd committed sins in hairdressing at the start, he had snipped a slice 'only a sliver' from a man's ear. He had also infuriated another of the prisoners, 'a man who liked looking at himself in the mirror', by cutting his hair askew. One or two prisoners, outraged at his inept scissors, wanted to throttle him. But he had improved. 'Evidently, Sophy, there is an art in hairdressing, or why would so many pretty women fall in love with their hairdressers?'

Talking of women, he said, he and one or two of his friends in the camp were given 'city leave' later. They were allowed to visit the nearby town of Rothëburg. They went twice a week and met some girls who were 'very good to us. They fed us like birds in winter. I became quite fat.' He smacked his flat stomach.

Now he was home at last and painting again. He had a notion he was going to succeed with his pictures. 'They are still flower studies. But what an enormous subject that is proving to be.'

Sophy remembered Alexis's paintings; he had sometimes brought them to Les Hesperides, and once he'd given a study of palm trees to Yvonne Dufour who had been effusively complimentary about it and had it framed.

Sophy had never admired his work. There was something

amateurish and crude about it. It reminded her of paintings in art class at school.

But she knew she must ask to see them and be nice about them.

He did not demur with some remark about her not wishing to look at his stuff which would then demand in turn the declaration that she did. He apparently expected the request, went over to the wall and began to turn the canvases round for her inspection. There they were. The flowers of the south. The long sprays of bougainvillaea with red or purple petals, a silver cupful of thin poppies, a vase of summer flowers, peonies, branches of flowering rosemary. There were blue campanulas with purple veins, roses as bold as full-blown women, tiny wild orchids. There were flowers striped like tigers and daisies simple as innocence itself. The canvases glowed with the changes of colour and season. Alexis had experimented with technique, some almost Impressionist, others minutely and delicately drawn, as if every trembling pollen-covered stamen must not be missed.

'They're beautiful, Alexis.'

He looked at the paintings critically as if they were not his.

'There is a good deal of emotion in nature.'

She picked up a small canvas, an earthenware jug of yellow roses standing on a stone ledge.

'May I buy this one?'

'Of course not. It's a present. But you need another to remind you of the Midi. What about this one?' He picked up a large painting of mimosa, cut it from the frame with a knife, rolled it up and presented it to her as if it were an umbrella.

Sophy laughed.

'Oh Alex. You haven't changed.'

'Oh Sophy. You have.'

'You mean I am older.'

'And that is what suits you. When I knew you before the war you were just an attractive romping English girl.'

'Rather a foolish one, I think.'

'Not exactly. A dazzled one. Daniel Vergé's dazzled girl,' he said dryly.

She was not sure if she was glad or sorry to hear the name. She smiled slightly but said nothing.

He began to turn his paintings back with their faces to the wall. Then returned to his high stool, and folded his arms.

'For a young woman whose face used to light up like the Cannes illuminations when Vergé appeared, I'm surprised that you have not asked for news of him. I don't know much, but I'm pretty sure he managed to get to England and join de Gaulle there.'

'Yes. He did.'

'Sophy! Why didn't you tell me you had heard of Vergé?'

'Because I preferred to hear about you.'

'Charming,' he said, disbelieving her.

She was still uncertain if she wanted to hear a word about Daniel, but Alexis had no intention of letting the subject drop.

'How did *you* know he was with the Free French?'

'I saw him once or twice.'

'You *met* Vergé. In London!'

His astonishment was very satisfying.

'Once or twice,' said Sophy, with English understatement.

'Come along, come along. You can't appear in my studio after heaven knows how many years, and tell me about an old friend from the past in a few words. So he was with the Free French? Excellent. As a war photographer, naturally?'

'No, he managed to get out of that and persuaded them to let him join what he called the real war.'

Alexis was deeply interested. He understood, he said; but the fact was Vergé had been a remarkable photographer. His photographs – Alexis spoke like a painter – had a hardness, a lack of compromise.

'They were disturbing,' he said thoughtfully.

'Yes, I do remember that,' lied Sophy. She had an idea by the quick glance he gave her, that he knew she remembered no such thing.

He returned to the 'astounding fact' that she had met Daniel in London during the war. She told him a little about the French at Queen's Gate. She spoke of them warmly, thinking mostly of Violette. He listened and questioned and nodded and looked pleased.

'How good to hear all this, Sophy. How good to see you. You can't know the joy – to be with a friend. A dear friend.'

'That's nice.'

'And what is more,' he added, 'a beautiful woman who is not chasing after me.'

She couldn't help laughing.

'How can you be so conceited? I said you hadn't changed but you have! What women run after you?'

She went on laughing, and Alexis was perfectly willing to join in. Did she think he exaggerated? It was scarcely something to be proud of, having to dodge proposals of marriage. There was a girl in the village who came to his studio to do the cleaning. 'Ripe as a Reine Claude plum'. She was very disturbing, so luscious. But had recently told him after a glass of pastis that she wanted to bear him four children.

'Imagine my studio with four little Alexises. How could I work?'

'You poor man.'

'I am serious,' he said, shaking his head. 'There are others. Madame Blanche owns a successful cleaning business in the village. She's offered me the apartment over her shop for a rent which even an unpractical painter can see is far too little. I am fond of Blanche and when she dances she wobbles. But somehow ... then there is Annette.'

'Do tell me about Annette.'

'You didn't happen to notice a girl at the Méditerranée who visits the hotel in the evenings during dinner? She goes from table to table, showing her paintings.'

'Why yes, I did see her. Dark and pretty? She was there last night.'

'Did you ask to see her work?'

'I didn't like to – I thought I probably wouldn't buy anything and it would only disappoint her.'

'It is my work Annette is selling,' he said severely.

'Alexis, I am so sorry! I had no idea. But you know, I live with my in-laws and the two lovely pictures you've just given

526

me will have to be propped against the wall in my room. My mother-in-law has absolutely crammed the walls with pictures.'

'There's always room for good work, Sophy. Tell your mother-in-law to buy more.'

'I shall tell her about you. She'll have to take some of her old engravings down and buy six or more of yours.' She leaned towards him as he had done to her and gave the old radiant smile.

'Ah,' he said. 'There is the girl I remember.'

The evening had grown cold. He closed the window and knelt down to light a paraffin stove. It shone with a blueish glow and smelled abominable.

Dusk fell faster than in England. They sat on in the fading light, Alexis on his high stool, Sophy leaning back in the shawl-draped chair.

During the pause which followed, Sophy thought she could perhaps mention one of the reasons she had come tonight. She said tentatively, 'Will you do something for me?'

'Name it.'

'You see, I'm only staying in Cannes for a few more days. Do you think it might be fun if we organized a little reunion?'

'Indeed, yes,' he said with a speaking look.

She saw that he misunderstood her.

'I meant you and me, of course. But what about the others? Anne-Marie and the Dufours and Paul and Claudio. We could make it like old times. When I went to Les Hesperides, and met the lady who gave me your address, she said you were trying to trace the Dufours. Have you had any luck? If not I could help. Surely we can find them somehow! They must be living near here.'

Even as she spoke she was aware of the silence. A vague horror went through her.

Alexis put one hand up to his mouth.

'So you don't know?'

'Know what?' She was filled with fear.

'That they're dead.'

'What are you saying? Who is dead?'

527

'Three of them. Anselme Dufour. Claudio. And Paul. But that is different. As a Frenchman I am proud that Paul died.'

'I don't understand – you left your card at Les Hesperides because you were trying to find –'

'News of Yvonne. And Anne-Marie if she is still living which I doubt. God knows what happened to either of them.'

She crouched down as if he had struck her.

'My poor girl. Let me tell you what I know.'

He began by speaking of Monsieur Dufour who had died of a heart attack at the end of the war, in 1945 he thought it was, he could not be sure. Alexis had visited the hospital and spoken to the nursing sister. The Reverend Mother had said, 'When that poor one died it was a mercy of the good God.' Alexis sensed she did not wish to tell him more.

While he talked Alexis did not put on the lights and by the time he finished they were in complete darkness except for the ghostly blue of the paraffin stove. He spoke without emphasis, without drama, in the way people do who have terrible things to describe and have worn out the very voice of tragedy.

When Alexis eventually came back to the south, it was after more than five years. He tried uselessly to find the Dufours. Nobody would talk about them. He'd spent days – weeks – trying to discover where they had gone. Their 'so-called friends' denied any knowledge of them. What they did talk of, still viciously, were the crimes of Claudio Arrighi. Had Sophy known, Alexis said, how high Claudio had been with the Fascisti? Returning from Rome he had been in a position of great authority. He had married Anne-Marie in the winter of 1940.

'It was a great formal wedding, everybody important attended the ceremony. Collaborators. People who knew Claudio was a man of power. Weak people who were rich. Officials of many kinds. The Italians were pretty well hated here on the coast, but that didn't show at the wedding.'

Alexis paused for a moment.

'What Claudio Arrighi did was very terrible. He organized the sending of all the food from Provence to feed the

Germans and Italians. The people here in the region were near starvation. A French soldier I know who served in the army for the Vichy lot, poor creature, watched wagonsful of fruit, meat, fuel, olives, taken out by train every night. Claudio did his work well.'

'But Anne-Marie?' said Sophy pitifully.

'She was much sought after. The wife of the big man. Les Hesperides was a place to be invited to – it was crammed with black market goods. Yes, Sophy, it was so. Yvonne was complacent enough and old Anselme, they told me, was unhappy and afraid. Specially after Paul –'

'*What about Paul?*'

'He disappeared in the winter of 1940. One day he was working at the office of Dufour et Cie in Nice. The next day, who could find him?'

'You mean he went into hiding?'

'Sophy, you don't know much, do you? Didn't you tell me just now that it was Paul who got you away? He joined the maquis, of course. He lived in the mountains near Sistéron and he and his comrades organized their campaign from there. I'm glad to say they succeeded in destroying the food trains scores of times. The story is that Paul was an expert with plastic explosives. He became too confident and actually blew the finger off his left hand. They called him Quatre Doigts after that.'

It was so dark as Alexis talked on. He called it a story of shame. When the farce of Vichy France ended and the whole of the country was occupied by the Germans, Claudio managed to protect his wife and the Dufour family, although Paul Dufour was known to be in the Resistance. Claudio's record for feeding the Germans and robbing the French kept his reputation high. Besides, it was hoped that he might help to catch his brother-in-law. Paul had murdered at least four German guards. It was time he was stopped.

And Paul was caught. There were rumours, Alexis said they might be lies, that Claudio baited the trap. Whatever the truth was, Paul was betrayed through a man posing as a member of the maquis. It was a few weeks before the

American invasion, and Paul and six of his companions were taken near La Turbie in the mountains one early morning. They were stood up against the church and shot.

'I took a bus up to La Turbie the other day. Apparently the Mayor is to put a plaque on the church wall soon. Paul's name will be there and the Cross of Lorraine and the Croix de Guerre he was awarded after his death ... It was so peaceful that morning by the church. But I saw the bullet holes.'

She gave a violent shudder. He put his hand on hers but she did not know he had touched her. She said in a trembling voice, 'Oh Paul.'

'Yes. A tragedy. Not a waste. Such deaths are never wasted. The men who died gave us our honour back. Who would have thought that speechless boy who went to the fish market every day in Nice and who used to look at you with his eyes when you flirted with Daniel Vergé in the grand salon – that he would turn out to be a saviour of France? He was twenty-three.'

He had another pause. Another de profundis.

Sophy did not speak. To be killed in London during the blitz as so many had been, to drown at sea like Bob, to be shot down in the air or on the beaches of Normandy, she knew about those deaths. They belonged to war, useless and terrible and somehow understandable. But to be murdered against a church wall in your own country ...

She began to think about the moment when he had taken her in his arms and said, 'Ah, *mignonne.*'

Why do we remember kisses? she thought. Kisses are so brief. They don't mean much. She could feel again the touch of Paul's lips and see the embarrassed smile which reached his dark eyes. Everybody in the south had brown eyes.

She thought of Daniel's kisses, his hair like the feathers of a blackbird, his eyelids which she used to kiss when he lay looking at her after they had made love.

'I will kiss your eyes,' she'd said.

'You only want to shut them because I can discover your secrets.'

'I haven't any.'

'Then you ought to have.'

There had been the chance to love Daniel, to keep their son, she had refused it. In this awful story, this lament, she wondered fearfully if Daniel, too, was dead.

'I come to the end, to the worst part, Sophy. Are you strong enough to hear it?'

'Is it so bad, then?'

'Yes. Hideous. An indictment of my country.'

'You mean Claudio?'

'No. Claudio was a traitor. I don't give a sou for Claudio Arrighi. He betrayed us and starved us, he was a pig and deserved what he got, though not the way it was decided. Did you know about the Courts they set up down here after the Liberation? Courts that were no more legal than if the grocer and the butcher had put on the wigs and robes of office. They collected together in groups, some men of honour, no doubt, some the opposite. They condemned people to death without trial, without law, without witnesses – do you know how many French people were murdered in their so-called courts? Thousands.

They are never spoken about now. The fashion is to claim you were in the Resistance. Nobody disagrees, even if they know what you used to be. And many French people begin to believe their own fantasies.

'I found out that Claudio was captured hiding at Les Hesperides in June 1945. Or maybe it was later. Nobody wanted to tell me about the Court that was set up or what was done to him. I discovered in the end. He was condemned the same night, and they hanged him.'

He looked across at Sophy; he could see nothing but the pale oval of her face.

'You are thinking about Anne-Marie. She was pregnant then. A woman I talked to in a shop in the Croisette not far from the house, remembered the family, and seemed to know them. Anne-Marie was rather ill about the time of the Liberation. When they came to take Claudio, they dragged the poor girl into the town and took her to where her husband was condemned. I don't know if she was present at the hanging. I pray God she was not. But the women surrounded

531

her' – he made a noise like vomiting – 'and scratched her face until it bled and screamed at her and chopped off all her hair. She was nearly bald. They would have lynched her there and then but somebody got her away from the women who were like Furies, tearing at her with their nails. Whoever it was, the holy Samaritan himself, knocked some of the women down and took Anne-Marie into a house and barred the door. That night she had a miscarriage.'

'Oh no. Oh no.'

He seemed to come to himself. 'Christ, what am I thinking of, sitting here with you in the dark telling you such things?' He sprang up, turned up the stove so that the room immediately became insufferably hot. He came to her and knelt beside her.

'Dear girl. My English girl. I wish I had never told you.'

'*It is unbearable.*'

'I know. I know. What had the poor child done but to honour a husband who had been a respected friend here before the filthy war? She was the victim of the man he became. Could she have left her husband and family and taken to the hills with Paul? Can you imagine timid Anne-Marie doing such a thing? She was a victim.'

'Is she still alive?'

'I wish I could say yes. I do not know. I've asked so many people, Sophy, but now I must give up. I can do no more. Sometimes at night when I've worked too long and can't sleep, I sit and think about Anne-Marie. She comes into my mind, I don't get free of her. Not long ago in a bar where Vergé and I used to drink sometimes, I heard an odd rumour. That he was with the Free French when they came here and that he was the man who saved her. But people tell you things like that and want to believe them. All I remember is how they dragged her into the street, those Furies, those bitches, and spat in her face and cut off her hair, and how terrified she must have been, pregnant and alone, her husband hanged, with nobody, nobody to help her until a stranger fought his way through that screaming crowd. God reward him, whoever he is.'

532

Sophy shut her eyes. It was not until now that she knew in her heart and in the body which had borne a French child, the tragedy of what had happened to La Belle France.

PART FIVE

23

The rain had stopped, the day had changed, brilliant sunshine came flooding through the château windows bringing with it a summer warmth. Sophy's fire had fallen into ashes and Thierry undid the neck buttons of his shirt. The room was almost too warm.

Roz looked across at him with curiosity. What was one supposed to feel, she thought, when presented with a ready-made uncle? He hadn't changed because of what her grandmother had told her. He was still a middle-aged Frenchman she had only met early this morning, a stranger. She had no sensation of kinship, why should she have? He met her eyes and smiled slightly.

'Did you bring a swimsuit, Roz?'

Surprised, she said yes, it was among her things.

'Then how about a swim?'

'Has this château got a pool?'

Sophy and Thierry laughed and Sophy said, 'Where could we fit it in? Thierry means he could take you along to the club. It's only ten minutes away.'

'Will you come too, Gran?' Roz was attracted to the idea of cool water away from this oppressive room, but dismayed at being alone with her new relative.

'Oh lord no! I shall have my usual lunch on a tray and a siesta. It's my new thing,' said Sophy. 'I never sleep in the afternoon in London. You go with Thierry. Give her some lunch, will you, Thierry? It will be a chance for you both to get to know each other.' She gave a bland, deliberately radiant smile.

Thierry settled Roz in his car, and drove away along a steep mountain road which steamed from the drying surfaces exposed to the hot sun. The windows of the car were down and a sharp herby smell came into the car. Roz sniffed with pleasure. She looked across the valley and caught a glimpse of the château, a toy on its vertiginous rocks.

Both she and her companion were silent during the drive. It was as if the past which Sophy had conjured up, which touched and did not touch them, had squeezed itself into the car and sat between them. Roz was still occupied in wondering how to treat the man beside her. It wasn't easy, however cool she felt.

Slowing down, Thierry turned through handsome gates into a drive of what might have been an expensive British golf club, with carefully tended lawns as soft as those at Hampton Court. But the flower beds filled with colour and splashed by the earlier heavy rain, were set about with bushes of blue flowers Roz did not recognize and the lawns were handsome with umbrella pines. Thierry took her into a rambling building, a modern version of a Provençal farm. There were acres of pale tiled floors and enormous picture windows wide open on to a pool of brilliant water.

'Shall we swim first? Then you must let me give you luncheon,' he said.

Roz muttered something; she thought he sounded like a father or perhaps a headmaster. He gave her the impression that he considered her too young to manage for herself, and too foreign to stutter a word of French. With unnecessary kindness, he accompanied her to the changing room and spoke to the attendant.

'See you in a moment,' he said, with a paternal nod.

He was the first out to the side of the pool, and stood watching his new niece when she emerged into the dazzling sun. He thought her figure too slim, not his style at all. She had no hips. But he approved of her neat jack-knife dive, and the strong swift stroke as she swam away to the far end of the pool. He himself walked down the marble steps into the water and followed more slowly. Roz, he thought, was a problem. His own children were too young, thank God, to give his wife and himself anything but delight or annoyance, resulting in kisses or slaps. The girl who now wandered over to join him when he sat down by the pool's edge was a grown woman. Her youth made her more formidable than if she were older. She was too confident, too easy to hurt. He was glad she was Sophy's responsibility.

Poor Sophy, thought Thierry. She had come running to France as full of hope as a girl younger than Roz. He often felt years older than the elderly foreign mother who had appeared out of the past. This girl did not have Sophy's happy mixture of thick skin and soft heart. She'd looked stormy when he'd found her in that disgusting place which called itself a hotel. And except for the moment when she had thrown herself into her grandmother's arms, the clouds about Roz, unlike those surrounding the château, had not dissolved. They were rather thicker than before.

He stretched out long tanned legs. For a man in his mid forties, he was pleasantly thin but it was a figure which looked better when clothed. He was bony and too tall for grace. It was his amusing amused face which women found attractive.

'Well, Roz?' he said, breaking the silence. Roz had dipped her feet in the water, stirring it to and fro. 'Do you intend to forgive her?'

She looked up and said coldly, 'What do you mean? I am not angry with Gran.'

'Mmm.'

She ignored that.

'Come along, Roz. We both know that you are. What Sophy told you this morning hasn't worked, has it?'

Again she said nothing. The pause, the unfriendly pause, was filled with the splashing of a fountain at the other end of the pool.

Thierry rubbed one hand along his still wet arm.

'Sophy caused you a lot of pain,' he said. He spoke as if he

537

knew her, had some kind of rights over her. He had none.

'She behaved very badly,' he went on, 'and she knows it. So do I. And what's to the point, so do you. But surely Sophy's behaviour can't have been all that much of a surprise?'

Roz, stung out of her silence, exclaimed, 'She's never done anything like that before!' Immediately the man at her side made a sudden, bitter face.

'Oh, I'm sorry,' she burst out, 'I'm sorry. I didn't mean that!'

'Of course you did. You meant she's never done anything like that before *to you*. I don't expect you to shed tears over something which happened to a total stranger nearly fifty years ago. I had thought perhaps Sophy had always been a sudden person. Impulsive? Selfish? Something like that. And in consequence her disappearing act was less of a shock than if she'd been somebody different. I see I was wrong. Sophy,' he said musingly, 'is full of surprises. Well, now. Shall you forgive her?'

'She doesn't think there is anything to forgive.'

He sighed, looking at her as if he thought her obtuse. She wasn't getting on very well with this man, uncle or no uncle. She had a moment of longing, simply longing to be with her old tortoise, her inhospitable grieved-for Jack.

'My dear child, she's filled with guilt. And penitence. Mary Magdalene herself couldn't be more penitent than your grandmother is about you.'

'Oh yeah. She feels like that at present. It won't last.'

'And you don't understand what made her do it? How mixed up she's been? All she went through?'

She gave a kind of shrug, and Thierry shook his head.

'You think poor Sophy's sins are a lot of nonsense. Not sins at all. You can't imagine how frightened women used to be. Helpless, too. It seems to me that your generation only admits to one sin: cruelty. No, now I come to think of it, there's another, any crime against the environment. Your judgement against those sinners is very severe and you're right. But you have no idea of the terrible power sexual sins used to have over people.'

'They committed them just the same.'

'Of course they did,' he said patiently, 'but knowing they *were* sins, and mortal ones. So they suffered. You've shrugged off the old moralities.'

'I know all about that. I'm not quite a fool. Women did have a pretty awful time. But we're free now.'

'So you are,' he said, very dryly indeed.

She drew a circle with a wet toe on the marble edge of the pool.

'You think I'm completely unsympathetic about Gran's past.'

'I think you underestimate its effect. And are still angry with her inside. Which brings me to the point, since we're discussing Sophy (I really can't call her my mother, I had a beloved mother of my own). Wouldn't you say, looking at it fairly, that I have rather more to forgive her than you have?'

The question was perfectly cool.

'You were happy without her,' was Roz's clumsy reply.

'What's that got to do with it?'

It was Roz's turn to look at him as if he were a fool. She was quite dumbfounded.

'Everything. Everything. She didn't hurt *you*.'

'That's true.'

'So why did you look like that when I said she'd never done it before?'

'I don't know. It was instinctive. Stupid, really.'

She felt slightly more friendly towards him and said with curiosity, 'Did you really know nothing about her?'

'Very little. Apparently my mother, Anne-Marie, was ill for a while after that ... that thing happened to her at the end of the war. My father looked after her and then they married. In the meantime he'd been to England and got all the permissions to adopt me. I remember my foster parents, they were very good to me, but, do you see, I always had a real father who used to come and see me sometimes. I was proud of him. When he finally brought me to France he explained things but only in a way and scarcely mentioned Sophy. He said I was now a French boy, and had been adopted. I boasted about that at school and then more or less forgot it. One is so busy as a child. My mother never once mentioned it to me. It's odd. I knew instinctively that it was something I mustn't ever speak about to her and must try and put out of my thoughts. I swear that for months, even years, she forgot I wasn't her own son.'

When he spoke about Anne-Marie his eyes were different.

'It must be peculiar, having two mothers,' remarked Roz, after a moment or two.

'I only had one. And it wasn't Sophy.'

'But –'

'No, Roz, you must get this right. Who looked after me? Who rose from her bed at night, when I came crying to her in the dark because I felt unwell? Who bandaged my knee when I fell off my bicycle? Who dressed, looking so very chic, in her best when she came to the prize-givings, and framed my certificates and hung them in her salon? Not the delightful Sophy, appearing from Albion with embraces and guilt.'

'You sound so hard. I thought you'd have been knocked out to meet your real –'

'Please, Roz, not that "real". What Sophy is to me is very unreal. Certainly she became pregnant by my father, and had a little son, and subsequently gave him away. That is how it was, nearly fifty years ago. As a mother she has no reality for me, and I'm pretty sure I don't for her either. We begin to like each other a little, though. She is very engaging.'

'She loves you!' cried Roz.

Thierry leaned back and gestured to a passing waiter and ordered – would that suit her? – two glasses of white wine.

'I arrive,' said the waiter, disappearing.

'What the impulsive Sophy loves,' went on Thierry, as if looking at the thought hard, 'is the idea. The long embrace at the end of the movie. The audience deeply moved.'

Roz looked askance for a moment. He took no notice.

'I do believe she was in love with my father. Many women were. He's always been very attractive to them.'

'Don Giovanni.'

He couldn't help laughing.

540

'I don't imagine he had one thousand and three. And he's certainly not destined for hell.'

French confidence, thought Roz, is unending. Why has he got to build up Daniel Vergé to me? What do I care whether his father went to bed with all Paris? Thierry's half smile, the expression of his eyes as he slightly lowered his heavy eyelids, stopped her from feeling friendly, or warming to him. It was the reverse of the sun which burned hotly on her back.

'We've been together, of course, since she arrived. At first it was quite boring, to me at any rate. But now it has changed and there are occasions when, just for an instant, I do feel a sort of familiarity with Sophy. As if I know what she's going to say, how she's going to react, not with my head but with my blood. By a kind of peculiar unexplainable instinct.'

'Well, that's something,' said Roz with a flick of sarcasm.

He hung fire for a moment.

'You think she came to France entirely to find me. That isn't how it was at all. What brought her running, I'm sure, was the notion that she would find my father *in* me. Apparently she does. She has often said so. I am not nearly as handsome as he is, but there's a certain resemblance. When I knew Sophy and I were going to see each other, I brought some photographs from Paris. I must show them to you.'

'But I don't understand! If all Gran wanted was to see your father, why hasn't she met him?'

'No,' he replied fairly, 'I didn't mean she came only for his sake. She was also intrigued at the idea of meeting her son. It was so new and dramatic. She still has fits of being sentimental over that and I laugh her out of them. But yes, I suppose we must say that it was more for my father she really came.'

'Did you ask her if she wanted to see him?'

'Of course. After Alexis Lucas wrote to me, I telephoned Sophy in London. I said I'd be happy to bring my father here, so that we could all three be together. She refused. Every time I've brought the subject up again, she goes on refusing.'

'But why?'

'When I ask, she won't say.'

Roz was bewildered. She couldn't solve such a sexual puzzle. It seemed to her that a woman who'd once been in love – even at a time as unreal to Roz as Ancient Rome – wouldn't be able to resist seeing her lover again.

They remained by the water for a while, then swam a second time, returning to sit in the sun while the water dried on their wet shoulders and backs. Eventually Thierry roused himself and suggested they should dress and have luncheon. There were people lunching on the terrace under parasols, but he said it was cooler indoors.

'We won't go back to the château yet,' he said, accompanying Roz into the spacious lounge which was blissfully cool, as he had said. 'Sophy has a routine. The lightest of lunches (so unlike people in France, we have a hot repast at midday whatever the weather). Then she has a siesta during the afternoon heat. She livens up at five in the evening when it begins to be less tropical. I bring her here for a swim, if I'm at the château, or we sit in the turret gardens and watch the world go by.'

'How did Gran find such an astonishing place?'

He was surprised.

'Sophy didn't find it. The Château de Favergés belongs to my father. He inherited it from *his* father who bought it in the Twenties when it was a ruin. It was repaired and also rebuilt in places. The Vergés are related distantly to the de Favergés, an ancient family which died out in the last century ... I thought you knew the château belonged to us.'

Roz took in the fact of a château 'belonging to us'. It sounded so grand. She asked if he'd been staying here all the time since her grandmother had arrived from England.

'Oh no. Weekends, mostly, when I can arrange my work in Paris and my family can spare me. When Sophy is alone she seems content enough. She gossips with Marguerite or goes into the village or listens to the radio to polish up her French. She is very philosophical when I am away.'

'That shouldn't be difficult,' said Roz cattily, 'considering that for the last forty years she didn't even know where you were.'

'But it isn't like that, surely. When you lose something you put it out of your mind, if you have any sense. You don't miss it. But if it reappears you start to thirst for it to stay.'

'Thirst for you?'

She was like a spitting tortoise-shell cat.

'No, Roz, not for me. For the idea. Now. Why don't we get something to eat?'

The contrast between the delicate food served by polite and skilled waiters, and the appalling meals she and Michael had been given at the Jardin Fleuri was enormous. But Roz had no appetite. Her uncle talked urbanely of life in Paris and his wife and two children. He talked well. He told her one or two stories which made her smile. But she was only half listening. A part of her mind was uneasy. Why didn't she seem able to be happy any more? She had fretted and lost sleep over Sophy, whom now she found safe. This new uncle for all his French male chauvinism wanted to be good to her. But when there was a pause in the conversation, Roz's thoughts turned to the days in Erith Road. They, and she, had been light-hearted. The place and her friends were all a picture together, a picture that shimmered in different colours, bright quadrangles and grey towers, Ally's Pre-Raphaelite figure in turquoise blue and time itself a kind of unending spring. She thought of Michael leaning against the front door at Erith Road one morning before this adventure began. She remembered the anguish over their Finals and the euphoria when it was over. A sense of unity, a bond so close. It seemed unbearable that it was broken. By Michael who was gone, and by her two friends who had disappeared without Roz even saying goodbye, towards their own real future and their love.

The afternoon advanced, the light outside deepened as she and Thierry lingered over their meal; more people arrived to swim or sit in the shaded gardens. Their voices were cheerful and now and again there was a ripple of laughter.

Thierry gave the girl opposite him one or two attentive glances, lit a cigarette and left her in peace. He asked himself if there were things she still wanted to ask him and would be unlikely to ask Sophy.

She roused herself from her reverie and said, conscious that he was looking at her, 'So it was very dramatic, was it? Meeting Gran that first time?'

'Not exactly. I was dubious when I heard about her. Not at all sure I wanted to meet her. When Alexis Lucas wrote to me, he explained that the only reason he was sending the letter after all these years was because he'd heard that my mother had died some months ago.'

'Anne-Marie Dufour,' murmured Roz.

'Yes. Dear Anne-Marie.'

'I thought Gran said they were such friends.'

'Once upon a time. What she was for the rest of her life was my father's wife and my mother. She was the centre, the heart of our family. Alexis Lucas got it right. She couldn't have borne to see Sophy again, even to hear her name. I'm afraid she knew my father had loved Sophy and asked her to be his wife and so on.'

'What's "and so on"?'

He really laughed.

'Is my English so bad after all? I mean that my father told my mother everything when they met again in Cannes. It was during that time of the Liberation, so shameful to her, and at first after she lost the child she was very ill. But he looked after her and when she recovered he told her the whole story. The little boy was still in England, you see,' he said, as if speaking about somebody else. 'I'm sure my father must have told her he loved Sophy, had treated her badly and later wanted to treat her very well. And that she wouldn't have it or have him. Or the little boy – me. Sophy abandoned me very much in the way she recently abandoned you. One set of rules for herself, another for the rest of us.'

'She has a warm heart!' exclaimed Roz, turning on him.

'Who denies it?' was the annoying reply.

She shot him a dark look which was met by an innocent one. He doesn't love Gran, she thought, but why should he? She could not stop herself from asking.

'What did happen when you met?'

He turned the question over.

'It was my idea that we should meet at the château. I thought the little place would amuse her.'

'She was not in the mood for amusement.'

'Or to use her head either. She didn't remember to let me know the time of her plane. I gather she was thoroughly disorganized when she left London.'

'You can say that again.'

'So of course I could not meet her,' he continued, ignoring the interruption. 'Fortunately I had told her the address of the château. She hired a car. All I knew was that after I'd arrived and was waiting for a telegram or a call about the plane time there was a ring of the bell. And Marguerite showed this lady into the turret room.'

He reflected, like a man looking at a painting.

'It was more of a comedy than anything else. We stood on either side of the room looking at each other. I remember thinking the accident of birth really is an accident. A thing of chance. My father and this English grande dame went to bed one night or another and that long-forgotten sex had created me, the human being she hadn't set eyes on since he was an infant in arms. As for Sophy, she burst into tears. Naturally I liked that.'

'You do sound a cold fish, Uncle Thierry.'

He looked taken aback but she was not sure if it was the title she'd given him, or her criticism.

'One can't manufacture emotions unless one happens to be an actor. Take you, for instance. You can't manufacture happiness because you've found your grandmother. Of course you were excited when I first spoke to you in that disgusting *logis*. But you've been sombre ever since. I have a notion it's more than just being angry with Sophy. However, you want to know how I felt. Plain curiosity. It was so interesting. I still can't believe I have a drop of English blood. I often wonder where the English half of me has got to. Do I annoy you?'

'Of course not,' said Roz. Ah, she thought, the French are different from us with their staunch patriotism. Is that the way *we* should be and apparently only are during wars?

545

'How does Gran feel about you being so totally French?' she wanted to know.

'She likes it.'

Roz looked for a minute at the tablecloth. Then raised her eyes. 'From the way you describe the meeting, Gran was knocked out and you were merely "interested". All I can say is – poor Gran.'

She'd broken through his façade at last.

'But you're wrong!' he exclaimed. 'You imagine Sophy, her warm heart filled with love when she meets a cold unfeeling foreigner. You called me cold just now. Be realistic, Roz. She can no more produce a ready-made love than I can. What is maternal love made of? Tell me that.'

'Instinct.'

'Yes, yes,' impatiently, 'a young woman with a baby, a lioness with a cub. That's obvious. But we're speaking about people of Sophy's age or mine. Passion, of course, can happen in a matter of minutes. Not the other love which is all made up of time. Of steady love and sharing – in French we say "dividing". By a thousand things. How could Sophy have those? They belonged to Anne-Marie.'

Silence.

'I see,' said the girl at last.

'Yes. You must.'

They returned to the château, and Roz showered and changed and tried to make herself look as good as she could manage, with a clean T-shirt and a pair of jeans which she had shoved into her travelling bag at the hotel.

Sophy and Thierry were in the small garden which had been created at the top of one of the towers. It was quite circular, and aped in miniature every great château garden, even to a lead statue of Mercury balanced on one toe at the end of a gravel path, and a tiny fountain in a circle of green turf. There were white rose bushes and prim box trees in tubs; the trees were circular too. It was a doll's house garden, commanding a sheer drop into the valley. Far below wound the ribbon of the river, in thin silver, and tiny figures making their way along a thread of road leading to a match-sized bridge. The sun was low and any moment would disappear behind the mountains.

Thierry poured drinks and talked to Sophy while Roz stood gazing down at the extraordinary view. The old housekeeper Marguerite poked her head round the garden door.

'Madame from Paris on the telephone, Monsieur.'

'Excellent,' cried Thierry, springing up.

When he had left them Sophy looked towards her granddaughter. She patted the seat beside her.

'Come and sit.'

Roz obeyed in silence. Sophy took her hand and kissed it.

'Have you decided to take me back into your good books?'

'Maybe.'

'Very grudging. But you do understand a bit better now, don't you?'

Such a blackmailing question, thought Roz, and all the old charm at work again. But when her grandmother began to disengage her hand, she clung.

Sophy squeezed the hand tightly for a moment.

'Darling Roz. I know I shouldn't have rushed off like that. I can't tell you how Jack tried to stop me. He was dead against it. He said he couldn't see the *point*. He kept looking at me and saying, the way he used to, that it would all end in tears. The thing was he was a lawyer in his bones. Those locked boxes in the Temple, and the locked promises not to be revealed for fifty years after a person's death. He didn't believe you could revive things, go back on decisions taken ages ago. He spent an entire evening trying to dissuade me. He was very blunt, for Jack.'

'What do you mean, Gran?'

Sophy's voice was strained.

'You know how he sort of dodged things by making jokes or bringing out corny old aphorisms. It was his way of avoiding subjects, even hiding his own emotions. Usually you could never get him into the open. This time he did come out. He said how could I be naïve enough to expect a man of Thierry's age to care twopence for me. Thierry had agreed to meet me but so what – did I expect filial love? If so I was a fool. He hadn't met Alexis Lucas but he considered Alexis's letter to Thierry was the action of an interfering busybody. Why dig all this up? he said. It couldn't work.'

'But you came to France just the same?'

'I couldn't stop myself. When I got back to London I *knew* I couldn't stop myself. I didn't ring Jack, there would only have been another long argument, this time on the telephone. And I didn't want to hurt him because Jack loves – I mean loved – me more than anyone. So I wrote and posted it at the airport. I gave him the château address. I rang when I got here. Poor love, he did sound so tired. I said how were you, and he said okay and I told him I'd met Thierry and things were fine. Jack sounded more like himself then. He gave a sort of chuckle and quoted Napoleon's mother. He said "as long as it lasts".'

Sophy gave a smile which was not a smile.

'I shall miss him for the rest of my life.'

And Roz remembered an old man who'd said to her, when she was happy, 'Don't look like that. Nobody should look like that.'

'I can't win with my children, can I?' Sophy said, with the air of wishing to revive more cheerful prospects and make heavy things light. 'All those years of feeling I had committed a sin. When I thought of Thierry (of course I tried not to), in my imagination he was called David, an Englishman who played cricket at weekends and lived in Sussex and commuted. I used to think – that man driving past might be David. He could be anybody, he could be anywhere, and I shall never know. All the time he was Thierry Vergé, growing up in Paris with Daniel and Anne-Marie. Isn't that strange?'

'Very.'

Sophy glanced at the girl, thinking the pause was discouraging. It was not a shock, although she slightly flinched, when Roz flared out, 'Why did you bugger off without telling me? Did you think I'd try to stop you, the way your brother tried? You couldn't have thought any such thing. The truth is you didn't spend a single minute thinking about anybody but yourself.'

How pitiless the young are, thought Sophy. She and her daughter's only child certainly shared their affection and their red hair. And what Jack used to call a filthy temper.

'So why did you disappear?' demanded Roz.

Sophy refused to be unnerved by the accusing brown eyes. She was too proud and too wise to say that in the last two or three years Roz had shown many signs of longing to escape. The company of anyone not her own age had seemed to bore the girl. And Sophy was old. It would have been humiliating to say so, just as it was to love, too much, someone who wanted so obviously to shake herself free. Sophy had truly believed Roz would not mind very much after the initial shock of surprise at finding her grandmother was gone. She might even welcome being queen of Bowling House, with sufficient money pumped into her bank account. Surely some girls might enjoy such lavish liberty.

But she had been wrong. Wildly wrong. Greedy for love, Sophy began to think that her misjudgement had lost her platefuls of the precious stuff.

She wanted to persuade. To coax. To bombard Roz with fondness and penitence, but for once she managed to hold her tongue, looking at the girl a little humorously.

As for Roz, she was affected by Sophy. There was something in her grandmother's aura, warm, welcoming, a little shallow, which moved her. She was struck by Sophy's mixtures of passion and selfishness, naïvete and sophistication. More than all that, by the hope in Sophy which nothing seemed able to destroy.

'Gran. Why don't you want to see Daniel Vergé?' she suddenly asked.

Sophy made a face.

'Thierry keeps saying that. I don't seem able to get it into his thick head that the answer is No, no, no. I absolutely don't want to clap eyes on Daniel, and I am sure *he* doesn't want to see me.'

'But he knows you're in France.'

'Of course he does, my dear child. This ridiculous house belongs to him and he lent it to Thierry so that we could meet here. That's funny, isn't it? They've got a little picture gallery and there are loads of Daniel's photographs there. I must show them to you. He's still working in Paris. Very looked-up-to now. You know how it is when you get old, you get canonized. What a laugh.'

Still curious, Roz was not to be distracted and said again, 'But why don't you want to see him?'

Sophy thrust a loose hairpin into the knot of hair on the top of her head. Oh, she said, Roz would think it a load of nonsense, the fact was she couldn't take the idea of him seeing her now.

'But —'

'No, Roz. Don't pay me some corny old compliment, the point is Daniel remembers me when I was twenty-two. I was rather beautiful then. I'd detest him to see how time has changed me.'

'It's changed him as well. Who's he to expect people to be eternally beautiful?'

Sophy looked pleased to find the girl on her side.

'But Daniel's looks and his age are nothing to do with it, darling. If Daniel looks old and wrinkled, and I'm sure he doesn't, that's not important. What I'm not going to do is to murder the girl in his imagination. Because perhaps she is living there still.'

'You're so sentimental, Gran.'

'Aren't I just?' Then coaxingly, 'Are we friends? I suppose I was rather a pig but I am doing penance now. I never meant to make you unhappy.'

She gave her granddaughter a beseeching glance, and the thought came to Roz that not meaning to make somebody unhappy yet doing so, could be worse than deliberate cruelty. She was judge and jury at the moment. She had the self-righteousness of somebody who had been cruelly hurt. She did not wish to relinquish it yet.

The diamond-clear light of the day had gone, the little castle which had been menacing once, filled with men and weapons, had turned into a brownish gold study as romantic as a Gothic painting. The prim trees developed elongated shadows like statues with narrow heads.

Sophy ventured again, 'I truly thought you'd be okay, Roz. Even rather glad I'd gone. I mean, you've never been sorry for the chance to have the house to yourself.'

Hidden in the words lightly spoken was the sadness of the old when they lose the young. Roz heard the sound but it was music through a closed door.

'After all, I did send Thierry for you in the end, didn't I?' added Sophy, vaguely retrieving another hairpin. She wondered if she should have held her tongue. Jack had told her about that. 'Talking too much is like hitting a nail in the wall. At first it grips but then if you go on, you loosen it. Your trouble, Sophy, is when you've persuaded someone to your point of view, you repeat yourself all over again.' 'How boring of me.' 'No. You are not boring. But you can be silly.'

It was an effort to keep silent this time but Sophy thought she discerned a softening in her granddaughter's face. The worst resentment was nearly gone. Oh, I'm at her mercy, thought Sophy. But with love you always are.

'And you're going to stay in this place, are you?' Roz finally said with a scornful glance at the battlements.

'Stay here? Of course not.'

Roz was moved to scold again.

'I thought that was what it was all about. Didn't you leave England and rush here to find your only son. And now you've found him won't you want to hang around and see him any time he can spare half a day?'

'Oh darling, I did hurt you, didn't I? How many times do I have to say how sorry I am. But you must try and understand something important. Emotions don't cool down, for some of us anyway, because we're old. They never have with me.'

'I'm glad. I'd hate you to be old and weak.'

'Well, that's nice,' said Sophy, with no idea where they had got to but aware she had somehow landed on her feet.

'So you are not going to stay with Thierry and turn into the lady of the château?'

'No, I am not.' Sophy felt it safe to laugh a little. She was thinking just then how the love of parents and children resembled sexual love. Didn't it hold inside it the same awful power of wounding you to death? Didn't it spring up in piteous hope and fall down as if it had been shot through the breast? Wasn't it bliss and slavery so that you sometimes longed not to love a single soul – and to hell with the lot of them.

'I'm certainly not going to remain in Daniel's château,' she said. 'Later when Thierry and I meet, I expect it will be in Paris. He says he'll introduce me to Claudine and their children. I feel quite scared.'

'You poor thing.'

'Don't mock. I know it's funny in a way.'

'I didn't think so,' said Roz more cheerfully. She hesitated, as if she had more to say.

'Gran ... I've been wondering. Do you think Anne-Marie made Thierry a good mother?'

It was odd to hear the girl talk of Sophy's dead friend as if she had known her. The young rarely cared a pin about the past. The sun was sinking, the sky turning from crimson to lemon yellow, the mountains already black. Somewhere in those great rising hills, Paul had been killed. How had Anne-Marie felt when her brother died, perhaps betrayed by Claudio? Impossible to guess.

Sophy's reply was different to her thoughts.

'Anne-Marie was born to be a mother. So domestic and affectionate and serious about homely things. Why, she used to talk about marriage and having kids even at school. And then that unspeakable thing happening to her ... Claudio murdered. I don't think she saw it, I pray to God she didn't, but she was there held by the mob somewhere and knew what was happening and then she lost her child. Thierry said later she was very ill. So she must have been so happy to marry Daniel, mustn't she? And have Thierry as her son. Perhaps she couldn't have other children, who knows? It would make him even more of a blessing. He was happy and cared for by his foster parents apparently, but Daniel used to come and see him when he got leave and make a big fuss of him. Then at last Daniel claimed him and took him to Paris. To his real mother. That's what Thierry calls her.'

'Do you mind?'

'Yes. However, there can scarcely be a tug of love between Anne-Marie and me. She wins all the time.'

'Did Uncle Thierry tell you anything else about the Dufours?' Roz wanted to know, still unwillingly interested.

'It isn't a subject he talks about. It's like that in France now. Nobody admits to having been a collaborator, in fact everyone claims to have been in the Resistance or that their parents were. If they mention it at all. When Daniel married Anne-Marie in Paris none of his friends knew what had happened. They didn't even know she'd been married before. She just lost her past like throwing it over there –' said Sophy, pointing at the castle wall. 'Her father had died. Yvonne is still alive. She's settled in Bordeaux somewhere, very ancient, still keeps her figure and apparently has made a positive shrine to Paul. She's known locally as the mother of a hero.'

'Well. She is,' said Roz disliking the irony.

'True,' said Sophy hastily. 'Well, my darling, are we friends again?'

'We were never anything else,' said Roz not speaking the truth.

'I'm glad. I think I'll be back in London in a week or so. How quickly it gets dark here. We must go in.' The windows of the turret room were open, the nail-studded door propped to stay ajar; a faint wind, fragrant, soft, blew through the high room. Sophy settled into a favourite chair.

'You know a lot more about me than you used to do. What about a swap?'

'What do you mean?'

'Something's bothering you. And I don't mean all the stuff about me.'

'Oh Gran.'

'It is no use,' said Sophy, 'wearing that what's-she-on-about expression. What is the trouble? Is it your Finals?'

'Gran, *really*.' The pitying tone had no effect.

'Then it is something to do with a man.'

'One's entire life does not have to hinge on a man.'

'Come on, Roz.'

The familiar presence, the sympathy and humour, reached Roz. Michael was heavy on her heart. But all she managed was a graceless, 'Yes. Sure. It's a guy, if you must know.'

'Of course I must know if it is making you miserable. Tell.'

Roz said nothing, and Sophy found herself again having to remember her brother's advice. At last Roz began to talk. To speak about Michael was a solace, even if she was angry with him and he'd hurt her. She talked now because she couldn't throw her arms round him. She forgave her grandmother because she listened so quietly and because now and then she sighed.

Wanting Sophy to see the sort of man she was in love with, Roz described him as best she could. His nature. Himself. She spoke of all that had happened since the night they'd found Sophy was gone. She told her everything, even the fact that Michael had paid the detective.

'He took on such a lot,' muttered Sophy at one point.

'He is, I mean he was in love with me,' was the flat reply.

'Men have fallen for you before. I bet they wouldn't have got up to their necks in your problems the way he did.'

'But if you really love somebody, you want to take them on completely, don't you?'

The enormous question hung in the turret room like an iridescent bubble. Sophy did not dare to prick it. It burst by itself.

She studied the girl for a moment, her eyes more serious than her manner.

'I take it you've been quarrelling.'

'Yes. We did. It usually worked out okay in the end.'

Sophy recognized in the euphemism, anger melted by sex; she knew that kind of love.

Questioned a little more Roz finally admitted that what had parted Michael and herself had been this morning's bitter dispute. Even speaking about it made her catch fire all over again.

'He flatly refused to spend any more time in Cannes. He said it was absolutely useless and we had to pack it in. He'd

554

done his best, that's what he *said*. How was it his best when we'd got nowhere? It was obvious he was bored with the whole thing. I could have killed him when he knew how I felt –'

'And how was that?'

'Well, I was really miserable and it was all your fault. Sorry, sorry! I won't go on about it any more but you did ask.'

'So I did. What happened at the end of this row about me?'

'He walked out, of course.' A pause. 'I don't expect he's actually gone yet.'

'You mean he's still in Cannes?'

'No, I don't mean that at all,' said Roz irritably, 'I mean after walking out, naturally he'll go back to London. But he couldn't take a flight right away, he only has a standby, and anyway he's run out of money. He left practically all his remaining cash on the dressing table for me. One of those masculine gestures.'

'Oh God. I don't think I can listen to any more.'

Roz looked at her in derision.

'You're only upset at us being skint. Having no cash didn't matter, we would have managed somehow. The point was he threw me over, didn't he? Me and my boring problems. He absolutely yelled. We had a furious row and he wouldn't listen to a word I said –'

'Because you were going on about me again. I don't blame him. It must have been sickening.'

'Oh, stop being so bloody open-minded.'

Roz was white under her sunburn.

Sophy stared at the young face.

'You rather love this guy.'

'Not really.'

'Roz. You do.'

'That's just rubbish.'

'Which means yes.'

'I wish you'd shut up.'

'I never have shut up,' said Sophy reasonably, 'but it does seem to me that since you read those dear old diaries which I thought Jack had put into the boiler, and since I told you the rest, *some* of it must be of use to you. What are we good for, Roz, if we aren't useful to the young when we're old? It isn't as if human ashes make the flowers grow. When forests get burned down, eventually the trees and bushes which grow up through the blackened mess are tremendously healthy. It isn't like that with people. No, I don't think I will shut up. If you love this man, go ahead and love him. It is horrible of me to say this, the truth often is horrible. But I didn't love Bob at all. Not love d'amour, as they say here. I loved him because he was so mad about me and was so sweet and vulnerable and strong at the same time, and because I felt safe when I was Bob's wife. But with Daniel ... it was the way it ought to be. When your legs give and you can't sleep and you think you'll die if you don't have him. And so on.'

The strangest of laughs came from Roz.

'You got that from Thierry. "And so on". It's an awful cheat.'

'It's handy. I don't mean to maunder on about love, so unsuitable, the old to the young. And I know you think it impossible that someone like me, as old as God, still *can*. As if love is a sort of secret you are told in your teens and allowed to know until you're thirty, and after that you totally forget it because you've been brainwashed. Anyway,' firmly, 'I did love Daniel, I was crazy about him. In a muffled sort of way I suppose I still am. No, that isn't right. I remember being in love and just how it felt, he was such a difficult, sexy, devilish, irresistible man. That is the one who is still somewhere in my thoughts. And only his living self could kill him.'

She added without emphasis, 'If I'd married him I'd never have had Polly, would I? Or you, darling.'

'It's no good smearing on the soft soap, Gran.'

'But I like soft soap. I love you a lot, Roz. Because I treated you badly doesn't disprove that. We're two peas out of a pod. If you love this guy of yours, get him back. While there's still time.'

Like grass long-withered in the heat on which a man inadvertently throws a still-glowing match, Roz went up in flames.

'Run after him? Beg him to do me the favour of taking me on again? Why should I chase after him when he's a shit and walked out when I was in trouble?'

'Poor Roz.'

'Don't give me that,' cried Roz, the note of pity in Sophy's voice working like petrol on the blaze. 'I was worried and unhappy and I didn't have a bean. I'll see him to hell before I try to make it up. I don't want a man like that. A man who marches out when things are difficult –'

'Perhaps it was you who made –'

'Gran, I've told you to *shut up*. He laid down the law. He refused to let me run up bills with my blasted plastic money. Why shouldn't I? It was ludicrous. I don't want him. He's a selfish sod and I wish he was dead!'

She sprang up in fury and rushed to the door which opened as Thierry came in. He caught her as they collided, and made some laughing remark. Roz shouted, 'Leave me alone!' and fled.

She had no idea where she was going. She ran from reason and resented advice, she couldn't bear to be understood, to be loved. She ran up some stairs and into the first room with an open door and found herself in a tiny medieval chamber turned into a bedroom. On the top of a small chest of drawers was a photograph of a man.

He regarded her sardonically. Black haired. High cheek-boned. The sort of looks she had never been drawn to, dramatic, actorish.

'To hell with you,' she said and slammed the picture face downwards.

24

Nobody came for her. Nobody tapped on the door and suggested a meal and Roz, ready to refuse, stayed in the room, lying on the bed. She stared at the stone-edged castle window outside which the sky turned steadily a darker blue, pricked out with stars. She knew her grandmother and her uncle had deliberately left her alone and she was half angry at not being sought out, half relieved at the blessed solitude. At present she could not have borne elderly sympathy.

When she looked at her watch, she saw it was already half past ten. She had been lying in a trance of misery for hours. She was sure Michael had not yet left France. He must be still here, twenty or thirty kilometres away, she supposed, sitting in a dreary airport lounge reading a French newspaper. She had teased him because he bought a local rag every morning: he read bits aloud to her. Horror stories, murders, a good deal of sex. Michael said it was the Cannes version of the *News of the World*. What beautiful French he spoke. She remembered days of telephone calls, how fluent and polite he sounded when he talked to strangers. They had stood together in the telephone booth pressed close, there wasn't an inch of room, and in between calls or waiting to speak to somebody, he would kiss her cheek or her nose and mutter 'I love you'. She thought of their sex together, its rising excitement, its final bliss, her own voice gasping his name.

She sat up and switched on a bedside light, trying to get away from him.

Gran said she's coming back to London soon, she thought. I will go with her. Does that mean staying here till then? Roz felt she did not want to stay another day – an hour – in this claustrophobic toy castle haunted by Michael, a ghost clearly seen by Sophy as well. I know Gran will go on talking about him to me. She will try to persuade me to get in touch with him. She is already on his side although she doesn't know him. It's typical of a woman of her age; they're always for the men.

Still trying to avoid the figure in her thoughts, Roz began to imagine what the future would hold for her. For the first time since she had driven away from the city, she had a sense of loss, a hollow in her stomach, to realize Oxford was finished for her. She and her friends used to discuss their prospects for hours when they were not worrying over their Finals. What lay ahead? they would wonder. Travel? Work? Ally and Huw were ambitious and already had plans for their careers, but Roz had once said 'All I want is liberty'. The word, beautiful to so many, meant nothing to her now. She wanted to be imprisoned.

Where is my feminine pride, she thought? I wish I had more. I wish I had any. She looked at her watch again. After the hours in a trance, time had begun to crawl.

Outside the turret window a pale glow meant the moon was rising; she climbed from the bed and went across to lean on the sill. There was the cold goddess floating in the sky above the hushed countryside. The room was too high and too far from the drop for Roz to make out the strip of road. All she had was the sky and a ruffle of trees on an outcrop of rocks. The village behind the château was hidden by other turrets and rooftops. She stayed at the window for a while, looked at her watch again, sighed and went back to lie on the bed. Michael is going to forget me, she thought. Can he? Is it so easy? I suppose I must undress and try and sleep. Would the standby plane leave very late, as theirs had done? And when he finally arrived at London Airport would he have a splitting headache? Her head had ached for hours after they'd landed at Nice.

Propping herself on the bed, she looked blankly round the room. The photograph of Daniel still lay on its face. There was a crucifix on the wall on the other side of the room and the strange certainty came to her that Anne-Marie must have hung it there. And then she noticed a book on the bedside table, a shabby old album tied with frayed silk cord. She wondered if it contained the photographs Thierry had said he had brought from Paris.

She opened it and began to turn the thick pages.

All kinds of pictures. Over-dramatic intensely lit studio portraits were signed Vergé. They must be Daniel's work. There was one of a plain plump woman looking solemnly at the camera, her arm round a far-too-neat child dressed in silk. Underneath was written, '*Thierry et moi*. Paris,' in purple ink. There was Thierry, a little boy in the Tuileries gardens, and Thierry, holy and with a priest, at the door of a church. '*Sa première communion*' Anne-Marie had written. Page after page, picture after picture, the records of a happy life. Now and then the man in the face-downwards picture appeared. He looked, thought Roz, a right bastard.

The album gave her a spasm of the heart. Like the diaries in Uncle Jack's attic, it was yesterday. Shut into books, made small by distance, the past was powerful. It was like a poison which, congealing in the dustiest bottle, thrust at the back of the highest shelf, still retains its danger.

She shivered to think Michael was receding into that lost world. Why did I let you go, she thought, closing the book on people who stood, immortal, frozen in their moments of happiness. Was her grandmother right and should you rush at destiny even if it was in the hands of somebody you fought with? Her grandmother was old, what right had she to counsel Roz not to be guided by her head?

Roz got up and went outside. In the parapet garden under an enormous sky flung with stars Thierry was leaning on the wall studying the view. The faintly glittering lights of St Paul de Vence were on the horizon, the shoulders of mountains dropped into the Gorge du Loup. His back was to Roz and without turning he said, 'Hungry?'

'No, thank you.'

'I could find you something to eat.'

'No, thank you,' repeated Roz, adding, 'Uncle Thierry.'

'Your grandmother has gone to bed,' he said, turning round, 'she was tired. Come and admire our view.'

She joined him. A night pause followed. A profound stillness. Then, 'I wonder if I might ask you a favour?'

'My dear English niece, ask me anything you like. I can't persuade you to eat, it seems. What else may I do for you?'

He threw his cigarette into the drop. It plunged, a red spot of fire, and vanished.

'I need a taxi to get to Nice airport.'

'*Dieu,* you are leaving very precipitately. You hate it here so much, do you?'

'No, no, it isn't that, I didn't mean — I only want —' stammered Roz, deep in embarrassment, 'I'm not leaving, but there's the friend I was with in Cannes. He's catching a plane tonight and he doesn't even know I have found Gran. If I went to the airport I could explain . . .'

He was evidently touched. He, in turn, consulted his watch.

'What time is his flight?'

'That's the trouble. I don't know.'

'Then,' began Thierry, 'perhaps his plane has gone.'

'I realize that.'

'You still want to try?'

'Please.'

Only somebody of this girl's age, he thought, would suggest driving off in the middle of the night to catch a friend who was now halfway across the Channel.

'Is it impossible to ring for a taxi?' asked Roz, trying to hurry him. She didn't know where the telephone was.

'Probably,' he said, smiling. 'I shall drive you.'

'Oh, I didn't mean!' blurted out Roz for the second time.

He interrupted with a brisk, 'I know you didn't but it looks as if we ought to move. Shall we go?'

They went out of the château, Thierry walking as swiftly as she did; his car was parked in the lee of the castle walls.

'Cross your fingers that we don't get bad traffic.'

He started off along the mountain road and within minutes was driving very fast, knowing every twist and curve and taking the centre of the road to save seconds. Later they were forced to slow down, frustrated by a large and lumbering lorry which belched exhaust fumes. Time and again, cursing, Thierry tried to pass. At length he got by, driving out on to a brushwood verge, then back with a grinding bump on to the tarmac.

During the journey neither of them spoke. Roz kept looking at a square of light on the dashboard where there was a digital clock. The figures slipped by so quickly. There was scarcely a quarter of an hour to midnight when they reached the autoroute. Mountains on either side were pricked with lights no brighter than the bowlful of stars. They had to slow down for Thierry to get a ticket at the autoroute barrier. That took three minutes on the digital clock.

The final stretch to the airport was uninterrupted and Thierry put his foot down. At five minutes to twelve when they were almost there he said, 'This is the one, is it? The man you care for.'

Tensed, taut, Roz still had her usual reaction – she did not want to answer the question. But her uncle had driven her here, expertly, generously and as fast as he dared. She muttered, 'Yeah.'

He raised his eyebrows, but she didn't see that.

'You love him with all your heart?' enquired Thierry.

Roz's eyes were fixed on the clock like a condemned man awaiting the death hour. She was forced to say, 'I suppose so. We quarrelled this morning.'

'That was very obvious when I met you. I'm afraid it's the trouble with red hair. Always this fighting. Sophy too.'

'*She* never quarrels.'

'Indeed? From one or two things she has told me about the past ...'

He had effectively silenced her and rather wished he hadn't.

'If he's at the airport he will be glad you have come,' he

remarked encouragingly. 'It would certainly be so for a romantic Frenchman.'

'The English are romantic too,' said Roz. He had turned into the airport entrance.

'That's a myth,' said Thierry and drew up with a screech of brakes. 'I'll wait for you over there under the trees. The police don't allow parking along this pavement. Don't worry, I won't leave.'

'I'll be quick –' said Roz scarcely knowing what she was saying. She threw herself out of the car.

She ran into the enormous spaces of the airport, looking for the Departure Board and not finding it. Racing across acres of slippery marble floors, all she saw were rows of shuttered boutiques and unmanned desks with their lights extinguished. Names stretched out in a bright procession, TWA, Air India, Lufthansa, Pan Am, British Airways. Urgent. Important. Not a soul to be seen. In daytime the place was crowded with travellers, staff, families meeting or saying goodbye, haste and happiness and work, perhaps tragedy. Now it was almost deserted. A couple went by, but when Roz hurried over to speak to them, they smiled and shook their heads. They did not understand either English or broken French.

Turning in desperation, Roz made out one light still shining. There was a girl in uniform sitting at a desk, going through a sheaf of papers.

'Could you tell me if the standby flight for London has gone? I'm not sure of the time it's due to leave –' gabbled Roz.

'Twenty-three forty,' said the girl, not looking up.

'You mean it has gone.'

A pause.

'Mademoiselle,' said the girl, finally raising her head and speaking with exaggerated patience, 'it is five minutes past midnight.'

'Are you sure?' The stupidity of the question deserved no reply.

Roz turned away feeling sick. With disappointment. With

563

grief, even. Thierry's kindness, the hurried journey, her hope, her longing, all collapsed round her feet. She couldn't return to her uncle yet, she simply could not. He would be so sympathetic. He would point out that it was not such a tragedy, she could telephone Michael tomorrow, couldn't she? He might even laugh.

She went slowly across the lounges and found a small bar. Parasols were set about, giving a foolish impression of sunshine in a windowless electrically lighted place as large as a hangar. A bald fat man was the only customer. He had a red face and a shiny head and a crumpled shirt and was sitting in front of a dish of melted ice cream. He was so tired that he kept falling asleep, his elbow on the table, chin on his hand. As he lost consciousness the elbow slipped and jogged him awake. Then, replacing chin on unsteady hand, he dozed off again.

Roz bought a coffee and sat down under a plastic parasol, huddling into herself. She was worn out and sad. Michael was gone. She knew it would never be right between them again. Every mile he travelled through the night sky took him further away, separating more than their physical selves.

She had no shred of hope to believe that tomorrow was another day, she did not even know where to find him. She had the Hammersmith telephone number, but telephoning a place where somebody occasionally stayed, and asking strangers if they knew where he had gone was sure to be pointless. Who kept addresses, who kept tracks, except your family or your closest friends? She did not even remember the name of Michael's friend at Hammersmith, and she had no address for the cousin he had said he might stay with in the Lakes. If you were not careful, people in your life simply disappeared. It happened all the time.

She had lost him. Now, tonight, if she had seen him, it would still have been in time. Later, if they happened to meet by chance or design, he would be hardened and changed perhaps, and so would she.

The airport lounges were so quiet. There was a lull before a later flight, the place had an eerie feeling. It was meant for bustle, for meetings and goodbyes. The shining floors were swept religiously three or four times a day. There was nothing to look at now but the ghostly ghastly cleanness.

She sat thinking about Michael; of how he had helped and supported her and taken her distress as his own. He had made love to her with passion and fallen in love with her, and all the time her hurt and her obsession had been fixed on finding Sophy. Michael was the one who came out of it well. Not Roz. Not Sophy. Like the man whose malicious smile had looked out at her from the old album, he was strong.

But he left me, she thought, arguing against misery.

In her despondence, she began to wonder if their quarrel had been the only reason he had walked out. Had he begun to believe that, after all, she wasn't worth all he wanted to give her?

It was too late for such thoughts, too late to judge Michael or herself or even her grandmother. She sat thinking about him.

'Roz!' said a voice.

She gave a shuddering start.

He was standing at a distance, bending from the weight of a heavy shoulder bag. He was as pale as she.

'*Roz, what are you doing here?*'

'Michael, you missed your plane!'

At her hoarse exclamation there was no welcome or warmth in his face. He stood glaring at her, then sat down at the table dropping the bag with a thud.

'No. I didn't miss it.'

'What do you mean? The girl said it left at twenty to twelve.'

'So *you* missed it, did you?' he said with a smile which was a sort of rictus.

'Of course I didn't miss it. I came to find you.'

'Really?'

What had she imagined in the first shock of seeing him here? Open arms? His whole face changing as they rushed into an embrace. He looked at her as if he literally disliked her, his expression so chilling that she couldn't find a word to say.

565

'You came to find me,' he repeated satirically. 'Great. Very thoughtful of you. But the plane you imagined I was taking had gone, hadn't it? You didn't bother to find out the flight time supposing I had been on it. What the hell was the point?'

'But I didn't even know if you'd ...'

'Look, Roz,' he said wearily, 'don't let's start this all up again, we had enough this morning. As a matter of interest, I'd like to tell you how I have spent today. Would it be too much for you to listen? Or to expect you to care a shit? Yes, I walked out this morning, you made me very angry but I came back less than an hour later and where were you? The girl at reception said you'd gone off in a car with some man. Who was he, for God's sake? Somebody else you picked up to help your quest for the Golden Fleece? And where have you been since then? I spent hours in that bloody awful hotel waiting for a telephone call.

'You never thought to ring me. Oh no. Then I began to stand at the door, thinking I'd see you coming through the garden – I couldn't believe even you were capable of doing anything so disgustingly selfish. My God! You carried on enough about your grandmother disappearing!'

'I didn't know you'd come back!' cried Roz in despair. He took no notice.

'Do you know,' he exclaimed, 'that I finally went to the police? I thought you might have been killed in a car accident or be in some French hospital. Christ, I didn't know what I thought –'

She had been beyond tears, but now they filled her eyes and poured down her cheeks; she gave a loud sob.

Michael said absurdly, 'Sh!' looking in the direction of a distant waiter. He thrust a handkerchief into her hand. Having caused the storm of grief he looked more furious.

She emerged from the handkerchief and said through hot tears, 'I'm sorry. I'm sorry. I never thought –'

'You don't need to tell me that. You don't, do you? Think, I mean, except about yourself and that missing grandmother. I felt I'd go mad. Okay. I've had my say. So where were you?'

He sounded as if he didn't care if he never saw her again.

She had the dazed expression of a boxer who has forgotten how to defend his head and Michael, looking at her, suddenly spoke her name differently.

'Roz? Where were you?'

'With Sophy. With my grandmother.'

'*What?*'

Still shocked and speaking in a low voice, twisting and knotting the handkerchief, she said, 'That man you said I picked up had come to the hotel to find me. He's her son. My uncle. He took me to Gran and that's where I've been all day. I never knew you were looking for me. Oh Michael, I truly thought you were so furious you wouldn't go back to the hotel, and I missed you so, and just now when I got to the airport, I thought – I thought –'

He seemed at first as if he could not take it in. They stared at each other in a kind of mutual dismay, and when he leaned forward to touch her, she reacted in a movement of violent longing and grabbed his hands.

'I'm so sorry –'

They spoke the words together, both stopped, both shakily laughed.

She began to speak again but he wasn't listening. He threw his arms round her and kissed her and she thought there were tears in his eyes as well.

They drew apart, talking at once, speaking in passionate broken voices. The fat man, jogged awake for the twentieth time, heard them and positively grinned.

LOVERS

Suzanne Goodwin

She was born in the slums of London. He was born into one of the most noble and ancient families in the realm. They met by chance – and they witnessed the scandal that shook society. Banished to bohemian Paris, they fell wildly, passionately in love. . . . But the legacy of his ancestors proved too strong. Edwardian England, family honour, and a crumbling stately home awaited.

And so did a stunning American heiress . . . All she had left was ambition. A driving ambition that made her the darling of the London stage. Her name became known to princes and poets, to queens and courtiers – and it was engraved on his heart. They were destined to meet again, to share a secret that only lovers can know. . . .

FICTION

TO LOVE A HERO

Suzanne Goodwin

There were few mysteries in the life of Sorrel Scott's
mother. So when death came to her during the Blitz,
there was little in her effects to arouse Sorrel's curiosity –
except the identity of 'George', the man who had been
inexplicably sending her money.

Taking leave from the WRNS, Sorrel embarks upon a
search that takes her to Evendon Priory and its owner,
George, Lord Martyn, the mysterious benefactor. There
too she meets Toby, his darkly handsome son and heir,
already a war hero with an MC to his name. And there
is no mystery about Toby and his feelings for Sorrel. . . .

After a whirlwind courtship, they marry, only to be
separated by Toby's overseas posting. And then disaster
strikes; Toby is reported missing in action. Overwhelmed
by grief and the violent aphrodisiac of war, Sorrel has a
wild, passionate affair. And, echoing the nation torn by
war, her new love is destined to change her life for
ever. . . .

FICTION

'A cracking story' *Sunday Times*

A CHANGE OF SEASON

Suzanne Goodwin

Penniless and orphaned, Lisa and Charles Whitfield find postwar Stratford-upon-Avon drab and unwelcoming after the exotic East. The highlight in their cheerless life is the colourful bustle of the actors arriving at the theatre. But for Lisa, secretly mourning a lost love, the last straw comes when her wayward brother elopes with young heiress Jenny Bowden.

Then Lisa's mysterious journalist friend Peter unearths a modest fortune in her father's forgotten investments, and Charles and Jenny return to share this unexpected prosperity. With her growing interest in her work at Perdita's eccentric antique shop, and Peter's devotion, Lisa should be content. But Charles's roving eye lights on Gemma Lambert, a leading actress of the new season, as sensually wayward as himself – and married to Lisa's lost love. . . .

A Change of Season is a moving, absorbing story of love and misunderstanding, of powerful passions and the final reward of a steadfast heart.

FICTION

'Compelling' *Sunday Times*

Warner now offers an exciting range of quality titles by both established and new authors. All of the books in this series are available from:

Little, Brown and Company (UK) Limited,
Cash Sales Department,
P.O. Box 11,
Falmouth,
Cornwall TR10 9EN.

Alternatively you may fax your order to the above address. Fax No. 0326 376423.

Payments can be made as follows: Cheque, postal order (payable to Little, Brown and Company) or by credit cards, Visa/Access. Do not send cash or currency. UK customers: and B.F.P.O.: please send a cheque or postal order (no currency) and allow £1.00 for postage and packing for the first book, plus 50p for the second book, plus 30p for each additional book up to a maximum charge of £3.00 (7 books plus).

Overseas customers including Ireland, please allow £2.00 for postage and packing for the first book, plus £1.00 for the second book, plus 50p for each additional book.

NAME (Block Letters) ....

ADDRESS..

....

☐ I enclose my remittance for _____

☐ I wish to pay by Access/Visa Card

Number ☐☐☐☐☐☐☐☐☐☐☐☐☐☐☐☐

Card Expiry Date ☐☐☐☐